KIN

A NOVEL

ALAN GRAEBNER

KIN: A Novel

Copyright © 2023 Alan Graebner

ISBN 9781948509480

Ice Cube Press, LLC (Est. 1991)
1180 Hauer Drive North Liberty, Iowa 52317
www.icecubepress.com steve@icecubepress.com

The paper used in this publication meets the minimum requirements
of the American National Standard for Information Sciences—
Permanence of Paper for Printed Library Materials, ANSI Z39.48-1992.

Made with recycled paper.

Manufactured in USA.

9/24/21, Iowa City

Dear Children,

You are holding what I warned you last week was on its way. It's a copy of part of a manuscript assembled by a cousin, Lewis Hollis Warden, left sure to be discovered after his death (from covid, in June). Family, cleaning out his place, came on it and sent a copy to me, wondering what "the history professor" made of it.

In my memory, Lew is irrevocably associated with antique cannon and porch pissing. When I was ten or twelve, during one of our family pilgrimages back to Tennessee mountains, my father took me along on visits to cousins. There were so many cousins. I could never keep them straight—let alone who was first cousin and who was second, much less "once removed." Except Lew. He was the cousin in stained Levi overalls, shirtless, his shoulder-length hair flying loose, unabashed by bare feet or the mason jar of brew.

Lew welcomed us cordially. August heat was suffocating, as usual, but heat was not the reason we three sat out on the porch. There was no room inside. Lew's place was jammed with teetering stacks of old books and piles of papers. His archive—or debris, for all I know—half-hid a massive antique artillery piece inexplicably parked in the kitchen. Detective mysteries with lurid paper covers (forbidden me at home) were scattered at random.

We talked along, mostly about family history; I was smart enough to decline Lew's repeated offers of his mason jar. Shortly after Lew perceptively invited me to join in a piss off the back porch, my father allowed we needed to get on to other cousins.

I wasn't surprised to hear my uncles refer to Lew as a COD, Certifiable Odd Duck. As I grew older I learned eccentricity ran in his lineage. Both his grandfather and his father were widely known for their virtuosity on banjo and mandolin, famous for their eclectic repertoire—hoot'n'holler to Bach—notorious for their disdain of audiences. I never met Lew's older brothers, the twins Walter and Wallace. Both died in their teens. They were remembered as right

1

smart, but as more than a mite peculiar—assuming it's odd to teach yourself Egyptian hieroglyphs.

Lew's mother suffered a series of mental breakdowns after their deaths; his upbringing was a scattershot affair. He drifted off to California and found a living there writing about music, and was flack for some famous bands. The deaths of friends from overdoses persuaded him, he said, to return to his roots in Tenn, where he lived a retired life, occupying himself chiefly by tracking down Hollis family lore. In recent years, when he spoke of trying to unravel a puzzling Hollis thread, he aroused some curiosity, but he seemed to enjoy remaining enigmatic.

In a note stapled to a cover page, Lew explains he found in "family papers" several substantial numbered manuscripts, the first titled *Quachasee*. All had "WHC" in the by-line. The initials are those under which his grandmother, Crotia Hollis Warden, wrote a popular newspaper column, somewhere between journalism and fictionalized accounts of mountain life and characters. (I read them years ago on microfilm and found them very entertaining; the mountain dialect, however, dashed any hope of bringing a talented regional writer named Hollis to the general public. Anker Osterude, a colleague here, told me he had an analogous experience with Norwegian-American writers of the early twentieth century with their Norwenglish in the Upper Midwest.)

Prefacing the *Quachasee* manuscript, the author thanks Henry Hollis, Henry's sister, Audrey Ann Hollis, and their intimate friends, John and Lydia Bright, for extensive interviews that formed the backbone of her work.

While Lew assumes an editor's role, he does not annotate Crotia's tale (no footnotes here), but inserts various texts in corroboration. He folds in private letters, extracts from a remarkable variety of documents, as well as passages from *Plowing with Greek* by HL [Herodotus Lucius] Hollis, Crotia's brother.

That sprawling memoir is a vast trove of antiquarian material (invaluable for Appalachian reenactment buffs), but it also includes many passages about Hollis family history. The latter is quite familiar, at least to my generation. Some of my cousins and I used to joke about it being inflicted on us already at the baptismal font.

What, then, do we have here? Lew unearths a lost family history. Its author is a thoughtful and talented writer. Her source is many interviews with central figures of the preceding generation. Lew presents the history, buttressed by a surprising variety of other, supporting sources. In the process he unravels the most difficult of all mysteries, a puzzle no one had previously suspected was a cipher, let alone decoded it.

On its face, admirable and invaluable. Who could object?

Quite a number of Hollis kin, it turns out. The Hollis family, like this whole country, it seems, has fragmented. Lew's work is the flashpoint. Certain Hollis cousins are up in arms about it. Reading their screeds, you would think a bloody, incestuous history of a warring moonshiner gang might be more palatable. Lew was certainly prudent to hold his assemblage for posthumous release.

Some unidentified person(s) sent underlined fragments to the like-minded, and the fat is in the fire. Their keyboards are curiously programmed, *able* to **produce** *only* BLARING **RESULTS**. An insinuating ? is their favorite, second only to ! or !! or even !!!. No fabrication seems too outrageous. They wax apoplectic at the hint (this volume was labeled "1") there may be more of Lew's work to follow.

They claim, of course, never to be talking about race. Most of the common whistles, however, are all too audible. Some talk of crowd-funding to finance a "true" Hollis history—and not incidentally to dig up dirt about Lew and Crotia. Certain cousins, graduates of reputable universities I know were taught better, and individuals whose alleged connection with the family is tenuous at best, scream *fraud* and *hoax*. Their rightful Hollis history, they say, has been **STOLEN**. It all mirrors the national scene but for one important detail: no Florida idol.

The agitators are so vocal and insistent that, as you may recall in this summer's mailing from the gentle and courtly J. B. Hollis, the annual family reunion at the usual state park pavilion was abruptly cancelled. J. B. mentions covid. The unstated reason, I'm told, was fear the reunion would be more fight than food, given hotheads with ready access to illegal liquor and to legal guns openly carried. Such is the state of Tennessee these days.

You may be gratified to hear of division within the hoaxer ranks. There are Crotia hoaxers and then there are Lew hoaxers. Both use Facebook postings to spread their calumnies. Crotia hoaxers argue that, just as she once invented a fictional mountain town, here she invented this story, not caring that she shames her whole family. Lew hoaxers insist, though, the Crotia/WHC manuscripts never existed for Lew to "find." Instead, he wrote the whole thing himself, inventing books he quotes. To my knowledge, no hoaxer has revealed that this plot to disgrace a fine, upstanding family is masterminded by the creators of the New York Times 1619 Project, but the din has yet to subside, so there is still time.

In the meantime some cousins allude to (actually, they harp on) *obviously* incriminating facts: the Warden family history of mental instability, Lew's familiarity with the West Coast Rock Scene (hair! drugs! sex!), his affinity for detective stories, and his Warden resentment of Hollis prosperity. Accounting for their credulity and diehard conviction is as difficult as explaining similar phenomena manifest these days in various capitol buildings.

Of course having such critics should not give Lew's work a free pass. His pages deserve close scrutiny, especially into the sources he quotes. The provenance of at least some seems dodgy. One can prove (or so I used to think) that a book is or is not quoted correctly. But how do you prove a book never existed? Regardless, I've started working through Lew's sources in his first volume. The university librarians already smile (or grimace) when they see me coming. So far, all I know is not to expect quick answers.

In the meantime, I look forward to your reactions.

Love to you all, spouses too, and dear children doubly so.

Dad

William H. Hollis   Director, Interdisciplinary Studies Program

QUACHASEE

WHC

Henry Hollis might have stayed in the high Quachasee valley all summer, working with the hands clearing at the new farm, except for the note the boy, shirt soaked through and breathing hard, carried up at dusk.

Tulips, Wed. morn.

Dearest brother, Father had a bad attack at his desk. Still insensible. The doctor bled, is worried. Come before it's too late.

Aud. A.

As he finished reading, Henry started loading a small bag, then spoke with his foreman. "Lem, my sister writes our father's taken sick bad. I'd better go down to the homeplace. While I'm gone, there's plenty of work clearing at the high field."

"Damn shame, Mister Hollis, an' sorry fer hit. Wisht thar was a nigh way down. Step kerful. Them Snake Sheer drop-offs is right easy fer t'go o'er, ye know, e'en wit' fulled moon t'night."

The moon had moved past midnight before Henry reached Tulips, but lamp light still shone from his father's bedroom. The ample figure in the doorway was Sally, the servant who had ruled the household almost as long as he could remember. She greeted him with a welcoming smile. "Yuh in tiam, Marse 'Enry. De doctah jes' lef. He say Marse Samuel's tough, an mebbe come 'round." Her smile faded. "Righ' now he not s'good."

Henry dropped into the upholstered chair near his father's bed and studied the old man. Laid out neatly, like a corpse, eyes closed, mouth slack, breathing hoarsely. Henry almost averted his eyes; he had never before seen his father in bed.

"Seem lahk he ken' move he lef' side a'tall," offered Sally. "An he nebbah say nuttin, 'least aftah I heah. Miss Audie wore out; say, wake she iffen yuh cum, Marse 'Enry."

He shook his head. "No, let her sleep. You'd better go to bed too, Sally. Plenty of work for all the women in the morning."

Sally's receding footsteps left the house so quiet Henry heard the stately cadence of the tall clock in the downstairs hall, a sound from his childhood. In all the east Tennessee mountains few clocks like that marked time, precious cargo when his father left the Shenandoah decades ago to seek his fortune. As he recounted many times, he had stopped at a scraggle of cabins (one day to be Asheville), decided it had no promise, and headed westward. He kept going until he came to a pleasant little valley with densely wooded slopes. It eventually was in Tennessee.

Yessir, God gave me fine land here. Good for crops and timber both. But God gives and God takes away. I've buried two wives, a daughter, and five sons on this land, sir. God willing, I'll be buried with 'em. The home place, Tulips, goes to my older boy, Sam Junior; the Quachasee goes to the younger, Henry. Thank God there's enough to provide for the wife, Sarah, and for my daughter, poor Audie Ann.

Henry could slip effortlessly into the rhythm of the old man's often-repeated litany. His God; his family; his land: the patriarch's triumvirate. Whigs or Democrats in the state house; Jackson or Van Buren in the White House: passing enthusiasms for Samuel B Hollis.

Since Henry's return to Tennessee that spring, he felt no premonition of what so abruptly felled his father. *Buried two wives, a daughter, and five sons* . . . the elderly's forgetfulness in that repetition. Otherwise, though, his father seemed only a little mellowed from the time, nearly seven years ago, when Henry, furious, left family and homeplace for New York. He intended his move to be permanent. But the recent deaths in New York of three intimate friends, his sister's artfully worded letters hoping for his return, and then his father's olive branch, the gift of a large tract at the head of the Quachasee: these had brought him back. He did not return, however, without memory of his departure. He stayed but a single night at Tulips on his way to the remote Quachasee.

True, his father had surprised him by braving the strenuous trip up the Quachasee several times recently to inspect Henry's progress. There, in his own rough way, he apologized for their quarrel. After inspecting his son's hard work, hearing Henry's painstaking plans, he hinted he now thought he made a mistake in bequeathing Tulips to Sam Junior instead of to Henry. He pledged to deed servants to Henry once the new farm's long-term needs came clear, adding that he had told Sam Junior explicitly of his intentions, so there'd be no contest between the stepbrothers if God took him unexpectedly.

The clock tolled. Two. Three. Henry rubbed his eyes, remembering the previous sick beds he sat by through the night. In New York, caring for friends. Pru's bed. Her deathbed it turned out, in that shabby boardinghouse. Before that, Pru and he sat at Isaiah Choker's bed, slipping out to beg a harried doctor for any palliative in the midst of epidemic. But begging medicine, night sitting, praying—none warded off death. Just as long ago in this very house when he sat—as much as a frightened little boy could sit—at his sister Emily Jo's deathbed, and then at his mother's.

A regular thump and scrape roused Henry from his doze, Audie Ann placing her crutch and dragging her crippled foot along the hall floor. Thump-scrape. Thump-scrape. She entered the bedroom, and Henry gave his sister a long hug. Over her shoulder, he glimpsed another figure in the shadows: Audie's maid, Carrie. He recognized her, a girl bought after he'd left Tennessee, from the background in the likeness Audie sent to him in New York.

Red fringed the sky as Audie Ann pulled the small slate from the cord around her neck. "Didn't wake me," she scribbled, scowling. She handed the slate to him, her way of demanding an answer.

Too impatient for the slate, Henry instead started to explain by the hand movements he and his sister used since early childhood, but his memory failed. Slow hands, long pauses. With the appealing little smile that had always touched Henry, Audie Ann shook her head. She did not understand; he must find another way to communicate.

"Should I help, Marse Henry?" Carrie stepped forward so Audie Ann could see her.

"You know the hand talk?" The possibility had not occurred to him.

"Yes, Marse, some."

"Well, then, can you try to tell her I didn't wake her because I knew today will be a long day? And what did the doctor say? I guess that's way too much too fast for you?"

"No, Marse," she answered Henry. For Audie Ann, Carrie's face became animated, her hands and arms moved in rapid, confident succession. Studying her intently, Audie Ann responded silently with her own face and hands.

"The doctor thinks," Audie Ann in Carrie's voice, "he thinks if Father–I mean, Marse Samuel–doesn't die in the next few days he may recover. At least some. He left medicine for Father in case he wakes up."

Henry nodded. "I understood some of that, but you two talk fast." He turned to Audie Ann. "Where's brother Sam?"

Carrie's words: "Marse Sam's in Knoxville with Miz Elvira, visiting her sister, Marse Henry." She moved her hands for Audie as she spoke and Audie Ann responded in Carrie's voice. "I wrote Sam a note when I wrote you, but I'm only telling him about his father, after all. Of course, no word from him or his Elvira."

After trying to imitate the women's hands, Henry grumbled, "I've forgotten so much. I remember the long ears means 'mule,' and we used to touch here for 'head.' But mule-head? I'm lost."

"No, you're not lost, Marse Henry." Carrie's dark eyes beamed encouragement. "That's Miss Audie Ann's name for Sam, for Marse Sam, I mean." Her face spoke sudden alarm. "Oh, Marse Henry, I'm out of place. Miss Audie Ann probably didn't want me to tell you that."

Henry chuckled. "Mulehead? She's got our stepbrother exactly right." Catching sight of his father's bed, he sombered. "Audie, when did you see Father was sick?" .

With Carrie between them, Audie Ann described coming on their father slumped over his diary, running to Sally for help, sending for Dr. McCaffee, dashing off notes to Henry and to Sam, calming the servants, while their stepmother, Sarah, retreated, tearless, to her bedroom.

After Henry smothered several yawns, Audie insisted he go to rest. She would keep watch and call the moment of any change. Henry resisted, but another yawn betrayed him. In his former bedroom he stretched out to rest his eyes "just for a moment," and fell soundly asleep.

❦

Mid-morning sun blinded Henry. Wincing, groggy, he needed a moment to place himself. Tulips. Audie Ann's summons. His risky after-dark walk down to Tulips. He reached hurriedly for his clothes; while he slept his father might have improved. Then he slowed. Audie Ann would never have let him sleep on if his father began mending.

On the way to his father's room, he paused at the open door of Audie's little suite. Carrie worked there alone, tidying, unaware of his approach. Her black hair tied back, but falling straight to her shoulders, she was so light for a servant she made Henry vaguely uneasy. He suppressed a rueful smile. The old patriarch, epitome of stern rectitude, of upright godliness—how did his father never fail? Wife, friends, even servants: most of the women around him were uncommonly fine-looking. Accidental selection? Divine intervention? Adroit manipulation? Henry could never decide.

Now Carrie. Henry tried to dredge up memory of his father's letters. He retrieved only fragments—purchase of a fine new cook and her daughter from some lawyer named Dinkins under peculiar circumstances, scandalous, but the details eluded Henry. How could you go off one morning to consult your attorney, and come home with likely the most attractive servant in the county? Dark eyes, a complexion that could have come from being merely careless about the sun. Of course she lacked the green eyes and translucent skin that always drew appraising stares in New York for Pru and for her sister, Charity, with the flaming hair and the birth mark. Carrie's style was darker. Still, given fashionable dress, she would have held her own with Pru and Riti in any comparison of face and form. Silently, Henry marveled.

Carrie looked up.

Henry stepped into the room. "Have you seen my sister?"

"She's been sitting by your father, Marse Henry, but he doesn't move. She went to stretch her body. Said she'd be right back. She sure didn't want to miss you a moment." Carrie hesitated, then continued. "I've never seen her face light up so bright as when she talks to you."

"We've always been close. Our stepbrothers were so much older that we younger children—Emily, Audie and I—were tight as thieves. Father bought Solomon and told him he had to look out for Audie. When we wanted to go somewhere Audie couldn't manage with her crutch, he just picked her up and carried her. We had our private world with our own language that kept out all the grown-ups except Mama. Solomon learned it because he was with us so much and we wanted to tell him things, but none of my brothers would."

Henry carefully moved a stack of books from a chair to the table, and sat down. "She could *feel* low sounds, though. We used to stand in front of the clock—its face seemed miles above us—and wait for it to strike noon. Those loud, low strikes she could feel."

"Oh yes, Marse. I used to think it must be near the end of the world. Miss Audie Ann says you taught her how to read and write."

"She taught herself." Henry dismissed praise. "Anyway, once she could read, things seemed so much easier. My stepbrother Sam used to say she's stupid because she didn't understand him when he shouted at her. But she isn't stupid."

"No, Marse. Maybe," Carrie picked her way with the wariness her mother had instilled from her earliest years, "maybe Marse Sam doesn't realize that with hands sometimes we can talk faster than I can say words out loud. She's smarter than the rest of us who can hear."

"She has to be smart to read everything she does." He gestured at crowded shelves. "Every time you dust there are more books."

"Yes, Marse." No need to confess how Audie Ann had once discovered her so tearfully engrossed in Charlotte Temple's pathos that she had lost track of the hall clock's strike, had missed even her mistress's unmistakable approach. Caught red-handed, caught sitting down, caught *reading*, she had expected harsh punishment.

Audie Ann had seized the book. But then she carefully turned pages to show Carrie faded handwriting inside the cover. There at the top: *Louisa Addison*. And on some inner pages, faint tiny stains. My mother's tears over Charlotte are here, too, said Audie Ann. So are mine.

Later, Audie seemed intrigued when Carrie cautiously ventured judgment. Miss Audie, that story is sad, but, in real life I don't see girls die when they aren't married and have babies. Audie began encouraging her to devour more volumes on her shelves so they could compare judgments. Audie made her maid duties light. Carrie read omnivorously, asking questions, offering opinions. It's almost like having Henry here to talk to, Audie would burst out.

"Audie Ann. How is Father?" Henry rose to embrace his sister. Distressed, she moved her hands far faster than Henry could follow.

Carrie saw his confusion. "Marse Henry, she's saying your father hasn't changed since you saw him. If she knew you were awake she'd have come back a lot sooner. I should have gone for her. Marse Henry," she added, "she's not happy with me."

"Not fair. Tell her I just now walked in. You're faster with hands; tell her that."

"Yes, Marse."

Audie Ann's face cleared as she understood. She locked one arm into Henry's, the other into Carrie's, leaned her head first on Carrie's shoulder, then on Henry's with the impulsive demonstrativeness that was part of her deafness or of her personality, who could say? She repeated her report on their father's condition, worried she was remiss in not sending a boy to fetch Pastor Berkemeier.

Carrie spoke respectfully from the window while her hands moved for Audie. "Marse Henry, I believe that's Pastor Berkemeier's buggy just come." Audie Ann took Henry's arm to go downstairs.

Had Samuel been the poorest or most wayward of his flock, at such distressing news Berkemeier would have come without delay. In fact, Mr. Hollis was one of the founders of Bethel Lutheran Church near Ginners Ford, a generous benefactor, long a congregational elder, active in the Tennessee Lutheran Synod, outspoken in supporting his pastor. Berkemeier came without delay.

By the time Henry and Audie Ann reached the parlor, the pastor had already greeted their stepmother, now with a lacy handkerchief dabbing her eyes. She accepted an awkward embrace from Henry and slumped forlornly in a chair. "How can a merciful God take dearest Samuel and leave a helpless woman all alone, tell me that."

"My dear Sarah, our loving Lord has not yet taken Samuel, and He never forsakes His children," Pastor Berkemeier remonstrated in a tone Henry thought surprisingly firm. Perhaps the pastor also reprimanded her "helpless woman" keening. Sarah only pressed the lace closer to her eyes and sniffled.

While Audie Ann and Carrie answered the pastor's solicitous questions about Samuel, Henry tried to distract his stepmother. "That Carrie talks with her hands a whole lot faster than I ever could," he murmured.

Sarah lowered the handkerchief. "Of course she's fast. Because poor Audie taught her. She's Lilly's, Cook's, daughter. When I came to this house I told Samuel the food wasn't fit to put on a respectable table, so he bought a new cook from that lawyer. Dinkins, I think his name is. He didn't want the bother of a useless, moping little daughter left behind, so Samuel bought her too, for poor Audie. Wasn't that just like him? Oh, what's a sickly woman going to do all alone without him?" She spread the handkerchief over her face.

Grated by his stepmother's self-absorption, Henry turned back to the pastor, a man he had known since boyhood. Henry was grateful for his comforting words and quiet prayers. Years ago Pastor Berkemeier had pressed him to consider the Lutheran ministry, to harken like the biblical Samuel for God's call. Henry listened attentively, but he was never certain he heard a call. Besides, he sensed his father's early endorsement became ambivalent as death reduced male heirs. Before Henry left for New York, Pastor sought him out to warn in a kindly way of snares the city set for young men. In fact, except for temporary curiosity, Henry did steer clear of the rowdy places. Though there was Charity. Riti with the red hair. Riti with the birthmark on her left hip. Was she a special snare or a special blessing? It did not matter; she now lay in the same Brooklyn cemetery as Pru and Isaiah.

The hall clock struck. ". . . and remember, Sarah, Audie Ann, Henry, remember to open Stark's prayer book when you feel overwhelmed. There is much holy balm there." Berkemeier was skilled at pastoral visits: not abruptly short, not tiresomely long. "Now I believe I'll go up and pray at Samuel's bedside. We don't know but what it may bring sacred solace to him."

The pastor, and the doctor too, came again the next day, and days after. Sam did not come. Instead he sent a note: *hopped Father wel naw; they thimselvs felin porli; be hom soon ez they up to travilin.* Audie Ann passed the note to Henry, rolling her eyes at the spelling, and flashed at him the lop-sided grin they used years ago as they made secret fun of their stepbrother.

Perhaps Sam's absence made no difference, at least to his father. Sally made the same pronouncement whenever someone opened the bedroom door. "Marse jes de same."

Plowing with Greek, My Life

HL Hollis

To some acquaintances, I am That Damned Hollis. To my wife, I am Harry. To my children, Daddy. To baptismal records, Herodotus Lucius, honoring my maternal grandfather, a distinguished jurist. Herodotus Lucius, however, seems pretentious for a mountain farmer. Unauthorized shortenings of Herodotus include Herod, no hero in the Gospels. My father preferred HL. As do I.

Presently, strong intimations of mortality impel me to write about my life and times, for the edification, or at least amusement, of my children, grandchildren, and those beyond. If not now, when? The first day of the eleventh month in the year of our Lord, 1938, seems high time to start.

My sister Crotia is a far more gifted writer than I. She writes stories, and wonderful stories they are. Under the initials *WHC*, she produces monthly a popular feature in the local newspaper reporting fictitious events in a fabricated mountain town. I look forward with great anticipation to her columns and take fraternal pride in her acclaim.

I fear, though, that our grandchildren and their grandchildren will not read her, no matter how entertaining. The stories are written in what for them will be a foreign language. There is mountain talk mixed in—"kindly" doesn't mean "to be kind,"—and there are terms for objects unused, even unknown in their lives, as well as a set of mind, assumptions, that will be long gone. Will our grandchildren's grandchildren know what it is to rive, know the shape and heft of a froe, know at a glance when harness lines are askew? Will they instantly know "staving" is a good thing, and "swarp" probably not?

They won't. The reason I am so assured in my prediction is the arcana of radios and aeroplanes. I recall, too, my bafflement when I first examined the engine of a Model T. And then all over again when I recently joined a young curbside crowd in Knoxville gathered around a Duesenberg automobile, appreciatively discussing its multiplicity of enviable features—to my utter mystification.

I peer uncertainly into the future. Hollis descendants will peer into the past with vision equally clouded.

What our grandchildren's grandchildren will need is some practical guide to describe people's lives, the objects they knew and used, the words they employed to communicate. To produce such a guide is prosaic work, but because it is prosaic, it is something I, a farmer, not a writer, may attempt.

I write also because I would like my descendants to know their Hollis forebears. So I hope to include them as I proceed intent on broader goals.

I was born at home, as was everyone my age, on April 17, 1869, here at the homeplace we call Tulips, built by Samuel B(enjamin) Hollis, my paternal grandfather, the first generation of the family to settle in these mountains of far eastern Tennessee. He arrived from the Shenandoah with some favorite tulips bulbs, a few slaves, a small money box, and a zealously protected, awkward bundle—the tall clock I rely on through the night. He allegedly claimed, with a wink, that he constructed here a clock container and it turned out to function as a house as well.

A special word for punctilious genealogists regarding this grandfather Samuel. Baptized Samuel Benjamin, he conceived a particular abhorrence for "Benjamin." Since a distant relative was Samuel B. Hollis, that shortening was not available as escape. Apparently plain Samuel Hollis did not pass the resonance test. So he identified himself as Samuel B, eliding the period. On legal documents his signature "B" includes ornate flourishes, but is ungraced by any punctuation. Samuel B was his preference. Samuel B is what I shall employ here.

In point of fact, without exception all of us are a dismayingly sorry lot before God, but specific facts explain familial peculiarities. The first American Hollis, Peter, arrived from England in the 1670s, an indentured servant. In other words he was so impoverished he could not pay upon embarkation for his passage, but had to cover the cost by selling his future services. Assuming (we have no proof) he was literate, any account he may have left of his antecedents evaporated.

Peter's son, Andrew, lived a rags-to-riches story, rising in tidewater Virginia to own a substantial plantation he christened Tulips, after a favorite flower. Andrew's son Jacob prospered as well, but these families confronted a common constraint—a son surplus. As solution, sons persistently removed west. In that migration, Jacob's son, Samuel B, my grandfather, arrived in Tennessee with tulips, cash, and clock.

Three wives, Judith, Louisa, and Sarah, did grandfather Samuel B bring in turn across the Tulips threshold.

By Judith Gall, he fathered six sons, Matthew, Luke, John, Mark, Jacob, and Samuel Junior. Judith Gall was killed by a horse shying at a handkerchief just as she was about to use an upping block, that is, a step or sometimes steps set in the yard to help women mount (or dismount from) their steed. Of her six sons, only Samuel Junior survived early manhood and married, to Elvira Gant.

By Louisa Addison, Samuel B fathered three offspring, of whom two survived childhood: my father, Henry, and my aunt Audrey Ann, though she lived a life sadly impaired. Louisa and her elder daughter died the same day "of a fever."

By Sarah Prescott, Samuel B had no children. She outlived him.

About these three wives: a legal document in my possession signed with an X indicates Judith's illiteracy; oral tradition strongly suggests she married distinctly up. Much evidence testifies to Louisa's native musical talent. Of Sarah only, we possess a portrait, confirming local gossip regarding her physical charms.

As a young man, Henry, my father, may have argued bitterly with his father, Samuel; the evidence is ambiguous. For whatever reason he first sought his fortune in New York City, under the business tutelage of a distant cousin, Hurley Hollis. At length, perhaps disappointed in love there, he returned to Tennessee, where Samuel B, his father, gave him land high up the narrow, remote valley of the Quachasee. There, for several decades, Henry cultivated a farm alone before moving down to inherit Tulips, where he married. I, his first-born, have lived here and farmed this land all my life, except for my years at Vanderbilt University studying Greek and Latin.

I am the eldest of the nine children born to Henry Hollis and the former Elizabeth Coyner, originally of Nashville. Following me are Dorinda, Marcus, Crotia, William, Samuel, Annie, Audrey, and

Lowe. All but Marcus and Samuel are living and reside at no great distance, except Lowe in Memphis. Grandchildren, however, have dispersed widely. A familiar refrain in this chronicle: too many children for the land, all the more so in these seasons, I should say years, of adversity.

Herodotus-Dorinda-Marcus-Crotia-William-Samuel-Annie-Audrey-Lowe—our mother enunciated one name, then another, when she intended still a third. You, too, may despair about maintaining all those names in proper order. Be of good cheer. When I discuss family, I shall mention here chiefly my sisters Dorinda and Crotia and my brother Bill because we older children formed a union somewhat separated from the confederacy of the younger children.

When he finally married, my father took as wife a woman much his junior—he could have been her father. My sisters, Dorinda and Crotia, sometimes teased her. *Mama, didn't that cause talk?* She always feigned otherwise. Her claim may have been honest ignorance, for she preferred books to people outside her own family, and I doubt she was even cognizant of town gossip. Father's considerable seniority shaped our lives, but that gets confusingly in advance of a coherent progression in this story. So my expository responsibilities require that I give precedence to relating other matters.

Dorinda Hollis Henderson to Crotia Hollis Warden

Collection of Lewis Hollis Warden

Nov. 11, 1938

Dear Sister,

You're sure to remember Justus Belvor, who was sweet on you in, maybe, sixth grade. He's still a gentle, kind man. Ran into him in town so we talked for a while. His favorite granddaughter eloped last week with Hank Hollis. I thought Hank was the boy's nickname, but Justus said it's his given name. Fits. He's Caleb's great-grandson. Yet another mean drunk in that line of them. She's a pretty girl, but a lot dumber than I thought. God only knows why she ran off with him. Justus is nearly heartbroken about it. "Fly around all the pretty flowers and land on a low crap" used to sum up that situation as well as anything. Still does, I think, though I haven't heard the expression used lately.

Most days I've been going over to Tulips to lend Caroline a hand with housekeeping since she is busy all day nursing HL. She's holding up pretty well, considering her husband, whom she's known since age two, is dying. HL doesn't complain, but looks a little worse every time I go. Dr. Bill says he can't do much any more. Make the patient comfortable is all. Or at least as comfortable as possible. Did I already tell you they went to see a special specialist in Knoxville last month? Specialist looked, shook his head and just sent them home.

HL decided he will distract himself by writing a — well, I don't know how to describe what he's writing. Some is continuation of the mountain talk lexicon you and he started decades ago. Some is description of life here when we were young. And some is genealogy and family history. If you ask me, it is a huge project—probably a whole lifetime's work. But I'm sure having some project is good for him, even if he'll never finish. It would be for me.

Yesterday when I went over, he already had neat stacks on the floor. This pile was about old farm implements not used any more. That pile was all about swine, from those wild tusk hogs that used to scare me witless to modern pigs by the careful breeding he's so good at. This pile was about horse-drawn wagons, carriages, and buggies and what to be careful about when you drive each kind. Over there was the start of a pile on rifles and Audie's pistols. Caroline says he's been writing nearly nonstop.

He admitted, though, that genealogy and family has slowed him way down. Words don't come as easy to him as to you. (I'm smart enough to stay out of it for I'm sure to make a bobble of the whole thing.) He strangles himself using silver dollar words when nickel words are better. If he wavers he tacks on more syllables. I encouraged him to use more four and five-letter words—Anglo-Saxon, not Latinate. Write like he talks, which can be pretty droll (you know what I mean). He had trouble swallowing my writing medicine. He's too scared of sounding like a mountain hoodger. I told him, If writing makes you grumpy, quit. Nobody is <u>forcing</u> you to write.

Shouldn't have said that. Set him off. Said <u>someone</u> has to write so people in the future understand things like Crotia's stories or appreciate the skill it takes to drive a four-horse team. Then he got on to why is Crotia signing her columns "WHC" instead of Crotia Hollis Warden? (Of course he'd prefer Crotia <u>Hollis</u> Warden, or Hollis italicized, maybe boldface <u>and</u> italicized.) I tried to calm him down—told him again how peckish Gates is about charity even when he's laid up and can't work, his hand so mangled he can't play the banjo he tunes, so why would he want his wife's full name all over the paper to show everyone she's bringing home the bacon now?

HL went on bitchin 'n bellyachin, as Father used to dismiss our complaining. I wanted to tell him, Jes stop yer yarmin, but he's a brother and he's slowly dying, so I held my tongue.

Then he started worrying that grandchildren wouldn't realize how unusual Audie Ann was. I admit I <u>thought</u> of telling him outright that in her family history manuscript Crotia spent many pages on Audie. Now, Crotia, relax. I kept our pact, sister: not a word about your manuscript until you say so. Good thing I spotted a bottle of the pain pills Bill left. I gave him one while I talked. Me or the pills, he got off his high horse.

By the way, I don't see writing competition between you — though he might disagree when he's not feeling good. You wrote about family and he's trying to write about family, but you're a story-teller and he's an encyclopedist. Each has its own place. They are different things, not superior-inferior. That's the way I see it.

Your admiring sister,

Dory

QUACHASEE
WHC

"He jes de same, Marse Sam." Sally greeted Sam and Elvira, back at last from Knoxville. Sam, however, did not waste much time at his father's bedside. He had other things on his mind. "Hit jes kills me t'come back t'Tulips an see all sorta weeds them boys dint chop in the crops. What the hell they thinkin? They gonna git rations when they jes relaxin on easy street?"

Much in his universe vexed Sam. He upbraided his stepmother for not changing her daily attire to mourning, then complained to Elvira that Sarah was sure to bankrupt Tulips by buying new fancy dresses excused by their required color.

He questioned the doctor peremptorily, listened impatiently to McCaffee's carefully hedged prognosis and settled on conclusions about Samuel B's condition the doctor never implied.

Sam ridiculed Berkemeier's kindly manner, and explained to Elvira that the Pastor came so often because he was actually courting Sarah, soon a widder woman, well off, and young 'nough to warm her ole man 'gainst Jan'ray chill.

If he noticed buggies out front, he retreated to the barn. There he fumed to himself about the ole man's reception of Henry just back from New York, like some damn prodigal son. Henry an' his citified talk, too good fer whur he birthed. Henry an' his clean, desk-soft hands (work up the Quachasee valley change thet damn soon an serve him right). Henry paying no proper respect to Sam's shouldering the ole man's responsibilities, even winding thet damn noisy clock ev'r Sat'day night, keepin' Hollis fambly ways goin. Henry pretending to love their deaf sister, lame in the brain as well's the foot, with them wavin hands an scary faces like some savage, making animal sounds 'stead of speechin like a human be-in, a sister who had orter stay in a back room outta decent people's sight.

When Henry once remarked on Tulips' rare luck to boast both a superb cook and a maid who could communicate easily with their deaf sister, Sam replied with a sneer. The ole man bought the cook, Lilly, an her datter from Lawyer Dinkins fer nuthin more'n a whoop an'a holler. I ax ye: why y'think a cheap, mean bastard like Dinkins sell low? Sam hyar ken tell ye. Latchstring is Dinkins' ole woman, ugly as a mud fence, she is. Some busybody whispers up in thet scarecrow's ear thet Dinkins boughten Lilly in Nashville, an is keepin her, fer *private* enertainmen lez say, out on hisn farm. Dinkins' woman go out and, sure 'nuf, thars Lilly, lookin jes' like the neat piece people sez. So Dinkins' woman she took a duck fit, screamin, throwin stuff, givin him the real what for. Dinkins is in a helluva jam, 'cause his woman has her fambly land, an he ain't figgered out yet how he gonna git his han on hit.

Dinkins has t'sell, an sell quick. I mean, sell afore sun 'n shadow switch. An it jes happen thet's the same damn day Samuel B Hollis show up 'bout some damn contract er'tother. Dinkins is shakin like a leaf. Gits rid'a Lilly faster'n a ratttler's strike, an' throws in Lilly's datter fer nuthin 'cause his ole woman hate light niggers, an Carrie's e'en lighter then her ma. Carrie's pa is one'a them gold-plate lawyermen at the state house. He fixin t'marry the gov'ner's datter but she get wind'a his good-lookin New Orleans sportin woman. An then she heered sompin 'bout a datter mebbe. So he has t'sell ma 'n datter. Quick 'n quiet, meanin dirt cheap.

Dinkins is visitin Nashville 'bout then, an snaps 'em up. He sneaks 'em to his farm, way, far way outta town. Figgered to double his fun purty soon. Have th'woman *an* th'girl, in the same bed, wouldn't thet be sumpin?—dinner 'n dessert both—but then his ole woman start screamin and he's a treed coon sartain. Has to sell quick, so he sell cheap. But he boughten cheap, so he don' lose e'en one thin dime.

Thet's why Samuel B Hollis got a big bargain. Trouble be, he give Carrie to poor Audie fer a maid, an' she ain't no maid, 'cause Audie spiles her damn rotten. Treat her like she white. When the ole man want Aud's likeness token to send t'ye in New York, she wont do hit lessen she git Carrie t'be right in the pitcher too. Whoever heerd'a gettin a nigger in wit' yourn likeness? Make her look like a sister. Tain't fittin. Thet make her look like she *my* sister. Jes riles a man damn mad, gittin *any* nigger's likeness, let 'lone gittin a nigger in wit' yer own likeness. Cain't hep but give a nigger airs. They soon fergit they's niggers.

An 'nother thing, Brother," added Sam after a long pause for his coffee, "has ye seed the hay cuttin at the ole Haney place?"

Henry nodded, though puzzled by the leap in logic from servants to hay.

"Ye seed how them boys is workin?" Sam's voice rose incredulously.

Henry's confusion cleared instantly: no leap after all. He tried to deflect the venom coming. "Best hay crop I can remember."

"Lazy niggers. They takin they own sweet time at hit, knowin I stuck up hyar in the house. I'm jes gonna tell the wemen straight. I, an ye too, prob'ly, cain't be waitin 'round ever dey fer thet damn doc an preacher. I needin t' be out, 'cause Tulips is goin t'hell. An yer Quachasee, too, fer all I know. I jes gonna tell t'wemen flat out, an they kin like hit er lump hit."

❧

Gathered in Samuel's bedroom after McCaffee left, Sam cleared his throat. "Henry hyar bin sayin, ah, an I kindly agree wit' him, thet, ah, his hands need him out in the fields, 'stead'a sittin in the house. The ole man would want us t'get back t'farmin. Ah, whatcha think?"

Elvira nodded. "Purty clar. Farmin's ourn food, an ye cain't be farmin inside."

"When you go back to your farm, Henry," added Sarah, "take a cook with you. Poor Audie Ann is right. You're so thin you look like a scarecrow. Your crew probably needs a cook as bad as you do, or you'll all die of starvation."

"I don't need an extra person to keep track of," Henry protested.

"Your loose clothes say you *do* need a cook," answered Sarah, warming to her subject. "Best a woman. Lilly I think. Carrie can be the cook here. She cooked fine last fall when Lilly stayed in bed all those weeks." Sarah almost derailed herself with the resentful memory of Lilly's claiming a high fever instead of keeping to her kitchen duty, but this time remembered to recover her maternal pretensions. "You need a real cook. We'll send Lilly."

More than anything else, from girlhood Sarah Prescott had feared pregnancy. She had rejected a hearty young suitor in favor of an elderly widower because she planned a marriage of cosseted security punctuated by few, very few, distinctly chaste kisses. When she discovered, too late, that her elderly, but still virile new husband expected conjugal union of an alarmingly corporeal nature, she suddenly developed debilitating complaints, mysterious disablements that defied medical attention.

Small wonder that Sarah sang silent psalms on her initial glimpse of the cook Samuel brought home, rejoicing at Lilly's light skin and a face that many a woman yearned for in her mirror. A Hagar for Sarah's Abraham—mistress's maid servant sent to the patriarch's bed—could only be providential. Sarah's sound health might return when at night she did not have to listen for her husband's approaching footsteps. She ensured Lilly wore flattering dresses and delicate under-things, delighted in housing her close at hand in the comparative luxury of the kitchen building loft—would have lobbied for a room adjacent to Samuel's had only there been one. She still worried, however, about what horrors her husband's solicitous search for medical advice might turn up.

Now, though, now that God rudely deprived her of Samuel, Sarah saw in Lilly, not a Hagar, but a Bathsheba. "Lilly will feed you proper meals. We'll send her."

"Sarah, we shoulda done thet month past," agreed Sam. "Sen Lilly up. She's not doin 'smuch fer Tulips as she ken fer Henry."

"You have some complaint about Lilly?" asked Henry in surprise.

"No, brother, jes lookin out fer ye."

In fact, Sam did harbor a secret complaint about Lilly. He knew right off Lilly be a special piece. He let her get settled in her cooking. Then, confident Lilly worked alone, and business took his father to town, he cornered her in the kitchen betwixt the cupboard and the long table, too heavy to move easily, plenty strong to bear her bending over it. Stroked her ass to check it be firm the way he favored. Showed her the hard soldier he tugged outta his pants so she unnerstan' he serious 'bout this.

From Jenny and Hannah, he knew there'd be cryin'an'shyin'. But not a bit from Lilly. Whilst he rubbin' her, she eased herself tight agin him without him never pullin her, so friendly ye ken tell right off this mare's been with stud afore and liked it plenty. She even stroked his stiff soldier so thorough-like he come parlous close to shootin his wad right there. A breather when she moved a hand to the table, likely to steady herself some, givin him time to cal'clate how often he could be back in this hyar kitchen. But she soon at hit agin, an he hed t'look sharp, so damn close to firin.

Perhaps it had been better so, for inexplicable, unquenchable flames shortly felled his soldier. Doubled over, gasping, Sam fled to the bushes near the well, his pants at half-mast, dousing his burning stalk with the coldest water possible.

Time gradually cured Sam's disablement, but not his shock at the desertion of a treasured comrade he always trusted to rise reliably for whatever a situation required. Sam brooded on Lilly's hex, for he did not question, except in the small morning hours, that her evil spells explained his humiliation. He avoided the kitchen house, convinced Lilly secretly smirked at him, a cat after stealing cream. He plotted reprisal—to no end, for his father's pride and delight in Lilly's cooking prevented retaliation. Sam could only take anticipatory satisfaction that Carrie blossomed with her mother's looks.

Henry's Quachasee farm offered opportunity, at last, to settle scores, even though it required joining forces with Sarah, a galling prospect. Jealous that his father could win the favor of a younger woman, Sam was of two minds. Some nights he entertained vivid fantasies of caressing Sarah's ripe bosom and shapely hips. Some days he begrudged the unproductive maintenance Sarah thoughtlessly required, and feared she might produce new heirs to displace him.

Still, better gnaw on tough crow now so as t'swaller tender hen later. That required agreeing with Sarah: send Lilly up, so Carrie cook at Tulips.

Plowing with Greek, My Life

HL Hollis

I never knew my grandfather, Samuel B Hollis, the Tennessee patriarch, since he collapsed of some kind of stroke a quarter-century prior to my birth. Had our lives overlapped, I think I might have found him inflexible and choleric, "testy," as some in these mountains say. He exemplified, though, great fortitude, for he mourned two wives and six children. Their gravestones were testimony to tragedies, speaking a language I should have understood, but did not until our own inconsolable loss in the Great War.

In his diaries, bold script marches past margins with fervent prayers, more meticulous examination of his soul's health than is now customary, resolutions to live a more godly life, and fatiguing detail. Painstaking records, in consequence of which we can ascertain what occupied him on a given day in a given year, which of his ethical lapses most troubled him, whom he met, traded with, and entertained at Tulips. One can, for instance, eavesdrop on his courtship of Sarah Prescott, to be his third wife. He itemized reasons favoring and opposing marriage to someone much younger, a list I deem sensible and sound, though "Appearance" seems a meager summary of Sarah's physical attractions. That the union was childless may have been a disappointment to him, since he wrote and underlined in the list, "Be fruitful and multiply." But that is only my speculation. He worried in his diary about Sarah's health, and perhaps was actually relieved not to find her pregnant. We can assume, I believe, that she mourned her childless state. Perhaps she regretted not having wed a younger consort, but she kept no diary I am aware of.

Grandfather's account books are equally detailed. I doubt my grandchildren will one day be able to follow my farm (mis)fortunes as well as I can audit Samuel B's. Of course no radio lured him from ledgers. Friday evening he appointed for laborious recapitulation and consequent reflection, not a movie the next town over.

Frustratingly, my narrative thereafter dwindles because the record thins for Samuel B's son, my father, Henry. His decades up at the head of the Quachasee valley remain perplexingly undocumented, save for his painstaking records of fruit tree grafting and swine breeding. For the majority of his life, one cannot state with specificity what his aspirations were, nor his opinions about phenomena in his purview. The Quachasee farm, now long abandoned in consequence of its isolation and laborious access, is tailor-fabricated for an extreme recluse. But my father never struck me as a hermit. Why then, I have long pondered, did he continue there? How could that extraordinary solitude content him?

Papers to those who write history are like rain to those who till soil. You seek a steady flow. Farmer or historian, what you most likely receive is flood or drought. I could write extensively and confidently about Father's few years in far-off New York City, for we treasure hundreds of his Manhattan letters. From the Quachasee we have—I was prepared to write, a paucity of evidence, but, in candid truth, we possess barely a scrap from his personal life.

In consequence, for Father's decades on the Quachasee land I can note little more than, he farmed, which, though indisputably the truth, hardly satisfies me. I do not imply some secret scandal. The full truth is as prosaic as "he farmed," though admittedly I search in vain for flesh with which to give body to those bare bones.

My frustration, however, overwhelms my narrative. I must record, admiringly, that Grandfather Samuel B displayed much energy and strong conviction. According to the public story that Samuel B told with self-deprecating humor, on his way west he did not dally at the future Asheville because he thought it obviously had no future. Close study of his diary leads me instead to believe that he concluded the opportunities for his political ambitions were far fewer in Buncombe County, North Carolina than further west.

He evaluated politics correctly, for he captained this county's governmental organization, though he failed in warfare worthy of an Iliad to retain the county seat at Ginners Ford. He served several terms in the early state legislature, back when the capitol of Tennessee was in Knoxville before being moved to Nashville.

About those Knoxville entries: at several points, pages have been painstakingly removed, I discovered by accident, neatly sliced out of the bound book. Whether these once spoke of the wheeling and dealing common, I gather, in those early days of statehood, I don't know. It may be that the absent pages once revealed some personal anguish, as may be hinted by entries before and after the missing pages. In any event he resisted strong pressure to extend his incumbency, and returned to a position of high regard, though no office, in Ginners Ford.

He was prominent in the founding of Ginners Ford, the now dejected hamlet near Tulips. (Truthfully, the town's aspirations ever exceeded its reality. Only by backroom shenanigans did the place narrowly escape engulfment by the national park lately established, but the effect of Mr. Henry Ford is now the town's death.)

He donated the land for, and helped found, the Lutheran congregation, Bethel Church, where his descendants still worship. He wasted no sympathy for antebellum politicians who questioned the Union, but he nevertheless owned slaves with a belligerently clear conscience. When the old Lutheran Tennessee Synod officially condemned American slavery, he demanded our Bethel Congregation's minutes incorporate his dissent and his contention of biblical support for slavery. On a hunch one winter I labored over Grandfather's Bible and a concordance, intent on every reference to slave or slavery. In so doing I confirmed that Samuel B had always anticipated me, underlining every passage, inserting lengthy, opinionated marginalia.

His ledger book entries for slave purchases parallel those for livestock purchases. Mule, bull, or slave, the columns display identical headings: date, name, source and cost. The high totals in the cost column quickly clarify why Samuel B did not acquire scores of slaves, despite chronic labor shortages.

He used "the hands" interchangeably for slave and for hired labor in his daily logs, but other records speak to slave status at least for Tulips domestics: Sally, Hannah, Jenny, Lilly—the last a cook, purchased with her young daughter from a "Lawyer Dinkins" for only one hundred dollars, the two of them. The price indicates Lilly arrived at Tulips sorely limited in some capacity. Presumably Samuel B could nevertheless not resist the bargain, though how the cook was incapacitated I have never ascertained.

Many of the slaves named in Tulips' records fled the area at Emancipation, never to return. A few—Sally Walter and Solomon Haller for example—maintained physical proximity but died before

I achieved the maturity to make intensive inquiry of them. Consequently, for me, people such as cook "Lilly with her young daughter" remain only fading ink in Samuel B's notations.

QUACHASEE
WHC

After Pastor Berkemeier finished his daily visit to offer prayers and consolation, Audie Ann and Carrie walked him out to his buggy, but the rest of the family lingered in Samuel's bedroom.

Sam nodded at Henry. "Brother, ye lookin mighty peaked. Yer pants'd fall right off 'cept fer yer belt. Doncha think, Sarah?"

Sarah nodded vigorously. "You need better meals and that means a cook. Lilly can go. Carrie can cook here."

"But Audie Ann needs Carrie," Henry objected.

"Oh, Audie won't mind giving up Carrie," Sarah assured him.

"But with Father sick," Henry put up a dogged resistance, "you need Lilly here for a lot of special cooking."

Sarah shook her head and Sam backed her up. "Not near much as y'think, Brother." Sam jerked a thumb at the bed. "He ain't eatin hardly nothin. Carrie'll do jes fine hyar. She's not no young'un no more."

Elvira watched her husband with a skeptical eye. Just a week ago, she prepared for bed after a hard day correcting the servants' laziness. The clock struck, with no sign of Sam. "Gotta work late on them accounts, woman. Ole man lef 'em all messed up." Elvira extinguished the lamp, opened the curtains and idly looked down. Shadows deep in one of the house's odd inside corners formed what seemed almost a human figure. As her eyes adjusted to the dark, Elvira saw an actual man standing there, stock-still, apparently staring up at the dimly lit, uncurtained window of the kitchen house loft. He disappeared, but Elvira knew what was afoot—one of the nigger men spying on Lilly and Carrie undressing. She would tell Sam later. But by the morning, she had changed her mind. What better than a black nigger man to brung them light nigger women offen theirn airs?

Now, though, she knew the shadowy figure's true identity: Sam. Sam everly up to his barnyard tricks, fixin to mount Carrie.

"Mister Hollis," she'd nip this bud damn quick 'n clean, "ye ne'er so much's biled water. Cookin is one thaing fer Carrie ifen her ma is nigh to ax. But thet Quachasee farm's too far up thet moun'in. Ifen we hafta sen sum'un—"

"Well, we do," Sarah interrupted. "But we can't spare Sally. I need her when my spells hit, and of course Samuel . . . "

"Carrie's a great cook." Sam declared. "She's made as good of biscuits than ye ever stuck in yer mouth. We'll eat good hyar. I made up m'mine. We sen Lilly."

That faked heartiness, false decisiveness. Elvira could spot in a blink when he tried conning someone. She knew now, positive. He was sniffing after Carrie, pawing another nigger girl; him an his filthy idear. Like Lilly when she firs' boughten, 'til sumpin happen. He hardly look at her now.

"Better t'sen Carrie up," Elvira insisted.

"Dammit woman," Sam roared, "since when don' my say mean noways hyar?"

"Mister Hollis, ye got charge'a impor'ant man-thaings." Elvira threw down her best card. "But not whur wemenfolk know. Don'cha 'gree, Mother? Henry's eatin is fer a ma's mine."

"Of course it is," snapped Sarah. "And I'll thank you, Sam, to keep a cleaner tongue in your mouth in front of ladies and in your father's sick room. In all our loving marriage I've never heard a single curse pass dear Samuel's lips. I remember . . ."

"We sen Carrie," repeated Elvira.

"There's no place for her to live," Henry protested. "It's just a camp. No privacy. Falling-down old shacks. And I can't take time to build something new." Henry paused, searching for even heavier ammunition. "Believe me, it's no place for . . . a . . ."

"Wal, Carrie ain't no lady. Ye keep fergittin' whur she come from. An jes 'cause Audie spile 'er, don' make 'er one. Hell—ah—heck, stick 'er in some shed wit' thet buck Jefferson . . ." Sam glanced sidelong at his stepmother. "I mean, jes put 'er anywhurs. Damn—hang hit all, 'pears I t'onliest one 'round hyar thet recollect Carrie's jest a nigger."

"We'uns know she a nigger, Sam." Elvira dismissed his objection. "On accounta thet Carrie goes whur we sen 'er. And we'uns a-gonna sen 'er up wit' Henry."

"**No.**"

Startled, everyone turned to Samuel's bed. "Did he say no?"

"He jes groaned."

"I didn't hear words."

"Jes' a sound."

A knock, and Sally entered, carrying a bowl of water and a towel. "Look lahk Marse Samuel cryin."

"Jes his eyes leakin," Sam huffed.

"We don't know," Henry puzzled. "We can't be sure he understands anything."

"He don' know 'smuch's thet bedpost," Sam snorted.

Samuel knew. It was true, sir, something had gone awry with his body; his limbs ignored commands. His mind, though, his mind still worked perfectly sound. He knew night from day. He counted the clock hours as he had since earliest boyhood. He prayed mentally along with Berkemeier on his visits. Incapacitated he was, not demented. Some doors had closed, mores the pity, but he had not vacated the premises. The proof, sir: he could recognize unanticipated catastrophe when it loomed. And he had only himself to blame.

He remembered the unexpected negotiations, if one could call them negotiations. Lawyer Dinkins, sweating his shirt through, lowering the price faster than Samuel could counterbid. Then Samuel's first glimpse of his bargains, the two waiting figures at the Dinkins farm lane. Shapeless drabs and large kerchiefs could not disguise their light color or fine features, so alarming he almost drove right by, abandoning them. Small wonder Dinkins hid his vixens far from town. No surprise Elsbeth Dinkins raised hellacious thunder when that hatchet-faced termagant ran the rumors down. Even gossip exaggerated did no justice to Dinkins's Nashville prizes.

Your name Lilly?

She pushed their little bundles of clothes onto the back of the wagon hurriedly, as if in flight. Yes, sir.

What's the wood box?

Cooking spices and kitchen things, sir. She didn't look up as she took hold of a handle, her haste a contrast to most servants' usual maddeningly lackadaisical pace.

It not verra big, Marse, added the girl with a dazzling smile as she heaved at the other end. The two scrambled up, sat in back on bundle and box, far more eager than he to be rolling.

He drove home chastened, humbly confessing to a just God his cupidity, his venality. Of course he enjoyed attractive females, wouldn't deny it. The last and best of God's creation, he always said. But would he never learn? With Judith, his first wife when he was young in these mountains, flirtatious eyes and unreserved complaisance enticed him, too besotted to heed warning signs of her indefatigable wrong-headedness. Later, she laughingly, passively, defeated his campaign to correct his mistake, to educate, to refine her. There were the dark times of messages from home when he was away in Knoxville as a rising young state legislator, times he had sworn to forget and would not revisit even now. Sam Jr., Matthew, Mark, Luke, and Judith's other sons—they all grew up with the same amiable, incorrigible disregard for responsibility, for consequences, their fecklessness imprinted indelibly already in her womb.

And now this Lilly. Lord have mercy. He carried home nettles to sow in his wheat. How many kingdoms of old did a foreign beguiler wreck? He ruled a kingdom in land, to be tilled by Hollis lineage for countless generations to come, manifestation of God's goodness, and credit to the Hollis name. But a servant, too comely, from the papist, sewer end of the Mississippi: how could she be anything but an ominous threat to the future he planned? The Israelites' history testifies to God's patient faithfulness. True, as Pastor preached. But it warns that corruption lies tirelessly in wait for the righteous.

In his Tulips day book he entered a new line: *Lilly, cook, and young daughter. Bo't from lawyer Dinkins. $100.* His hand slackened. His heart knew no joy at the bargain. Duty spoke clear. He must ever be the watchman on the ramparts, the alarm trumpet always at hand.

Instead, too quickly did he abandon his office. Too readily did he welcome the fine meals which soon distinguished Tulips hospitality known far and wide, enhancing his proud reputation as generous host. Too thoughtlessly did he enjoy this melodious-voiced servant, with grammar and manners more suitably seated at the table than those she served. Too easily did he accept the presence of this trim-figured woman, attentive to his needs, solicitous of his wishes, who, when she addressed him as Mister—not Marse—Samuel, barely sounded the title.

Not one of those dour Calvinists, he rejoiced in his Lutheranism, commanded to enjoy God's magnificent creation. God manifestly intended gentle, lovely women central in His handiwork. Last made, best made. True, the Lord takes away, as the unreliability of stirrings in Samuel's loins reminded him. But he saw with greater clarity that the good Lord also gives—age banks the fires of concupiscence. He could admire without coveting. So, innocent, he enjoyed.

Changes seemed to unfold providentially. Sam Jr. was seized by some uncharacteristic concern for decorum, objecting in fury at his father assigning Solomon to carry Audie Ann in his arms from place to place. "Hit make a man vomit to see his own flesh and blood wit' her arms 'round a nigger, an his hands doin what ye ken spec'late easy e'er time he lift an set her."

With Lilly's arrival at Tulips, Samuel was able to mollify Sam Jr. by assigning her daughter to Audie Ann, and shifting Solomon away from the house. And when Sam Jr. in a new paroxysm of propriety objected to Audie's desire that Carrie pose with her for a likeness to send Henry, Emmer Pruitt needed a supervisor for a freight trip that kept Sam Jr. away from Tulips for weeks. His outrage on his return was small price for a fine likeness of both girls, which incidentally gave Henry proof his sister thrived, attended in his absence by her very own maid.

With Carrie as maid and companion, poor Audie Ann looked happier than for years. Despite Samuel's fervent prayers, he could provide for his daughter neither hearing nor husband. He thanked God he could give his crippled child this one small solace. But *now* he recognized he had been as insensible in his own way as deaf Audie Ann. A woman's graceful form, pleasing delicacy in manners, savory food: how little lulls a sinner from vigilance.

Only *after* his body failed did the serpent reveal itself. Easy to see— now. He *had* brought a viper to his bosom. A cunning viper, even slipping in a decoy. He feared the mother. But the true menace was not she. No. Instead, the girl!

He had followed his sons much more closely than they realized, all the more since Sarah, wed in hope of fecundity, had disappointed him. His own shrewd observation at Tulips coupled with Cousin Hurley's regular confidential reports from New York firmly grounded his clear-eyed conclusions. Resolutely setting aside paternal vanity, he judged his sons with stoic dispassion. Sam was a stupid hog, headed before long to butchering. Henry was an admirable workhorse, but his reins were held by those red-haired city strumpets with their woolly-minded good causes.

The girl checkmated him either way: at Tulips and a Sam eager for adultery and dissipation. Or at Quachasee and a Henry converted to New England isms, diverted from aggressive aggrandizement, necessary to ensure Hollis hegemony. Either way, the girl insured the patrimony bequeathed by Samuel B Hollis would be squandered.

He viewed it all with perfect clarity as if through a telescope at far distant figures. Scream warning and no one heard. Wave madly and no one saw. By mobilizing all his energy, he shouted a mighty "no." But hearing, what did his family understand? He wept in helplessness. Heartbroken, beyond any solace the pastor's prayers provided, Samuel willed his end.

His body, though, a powerful machine, could not fail merely by wish on a specified day of June in the year of our Lord, eighteen hundred and forty-three, however fervent that wish. A lever here, a drive gear in this train, a cam there, a delicate spring at that pivot—yes, these stilled. But those impedances totalled only minor inertia against the momentum of the whole. Heedless, however, was now that momentum. As the hall clock sounded the hours, Samuel B Hollis refused any longer to count.

Plowing with Greek, My Life

HL Hollis

My grandfather's diary breaks off mid-sentence with a great ink smear at June 14, 1843, when he slumped over at his desk. You will find nothing comparable from a lesser mortal in 1938, merely quiet dismay as a junior scribe copes with the realization of how much effort his few pages require.

Samuel B never wrote another word after that spoiled page. To what degree and duration he remained impaired by his stroke I am uncertain. When, long ago, I asked Aunt Audie Ann, her response seemed ambivalent. In point of fact it may well be that after many decades, she herself could not recall details of subordinate importance.

Farming being farming, my assumption is that the incapacitation of Tulips' most superannuated resident—already too senior for strenuous chores—made little real difference, however heartless that sounds to put into words. The next generation strode forward without misstep, decisions were shaped by familiar precedents, and life at Tulips continued much as always, albeit absent its most faithful diarist dutifully documenting the grand annual solar cycles.

Though Grandfather Samuel B defended slavery throughout his life, his son Henry (my father) opposed it implacably, as I learned at an early age. Beginning approximately in my twelfth year, Father often requested I accompany him for business matters. He assigned me the arithmetic because, he averred, he left his strong glasses at home and anyway, his mind got creaky on long sums, something I at first believed. (You apprehend why I required a prolonged apprenticeship.)

In one instance we drove a considerable distance to meet a man, Clement Salter, who offered to buy certain of our stock at, I laboriously calculated, an unusually good price. He and Father chatted inconsequentially, since it was not fitting back then to conclude a deal expeditiously, as one does now, even on the telephone line, in this more hurried-up era. A Confederate veteran who served under General Lee, Salter reminisced regarding battle maneuvers, compelling stuff for a lad my age. This somehow led him to praise slavery: good profits, kept the darkies in their place, suited them, they had it pretty good, too bad we can't go back, and the like.

Initially relaxed and affable, Father stiffened perceptibly. He challenged Salter mid-sentence. "Clem, you don't believe that nonsense, do you?"

"Tain't no nonsense, Hollis. Ye believe hit too, 'cept ye cain't admit hit. Them the bestes' year."

"Clement Salter, you're a goddam fool." Father spat out opprobrium he rarely employed. "I'll do no business with goddam fools." He turned on his heel, stalked away from a lucrative deal so precipitously I had to dart after him to catch up; he whipped the buggy homeward at such manic velocity I gripped my handholds with white knuckles, convinced we must sheer off a wheel on some tree we whisked by.

After Father slowed—in truth, the horse faded—he addressed me. "Don't you ever live in that past. I did. Believe me, slavery was hell for slaves. It was hell for masters, though most of 'em were too blind to see it. Everything about slavery was much worse than you can ever imagine. A terrible sin before God. The Catechism says it all: that sin will be visited on the third and fourth generation. Your children's children will be old before they escape it. *If* they escape it." I recall his prescient words with sad clarity.

One more such story which I well know I have related sufficiently often to anticipate listener fatigue. I nevertheless feel compelled to place a record on paper to ensure its indelible permanence.

As the young lord presumptive of the manor, too full of myself at fifteen—even my charitable sisters Dory and Crotia heartily concur—I once entered the kitchen to snatch a snack from Edie, our much-loved cook of many years, the epitome of kindness and indulgence. Rushed with dinner preparation, she politely fended me off. To show I was no longer a child, I converted a whiney appeal to a steely order. She apologetically demurred. I perceived she recognized my order originated in an appetite, not for food, but for authority. Realizing my motivation was transparent embarrassed me so acutely I succumbed to that common human temptation, and converted embarrassment to rage. I lost all self-control. I informed her she was merely a servant, to take orders. Further, she was—I shrivel inside at the memory still—only a nigger, coal-black at that. I reduced a gentle soul to tears.

Fortunately, though I concede this "fortunately" only in long retrospect, Father overheard my rant, including that terrible pejorative, forbidden in our household. By that age, feeling my oats, taller and heavier than he, I considered him rather frail, but he seized my shoulders and hurled me back so forcefully I collided painfully with the wall behind.

All the while he raged. "Never, ever, do that again. Never. You have no right. Nobody has that right. You treat her like she's your mother. The same as your mother. Do you hear?" His voice became so fearsome and foreign I hardly dared look at him, but when I did, I saw tears streaming down his face. "Ask her forgiveness. And then beg God's forgiveness. On your knees. Do you understand? Beg God's forgiveness on your knees."

I have reflected much about that scene long ago in the Tulips kitchen. Turning the details over in my mind, as I lately do, is painful, for their edges remain razor sharp, unblunted by time. My role discomforts me so acutely I have sometimes attempted to elide my arrogance by reshaping the telling, but that vitiates the story. I have even considered suppressing the entire episode. I am the sole survivor; there exists no other record.

The essence of the story is such, however, that if, many decades hence, I were somehow to give a sworn deposition before grandchildren's grandchildren concerning their Hollis patrimony, my testimony must be this: the tale about a callous fifteen-year-old, a hard-working, loyal servant of a despised skin color, and Henry Hollis, their remarkable forbear, who raged and even wept at what could never be right.

Dorinda Hollis Henderson to Crotia Hollis Warden
Collection of Lewis Hollis Warden

Nov. 18, 1938

Dear Sister,

Jes set yersef sum, as the old timers say. I've got all kinds of (mostly trivial) news.

Was over to Tulips again yesterday and visited with HL while Caroline took a lie-down from nursing him. We talked about his writing, of course; that's all he wants to talk about these days. He said he got on paper his I-insulted-Edie story. So we rehearsed that. <u>Again</u>. Crotia, it isn't Christian to say this, but I am sick to death of hearing that story. In the first place I've heard it so often I know where the commas go. In the second place poor Edie was a complete misfit in the kitchen. She lacked the faintest hint of culinary imagination. I am convinced her tongue simply could not detect any flavors but salt and sugar. And she was stubborn in her deprivation. I remember once — you were visiting in Knoxville, I think — some friend in California sent Father a little box of artichokes. Artichokes in Tenn!

I was entranced. I'd never even seen one before. Edie? She treated them like dog dirt, wouldn't have anything to do with them. They were outside her (and Mother's, of course) standard repertoire. Bill and I looked artichokes up in an old cookbook; I remember him standing on a box because he was still too short for the stove. If we hadn't, we'd never have known how good they taste. To tell you the truth, I think I've eaten them only twice since.

I recall complaining about Edie to Sally once. Now <u>she</u> was a woman who loved to eat. She enjoyed flavors. Maybe that was the reason she was the one I complained to. Anyhow, I remember her telling me — kind of guardedly; you known how she was about telling us anything of slave days — she told me Edie was pushed into the kitchen as a mere girl when the real cook named Lilly died suddenly. It was a catastrophe for Tulips because this Lilly was an exceptional cook. "Makes mah mout watah jes to <u>tink</u> 'bout Lilly cookin. Breads 'n pies 'n cakes. Lilly puts in spices 'n ting yuh nebah hears of in no udder kitchen. She cums from Nuh Or-lins, an dat dahky, she could cook, believe yuh me, she could cook. Marse Samuel, he so proud ob she. Lilly 'n me, we wuz bes' frens, but den one nigh' she go t'sleep an she jes nebah wakes up. So we gits dat girl Edie. She doan know nuttin. She doan eben know how ta bile watah." (Have I got her right, Crotia? I did love that woman.)

Alright, now I've let off all my steam about Edie. It's not her fault HL tells that story so many times I could scream. Even though I admit the story needs telling again and again to the people around G. Ford. Actually I'm upset at seeing so much of what we knew and loved — my Mike, HL, your twins, Edie, Sally, Audie Ann, Solomon — they all disappear through our fingers like sand.

I need to change topics. I'm on a committee at church for the outdoor Christmas manger scene. Thought I aged out of jobs like that, but Pastor asked me as a favor because he doesn't want a repeat of last Christmas. I never wrote you about that disaster because it was right at the time when you had that fire at your place. I was worried sick about you and Gates. And then about whether your family manuscript got burned. I don't know whether I ever told you, but when I got the first word (it was that your place burned to the ground) I dug out my copy of the fragments you left here and tried to figure out if I could reconstruct the whole from what I had. I couldn't, so I was pretty relieved the first word was wrong. Bad enough as it was, I know. Bad enough that I didn't write then about Christmas here. But I knew to keep notes for my sister's Mtn. Springs column. It's soon Advent again, so here are my notes.

The whole problem started this way. First Sunday in Advent, Pastor took to bed with one helluva cold. Mr. Holms stepped in. He was our seminary student assigned here for his practical year. Trouble is, Pastor says, the seminary hammers on students to delegate, delegate, delegate. But they don't say anything about checking up after delegating.

The committee voted to have a live outdoor reenactment of the Bethlehem adoration on Christmas Eve. Unanimous vote. So Mr. Holms delegated one person responsible for the animals, another person for the sets, a third person for actors, a fourth for costumes, and so on. So far so good. (Except it really wasn't because Mr. Holms didn't know these people's histories. You're right to think of people like Brian Cays and Dwindle Habermost and Abby Comfort and Cindy Trost, and say uh-oh, several times over.) Mr. Holmes delegated, but didn't ask for reporting.

Come Christmas Eve, David and Tina drove me in to have a look. There they were. Joseph, Mary, the Babe — all in costume. Joseph was wearing the bearskin off the wall that his Daddy is so proud of. Mary — I almost wrote 'Eve' — had on some of her ma's lingerie that should never have left the bedroom, much less the house.

Baby Jesus in the manger got to crying. The louder the crying, the louder the narrator to drown it out until Tom was nearly at his livestock auction voice (you remember Tom's auction voice has a nasal twang and auctioneer's mumble; it's hard to fit with King James' St. Matthew). The crying baby was mercifully rescued by his mother.

But that left the manger obviously empty. How do you have an adoration of an empty cradle? They quick borrowed Hetty Tilton's baby. Baby's name is Alice. In the manger. (Crotia, I couldn't make this up, but my women's suffrage friends in Nashville should take note of it, right here in G. Ford. They think we still spell it women's sufferage.)

The stable building they put up would have benefitted considerably from the advice of dear old Herr Schmidt, rest his atheist soul. Ours instead owed a good deal for architectural inspiration, in my eyes, to the Taj Mahal. Not humble. Nor lowly. Ornate and large.

Large, it needed to be. We had geese and ducks. Chickens and roosters. Lots of crowing for a silent night when all is calm for heavenly peace. Sheep, of course, and also their shepherds, in from watching their flocks by night. Unfortunately the shepherds forgot and left their crooks in the fields. Maybe they were too overcome by the appearance of the angel choirs. So they substituted pitchforks. Crooks and pitchforks are both agricultural tools, aren't they? Our shepherds carried their crookforks tines up, which made them look more like sentries at the gates of hell.

Then there was the cherub choir. Effie Keller made wings for each little child. Trouble was, the glue hadn't quite had time to dry hard—you know Effie and deadlines—so parts kept falling off. Which upset some cherubs so much that they were in no voice to sing, let alone remember the hymn.

Cows lowed their adoration, as did their calves. Small mules stood in for donkeys. Vi Abrams snuck in her cage of cockatoos.

Also adoring were pigs. Crotia, I could not believe my eyes. Pigs in Bethlehem. I know all of Creation is to worship the Lord, but, but, but. Do these people never read the Jewish dietary laws in Scripture?

I near forgot the Magi. We knew they were Magi because they wore crowns. Furthermore each had his name stenciled on the back of his robe. Caspar, Melchior and Balthasar. It was a good reminder, though the stencil font made it obvious the stencil set was borrowed from the athletic department at the school, and its R unfortunately needed major repair.

Each King had his own camel, of course. Camels probably being as rare as cougars in G. Ford these days, someone thought to strap a very large stack of hay on a mule's back, and cover it with blankets. Lo, a G. Ford camel. Good in theory, but no one was delegated to cinch the hump girths tight. In their solemn approach to the manger, the Magi found their camels' humps sliding in various non-camel-like directions.

Westward leading/ still proceeding, the Magi came to present their gifts. Someone was inspired to add authenticity by having the Magi carry burning incense. Sister, do you have any idea where, short of Knoxville, one can beg, buy, or steal incense? But incense it was. Pungent smell. Smoking very heavily, the incense.

Overall, a bad idea, considering this was a bunch of Lutherans not handy with incense. Incense burned too hot. Burning incense lit the stable hay. Loose, dry hay. Someone threw water (brought for the stock), but missed and drenched Caspar and Melchior, I think it was. The Magi King Balthasar was by then doubled over laughing, a peculiar posture for presenting his myrrh. Fortunately the shepherds had pitchcrooks handy to evict burning hay. Fire out, we quick went home before we could witness another catastrophe.

That's why Pastor got together this year's "coordinating committee" for Christmas. During which he mentioned that he had a letter from Mr. Holmes, back at the Seminary for his last year. Holmes wrote that one thing he learned at G. Ford was never to have an Adoration Enactment. We know better than such cowardice. We've had our first meeting and got well started. Established Rule #1. NO PIGS.

You ought to be able to use at least some of this for a Mtn. Springs column, don't you think? Just be sure to make it a Baptist church, Crotia. I can't bear to advertise such Lutheran biblical illiteracy.

Ooh, Sister, you're going to ship me off to the county home soon, for sure. I got so involved with Bethlehem pigs, I nearly forgot to write at the very top of this letter what I missed last letter and told myself after I sealed it that I'll just mention it first thing next time I write. Now I've almost done it again. Senility is catching up. I don't even have to look over my shoulder any more.

What I wanted to write is that the last time I was in Ginners Ford, Ed Tower crossed the street to give compliments—not to me, but to you. He says he didn't "want to throw off on any other writer," but he goes to your stories about Mtn. Springs before anything else in the paper, even though he has to open the dictionary for some words you use. He said "he knowed he cain't find no Mtn. Springs town marked somwhur's on no map, but hell thet don' mean it ain't all 'round us. Thar's more'n one kinda true."

Crotia, you're not ever going to get more genuine praise than that. No better confirmation, either, of what you decided years ago about your interviews with Father and Audie. I remember you going back and forth between a bare transcript of questions with answers, and using those answers to construct their story. More than one kind of true. Your choice was a lot more work, but aren't you glad you went with the stories? I am.

To return to where I was—just to prove to myself that I'm not completely batty this morning—HL said the next time I come he'll have me read some of his pages—the family ones, not the pages on mountain living fifty years ago. Talked about sending some to you, too. Be kind, Crotia. He's dying.

Your loving, scrambled-brain sister.

Dory

QUACHASEE

WHC

Elvira marched into Audie Ann's room without knock or invitation. She remained standing, Audie knew, to say hers was no sisterly visit, but strictly business, to be disposed of quickly, at least as quickly as possible given Audie's severe mental limitations. Seeing Elvira motion peremptorily toward her while speaking to Carrie, Audie faced Carrie for hand talk.

"What's The Witch ordering you to tell me now?"

Carrie's bland smile gave no hint of her sarcasm. "Assuming you have not the faintest inkling of family debates, The Witch, with her customary gentle grace and ladylike demeanor, humbly inquires of her beloved sister-in-law whether she favors sending Lilly or me back with Henry to cook for his crew."

"I think," Audie pursed her lips, "you're dressing up what she said."

"Maybe a little here and there," Carrie grinned.

"A little here and a little there makes a sow into a mare." Out of the corner of her eye, Audie saw her sister-in-law watching the hand talk with the sour expression that spoke disbelief it could be actual communication, scorn for whatever it was, and resentment about her exclusion. "What she wants is my help fighting stubborn Mule-Head who is so set on Lilly going."

"You're right. Sally says there've been shouting fights between Sam and Elvira."

"Sally been listening outside the door again?"

"The fight is fierce. Way beyond who's cooking where. Elvira wants to go into business with her sister in Knoxville. Make it Holt and Hollis. Sam is against it."

Audie was idly curious. "Selling ribbons and trinkets?"

44

"It's not trinkets, but slaves. Her sister, Miz Holt, has gotten into the slave trade from Knoxville. She is making a lot of money specializing in maids, cooks, and wet nurses."

"Slave trader! Elvira is even lower than I thought. I'd disown her if I could. But Sam isn't against buying and selling people."

"No, that part doesn't bother him. He doesn't like how it looks if his wife makes more money than he. Now he's offering to cut a deal with Elvira."

Audie saw Elvira speaking. "What she want now?"

Again Carrie's bland smile. "She wants to know how I can stand so much moving hands and face to ask her simple question. But she guesses I have to keep repeating before you catch on. She's getting impatient. What should I tell her?"

"Tell her," Audie paused, not uncertain but reluctant to say what she must say. "Tell her I think you're the best one to help Henry."

"Should I make it endearing and sisterly or—" teased Carrie.

"Don't you dare make sisterly," interrupted Audie. "Keep it all business. She does."

Carrie spoke briefly to Elvira, earning a triumphant smirk Elvira barely suppressed. She turned on her heel, saying a few words without a glance at Audie, and was out the door.

Carrie picked up even before Elvira disappeared. "Guess she hasn't had her daily dose of Ahler's Tonic yet."

"Sweeten a lemon?"

"I doubt Ahler's is ever called sweet. Sally says it's got more kick than Sam's brew. That's another reason Elvira keeps it under lock in the storeroom."

"Ahler's? I'll have to try some, next time I'm in there."

"Oh, Audie, be careful. You could make a lot of trouble for the women. Elvira marks the bottle after every dose she takes."

"She does? Then I'll fill back to her mark with piss. On her way out she turned so I couldn't see her mouth. What did she say?"

"That fighting her husband is like dogs hounding a bear."

"More like a fight between skunk and rattler."

"And Elvira is the skunk? Or the snake? Uh-oh, I almost forgot, Audie: Mama wanted me to help with pies this afternoon."

Audie waved her away to the kitchen house, relieved not to have witness for her tears. Was it ungrateful to God to look back and see mostly one loss after another? First, her mother and sister called to heaven before she could fully remember them. And after that, in different ways, she lost Henry, then Solomon. And now Carrie.

She remembered Henry teaching her to count; he made it a game, like putting her head against the tall clock at the hour, and raising a new finger at each strike until she connected the reverberations, the symbols on the dial, the numbers in ascending progression. Then he taught her to read and write. Henry tried to protect her from the big boys, her stepbrothers, who did cruel parodies of her hand talk right in front of her. Henry let her fire his pistol and exclaimed so admiringly about her accuracy that Father came to watch, astounded—having no inkling that, God forgive her, she imagined her stepbrothers' faces on the target. Henry proposed she explore with him beyond what she could see from the Tulips porch, struggling to lift her when in exhausted tears she bogged down with her crutch. Henry badgered Father for some helper to take her wherever she wanted to go. He kept badgering until Father bought Solomon, still a boy himself, but big enough to carry her adventuring beyond the porch.

When fears gripped her in the night and dogged her in the day, Henry comforted her: he would always be there. He could not inherit Tulips, of course, but when they grew up he would have a farm nearby and she could visit him or live with him, and Solomon too. That's what she looked for, prayed for, until the needless quarrel between Henry and Father, which she worked so hard to patch over, and Sam tried so hard to fuel. The evening came when Henry stood at her door, telling her he did not want to be separated, but he could not stay at Tulips any longer, and had no means to take her with him.

In her desolation, Solomon, now a strapping man, became her solace, ever ready to help her escape the limits of her crutch, as he had since she was a girl. With him she ventured much further than her family could imagine, leaving behind not only the geographical but also the mental confines of Tulips. She never stopped being Samuel B Hollis's daughter: no one could have prayed more fervently when she and Solomon said vows before God. She lived in blessed euphoria, her happiness alloyed only by the impossibility of publicly sharing it. But, despite all her precautions, her idyll ended abruptly.

From brother Sam's eyes, she knew to the day, the hour, when it first dawned on him that his crippled little sister was somehow become a woman. To Father he protested vociferously the impropriety of a nigger buck serving a young mistress now of age, but too dim to distinguish right and wrong. He pressed his argument even in a letter while on a trip freighting harvest to market. With despair and dread Audie read those crabbed lines on her Father's desk. Frantically fearful about what could befall Solomon, she feigned indifference about Sam's urgings, though she never took off her mother's ring, tangible proof of her vow.

Solomon was sold to a neighbor who rented him out for day labor. Once again Audie listened to a man she deeply loved tell her he could not stay but had no means to take her with him. That his new owner was indulgent, and Solomon, stealthy as an Indian, spent much more time with her than anyone knew did not lessen her mourning what could never be.

Father's gift of little Carrie, to "replace" Solomon, was at first hardly consolation. Yet the girl proved discreet far beyond her years, greeted Solomon's noiseless appearances calmly, intuited when Audie wanted privacy with him, and more than once cleverly distracted an unexpected visitor.

As Carrie grew older she grew in other ways as well, until Audie took great pleasure in her company. God had taken from Audie her big sister, but gave her a little one, a loving sister, quick, with a sharp eye and sense of humor as wicked as her own, though—good thing—less mordant. With tutoring from Solomon, and coaching from Audie's slate, Carrie learned to talk with her hands and face as fluently as Henry and Solomon. Being together from rising to retiring made it easy to provide Carrie practice in the reading lessons her mother had surreptitiously taught her. She became so thoughtful a reader that for Audie to share books seemed a self-indulgence to gain intelligent company.

How could Audie fail to show to a sister the letters from Henry, letters their older brothers refused to read, ridiculing them as young Henry putting on airs. His painstaking pages, implicit apology for his absence, intended as eyes and ears on the world for his lame, deaf sister, served also to educate a girl physically sound but as unable to escape Tulips. Watching Carrie slowly rereading the stack of Henry's letters neatly piled next to the thumb-sized likeness from New York, sharing with her their impressions of his reports, Audie felt a sibling bond, not between two, but among three.

But those she loved most, she lost. For Carrie, Tulips was impossible. Audie had known it, unwillingly, resentfully, for years. Sam, convinced his stepsister was feeble-minded, never bothered to conceal from her his lusting after servant girls, something that left her sleepless many nights, raging over her inability to intervene. She watched him study Carrie lecherously, knowing that Audie saw him, dismissing her with a contemptuous glare, a dare to stop him. She could not. She depended on Father to keep Carrie safely by her.

Now that Father lay insensible, though, Sam would make his move. To protect a sister, she must lose her. Audie's tears fell, not soundlessly, but unheard.

Plowing with Greek, My Life
HL Hollis

Somewhere I once read that each generation seeks to avoid what it perceives as the errors and deficiencies of the previous, but in its correction, each makes its own mistakes, which the following generation avoids. So if you could observe a family intimately across many generations, you could see it zigging and zagging through time. I am minded of learning to drive an automobile down the Tulips lane, overcompensating with the steering wheel as I barely first escaped the yawning ditch on one side then the unyielding oaks on the other.

The theory makes good sense to me. Because my father, Henry, seemed oblivious to family history, and rarely discussed his early life, I suspect his father, Samuel B, often spoke at length about family and early struggles. And in reaction to my father's willful amnesia, I fix on place and preserving a family record. My children will therefore respond to my excess by silence about family and carelessness about place, which failings my grandchildren, I predict, will one day correct with exhaustive genealogical research, industrious rehabilitation of family artifacts, and who knows what other ancestor idolatry. Well, then, we each must work as our generation dictates. My lot is to preserve to the utmost of my ability the memories I foresee shall otherwise expire with my last breath.

Accordingly, I write about Father's unmarried sister, Audrey Ann, who resided at Tulips her whole life, in consequence of which I knew her as well as my parents. As extraordinary woman, in point of fact, Audrey Ann Hollis was born lame, the result, believes my brother Bill, William Hollis, M.D., most likely of a midwife's blundering delivery. In consequence she perambulated poorly; without her crutch she was unable to advance a yard.

The crutch, however, counted as nothing compared to an early childhood illness that left her insensible to any sound. Crippled and deaf. Deaf and crippled. I cannot conceive how she collected courage to continue. In stammering fashion, far more clod-footed than I care to reveal here, I once inquired of her about despair. How, considering her infirmities, did she escape it?

She didn't, Audie answered calmly. After her brother Henry departed for New York, she felt so overwhelmed by her situation she entered a time of blackness when she questioned the goodness, even the very existence, of God. She escaped this hell, she disclosed, only with the help of her pastor (Eusenius Berkemeier at the time) and solicitous friends.

Audie said she thanked God daily for providing these people to pull her back from the abyss. I wish now, of course, I had pursued the subject, for she confided all this as matter-of-factly as she evaluated rifles, but I failed to ascertain the identity of the invaluable friends, and I was yet so immature I hardly recognized an abyss existed, let alone how proximate to it one daily treads. Instead, our conversation terminated when Audie Ann smiled sadly and said she hoped, in the glorious hereafter, to comprehend enough to thank God too for making her lame and deaf, which must have served some divine purpose.

In point of fact we communicated well with Audie Ann, despite her deafness, because in her early childhood the family invented a versatile system of hand and facial signals, developing a substantial vocabulary, expandable, including prefixes and suffixes, that facilitated discussion even of abstract ideas. When I once described this to a professor at the University, he erroneously imagined some primitive system of pointing, essentially mere pantomime. The Hollis system, however, as other sign languages, employed finger positions and motions, along with hands and facial expressions and subtle changes in body position, to signify concepts and actions, just as articulated sounds are not the essence of, say, an object, but stand for it. I was not fore-sighted enough ever to garner a coherent account from her or Father of the origins of this sign language, but I believe their father, Samuel B, must have been prime mover in this, as in so many matters.

Both my parents knew the hand talk, though Father spoke much more fluently, having used it many more decades. We children absorbed it as we learned to speak with sound. When I inquire of my brothers and sisters, none of us recalls consciously initiating this silent language, any more than we recall our initial babbling aloud. The hand language (I use that term for convenience, though in point of fact hands were only a part) seemed so natural to us, we resorted to it even in Audie Ann's absence. Miss Deborah Ebbers sent home urgent notes—Crotia informs me she has them still—pleading that Mrs. Hollis please forbid her children the silent language at school.

With this language we said some things quicker, perhaps better, than in English, just as any other foreign language provides some perfect word without English equivalent. To this day, at family gatherings, one may occasionally observe a quick sign from my brothers or sisters—though after Audie Ann died (at her funeral Dorinda gave an eloquent and moving appreciation of Audie Ann, gave it entirely in her hand language, with Crotia translating for the crowded church), a majority of the hand language slowly atrophied. I just now attempted to translate the previous sentences, and must sadly confess my failure, a lapse that grieves me greatly, for it is as if Audie Ann herself has slipped still further into oblivion.

Though Audie Ann rarely left Tulips, most people around here knew her, partly for her spunk and silent language, but mostly as our own Annie Oakley. In her girlhood she became enthusiastic about target shooting, an absorption easily understood, as it surely gratified to surpass everyone else at *some* valued activity. Samuel B at first merely humored her, she once confided to me, because of her physical burdens. As she proved herself, however, his boasting of her prowess itself became part of local lore. (N.B. I must place that fact, too, within my imagination's portrait of a stern Grandfather Samuel B Hollis.) His pride was entirely justified. I can attest that repeatedly I personally witnessed Audie empty a revolver, consecutive rounds fired so quickly one could hardly count them. The target displayed a single, centered hole.

Some enthusiasts proposed issuing a formal challenge to the Annie Oakley of international renown, but that would have been out of character for Audie Ann. She never married; she was one of those women whose affections are diffuse rather than concentrated on a husband. She remained the quintessential homebody, perfectly content only at Tulips; she left but once a week, to attend church.

I believe she could be so resolutely homebound without mental stultification because of her incessant, thoughtful reading. She and my father disputed favorite authors, about whom they differed. Her hit-and-run attacks on my father's stalwart defense of James Fenimore Cooper seemed to us eavesdropping children deliciously

sly, high entertainment. For all her isolation Audie Ann always struck me as much more world-wise than my mother. To my knowledge, no one in Ginners Ford kept better informed about Nashville and Washington politics.

On occasion our bolder childhood friends ridiculed her, though not for long. My siblings and I never tolerated that. Action forbidden outsiders, however, may be permitted intimates. Bill, the devil in him, once caricatured Audie wickedly—and hilariously—behind her back. Then Father spotted him. "I shall see you at the barn before supper." No laughing matter that.

In the barn Father picked up, not a strop, but softened beeswax, which he molded into Bill's ears. Then he employed heavy cotton batting to fasten layers of cork over the beeswax. Finally, Father required Bill replace a shoe with a kind of sandal that Ben, one of the hired men, contrived on Father's specifications, small nails driven through the sole, sticking up. The nail points did not cause much pain—unless you applied appreciable weight. For stability, Ben fabricated a crude crutch. Four fingers, Father raised. Four days so confined.

Father issued an unappealable order: nobody was permitted to assist Bill. For sympathy's sake, Audie Ann and Mama could not look at him, but I confess his brothers became zealous in sanctimonious obedience. Though Bill stayed stoic during the day, he gave me qualms at night when I heard him stifle sniffling in bed.

After the prescribed duration, Father freed him without ceremony, censure, or counsel. Bill claims insistently and unhesitatingly that the experience was decisive in aiming him down the path to medical career. When on his most recent visit I recalled this episode for him, he nodded. "Science is a wonderful thing, HL. But without empathy, a doctor is merely a scientist, not a physician."

Long ago my wife's postmortems after social gatherings made me aware I can exhaust a captive audience with an especially favorite topic: esoterica of Greek grammar, mountain-talk I have collected, and perhaps, here, my phenomenal aunt, Audrey Ann. Still, I cannot conclude without emphasizing the startling quality of Audie's communication, given such isolation in these mountains. She is reminiscent of the Cherokee, Sequoyah, completely alone, creating a written form of his native language. Astonishing.

At Vanderbilt University in Nashville, when a deaf man once entered Old Main and attempted unsuccessfully to make himself understood, the professor to whom I had described our silent language summoned me. "Here, Hollis, use your hands to find out what this poor man needs." I stepped up with confidence, and we both employed hand talk, but we were as the Medes and Parthians in the New Testament Book of Acts—spoken to each in their own tongue, only this time without the Holy Spirit's mediation. In point of fact he could not comprehend my signs and I understood his so ill that we perforce retreated ignominiously to paper and pencil. The language Audie spoke was a Hollis invention, patently different—whether superior or inferior, I cannot say—from that taught the deaf elsewhere.

That Audie Ann died so soon after my father was killed was saddening but not unanticipated since we older children well knew she nearly idolized him. Bill, I think, displays his usual perspicacity in observing that *two* crutches supported Audie Ann, one wooden, the other, our father. When my mother and sisters later sorted through her effects, they discovered the great treasure Audie Ann preserved, a box of nearly three hundred letters Father wrote to her from New York. They include his elated news—Crotia exults in this—announcing his engagement to the daughter of a wealthy banker.

The paper of the letters is fragile now, showing evidence of much wear in consequence of many readings—no surprise since we may safely surmise the letters from far-off New York eagerly passed from hand to hand among his brothers at Tulips.

(Some years ago, to prevent loss by fire and reduce contention over custodianship, I commissioned a typist to produce copies which I distributed to all my siblings. I once hoped to summarize the letters' contents in these pages, but now see that is beyond my strength. Those letters provide fascinating glimpses of a burgeoning metropolis, and of Henry Hollis as a very young man.)

Among the things Audie had stored away we discovered sketches she made when young ladies demonstrated their gentility by inflicting Art upon their family parlors. To be candid, the world is little impoverished that these sheets were secreted away so many decades. It must be said, however, that Audie documented Tulips at a time when the oaks surrounding the house, a towering arboreal canopy now, were slender saplings. One can see in her sketch the rawness of this country that Grandfather Samuel B settled. The shift from forest primeval to agrarian cornucopia, backdrop for these reminiscences, included a phase as awkward, ill-proportioned, and badly-complected as any adolescence.

Crotia instead concentrates on Audie's penciled drawing of a young man's head and shoulders. There is in the portrait an incongruity: technically the artist was not highly proficient, but the subject is very closely observed. The young man we recognize as Solomon Haller, once a Tulips slave, and in his old age a familiar figure frequently sitting on the Tulips porch talking with Father and Audie Ann. He was the only person outside the family who had the ability to converse fluently in Audie's hand talk. Why, asks Crotia, of all people did Audie choose Solomon to sketch? A special relationship, she announces, existed between them, a relationship that Audie never divulged.

Brother Bill, the family rationalist, nods his head in treachery's agreement. "Of course there was something between them, Crotia." He pauses. "Slavery. Audie was a novice artist; she needed unmoving subjects, like tulips at Tulips. Or a slave, like Solomon, who had to stay still when ordered to do so."

Crotia sputteringly rejects such obtuse skepticism and predictably cites the simple gold band Audie wore, which had been her mother's wedding ring. To questions of why she wore it on her left third finger, she answered, That's where her mother wore it. End of subject. After her death, we found "SH" engraved inside it. Crotia deduces SH to be Solomon Haller.

Bill erupts at this. "Crotia, haven't you ever heard of Occam's Razor? Use it, Crotia, morning and night. I prescribe it. Think, Crotia: It was Louisa's wedding ring. Louisa's husband is Samuel Hollis. That's S-H."

Crotia is unperturbed. "Louisa's husband was Samuel *B*. Samuel *B* Hollis. That's S-*B-H*. Or did Occam invent a new alphabet?"

Bill and Crotia argue as ferociously over a few undated notes she found inserted (and I assume forgotten) in one of Audie's books. They are addressed "Audie" and signed "C" or, sometimes, "Cora," a name unknown to anyone in the family still living.

They also argue over an unlabeled photograph. An older woman is posed seated, surrounded by a standing young woman and two younger men, all three attractive—from Cleveland, if one assumes the photographer's frame is original. Even Bill and Crotia agree similarity in features indicates this probably is a family grouping, missing the father.

Beyond that agreement is contention. Perhaps the father had died. Or deserted. Or perhaps the portrait was taken to send to the father, then elsewhere. Who can say? The family's very identity is at issue. Further, the portrait may be connected to the letters. With equal chance, it may be entirely unrelated. Did Audie value it, or did she preserve only accidentally as a bookmark something that happened to be readily at hand? The answers are equally plausible, though, as is her wont, Crotia appropriates the one with most romantic possibilities, and spins out scenarios intricate, improbable, impossible.

I prefer a different route. We shall never ascertain the identity of those people. We should employ the photograph as a reminder that one must consistently date and place letters, and inscribe identifications on the backs of portraits, even of those closely familiar, an obligation easily overlooked, since transgressions of omission usually seem less egregious than those of commission.

Fisk University Project on Ex-Slave Reminiscences
1931
Interview 731
Mr. Solomon Haller

Note: because Mr. Haller has a speech impediment and an unusual accent, he was at times difficult to understand without much repetition. Accordingly, the following violates the Project's customary practice. Mr. Haller's answers are rendered as a very close paraphrase with no attempt at a stenographic transcript.

Mr. Haller, I would like to ask you about slavery as you knew it. Do you remember that far back?

Of course I remember. And I will tell you the honest truth about it. Many old Negroes, when they are around white people, they bow their heads and shuffle their feet: Oh, yessem, we all loved our master and missus. They were so good to us. We made just one big happy family. Those were the best times.

Solomon Haller won't tell you that, because it wasn't true.

Have you lived here in Nashville all your life?

Oh no. I'm here now because my granddaughter lives here. She takes care of me real good, you know. I used to live in east Tennessee, spent a lot of my life there in the mountains. Born and raised near a little town called Ginners Ford.

Ginners Ford? Where is that?

I'm not surprised you ask. It's just inside the state line, so it's not Carolina. So itty-bitty small nobody ever heard of it. It's right at a ford in the river there. No bridge, you see. But I didn't live in town. We were out from town on a big farm, big for those parts anyway. That's where I was born and raised.

Do you remember the owner's name?

Do you think I forget the name of the man who beat my back bloody? Hollis, it was. Rich family there. This Hollis Junior, he was a plain bad man, plain bad. Say you're in the field working hard and you straighten up, you need to ease your back, he's shouting at you right away, maybe on you with his stick. My father—he was Old Solomon, so I'm Young Solomon—he told me this master's father was a good man, God-fearing and all. That was the father, but he took sick sudden-like. His son, this Junior I knew, he was the devil. His wife just the same, worse. She was filled with hate against Negroes, especially the women. Some folks down in the quarters, they said she was trading in slaves, like on the side. But I didn't see her do that with my own eyes. All I know for certain is she hated Negro women.

A woman trading slaves would have been unusual, wouldn't it?

Maybe so. But maybe not. I don't see much difference between trading and owning. And a lot of women owned.

You mean widows who inherited their former husbands' slaves?

No sir. I did not say widows, did I? I knew plenty of single white ladies who owned slaves for their farms or to rent them out. They could be just as mean as the men, no difference. They'd say, Look here. I'm tired of fighting with you. Either you straighten out or I'm going to sell you south. And they'd sell them too.

There was just a small family in the big house?

No, the master's sister lived there too. The sister was deaf and dumb, and needed a crutch. The master and the missus, they didn't get along with her. They made his sister eat in her own room, some times didn't even send her dinner. Made fun of her in front of everybody because she didn't hear them. But when Hollis Junior drove us Negroes too hard, she and the cook came down to the cabins after dark with extra food she took right out of the store room; she had a secret key. When one of us was sick or mistreated, she'd get my father to carry for her because she had that crutch, and they'd bring medicine and things to rub on when your back or your arm is sore. A few times her brother caught her coming home, but she just acted crazy-like, wandering in the night, deaf so his questions make no difference even when he shouted. He's suspicious, but what could he do? If he locks the door, she just goes out the window.

That wasn't usual, was it?

No, no, not usual at all. Once—I didn't see this with my own eyes because I was away cutting timber, but I heard about it from people who were there—when the missus was in town visiting, Hollis Junior got mad at Miss Sally for something and tied her up to give her a whipping. The sister could see what was coming. Didn't like it. Waved her hands, shook her head, but he shouted at her, pointed to go into the house. She ran inside, but right away she came back out with a big, long pistol—she liked to shoot at targets behind the barn—and when Hollis Junior lifted his whip up to thrash Sally, she aimed the pistol and shot the whip in two, so all he had in his hand was that handle. He turned around and saw her on the porch with the pistol pointed at him. They looked at each other, but she kept aiming the pistol. Finally he just threw down the handle and stomped off, shouting a bunch of bad language. So she went and untied Sally, and everything calmed down. I tell you she was white outside, but inside she was black.

Why do you think that was?

I've put my mind to just that question many times. Many times. I think it was because she was deaf and dumb and needed a crutch. She had such tribulations, you see, tribulations just like us black folks. So she was just like us even though she was white.

Where did you work, in the fields or in the house?

In the fields, mostly. It was women who worked in the house. We worked in the fields, but also in the woods. You see, in east Tennessee up on the slopes there were a lot more trees than here around Nashville, thick woods. When the crops didn't need tending, we'd be working timber. I was just a boy then, so when the tree came down they set me to chopping off the limbs and dragging them out of the way. Some of those limbs seemed mighty big, I remember. But it was my job so I chopped and dragged.

Was cutting timber dangerous?

You've never cut timber, have you? Otherwise you'd know it was dangerous. Very dangerous. Could kill a man. Lots of trees we called widow-makers. I remember one time just a little tree fell the wrong way; it knocked old Cyrus down. Down flat right to the ground, broke his arm. But the master didn't give Cyrus anybody, even me, to help him go back to the cabins. Master told him to walk back himself. Master didn't want to lose any cutting time. And then he wouldn't call a doctor, except that the sister wrote a note and told my father to carry it to the doctor and it made him come. Master nearly had a fit about that.

Was he typical?

Eh?

Were other masters like that?

About all of them, yes. Only a choice one or two were different. Where all of us wished we worked was like a place that was up a narrow valley, way back up in the mountains, clearing for a new farm. My father worked up there for a time; he said it was the best place he ever worked. They went sunup to sundown, hard, but nobody worked harder than the master. That makes all the difference, don't you know. Besides, the master up there took care of them, fed them good. And no whip neither. They built a nice little farm up there. My father liked to go up there to work or just visit. He sure liked to visit up there, good friends there.

What was the owner's name?

Hollis, it was.

I thought you said your master was named Hollis.

Maybe you're not listening so good. There were two Hollis masters. They were brothers—half-brothers. My father always said, that half made all the difference. There was Hollis Junior, my master. And there was Hollis, his half-brother, who opened this farm way up there in the mountains. He was a good man. But Hollis Junior, my master, that man was the devil. He corrupted my sister Mabel.

How did he corrupt her?

Every time his missus was away, and sometimes even when she was home, Hollis Junior was on to one Negro girl or another, making them satisfy him. When he gave Mabel a big belly, that's when he quick sold her off and I never saw her ever again. I looked for her, looked all over, but never could find her. Terrible. Jesus must have tears in his eyes for her. Like I did.

Sometimes he told a Negro girl, Joe here or Jim there, he's your husband now, and they had to sleep together, and if she said no, he gave her a beating til she did. That's how I'm here, from what Hollis Junior told my mother and father.

I think master was part of what made his missus so hateful to our womenfolk. She knew he was after Negro girls. But she would have hated Negro girls even without him. Otherwise why would she buy and sell them? I think the only one on the place master didn't mess with was the cook. She was one powerful woman.

Big and strong?

No I didn't say big and strong. Why do you think I said big and strong, when I didn't say that at all? Fact is she was kind of skinny, not much flesh on her. I said she was powerful. From New Orleans. Very light. Very light. She could speak that language they have down there. If she used those words to put a hex, people said no matter what you did, that hex stuck until somebody used the same words to lift it. And nobody else around there knew that language. So you were stuck. Besides, I expect master saw that being cook, she could poison him easy. No one would know if she put poison in with all the spices and things she used in the special dishes she cooked. She could poison him easy. And she would have, too. She had fire, that Negro, fire, yessir.

Did you or other slaves offer any resistance, object to your treatment?

Of course we objected. What would you expect? We objected. Like if they work you too hard, you go out into the field to hoe, and maybe you can't see so good what is crop and what is weed. Or maybe you can see, but your hoe keeps slipping. And if the missus calls, you don't rush up right now like it's some party. If things get too bad, you can run away, at least for a while. Of course you get a beating when they track you with the dogs. Or if you come back on your own because you get too cold. But at least you have a spell away from them to put your mind at ease. Things like that.

One time the cook got angry at Hollis Junior, I forget what about, and called him a bunch of bad names, some of them in New Orleans language. He grabbed her, told her to pull up her dress because he was going to beat her raw. But she kicked him where it hurt him bad, so he had to let go. She ran into the big house, straight to the big, fancy cabinet where the missus kept all the special dishes and things. She pulled and pulled and tipped that cabinet down to the floor. Crash. Things that didn't mash up she picked those dishes up and threw against the wall.

What was her punishment?

I told you, she was one powerful woman. I expect she must have put a hex on that man, and it was too powerful for him. When the missus came home he just told her some lie.

Where were you when the war ended?

On that same farm. Hollis called us up to the big house and told us the war was over and that made us free. I knew that already. I just wanted to hear him have to say it. He told us we could work for wages now, but we would have to pay rent for where we lived. Pay money for shacks with holes everywhere! I was so sick of the place, I left for Georgia. That was where my mother got sold to. I never did find her, so I went back to live some places in Tennessee, but not anywhere close to Ginners Ford, except the times I went back to see my father. That's how I heard the old devil died one day right while he was corrupting another maid. I don't know that for a fact, because I didn't see his dead body, but if it was true, he deserved it. I said, I hope master and missus both burn hot in hell. I still think that. Jesus says to love your enemy, but those people weren't my enemy. They were the devil, and that's the truth.

You went back to see your father. Did you miss him?

Of course I did. He was a wise man, just like in the Bible, a very wise man. Everybody came to him for advice, Negroes—even some white people. He and the master's deaf and dumb sister were close, very close. They could talk to each other with their hands, no sounds.

A sign language?

No, they didn't hold up signs. They knew that some move with a hand or even just a finger meant something. So she could tell him where she wanted to go, and he understood with no one saying any words with their mouths. Maybe he made up the hand talk, I don't know. I wasn't alive yet so there's no reason for me to know. All I know is that when she wanted to go somewhere fast, she'd talk to him with her hands, and he'd know to pick her up and carry her, except when the master was around, because Hollis Junior, he'd throw a fit.

For what reason?

Because of a Negro man touching a white lady, of course. So when my father visited her, I know he did what he could do: he could move quiet as a shadow. You'd be sitting all alone, and then he was right beside you. Happened to me lots of times. He visited in her room for years, and nobody knew. I think she was good to him, and my father was good to her—if you catch my meaning. She died only about a week after he did, which tells a lot, except to a body that doesn't want to hear it.

Is there anything else you want to say about your time in slavery?

Yes. Some old Negroes look back and say, Well, at least back in those days we always had food and a roof over our heads. I don't ever say that. The best day of my life was the day I walked away from that farm. A free man. The only way I would go back is dead.

And another thing I want to say: I'm old now and don't sleep good always. Sometimes I wake up in the night and think back on where I've been, and I ponder why God put some white people on this earth, to do so much evil to us Negroes. Maybe, I think, He made a mistake. But God can't make a mistake. He's God. So I think that He put white people here, most of them, just the way we have thorns and thistles—to mess up the crops.

That's all I want to say. Now you be sure to get down right everything Young Solomon Haller told you, because it's the truth.

Dorinda Hollis Henderson to Crotia Hollis Warden

Collection of Lewis Hollis Warden

Nov. 20, 1938

Dear Sister,

Went over to Tulips today, as usual. HL seemed a little better. Most recently, he says, he's been writing up how the old timers used to grow and process sorghum. But what he asked me to read is about Audie Ann.

I sat right down and read it. He dodges some — you would have featured more of Audie's downright bawdy humor. You won't catch HL retelling Audie's favorite jokes, like the one about the difference between farm whores and city whores. Did she relish those jokes all the more because they were off, or did her deafness mean she didn't get some social nuances? I was never sure, to tell you the truth. (Too busy laughing, I guess.)

Another thing HL doesn't mention is Audie's colorblindness. I mean about people. Was that related to her deafness, too, or was it because she took the New Test. seriously? Anyhow, aside from that, you'd recognize HL's Audie Ann. He even included Bill's punishment, which I had completely forgotten, to tell the truth.

You'll be relieved he doesn't say a word about when you were so moonstruck over that smooth Tom Faricy, and Audie got you back in the house through the upstairs window. Maybe he never knew. I certainly wasn't going to risk asking him. I'll bet he could never have even dreamed one of <u>his</u> sisters could be <u>that</u> dumb. Crotia, you have to admit, it was pretty dumb. Audie Ann leaning too far out the window, barely holding on to the top of that ladder, telling you it was perfectly safe. Well, you lived to tell the tale in one of your columns. I admit, you got wiser. About Tom, anyhow. You hear he's in jail again?

I shouldn't pretend superiority over HL. After all, back then neither you nor I were smart enough to wonder how Audie Ann of all people knew those little details. The Tulips wall most screened from sight has only one window upstairs big enough for someone to scramble in and out. There were two ladders at the far end of the orchard. And one, but not the other, was tall enough (barely) to reach that window. You and I just took for granted Audie knew that. How dumb could we be?

HL worries you are holding back some family tidbits he should be putting on paper. I guess it's easy to get paranoid when you're trapped in your bedroom every day. I don't know which is worse — linger on like HL, with no strength to do much except think back and write about it, or get taken suddenly, like my Mike, out in the fields he loved so. Both are so bad I'll stop here. I shouldn't fix on it or I'll start crying.

Received a newsy letter from our big-city littlest brother, Lowe. He's breathing easier now. His new store is "doing good" — well, too, I assume, to be schoolmarm-ish. His hours sounded awfully long. I wouldn't be happy with <u>my</u> husband gone that much, but he says Elizabeth is very content in Memphis, making many friends, etc. Meaning — I can read between lines — his darling nose-in-the-air wife got where she wants to be, at the other end of the state, as far from Hollis territory as she can still be in Tenn.

What do you expect of a city woman? Lowe's choice. I'm only sorry their children grow up thinking the rest of the Hollis family are mountain rubes. Now I know, when Elizabeth asked where the name Lowe comes from, of course Bill shouldn't have announced that Audie Ann always said it came from the height of the chair where he was conceived. But another of course, Elizabeth could have at least smiled, instead of being such a prune face about it. You know for sure their daughters will never enjoy that story because they'll never hear it.

Have you seen Lowe's new store stationery? When you do, you'll get a good chuckle. I think I won't tell HL. Our youngest brother is not Lowe anymore; he's L. J. Hollis! Hah. So much for a special chair.

Caroline says she's ashamed — not staying in touch with everyone about HL. Believe me she is running ragged all day long. I had the shock, but at least Mike didn't suffer. I only wish I had a chance to tell him goodbye before I can join him again. Caroline will be able to say goodbye, but she has the care — day after day after day. I told her not to worry. I'll try to write to family. So I'd better stop here for other letters.

Your loving sister,

Dory

Plowing with Greek, My Life
HL Hollis

I regret that I never conversed in person with my grandfather, Samuel B Hollis, for he could have told me much that would be informative as I write on other pages about farming during the early opening of this valley. His papers testify that family ever occupied his mind. He apparently preserved every scintilla of information that came his way about earlier generations. His sense of loss in his diary during the few years that five sons expired of careless accidents and unfortunate incidents is painful to read. He mourns his wayward Absaloms, forfeiting their (and his) glorious Hollis future. When he itemized reasons for marrying Sarah Prescott, his young third wife, he included the prime consideration "Be fruitful and multiply."

I recall hearing that people routinely offered Grandfather magnificent sums for land parcels he acquired early on, especially in the fertile valley where Tulips is located. Despite his chronic shortage of capital, Samuel B summarily rejected offers, though his total acreage seemed wildly in excess of what he could ever bring to plow. "Can't sell it," he confided to his diary. "My grandchildren or their children will need that piece." In this he prophesied with absolute accuracy.

Though he did not live to observe all his wilderness acres in farms, Samuel B surely died confident of the Hollis future, for he must have anticipated, reasonably so, that Sam and Henry, my father, would produce multiple heirs to occupy the Hollis holdings. At least in my father's case, things eventuated as Samuel B anticipated. His only miscalculation was not acquiring still more land when it sold cheap.

I confess that I would like to hear him explain why he arranged Tulips' rooms as he did. I would have to inform him the structure is far from convenient as a residence. My children occupy houses nearby (and some faraway) much more comfortable. Yet, I confess that when I'm in my children's houses, as hospitable, up to date, and convenient to live in as they are, I feel I've entered a hospital, everything sanitized and scrubbed clean of associations and connections with the past. Not so at Tulips.

Out in the building which once housed Tulips' kitchen (when the cook still suffered at a hearth), stands a monumental work table, its top an astonishing single board, the widest I have ever seen, sawn from a prodigious tree when giants walked this land. If I put my nose close to that table I smell the faint trace of spices. I am unable confidently to identify those spices, but no wood species is naturally redolent with such exotic scents. I wish I could put to that wood some earpiece, one of Bill's stethoscopes hugely amplified, to hear what that table once heard: the cook's conversation with her helpers and friends as they trade opinions, gossip, confidences, and complaints about the people out back, and, I'm equally certain, about those in the big house.

QUACHASEE
WHC

At the massive kitchen house table, Carrie helped roll out pie dough. "Mama, how can stepbrothers be so different? Marse Sam is . . ." She paused as Lilly nodded warningly toward the open door. "Marse Henry seems like he's from a different family. Don't you think so?"

"What's the difference?"

"Sam never visits Audie Ann. Henry's always there. He's so loving and patient, laughing at himself when he gets his hand talk mixed up and says what he didn't mean." She took another dough ball to roll out. "Every time she asks him to go pistol shooting with her out back he goes, even when she always beats him. He's a much worse shot than I am. He's so interested in her opinion about what they've read. He even talks to me almost the same as he talks to her."

"Carrie, you're minding Henry, not that crust." Lilly's voice became sterner. "What's this 'a much worse shot than I am'? You never told me that Miss Audie Ann let you shoot. Back in that closed-in place Mister Samuel told Jim to fix for her?"

Carrie stammered, "Well, maybe I forgot to tell you." She trailed off. "Mama, Audie Ann wanted me to learn. So I could be some competition. She makes me be very careful."

Lilly hesitated. "I guess knowing a pistol might be needful sometime. But, daughter, you keep that knowing real close to yourself, mind? Real close."

Carrie nodded at the obvious and tried to turn the topic. "Henry says please and thank you, I mean, to me. And talks with me about all kinds of things. He treats me almost like his sister."

Lilly moved quickly to the door and swung it closed with a crash. "Caroline LaCroix, are you gone blind? 'Treats me like his sister.' He'll *never* treat you like a sister. Because he's white and your great-grandmother wasn't quite white. So he's a marse—and you're property. Oh, he's a please-and-thank-you marse. But he's still a marse. He doesn't need to carry a whip or a stick to be a marse. Don't you ever forget that—always a marse—all the more when you're feeling like he's treating you good. Never forget that."

Lilly seemed to finish, but then continued with a further point. "The difference between Sam and Henry? There's *no* difference between Sam and Henry. Neither one has trouble buying and selling human beings like stock whenever it suits 'em. No matter those people crying and begging to stay with their families."

Lilly's tone softened slightly as she saw its effect on her daughter. "I admit Henry is a gentleman," she conceded. "If you have to have men around, a gentleman is a big improvement over the usual run in these mountains."

Carrie could manage only a subdued "You think all men are bad?"

"No, men are God's creatures too, but sometimes I'm not sure how. Remember, the gentleman has fine boots, but inside are *always* clay feet." After a pause she added, "Like the rest of us sinners, I guess," as she glanced at Carrie's work. "Put more flour on the rolling pin, child, or that crust won't ever come off."

Carrie bit her lip. Fitting crusts into the tins, she spoke slowly. "You don't . . . think . . . I'll do a good job . . . cooking for Henry, Marse Henry up the mountain, . . . do you?"

"All you need is experience, child. You'll get plenty of that up there."

"Ever since they told me I'm going up the Quachasee, you haven't seemed very happy with me."

Wiping spilled flour from the table top, Lilly shook her head. "I'm a poor mother."

Carrie squeezed her with as close a hug as dough-sticky fingers allowed. "Mama, you're the best mother I—"

"I know," Lilly added dryly. "The best one you ever had. But not good enough. I worry so much about you up there that I spoil our days together down here."

"Mama, I'll be all right. I'll take my little book of things you told me about cooking."

"It's not the cooking. I'm talking about being up there with no older woman to warn you."

"About what?"

"About forgetting you're the only woman up there with a whole crew of men, about forgetting that a marse is a marse."

"Mama, you worry too much. Remember, you've been teaching me all these years about handling men."

"And a poor pupil you've been."

"No, Mama, no. I studied hard. Studied on how you sewed up Pruitt's man, that Monroe."

Lilly eyed her daughter sharply. "That's years ago. What do you remember about Roe?"

"A lot." Carrie launched one of her teases. "A whole lot. You know," she leaned close to confide, "you sat on the kitchen stoop with the bedroom window in the loft right above you, and wide open."

Lilly wore an arch look that almost concealed her smile. "How could I forget that window, when I knew you were about to fall out of it right on top of us, trying to hear?"

Both began laughing at memory of the time soon after they first arrived at Tulips. Monroe, neighbor Pruitt's personal servant, sent from Chestnut Hill first on an errand, returned with flimsy excuses, then continued to moon about Tulips' kitchen, increasingly bothersome.

Lilly dallied with him on the stoop, shrewdly taking his measure. Monroe, she decided, was no equal to Sam Jr., so dangerous a threat she had rubbed on his privates the hottest Scotch Bonnet pepper sold by Moishe the itinerant Nashville peddler. Relieved by her conclusion, she offered Monroe her rarest favor, a private reading of his individual fortune. A gift so special demanded unusual requirements: Marse Pruitt's biggest rooster freshly sacrificed, a full moon bright, a mirror uncracked, a holly stick forked.

A huge moon dazzling white, fresh-wiped mirror, night dead calm. They counted the strikes of the great clock clearly audible from inside the big house. As its midnight stroke died away, Roe hunched on the stoop beside Lilly, a breathless Carrie leaning dangerously far out of the window above. She nearly fell from choking back giggles when she recognized Lilly's hoarse-whispered, *Guégué Solingaie, balliez chimlà, m'a dis li, oui, m'a dis li* . . . Words of the Creole tune Lilly taught her to charm Marse Philip back in Nashville, but now in a monotone.

Monroe's eyes widened at the mysterious spirit-summons. Lilly pushed the dripping entrails into the moon's mirrored light, her voice a droning incantation. *Ah, Suzette, chère, to pas l'aimain moin, chère, Ah Suzette, z'aime, to pas l'aimain moin.* At the window above, Carrie wanted to add melody and hum along. *M'allais in montagne, z'amie.* Roe was trembling when, with reluctance, with a barely-stifled gasp of sympathy, Lilly turned to him with a fate so dire she could only whisper it. The signs allowed no mistake, at least to someone with her gift to read them. But maybe his strength could not bear what no other living creature than she could tell him.

Whud id say, Lilly? Whud id say?

Lilly shuddered. In a year or two or three, Marse Pruitt would bring to Chestnut Hill a maid for his wife. The girl would work inside so Roe would see her every day. Lilly shuddered again. The new maid would be young. She would be beautiful. Yes, and she would cook dishes to make any man's mouth water. In commiseration, Lilly locked eyes with Roe.

Eatin good. Whud de matter wid dat?

Lilly shook her head slowly, ominously, looked down for more sign in the mirror's eerie light, and in pain answered with a groan. She gonna hate . . . Monroe . . . yes, it's our Roe she'll hate, and she'll hate him so much she'll . . . Lilly's voice was barely a whisper . . . she'll poison Monroe.

Pie-son Monroe, repeated Roe mechanically in petrified dread.

Lilly nodded, horror on her face.

Pie-son 'im da-id?

M'allais fait l'argent plein, Pou porte donne toi. . . . Mumbling her chant, Lilly hunched back over her black art, adjusting the mirror yet again, poking persistently with the forked holly stick through the bloody organs in front of her. There is only one way to escape . . . She peered again, then shook her head with regretful rejection. No, never, that would be too . . .

Whut 'scape? urged Roe.

Lilly shook her head despairingly without lifting her eyes.

Whud id be, Lilly? Yuh ken tells me. Roe doan wan no pie-son da-id.

Your sole alternative . . . an interminable pause while Lilly scraped blood together . . . de onliest 'scape is, Roe doan touch no woman, an' foah a *hull* yeah.

No womans, a yeah, echoed Roe.

Yet again Lilly plied her holly stick and tilted the mirror for the best reflected light. "And, Roe, if you want her to be your friend . . ."

'Course I wans dat, Lilly, 'specially iffen she booful . . . an a cook?

Lilly nodded sternly. If you want her to let you into her bed, Roe, you must prepare now.

Yuh tells Roe how, Lilly, and Roe, he do id.

Lilly leaned down and squinted for the most focused view. A final decisive poke with the stick before she raised it to snap dramatically in two, inches from the man's bulging eyes. Now listen, Roe. In the evening—yes, *every* evening—you wash your privates in a mare's water. It has to be fresh horse piss, remember that. Warm. Fresh. You can't skip a single day. And Roe . . . you need to know this . . .

Roe looked at her expectantly.

If you ever tell someone about this horse piss, it won't work for you—but it will work for him.

Dat easy, exalted Roe, his reach to hug Lilly in thanks barely forestalled by her warning finger. Oh I fo'git, he recoiled as if stung. I doan touch no womans de hull ye-ah. I sho dank yuh, Lilly. Yuh mah bes fren. Doan skip no dey. Fresh keched. Doan say noddin.

"And remember, Mama, how tough that rooster was when you roasted it." With the antics she learned years ago might cheer her mother's recurrent melancholy, Carrie lifted the biggest empty pot and began chanting into it for the muffled echoes. "That's what he say: 'Doan skip no dey, no ma'am.'" She seized a wooden spoon and beat out the syllables on the flour-dusted worktable. "Say, doan skip no dey, no ma'am. Say, doan skip no dey, no ma'am." She laughed so hard she made her mother's smile broaden.

"I was watching you," Carrie confided, "and you had to stop so often because you were about to burst out laughing and spoil the whole show." She countered her mother's feeble denial. "No, I know because I was watching."

"And, Mama, don't forget what Sally told you later." Carrie moved away from the table to puff herself up, imitation of Sally's bulk. "Marse Pruitt," a behind-the-door whisper, "he gag so at Roe's stink dat he make Roe take a bad." Louder. "But de nex dey Roe stink moh. So 'nother bad." Continuing crescendo. "But moh stink. Moh gag. Till Marse Pruitt say," a strangled shout, "HE CAN' STAN DE STINK NO

MOH." An evil smirk and growl. "Send Roe 'n his stink off t'some cuz o'er neah Knoxville."

Carrie raised the spoon high to lead a chorus. "And don't forget neither what Buck told all the men folk: 'Dat woman, she ken hex a man near daid. She one pow'ful woman.'" Carrie pointed at her mother triumphantly. "And, Mama, dat woman be you. Dat-woman-be-you-dat-woman-be-you." The spoon invited Lilly to join the choir.

"Hush your noise, girl," Lilly tut-tutted, but how could she be stern? At last, she quieted Carrie's hilarity. "I wouldn't worry if I thought a simpleton like Monroe will be your worst problem."

"What could happen, Mama? If I take sick or hurt myself, Marse Henry will send for you or Aunt Sally right away. I know he would. He's not Sam."

Lilly shook her head, affirming, Carrie thought, her comparison of the stepbrothers. Carrie looked forward with high anticipation to the Quachasee. She had never traveled more than a mile or two from Tulips since the day she and Lilly jumped down off Marse Samuel's wagon from the hated Dinkins hideaway. Before that, she remembered a man who always indulged her when she sang *Si l'amour vous si fort, faut plein d'argent dans poche*. Lilly said he was her father, though she must never call him that. Marse Philip. Philip Henkel, a name she saw occasionally in Audie Ann's newspapers reporting on intrigue at the state capitol. By books and Henry's letters, she journeyed far, but she wanted more than imaginary journeys. She longed for real travel, and with as congenial a companion as she had seen in Henry's letters to Audrey.

A low noise awakened Carrie. In the faint early dawn light, Lilly was kneeling by her bed. Carrie slipped over to put her arm around her mother's shoulder.

"Mama, I'm not going a thousand miles away."

"Your body isn't. But your mind is. And I can't be there to help you." She hugged her daughter. "Oh Carrie," she whispered, "look out for yourself."

"Carrie, I knows yuh nebbah fo'gits ole Aunt Sally." Sitting on the doorsill of her tiny cabin in the twilight, Sally saw Carrie approaching.

"'Course I wouldn't forget you, Sally."

"Cum t'say goodby foah de tiam?"

Carrie nodded.

"Yuh goin up de valley?"

"Right soon, I guess."

Sally rose to wrap her in a hug. "Gal, yuh taller den me now." She pointed inside. "An I 'membahs yuh jes wah a teen-ee slip o'a chile; yuh cum an sid quiet as a lil' mouse in de conah, lissen t'de wemans talkin. Yuh 'membahs?"

Carrie nodded. She used to sit in the darkest corner, forgotten, while, in the flickering light of a few fireplace coals, Sally held surreptitious court for aunties from the area, each ready for a white man's interrogation, prepared with some story of nocturnal emergency summons to nurse at an accident, a deathbed. Carrie listened as talk drifted from a mistress's secrets to heart's laments to darker matters. *Fust yuh needs de leg bone ob a black cat—black, onlyist black, wid no odder colah. An yuh biles some of dat dere root fum de conjerman ta mush. And den whut yuh does is . . .*

Sally shook her head. "Yuh doan cum too offen 'cuz I tink Lilly doan lahk yuh heah."

Carrie smiled to avoid confirming Sally's suspicion.

When she returned, sometimes terrified, from listening to the aunties in Sally's cabin, running wildly to the kitchen house in the dark, blindly, heedless of obstacles, her questions always set Lilly off: Sally is my one true friend here, but that cabin is a sink of ignorance. All that talk of spirits, child, just talk. Talk that can't stand light of day or of the Gospels, either one.

And where did you learn those manners? You know better than to eat out of the skillet like that. Caroline, no. Animals eat standing up. Humans eat sitting down. A dining chair is a mark of civilization. So bring yourself a chair and sit in it, with your back straight as a board. Caroline LaCroix, you set a place at the table with a dish and a fork and a knife. *And* a napkin, child, *and* a napkin. That's what people with proper manners always do. And get your elbow off that table, child. Sit up straight, not hunched over your food like some poor mountain trash. Remember, posture in a dining chair is a mark of better people. Daughter, we may eat in the kitchen, but that doesn't mean our table manners aren't fit for any dining room all the way to New Orleans.

Once set off so, Lilly was hard to stop. And another thing, child, what has happened to your tongue? You know perfectly well how to make a T-H sound. When I was your age in Miz Angela's New Orleans school she kept a hard paddle to use if we forgot our T-H. I can make myself a paddle just like it, I assure you. I've taught you correct English and that's what I want to hear. Not, dass wad Ah wons t'heah. What's the word from the Bible story? Say it, child.

Shibboleth, Mama, Shibbo*leth*. But Mama, when I talk like this out back, they don't like it.

Das alrigh, das alrigh. Law, chile, we jes gonna talk lahk dahkies does, ain't us?

Ma-ma.

Whut yuh 'jectin' to, chile? Whooee, lookit wid yuh eye on dis messa bean. How us gonna get dem fix in tiam foah dinna? Ken yuh tells I dat? Hul lotta wok.

Ma-ma.

Yuh git back to yuh wok on dem bean afoah I wallop yuh good.

MA-MA

Whut de mahda? Yuh ken unnerstan jes fine. Why yuh nebbah lahk I speakin so? Yuh stuck up'r sompin? Why yuh doan lahk mah speakin?

Because it's not *you*, Mama.

And it's not *you* either, Caroline LaCroix. Remember who you are.

"Now Carrie, honey, up dere on Marse 'Enry's new place," Sally could not part without admonitions, "yuh make sho Solomon an' Jake gets 'nuff t'ate. I doan wanna see 'em back heah lookin ghosty."

Carrie's smile was for an overly-cautious senior.

"Id ain't gonna be easy up dere," Sally warned.

Carrie smiled again, confident.

"Yuh sho has growed up, Carrie." Sally viewed her closely, sighed, her face grave. "Be kerful, honey. An' Carrie, 'membahs who yuh is."

Plowing with Greek, My Life

HL Hollis

A distant tractor's chugging—John Burke's, to guess from the extra, intermittent growl—is audible reminder, confined as I lately am, of how closely observant of sounds I have become. Someone driving up, car door slammed shut, house door opened and closed, conversation downstairs, footfalls on the stairs—I follow intently a visitor's progression to my bedroom.

My own aural attention makes me ponder other generations. Youngsters' addiction to inharmonious bleating on radio and victrola makes me grumpy, so I prefer contemplating those who came before me. My father, Henry, and my grandfather, too, counted the hall clock's marking hours; they instantly recognized Aunt Audie Ann's thump-and-scrape gait; they identified buggies and wagons by size of the team and wheel squeaks. I wish I knew what else was familiar to their ears.

My little grandson's cherub voice downstairs is more evidence that sounds at Tulips have been cyclical as certain as the seasons, though on an even more cosmic scale. Tulips, now muted, resounded with cries and laughter when my children grew up here. Before them, somnolence in the house. Tumult preceded that lull, the chaos when my eight siblings and I grew up here. Then, before we arrived, tranquility.

Prior to that calm, boisterous clamor when Father's stepbrothers all resided at Tulips—Matthew, Luke, John, Mark, Jacob and Sam Jr. (What angelic blundering at the font, grumbles my sacrilegious brother Bill. Surely God intended the last two boys baptized Acts and Epistles.)

A hell-raising fraternity, those six brothers. Notoriously pugnacious, they'd fight a circle saw, as the saying goes, and if no saw was available, they'd fight each other, just for the practice and the joy of it.

They once, the rest of the family absent, staged an impromptu shooting contest at Tulips, involving firing <u>through</u> the house (by opening front and back doors of the center hall), ricocheting off an old plowshare to strike a target out of sight on the kitchen building wall. An all-clear signal. The shot. It ricocheted off the plowshare. But not off Matthew's chest. He good as gone—though Death waited out eleven days of delirium. Luke, who fired the shot, brooded for a year, then concluded a week-long binge with a pistol in his mouth. Who gave the all-clear signal? Their cousin Caleb, though he never brooded over it, much less brought a pistol to his head.

Luke lay buried but a few years before the notorious incident at Krugel's Gap, that sheer cleft clear through Blackstone Ridge on the other side of the mountains. A fine horseman from Asheville famously jumped the gap with room to spare, pocketing a thousand-dollar purse and fantastic offers for his mount. His feat still animated admiring talk when Mark and Jacob happened by, culminating an epic fortnight of cross-country carousing. Tennessee honor required they demonstrate the North Carolina rider no prodigy, though they rode horses of livery barn bloodlines and spavined besides. Mark tried the jump first, but his plug balked right at the edge, nearly throwing him over its head into the gap, and considerably discomforting his manhood on the saddle horn. When Mark trotted back, in pain, well ready to abandon glory, Jacob shouted encouragement, "Here, I'll lead. Spur hard and follow close. That damn nag will come along."

Mark did. The damn nag did. And both brothers ended their jump on the rocks at the gap's bottom, near eighty feet below.

Who put those boys up to it? Their cousin Caleb, while providing a large jug and a small harem. Those loose women teased the brothers lewdly about their masculinity when they hesitated over Caleb's dare. Witnesses swore Caleb sounded stone sober, rode close behind the brothers to encourage them—until he reined in sharp at the gap. The whole story came out at the inquest, or as much as could come out, given women witnesses long fled. Anyway, in these mountains, how could you haul a man to court for proposing an equestrian contest, even a damn fool one? After all, Caleb was kin, dutifully sorrowing among the mourners at his cousins' wake and funeral.

"John died whoring," said Father, but not a word more. Mystery mercifully clouds a distasteful matter. Whether death was due to a social disease or, as Bill guesses, some aneurysm, remains a question. (Another question is whether Caleb enticed him to the temptation.) By John's death, seven male heirs had shrunk to just two, Sam Jr. and Henry.

After fraternal commotion at Tulips and city racket in New York, Father most likely found the solitary silence of the Quachasee farm a great relief, at least initially. There isn't—wasn't—much up there to hear, other than wind and birds.

In similar situations some men single in the mountains compensated by lengthy conversations with their animals or with themselves. During my boyhood Walt Ham reported his chats with Ruther in such detail at the Mercantile I looked outside to assure myself of Ruther's mulehood. Bailer Benjamin did not converse with his (four-footed) Florence that I knew, but he always threw a retort when Mercantile porch regulars ribbed him for talking excessively to himself. "Heap sight better'n yourn jabberin. Better'n some damn woman's too. Flo ain't offish. Talks when I wants a body to liven me some, an' lissens kerful when I talks, an' shuts up ifen thars nuttin t'say." Good company indeed, but Father never to my knowledge conducted conversations with his stock or with himself.

Lowe in Memphis sends a kind, brotherly letter, lamenting he cannot provide some miraculous drug from the new pharmacy he just opened. His proud description of a mirrored soda counter, gleaming with chromed fixtures marching along one wall dazzles me. In lieu of miraculous drug I covet some multi-hued, towering, fudge-capped confection topped by one delicious maraschino cherry. Or even two.

QUACHASEE
WHC

Audie Ann sat at her father's bedside, watching, and occasionally reading to escape worry and tedium. Henry often joined her, benefitting from refresher lessons in her hand talk. At intervals he made rapid trips up the Quachasee to check on his crew. Sarah relapsed into her customary lethargy. Sam, become comfortable in enforced idleness, loitered near enough the barn to disappear the moment he spotted the buggies of the pastor or the doctor. Elvira assured storeroom and smokehouse were secured against thieving servants. Her unease at the inexplicably rapid reduction in reserves of Ahler's Tonic was more than offset by her relief at no longer having to conceal her pipe.

Henry returned from a quick visit to his emerging farm with a new worry. The crew there had progressed so that his daily presence was required for timely decisions. He must go up and stay until summoned by the women about some change in his father's condition. The triumvirate of Sarah, Elvira, and Audie, however, was formidable, insisting he take up a cook. He had so many more important things to keep straight. If he was lucky they had forgotten their earlier concern, or discounted it in view of his voracious appetite at the Tulips table. If he wasn't lucky, he knew he had a problem, for he was reluctant to force a family battle while his father lay sick.

After Berkemeier's visit and prayers, Audie and Carrie saw him out. Sarah drifted off. Henry grasped his chance with more even odds. Catching Elvira in the hall before she went down to check the kitchen house, he announced his decision. The crew needed him as soon as possible to maintain momentum.

"Guess I'll go this afternoon," he said, mostly to emphasize the urgency, as they started down the steep back steps.

Elvira waited until the first landing to shake her head. At the next landing, "Sundown'll catch ye on thet trace wit' them dropoffs." At the bottom, "Carrie ain't ready. Better a soon start tamarrah. Supplies is all put aside. More then two ken carry. Ye needin a mule."

"But," Henry called after her as she headed for the back door, "what would Audie do without Carrie?"

Elvira did not pause at the door. "She ken do jes fine. Already talk w'poor Audie—hed Carrie doin the hands an fingers. She sez Carrie orter go an take care'a y'all. She worried 'bout ye, same as me—an Mother." She pulled the door shut behind her.

"Henry, she is exactly right." He turned to see Sarah coming down after them, cautiously testing each tread. She finally reached the bottom. "I cannot understand why Samuel did not build better stairs. But I agree with what Elvira said. You must take Carrie up with you."

Discouraged at these setbacks, Henry still hoped for a different story when he checked with Audie Ann. But he found that if anything Elvira underplayed Audie Ann's concern—for Carrie. "Promise, take good care of her," Audie Ann wrote on her slate to avoid misunderstanding. He replied by a tap on "promise" and a finger on his chest. Inelegant, but unambiguous.

He stepped outside to clear his head. Three out of three allowed no maneuvering room. To keep the peace he would take Carrie up with him. Defeated, Henry did not sulk, for his capitulation included an unstated proviso: bring Carrie back in a week or two.

Low clouds were pearly, but the highest clouds showed a faint rose. Doves had just begun tentative cooing. A rooster's first crowing turned to a squawk as Henry stepped out Tulips' back door for a soon start. Eager for return to work, he expected to chafe at the women's tardiness. Instead Carrie was already leading Elton from the barn. Audie Ann checked a list against the parcels and bags Lilly carried from the kitchen house. Carrie intuitively grasped the logic of mule-packing. Hugs, kisses, waves. They set off before sunrise.

Carrie, tired of trailing Elton, strode sturdily ahead, despite a heavy bag over her shoulder. Henry caught up with her when she stopped to survey the valley below. "I've never looked down before, Marse. Only up."

At one bare promontory, he halted to give Elton a breather. "The cliff edge you're standing way too close to is Snake Sheer. So we're halfway."

"Half?" She stretched to peer over the vertiginous edge, retreated a scant inch. "However did you find this, Marse Henry? Some places the valley's so narrow you near rub both your shoulders."

"Was up here a lot as a boy. I wasn't the first, though. Obediah Oppdyke—easy to remember with those initials—Grandmother's distant kin, brought family and started a farm up at the top years ago. Cleared some. Built a cabin, sheds. Lightning burned the cabin, and the typhoid took 'em. Obediah lost five children. He gave up on Tennessee. Sold cheap to my father and cleared out. For Missourah, I think." He hurled a small rock out over the edge. When they did not hear it land, he turned. "Time to move. Come up, Elton."

The primitive trace ascending the close valley faded at some places into stretches barely allowing even a pack mule. At the worst, they had to unload, push and pull the unhappy Elton up a steep way, scramble the load up bag by parcel, then reload the pack. Carrie worked without pause, hauling her share. When they again stood with a secured pack, she stroked the mule, marveling, "Have to do all this for every load."

"Until we get time to fix this part."

"Lot of work either way."

"Yup."

As they stepped out of the trees into the great bowl at the top of the valley, they stopped. Henry looked for his crew. Carrie slowly turned a complete revolution. "I see now why you're here, Marse Henry," she breathed, so softly he almost missed it.

Approaching the higgledy-piggledy scattering of dilapidated open-front sheds, Henry slapped his hat against a leg in frustration. "Damnation." He pointed to a jumbled pile of rotted boards. "That's where I figured you could sleep. Looks like the shed just collapsed since I was here last. Good thing you weren't in it." He rubbed his forehead slowly. "Alright, the new plan is Solomon and Jefferson sleep in the open tonight. Put your things in their shed, the low one there. I'll get 'em to start building some shelter for themselves . . . well, first chance we get."

"No. No, thank you, Marse Henry." From Aunt Sally, stationed at her favorite eavesdropping spot, Carrie had a nearly verbatim report of Sam's *Carrie ain't no lady*, and Henry's *Can't take time to build for her.*

"I'll just fix up something for myself." Looking at Henry's face she realized too late he was not Audie Ann at Tulips. "Marse Henry, if you treat me special at the start, the gang will always hold it against me." Still too undeferential, directive. Marse Sam would have taken angry offense. She held her breath in apprehension.

"Hadn't thought of that," he replied. "But Audie Ann won't approve if I put you in with Solomon and Jefferson."

She exhaled softly while scanning the sky. "Don't look like rain tonight. I'll be fine. Get some shelter together tomorrow."

Henry nodded, already moving off to check the crew's progress.

Solomon approached, a broken harness trailing from his arm. He hurriedly helped Carrie finish unloading Elton, then stood at a large stump, using its flat top as work table for harness repair.

"I'm here to cook, Solomon."

"We sho needin dat."

Carrie looked for a chimney. "Where's the fireplace?"

Solomon jabbed a thumb at a ring of blackened stones.

"What do you work on when you have food to fix?"

"Sum boarh's 'round sumwheahs."

"Water?"

"Ovah dere." He nodded toward an overgrown path meandering out of sight.

"When you eat?"

"'Bout dusk, Carrie. Marse 'Enry jes keep goin til nobody ken see no moh."

A distant voice bellowed something indistinguishable but urgent from the field.

"Carrie, dey callin. Ken' talk no moh now. Dey needs dis." He gathered up tools, harness, and hurried off.

Carrie watched him go, then surveyed the camp. "Hired crew's sheds there. Servant's shed there. Marse's, there. No other roof in this corner of God's creation. Fire here out in the open. Work-board somewhere. Water there. Caroline LaCroix, this might be harder than you thought."

The high western ridge forced early sunset, but twilight seemed endless. Well before the men straggled in, she coaxed a kettle to simmer with a savory smell, filled water buckets for washing up, and sorted new supplies.

Perhaps Henry called day-done early, for enough light still shone to distinguish faces. Henry took charge, rattling off LemDallmanJakeHilpertFranklinJeffersonSolomon too fast to follow. "This is Carrie, our *temporary* cook."

"Some cook," came a suppressed mutter. "Thank God we don' have t'ate nary none a Lem's damn stew." "Whur she stayin?" "Carrie, honey, how 'bout sleepin in my bed?" "Mine's better." "She-it, what better 'bout yourn? Men like you'uns too ole t'git hit up fer her." "Hit's not gitten hit up, hit's keepin hit up." "She kin hep a heap w'thet."

Carrie did not consciously think things through. She did not say to herself, if Henry is the gentleman Mama said he is, he is going to spit out warning to watch your tongue in front of a woman, but he'll be too annoyed to say it right, and then my goose is cooked with this gang. She knew it all instantly. She saw Henry frown and inhale to speak sharply.

She cut in half a beat ahead of him. "Oh, Aunt Sally tole me all 'bout yuh boys." She dropped into Sally's husky drawl, "Carrie, honey, dem boys up dere, dey woks mighty ha'd, but when dey cum in, wash out. Dey got de-lusion. An believe yuh me, de-lusion am *all* dey got."

"Delusion?" a skeptical voice from the shadows.

"Solomon, ain't dat whut Sally say?" Carrie called. "She say, 'If dey gibs yuh trubble, jes send 'em down t'Tulips, an Aunt Sally doses 'em par'ful wid lobelia.'"

"Yessem. 'Xactly whut she say." Solomon chuckled, delighted to hear Sally imitated so well. "Heered id wid mah own ear."

Amid laughter, Carrie took the lid off the kettle. "Who first plate?" A line formed. After a time a voice came out of the dusk. "This hyar eats the goodest." A long sigh from another voice: "Thet's a real bait." A third agreed. "Mighty fine an' I thankee muchly." Murmurs of assent followed. Carrie did not suggest they thank Lilly, who had urged her to prepare the first meal before she left Tulips. She heard no more about sharing beds. She did hear a brief argument closed with, "sen 'im to Aunt Sally fer thet thar lobelia."

The men snored long before she finished cleaning up, stacked more firewood close, consolidated water buckets, sorted things for breakfast.

She spread quilts over the small branches and pine needles she hastily pulled together in the afternoon, lay down fully dressed, fell asleep mid-yawn.

Stars still twinkled bright when Solomon tugged at her skirt hem. "Bes be stirrin, Carrie," he whispered. "Marse Henry lahkes t'be goin early."

That night she again dropped to her quilt long after sunset, and slept dressed. The third day the same, except in the afternoon she hurried to the spring pool for a quick sponge bath, a requirement Lilly enforced no less than a napkin, a civilizing chair, and the T-H sound. The fourth day almost the same, though her work seemed easier. Had she become more efficient? Less anxious? Had Henry given quiet orders about assistance? She knew only that she could catch her breath sometimes during the day.

Solomon built her a rough table, hardly the equivalent of the worn-smooth expanse in the Tulips kitchen, but at least a surface at waist height. Lem cut saplings and got her started on her own lean-to against one of the shacks, so she could pile up brush and bark slabs for a roof. Jefferson adzed out a short length of a thick trunk for a water trough. Dallman and Hilpert hauled buckets from the spring. Nightly she heard murmurs of appreciation for her cooking.

A midnight thunderstorm echoed mightily through the mountains; close lightning bolts revealed spooked teams and men braced against the gusts, trying to hold down loose gear. An hour's deluge soaked Carrie through. She shivered by the hissing, smoking fire until dawn. When the sun rose on a sparkling clean day, she did too. "Marse, I need some supplies from Tulips. I can be back before dark."

Henry shook his head. "Can't spare a mule from any team."

"Yes, Marse Henry." She expected as much. "But I can carry what I need, leave word about leftovers with Solomon in case I'm late."

Preoccupied with work assignments, Henry barely acknowledged her. "You won't get lost?"

"It's all downhill, Marse."

"Remember Snake Sheer."

At Tulips, Carrie went straight to the kitchen house. After a fierce hug, Lilly stepped back. "Well?"

"Mama, it's so-o-o hard." Carrie laughed ruefully. "I thought I knew cooking, but I never have time to sit down. How do you do it all these years?"

To Lilly's knowing smile, Carrie added, "I didn't see I'd miss you and Audie Ann so much. But it's good land up there, Mama, real good. It'll make a fine farm. And the mountains all around, you have it to yourself. I just feel different up there. I almost forget the way things are down here—and everywhere else. Some times I almost feel free. It's a little world. All by itself. Those ridges high around keep out . . . everything, I guess, except the birds. It's hard work, but I could stay up there, well, forever."

She fished for her list, put it on the table. "The only reason I came down now is I need so many things. But I don't know whether Sam and Elvira will part with them. Maybe. I see Elvira got you the bedroom curtains you've been asking for since we came here."

Without warning, as usual when checking up on servants, Elvira strode in. "Carrie," she scowled, "you're back."

"Yes, Miz Elvira, but just—" Carrie began brightly.

"Things are hard up there, Miz Elvira," Lilly interrupted dolefully, casually sliding a plate over the evidence of Carrie's literacy. "She needs so much, with all those men to feed. And every rain, Carrie gets soaked through. I'm afraid she'll get sick and have to come back here for nursing." Carrie felt Lilly's grip on her elbow, the old signal for the daughter to keep silent.

Elvira nodded. "Jes like menfolk. Sound like them men up thar, they don' take care'a theirselves—ner nobody else neither. Henry ain't thinkin. Wemen hefta take o'er. Don' wan'er ketchin 'er death'a cole so she cain't cook up thar. Carrie, go git poor Audie Ann. She don' have no new i-dee, but 'least she kin hep carry."

If the trace to Tulips wound all downhill, the return wound endlessly up. Carrie plodded wearily out of the dusk just as Lem lit a lantern to search for her. She eased down a heavy load, and turned to go back. "Left some a ways back."

"Stay hyar an ate; we'll fotch hit," said Lem. "We'd near give you out a'comin."

"I'd better go too; there's more than one carry back." She sounded drained.

"Jefferson an Zeke," ordered Lem, "go back fer hit."

"What happened?" Henry asked as Solomon handed Carrie a heaping dish. "Visiting too long with Audie?"

She shook her head. "No Marse, no time for that," she slurred around her spoon. "I started out with twice what I could carry. So I'd go a ways and set down, go back and bring up the other part, set down, and go ahead again. But the trace got steeper or maybe I got tireder. I had to break it into thirds. Takes still longer."

Zeke and Jefferson materialized, laden, out of the dark. No one said much. Solomon did cleanup. The next morning Carrie woke late, guilty that none of the crew had awakened her. Despite aches in every muscle she knew of, she hurried to get to work. By midmorning, when Marse Henry checked on her, she was struggling with rope, hatchet, saplings, and a large piece of canvas in the spot her lean-to had occupied.

"Where'd you get the cover?"

"At Tulips, Marse Henry, folded up in the barn."

"Sam gave it to you?" Henry's tone spoke his skepticism.

"Miz Elvira, Marse. She said, 'Sam sure as hell don' need hit,' so I should . . . borry hit."

"Just like she said you should borry them hams you brought up in the big tote?"

"Yessir. Audie—Miss Audie Ann, Marse—wanted me to bring a whole lot more, but it was too much to carry. Miz Elvira said she's worried we take down with sompin bad."

"Worried mostly because she doesn't want to nurse us?"

Carrie could not resist repeating Lilly's observation. "Marse Henry, the only things Miz Elvira nurses are her own complaints."

"Mmm. Why's she so ready to help?"

Carrie shook her head in bewilderment. "But Marse Henry, you milk any teat that fills the bucket, is what Aunt Sally says."

"Next time you go, take a mule to carry up a proper milking."

Henry sent Hilpert to help Carrie and by nightfall she boasted a well-anchored, neat tent. Small it was, but dry and private, with a place for a tiny mirror and a board up at the back with pegs for clothes. She felt settled in. At last she had secure shelter.

She also had friends. As the men waited to be served one evening, Lem perched on a log close to the fire and spoke so everyone could hear. "Boys, I made a dis-cov'ry today. A real interestin' dis-cov'ry. I sorter suspicioned hit." He glanced at Carrie, then turned to face Franklin. "So I come in an found Frank, hyar, fixin t'spy on Carrie when she goes t'the spring t'warsh herself."

Had Lem shouted FIRE, the reaction would not have been more urgent. Henry's, "Franklin, is that true?" came simultaneously with tin plate clatter as Carrie knocked over the stack while jerking around to face Franklin.

"Dint mean no harm," whined Franklin.

"Wal, what in God's name *did* ye mean?" roared Dallman, renowned as lay preacher for the strength of his voice and for his denunciations of sin. "Carrie's ourn *cook*. Ye unnerstan? Yer pappy gonna hide ye sompin awefullest when he fine out ye messin wit' ourn cook. And thet ain't nuthin to what God has on store fer ye."

The laconic Hilpert did his part by retrieving the noisy tin plates, using a sleeve to brush them clean of dirt as he restacked.

"Frank," broke in Henry, "we don't need you after your week ends. I'll give you a note to Mister Charles at the bank for your pay."

Dallman had not finished with Franklin's transgression. "We'uns—our Inners an ourn Cook—made a covenant, one wit' tother. Ye has vi-o-lated thet covenant. Ye has abandoned the ark of ourn pro-tect-shun to jump into the sinful sea. An ye cain't swim."

Lem was not finished either. "Beggin your pardon, Mister Hollis. The men hyar feel thet a body what don' respect women's privacy don' be collectin no pay."

"Sen' thet sumbitch to Aunt Sally right *now*," urged a disgusted voice.

"An tell her she use *triplest* lobelia." An emphatic voice in the shadows.

Lem faced Franklin. "Ye heered 'em, Frank. Best ye go now. Moon's about to full."

A figure rose and walked into the dark. "Dint a-mean no harm."

"Repent, foul sinner, repent, a-fore ye be fergiven," boomed Dallman.

"Jes *keep goin*, Franklin," called Lem, "an don' ne'er come back. Somebody mebbe bring yer kit down later."

"Ye done persackly right, Lem. Cain't have *nobody* messin' with ourn cook nohow." Hilpert lavished a fortnight's words as he restacked the tin plates.

"Wal, Carrie," Lem lowered his voice for quiet conversation. "I'm sorry fer hit, but thet's done an finish. I guarantee, Miss Carrie, thet ye ken warsh'n not worry none." He took a plate from Hilpert. "What ye dishin fer us'un t'night?"

⁂

Appreciative of Carrie's cooking and pleased to have a pretty woman among them, the crew joked and teased her, half-admiringly, on her domesticity. But the men gathered in the dawn's fog after an all-night drizzle grumbled morosely.

"Damn, thet ole shed roof leaks like a busted sieve."

"Ourn too."

"Had me 'xtry bad this mont' on accounta thet roof."

Carrie filled their coffee mugs, reluctant to admit how well her canvas roof shed water. "Marse, last time I went down, Miz Elvira looked at me real hard and said, 'Mister Hollis usually goes to town on Saturday, you know.' I think she was telling me something. Isn't today Saturday? Maybe it's a good day to visit Tulips."

"Milking?" He swirled his coffee. "Take Elton," he muttered. She and the mule soon disappeared into the fog wisps.

The sun had slid behind the west ridge long before she reappeared. Elton moved slowly under a load piled high. Incredulous, Henry inspected the goods that came off the mule's back. "Froe and mallet?"

"Marse Sam picked them up when Judah Rainey's men reshingled the old wing. He said they left 'em."

"And what got picked up once can be picked up again?"

"Marse Henry," Carrie grinned, "That's exactly what Miz Elvira said."

Henry made a face, but the parallel did not distract him. "I'm all in favor of milking, Carrie, but what do we need a froe up here for?"

"To make shingles, Marse."

"I don't have enough hands to do what I need to do. Who's gonna make shingles?

"Me."

He erupted in laughter.

"Marse Henry, when Judah Rainey reshingled the old wing at Tulips, Miss Audie Ann and I stayed outside every day watching them. She wanted to try the froe. Marse Samuel made one of the men give us lessons, but then it took practice. I figured maybe I could try it again."

Still laughing, Henry headed past the cleared Low Field toward the men downing trees.

Elton's load stowed, Carried embarked on a delicate diplomatic mission. That evening, Jefferson and Solomon came in carrying log lengths already split into shingle bolts. The next morning, some of Lilly's sweets found their way into the basket carried to the field for a quartering time.

When the men were far from camp, Carrie hefted the froe. Her first trial ended in tears. She burned the whole lot in the cooking fire. There was much extra kindling the next day, too. Two days later, though, recognizable shingles were scattered about, perhaps as a tentative base for a pile.

As Lilly's sweets supply ran low, Carrie had to reopen negotiations in order to assure a continuing supply of bolts. The shingle pile grew enough to tip over. Henry watched, wordless. When he saw the daily supply of incoming bolts double and the shingle pile rising appreciably, he paused in the dawn light on his way out to the new field. "You don't go up there," his unsmiling face reinforced his admonitory finger pointing toward the shed roofs, "you do *not* go up there absent Hilpert here. Carrie, do you understand that?"

"Yes, Marse." A pause. "Marse Henry, when'll Hilpert be around?"

Henry surveyed the pile, "Maybe next Tuesday."

"Next Tuesday be good, Marse."

On Tuesday the elfin Hilpert crept cautiously over half-rotted rafters to patch the worst holes in the roofs with new shingles Carrie handed up to him. Finally safely back on the ground he stood beside her to inspect their work.

Carrie shook her head. "I'm afraid it doesn't look very pretty, Hilpert."

"Dry beat purty."

The crew said even less than Hilpert, but Carrie grew accustomed to having always at hand ample full buckets from the spring.

Plowing with Greek, My Life
HL Hollis

Writing about Audie Ann has prompted me to locate and scrutinize again several old photographs of her. In one she sits on the Tulips front porch. The porch railing is remodeled, but the wicker furniture is not yet retired as too wambly. I therefore date the photograph to about 1890. Standing deep in the porch shade is a rather shadowy Solomon, looking like a family retainer, for he carries a tray with a glass. Audrey, much more clearly in focus, projects no remarkable aura. In point of fact, she's an old woman shrunken inside an unadorned black dress, her heavily lined face set in what could be reproach. Perhaps the sun was hot or the photographer peremptory.

The other picture, likely done by some early, itinerant photographer with a portable studio, captures a much younger Audie. Stored with the few papers my father saved from his New York years, the photograph was probably sent to him there. Audie Ann is seated beside a rug-draped table on which are a vase of flowers and a book. Her dress boasts more ornamentation than any I ever saw her in, its skirt arranged to hide her lame leg, crutch removed from view; her hair is in that tightly pulled-back, center-parted style of the era, a choice which has always puzzled me, for I have yet to see a face it flatters.

Much unresolved contention, especially among my sisters Crotia and Dory, and my brother Bill, centers on this photograph, which includes a second woman, debatably younger than Audie Ann, undebatably very attractive, who stands as if about to reach for the book on the table, perhaps to give it to Audie Ann. Crotia speculates that this woman was a magnet to pull my father home from Manhattan exile.

In point of fact, the stranger standing in the photo could certainly catch any young man's eye. Bill admits that but nevertheless rejects Crotia's "loony logic." Name one time, he demands, that Father even hinted feminine magnetism drew him back to Tulips. And how do you explain he did not marry until decades after his return?

For my part, I tick off photographic clues that contradict Crotia. The unidentified woman poses in the background, behind, not beside the table; she faces Audie Ann, not the camera; she does not share Audie's sofa, but stands; and she wears a noticeably plainer dress than Audie's. She is, I therefore confidently deduce, Audie Ann's maid, some young woman hired for a time—maybe when Samuel B could not locate (or perhaps afford) a suitable slave—a hired maid of such abbreviated tenure she evaporated from family lore.

Such prosaic nitpicking disgusts Crotia. Dory, ever judicious, mediates with one word, "Hollywood." Our vision is both enhanced and blinded by movies. From Saturday nights, we know about "minor" characters early in the plot—you see that uniformed lady's maid? You notice how artfully the camera lingers on her face and caresses her figure? Watch her. Before The End, she will be the beautiful heroine in a sumptuous gown. The nineteenth-century photographer, though, did not see (through Hollywood) as we do. Intriguing as that idea may be, it does not lead to identification. Bill and I stick doggedly to the facts before us.

I must mention rare unanimity about one entertaining detail, something Crotia first spotted. The portrait contains an in-joke. The book is placed so that its reader behind the table would find its pages upside down, meaning it is right side up for the portrait viewer. If one studies the cover with only minimal magnification, one can discern the name Cooper, as in James Fenimore, as in *The Last of the Mohicans*, among Father's favorite reading and butt of much teasing from Audie.

I am cognizant I have strayed from my original point, Audie Ann's portraits. In both she sits stiffly, staring down the camera. My siblings and I do not argue about *her* image because we tacitly fill it to overflowing with our favorite memories of her. Someone who did not know her, however, would never be able to reconstruct from either photograph the occasionally ribald, always animated, demonstrative Audie Ann we knew. In neither photograph does the actual person spring from the paper, and I sadly anticipate the same shall prove true of these pages.

QUACHASEE
WHC

"Hello?"

At an unfamiliar male voice, Carrie stepped out of her tent, relieved to have clean hair, to be wearing a fresh dress. The voice belonged to the stranger walking toward the camp. A hunter, to gauge by the long rifle he carried and the bag over his shoulder, though well groomed for his trade. "Looking for Henry Hollis." Not a mountain man, said his speech.

"He's out there, sir." She pointed to distant figures. "At the far edge of the field." A tree went down as they watched.

"There went a fat coon," the man grumbled. He turned to Carrie. "I'm John Bright. And who are you, miss?"

"Just Carrie, from Tulips, sir. Cooking for Marse Henry."

"Well, Just Carrie, I'm happy to meet you. At Tulips the cook is Lilly. Lilly LaCroix."

She was surprised enough by the LaCroix that her "Yessir" came delayed.

"You're her daughter."

"Yessir."

"And even more attractive." He spoke without insinuation, so matter-of-factly she almost replied with a yessir. "Is your cooking as good?"

"No sir, but I keep trying."

"You're much appreciated here."

Carrie foundered: a statement? a question? a compliment? "I hope so, sir."

"Like it here?" Bright's friendly interest reminded her of Audie Ann and of Henry, too, when he wasn't so busy or tired.

93

"Good land. I like listening to the birds singing and the wind in the trees. The mountains seem like walls."

"Keeping you in?"

"Oh no, sir, keeping the world out. When Marse Henry doesn't need all those men for clearing, it will be even better."

"The men give you a hard time."

"Never at all. I just like working by myself with the ridges around me."

"Some people might get lonesome up here."

"I guess. But you can climb up that ridge over there, and the whole valley is laid out like you're a bird flying free." He studied her with a look she did not understand. "Want me to run and get Marse?"

"If I'm not mistaken, Just Carrie, Henry's on his way already." He had only glanced at the field, but when Carrie focused, she could distinguish Henry walking back, occasionally waving his hat. The visitor must enjoy keen vision.

"One of his crew must have spotted me. Henry can't see to hit the side of the barn at twenty paces."

Carrie giggled. "I know. His aim is hopeless." Bright turned to look sharply at her. She had revealed far too much. "I mean, I guess that's what I've heard," she stammered. "From . . . Marse Sam, maybe."

He shook his head. "Daresay not. Sam is as poor at targets as Henry is. Sam can see better, but his bad temper makes him rush his shots." Carrie checked her agreeing nod too late to escape his notice. "Do you perhaps have some coffee, Just Carrie from Tulips? My breakfast seems long ago."

Ashamed of her inhospitality, Carrie hurried to the fire. By the time Henry walked up, two steaming mugs and plates waited.

Bright inspected Henry sternly. "You look not so citified, oh son of the great chief, as the last time I saw you."

Henry stopped stone-faced a few feet away. "Hail, Deerslayer. What game did Killdeer find?"

Bright answered, his face immobile. "Only the pitiful remnants left from the white man slaughtering trees and bringing civilization."

"Ugh."

"Ugh."

The two men grinned, stepped close for a hearty handshake reinforced by left hands. Bright noticed Carrie's mystification and paused to explain. "When we were growing up, he and I read a book by a man named James Fenimore Cooper. I grew out of it at last, but Henry never did."

"No, the other way around, Deerslayer. Look at that rifle. Killdeer for sure. You can't tell me you've gotten over the last Mohican."

The teasing felt so much like Audie Ann's room that Carrie unconsciously let down her guard. "You ever move up from Deerslayer to Hawkeye?" she laughed.

Bright shot Henry a startled glance, then nodded for Carrie. "But I had a hard time getting Henry to be the Hurons, so I could kill 'em off. He thought he should be Uncas."

"Except at the end I always wanted to be someone else," Henry corrected. "Didn't like all that stabbing."

"But I have to admit," Bright confided as if behind Henry's back, "he acted out Uncas's death very convincingly. Slumped most dramatically and staggered as someone soon dead." He gave Carrie a sidelong glance. "I suppose you were Cora," he asked casually, looking into his mug.

"Oh, of course," exclaimed Carrie. "Except I wasn't happy about that 'knife in the bosom' just on the verge of rescue. That's where I quick switched to being Alice, even if all she can do is . . . faint . . ." She trailed off, realizing that Bright again studied her intently, that she wasn't safe in Audie Ann's room, comparing her reactions to Audie's.

"Bloody book, isn't it?" he smiled.

"Was it written for boys, do you think?"

"If so, it gave these two boys problems. We thought Henry and Audie Ann could be Heyward and Alice. Took us a while to grasp that Heyward and Alice shouldn't be brother and sister."

He grinned and pointed to Henry. "So he had to be Uncas. A pity you didn't know to be there. A perfect Cora. Maybe we could have dropped Magua over the cliff about five pages before the end so you could live happily ever after."

A faint crack and heavy wump in the distance as a tree went down. "Another fat coon," mourned Bright. "By the way, Henry, how did you know I was here?"

"To tell the truth, the men keep close watch out for Carrie. Nearly unhitched a team to ride in here like thunder to protect her. Then they mentioned a long rifle, and I guessed it must be you. They won't have nobody messin none with their cook, so you'd better be respectful."

"An enviable status," said Bright, saluting Carrie.

"Spooks," said Henry, "we go 'til nearly dark. You'll eat with us then?"

"Assuming I can bring some squirrels in for Miss Cora. I need to eat here so she can explain to me why Deerslayer never attracts any of those beautiful women. And why Cora and Uncas can't be paired, matching Alice and Heyward."

"And you can explain to me why the girls never do anything heroic; they always need rescuing." News of the crew's compliment loosened Carrie's self-restraint. "It's so boring. Half the time I had to be Hawkeye."

"Henry," Bright waved a dismissive hand, "go back to your men with a clear conscience. Don't mind us. Miss Cora and I have many important matters to thrash out here. I shall see you as the sun lies down to sleep beyond yonder mountain, oh noble last son of the Delaware." He turned to Carrie. "Now Cora Hawkeye, you pose an interesting question that never occurred to me before. I'd like to investigate this more after I have decimated some herd of buffalo or barked a mess of squirrel."

As he walked off, Carrie checked shadows. The sun was still high enough for her to revise the evening meal, if she hurried.

She was lucky she had not miscalculated, for the gang came in early, just after Bright's squirrels went into the stew pot for the next day. Carrie noticed the warmth in their deferential greetings. "'Lo, Mister Bright, sir." "Right glad t'see yer back, Mister John."

After thumb or crust scoured the last morsel from plates, Bright moved next to Lem. "Now Mister Lem, with a meal that tasty from Cook Carrie, why don't you have armed sentinels posted night and day to ensure no one kidnaps so rare a cook?"

"Wal, Mister Bright, sir, we'uns heared us 'bout cook-thieves. Low no'counts, they is." Lem paused to spit and meditate. "Yessir, we heered'a 'em. An we knowed we'uns got us a stavin' cook. We pondered on hit consid'ble. Dint hardly know us'un what t'do."

Another pause to pick vigorously at his teeth. "The answer, hit come to us'un all a-sudden: ary'un fixin fer t'steal 'way ourn cook, thet thievin body got to *know* 'bout Carrie. So we'uns give out thet ever'body up hyar git double-swored fer secret. Evern some ferriner body—like, mebbe, some lawyerman," he squinted sidelong at Bright—"some ferriner come an tas-tes ourn cook' food, hit everly happen thet he jes dis'pear goin home."

Lem shook his head sadly. "Mebbe he take a tumble at Snake Shear, mos' likely. Nobody never heared on him agin nowhurs nohow."

"Either thet," a voice from the dark, "or he tie up to starve daid."

Another flat voice: "Jake's jest guyin ye. Trut is, evernwhen some cook thiever's starvin daid with only mast t'ate, he fernent the cookin fiah, so he mus' smell all'a them good scents 'til he drop off."

"Gentlemen," Bright darted looks about in mock nervousness, "I see I've strayed into a dangerously exposed position."

"Yessir, some'd say yer most pintedly is. But myself, I wouldn't want t'spend no 'pinion on thet."

"I'd take your oath of secrecy most willingly."

"Cain't." Lem answered with regretful finality. "Oath take 'bout eleven an a half drop'a painter blood under a fulled moon to seal hit solid."

"And I haven't spotted a prowling panther in years."

"Nossir, nary'un," Lem sorrowed. "I seed a wumpus cat hyar'n thar some time, but wumpus cat blood, hit jest too thin fer sealin ofa oath."

"Blood of wumpus cat, you can just see right through it," agreed Bright with a wink. "Perhaps I could substitute a mess of squirrels or some venison for the panther blood?"

"Wal, I dunno 'bout thet. Nary none'us hankerin t'have some lawyerman outsharp us'un."

"Ifen hit's young venison." Hilpert offered escape.

"Oh, only young venison, of course," answered Bright.

"Nary nothin else," growled a skeptic from the shadows.

"Wouldn't consider it. Should we declare this an oral contract?"

"Better we'uns study hit out." The skeptic in the shadows.

Lem was finally receptive. "I don' care ifen we do. Good thing ye a smart lawyerman, Mister Bright," Lem sealed the deal, "er ye'd ne'er git outta hyar 'livin."

"Thank the court, indeed. It's not every crew protects their cook so zealously."

"Ye hain't ne'er ate Hilpert's damn cookin, Mister Bright."

"An not much'a Carrie's, yet," added Hilpert.

While the men drifted off to their straw ticks in the sheds, Bright and Henry lingered by the fire, discussing the farm, chuckling at memories of playing Uncas and Hawkeye. After a prolonged easy silence, Bright broached a new subject. "Your last letter seemed to me a bit cryptic, Henry, but I gather your Elise became a great disappointment."

Henry hurled a log into the fire. "She pledges to wait for me until I have the stake to satisfy her father. She goes off to Newport with her parents to escape the fever in New York. I stay and get sick like to die, but somehow don't. The first news I see after I can read again is the announcement of Miss Elise Vail's betrothal to some nabob from Newport."

"That was before Isaiah and Prudence died?"

"No, after. Pretty much the last straw for me and New York."

"I'm sorry, friend. Hard blows, those."

"From this distance I've decided it's just as well. I don't miss her. Not like the Kendall sisters."

"Prudence and . . . ah . . ."

"Riti. Charity."

"Charity, yes, sorry. For a time I guessed that you might make her your wife."

Henry nodded. "Except for the Grim Reaper. Three of them—my friend Isaiah, his girl Pru, and Riti—all gone in four months." He stared at the fire. "I'd have married Riti, no matter Cousin Hurley warning me she wasn't 'suitable' for a Hollis. He's the one who urged his banker's daughter, Elise. Not that I hold it against him; the Newport news shocked him more than me. Pru and Charity weren't refined enough for Cousin Hurley, just good looking and smart."

"Smarts and looks go a long way," observed Bright with a smile.

"That's what I thought. But what I remember most now is how they made me think about things I had taken for granted. Slavery, for instance. I even wrote out one of our conversations about slavery, just to see if I could spot some flaw in the reasoning. I was going to send it to you, but then I got sick and never mailed it. I think it's still with my New York things at Tulips. Next time I'm down there I'll dig it out."

"No hurry," Bright assured him.

"What I don't understand, old friend, is why, when you and I grew up here, *we* never thought about these things and tried to change them?"

"Did you think about the air you breathed?" answered Bright. "You have to be under water before you genuinely understand."

"I think slavery isn't right," said Henry slowly.

"No, it isn't." Bright answered briskly. "But I want to live at peace in these mountains, so I'm afraid I compromise. I keep as clear of slavery as I can, and hope others do the same so that it finally withers away. But you have had a very long day. We must talk of this again."

"Yes, we need to." Henry then shifted to a suspiciously mellifluous voice, "And so, gentle reader, our hero—disappointed by a faithless woman unworthy of her sex, and sorrowing over the wide swaths mercilessly scythed by the Angel of Death, tried beyond capacity by ceaseless striving after Mammon—returns at last from his trials in the hurrying, scurrying metropolis. He arrives, crushed and fainting, to the sylvan recluse of his ancient estate, hoping there to find refuge from Evil, and sustenance for his wearied soul, though he does not escape humans' cruelty to others."

"To stand," Bright took up the narrative, in an even more theatrical voice, "to stand at the noble brow of lofty peak and ominous precipice, feast for his eyes. To stroll through forest glades and stride the broad and fertile sward, there to survey the . . . ah . . . the . . ." He faltered. "To survey the . . . " his hands appealed for assistance.

"To survey the," Henry tried to help, "the shit-end of a mule from sunup to set, tryin t'make a livin outta them damned rocks."

"True, though the declamation perhaps lacks a certain refinement." Bright poked the fire. "Uncas, I fear we're not meant to write novels from our lives."

"They'd be bad," Henry laughed. "No gloriously hopeless rebellions, no forbidden love for a beautiful lady with a besmirched past, no hidden illegitimate offspring."

"Don't forget switched babies and malevolent uncles."

"No switched babies. Nothing dramatic. Except my father's collapse and . . . and recovery, I hope."

"All of us hope and pray, Henry," Bright added quietly.

MOUNTAIN SKETCHBOOK

A Journalist's Travels

and

Observations in Parts of

The Southern Appalachians

August N. Graves

Liverwright & Sons
New York, N.Y.
1887

V. "General Store"

August, 1881

Dog days. All the mountains in east Tennessee cannot hold back suffocating August heat. Wise farmers invent chores to justify work in deepest shade. Prudent housewives postpone laundry day's fire and steaming tubs. In town, Mercantile porch regulars suspend the usual checkers for listless contemplation of the sun-baked street.

Nothing new is there to see. Opposite the Mercantile a flag hangs limp, covering part of the fly-specked window sign.

U.S. POST OFFI
NERS FORD, TE

The Mercantile sitters chew at lengthy intervals. They spit after prolonged deliberation. They scratch without urgency. They stare unfocused. They blink solemnly as owls.

A door opens on the building across Ford Street, the building with GINNERS FORD COMMERCIAL BANK. LINWOOD LEDLEY, PRES. painted high on its false front. Swiveling only eyes, the Mercantile sitters follow a white-haired man as he leaves the bank. He waits, back in the shade, for a mule team to shuffle past. Braving direct sun, he angles toward ELLSWORTH THOM, ATTORNEY AT LAW, the sign next to the Mercantile. For the porch he pantomimes an exaggerated mop of his brow.

From the Mercantile porch sound some murmurs and a lone 'Morning, Mister Hollis. Mostly only low-voiced Yessirs, meant to endorse the brow-mop, though with minimum exertion. Elmer Slack spits a powerful stream off the porch, close enough to a dog lying on its side that it rises with awkward effort, turns a full circle, and flops heavily back down, jowls seeking the coolest ground. Mister Hollis vanishes into Lawyer Thom's office. The mule team disappears around the bend at the Methodist church. The dust raised by the passing team settles back. The street is again empty.

On the Mercantile porch Elmer wipes sweat gliding down his temple, nods in agreement with himself. Elmer says he looked fer thet soon as Hollis come outta thet damn Ledley bank. Goin di-reck from Banker Ledley to Lawyer Thom, thet Hollis is mebbe cooking some deal oreither other.

Russell Platt makes a noise that might be dissent, but he is instead addressing a bothersome fly, which he swats hard. He flicks the corpse away, looks up with a victorious smile, and says thar ain't no mebbe 'bout Henry Hollis's cookin. Henry Hollis is buyin more land 'cause Henry Hollis is everly buyin more land, which e'en the goddam flies know because that they are burdened to fly so far o'er all thet Hollis land t'plague poor men like Russell Platt.

A mule drowsing at a nearby rail shakes its head and neck with irritated vigor, jangling the harness, then stamps a hoof. Garris Falt says what fer, 'specially on a damn hot day, is Russell quarrelin at Hollis. Hollis's shifty: he don' steal no land; he buys him hit legal, an makes a big lot offen hit, an then uses thet money t'buy him more land t'make a big lot more. A cloud of flies rises from the mule, buzzes about briefly, descends to torture its host anew.

Wilber Tabbet says what sortta life be thet, buyin land t'buy more land. Garris says Wilber would admire to have thet very life ifen he, Wilber, owned all'a Henry Hollis land. Wilber right quick says ever body know thet ain't true, elseways . . . But Wilber stops there, searching vacant cranial recesses vainly for some snappy comeback.

Garris says mebbe thet Wilber he a smidgen contrarious on account of at las' year shootin match Miss Audie Ann Hollis show thet some people, like mebbe Wilber, talks way better'n they shoots. Wilber says ever body know Hollis's sister's damn shootin don' have nary t'do wit' Hollis's land. Garris says um-hmm.

Russell says don' throw off on Wilber. He cain't holp hisself shoot. Elmer says Hollis land minds him 'bout a story belongen to tell, which is at the post office oncet he ax Hollis right out, how much land he want and Hollis says jes my land an' what's next t'it. Which is a right good joke when ye study hit some, that is, ifen Hollis jokin.

Wilber says whatever land Hollis has, hit's a whole mess, and tain't right. Garris rolls his eyes and says Hollis's land is not no whole mess, hits what he hurtin fer. Garris is fixin to go on, but Lemuel Shetcliffe sets to his murmuring or mumbling or stammering, trying to get words out. Lem is senior by maybe three or four decades to everyone on the porch, quair, most say, so he lives by his granddaughter. She dasn't leave him alone on his tick fearin he might get up and hurt hisself somehow. So she brings him to sit at the Mercantile when she must be away from the house.

Words come terrible hard to Lem or he has struggles pronouncing them or something else is troublesome inside his head; nobody knows for sure, though everyone has his own separate opinion—and certain cure. I . . . I . . . worked . . . worked . . . foreman . . . fer . . . Hollis . . . Hollis . . . way . . . up . . . up . . .

Wade, always kind to Lem, often tries to birth his words by paying him close attention and nodding, which he does now.

The effort of speaking strains Lem so mightily that Wade, as usual, pats his shoulder and gives some reply so Lem can feel sure he did get in his two cents and can relax. Wade says yes, them as has memory knows most ever last body sittin hyar work fer Hollis, one time t'other.

Work isn't what Lem wants to talk about. . . . fer . . . fer . . . fer . . . Hollis . . . when . . . he . . . was . . . up . . . the . . . high . . . high . . . Qua . . .

Not patient like Wade, Garris talks right over Lem. Garris says any man ken see Hollis need all'a his land and then some, on account'a future days. Hollis is good to plan fer nex' gen'rations, Hollis is, not lettin chillens run like rabbits, the way Wilber hyar does.

Wilber says my chillens don' run like rabbits. Garris says ye have so many rabbits, how ye know? Wilber says I only has fourteen rabbits—an one on the way. Garris says mebbe more when ye tearin up jack everwhen ye take a notion.

Nace Johns has been looking for open water to stick in his oar. Nace says I don' have no nary use fer how friendly Hollis cozies to the damn— A huge bumblebee interrupts Nace, bouncing noisily off the Mercantile window, clumsily diving at ears or chins, and at Nace's thick long beard. A bumblebee in a beard might inconvenience and preoccupy most any man. Nace can't be an exception. He waves his arms, ducks the bee. Howsomever, it keep coming after him, even crawling into the privacy of Nace's beard.

Elmer says Nace, ye might think'a gitten a razor er a skissers fer thet goddam beard. Hits a fright, thet beard. But Nace is concentrating on the bee-ed beard too much to pay heed to Elmer, let alone return insult from a man who also has a big beard hurtin bad for redding up. Russell says don' a-put on Nace. He the sorter man which need t'think one thang at a time, not all together at oncet. Bees'n thinkin'n talkin—hit excess fer one good brain, leastwise Nace's.

The bee escapes Nace's beard and zigzags noisily off into the Mercantile. Elmer says I heered some feller in Nashville's gonna git them bicycle machines t'Tennessee. Russell says he heered thet too. Ye kin know right off thet crazy man is fotched on. Has t'be. No sense in'im.

Staring straight ahead, Lem continues his monotone. . . . worked . . . worked . . . long . . . days . . . from . . . can-see . . . to . . . cain't-see . . . livin . . . in . . . leakin . . . shacks . . . 'til . . . she . . . fix . . . fix . . .

Elmer says I don' see what being a ferriner has t'do with bicycles. Garris says if ye ken ride em—an I 'spect ye needin t'be some kind'a acribat t'balance thet way; ye not ketchin me e'en tryin—then whur ye ride? Tell me whur. The goddam roads they ain't fittin fer wheels, sartain not fer no two wheel, one front'a t'other. Tain't nary'un hyar thet's smoothed off 'nough.

Reliving his bumblebee encounter, Nace smooths his beard and shudders. When smoothing and shuddering's done, Nace says Hollis ain't sound 'bout niggers. Ye cain't look o'er hit. He cain't be sound, not ifen he willin to shake a nigger's hand, which Nace has seen him do just thet.

Russell says an when it rain on them trails called roads, ye mudded up past yourn knee. Man might despise mud t'hisn knee.

Lem sweats from his effort in this heat. an . . . an . . . Hollis . . . found . . . a . . . real . . . fine . . . cook . . . Carrie . . . Lilly's . . . datter . . . an . . . near . . .

Nace says sumpin ain't right. His granddaddy tole him when Hollis young he were a big Ike sort, dint try'ta hide he were a damn nigger lover. Nace says his granddaddy got a little offen in t'head, quair, same as Lem hyar. Thusly Nace warn't sure then. But he know sartain now. A man ken see hit easy ifen he spies Hollis talking with a nigger. Take thet damn Amos White. Nace watch 'em oncet, an when Amos he walk away he has his haid so high an walkin down *the boardwalk*, anyone ken see he forgettin a free nigger's still a damn nigger, no matter his name is White.

Wilber says even a rich sumbitch like Hollis has to start somewhurs so how thet Hollis git from a dirt farmer like e'er body to bein' a rich sumbitch? Wilber says I plowed a steer fer four year afore I git a mule, an lookit them teams thet Hollis drive.

Garris fixes to say something vexed to dumb Wilber, but Wade is kinder and quicker and says Hollis heired his land from his father. His father, name'a Samuel B which come into this country right when hit open up. With cash money t'buy whole valleys.

Nace says thet ain't the nub'a hit. Nace says this Samuel B Hollis came a-purpose to cheat honest men outta their rightful. Them Hollis people don' git whur them is withouten a-doin things the sheriff should'a look at. Dint make no difference if ye was a widow. Er some orphan chile neither. Ole Hollis treat ye jest the same. Real sharp, he treat ye. Put yourn name on a paper an later Ole Hollis change hit. Ye sold ten acre. Now th'damn paper say ye sold a hundred acre. Or ye owed seventeen dollar. Now paper say ye owe hundred an' seventy dollar. A body objected, Ole Hollis jes pint at the paper in black'n white. Nace says Ole Hollis smelled like thet kind of skunk, an' blood's thick when hit come to th'son.

Wade says hokum. Them stories is plain damn hokum. Belong in a spittoon. Wade says him, nor his daddy, ner his granddaddy neither, never saw no problem with a Hollis. Father ner son neither. They rich, but honest rich.

Nace says no such thing's honest rich. Wade says ye a-bring me some real show, not no gossip. Nace growls deep in his throat. Garris says Nace, what ye tryin t'be, some severe huntin dog, mebbe Plotts, from t'sound a'hit. The day's too damn hot t'be all fire an tow.

Wade says ye ken see Hollises hed t'be sumpin whur they come from, by the way they give a name to thet thar homeplace. 'Course nobody else 'round hyar live in a homeplace like Tulips, not since thet fancy Pruitt place burnt down.

Wade says he hoofed out t'Tulips oncet to col-lect pay he owed. Worth the walk t'study thet clock they put down plumb in the front hall thar. An lissen at hit ringin on t'hour. Hit stand nigh akin t'twenty foot high, seem like, wit' thet huge wide case fer the mighty pend'lum, swingin back'ards 'n for'ards, back'ards 'n for'ards, . . slow . . . 's . . . death.

Garris spits quick to say 'most any clock be tall to a feller like Wade, which is hurtin fer reach. Hits jest untelling what Wade'll say. Thet he found a madstone in ev'ry deer he kilt. Or mebbe he heared the damn clock strike thirteen.

. . . cooked . . . cooked . . . fine . . . eats . . . an . . . took . . . care . . . a . . . us . . . real . . . good . . . an . . . she's . . . pretty . . . pretty . . . like . . . like . . .

Wade says he ain't gonna fool up nobody. Anyone, excepten some poor bastard like Garris Falt, shammuck 'long from ahind the moun'in, anyone know clocks they don' ne'er strike thirteen, lessen they bust, an this hyar clock ain't bust. Hit tick jest fine. The way ye sartain this clock hit run right is when hit strike midnight.

Wade says now thet poor Garris cain't know this 'cause he cain't count thet high. But fer the rest'a us'en, ye wait 'til it gittin on t'midnight. Thet clock boom out ten near loud 'nough t'wake the daid. Hit boom out 'leven e'en louder. Then hit boom out twelve an t'hul house shake like one'a them thar quakes ta t'yearth. An then all to oncet thet clock case door open up an' some gorgeous young female come outta thet big ole clock, stark neked, skin soft's a baby, sweet's a ripe peach, white as milk, ready to do a man whatsoe'er he want. But he better a-be quick 'bout hit, on account of, sartain as hell, she mus' be back inside the clock case—an the door close, close tight, mind ye—afore hit strike one wit' thet big boom.

. . . real . . . real . . . beautiful . . . and . . . near . . .

Wilber says nobody's telling me sartain sure proof Hollis got Tulips an all hits land offen his daddy. Garris is quicker than Wade this time and says Wilber got things balled up hopeless an' helpless, as he everly do. Wade is kinder and says Tulips passed fust to Hollis's older stepbrother, Sam Junior.

Garris says now thet Sam Junior: one damn cheap sumbitch. Two peas in a pod wit' his damn no'count cousin Caleb, thet Sam Junior. He so cheap he chews his 'baccy twicet. Real mean t'all hisn help, don' matter white er black.

Garris says he ain't fergetting when Sam Hollis Junior tries to dock pay fer a busted . . . a bust . . . a bust, dingus, ye know. Wade, who has this story memorized, says dingus? Ye meanin axe han'le. Garris says thet's what I sayin, axe han'le. I ain't fergettin Sam Hollis Junior tryin to dock my pay fer a busted axe han'le, which han'le is cracked a-fore I e'er touches hit, fer God's sake, but Sam Junior give me down the country fer thet. Sam want me t'buy him a bran' new han'le. Garris says damn, thet's the last time Garris Falt e'er work up fer Sam Junior. Thet sumabitch's so tight he screaks when he walk.

Wilber says was you jokin 'bout Hollis comin nekked outta thet clock? Garris throws up his hands and flings back his head like he's been shot with a rusty ole hog rifle. Then Garris says Wilber, fer God's sake, say ye was jest a-joken us. Ye jokin er dumb. An ye jes' cain't be thet dumb.

Under his breath Russell Platt says yessir, Wilber really really is thet dumb. Wade says Hollis come home from

New York City, by what Wade heard. Wade says thet's how come him to git thet big scar clear 'crosst hisn throat. Stand to reason on account'a New York City's a danger place.

Nace Johns forgets the heat so, he slaps his knee. He says New York, a-course. I ne'er did know hit a-fore, but Hollis taked his damn ideas 'bout damn niggers from up nor' to New York. Nace says I see hit now. What I tell ye boys?

Garris spits at the post. When he nails it square, as he always does, as anyone can see from the pool of 'baccy drool at the post base, Garris studies an ant scurrying along the rocking chair arm. He keeps his eyes on the ant and says Nace hyar practically a cock a-crowin on t'porch, what Nace sayin is thet the to-tal en-tire-rity a'what he think 'bout, talk 'bout, dream 'bout is niggers, an niggers, an niggers.

Garris quashes the ant and looks up. Garris says thet might could'a happen to some'un which has young Sadie Krebs 'scape him on the river trace. Elmer snickers. Russell Platt too.

Nace says Sadie dint 'scape. Elmer and Russell and Garris hoot, all'a'em. Nace says he let 'er off, he let Sadie go. Garris and Elmer and Wade howl.

Nace says yessir he let damn Sadie go. Hootin and howlin so loud the mule lifts its head to stare. Nace says he let 'er go on account thet he found out the damn woman got 'er monthlies and he dint want nary none of thet damn pollution.

Garris spits again with the same sure aim. Garris says Nace should try a willin woman nex'time, thet oreither some woman not strong as Sadie. Mebbe git a body like Wilber hyar, t'holp him. Wilber is not so bright, thet true. Howsomever he holp some.

Nace says he don' need nary no hep. More hootin an howlin.

Russel says Nace, ye is right puffed up. Ye shouldn't git so het over no woman. But then both Russell and Nace see Hollis coming out of Lawyer Thom's office. Hollis' hearin's fadin, seem like, so he and Lawyer Thom talk louder than most people would, 'leas out in public, 'bout theirn privit bus'ness. Nace and the hooting cease, fast's they swat a fly. The porch falls silent as death.

. . . she . . . she . . . looked . . . white . . . an . . . up . . . up . . . up . . . on . . . on . . . the . . . Quachasee . . .

Lem is too much even for Wade. Wade hisses dammit Lem, shattup. How ken a body hear Hollis consultatin Lawyer Thom wit' ye jabberin?

QUACHASEE
WHC

Again John Bright appeared unannounced at the Quachasee camp, this time bearing young venison. He also delivered spices from Lilly. Again he traded straight-faced tall talk with Lem Shetcliffe. Again he debated questions about James Fenimore Cooper with Cora Hawkeye. Again he sat up late talking and laughing quietly with Henry. He slipped away before sunrise, game he left the only tangible evidence of his visit.

A day or two passed before Carrie had opportunity to pose her question. "Marse Henry, it's not my place to ask, but does Marse Bright have two names? Sometimes you say 'Bright' and sometimes you call him a name that sounds like 'Spooks.'"

"Yes. Spooks." Buoyed by his friend's admiration for his new farm, Henry could not resist continuing. "When he was little he always played the game of sneaking up on his father. They started calling him Spooks and it stuck, at least for his close friends. We grew up together. My stepbrothers were so much older they were family, but not brothers. Spooks was a brother.

Henry smiled in recollection. "The Brights owned the house that Emmer Pruitt bought and named Chestnut Hill—after he fancied it up considerable. Our fathers were alike in a lot of ways—except that Spooks's father bought more than half of two counties. When I headed north, Spooks went off to college, then read law. Just came back to live here. He doesn't need law for a living. He loves to be out in the mountains, so he tells people he's scouting land for clients. He's a first-rate shot."

"I'd like to watch Miss Audie Ann and him in a shooting contest."

"That'd be interesting, but I don't think they'd agree to compete. They're too close. He helped me teach her to read. He learned hand talk from her and Solomon. She'd be happy you happened to cook a special stew that night he first came."

Carrie curtsied to acknowledge the compliment and did not mention her last minute switch. Her mother's example. Forgotten pies hastily pulled from the fire barely in time, fruit ingeniously stripped of rot and mold, rock-like biscuits quietly scattered for the chickens, elaborate frosting camouflaging an injured cake, a mis-remembered recipe watered to swill for the hogs: "Daughter, all they need to know is what's on their plate."

Was Lilly correct as well about gentlemen's clay feet? Carrie looked forward to more visits. Though she tried not to dwell on the thought, at the high Quachasee there lurked one disappointment. She expected to continue the happy conversations at Tulips she translated, sometimes even entered, when Henry visited Audie Ann's room, discussions about books or interesting people. But at his new farm Henry barely waited to drink his coffee at dawn. At dusk, worn out, he could barely do anything but plan the next day with Lem. Carrie understood, but still missed the talk. Marse John—Marse Spooks?, no, Marse John—promised conversation.

❧

Bright came yet again, this time with company. A representative sent by English investors asked to go hunting. Seeing the English visitor's finely wrought shooting piece, Henry turned to Bright. "Another Killdeer, Hawkeye?"

"Wait until he spies the villainous Hurons, Uncas. Where is your Cora? I have a note from Audie Ann for her."

Courteous, observant, the visitor inquired about everything. He searched for a large parcel of land, he explained, a sweep of land suitable for junior sons of English gentlemen to settle near each other in congenial proximity, young men who would farm—and ride with their hounds on fox hunts when farm work was done.

Henry did not hide his skepticism about such a dream. Tennessee, this part at least, was too mountainous and timbered to offer the cleared fields and gentle terrain of the England he had read about in books. Further, especially on a newly-opened farm, work is never done enough to allow something as frivolous as chasing over a fox.

The visitor listened patiently, and posed more questions. "I must inquire, Bright, why you sometimes address each other as Deerslayer and Uncle. Is this some kind of Americanism?"

"Less Americanism than affectation. In truth it is not uncle, but Uncas. Uncas and Deerslayer. They are bosom companions in an American novel, *The Last of the Mohicans*, very popular in this country."

"Ah yes, a literary friend suggested I read that on shipboard to while away the time when we were becalmed, but we enjoyed fair winds and very fast passage. Deerslayer and Uncas? I expect the story is convoluted?"

"Not very, no. On almost every page someone is chasing someone. Almost unendurable suspense. It's in New York State, far to the north of us here. Seventeen and fifty-seven, when we fought on your side. Or you on ours. The British commander, brave of course, under enemy siege, is unwisely visited by his two daughters, beautiful of course. Fair Alice is, alas, insipid. Dark Cora possesses more fire. Naturally the beautiful sisters must be captured by the evil Magua. Deerslayer and Uncas must, of course, lead the pursuit. Deerslayer— he's also called Hawkeye—is an American frontiersman, armed with a trusted rifle, Killdeer. Uncas, wily with forest lore, is the last of his tribe. But just as the daughters are rescued, a Huron fatally stabs dark Cora. Uncas is stabbed dead by the perfidious Magua, at whom Deerslayer fires his Killdeer, which never misses. Fair Alice may live happily ever after with Heyward Duncan, her loyal officer."

"And Deerslayer?"

"He goes his solitary way. On and on. Cooper kept adding volumes, though not in chronological order."

"Thank you. I see why Symington recommended the book. I can also see why your situation here brings it to mind. Over there in the deep shadows behind those magnificent trees might lurk bloodthirsty savages seeking our scalps. Close by we see the beautiful, raven-haired Cora of sun-blessed complexion. But," he looked around, "where is her sister, the fair Alice?"

"She and Duncan should soon arrive, I trust, sir. They're delayed. Some mix-up with the page proofs, I'm told."

The visitor saw Carrie smile, and turned to Bright, "She comprehends your jest, sir?"

"Yes, of course, poor as it is."

"Puzzles every place I go in this country."

Bright came again. They argued Cooper compared to Longstreet. He left a new volume by a writer named Simms, and a sea story. She objected to not getting a heroine. He claimed the realities of sailing. Why then, she asked, were Cora and Alice on a dangerous battlefront? He countered that Cooper's Judith and Hetty on Lake George lived not so far from Carrie at the Quachasee.

He came frequently, welcomed respectfully by the men for his wit and the tasty game he tendered in lieu of painter blood. Welcomed by Henry for their talk about politics and books. Always he inquired solicitously of her welfare. Try as she might, Carrie detected no clay feet.

ABBOTT'S STUDENT GUIDES

Plot Summaries and Characters
For the Convenience of
Readers Studying Major Works of Literature

LAST OF THE MOHICANS
James Fenimore Cooper

PLOT SUMMARY
Chapters 1-3

Action is set in upstate New York during the French and Indian War (1754-1763). General Montcalm (Fr.) has led an invading force south to attack the British at Fort William Henry, under the command of Col. Munro.

Traveling to meet their father, Munro's two daughters, escorted by the young Major Heyward Duncan, attach themselves to the force sent to reinforce Munro.

The two daughters are half-sisters. The timid, naive Alice, younger by four or five years, was born of Munro's second wife, a Scots woman. Alice has a "dazzling complexion, fair golden hair, and bright blue eyes."

Her more mature sister, Cora, was born of Munro's first wife, a woman Munro married while on duty in the Caribbean. Cora's mother was descended generations earlier from African slaves. Cora has hair that was "like the plumage of a raven. Her complexion was not brown, but it rather appeared charged with the color of the rich blood, that seemed likely to burst it bounds. And yet there was neither coarseness nor want of shadowing in a countenance that was exquisitely regular, and dignified and surpassingly beautiful."

Led by a treacherous Indian guide, Magua, Major Duncan and the sisters are imperiled when they imprudently choose a short-cut to the Fort. In the vicinity are Deerslayer, his friend Chingachgook, and Chingachgook's son, Uncas, the last of his Mohican tribe.

Deerslayer, also known as Hawkeye, has the frame of "one who had known hardships and exertion from his earliest youth. His person, though muscular, was rather attenuated than full; but every nerve and muscle appeared striking and indurate by unremitting exposure and toil. A pouch and horn completed his personal accoutrements, though a rifle of great length leaned against a neighboring sapling. The eye of the hunter, or scout, was small, quick, keen, and restless, roving while he spoke, on every side of him, as if in quest of game, or distrusting the approach of some lurking enemy. Notwithstanding the symptoms of habitual distrust, his countenance was not only without guile at the moment at which he is introduced, it was charmed with an expression of sturdy honesty."

When the two women and Duncan view the resting Uncas, they see an "upright, flexible figure . . graceful and unashamed in the attitudes and movements of nature. Though his person was more than usually screened by a green and fringed hunting shirt . . . there was no concealment of his high, haughty features, pure in their native red; . . . together with the finest proportions of a noble head."

Alice and Heyward weigh whether Uncas, a possibly savage Indian, can be trustworthy, but it is the richly complected, surpassingly beautiful Cora who brings the discussion to a dead stop with an impassioned, "who that looks at this creature remembers the shade of his skin?"

Plowing with Greek, My Life
HL Hollis

The document below originates in a small cache of papers my father kept from his New York City days, all wrapped in a long sheet of ledger paper, headed **Hurley Hollis, Merchant, New York, N.Y.**

Years ago I misplaced the following document, and was therefore greatly relieved last week to discover it a second time. I look forward to sharing it with my sisters and brothers.

I wish I could assert that the document is self-explanatory. But, like so much in the past, it resists easy interpretation. I discovered it untitled, undated, unsigned, uncertified. Readers are certainly left much on their own. It piques my curiosity.

The inclusion of a stock New England figure, "Prudence Kendall," and the antiphonal teacher-student exchange remind me very much of school textbooks from the previous century I once unearthed in the attic. I am inclined to believe that this originated in some instructional extract (perhaps from an abolitionist newspaper?), an effort to combine in daily pedagogy moral guidance with reading instruction.

Whether Father composed this himself as a sample lesson or borrowed it from somewhere is a question the document does not address, much less answer. He did, though, think enough of it to leave a fair copy in his hand. Thus I consider the most important conclusion is that here is evidence that Father was committed long before his children knew him to instructing his peers about the evils of slavery.

Prudence Kendall. I thought you were from Vermont, like Isaiah.

Uncas. No, a little state like Vermont wouldn't do for me. I'm from Tennessee. It's as long as its name. We have flatlands and many mountains.

Prudence. Oh, a Southern Planter. Big mansion, carriages, piano, whole village of slaves to tend the cotton.

Uncas. No, you're thinking of the flatlands. My home is in the mountains.

Prudence. You do have slaves in those mountains.

Uncas. Just a few.

Prudence. Just a few is too many. Tell me, Mister Slaveowner, after you flog your *few* slaves, which do you rub in, salt or sand?

Uncas. I've never hit a slave my whole life. I don't think my father has either.

Prudence. Oh, I'm so sorry. I forgot. Planters don't flog. They have the overseer do the dirty work.

Uncas. My father never hired an overseer. We and the hired men worked right alongside our boys. Even if he had an overseer, there wouldn't be any whipping. My father says that's like burning down your own house. If a slave is a problem, don't whip, sell him off.

Prudence. That's what Aunt Clem said: 'Evil masters lash with the whip; good masters, their tongues. But they both lash.' I bet your father read Ephesians to all his slaves, to make sure they knew God wanted obedience from 'em.

Uncas. He read a whole lot of Bible, including Ephesians, my father did, but he always included the part telling masters they better not threaten, because Christ doesn't distinguish by persons.

Prudence. The Devil quoted Scripture, too. Whenever the master wants: sell the slave and ignore any family or kin they might have.

Uncas. Slavery in East Tennessee is different.

Prudence. Tell that to the slaves. I'm sure they'll be relieved to know that you're paying wages, and they can leave any time they want.

Uncas. I didn't mean it was different that way.

Prudence. How many half-brothers with slave mothers do you have? Or did your father sell them off before you knew about them?

Uncas. How can I answer that? You know that's not a fair question.

Prudence. Seems to me slavery is what isn't fair.

Uncas. What you're not understanding is that my part of Tennessee isn't cotton country. A lot of owners even let their servants—

Prudence. Not "servants." They are slaves, and don't use pretty words to dress up the horrible evil.

Uncas. In my east Tennessee some owners even let their servants live away from the homeplace as long as they get to work on time. There used to be an antislavery paper over in Greeneville.

Prudence. Sure, and Noah used to float around in his ark. But the waters receded, and I bet that antislavery paper is just as far gone. Right?

Uncas. Well, yes. But I've seen free white people in this city living worse. My father's people don't go hungry.

Prudence. They're God's people, not your father's people. You're just a puppet repeating slave owners' excuses. Attacking the North doesn't erase the sin of slavery. Anyhow, at least poor people here can come and go.

Tell me, Mister Southern Planter, how is it that free people inherit through their fathers, but slaves only inherit through their mothers? If the mother is slave, so is the child. And how does the master get himself more slaves cheap? It's an iniquitous system.

Uncas. "Iniquitous system." Where did you get that fancy phrase?

Prudence. It's not fancy if it's true. And this is true. I learned it from my Aunt Clementine. She was the only woman I admired. Aunt Clem read for herself and thought for herself. When she started talking about slavery, I listened carefully and started thinking hard. Same thing when she started talking about women's rights. Bet you've never once thought about women's rights, have you?

Uncas. I think about women all the time. But not about women's rights. Should I?

Prudence. Yes you should. And when did you start thinking about slavery?

Uncas. I guess, to tell the truth, I never did before.

Prudence. Do you see now? A Southern Planter for sure.

QUACHASEE
WHC

"Solomon, pretty soon I'm gonna use words real ladies don't use." Enveloped in smoke, Carrie was trying to dish out food for the waiting men.

"I sed em, Carrie." He fanned a plate at the fire to no effect. "Dis be t'reason God say, 'Idolaters, dey is smoke in mah nostrils.'"

"What? Solomon! Where did you get that?"

"Bible. Isaiah." He fanned still harder.

"Awwg." Strong gusts swept the fire hard one way, then another. No matter which side Carrie chose, it became downwind. She could barely see the kettle.

"We need a chimney," she coughed. "Why can't we build a chimney?"

"Takes rocks." Hilpert helped fan smoke away with his plate.

"Rocks! I can't walk three feet without stubbing my toe."

"Rocks in a pile."

Carrie's eyes beseeched heaven.

"When yuh biles a mess a'bean," Solomon wheezed, "yuh doan go an pick won an put he in de pot, den go t'de ga'den foah 'nuthah won. Yuh picks 'em all, an wahshes dem t'gedder, an puts dem in de pot all one time."

"Rocks in a pile," repeated Hilpert, vindicated.

"Alright, how many rocks I need, Hilpert?"

"'Nough."

"How many is enough?"

"To finish the chimly."

"Hilpert!" Carrie looked around to see smiles politely swallowed. She turned to Henry. "Marse, where should the pile be?"

"What difference does it make?"

"Marse Henry, I don't want to pile rocks some place where they'd be troublesome later."

"Your pile can't be much to move. But if you put them there," he pointed, "that ought to be near where I think a chimney might go—eventually."

Spurred by the men's patronizing grins, Carrie started the next morning just after the crew left. Fast at first, when she simply dismantled the old sill supports of the original burned-down cabin. Still fast when she could pitch small field stones from close. Slower as the throw grew longer. Slower still when she had to carry bigger ones. The men returning at dusk said nothing.

She kept the circumference small to make the pile grow high quickly. No comment. Grunting and heaving, scouting for small rocks to serve as solid fulcrum, she pried large stones end over end with a sapling lever, buttressing the pile's base, and threw more on top. Not a word.

Came Saturday, time for another expedition to Tulips. Elton's precarious return load included nervous hens and a rooster in cages. On top, an outlandish profile she hastily dismantled. She pushed the wheelbarrow behind one of the sheds and dropped the long steel prybar in tall grass before anyone saw them.

When Henry came in to inspect her haul, he pointed to the chickens. "Eggs or drumsticks?"

"Eggs, I hope, Marse Henry."

"Drumsticks. No time to build a hen house."

She opened her gambit with a large slice of Lilly's peach pie. "I know you're busy, Marse. So I brought up all those cages. Figured I could make something that would do for the time being."

Silence conveyed his skepticism.

"If I can't, Marse, into the pot they go. Would you like more pie?"

A second piece of pie on Henry's plate raised the stakes.

"Marse Henry, did you say you're pretty close to putting some men on trail work?"

He put down his empty plate thoughtfully. "All right: two pieces of Lilly's peach pie. From the smell of it, my favorite squirrel dish. Where's this going, Carrie?"

"Wait 'til you taste Mama's icing on the cakes."

After the plate had only crumbs: "I wasn't going any place special, Marse Henry, except if some men work on the trail this coming week, it will be a lot easier to bring the cow up next Saturday."

"Cow?" Henry's pitch and volume both rose rapidly. "Carrie, a cow isn't petty stuff. That's major theft," he lectured. "Sam'll have the sheriff on me. Leave the cow. Figure to buy one next spring."

"Yes, Marse Henry." Another of Lilly's cakes. "Miz Elvira just thought it would be nice for you to have some custards sooner than next year. Those custards you liked so much at Tulips."

"Carrie," Henry shook his head. "Sam counts real well."

"Oh, I knows 'bout Sam, Marse Henry. 'Specially ifen hit's hisn, he alwuz counts twicet. Thet's why he'll git the 'xac same numer e'er night."

Henry had to grin at the mimicry, not the idea. "Carrie, what's the plot?"

"It's a mite complicated, Marse Henry."

"Carrie, the plot."

"Miz Elvira made some . . . arrangements."

"Carrie."

"Miz Elvira will take her eggs and butter to Mister Abner at the Mercantile, like she always does."

"And?"

"Only her credit he'll give to Miz Pruitt at Chestnut Hill. Elvira says Miz Pruitt will send a thrifty young cow to Tulips."

"And?"

"And Elvira said I should take Daisy up here."

"But isn't Daisy her best milker?"

"Nossir."

"I thought sure she is the best."

"Nossir. . . . Second best, Marse."

"Sam won't see the difference between Eleanor Pruitt's thrifty young cow and second-best Daisy?"

"Miz Elvira says their coloring's the same, Marse. And of course the thrifty young cow will get to wear that fancy collar that Daisy wouldn't need up here."

"Elvira doesn't consider that theft?"

"Nossir. I asked her. Figured you would want me to. She said half the cows belong to her anyway, and all the milk and eggs. She said," Carrie switched to Elvira's distinctive nasal, "'I jes lookin out fer Sam's good.' I don't know what she meant, Marse Henry, and Audie Ann neither. But Daisy *will* be waiting to travel next Saturday. I *could* use fresh milk, Marse. Butter *would* be good to have. You *already* have all that tall grass you cut and stacked, Marse Henry."

That evening Henry called Lem over. "Any reason we shouldn't work on that bad stretch in the trail soon?"

❧

Contriving a primitive chicken coop took time from rock harvesting. So did Daisy. But in time the rock pile resumed its rise. It became near as big as a doodle. The men gave no notice.

With a wheelbarrow Carrie could range farther and trundle in larger rocks, too heavy to heave to the pile's center. She stacked up a rudimentary stairway so she could carry rocks higher and heap them to the angle of repose. The men said nothing.

Rocks too big even for the wheelbarrow she pried by great effort to roll over and over to the pile. The stairs crept higher. So did the pile, a cone of field rocks with a stairway to its peak. On a rare afternoon the men quit early, Solomon studied the silhouette cast by the setting sun. "Now I knows: id lahk in de Bible."

When Spooks returned in a few weeks, the crew referred to it familiarly as "Carrie's Tower of Babel."

"How high will it go?" Spooks inquired.

"To t'top," Hilpert assured him.

One evening Hilpert slowly circled the pile several times, climbed the stairs, hefted some of the stone. At last he sought Carrie. "Got 'nough."

Returned from a brief trip down the valley, Henry spoke long with Lem, then called Carrie over. "I think it'll be about even for food. Lem and his men leave for a while at the end of the week; they're promised near Claytown for a time. But I talked Judah Rainey into coming up with his crew."

"I remember Judah Rainey worked on the new wing at Tulips. But no one ever said why he always gets two names."

Henry shrugged. "The story I heard was there come to be two Judahs in the cove where he grew up. So they included mothers' names to keep 'em apart, and this one was Judah Rainey. It stuck."

"A nice sound to it," Carrie nodded, but still puzzled. "Marse, I thought Judah Rainey just builds houses."

"He does. I planned to wait until next spring or summer. That's too long to stand reproach from the Tower of Babel."

Carrie rose heavy with sleep the morning Lem and his men left. By rote she set out coffee, corn bread, ham and pie. Should she have checked the mirror better before she left the tent? Some of the men seemed to be watching her closely. Solomon called. She turned and saw it. A stick atop the Tower. Tied to it, a tiny Tennessee state flag greeted the rising sun.

❧

Judah Rainey spat as exclamation as he viewed the flag-decked pile. "Mister Hollis, I knowed ye tole me all the stone wuz heap up a-waitin. But lotsa people tell me thet. They jes tryin ta hustle me. I git thar, an she-it, hit's jes a lil pile weeds is a-gonna kiver quick. Nuthin like this'un. An I not fleechin ye."

Judah Rainey was a short man made shorter by a habitual stoop from close application to his work. The stoop and grey hair going white might have made him seem elderly, except that he was in constant motion. His features were sharp cut, which seemed to match his staccato speech.

"My crew's a bit ahind me. On thet damn path ye calls a trail. Five men an four mule. Fer tools an supplies we needin. 'Cept the winders wit' glass. Get 'em later. Hired me a bran new mason. Ye ken spy him a mile off. Thet boy borned wit' the redistis hair ye e'er did see. I jes hope he pay as much attention t'rock layin as t'hair."

Judah's eyes darted around the camp. Carrie thought she could tell from his grunts what he was absorbing. Umm: the shingle repairs on the dilapidated sheds. Umm: the rickety table near the fire pit for food preparation. Umm: the water trough and path to the spring. His eyes moved to the partially-cleared fields. Umm: the bare limbs of girdled trees to be felled as time allowed. He raised his eyes to the serried ridges surrounding them and turned a complete circle. He looked at Henry. "Right purty place."

They heard the noises of the mule train approaching.

Judah Rainey cleared his throat. "Mister Hollis, I ain't like people I might mebbe mention. Them men don' want no owners 'round. 'Least not 'til the place is all done up. What I everly want is reg'lar visitin. So as to head us off ifen we'uns buildin somethin ye not approvin."

He looked squarely at Carrie. "Ye come too," he ordered. "I 'member ye was jes a girl wit' Miss Audie Ann at Tulips. Usin yer hand to talk. Look like magic how ye done hit. An ye takin care'a the speechin side so the rest a'us ken unnerstan Miss Audie."

Carrie smiled. "What I remember is how patient you were when we were in your way."

"I was a-wishin ye was 'round sooner. Fer my lil' sister. She borned deef, she was. But thar warn't nobody fer to teach 'er. No talkin wit' her hand. So she kinda trap thar in'er haid. Real hard, she had't. I felt bad 'cause I played lots wit' her. But I dint know no way t'hep none."

"I wish Miss Audie and I had known. Maybe we could have helped her," said Carrie earnestly.

Judah Rainey studied his shoes. "Afore yourn time. An my ole man, he dint want nobody t'know. Thet we had a de-fek in the fambly. Died young. Run over, she was. By some team she couldn't hear comin."

Shocked, Carrie exclaimed. "That's terrible."

"Anyhow," Judah changed the subject. "Thet Miss Audie, I 'member she want to know everthin 'bout buildin. I was afeered I got to get her down from the damn roof."

He turned to Henry, thumbing toward Carrie. "Them two was sumpin t'watch. Ever'damn thaing agin 'em, one way or'tother. An they jes keep goin. Thar's a lesson fer a body."

Clearly audible now, the pack train's mules began greeting Henry's.

"Mister Hollis, in my 'pinion, the bestest plan is fer ye t'tell me right hyar 'xactly what ye got in mine."

"Nothing fancy, not another Tulips. I'd like a main room with the fireplace, a small sleeping room in back, a low loft above and a wide front porch."

"Nary no dogtrot?"

"No."

"Winders?"

"One or two in front beside the door, and one in back."

"Whur ye wan hit? Nigh on them rocks?"

"Yes, to make it easier for the mason. I've put stakes to mark corners."

"Look like my mason right hyar." Judah Rainey waved over a young man with flaming hair and a sullen mouth. "This hyar's Jim, what I tole ye 'bout. Now Jim, Mister Hollis desirin a room wit' fiah, a chile-standin' loft above, a lil' sleepin room pooched out back, an a front porch wide's the house."

"That's it, Judah Rainey," confirmed Henry. "You've done that maybe before."

"Twicet as I can think of."

"More like a hunert times," muttered Jim, as he carefully stroked a lock to tuck it behind an ear.

"An, Jim, Mister Hollis want nary no chimly carry up with cats and clay, but a real stone chimly up all the ways. A fireboard nigh onto this high?" He paused for Henry to confirm height of the mantle. "This hyar rock, hit make the lastiest chimly they is. So, Jim, ye git hit right an yourn chimly be hyar a long time when my logs is rot out."

Jim nodded, distracted by a red lock out of place, as well as the sight of Carrie at the fire.

Judah Rainey glanced at him sharply, then turned to Henry. "I 'spect we done quick, Mister Hollis. Lessen the weather go bad, an rain set in."

"I'm told you're a master hand at a puncheon floor, Judah Rainey."

"Boastin ain't my line, Mr. Hollis. When I done wit' thet floor, it be baby-ass smooth. Tight's a drum. Now les' us'un look at them karners ye staked."

❧

Carrie's cooking duties stayed the same, for Judah Rainey's crew was no larger than Lem's. But instead of faint cries far distant, she heard men working close in to the camp all day. She enjoyed watching the men at work, so deft with their tools, also a reminder of standing with Audie, watching work on Tulips.

Watching, she became aware, had consequences. Jim the mason was forever adjusting his cap to get his flaming hair just so. After he noticed her surveillance, his hair adjusting did not cease; it became a performance, one that used all reflective surfaces as props. Further, at any time she might look up from her food preparation to see Jim studying *her*, oblivious even to Judah Rainey's impatient direction.

After a hot day when, as a special favor, she carried fresh cold water from the spring to the house crew, Jim began addressing her as "woman" when he called for water, the only one of the crew to do so. She even overheard "my woman" when Jim was talking to the carpenters, and suspected she was meant to hear it.

With heightened awareness that she no longer had Lem's guarantee when she went to wash, she triple-checked where the men were before she set off for the spring. Whenever possible, she left the camp entirely, climbing the back trail to the first ridge overlooking the camp, but her cooking duties usually prevented such escape.

Late one night, she woke to an unfamiliar noise. She lay still, listening, all senses acute. Not the gnawing of some rodent. It was ripping. She rose, knife from under the pillow in her left hand. Just inside the front flap she picked up the piece of firewood she kept there; splitting had left one end a good size for her grip and at the other, a rock-like knot.

Barefoot, she eased silently out of the tent and along its side. She peered around the corner: there, a shadowy human figure, crouched close to the ground. She moved like a game, three quick steps, a full arm swing, her maximum strength on the downward arc, the knife in reserve. A dead-on blow. She raised her arm for another, but the crouching figure was now collapsed, unmoving, on the ground.

Fearing any light would call attention she wasn't ready for, she dropped the firewood club and reached down gingerly. Her patting hand felt a shoulder, a head, scalp. She felt long hair. Wrapping a few strands around a finger, she pulled.

At the still-burning fire, she carefully opened her fist. Across her palm hair strands glinted red in the firelight. She closed her fist and dozed fitfully the rest of the night by a high fire she fed with her free hand. In dim light of early dawn she saw a man crawling unsteadily toward the sheds where Judah's crew slept. He barely made it. Sun nearly up, she opened her fist again. No doubt about the color.

"Gotta problem, Mister Hollis," Judah Rainey reported as the sun, now just above the horizon, greeted the camp's earliest risers. "Thet boy Jim go out to piss in t'night. He *says* he tripped, hit his head on a rock. How ken a body hit the *back'a* his head trippin? I jes cain't unnerstan hit. But he's in a bad way. I'd best take 'im fer some doctorin up. An fine me 'nother mason."

Henry asked Carrie if coffee was ready, but she seemed distracted, and he walked over to the cabin site for yet another inspection while a complicated breakfast required her undivided attention. Soon after Judah Rainey left, steadying Jim astride a mule, John Bright appeared. He knew the story from Judah Rainey on the trail.

"Deerslayer," Henry grumbled, "I suspect Jim went out in the night to drink, against Judah Rainey's rules, against my rules. Think we can find any trace, maybe a bottle or flask?"

They began at Judah's sheds, but Henry's patience quickly ran out. He left for the fields. Spooks sank to hands and knees, moving inches at a time. He progressed to behind the sheds, then toward Carrie's tent. She was sipping coffee by the fire when he came over, poured himself some coffee, and sat down on the log beside her, dropping the knotted firewood piece at his feet.

"I admit bafflement until I saw the cut canvas. And bright red hair somehow caught on this ugly knot. Might explain your remoteness this morning. Please pardon the liberty, Miss Cora." He lightly touched her shoulder, then upper arm. "Nothing like carrying rocks to build muscles. Strong enough to kill him easy," he mused. "Why not?"

"Never meant to."

"Why didn't you tell Henry?" Bright might have been questioning motives in James Fenimore Cooper.

"Because from the beginning he never wanted me up here. He said I'm a temporary cook. If he finds out about Jim, that'll be an excuse to send me back to Tulips. I want to stay here."

Spooks nodded pensively. "Speaking of Tulips, when I stopped there two days ago, I heard a whole army out back. So I went around to the barn and found Audie Ann at her shooting range, firing away. I had no idea what a marks . . . markswoman, she has become."

Carrie brightened. "Did you see her split a playing card edge-on?"

"You've seen her do that? All the more reason I must be thankful we'll never fight a duel; I'd have to forfeit my honor and flee to the wilds of Arkansas. We visited a nice long time because I remembered more of her hand talk than I expected. She worries about you up here, a young woman alone with a crew of men."

"I wish Audie wouldn't worry." After both sipped their coffee, Carrie gestured toward the knotted wood at Spooks' feet. "You gonna tell Marse Henry?"

"This firewood? Looks dry to me. Jes' righ'ta reheat coffee." He pitched it into the fire. "Audie Ann required me to bring you a dress she thinks you can use. I put it in your tent, all rolled up. You'll want to tend to it. I know you women don't like creased skirts."

That night Carrie found the rolled dress in her tent. She caressed the familiar fabric wistfully. It was too fine for an open fire; the dress wouldn't fit after her weeks of rock hauling. When she lifted it to fold properly, its weight seemed not right; something heavy and hard inside. Unrolling it, she came first to a note in Audie's hand. *Under your pillow to sleep better.* At the innermost roll, one of Audie Ann's best pistols.

Judah Rainey returned at dusk with an unfamiliar man. He brushed off Henry's questions about Jim. "Mistook 'bout thet boy, I wuz. Real no'count, Mister Hollis. We'uns better off now I got shet'a 'im. George hyar's a gooder mason nor Jim. Worked wit' him many time."

At the cabin site, heavy sills on solid stone defined perimeter. Walls enclosed space. Thick puncheon offered smooth footing. Openings framed views. Rafters promised shelter.

Judah Rainey was satisfied. "Checked ever wall twicet, Mister Hollis, down to a gnat's bristle. Nary'un thet's sigodlin."

Henry nodded to him with a smile as he walked the site, Carrie a step behind. "Good news, Judah Rainey. Mighty glad to hear that."

They returned to the fire. "Marse Henry, pardon me for bothering you, but what does sigod, or whatever it is, mean?"

"Thought you knew that," Henry had a dismissive expression, "from Tulips building years ago. It's good the new walls aren't afflicted."

A massive fireplace established permanence. As the fireplace gained a throat, the Tower of Babel towered less. Henry found excuses to come in from the fields to check progress. "Can't stay away," he admitted ruefully to Carrie. "And Judah Rainey said we should inspect regularly."

At the cabin site he called to George, poking among the rock pile. "Looks we have way more stone than you need."

"Nossir, hit jes right, Mister Hollis. A man need more at hand then he use, 'cause ye had orter fine jes the right'un fer thet hole starin' at ye. Mos' people reckon hit don' differ none which'a them rock I picks up. But they wrongous."

"You have a sharp eye for the empty places, George."

"Hit's tol'ble. Ye jes 'member this here'un so thet space o'er thar need havin a big 'un, an mebbe up thar needin too. I ain't kickin 'nother man's work, but lots a rock men fergits color. An color ken change how big a stone seem. So ye re-quire more stone then ye need. Then ye ken be choisey."

Carrie became too wrapped in the conversation to resist joining it. "Mister Hilpert, on Mister Lem's crew, told Marse Henry that the pile was big enough."

George smiled broadly. "I disremember ye knowed Hilpert. He my favoritist cousin. He have a powerful good eye, but after thet pile roll an crush his hand down in Claytown, he cain't do stonework so easy no more. But we consultate 'bout the hard places. Anyhow, even if a body cain't tell 'tother from which, there's allers a sure test—a chimly draw good as a bellows or it don' draw. And if it don' . . . ." He pulled a battered finger across his throat.

Looking about, Henry spoke in a low tone. "George, my memory fails me with age, though I hate to admit it." His voice dropped still more. "I can't seem to recall just exactly what sigodlin means. Can you give me a boost?"

"Sartain," answered George, with an affable smile. "Ye ken say sigodlin or catawumpus or slaunchways or outta whanker. All t'same. Oncet I heered a man from off say 'outta plumb,' but hardly nobody but me knowed what he mean, and I only knowed 'cause I work in Knoxville fer a time. So they's all kinda word t'mean the same."

"None of them mean good."

"Not ifen ye buildin ye a wall, ner a chimly neither."

"Of course. I just could not get my mind to it."

"Thet happin t'me 'most ev'ry day, Mister Hollis," George reassured him heartily.

"Oh, to me too," chimed in Carrie, keeping her eyes on George.

Another spare moment mid-afternoon, just time enough for yet another inspection walk. Carrie paused a moment beside Henry to watch Judah Rainey with mallet and froe. "He's so fast. I'm jealous."

"Just experience," Henry replied. "Day after day. Looks like he doesn't have many to hide in the fire." He looked at her with a sideways glance and perhaps a trace of a smile.

"No, Marse."

Smoke billowed into a cloudless sky from the chimney top. George came outside to study his success. "Reckon she draw," he finally nodded, just perceptibly.

Judah Rainey and his men built a solid table of wide cherry for the cabin as thanks for extry good eats, as they put it when they packed up to disappear down the valley. Even though Lem's crew soon replaced Judah Rainey's, so that food consumption remained nearly the same, the Quachasee farm was much transformed. Carrie moved Henry's things into the cabin. His old shanty became Daisy's barn. Carrie propped her tent as a lean-to against a wall of the cabin, and set up her kitchen in the cabin's main room. Instead of cooking and domestic chores outside no matter the weather, she worked inside or under the porch roof.

Granted, cabin details remained uncompleted. But Henry had marked a sunplank on the floor, in pencil to check before cutting in with a knife. True, no proper barns yet, not even a small one. But there were stakes to mark a large barn's future corners. Conceded, weather-tight shelter for servants hardly considered. Yes, a smokehouse and root cellar still a dream. But with cold water running clear in the spring year round, they needed no water witch for dowsing, nor risky well digging.

From the high ridge, Carrie saw smoke curling above the cabin chimney; she distinguished sparrow-sized chickens pecking the ground around the cabin. A few orderly rows of green in fields nearby. Daisy browsed grass to convert it to milk. The place looked a rough camp no longer.

Here stood a farm. Set a large barn right there, well-built sheltering sheds here and here, tear down that last old shed, plant an orchard protected by that sharply-rising hill. Plenty of chestnut, promising rails for zigzag fences to control the stock. Pale in a garden not far from the cabin. Nearby, gum tree hollows were already collected for hives. Yes, clear that field up to where the slope steepened sharply. No, don't worry about the hogs; they can run in the forest for the time, with an abundance of free feed, acorns and chestnut mast, to fatten.

Still much to do, of course, but the handsome fireplace in the main house with its massive fire board, the new table, shelves and hooks convenient, and, in the little back room, a thick tick on a corded frame, with shelves and hanging pegs on the walls—all this made comfortable residence palpable reality rather than future hope.

Henry seemed less tense. He did not drive himself and the men so late in the day. At dawn he had time for a few words, at dusk still energy to converse about something other than work. He found patience enough after supper to bring out a Bible and read verses aloud for all to follow, then turn to Starck's prayer book, as his father did at Tulips.

Bright noticed the change. "Uncas, the enemy seems not so hot on your trail these days." He turned to Carrie, "Cora, think you so?"

She nodded. "But Deerslayer, tell the brave warrior he must quiver his arrows so he has time for more than coffee as breakfast."

Bright maintained his stern face. "Lo, Cora thinks well, noble Uncas. And Cora, she too seems happier."

"A snug cabin and no cooking smoke in my eyes: what more could I ask?" Carrie burst out gaily. Bright looked at her, silent, for a moment and she bit her lip. John Bright made it so easy to forget she was not at Tulips, teasing Audie Ann.

Henry was too immersed in planning to notice the silence. "A question for Deerslayer, master of forests. Uncas retains recollection, though distant and dim, of a faint trace over that ridge, headed roughly toward Claytown and beyond. Do Hawkeye's well-traveled moccasins remember that?"

"Easily. They trod it last month. Over the ridge there," Bright pointed to a tree-less low saddle on the horizon, "then down, north through a gap, down, follow a creek. Why?"

"Been meaning to take the mare to Doc Sexton. Elton and Earl won't live forever. I'd like to have some young mules coming up. I believe the mare may be ready soon."

"If you go tomorrow, I can show you a good bit of the way. With a horse through the rough, though, it's more than a full day from here to Sexton."

"I didn't think it's that far. But Hawkeye is a trusted guide and pleasant company. As Cora says, what more can Uncas ask?"

Plowing with Greek, My Life

HL Hollis

Since I am, like generations before me, a tiller of the soil, in odd moments I revert automatically to the land and the multitude of decisions it entails. My mind's eyes survey the Tulips fields for weeds. They sweep the fruit trees for branches that need pruning. They follow fence lines for fallen rails (mourning again the blight, which decimated the invaluable chestnuts, and lamenting the incursion of barbed wire, that insidious invention of the West). I mentally inspect the barns, beam by board, itemizing repairs to maintain them sound at least a half-century more. As I do so I think of my father, who, also being a farmer, surely did the same here at Tulips, and at his first farm up the Quachasee, as well

In Samuel B's diary is the brief notation, "Bo't Quachasee tract from cousin O. Oppdyke, headed to Missouri." (Obediah Oppdyke was his mother's second cousin.) Some years ago, by happy inspiration, I wrote to the Missouri Historical Society, inquiring if they had any information on the man. To my astonishment, I soon had a reply, stating they held three letters written by him. To condense ensuing correspondence, in one of those letters, copies of which I possess, Obediah mentions that he had escaped from the rugged mountains of eastern Tennessee, where he had built a "tidy cabin" and other buildings.

Thus we have solid evidence that, upon Father's arrival up there, he benefitted from the advantage of cabin and barns waiting for him to occupy. Sound construction distinguishes these buildings, even by today's standards. (I should rather say, *especially* by standards today, when so many buildings are just cobbled up.) Walls stand plumb, rafters stretch sag-less, floors ring solid. and a magnificent maple slab as mantle presides over all.

The masonry is as fine as I've seen. Tutored by a retired mason, I have in another place drawn appropriate illustrative diagrams. One evaluates last century's masonry, I am informed, by assessing the percentage of rubble. The best work has a low ratio, and a substantial number of large stone arranged with an eye to symmetry.

The Quachasee cabin has no rubble visible inside or out. Chimney stonework is so balanced one would think some artist drew it on paper before the laying. Simply collecting those stones cost much time and great weariness. The laying demonstrates a master's hand. I'd wince at the bill today. Obediah did well. Having those buildings already in place surely saved Father great effort as he got started. He maintained them carefully, and required high standards of upkeep even subsequent to his occupancy. Barring fire, those buildings should endure indefinitely.

The Quachasee farm was much smaller than Tulips, of course, but Father worked there alone. Up there, level land is limited, but for a single man adequate, even a challenge, especially considering the tedious, backbreaking toil simply to bring a field to the point (free of entangling roots) that it could be properly plowed. Father not only plowed and hoed, but was active in growing and grafting fruit frees and in breeding swine. In the absence of any evidence to the contrary, I assume that Father plowed whistling, planted in prayerful hope, cultivated conscientiously, and harvested with thanksgiving, as I have done all my life.

An engine in the distance is also reminder I must mention one important difference between Father's farming and my own. My father (and everybody else) farmed mostly with mules. Early in his farming years, he relied much on a renowned mule trader located past Claytown, not far on modern roads, an inconvenient distance on trails. This dealer knew mules, though he was, I gather, more than slightly eccentric. He made a deep impression on my father, who took and profited from his advice. In consequence Tulips enjoyed a reputation locally for finely matched pairs.

By contrast, I have come to rely exclusively on horses. Perhaps the manner of my father's death played some role. I feel a much greater affinity for horses than for mules. Not having the wise counsel of the Clayton mule expert, I find mules unpredictable, intractable, and esthetically inferior. It is my lot to be caught as a between-generation insofar as my father ridiculed my aversion to mules, and my son brings tractors to Tulips.

My preference has led to some head-shaking hereabouts, but I suspect the neighborhood became inured to Hollis eccentricities prior to my time so my own go less remarked. My preference for horses is not an affectation; there's no better work than plowing with a nicely matched, well-trained, experienced team of intelligent horses.

My teams don't need reins; I can ride the plow or walk beside. We plow in Greek. They listen attentively whether I choose Homer or Thucydides. When they stop unbidden, I recognize they somehow sense a problem—not in hexameter, but a buried rock about to damage a plow tip, a harness out of order. Under no great strain, they move with grave, unhurried dignity and conviction, sensible to the task. There is time for me to study the clouds or sneak a look at the passage my memory lost.

To work with an experienced team in an orchard is equally a pleasure. The team steers down the orchard aisle slack-reined, stopping without command at the first tree, waiting for what requires doing, then at a quiet word moving on to stop without supervision at the subsequent tree.

A tractor is an abominable substitute. What tractor plows with Greek? What tractor inspires a sculptor? How could a mere machine be as handsome as a pair of live animals, with their swiveling curious ears and gentle eyes and powerful muscles? Besides, a tractor allows no books even in English, let alone the glory of Demosthenes or the adventures of Ulysses.

A tractor does not stop of its own at an unnoticed hazard. Its noisome chugging clashes with dactyls. It does not work automatically down the orchard row, steering, stopping, starting of itself. Instead it demands continual off and on the seat, watchful control of the steering wheel, and tiresome legwork on the pedals. Its tenaciously soiling grease and vaporous gasoline produce a lingering stench incompatible with a barn's mellow scent of wood and hay.

A tractor's fuel tank filling, bolt securing, belt tightening, linkage adjusting, and oil changing are a constant worry. In point of fact, four-wheeled propulsion requires more attention than four-hoofed. Further a tractor takes no pleasure in its currying. In early morning chill, it can be even more cantankerous than mules.

Thus do I find enmity between us, tractors and me. My father would certainly be as appalled as I, accustomed as he was to following the advice of his mule dealer.

QUACHASEE
WHC

Spooks had, of course, estimated rightly the distance to the Sexton place. Dark fell before Henry came even close. He begged a barn hay bed at the second farm where he stopped. No difficulty getting directions, though. Everyone knew Doc Sexton, the most respected mule breeder and trader in three or four counties. Henry had never met Sexton, but he recalled his father's pronouncement years earlier. "Boys, the man is either a master actor or raving mad. He belongs on the stage or in Bedlam, except for two things: he's honest and he understands mules like a mule."

"Look fer thet all-white barn, fren," Henry heard. "Cain't missit." He did not. Bright white, even trim and doors. In front, on a sign almost as large as the barn side, huge black letters.

DOC SEXTON. MULES

THEY SHALL BRING AN OFFERING ON MULES. ISAIAH, 66
ABSALOM RODE UPON A MULE. II SAMUEL, 18.

A much smaller sign on a stake identified a side door, hanging ajar.

OFFICE

PORTAL OF CREATION

ENTER HERE WITHOUT FEAR

Henry obeyed. A large man of dark complexion stood in the center of a low-ceiling room, immersed in a book. He wore black pants, a black long-sleeved shirt, a black hat. An enormous, curly mass of black beard hung halfway to a wide black belt circling his great girth. He looked up at Henry. Or he looked at something beside Henry. Or he looked at something behind Henry. No knowing. He looked with eyes severely crossed. Snapping the book shut, he dropped it atop a disorderly heap of books at his feet. He turned a complete revolution and again faced Henry. "And you, sir, you are?"

"Hollis. Henry Hollis. I'm looking for Doc Sexton."

"Aha, a younger son of Mister Samuel B Hollis at Tulips."

"The youngest, yes sir."

"Elton and Earl? Still well matched? Does Ezra still shirk? Can you depend on Ewald to get cranky in bad weather? Remind your father, and remind him again, Doc Sexton told him his next mare must have stronger shoulders than Sybil."

"You Doc Sexton?"

The man turned another complete circle. With a sly smile and conspiratorial wink he tiptoed ponderously to the open door, jerked it quickly away from the wall for cautious, thorough inspection behind it, then returned to his original place. Yet another revolution. "Doc Sexton so assumes."

"Since you know my father, I should tell you he's very sick."

Sexton sighed. "People appear problems, but in reality are easy. Mules appear easy, but in reality are problems. Your father may recover. Or he may die. As God wills. But you? You seek Doc Sexton for?"

"I brought a mare for stud. Shall I leave her with you?"

"A 'mare'? Is she nameless, sir?" Sexton thundered.

"So far. I've been too busy to think of a good name."

"This is unpardonable disrespect for our quadruped benefactors." Sexton's voice rose indignantly, but he stopped almost between syllables. Intense concentration led to a satisfied smile. "Aha. Doc Sexton says slight of words may conceal the infraction and repair young Hollis's reputation. The unnamed mare's appellation is surely Anonymous. Anonymous it is, a mouth-filling name. A-non-e-mous. But a name we shall shorten. The diminutive must be Anon. Anon will be much pleased."

"Shall I leave her?" asked Henry, less patiently.

"That depends. That depends. That depends."

"On what? On what? On what?"

Sexton's smile appeared, quickly broadened, then erupted in a bellowing laugh that seemed to shake the room. His roar stopped as if cut off. "The young Hollis and Doc Sexton get along splendidly. Splendidly. The young Hollis shall tell Doc Sexton, where did he acquire Anon?"

"A man in Clinton."

"So Doc Sexton don't know Anon. Doc Sexton must meet her."

Outside he hardly glanced at the mare before he shook his head. "Aha. The gentle mare, Anon, hails not from Clinton. Sold there from Claytown, she was. Doc Sexton knows Anon well. Knows her whole line well. All too small in the pipes to race more than a mile. But sound, sir, very sound."

He turned to Henry. "Doc Sexton has in his barn four possible jacks. Four, sir, as different as possum and coon. But to the young Hollis, Doc Sexton says the best for Anon is either Beelzebub or Bael. Bael's bloodline harks back to Spain via that famous gift to President George Washington. Beelzebub's line also traces there but not by so well recognized a sire. Not so recognized, but Doc Sexton knows that line to be excellent for generations. And most complementary to Anon. Doc Sexton recommends Beelzebub without reservation."

"Whatever you say. How long do you want me to leave her?"

Sexton ran his hands over the mare, threw her tail aside. "Nature, like youth, can be impetuous, young Hollis. Give Doc Sexton some small time to answer." He faced the open barn door. "Lazarus," he rumbled, "come forth," raising an arm to horizontal, extended forefinger pointing at the door.

Mystified, Henry's eyes followed Sexton's finger. Out of the barn's dimness limped a short man, squinting in the bright sun. The white of his pants and shirt exceeded even that of the barn.

"Lazarus, it is my privilege to present to you this fine mare, Anon," announced Sexton in a formal manner. "You must conduct her grandly down the aisle, like the beautiful bride she is, a wedding processional past the stallion Teaser's stall." He lowered his voice to a stage whisper. "It is, sir, a low trick, alas, but we must tempt the mare with the mate, not of reality, but of her dreams." Louder, "Slowly, I say, slowly, Lazarus, for I must observe her with the greatest care."

Inside the barn, the mare danced nervously, eyes wide, ears swiveling, her hind legs sidestepping, breathing soft whinnies. Lazarus steered her close to the box stall with the sign TEASER over the door. The stallion kicked hard at his stall door, threw his weight against the walls so the heavy timbers shook. He reared, lunging from side to side. Anon squealed loud, prancing wide around Lazarus, trying to keep her eyes on Teaser's stall, passing water in small spurts.

"Get her out of here," Sexton ordered. Distress on his face, Sexton spoke to Henry. "I feel guilty, sir, painfully guilty that we have enticed the mare under false pretenses. She would never respond so to Beelzebub. But we have now seen. Doc Sexton's opinion, sir: we must join our pair forthwith. There is not a moment to lose. What say you, young Hollis?"

"You're the expert."

"Young Hollis is most certainly correct. Doc Sexton *is* the expert! Lazarus! Lead Anon out to the pit. Shadrack! Meshack! Manifest yourselves, you devils."

Two boys sauntered out of the harness room, their black clothes matching their skin. "Yessuh, yessuh," one grinned. "I 'spect yuh needin Beelzebub foah won'a his preformences."

"Right you are, says Doc Sexton. One on each side as you go out. Remember, Shadrack, your foolish mistake last week."

Sexton turned to Henry. "And the young Hollis? Does he have self-possession enough to witness the generative act without losing his veneer of civilization? We shall test the young Hollis—after we pick up the fucking stick." He stepped into the office and went to a hook on one wall. Above the hook a painted label in six-inch letters declared FUCKING CANE. From the hook he lifted a stout four-foot rod, the two words repeatedly incised deeply its whole length. With speed surprising in a man of his girth, he strode around the barn toward its back, Henry at his heels.

"Here, sir, in this very place," he spoke without slowing his gait, "we encounter the mystery of the universe. You will agree 'tis a placid morning in the glorious mountains of eastern Tennessee, our great state, sixteenth to grace the grand union of these United States of America. But how is it that on this day, in specifically this place, whose latitude and longitude may be noted to the seconds of a degree, sir, how is it that precisely here," he pounded the ground with his cane, "nature erupts with force greater than storm's wind, mightier than ocean's tide, surpassing even globe's gravity—in short, sexual generation?"

He broke off as they entered an area closed in with high, solid walls. "Doc Sexton approves." Lazarus had led the mare into a narrow, blind trench. Its level floor was cut into a rising slope. Rough timbers lined the trench's sides, leaving barely enough width for the mare. In the rising ground, close on both sides of the trench, hoof marks showed deep in the bare dirt and topmost timbers. The mare wore a heavy halter over the one Henry brought, and a blindfold. Double ropes tethered her to stout rings bolted on each trench wall. Lazarus sat on the trench edge at the mare's head, quieting her with an apple.

Sexton circled the mare, inspecting her and her halter. He yanked one of the ropes hard against its anchor ring. "Doc Sexton asks Lazarus whether Anon is secure."

"Twicet-knotted, Doc."

First glancing at Henry, perhaps, Sexton faced the distant mountains. "Last month, a man—a foolish man, an overeducated man, a citified man—preened in just the space young Hollis there occupies, and inquired of Doc Sexton with a jeering voice: 'If the sexual urge is so strong, why do you tie her down?' Poor Doc Sexton despairs of mankind. Poor Doc Sexton must stoop low to instruct, must patiently tutor this ignoramus. Teaser, not Beelzebub, is Anon's dream. But she is the one subservient. She it is who must be bound for sexual congress with an ass."

Sexton's laugh rumbled up. "Not nymphs and satyrs gamboling carefree in the Arcadian wood, young Hollis will agree." He raised his voice. "Enter Beelzebub." The two boys struggled into the walled-off rectangle, one on each side of the jack, using all their strength and weight to control him. Sensing him, the mare neighed and threw herself against the ropes, then from side to side, slamming into the trench walls, tail high. Urine flowed down her hind legs and sprayed the boys as she kicked.

"Easy boys. Easy." Sexton shouted over the commotion. "Get him started on the right track." They worked to push Beelzebub in line so he planted a front hoof on each side of the trench's beginning. "Good work. Good work. Let him at her a little more so he gets his business end started," Sexton ordered.

The jack was trying to rear, nearly hauling the two young handlers off their feet. Once his rear legs straddled the trench, the boys let him go forward some. When he reached the mare's hind quarters, he reared, strained forward and reared again until, because he was on rising ground and she in the trench, he was able to mount the longer-legged mare.

"Enter, Beelzebub," commanded Sexton over the trumpeting, the neighing, solid mass crashing into timbers, hooves stamping hard. The trunk of distended penis swung wildly, striking the mare's legs as Beelzebub reared, his front hooves narrowly missing the two boys at his head.

"Enter, Beelzebub," Sexton repeated, as he deftly used the cane to lift and aim the blindly thrusting penis, his work aided by the deep incisions on the cane. Trumpeting, shaking his head wildly, Beelzebub bit at the mare's neck. As Sexton's cane succeeded, she strained against the tether ropes.

"Enter, Beelzebub." Sexton whacked the cane on Beelzebub's hindquarters as the jack drove into the mare. The great stiff hose disappeared as Beelzebub took in gasps of air, tossing his head, sweat flowing from his neck and shoulders when he shuddered, the muscles in his rear legs bulging under his hide.

Beelzebub quieted. "Repeating 'enter' three times always accomplishes the goal. Look sharp, Shadrack. Look sharp. This is where we look sharp. Back him. Back. Out. Out. Get him away fast. Watch out for the mare's kick. Back him down. Back him down. Quick. Quick. Good job, Meshack. Good job. Neither of them injured. Sexual magnetism safely released."

As the boys led the spent Beelzebub away, Lazarus soothed the trembling mare. Sexton faced Henry, holding the cane as scepter. With glittering eyes he fixed on Henry, or on some other audience—Henry was not sure—and began declaiming in his great bass.

"Friend, you have seen. With your own eyes you have observed. There is much to be learned from what you have witnessed. Consider what we glimpse here of the Divine. Yes, the Divine, for in this generative act we have much evidence of God Almighty."

He paused, apparently to savor his own broadening smile.

"Firstly, we see proof that God possesses a capacious sense of humor. Yes! Why should not God laugh, sir? God loves a joke. Doc Sexton knows. The Almighty has played a joke of infinite mirth, a God-worthy joke on His en-tire creation. God amuses Himself and His angels. Mark this, sir—God commands all life to be fruitful and multiply. Holy Writ so testifies. But Holy Writ is silent about means to that end. Why sir? Doc Sexton will tell you to trust your eyes. Our eyes testify that God provides to fulfill His commandment. What does he provide?"

Sexton's smile became a grin.

"Why, a *penis*. A penis, of all appendages. The most ridiculous of possibilities: a damn dumb *Penis*. The shriveled, wobbly, mis-aimed, stand-up, PENIS, for God's sake. Yes, truly, *for God's sake*, for God's great uproarious laughter, while the heavens look down on us, guffawing, truly *down* on us, all miserably equipped to answer God's command. Answer Him with? With a p-e-e-nis. God does not smile. God laughs."

Sexton suddenly raised the cane to hold it vertically above his head. He began slowly turning in place, bowing to Lazarus as they faced each other. Lazarus returned the bow. Then he faced Henry, again bowing, but Henry, mystified, returned only a nod. Sexton continued to rotate until he was back to his original position, something he looked about carefully to confirm. "Doc Sexton shall now proceed." He lowered the cane.

"A divine *joke* it *must* be. Doc Sexton will prove that. Consider, sir, a woman's breast."

Gripping his cane under his arm, Sexton cupped his hands at his chest.

"Essential to the suckling newborn, and admirably so suited, but also a pleasure to view, a delight to fondle, a dream to kiss: humble utility and superfluous luxury combined, you must agree, you shall agree, unless you are sinfully blind to God's blessings."

Again gripping his cane, Sexton pointed it at Henry. "Now, consider, sir: if God finds all things possible, as, being the Omnipotent Deity, He *must*, why could not God create the penis as comely as the breast? Why, sir? Doc Sexton knows: God creates a Holy Joke. God teases His creation for His own amusement."

Sexton flicked the cane point away from Henry, and flourished it high.

"And friend, another lesson here. A lesson against pride. Mankind speaks and sings and draws. Man cogitates, and reasons that he therefore is. He concludes therefore he is superior to all other creatures. Yet leviathans which dwarf even Doc Sexton, leviathans swimming in the sea and leviathans coursing the land, *they* prove otherwise. Consider, sir: whales, those leviathans of the deep—have penises, sir, penises thicker than your body. Elephants, those leviathans of Africa and far-off Asia—have penises, and longer than your leg. The buffalo, those leviathan herds of prairie and plain—have penises, and mightier than your arm."

And what," he inquired in an insinuating tone, "has man hanging in front of him, to remind him that though he communicates, though he cogitates, he is kin—albeit kin frail and fickle—to all these? What does he possess? Alas, his poor puny penis."

Sexton let the cane dangle, his wrist limp.

"The cogitating man in his pride, in his concealing garments, may deny this affinity to Whale and Elephant and Buffalo, may deny it adamantly. But to prove his denial he must sever this connection irretrievably. Sever, sir. But a severing painful even in thought. That disconnection means severing what no Zealot will ever preach, for it is too precious to man. Doc Sexton's case is thus proven, sir, proven beyond contention."

Again Sexton stopped, raised the cane to vertical as if he were balancing it on top his head, and began his rotation. When he reached Lazarus he stopped and in a monotone asked, "Lazarus, are you here?"

Lazarus replied, "I'm here."

Instead of continuing the rotation, the monotone again. "Anon, are you here?"

Lazarus spoke up again. "Yes, Doc, Anon is here, yes."

The rotation continued to Henry, who was too intrigued not to answer. "Yes."

When he reached—and again carefully confirmed—his starting point, Sexton lowered the cane, and, without explanation, continued his sermon. He again pointed the cane at Henry.

"And further—the young Hollis, sir. When *you* come panting to your mare? Will she be tethered, unable to escape? Will you be different from Beelzebub who drives heedless of effort to impale an available mare on the shaft he believes so magnificent? Will you be distinguishable? No sir. The same, sir, as whale and elephant and bison. I-den-ti-cal."

Sexton nodded, then leaned toward Henry.

"But friend, there is yet more to be learned. You witnessed the generative act. You saw. By trench and tether we ensured Anon was available to the Great Penis. Did Beelzebub hesitate when presented with the nubile Anon? You answer no. Correct, sir, no hesitation. Was this, then, an act governed by Nature? You answer yes. But Doc Sexton knows better. Doc Sexton says the proper answer is a resounding no. T'was *not* a natural act, sir. On the contrary, it was *un*natural, sir, shockingly *unnatural*. A *shameful* act. *You* know its shamefulness, for Doc Sexton marked your fixed stare, your quickened breath, your flushed face, sir—aha, the young Hollis did not apprehend he himself was watched, and as closely as he watched his mare. Doc Sexton observed all."

He pointed to his squinted eyes to emphasize his point.

"*Why* was it shameful? Doc Sexton knows. Doc Sexton will tell you. God made He male and female *of every kind*. Why would God go to that extraordinary effort, sir? Why should not God economize with a single male for all generative acts, sir? With such economy God could have rested an extra day. Here is a Divine Mystery that demands explication. Doc Sexton will solve this mystery. Doc Sexton tells you that God made He male and female of every kind to ensure there need be *no mixing*. Each kind has its own to propagate, sir. Kinds and colors, God desires separate. I repeat, sir: kinds and colors, God desires separate."

Sexton slowly raised his head as if to receive some divination, then struck the ground hard with the cane. He must have hit a buried rock, for the result was far beyond a soft thud. Thump. Thump. Thump. "Lazarus, are you there?"

"Here, Doc, and Anon. And thet Hollis feller, too."

Sexton nodded acknowledgement and continued. "God desires separate. SEPARATE SHALL WE KEEP THEM. Doc Sexton obeys. OBEYS, sir. Here in Doc Sexton's domain, white mingles only with white, and black only with black, sir. Observe the barn for proof: all white. The black sign is *separate* from the white barn. White skin demands white clothes, and black skin, black.

"Doc Sexton mates horses in *front* of the barn. And asses likewise. In front, in plain view. Why sir, in front, when prudes and ignorant women scold Doc Sexton for so doing? Doc Sexton points to the obvious—where there is no mixing, there is no shame. There can be no shame in the generative act within kind, sir, for it is of God."

He raised his face to the sun, as if receiving some special divination.

"But as you see, sir, this trench is well hidden, *in back,* for it is a shameful place. God is not pleased. The generative act here bears fruit, true it is. But because the act is unnatural, the fruit is flawed. Flawed, young Hollis, for the fruit, the jack and the jenny, may subsequently couple, but they are condemned by their guilty progenitors. Doomed to bear no fruit of their own. The Lord may tolerate. The Lord need not bless."

He opened his arms wide. "There, friend, we learn the ultimate wisdom of the Great God Almighty, for He governs and maintains order in all His creation. *Order*, sir. God keeps all of His creation *in order*. All that creep and run and fly and swim. All in their appointed *order*. Man tinkers with that order only at GREAT expense and imperilment. Cost and peril, sir, penalty in the Great Oeconomy of the Universe sufficient for bankruptcy and destitution. *Order*, sir, is what will preserve us until the heavenly trumpets sound God's *Great Last Call* to His chosen.

"So saith the Lord, and his humble servant, Doc Sexton."

"Neighbor," his voice and tone now conversational, he continued. "The stud fee guarantees issue, excluding birth. Lazarus it is who tends to details and handles filthy lucre. Good day, sir." Sexton shouldered his cane, turned, and trudged away without a backward glance.

Henry stared at Sexton's retreating back. "Is he at himself?" he asked Lazarus. "Does he preach so every time?"

"Nossir," answered Lazarus in a reverent tone. "He don' preach so as a rule. I ken tell: Doc's powerful moved this time. He's a seer, y'know. Mebbe he got wind'a sumpin in ye thet need talkin at."

"What the hell was all that rigamarole of turning and asking if we were here?"

"Oh," answered Lazarus, "thet's jest t'make sartain we're all awake an lissenin still."

"Even the horse?" persisted Henry.

"Wal, Doc say critters unnerstan." Lazarus paused, then added, "An he don' like nobody callin hit 'rigamarole' neither. He say hit's 'ritual.'"

"He's insane," Henry burst out.

"Mebbe he is," allowed Lazarus calmly. "But mebbe he *has* t'be a mite teched t'unnerstan mules like he do. A year an ye might think differen 'bout Doc. At least I notice thet happen to smart men when theirn mule's borned an standin."

He pulled on Anon's tether, then stopped to tug at his crotch. "Gawd-damn. I watch ole Beelzebub at work an hit jes makes me stiff as hickory. Ye see him slidin' thet great slick shaft in an out, in an out? Gotta be near a yard long. Think'a havin thet treasure in yer pants. My woman gonna get a poundin' t'night, thet's sartain. She'll say, 'Oh, Laz, you bin watchin Beelzebub, I jes knowed hit.' Then she damn near suck me dry."

He backed the mare out of the trench. "Doc thinks Anon's had it, but ye ken leave 'er a coupl'a weeks jes t'be sure. Got a long piece t'hoof now?"

"A day steep uphill."

"Don' mean to butt in yer bus'ness, but ye jes ain't gonna be tol'able lessen y'get a woman hyar. Whur y'hail?"

"Quachasee."

"Ye from off. So y'don' know these parts good?"

Henry shook his head.

"Mebbe y'be wantin sassy Carrie."

Startled, Henry looked sharply at Lazarus. "Beg your pardon?"

"Oh, her real name's Carolyn. I bin in her so many times I call her Carrie. Hot Carrie. I 'spect she's got some mixed blood not too fer back. She allers right accommodatin fer a man in yer sitiation. Live alone, a little cabin anigh the left fork yonder." Lazarus pointed down the slope.

"Thank you, Lazarus, but it's a long step home. I should get going."

"Ole Carrie, she don' take long," Lazarus laughed. "An' ifen a man be wantin second helpins a diffren way, she serves thet right up too. But dessert, she make you *dick-er*." He roared at his cleverness.

Henry smiled acknowledgement and turned uphill.

❧

By sunset, the lane back toward Quachasee narrowed to a trace. Farms became spaced at increasing intervals. The trace grew fainter, the terrain rougher. Rather than lose his way, Henry settled at a huge maple's base, waiting for the moon.

He drifted in and out of fitful sleep, dogged by persistent images. The crippled sailor's lecherous grin on that Manhattan dock as he held up scrimshaw of a whale's huge penis, urging Henry to buy. Doc Sexton's mad-eyed smile in that boarded enclosure as he wielded his cane to drive Beelzebub's great shaft full into the mare. Elise Vail's half-lidded eyes in that opulent Manhattan parlor calculating her mother's approaching stairsteps to the second as she seized Harry's hand, without warning, to push it hard into her skirt high between her legs. Riti's smile in that miserable Brooklyn boarding house room as she moved Henry's hand to her breasts while she stretched unreservedly, half atop him.

The fugitive Riti. When Pru learned her tyrannical father intended marrying Riti off to a neighbor, landed but a lout, she engineered her sister's escape disguised as a boy driving sheep (it must be a flock of sheep, Pru insisted) to market. In New York, Riti quickly threw her lot in with Henry, freely pooling her small resources with his. Henry could hardly believe his good fortune. He did not ignore Pastor Berkemeier's warnings. But did he stray into Gomorrah or stumble into Gilead? His father would have called her a wolf disguised as a lamb. But wolves did not shepherd the neighborhood's lost with the solicitude that Riti did.

Wolves did not demand unchaining slaves and feeding the poor as Riti did.

And yet. She undressed, herself and him, with no more self-consciousness than when she set the table. She referred to sexual appetite as if speaking about hankering for fresh bread. She demonstrated some new way of intertwining their bodies with the same curiosity that she studied a new map of the city. She laughed at Preacher Bulwer parsing Genesis and Eve's apple. "He skipped right over 'made in God's image.' He's wrong, Henry. Our bodies aren't to punish us. God wants us to enjoy them. All God's creatures enjoy their bodies, or should."

Heresy or new insight into familiar texts? Henry tried to weigh judiciously. He could argue with a pretty woman. Or with an intelligent woman. Or with a woman passionate in her convictions. But Riti was all three. Outnumbered, he listened and learned. Among his lessons, he learned to enjoy his body. And hers. He could hardly contain himself whenever he heard her footsteps running up the stairs to their room.

The flying steps one hot July evening were those of a wide-eyed street urchin with a breathless summons. Henry raced down the stairs and pushed frantically through the circle of people at an intersection to crouch over Charity crumpled in the mud, trampled dead by a cruel drayman's beating-crazed runaways.

He woke up fully at a loud tearing noise followed by heavy thud as a forest giant surrendered at last to gravity. He sat up and checked he still had an arm looped as reminder through the strap of the small bag he carried. He rummaged there fruitlessly for any morsel yet uneaten, then shook himself mentally. He should be thinking, not dreaming; and of the future, not the past.

Young man, when I see a failed firm, the first evidence I examine is the man at the top. Most often I find he did not think. Cousin Hurley's New York rasp, still fresh in Henry's mind. *I'm old school. When I was a little shaver, still a very junior clerk, almost all the clerks lived with the master. Not as much freedom, but the master could size up his people pretty well. He knew his true balance sheet included people. The numbers were the easy part. But the people . . .*

His first break in weeks from dawn-to-dusk labor, Henry told himself, was a chance to consider matters other than the day immediately at hand. Important matters, such as people. Lem, his foreman, was always accommodating to Henry's preferences, but often too stinting with praise for his men who deserved it. Too stinting, also, with correction. He must have a private word with Lem to encourage both.

Young Douglas was inexperienced, but willing. Recalcitrant Jefferson needed close watching; the most powerful physically, he was the weakest link on the crew.

Who was the strongest link? Lem, Dallman, Jake, Hilpert, Douglas, Jefferson, Solomon, Carrie: one by one Henry worked his way through the list, trying to assess each as Hurley would, judging without animus or favoritism. Cousin Hurley was right as usual; the man at the top had to think hard.

The central link in his crew, Henry concluded, was Carrie. Every man at the camp looked forward to Carrie's cooking. But more, Henry recognized, they respected her for taking duties seriously; she was an unconscious model. Her sense of responsibility led Henry to recall the amusing way she chewed her lips in earnest concentration on a stew pot, and the radiance of her smile at compliments on her cooking. He remembered how impressed Spooks seemed to be with her conversation about books. Henry admitted to himself that he was pampered; she made sure steaming coffee and some special savory treat were unobtrusively at his hand when he finished work assignments at daybreak.

Henry decided he had surely been too quick in his first impression of Carrie. He had missed the key to his crew. Damn lucky for him Elvira had been so determined to send Carrie up as cook. He had been careful, he remembered, to introduce her as a *temporary* cook. Crew reaction to her meals soon silently quashed his "temporary." At least he had escaped a very bad mistake for morale. What Elvira surely hadn't realized, and neither had he at first, was that he brought up much more than a cook. No one could have called his crew slackers before Carrie arrived. But her cooking, her lively spirits, her shingle splitting and rock piling, her pluck: with her at the Quachasee the crew was clearly happier. So, he reflected, was he.

He was surprised by his conclusion, but the moon's rise meant he could distinguish the path; he better not dally musing at a big maple. *Analysis, then action*, said Cousin Hurley. Analysis done, but action, whatever it was, would have to wait until he reached home. He rose to set off uphill again.

Dawn, however, showed he followed a mistaken trace. Too impatient for backtracking to the crucial fork, he struck out across rough country. When the sun showed few shadows, he wandered deep in thickety terrain, not exactly lost, but certainly perplexed about the quickest way home. Shadows were long and deepening as he trudged up to the cabin porch, weary, famished, scratched, and thoroughly irritated with himself.

What he heard there made him irritated with others. The crew had felled a tree wrong, gashing a mule's leg and damaging tools. Carrie had burned both biscuits and corn mush. A defensive Lem admitted that because Elbert had not been hobbled for the night he had cut up the bottom of the spring pool so badly their cooking and wash water was only beginning to clear. Hilpert, Dallman, and Douglas had eaten too many wild berries and were afflicted with debilitating cases of the runs. Jefferson had sulked for two days. Henry went to bed angry at the world. His fury prevented sound sleep but did not block disturbing images of softly rounded breasts and thighs.

As vexed as unrested, he rose at first light, determined to eliminate the mud threat at the spring once and for all. His call for a fortifying breakfast, however, produced only anxious helplessness from Carrie. "Why, Marse Henry, I didn't know you wanted all that so early. The fire's just starting to build, Marse."

"Bring me a good meal when it's ready," he ordered sharply, and left in a huff. At the spring he dropped shirt next to boots, and plunged angrily in.

Who could stay grumpy splashing about in cool water on a beautiful warm summer morning? Several hours later, the world and its humans seemed not so maddening. He was heartened by good progress moving rock underwater. The pool was gaining a hard bottom.

The project occupied him so satisfyingly that at first he did not notice Carrie, a basket over her arm. Ready to celebrate his pool progress, he climbed out in his dripping trousers and found a seat on a shaded stump. In a clean dress, her hair tied with a matching ribbon, Carrie perched on a log to dispense breakfast. Fresh biscuits, newly churned butter, lean bacon, pie, just-made coffee: ravenous, he demolished all, a bit abashed for being so gruff earlier.

"And this," she raised a large square of gingerbread, "is special." Laughing at his wolfish look, she appeared to him so light-hearted, maybe at his improved mood, that she seemed almost giddy, certainly saucy. "Since it's special, you have to say please." He recognized a mother teaching her three-year-old. She extended her arm above her head, held it a bit behind her to indicate no automatic access. "Please?" she prompted.

Shaking his head in mock boyish defiance, he made a broad swipe for the treat.

"No-o-o." Giggling, she ducked back quickly, denying him the gingerbread. Her log seat rolled. She clutched at him to save herself.

He tried hard to break her fall, but had not braced for her emergency grasp. With a tiny screech, she tumbled on her back to the ground, he mostly on top of her. Inviting smile overcome by silent appeal for help with lost balance, skirt flown far up, swellings at her chest now close, firm thighs opened on each side of him, much bared skin. *All God's creatures enjoy their bodies, or should.*

These two creatures should start enjoying their bodies now, he thought, as he sank onto her, frantically yanking on his belt to release himself. As he sought access, his wet clothes were an impediment. Her simple garments were not. He was soon where he wanted to be, pushed urgently into her, and after intense action found release.

Later, when he caught his breath, he opened his eyes. She stared up at him, watchful. He heard Doc Sexton's *Back off now, back him off.* Instead he slid to one side so he could admire her face. *And you, sir, will you be different from Beelzebub?* Sexton was not so mad.

"Thanks for the gingerbread. Delicious," he murmured.

"Never did hear a please, Marse," she whispered, watching him slantwise.

Henry winced at the "Marse." That wasn't what he had meant at all. Maybe Sexton had this right too: *not nymphs and satyrs gamboling carefree in the Arcadian wood.*

His eyelids seemed to be weighted. He had enough consciousness to know he was falling asleep. He thought she whispered, "A please and not so much hurry gets lots more." But he was too far gone to be certain. He tried to nod concession, but his eyelids were too heavy. He fell sound asleep. When, much later, a steady shaft of direct sun through the trees woke him, he was alone.

❧

She worked late at the cabin table, organizing supplies by a single candle. Henry, who dropped into bed immediately after yawning through the evening meal with the crew, appeared at the door to his back room. "Carrie, is it possible to enjoy some of your gingerbread?" Preoccupied with counting, she nodded and pulled a pan from a high shelf. When she turned around, he took it from her and put it on the table. "I was thinking of your gingerbread at the spring." He stood unmoving. "I understand please and not so much hurry's best."

"Um-hmm."

"Please."

She nodded. "That's the magic word."

He reached for her. She stood against him, motionless while he carefully unbuttoned her. Sexton's voice again: *and when you come panting to your mare? Will she be tethered, unable to escape?*

Henry blew out the candle, went to the door and opened it. Moonlight flooded in.

"Why're you doing that?" she asked.

"So you can leave if you want. There's enough light to find your way."

She stood beside him as they looked out across the yard, deeply-shadowed sheds and rough, partially cleared field to the mountains brightly lit by the moon. "Where'd I go?"

Plowing with Greek, My Life
HL Hollis

The original bounds and metes for the land parcel within which Tulips stands were specified in an archaic style: commence at the Great Oak, fire-scarred on its east side, thence NNE so many rods, thence E approximately so many rods to Hickory Creek, thence following the West Bank of said creek to the first dreen, thence following it to a chest-high boulder, thence W so many rods to a Sawed Beech Stump approx. 6-1/2 feet diameter, three ax handles tall, then NNW so many rods, thence N (and there my memory fades). Those are the directions my forebears followed each January to "walk the farm," the annual circuit to memorize, and clear underbrush from, the boundaries. The document is no more; it and a great deal else was incinerated in the courthouse conflagration of 1909. (I blame myself for not transcribing it when I first discovered it.)

The house still stands. Four Hollis men have claimed ownership since its original construction. My grandfather, Samuel B, the builder; successively his sons, Sam and my father, Henry; and I.

"Claimed ownership" is, on second thought, an inappropriate term when considering Tulips. "Assumed stewardship" is more seemly, surely for Samuel B, Henry, and me. I do not include Sam automatically because I know so little of him. I do know that from the day of Samuel B's stroke until my father moved down from his Quachasee farm, Sam was in charge of Tulips. Yet I cannot dredge up a single memory in which my father talked of him or of his wife, Elvira.

Neither I nor any of my siblings can recall Audie Ann ever speaking of Sam, though she lived in his household for many years. Crotia does remember the summer day when Audie Ann and she decorated graves at our family cemetery. My sister asserts categorically that Audie Ann dropped not blossoms but thistles on Sam's grave when she thought Crotia wasn't looking. Even guarding against uncharitable conclusions, there appears to have been some degree of bad blood between the stepbrothers, though the cause may in hindsight appear trifling. To be candid, even in this treatise given over to ancestor reverence, I am at a loss.

Troubling signs do exist. For instance not a single outbuilding at Tulips—barn, shed, or weather-cover—was erected during Sam's years of stewardship. The big house itself has been remodeled many times, but not single board or nail can be credited to Sam.

Then there is the gravestone matter. At the Hollis burying ground, Sam's grave lies at the extreme edge, curious in itself. Moreover his marker is modest in size. I must amend that. His marker is the smallest of any in his generation. And lonely in its severity. No epitaph, no Gospel verse, no artwork. More, there is no marker whatsoever for Elvira. Why is her burial place not beside her husband in the Hollis cemetery? Where in fact is it? I have no clue.

For other purposes, I have spent much time in the archives of our Bethel Lutheran Church. I noted there record of Sam's baptism at Bethel. But after that promising entry, he disappears. Could he nevertheless have been an honorable man? Of course. And active in his community to do good? Indeed. But in public records likewise he is absent.

One day early in her girl-reporter phase, Crotia ginned up the considerable courage required to mix with the Mercantile porch crowd of an afternoon to ask about their memories of Tulips. I have read the tablet on which she wrote out in advance her questions and, reporter-like, noted the answers. (In retrospect she wished she had not exhibited paper and pencil there, for she thought it inhibited free answers, but that itself must remain an open question.)

By happy inspiration she began with some throwaway questions about the venerable clock still marking time here in Tulips' hallway. That elicited admiring recollections of its tall case, the long door giving access to the mechanism. A number of the men enthusiastically described their anticipation of the clock striking twelve, a bit of forgivable hyperbole, for who of them would have been here at noon, let alone at midnight?

Checking off that subject with elan, Crotia proceeded to the nub of her interview.

Question. Were you well acquainted with Sam Junior?

Answer. I knowed him, Miss.

Question. How long did you know him?

Answer. Till he passed.

Question. Did you work for him at Tulips?

Answer. Of a time.

Question. Was he considered a fair employer?

Answer. Some might say so. [Long pause] But don' git crossaways 'a him.

Question. Did people easily get crossways of him?

Answer. No more then wit' another feller bent thet way.

Crotia labored mightily. She tried rephrasing her questions a half dozen different ways to elicit more details or greater elaboration, with no greater success. Finally, Wade Slater—the most thoughtful and kindest of the lot—shifted the plug in his cheek while keeping his focus on the railing. "Wal, Miss Hollis, it pleasures me to have you light hyar, but 'bout Mister Sam, the word with the bark on it is thet he were the troublesomist man hyar'bouts. Seem like he jes' bad to bein' contrarious. I never did study on why fer. He jes' was."

Wade shifted his plug again. "Now, Miss, you a-gonna wanna writ up ever fac' in thet purty book'a yourn, but I ain't a-gonna cheep, on account of I don' think hit right to bad-mouth a man which is gone dead an' cain't defend hisself neither.

Give Crotia her considerable due. She had courage and tenacity to face Wade and continue her questioning. "Well, what about Sam's wife, Elvira?" A muted joint chuckle came as reply. "His woman jes lef'," sounded from Crotia's right. "Hit were sompin 'bout a boy horse an mare," from her left. "Yer fergettin Holt and Holllis needin her 'cause whole damn bus'ness goin broke," from her right. "Better ax her hired man, Jim," from her left.

Turning back and forth, vainly trying to identify speakers, Crotia gave up note taking and asked, "Well where can I find Jim to ask *him*?" The answer came from her left. "Hell, mos' likely. He up an drop off." When she turned that way, a mutter on her right: "Ole Elvira, she mighta lef' lookin fer her Ahler's." Then silence. (Ahlers will be recognized only by those of a certain age; it was once a popular tonic, sure to cure your every complaint, until banned from the market without alcohol excise stamps.) Crotia looked hard, but to a man the Mercantile loafers were totally engrossed in petting dogs, swatting flies, or tending to their several tobacco needs.

Crotia recognized defeat deep in hostile territory. To avoid rout, she extricated herself from the Mercantile as swiftly as possible, eased only by Wade's "light agin, Miss, happen ye pass."

A final shard. After Samuel B's meticulous record keeping and Father's equally detailed notes for tree grafting and swine breeding, Sam's bookkeeping is a disorienting shock. His records are fragmentary and indecipherable. He either didn't care or didn't want to know his financial status. In my observation, farmers who attempt the task without records are headed ultimately toward loss of land and livelihood. Is that where Sam was bound or do I misconstrue his financial state?

To what do all these fragments add up? They are, in point of fact, too strong to ignore, too weak alone to condemn a man. I hope they add up to watchful expectation that one day this side of eternity, more evidence—exculpatory, I trust—comes to a future Hollis family historian.

During a cemetery cleanup some years after Crotia braved the Mercantile porch, Sam's gravestone prompted her to ask Father, how did he die and why was his marker so small and plain? Father answered that Sam was found dead in a Tulips bedroom by Jim, one of the hired men who did maintenance and odd jobs around Tulips.

Jim made repeated appearance in Father's stories. Tall and lean, he seemed an assemblage of arms and legs; his limbs were constantly getting in his way. He might, as mountain folk say, feather into a task, disposing of it summarily. But he always marched to his own drummer.

Among his peculiarities was apparently an aversion to scissors, for his scalp hair hung lankly past his shoulders. Father, always clean-shaven, described Jim's beard in detail. Dangling well down his chest, the tangled mass was downright dangerous. Several times Jim set it afire. More often he caught it in closing doors. He refused to trim it, however, because his beard was an essential gearwheel in his mental processes. When confronted by a problem, Jim would gradually chew his beard into his mouth. One might gauge the problem's difficulty by the amount of beard that disappeared. Finally Jim would unchew it to announce his conclusion.

Now, at the cemetery, Father added to his Jim compendium another tale: Jim's fabrication of a new fence around the graveyard. Jim installed pickets, some with point up, others with point down, all in determinedly random order. When Father reprimanded him for at least the inconsistency, Jim started chewing on his beard. In due course his mouth was empty enough for him to announce thet puttin all them pints up jes bored his mind too damn much t'stan hit. Tamarrah he'd take the whole lot offen an nail em back alternatin, pint up then pint down. Forgotten in our laughter was Sam's death and his puzzling gravestone. Our induced amnesia, I am reasonably certain, was Father's intention.

For the last few days I have been working hard to explain on paper what was required to plow a newly-cleared field. Plowing thus seems an appropriate metaphor here when writing about Tulips' boundaries, to return at last to where I started. It becomes clear to me that I initiated "plowing" this field before proper calculation of the work to finish the whole—all the more when my attention strays so easily to the equivalent of displaced field mice, bird songs, and newly budded trees. The reason why many old folks appear reticent is because, I see, it requires so much effort to cover everything necessarily explained, painstakingly explained. A glance back at these pages is intimidating because it gives me a yardstick by which I can measure the distance to my goal. To remember bright as noon is quick, but to explain so future generations understand even dimly is slow and laborious work indeed.

QUACHASEE
WHC

"Confound that woman," muttered Henry. He threw down his stepmother's note that John Bright brought from Tulips. *Your father is failing. Sometimes he seems ready to speak. Come before it's too late. You can combine it with the Pruitt's party at Chestnut Hill.* Sarah Hollis could never be called clever, but this . . . Predictable as the tall hall clock: time to look for a wife; time to think of a family; time to meet young women; time to; time.

Sarah wrote of Sophy Pruitt's approaching wedding. Many guests, including Sophy's sister, Alice, just home from two whole years at the ladies seminary in Lexington. Henry wrote back his no. Wrote no three notes running. Again this summons. He threw it into the fire.

What, though, if his father *did* want to say something before he died? Defeated, he took the trail down to Tulips. An hour watching flickerless closed eyelids at his father's bed. A minute questioning Sally. "No, Marse, he doan nebbah change, nebbah say nuttin." Henry could go home in good conscience.

No, not in good conscience. Given his sister's exhilaration at his company, her desperation for someone to talk to, the thought of leaving immediately made him wince. He resigned himself to attending the party. His New York clothes gaped at the waist, pinched at the shoulders, the material too smooth, too flimsy. His stepmother approved enthusiastically, which depressed him. But so did Audie Ann, which cheered him.

The Pruitt's Chestnut Hill, as grand a mansion house as stood thereabouts, flaunted Italianate brackets—at least in the front—and even an ornate wrought iron gate, a gate freshly painted for the party, Henry noticed. On the portico he congratulated the bride's mother, Eleanor Pruitt, standing with his stepmother. He needed no intuition to understand their conspiracy; they chose him as Alice Pruitt's informal escort. He resolved on graceful acceptance of social duty. Stoic, though with a sliver of curiosity. He remembered Alice as an amusing little hoyden, her mother's despair, given to climbing into dusty barn lofts and to running clothes-tearing races.

Alice seven years later transfixed him. Astonishingly blue eyes, delicate features, translucent complexion, blue dress that revealed a great deal of unblemished white skin. Little Alice was country clay; Miss Alice Pruitt, fine porcelain. Henry's impatience eased. Such a lovely sentry at the gilded cage's door almost erased his awareness of confinement.

Alice excused herself to help her sister inside. Henry strolled Chestnut Hill's extensive manicured yard. Some of the male guests made crude jokes about bride and groom. The women officially did not hear. Of course the women heard. The shy blushed and kept their eyes lowered; the bold answered in kind. Younger girls skittered in flocks, younger boys marauded in packs. Older boys and girls mingled self-consciously. An expectant atmosphere seemed familiar to Henry, but he could not place it.

The wedded couple appeared on the piazza to toasts, jibes, boisterous shouts, sometimes racy or slurred commentary from the crowd's edges. The groom began several jokes about Sophy, but, drunk, mercifully always lost his point. When she forgot she was on display, the bride looked apprehensive. Henry belatedly recognized his surroundings: he was again behind Doc Sexton's barn. Now tied in the trench, Anon could not escape Beelzebub being led out to her. Whales, elephants, and buffalo crowded around.

Alice reappeared. Complying with his watchful stepmother's signals, Henry ambled toward the gazebo to establish amiable presence. No competing bull shouldered in to challenge him. Alice's boarding school years and formal manners intimidated the younger. Her clothes and fresh beauty discouraged the older. Seven years earlier, his stepmother's selection of little Alice would have damned the girl in Henry's eyes. But now the dazzling Miss Alice Pruitt could make men even more sensible than Henry lose their bearings.

After the isolation of the Quachasee, at Chestnut Hill Henry felt almost back in New York crowds. He wished for Pru's practical guidance. Prudence, his friend Isaiah's companion. Now lying in that Brooklyn cemetery, the both of them. Henry had been their sole graveside mourner during the worst of the epidemic. In happier days, Henry spent summer Sunday afternoons with them. Isaiah liked that, for someone at hand to envy him his expensive mistress. He seemed unaware Pru cheerfully proposed to Henry that she seduce him, brought it up once or twice a month.

Along the way from farm to city, Pru learned perhaps more than a proper lady should. When they rested on a park bench to review the fashionable promenade, she played worldly aunt to Henry's mountain rustic. Just as she corrected his thinking on slavery, she provided pointers about New York ladies. She might do the same for Tennessee ladies if only Henry listened with an inner ear.

Now, Hen, your pretty Miss Alice spends a lot of time with a wide, tall mirror. How do I know? There, that flash of eyes: straight out of the mirror. And watch for the twist of her shoulders—there, Hen. That's to make her little bosom seem adequate. Watch her chest when she turns. Don't stare, silly. Hen, if we undress this china doll, all we're gonna find is two tight little rosebuds painted on its chest.

"Mister Hollis, did you leave many friends behind in New York?" Alice had been well schooled in making polite conversation. "My friend Betsy says city people are different. But I think people are the same everywhere. Don't you agree?"

"Yes, Miss Pruitt, I left three of my dearest friends behind in New York. I have to say, though, that they were a little different from here."

I can tell you're admiring that tiny waist, you clod-hoppin bumpkin. You're supposed to, Hen. She gets some help with that corset. A blind man could see that, Hen. What you have to notice is that she's used to it. She don't shift around when she thinks nobody's lookin. Wears it tight all the time—though she sure don't need it to hold up her rosebuds. It's good for her, Hen. Makes her walk slow and lean on men the way they like.

"Mister Hollis, is your dear father's health improving?"

"Kind of you to ask, Miss Pruitt. He does accept some liquid nourishment, which encourages us. But he is as yet incapable of intelligible speech, which is a disappointment.

Now that shade of blue in her dress, Hen. What? Of course her dress matches her eyes, dunce. But that means hours of lookin to get the right shade. So men will stare at her. You're starin' at her, ain't ya? Men don't invest in girls men don't stare at. Just get out your pocketbook, Hen. That dress cost a lot more'n you ever dreamed. And it's sewed by slaves. You know I don't approve. Their owners stole the money Pruitt paid 'em.

"Mister Hollis, I don't believe I've had the pleasure of seeing your brother, Mister Sam, and his dear wife this evening."

"Thanks to your father's hospitality, Miss Pruitt, there's such a crowd that two people can disappear."

And notice what your Miss P. ain't doin. Hen, how you gonna get rich enough to afford me when you can't see the obvious: she ain't always fussing with her dress. She ain't fussing because she can afford not to worry about her expensive dress. And she ain't worryin because she's got a whole huge wardrobe closet full of 'em. No tellin how many slave seamstresses went near blind.

"Mister Hollis, why are you smiling?"

"The little girl over there doing cartwheels—until her mother caught up with her. I remember trying to do that. Don't you?"

"I don't believe I do, Mister Hollis."

Hen, I think she's maybe a little young for you. She's not sure enough of herself to be plain Alice. She so wants to be Miss Pruitt and she wants to talk to Mister Hollis, not Henry, the boy who remembers her in short skirts. I can see you now, Hen: 'Oh, Mister Hollis, dear, please come to bed so your Alice can give you . . . a little kiss.'

"Mister Hollis, your mother says that you'll be building a house up at your new farm. Will it be like our Chestnut Hill, in the Italian villa style? That seems so refined to me."

"Chestnut Hill is elegant indeed, Miss Pruitt, but I'm afraid the style wouldn't fit well up the Quachasee, surrounded by rough mountains. May I fetch a flavored ice for you?"

Hen, this ice is downright evil of you. You're just trying to embarrass me for when Isaiah gave me too much champagne and I told you Pru's Law. But I shan't be shamed. Once again for the slow boys in the class: Pru's Law is that the girls who just take little licks on their ice are the ones who can't stand the thought of giving a man's soldier some special treatment until he stands up stiff at attention and fires a salute.

Flavored ice safely delivered, Henry could relax his guard against being jostled. *When you give a girl an ice, look for a girl who doesn't just lick, but gets her pretty lips all around her ice. Watch her sharp now, Hen. . . . Oh dear. Sorry, Henry, no cheroot on that one, as the circus man says. But it's not the end of the world. Maybe you're not so interested in that sort of thing. I'm sure I wouldn't know. Maybe she's talented in talking about all those books you read. You better find out what's inside that pretty head, Hen.*

"Miss Pruitt, tell me, what do you enjoy doing?"

"Oh Mister Hollis, I'm so busy all day. I help Mama in the kitchen, directing Jenny. And then, of course, I work on my fancy stitching and embroidery and . . ."

Henry recognized their destination, the dutiful recital of womanly accomplishments. He nodded polite encouragement while he scanned the lawn. No contest: in a yard full of pretty girls, and a good many plain ones too, Alice reigned.

". . . and I love to play the piano dear Papa bought for me. You know," she leaned toward him confidingly, "there aren't many girls who have a father who will spend, oh, I don't know how much money, to make his daughter happy."

Henry heard Pru snicker. *What did I tell you, Hen?* "You must be a much loved-daughter, you can be sure," answered Henry, his sorrowing eyes fixed on once-vivacious Laura Green, married to that drunk womanizer, Horace Gosler, after Henry left for New York, and now shockingly aged.

Henry tried a different subject. "And you enjoy reading?"

"Oh-h yes," Alice's wide eyes sparkled. "So-o-o much. I have so-o-o many books on my shelf, Mister Hollis."

Henry's spirits lifted. He had judged prematurely. She would know Cooper and the Deerslayer, just for a start.

She lifted her delicate hand to tick off her many books. "The Bible, of course. Papa says . . ."

A pimply-faced boy, his arms too long for his sleeves, walked by, touching the smiling girl beside him in a way that struck Henry as perhaps proprietary.

". . . and another book is my journal."

Glancing after the young pair, Henry glimpsed small stalks of hay clinging to the girl's back. Definitely proprietary.

"God's creation is so divine, isn't it, Mister Hollis? We set wickets up on the lawn the other day. I spent two whole hours out there, just enjoying nature, and winning three games."

"Nothing clears the mind like a walk in tall trees."

"Trees?" Alice looked dubious. "Well I do walk in the garden. Until I get tired. Papa takes Mama and me for drives when the sky is clear and we can have the top down."

The sight of John Bright not far off, a smile-mask fixed to his face, surprised Henry. Deerslayers avoid parties like they avoid cities. "Miss Pruitt, with your permission I'll get you another lemonade before it's all gone." He struck off in Spooks' direction.

"Crowded party." Spooks greeted him with a lopsided grin.

"Thick as fiddlers in hell," answered Henry jovially, sensing Spooks had more to say.

"What exceptional beauty." Spooks nodded in Alice's direction and murmured just loud enough for Henry's ear.

"Yes. Perfection. But she's an Alice."

"Alice Pruitt."

"No, Alice Munro."

"I see." Spooks steered him more apart from other guests. "For Uncas, she's Alice. Well, Uncas, the campfire's smoke may be thickening. I just sat in council with an old chief who seeks alliance, for he fears his warpath days soon end." Bright glanced casually around to make doubly sure no one could overhear. "Emmer Pruitt just caught my arm for a long private talk. He believes Sophy's brand-new husband, his newly minted son-in-law, is a hopeless idiot, lazy dolt, irresponsible spendthrift, hardly the candidate to take over Pruitt holdings."

"What? Then why let Sophy marry him?"

"Needed a father for Sophy's baby. Shhh, Henry, contain your naivete. Visiting in Chattanooga, Sophy flaunted a reputation as . . . Anyway, Emmer says he hopes Alice will snag a sound man to inherit the Pruitt enterprises. He specifically named you as candidate."

"He was drinking."

"Just enough to loosen his tongue. Though if this were the year of our Lord seventeen and thirty, he'd be negotiating a dowry."

"Too much punch."

"Doesn't matter if—"

"There you are; been looking for you, Bright." Asher Bingham took his arm. "Let me introduce you to some people who need a prime lawyer."

Henry braved the lemonade stand, but a knot of people blocked his way back with the too-full glass. He detoured. Another knot; another detour. Wound up approaching Alice's chair from behind a screen. Before he saw them, he heard a young woman's voice.

"Alice, c'mon." A giggle. "We're going to start a game out back, now that it's dark. Bring Henry Hollis, if you know what's good for you. There're lots of places to be alone."

"Bessie, Mama doesn't like me in those kissing games. She says—"

"Your ma don't need to know any more than mine. C'mon."

He took another detour and approached Alice so that he would be visible for yards. A girl he didn't know ceased tugging on Alice and ran off. The lemonade delivered, Henry managed to keep conversation afloat while he appreciated her face. Found charming her bell-like laugh. Admired her stunning dress.

He tried imagining Alice near an open fire ladling a savory stew to a line of tired, sweat-stained laborers. Impossible. He could, though, imagine a luxurious upstairs bedroom in Chestnut Hill; an undressed, passive-limbed doll lay tucked under the bed-covers, two miniature rose buds painted on its chest. Downstairs, in his office Emmer explained the complexities of farming, logging, the mill, the store, and the many tracts dotting the county, held for appreciation.

Henry swallowed a yawn. Tomorrow. He could think tomorrow about Alice and friends arguing over Uncas.

Cousin Caleb approached the gazebo with an ingratiating face for Alice, a sneer for Henry. Henry greeted him warmly. A perennial enemy might still be rescuer. Henry stood, introduced Mister Caleb Hollis to Miss Pruitt, lately home from far-off school. Moved just enough to allow Caleb access to his vacated seat. Joked with the two on the bench. Assured Alice that Caleb would take a gentleman's care of her. Avoided Mrs. Pruitt's eye. Slid out of his stepmother's sight. Evaporated.

Stretching out in bed at Tulips, Henry grimaced. Ole Caleb hadn't changed a bit. A skunk as a boy; a skunk as a man. Right about now, bland innocence on his face, he'd be easing a hand on Alice where it shouldn't be. He'd be so pleased to think he stole her from his hated cousin. Remembering Doc Sexton's barn, Henry wondered if he at least qualified as a Teaser.

He almost drifted off when a new thought brought him wide awake: perhaps his stepmother's machinations weren't her idea at all, but his father's. Samuel B and Emmer sometimes joined resources in Hollis & Pruitt Co. Perhaps Samuel dreamed of a tighter alliance.

Henry heard Cousin Hurley in that Manhattan office: *Now young man, in New York business, it's the numbers that count, not clothes and fancy manners. Do the sums.* Henry began a mental itemization of Pruitt's various operations, calculating estimates of income and expenses. He did the sums, whistled to himself. If Emmer intended to cut Sophy's new groom out, Alice's future husband would have bright prospects, profitable enough easily to indulge his wife in many dresses that matched her eyes. Few-books-and-painted-rosebuds. Yes, but maybe he decided superficially. Perhaps he had consigned Alice to cousin Caleb prematurely. Sleep came slowly.

Plowing with Greek, My Life
HL Hollis

As a young boy, I was impressed by what some called Purties, trinkets, in my friends' homes. With more maturity—and more reading—I wondered at the absence even of shelves, let alone books, at my friends' homes. With the eye of a new university man, I began to realize that the crowded shelves at Tulips were unusual in all but certain favored places. As a graduate I began finally to wonder at the cornucopia of books I enjoyed here.

Mother first found books a solace when she was growing up in Nashville, very much alone she recalled. How Father acquired his book addiction is another of those many details I failed to inquire about in timely fashion. I would nominate my grandfather as book instigator, but my understanding is that Samuel B's reading did not venture far from the Bible and devotional volumes. (By that I don't imply that Father was not also faithful in Bible reading and prayer.) Father's book habit did not likely come from Mama, for in point of fact she consistently adapted to him. I believe his Quachasee years produced the reader and book buyer. The intense solitude during those many years he farmed alone at the head of that remote valley would surely impel a man to booze or to books. Father read.

He read all kinds, including some pretty poor. Scandalized, Mama chafed him for wasting his time and mind on what she disdained as meretricious trash, but he always defended himself vigorously— sometimes, I think, for the sport of an inconsequential argument— claiming that a bad book cries out for judgment, so one's critical faculties get more exercised than on a middling book, let alone an excellent one. Besides, he always added, a good bad book can be fine relaxation.

In consequence of their reading standards, my parents differed greatly about their children's choices, though as always, Father had the last word. I discovered at the University that from my father's shelves I took for granted titles my peers considered daring or downright risque.

From time to time my father returned to James Fenimore Cooper, having as a boy virtually memorized *The Last of the Mohicans*, a youthful devotion he shared with Judge Bright, his best friend from boyhood to old age. Both of them told me more than once that when young they acted out the Mohican story scene by scene. Father urged the book on me almost before I firmly grasped the alphabet, but out of some recalcitrant independence I steadfastly refused or evaded—to his disappointment, I believe. And now I doubt I shall get to Cooper, and a good many other worthy authors, in whatever time is yet allotted me.

At every discussion of ordering more books—a frequent occurrence—Father always repeated, "But I already have *four* books," also our traditional refrain whenever any of us bought a book or gave a gift book or received one. To explain "four books," I must revisit my father's stories.

One day not very long before I left for Nashville, someone reported at the noon table that the big barn at the Gifford place burned the night before. (The original house itself, of proportions said to rival Newport, burned prior to my birth.) The news distressed Father, or at least made him unusually pensive, and he began reminiscing. Originally built by the Brights, he said, the place was later owned, and "improved," by a wealthy family, the Pruitts. They resided in seignorial splendor, at least for these parts, even installing in the wood fence enclosing their yard a wrought iron gate, direct from New Orleans. Its curlicues and flourishes were long the talk of the county.

The Pruitt family, Father recalled tangentially, included two attractive daughters. It did not occur to me then, but now I suspect him of baiting Crotia with these daughters. In any case, she could not resist such lure. She always teased Father much more than she teased Mama, who, though never dour, rarely seemed given to laughter; choosing between Jane Austen and George Eliot for quick instance, she always rejected the former for the latter.

To return to the Pruitts and their daughters. In answer to Crotia's instantaneous barrage of questions, Father described the younger, unmarried Pruitt daughter, Alice, as a china doll—dainty features, flaxen hair, peaches-and-cream complexion, beautiful blue eyes— easily the prettiest girl in the county. Crotia soon began probing about this china doll. Was Alice Pruitt prettier than Mama? Father didn't know because Mama was in Nashville then. (In fact she was not yet born, but even Crotia had not yet figured that out.) Crotia kept at him. "This pretty Alice, prettiest Alice, didn't you want to marry her?" Father conceded he thought about that some.

Talk of Crotia catnip! She pounced. "Thought about it? I bet you more than thought about it. I bet you fell madly in love with prettiest Alice, ready to propose to her." (Crotia was given to much romantic nonsense then, and since, I might add.) "In fact, maybe you did marry her and kept it a secret. Until she died in the bloom of her youth and you had to wait for Mama."

All of us expected Father to summarily quash such outrageous fantasizing. Instead, he offered his "Not quite" so mildly that all the older children snapped to close attention, though of course we pretended utter nonchalance. Crotia shifted into high gear. "Well you *did* think about it. I bet you thought about it a long time because you had to choose between *two* girls. Alice was fair. So stands to reason the other girl was dark. But how could the dark girl compete with Alice since Alice was the prettiest girl for miles around?"

Father grinned. "You tell me, Miss Smarty. There's pretty, prettier, and prettiest. Alice was prettiest. How can you have even better than prettiest, the prettiest girl in the county?"

Crotia argued there could be no one with looks superior to the prettiest girl. Logically impossible. She became increasingly adamant, until Father proposed a wager. If Crotia proved right, he promised to purchase the new shoes she pined after, and if wrong, she pledged to crank Father's favorite dessert that very afternoon, peach ice cream. The instant Crotia rashly accepted those terms, Marcus, Bill, and I tabled our forks, resolved to retain maximum capacity that evening. Henry Hollis, notoriously, never entered a wager until he eliminated all risk, something he demonstrated by then telling Crotia, "You forgot a possibility. The prettiest girl is trumped by the most beautiful woman."

After such ignoble defeat, the rest of us would have retreated tails dragging to nurse our wounds—and save energy for cranking the ice cream bucket. Crotia, however, though capable of bizarre fantasies, also possesses a formidable tenacity. Unperturbed, she renewed her attack, hypothesizing what attributes made the dark woman so superior, and throwing out guesses about which local family produced this beauty. (Crotia persisted in stipulation of opposites: the blonde Alice's beautiful competition was without doubt dark.)

Father did not follow Crotia crashing about in the thicket of her singular suppositions. Instead, he described a wedding party where he chatted with Prettiest Alice about reading. I would exceed the limits of veracity were I to claim Father possessed a gifted mimic's skills, but this time he reproduced voices and intonation with uncanny verisimilitude, and all of us around the table eavesdropped on the party.

He asked Alice if she enjoyed reading. Her eyes brightened enthusiastically. "Oh-h yes. So-o-o much." Father thought, that's promising, for Alice and he can enliven the evening by comparing reactions to the authors they both know. He was about to seek her opinion of James Fenimore Cooper when she launched in without prompting.

"Mister Hollis, I have so-o-many books." Alice started to tick them off on her fingers. "First the Bible, of course. Papa says I must read a chapter a day." Under cross-examination, she admitted she did search for the briefest chapters, or at least very short ones. "And my second book has the most beautiful cover. Sometimes I just sit and look at the cover, don't even open it. But when I do, it has the cutest little pomes."

Bill burst in. "Father, don't you mean po-ems? Mama always says, it's po-em." Under the table Dory kicked Bill.

Father replied, "No, Alice read pomes."

"I read so many good pomes there," breathes the pretty Alice, "and little sentences, it's so-o-inspiring." Her fingers moved. "My third book is my Woman's Treasury."

By then Father, whose mind had wandered, feared seeming rude by inattention, so he hazarded a friendly interruption. "Let me guess, Miss Pruitt. Your Woman's Treasury has intricate marbling, even inside the covers, and wonderful little stories about pretty little girls in fine dresses who have smart little dogs and cute little birds. But the pets die, and the girls are s-o-o sad."

That startled Alice. "Mister Hollis, do you have a copy too?"

"I regret not." Father advanced the subject. "What's your fourth book, Miss Pruitt?"

"Well, perhaps it's not exactly the same as the others. It's my journal, where I write down the most important things in my life and what I think about them."

"Would it be invading the privacy of Miss Pruitt's journal to inquire what are the 'most important things'?"

"Oh no, Mister Hollis, not at all. I *must* write about this party. This party is an important one, isn't it? It's such fun to read later what all the ladies wore."

"I'm sure it is, Miss Pruitt. I hear there's a lending library in Ginners Ford now. Do you find it's a promising source to crowd your shelves—novels and such?"

"*Novels*? I don't think so, Mister Hollis. Papa says novels have a lot of things in them that young ladies shouldn't know."

"All novels? Even by Walter Scott?"

"Well," Miss Pruitt hesitated. "I'm not sure of your Waterscott, whoever that is. Papa says a few novels *might* be acceptable for ladies, but you don't know until you've started them, and then what if it's too late? The safest thing is not to open any of them. Besides, I don't need more books. I already have *four* books."

Even Mama found *I already have four books* a fine line. We employed the phrase so generously we detached it from the original prettiest Alice Pruitt. *Four books* became a secret cipher when the boys (and sisters) in the family entered the age of evaluating eligible young ladies of our acquaintance, most notoriously when Bill brought home (he claims it was only a misconceived lark) a young lady exceedingly pretty, but vacuous in equal degree. I'll call her Peggy. Crotia communicated her opinion of Peggy by thanking Bill for introducing all of us. "I can see right away," proclaimed Crotia as she beamed at our visitor, "our dear Peggy is a *four-book* girl," in a tone so effusive that Peggy thanked her kindly for such a generous compliment.

I would give much to have at hand portraits of the prettiest Alice Pruitt and of her theoretical competitor, whoever she was, light or dark, but in point of fact we must be satisfied with *I already have four books*.

The story, I admit, is as long as the point is minor, but I excuse my self-indulgence by an instructive mystery. After Crotia's persistent inquiries, I now see, we didn't learn if Father decided for or against Alice and we certainly did not hear the fate of the woman whose beauty outranked "prettiest." Instead we were entranced by Alice's bibliophilia. As I write this I cannot decide whether passive voice is appropriate. Should I say we were drawn from one subject to another? Or should I say Father played the skilled magician at the verge of necromancy, distracting his audience's attention from pretty girl and beautiful woman, who then vanish before our very eyes without us realizing they're gone?

QUACHASEE
WHC

Since Henry had warned Audie he would return to his mountain farm after the wedding, she was ecstatic at the breakfast table the next morning when he said he would stay on at Tulips for a few days, helping with Father's care. Sam listened without comment, except a broad wink answering Elvira's smirk.

Emmer Pruitt trotted in that very morning with some story about needing to settle a small debt he long owed Samuel, something he could discharge to Sam Jr. With Emmer was Alice, "along for the ride," her blond hair tossed into fetching disarray by the wind. Once again her dress perfectly complemented her eyes.

Emmer said they didn't want to upset the household with Samuel lying sick and the ladies nursing; he could consult with Sam Jr. in the Tulips office. Alice would wait for him in the buggy. So did she, kept company by Henry, who traded talk about Sophy and her new husband. Alice seemed to glow with the excitement of gone to housekeeping. Henry need only listen, which was just as well, engrossed as he became in admiring Alice's face.

After a time surprisingly long for a simple transaction, Emmer returned to the buggy. He continued cordial conversation with Henry, though he had to check his high-strung trotter several times to do so. He pressed Henry to visit Chestnut Hill soon. Alice seconded her father with an inviting smile and a light touch on Henry's shoulder.

Sam snickered as Emmer finally dashed off. "Dresses like thet'll cost Henry Hollis a pretty penny. Like pouring money down a shet-hole," he grumped at Henry. "Damn foolishness, all them dresses. Any man ken see she ain't got no tits needin coverin. But, hell, wit' her ass up ye won't see thet. Anyways, wit' all'a Emmer's money, a man ken evern go out an buy big tits on the side. But I bet mebbe e'en Alice'll git hungry, oncet she find out how good a hard ramrod feel."

Disgusted, Henry nearly left, bound for the cleaner, clearer air up the Quachasee. On second thought, why should he allow Sam to control his actions? Fuming, he rode over to Chestnut Hill, mostly to show his independence of Sam. He left there much later than he intended, with Eleanor Pruitt's invitation to dinner the next day. He pledged to take Alice riding some day soon.

Henry conscientiously took his turns in his father's bedroom. In the pause following Pastor's prayer at Samuel B's bed, Berkemeier beckoned Henry to follow him outside. There, his foot on the buggy's step, the pastor turned to Henry. "I was called to be a healer of souls, not a healer of bodies. But in my experience, soul and body are mysteriously connected, and can affect each other. So I tell you what I tell everyone who cares for the gravely ill: do not allow this duty to consume you."

He pulled himself to the buggy seat. "Make time for an engrossing book or for some small project, and especially for friends. That is not selfishness, Henry. It will strengthen you in your care for your father."

"How is he today?" Henry signed as he entered his father's bedroom.

His sister put down her book. "He sipped a little soup this morning. But I can tell from Sally's face he still can't say anything intelligible. I'm afraid he's not improving, but I can't be sure."

At Henry's urging she finally vacated her station to catch up on sleep. Henry settled in as watcher. There was so much to keep track of when clearing for his new farm that he had put his father's health in the back of his mind, assuming that Samuel B would recover, as he had from previous setbacks. But high time now that he pay attention when his father was inexplicably not on his feet again.

Emmer Pruitt always greeted him with smile and careful inquiry of his old friend Samuel's condition. Eleanor came out with a worried face to welcome him with an embrace. Alice appeared—after a short delay—to reinforce her parents' reception. All three urged him repeatedly to return whenever he could.

After spartan living at the Quachasee camp, and quasi-mourning at Tulips, the Pruitt's Chestnut Hill smiled sunshine, a deft hand offering refreshments, luxurious pillows. a footrest, some adjustment of the light. Eleanor and Alice sought his preferences, ever gently solicitous of his comfort.

❧

"Mister Hollis, good day, sir." Dr. McCaffee made his visits early. "I have taken the precaution to bring in Doctor Keller, a very experienced practitioner in Claytown." He motioned to the dour-faced man beside him. "He, too, finds your father's condition serious. But not hopeless, we can assure you." McCaffee's face grew worried. "Yet the patient does not appear to be answering treatments that are normally efficacious."

McCaffee paused, apparently expecting Keller to speak, but when he said nothing, McCaffee hastily continued. "He . . . I . . . we feel that, in light of the patient's escalated pulse, cardiac perturbations, certain changes in respiratory activity, as well as heightened nervous manifestations, we should respond with a more . . . aggressive schedule of phlebotomy."

Keller cleared his throat, then spoke in a monotone. "As our eminent Doctor Benjamin Rush of Philadelphia has written, the human body contains probably twenty-five pounds of blood, so to withdraw seventy or eighty ounces over a course of days is not threatening the system. As some obscurantist populists would have us believe. Their way leads to death."

Still staring straight ahead, he cleared his throat again, his face continued an expressionless mask. "We face a morbid excitement of capillary tension, and we must relieve that tension in the vascular system."

When Henry did not applaud this revelation, McCaffee picked up. "As I mentioned, Doctor Keller's an esteemed colleague. Ah, Mister Hollis, we shall need space to do our work."

Henry took the hint and left his father's room.

❧

As nostalgic as he was about the house in which he was born and grew up, Henry had to admit that, compared to Tulips, Chestnut Hill was far more graciously laid out. Further, its wide halls and spacious rooms were complemented by the quiet efficiency of its large household staff.

Emmer Pruitt styled himself master of a lowland plantation, prideful of well-trained household servants. Years ago he had mounted a determined campaign to persuade Samuel B to sell him Tulips' cook, Lilly. He had given up only when Samuel B had agreed to let the Chestnut Hill cook apprentice some months with Lilly.

Audrey Ann had written to him in high glee when Samuel B had hesitantly broached the subject to Lilly, and received a surprising reply.

"Don't worry, Mist' Samuel. I'll teach that girl just a few things she doesn't know." A conspiratorial wink. "But I'm not about to teach her *every*thing."

Most of Pruitt's servants Henry recalled from years ago. When, making conversation, he inquired about the absence of Monroe, Emmer made a face. "Cousin Daniel in Knoxville needed a boy like Roe something desperate, so I let him go. Hard to replace, but I do a lot of business with Cousin Daniel. Last month I sent him eight wagonloads. Sometimes I think the profits of going on to Chattanooga might be worth the extra freight. Look at these figures, will you, and tell me what you think."

❧

"A good book, Audie? How was Father overnight?"

Audie Ann closed her book and put it aside with a sigh. "I'm not reading it anyway. Too upset."

She scribbled *McCaffee <u>more</u> blood* on her slate. Then her hands moved too rapidly for him to follow. With repetition, he thought she was saying the doctor urged more bleeding, but Audie had forbidden it. Henry called in Sally for confirmation.

"Marse, yuh right. Das what dat doctah say." Sally shook her head in disapproval. "Dat man, all he know is moh blood, moh blood. If de patience ain't bettah, dat doctah' doan *stop* bleedin, lahk a man wid sum sense do. He bleed *moh*. He say mebbe Marse Samuel hab too *much* blood, so he take whole big bowl ob id. Look t'me lahk hog-killin tiam. An Marse Samuel's not no hog. Miss Audie, she agin it."

Audie Ann picked up her slate. "I call Dr. Lyon. You agree?"

Henry answered with a nod, a shrug, and lifted shoulders. Not Audie's hand talk, but it conveyed his grudging deference to professional authority, but now also a loss of confidence.

ॐ

Hardened to Sam's grins, and mindful of Berkemeier's advice and the Pruitt's invitations, Henry returned often to Chestnut Hill, always warmly welcomed by an Emmer increasingly inclined to disclose details of his many astonishingly profitable enterprises. And an Eleanor who never failed to inquire kindly of Samuel's condition, to sympathize about the search for doctors, and to send sympathetic greetings to Audie Ann.

In his visits Henry gradually saw that Alice did indeed enjoy a whole big wardrobe upstairs filled with flattering dresses; all featured her tiny waist, all complementing the color of her hair or of her eyes. She leaned most dependently on her escort. In the privacy of buggy rides, she no longer found it necessary to address him as Mister Hollis when she sought his shoulder to steady herself on a rough road, and even after deep ruts were behind them.

ॐ

Henry returned to his father's bedroom with the last of his breakfast in his hand. A man he had never seen before stood beside the bed, gently flexing the patient's limbs. He finished without hurry, and finally looked up at Henry.

"I am Doctor Lyon, trained in all aspects of homeopathic medicine. And who are you, sir?"

"Henry." He pointed to Samuel B. "His son."

"A-ha. Then it was your sister, Audrey Ann Hollis, who wrote me an urgent note, begging me to take charge of your father's care."

He pointed disdainfully to the tray of medicine bottles. "I must insist these all be removed."

At Henry's raised eyebrows, Lyon continued. "I have examined your father carefully and must tell you that the previous course of treatment inflicted on him would have resulted in his premature and painful death."

"That's a pretty radical statement," said Henry, mostly to gain time to digest the news.

"On the contrary. It is extremely conservative." Lyon's hand swept the tray. "It is these poisonous compounds—calomel, arsenic, strychnine—that is radical."

"I'm not a doctor. What do you suggest?"

"The basic principle is simila similibus curentur." He smiled complacently.

Irritated with the man, Henry could not resist: "Sorry, Doctor, I don't follow French."

"It is Latin. Like cures like."

Lyon's smile might have been patronizing, but Henry ignored it. "I still don't follow you."

"To speak for laymen, sir, what in *healthy* people *causes* a condition that is similar to your father's current condition, that very substance may be used to *cure* your father. Like cures like."

Henry rubbed his jaw in skepticism. "Something strong enough to put a man as low as my father is now, that very something would kill him pretty quick."

"Except," Lyon raised a cautionary finger, "what we will henceforth give him—what I have *already* administered to the patient, for his is a very grave prognosis—is a substance subjected to scientific provings, in a dose calculated according to the laws of infinitesimals." He added as an aside, "Incidentally I prefer to work on the centesimal scale. But," his voice rose in triumph, "the dose is reinvigorated by *sucussion.*"

Sorry, I don't know the word. Succession?"

"Sucussion, sir. For the layman, violent shaking for a certain specific duration."

Henry peered around Lyon at his father. "If you've already given him this sucussioned medicine, it doesn't look like he's ready to get up and walk."

"Sir," Lyon drew himself up. "I am a homeopathic doctor, not Jesus Christ. My cure is not instantaneous, especially after what so-called physicians have inflicted upon your father. We must give his body time to recover from their cures."

"How much time?" Henry asked, but Lyon was out the door.

When Henry incredulously asked Audie about Lyon, she quickly produced from discarded papers her first note; she had spoiled it in her haste. She had asked only if Lyon was available for a consultation.

When, however, she prepared to write a note dismissing him, Henry counseled patience. "Maybe the man's right. I'm not sure any of these doctors really know what they're doing. Let's wait a bit and see if Lyon's treatment works.

❧

Emmer Pruitt always greeted Henry warmly; this time he was roaring with laughter. "You remember you asked about my man Roe that I let go to my cousin Daniel? Well I met Dan a few days ago and thought to ask him about Roe. He said Roe finally 'fessed up to why he always smelled so bad. It wasn't lack of soap and water." Emmer paused to check for who was in earshot. "It was the horse piss he was splashing in every day. Can you believe it? Roe thought it was some kind of sex stimulant."

"That's one I never heard of," laughed Henry.

"Daniel said Roe's got a woman now, so he doesn't need the piss bath any more." His face became serious. "There's Alice coming this way. Mum's the word in front of females, eh?"

Alice's greeting was always as warm as her father's. During his visits she solicited Henry's advice about books, and with his assurance even immersed herself, breathless, in the *Ivanhoe* he lent her. Alice, he decided, was not stupid, but badly educated and timid, just awakening to her ignorance. She listened raptly to his answers when she asked, as she often did, about his New York days, and said she must persuade her parents to take her there. They had spoken of going north sometime soon, perhaps even so far as Cincinnati. New York wasn't much further, was it?

❧

Henry woke from a doze beside his father's bed at the sound of footfalls on the stairs. Though it was still early, several people were approaching. Elvira appeared at the door. Trailing her were Audie Ann and a man with a long thin neck and a very scruffy beard.

Elvira began without preliminaries. "Henry, ye ken make poor Audrey unnerstan."

"What's the problem?" asked Henry, lack of sleep adding to his normal wariness around Elvira.

"The ole man ain't gittin no better. Fac' is, he slippin bad. Them docs ye got is jes pushin him into hisn grave."

She rubbed thumb and forefinger. "An they chargin ye a heep t'kill 'im."

Henry loathed agreeing with Elvira, but had to admit that here she was close to the mark. Still, he was defensive. "We've called in the doctors with the best reputations. Father is apparently a difficult case."

"Seem t'me, the problem ain't the patient. Hit's the docs. Coupla year ago I bought me a book from him." She jerked a thumb at Scruffy Beard. "Man named Thompson done writ hit." She turned to the man. "Tell 'im," she ordered.

The visitor stepped forward to expound the discoveries of his mentor, the late Samuel Thompson. Instead of poisons used by over-charging and arrogant doctors who boasted of their education, he said, Thompson used local herbs that were available to anyone. Lobelia as emetic was just one example. Thompson discovered the healing properties of heat, and cured people with cayenne pepper and sweat baths. Especially sweat baths.

Henry turned to Audie. "What do you think?"

Audie did not know what to think. She was certain of only one thing: Father was growing weaker by the day. Maybe the sweat baths could cure him.

Elvira beamed in triumph, but then slipped away. Henry found it was up to him to organize the complex undertaking. The elaborate heavy tent outside to trap steam. The pit not too close to the tent for the fire, but not too far for the steam. The fire kept high but even. Volumes of water. The door taken off its hinges to serve as pallet to convey Samuel B down the stairs. Hours with clouds of steam. Then reversal of the whole procession, back to the bed.

The Thompson book agent—his name Henry finally learned was Philemon—urged repetition for three days, in fact suggested "nigh up to a week," but Henry refused. What accounted for his adamance was not the work involved, but a glimpse when a sheet accidentally dropped away. His father's skin did not look human. His buttocks and upper legs bore burns where steam had been trapped too close.

❧

Eager for someone away from Tulips to talk to, Henry rode to Chestnut Hill. Emmer and Eleanor were shocked by his report, distressed by his difficulties in finding a successful doctor. But, almost to Henry's relief, they had no better alternative. Commenting on how tired he looked, they urged rides in the mountains for relaxation. The high road toward Howards Knob, perhaps.

"Take Alice. She needs to get out too, and you can cheer each other up."

Alice appeared sooner than usual. The buggy was standing ready. Off they went. Alice Pruitt had begun sweetly suggesting routes that happened, he noticed, to bring them home as twilight deepened. She guarded against evening damp by sitting very close to him. On their stops to enjoy mountain vistas she boldly braved the chill as she threw back her wrap to expose enticing shoulders. In every way a lady could, the adorable Alice showed she held his company in high regard.

❧

According to Philemon, who visited again some days after the sweat bath fiasco, in certain really desperate cases he had suggested leeches to draw off stubborn toxins.

Henry was incredulous. "You mean we're back to bleeding?"

"No, no," assured Philemon hastily. "Leeches is really part'a nature, nothin like thet unnatural scarifying steel. A differen thaing entire. Leeches," he patiently explained, "they know by theirselves t'draw off blood thet's full'a pison. They only sucks off the bad blood. They leaves the good. And when they bite they carries healing liquids in their bite thet hep a body recover."

"Sounds right, Henry," offered Elvira, who had reappeared once Samuel B was back at last in his bed. "Me, an Sam too, we thinks the ole man's in turr'ble shape. This could be our las' chance t'save 'im."

Audie Ann was too beaten down to make choices. Henry nodded to Philemon.

The many leeches, distended with blood, that Philemon carefully picked off Samuel B's chest and abdomen brought a confident smile to Philemon's face. "When I come tomorrah, we're a-gonna see a hull diff'ren man."

⁂

"Sally, I'll watch this evening. How is he?"

Sally's eyes were red from crying; her shoulders sagged from fatigue. "Wid dem ugly leech bugs, Marse Sam'l's not s'good. His breathin's not steady a'tall now."

Henry brought a chair close to his father's pillow. The family urgently needed to find some other doctor, but they had run out of ideas. Maybe in the morning someone—meaning he—should go to Knoxville. In the quiet after Sally's footsteps receded, the sheet over his father's chest barely moved. Henry lingered on his father's familiar profile, now reduced to caricature, thin skin stretched taut over sharp bone.

As he sat, Henry's mind wandered. He remembered Samuel's conversation on his last visit to the Quachasee farm, his satisfaction with the crew's work, his unanticipated promise to give servants to his son. Sitting by the fire after the crew dropped asleep, Samuel spoke obliquely about Sarah. "I worry about her, Henry. She's going to need help as she gets older, I think. I won't swear you to it, but promise me you'll look after her when I'm gone." Henry promised. How could he not?

His father took a breath much deeper than most, almost a sigh. Henry imagined him opening his eyes, looking around, speaking in a hoarse voice. He would ask first about the crops, certainly, then about Sarah, and Audie Ann, then church matters. Maybe he would reminisce. *Buried two wives, five sons, and a daughter* . . . He might well volunteer shrewd advice, buttressed by decades' experience, about how to handle contrary people they knew.

Henry scanned the familiar desk where his mother always sat to write letters. He and his sister Emily Jo used an old quilt to build a hiding place under that desk. He remembered their whispered confidences, their hand talk inventions to help Audie, their giggly planning of tricks to play on their father.

What opinion would his father have about Alice Pruitt? Alice Pruitt the china doll? Alice Pruitt the once shy girl? Alice Pruitt the heiress?

Henry looked again at his father. Voices outside the house died away. Again the room fell quiet. After preliminary clickings and whirrings, the hall clock struck the hour with solemnity, as if no further hours remained ever to strike. Henry listened in the following silence for his father's stentorious respiration, but heard only the clock ticking on toward the next hour. He held his breath to listen intently. Nothing. The sheet did not move.

Henry rose and leaned over the bed to put his ear to his father's chest. Listened long. Silence. Samuel had slipped away while his son sat close by but not there.

Henry sat down with a long sigh. He knew what would follow this instant. His urgent call for Sally. Her running steps. Her loud crying. His summons for his stepmother and Audie Ann. Their muted weeping. The black cloth drapery, black armbands, black veils at Sam's demand. The solemn faces of sunburned farmers in rarely worn clothes at the wake. The attentive faces listening to Pastor Berkemeier's summary of this man's life, Samuel B Hollis, Senior, God's child, simultaneously sinner and saint. The short walk behind the coffin-loaded wagon, the following mourners dividing expressionlessly around a mule's droppings in the lane to the Tulips cemetery. The open hole adjacent to two wives, a daughter, five sons. The mourners straining to hear as Pastor raised his voice for the committal prayers over the sound of dry clods falling against hollow wood.

The long conferences with lawyers, obscure language, signatures, parting handshakes, papers duly sealed and stamped. At Chestnut Hill the steady, firm handshake of condolence from Emmer Pruitt, and Eleanor's embrace. The sympathy from Alice, her face no less enticing for its tears as she offered solace. At Tulips the stoicism of Audie Ann. The nagging at every chance from his stepmother that now he must find a suitable wife, start a family, continue the Hollis line.

Everything followed. He studied his father. If Samuel had opened his eyes, spoken?

He rose, threw open the door, drew in a breath to call.

Plowing with Greek, My Life
HL Hollis

Last night I woke in the small hours, irritated with myself that thus far I have given no account of a very popular annual event in an era with less "entertainment" than today—and also, I think, an era more relaxed and neighborly.

Every fall, Father and some other men sponsored a shooting match. Bull's-eye targets, clay discs, a turkey shoot. A little stand, bunting, food, small prizes. Reen Molis happily brought his trumpet and the town band for a ready audience. Informal rules divided contestants into classes by age and shooting piece, and sometimes by sex. Ancillary socializing, crop-yield boasting, and courting added essential attractions. Women brought their best edibles; men, their best mules. Children vied for notoriety by pie-eating contests and watermelon consumption.

As in the old cliché, a good time was had by all. Father, however, once remarked that in the early years, after a fine initiation, participation in the shooting match suffered a precipitous decline. When pressed, Wade Slater confided, "Why Mister Hollis, thars nary no pint in contestatin' whur Miss Audie Ann's shootin. Hits like fighten a ba'ar wit' yer fingernails. Somebody 'tother gonna lose bad. And hit tain't a-gonna be Mister Ba'ar." For the next contest, Father added handbill lines that fully restored participation.

MISS AUDREY ANN HOLLIS

WILL GIVE A MARKSMANSHIP DEMONSTRATION

BEFORE THE LAST PAIR OF CONTESTANTS.

SHE WILL *NOT* BE COMPETING

Audie's demonstrations, as I knew them, required a perspiring man behind a thick sod shelter, sending up targets at breakneck speed. Audie Ann sat on a stool with a Winchester and effortlessly knocked them down as they appeared. Then two men sent up targets, at irregular spacing, mind you, which made her smile as she fired away—a little, white-haired lady in floor-length skirts, her habitual attire, I'm sure, to conceal her lameness. Her unfailing accuracy seemed machine-like, if not uncanny, except that she made it seem so casual.

Perhaps readers may indulgently excuse an Audie Ann shooting anecdote that includes me. As a boy, when Buffalo Bill's show generated international sensation, I read too many Wild West thrillers. I came to fancy myself a fast-draw expert, a Dead-Eye Dick, so fatuously self-absorbed I even challenged Aunt Audie Ann to a contest. On a signal we would draw from holsters and fire at a target. Mama, the timorous killjoy, required me to load only blanks. Father forbade any spectators, on pretext of safety, but in point of fact I think he desired no witnesses to the ignominy he anticipated for me. Audie Ann and I positioned ourselves at the line. Father gave the signal. Audie's bullet centered the bull's eye before I raised my pistol anywhere level to fire. Of course I claimed I wasn't ready, so we did a second round. A third. Skunked.

Father observed my resultant fragility and dispensed sound advice I've tried to bequeath to my children and grandchildren. "When you're whipped bad, you can slink off hangdog. Or you can stomp off mad at everybody. Or you can stick and study the man on top. Now," he said, "stick and analyze how Audie Ann does it." I stuck. I aspired to see my name below Audie's on the handbill as demonstrator, but did not fully achieve that proficiency before Father's death, and subsequently, a host could not fittingly participate in the shootings.

Remarkably, Audie retained her effortless accuracy well into old age. In fact, one of the most astonishing examples occurred only shortly before she died. At the annual competition, after Audie Ann's demonstration, several silly girls egged each other into asking her for pointers. My sister Dory had some inkling of what was afoot and offered to translate as safeguard against anyone making fun at Audie's expense.

Audie Ann treated the girls more cordially than they deserved. Rifle to her shoulder, she was demonstrating sighting down the field, when it unexpectedly went off. Bystanders jumped at the report and exclaimed in consternation—everyone except Audie Ann. She turned calmly to her interrogators and, via Dory, said, "I should have told you that the first rule is to make certain any gun you pick up is unloaded." She smiled ever so slightly and added, "I seem to have robbed Nace Johns of the big Havana he won at the guessing booth."

In point of fact she had shot the just-lit stogie cleanly from Nace's lips. Fortunately, he was then standing well apart from others in the crowd. Nace Johns was infamous for his blustering braggadocio, and ordinarily one would expect him to storm up the field intent on upbraiding Audie Ann, demanding compensation for his endangerment, or at least, for his stogie. Instead he disappeared. We Hollises considered that small loss, for Nace was a man mean (in both meanings), who mistreated wife, children, and mules. Father thought him so beneath contempt that he refused to hire him as day labor, contempt as I may later have occasion to otherwise illustrate.

Solomon asserted that as memorable as I considered Audie Ann's marksmanship, she was then beyond her prime. He maintained that as a young woman Audie could split a playing card set edge toward her, a feat he witnessed more than once.

I consider that no mere fable, for I knew Solomon to be a man of unquestionable integrity. Once, discovering that Father was about to send all of three dollars with Solomon to a merchant in town, I gravely volunteered my approval, guessing the money would be delivered safely. (A mere boy trying to act grown-up, of course, but 'twas ever so.) Father regarded me with barely repressed hilarity. "I don't *guess*. He's carried forty dollars in gold five hundred miles for me." (Intent on establishing my credentials as a mature man of business, I did not think then, as I do now, to ask why and where in the world Solomon ferried such a sum.)

In my youth I considered Solomon Haller a gentleman. I still do, to the extent that I have paused long here over matters of address. Aged former slaves were often "honored" by being called *Uncle* or *Aunt*. But in Solomon Haller's case, I find *Uncle* demeaning. *Mister* would be much more appropriate, except that in his case, *Mister* would fail to affirm the intimate place he had in our family. So I conclude an untitled Solomon he must be, with hope that my grandchildren's grandchildren will keep these reflections on respect and affection in mind as they read about Solomon.

But for his race Solomon Haller could have served with distinction in the judiciary, renowned for sagacity and discernment. He was born a slave and received no formal education. He spoke, though, as one who had read broadly. He picked up Audie Ann's hand talk, and used it with great fluency. I must rephrase that: in point of fact,

Solomon's hand talk was distinctively rapid and precise, cleanly "spoken." It was characterized by large vocabulary, clever coinages and imaginative turns of phrase. The result meant startling juxtaposition as he moved between oral and hand language.

I think I had better linger here to avoid misunderstandings about matters researchers far more erudite than I have studied with scholarly intensity. I was always surprised when Solomon shifted to hand talk. My surprise, however, was never at his capability, but at the juxtaposition. Just as I would be surprised should a gallused back-mountain farmer shift his corncob pipe to break from his dialect into fluent French, or a suave Parisian break into mountain English. Solomon hand talking was not the man who came to maturity a slave, with all that implied. Observant of the old deferential forms between servant and master in oral communication, in hand talk he abandoned elisions and slurrings to become expansive, precise, and eloquent, with no hint of his former status.

It was while he used hand talk that I first apprehended how handsome he was, even in old age. (The connection between communication fluency and appraisal of appearance is an interesting phenomenon I would like to expand on when the hour is not so late.)

Though he was much respected hereabouts, outside family, not even a half-dozen people in these parts were aware of Solomon's hand language. Audie Ann was primary, of course. I needed no unusual perceptiveness to grasp her attention to him (and his to her) when they sat on the Tulips porch. My brother Marcus was another; he engaged Solomon in long hand-talk conversations and told me that he absorbed much that later influenced his translation for Audie of Pastor's sermons.

Solomon appeased an apparent wanderlust by traversing large distances. He possessed a remarkable awareness of space and direction. I occasionally walked with him in these mountains, and noticed he navigated without trails, slipping independently, and near soundlessly, through the woods like a stealthy Indian of old; beside him I felt like the proverbial bull in a china shop. He revealed his range only incidentally, as when he described crashing waves on Lake Erie, or compared the Mississippi at Memphis with the Hudson at Albany. He lived in his own little cabin, but he was a fixture at Tulips, sitting with Audie for congenial conversation, often conducted over preparation of garden harvest for the kitchen.

Of course I don't accept Crotia's preposterous hypothesizing about Solomon and Audie Ann, but I concede his life intertwined with Audie Ann's and Father's at Tulips much more than I understood as a boy. How much more I cannot say; he died before I grasped there was anything to inquire about. Perhaps as a result of general nervousness about people his color and weapons, Solomon never, in my presence, fired a marksman's rifle, but at the contests he served as Audie Ann's assistant, and took complacent satisfaction in her incredible accuracy. Something—I cannot be more specific—about their relationship indicated to me that for an apple to appear atop his head, she had only to hint.

By describing Audie Ann's prowess with lethal weapons, I fear leaving the impression of mannishness. In point of fact, for us children she acted as a tender second mother, who moved a teething or colicky baby brother or sister into her room for the duration, untroubled by prolonged fussing and loud crying. My sisters, I must record (guided, of course, only by the imperative toward historical accuracy), used Audie Ann shamelessly to wheedle favors from Father, and, I suspect, to protect girlish secrets. No one could question her solicitous affection within the family.

QUACHASEE
WHC

Henry's men had never worked so long without him, yet his absence created no crisis, for their numbers were many fewer and priorities unchanging. Solomon directed continuing tasks ably, first among equals. Only Jefferson began to follow his own lights. He lingered on the cabin porch in the morning, came back ever earlier in the afternoon. He tried to make himself agreeable, fetching things he thought Carrie needed, issuing friendly observations about anything at hand. First he stood in the doorway of the cabin while she worked. Then he eased inside, settling with obvious satisfaction in the chair at the table.

"Carrie, doan be wokin so ha'd heah. It nebbah gits yuh nuttin. All dem rock? Nuttin foh yuh."

"Got me a fine fireplace," Carrie corrected him.

"But look'id whut id gits de wide man. Carrie doan own de fiahplace. Marse 'Enry do. Carrie work finger t'de bone an doan gits nut'in t'show foah it. Ease back, gal, ease back consid'ble. Dis ain't profitin Carrie nohow. Make Marse 'Enry re'lize who *really* puttin' bread in front'a he."

"If I ease back, who puts bread in front of *you*, Jefferson?" She exercised cook's prerogative. "Now get outta that chair, outta my space. No, no, you keep going outta this room. I can't be always walking 'round you to get my bread done."

A boy sent up from Tulips brought news as well as supplies. Because of the funeral and tending to Samuel B's estate, Henry would be more days away. "Bid-ness foah 'portan' lawyermens wif mighty fian hosses," reported the boy solemnly. He could not help adding gossip from Sally about a loud Hollis family conference. "Li'l Sam, he wanna sell off sum wemens t'raise cash, but de Hollis wemens, 'specially Elvira, squash 'im flat. Flat's a bu-ug. Elvira, she say she tinkin 'bout buyin moh sarvans, not no sellin, an rentin dem oud. An Sam, he near hab a connipshun."

Jefferson dawdled still longer over his coffee. "Dat dress lookin good on yuh, Carrie." He helped himself to more biscuits. "We hab 'bout de bes cook I ebbah meet." He snatched up a piece of bacon. "Any man be happy wif yore cookin."

That afternoon he filled the cabin doorway. "Carrie, I wan yuh be mah woman," he announced. He came in to stand behind her at the table where she was assembling baking ingredients. She felt his hands stroke her waist, then ease toward her front. She had seen a foolish delivery man do this on her mother once: Lilly did not resist, attempt escape, issue reproof.

As her mother had, Carrie calmly worked on. She cracked several more eggs into the bowl, dumped in pepper and briefly whisked the mix as she sensed Jefferson's breath close to her ear. A cupped hand, a quick jerk. Jefferson's smiling face, about to kiss her neck, dripped raw egg and oil. With a yelp he stumbled back, blinded, sneezing and coughing, wiping his eyes, which embedded the pepper and sharp shell fragments from the last eggs.

"Better hope you can find six more eggs," she shoved him roughly toward the door, "or no decent meal tonight." She pushed him through the doorway. "You're lucky I wasn't frying."

He fled, all the way to the spring, to rinse egg and shell pieces out of eyes, his nose, his hair. Carrie slipped a paring knife into the pocket of her apron. But a knife does not decide the basic problem, whether to become Jefferson's woman. He could be kind. She never heard jokes about him drinking on the sly. She remembered seeing him in the fields, his bare torso gleaming black with sweat, sloped sharply out from his waist to wide shoulders. The muscles in his powerful arms and back rippled under his skin as he worked. She had grasped his shoulder once when she tripped; what she briefly held on to was solid muscle that did not yield.

Yes. Yet when, soon after she arrived, she offered to teach Jefferson how to read, his answer came brusque and unequivocal. "Doan need no truck wid dat." The morning after Henry and John Bright disagreed jovially late into the previous evening about Longstreet's writing style, Jefferson spoke of them scornfully. "Whut foolishness. Dey stay 'wake jes to talk 'bout some book dat made up."

Hours later Jefferson stood sheepishly on the cabin porch to offer eggs he patiently hunted and to apologize. "I jes gets too 'cited 'bout yuh. I promises t'behave. I wans yuh be mah woman. I ken fix up a nice place in de shed or come in de tent. Yuh say whut yuh wans. Now how 'bou'id, Carrie?"

"Jefferson, I'm flattered. The problem is, I don't love you."

"But I loves yuh, Carrie. An yuh needs someone t'love yuh, 'cause yuh in foah some rough time. Any dey now Marse 'Enry gonna open him eye an see de dish dat's right front ob he. An he gonna grab dat dish wif bot hand. Yuh ken' jest trow egg at Marse 'Enry, Carrie, or he wop yuh hard 'til yuh happy yuh under he. But he won' love yuh. He jes use Carrie till he fine some wide lady. Den he get rid'a Carrie. Wide lady makes he do id. Yuh be lucky he doan sells yuh off long ways down sud."

Jefferson tapped his chest. "But Jefferson heah, yuh ken count on he. Yessem. E'en afta mah wok done heah wid Marse 'Enry rentin me, an bahk at Miz Hackett, she nebbah care iffen I cum see yuh on Sundeys, long's I bahk Mondey moanin fust ting. An I used t'walkin in de dahk."

He reached for her hand, but she drew away. "No, Jefferson, I just can't be your woman when I don't love you."

"But who' woman yuh gonna be? Solomon won' hab no woman. Zeke got Lucia. She'd 'bout kill yuh iffen yuh try t'take he. An 'Enry, he wide." Jefferson leaned closer and lowered his voice. "An yuh knows de wide man ken' sat'fy no woman de way de black man ken."

His wink and leer gave Carrie a face-saving escape. "Jefferson," she waved him back with a towel, "you get out of my ears with your trashy talk. And don't come back to me with sugar later. You've got plenty to do with Solomon and Zeke. I never heard such talk from a real gentleman." She pushed him hard with both hands. She thought his laugh sounded forced, but at least he left.

His words, though, were harder to push away. Mama always said that when you need to think clearly, you think while you make a soup. So she started peeling, slicing, dicing, rummaging in her memory for what her mother had told her.

Years ago, masters from three or four farms had given their servants permission to gather at Tulips for jollification. Carrie wandered mostly alone, aware other servant children mostly avoided her. Alone she slipped through a side door into the barn and heard men's voices. She crept in the shadows up a ladder to lie in the hay and look down on the ground floor. Their backs to her, men lounged on barrels and stools, facing the open wagon door. During a momentary lull in the laughing and gossiping, one stepped forward and turned to face the others. Carrie recognized Buck, someone she avoided because of the way he pawed her in teases. Now he swaggered in his best clothes.

"Now I ax all yuh dahkies, who de strongest," Buck began, "de wide man er de black? I ax yuh. Why, de black, a'course. Yuh knows de wide man ken' stay in de field all dey. Not in dat hot sun, nosuh. He fall over an die daid. Right? Right."

Murmurs and chuckles, especially from servants Carrie didn't recognize as Tulips people, encouraged Buck.

"An I ax yuh, who de smartest? De wide man er de black man? De black man 'gain. Yuh doubt dat, dahkies? Well, who take care'a de mules an de cows, an knows whut ailin' dem wen dey sick? Yuh 'membahs id de black man."

Solomon moved into Carrie's view as he walked to the door and looked out left and right. Buck continued without a pause. "De wide man wan give all kind'a bad stuff to 'em. Only 'cepshon be Doc Sexton ober de mount'n, an seem lahk he *mosly* black.

Appreciative laughter warmed Buck still more.

"An I ax yuh, who bes 'quipped t'keep wemens happy, de wide man er de black man? Tink ob it. Who best 'quipped? Yuh know id be de black man."

A gray-haired man Carrie recognized as one of the few servants she knew from the Pruitt farm stood to interrupt. "Mah ole marse 'fore he die, he hab a pitcher book'a statues, ole fum Rome tiam, gen'rals an sech. De statues, dey look jes lahk livin people. Dint hab much on, jes a sheet, 'cause id hot dere, I'spect. Some wuz fum Africa, but yuh ken tell dey wuz wide 'cause dere equi'men—id carve out right dere plain's day—dere equi'men s'small." He opened thumb and forefinger with a deprecatory snort.

"Dat jes be more proofs foah whut I *already* sayin," Buck broke in dismissively; he clearly preferred to perform solo. "I doan needs *dat* proof. He reached for his crotch. "I gots all de proof righ heah, an den sum." Encouraged by the laughter and yessuh, yessuh, he glanced outside, then opened his pants and supported his proof with an open palm. "Dis be whut de wemens wan. Dis be whut dey need, an doan dey know id." He opened his arms wide as his proof stood unaided. "*Dis* be whut all de cat'walin' be 'bout. An I ax yuh, do de wide man hab't? No, he doan. We knows who best 'quipped. De black man."

He peered around conspiratorially. "Dis be wad de *wide* wemens all wan, too. Right?" His voice went to falsetto. "Jes tink ob Miz Hackett 'n huh black boys."

Except for several loud guffaws, laughter from Buck's audience died mid-breath. Solomon again stepped out the door to survey the yard, but this time he spoke. "Bettah put dat 'ways, Buck." His tone accepted no argument.

The barn floor quickly emptied as men hurried away to the pleasantly shaded side yard where the women had laid out their best dishes on boards over trestles.

In the kitchen house loft, Carrie reported the episode to her mother. Lilly's response sounded almost angry. "Caroline LaCroix, when you see a bunch of men in the barn, you stay outta there." She relented a little. "I'm sorry you heard all that, especially from that Buck. He's a no good nigger."

"But Mama, was he right about black and white equipment?"

"Girl your age doesn't need to know about that."

"I'm growing up, you know."

"Know it too well. Lord, how do I explain this to a child?"

"Mama, I am not a child."

"No, you're not." Lilly hugged her. "But you're not a full-grown woman either. It's maybe like this. Let's say it's winter, freezing cold. You're not just a little chilly. You're cold clear through to the bone. You come to a fire outside with two people sitting by. I'm one and a great wide auntie like Sally is on the other side. We both say, 'Honey, come here against me and I'll get you warm.' Which one would you sit against?"

"You, Mama."

"But that great wide auntie would warm you up faster than I could."

"But you're my mama."

"Um-hmm. You know who loves you best. Buck doesn't have much brain and what he has he hides in his pants. He thinks the body gives orders to the heart. But it's the other way 'round. When a man and a woman are together, it's not his equipment, it's her heart that says she wants to satisfy him."

Carrie tried to sound grown up. "I understand, Mama."

"No you don't, child. But maybe you'll remember this when you *can* understand it."

"Mama, when your heart says you want to satisfy a man, what all do you do?"

Lilly threw up her hands. "Curse that Buck. Talk about Pandora's box. That's something you sure don't need to know."

"But Mama, Aunt Sally says—"

"Sally says? . . . She's been talkin? . . . All right child. If you promise not to ask Sally or anybody else again, solemn promise, then I'll promise you that after you get your regular monthlies . . . regular, mind you, then I'll tell you what a smart woman ought to know about satisfying her man." Carrie kept her solemn promise. So did her mother.

Carrie raised a tentative tasting spoon, and reached for spices. She knew now her mother was right about satisfying a man. That didn't guarantee she was necessarily right about their equipment. After all, perhaps Lilly had slept only with her white owners. Maybe she invented as cover. If you compared Henry—narrow chest, ropy arms and silly red collar of sunburn—with the muscles rippling in Jefferson's wide back beneath that even-toned skin, black won easily.

Of course, Marse John Bright, Hawkeye, was a handsome man in any company. Hawkeye led her to Cora, to Cora's passionate cry, *Who that looks at this creature remembers the color of his skin?* That led her to Cora's Uncas, and Uncas to Henry, where she had begun. She had not, though, merely gone around in a circle. Jefferson would not recognize Cooper's characters, in fact would scorn them. *Whut foolishness.* This soup needs more onion, for sure. Lilly must be right: thin mama or great wide auntie. White pepper too. Did she have any thyme left? This soup definitely lacked for thyme. Way more greens would also help a lot.

She didn't need Jefferson to tell her about masters selling off servant women who inconvenienced a marriage. In the small hours, Carrie tried hard to keep at bay her memory of Henkel and Dinkins, their impersonal messages that mother and daughter were sold and must leave immediately.

The boy sent up from Tulips with crew instructions also carried details 'bout big weddin doins at de Pruitts. 'Bout Marse 'Enry sitten all' tiam wit' Miss Alice in dat blue dress, huh haih lookin lahk honey. Ever'body lookin at she s'much's de bride. Jes lahk some prin'ess, sittin an givin ordahs. She doan hav'ta get off fum huh trone. Marse Henry, he gets huh all de lem'nade she ken drink. Marse Henry 'bout lived at Pruitts 'stead of Tulips. Ebbahbody say dey make de perfek coup'l, an dere be 'nodder weddin righ' soon.

A further thought added to Carrie's dread. When Henry married the beautiful Alice, he would have no reason to keep his little mountain farm, not when he could be at the Pruitt's palatial Chestnut Hill. No more mountain walls for Carrie. And she'd have a new mistress, a mistress she did not know. Maybe that's what Lilly really meant when she talked of being owned.

The perfect couple: Henry . . . with Alice, the fairy-tale princess. Who is the most beautiful of all? Look into the mirror on the wall, Caroline LaCroix. It doesn't lie. Alice smiles into a bright pier glass that reflects her glory from slipper to crown. Carrie peers into a shadowy hand mirror that reveals a nut-dyed homespun shift with a crack dividing its top and skirt. Compared to delicate Alice, Carrie is callused palms, wind-burned cheeks, and arms muscled by big rocks and heavy kettles. In her bright mirror, Alice Pruitt waves her magic wand. Look into your hand mirror on its nail, Carrie LaCroix, and see your stirring spoon.

❧

It was after sunset when Henry plodded up to the cabin. He sank down on the porch steps, quietly greeting the men who had just finished their evening meal.

"Yuh lookin' real tard, Marse 'Enry," observed Solomon.

"If I look it, I feel it even more. A long day with the lawyers and Miss Audie Ann, and the walk up here, but this morning I decided I wanted to sleep in my own bed tonight, no matter what."

"Marse Henry, if you can wait a little," Carrie anxiously pleaded, "I can get the kettle hot again soon."

"I'm home, so I don't mind sitting." At the trough he splashed water over his face. "By the way, Carrie," speaking through the towel. "I hope you saved some gingerbread for me. Please."

Carrie's voice became much lighter. "Oh yes, Marse Henry, yes, I did."

Late in the evening, after she made a good start on the next day's baking, he pulled her to his bed in the back room and held her gently with kisses. A rising moon flooded into the bedroom, lighting his face. "I wasn't sure you were coming back," she breathed.

"But this is home."

"I wasn't sure you were coming back to me," she corrected. "The boy you sent said Miss Alice is pretty as a princess." She tried to keep her voice neutral.

"She is indeed."

The catch in her chest tightened. "He said you would be marrying her."

"A number of people think that."

She tried to keep a calm voice. "He said the wedding be real soon."

"Our mothers have almost every detail settled."

She closed her eyes. "He said that after the wedding you wouldn't be stayin on this 'pokey lil place.' You'd move down to the Pruitt's Chestnut Hill."

"Emmer Pruitt has offered to build a fine house near Chestnut Hill."

She felt tears leaving her eyes, though she refused to brush them away.

"But all those people don't know one essential fact."

"What's that?" She swallowed the wail in her throat.

"I already found my princess."

A wide auntie or a thin mama: she instantly made her choice.

A faint glow in the eastern sky greeted a setting moon's farewell when Carrie stepped down from the cabin porch to her tent, a cat her only witness, she thought. At the open side of one of the sheds, Jefferson spat out *damn,* and lay back to close his eyes for the first time that night.

NOTARY PUBLIC ATTESTATION
ROCK COUNTY
STATE OF TENNESSEE

The undersigned, at the request of, and in the company of, Lewis Gates Warden, resident of the vicinity of Ginners Ford, Rock County, Tennessee,

Does hereby attest that I have personally inspected the original in situ and find the words on page 2 of this attestation to be a faithful, true, and complete transcription of the tombstone designated "Alice Pruitt Hollis," in the private burying ground locally known as the Ennis Hollis Graveyard, presently located on the property of John A. Packer, of rural Rock County, Tennessee.

Witness my hand and Seal of Office this 17th day of April, 1954.

SIGNED

Albert E. Cumb, Notary Public, State of Tennessee.

REST IN PEACE

ALICE PRUITT HOLLIS

JULY 23, 1825
MARCH 10, 1848

WIFE OF CALEB JACOB HOLLIS

MOTHER OF
GEORGIA JANE
JUDITH SARAH †
JACOB ENNIS †
RUTH ELIZA

FOREVER BELOVED

QUACHASEE
WHC

"Take a breath, Solomon." Henry absentmindedly brushed debris off the teeth of the two-man saw. "What's Jefferson's sulk about?"

"Dunno, Marse. All I knows, Jeff'son ain't pullin' he fair share a'de load. When yuh gone I talks 'bou'id, but he nebbah lissen."

"Good thing for me he's rented. I'm about ready to take him back to Miss Hackett. I don't like to because I've heard she's rough on rented boys who get sent back."

"She sho am."

"You've heard that too, eh? I'll wait a bit then. Maybe he'll come 'round now I'm here again."

Henry said the same to Carrie. Helpless, she worried. She heard Solomon, checking tools, ask where the best double-bladed axe was. Jefferson, who everyone knew had used it last, eventually responded with a lethargic "Guess id got lef' in de field." He gave Solomon a sullen stare when told to fetch it ahead of oncoming rain.

Carrie listened as Jefferson began dropping the *Marse* when addressing Henry. Or he managed a *Marse*, but made it sound so insolent that Zeke shook his head. "Dat boy," he confided to Carrie, "headin foah grief."

Impatient with the trash collecting around the camp, Henry assigned Jefferson one morning to clean it up. Later, when Carrie stepped out to the porch to catch the freshening breeze, she saw a large pile of brush burning furiously, igniting the tinder-dry grass. Rising wind drove flames toward the shanties and cabin. By instinct she jumped to the water buckets, filled at noon. Empty. How could that be? She threw the top off the cistern barrel, always a reserve. Empty. Wind-fueled, the grass burned at frightening speed.

"Jefferson! Fire!" she screamed. He appeared eventually from behind the cabin at a sedate walk. What was the matter with him? She knew the other men worked at the far edge of the High Field, well beyond her shouts. In the time she ran out to them the whole camp would be afire.

She rushed to her tent, pulled Audie's pistol from under her pillow, and fired through the canvas roof. She ran to Daisy, untied her, and shooed the last chickens out of the coup. Then to a shed for an old mule blanket. She beat it at the flames.

Jefferson materialized through the smoke, also beating, but casually, stopping from time to time to kick live embers ahead. "Doan fight too ha'd, er yuh puts id out. 'Membah, Carrie doan own nuttin heah." He beat at the ground slowly and randomly, avoiding only the flame line.

Carrie stopped. Jefferson spoke true. Let it go. She didn't own this. Her name appeared on nothing—except the papers documenting who owned her. Lowering her arms, she stood, breathing hard. Let it go. Cabin, sheds, haystack, everything. Wouldn't take long to be smoldering ruins, smoke curling up from the cabin floor beams. Only the fireplace and chimney, blackened by flames, would mark the spot. Her stones would remain.

They would be a grave marker. For whose grave? She pictured Henry's face as he ran in too late to save what he worked for. What *they* worked for. The first owners had abandoned the place. Maybe Henry would be so disheartened he'd leave too, same as his kin had.

Then what would happen to her? She knew: back, defeated, down the trail. To Tulips, where she must always be on guard for Sam. To Tulips, always at some one's beck and call. To Tulips, where there was no high place to be an eagle, scanning the landscape folded into one ridge and valley after another until haze and mountain became impossible to differentiate.

She suddenly was angry with the fire and again began to beat it frantically. No Tulips. No Sam. No Caleb. No Elvira. Surrounded by thick smoke she coughed uncontrollably. Tears ran down her face. She beat at her shins to keep her smoldering skirt from flaring up, but she kept beating at the fire. No bondage. No Marse. No whip. No walls.

She tried to stay between flame and cabin. The fire outflanked her. Only yards more and the rotten wood of the sheds would catch quickly. A long tongue of fire almost lapped at the cabin. Her arms felt ready to drop off. She could not hold the pace. Where were the men in the field? They must not have heard her shot.

A slight wind shift revealed ghostly figures. Zeke and Solomon were dousing flames on the other side of the fire. Then, working his way toward her, Henry. Jefferson flailed madly now. Fresh and able, the men moved efficiently along the fire line. Their all-out fight with rising flames subsided within a few minutes to a watchful patrol smothering fast-fading embers.

Carrie bent over, coughing hard from inhaled smoke. Her dress hung filthy and singed. Her face was tears and sweat runs smudged in ash. Exhausted, she sank to a boulder seat. Henry came over to check on her. He quickly sent Solomon and Zeke running to the spring with empty buckets.

He turned on Jefferson. "What happened?" he demanded.

"Well, Marse, fust I jes gath'in brush, lahk yuh tole me t'clean up heah, pilin up dis 'n dat. All kinda stuff, lahk yuh say, Massa. It gettin purty mess 'round heah. I cleans it up good, Massa. An den de wind, it takes hold ob de fiah, an de fiah jes gets 'way, I guess."

"Why would you light a fire when the grass is this dry?" demanded Henry.

"Marse, I jes tryin' t'do de bes I knows, an do 'xactly whut yuh tells me."

"You could have burned down every building."

"Marse Henry, yuh blame t'wind. Id cum up fum nowheres an blows de fiah. I wuz tryin ha'd t'fights id, but de wind too strong foh one man, I guess."

"I don't believe you. When we were riding in, the smoke cleared just a moment. Carrie's arms were going like a machine. You were swatting flies. You meant to burn us out. I'm taking you back to Miss Hackett."

Carrie's coughing spasms began again. Henry looked around in irritation "Where are those boys with water for you?" He seized a bucket and ran toward the spring.

Jefferson turned to Carrie. "Doan give me 'way. I sees whut he doin' t'yuh nights. I'se payin' he back. Wy yuh shoot dat 'larm? Iffin dey din' come in, we coulda burn alla id. An yuh hab pun'shmen foah dat marse."

He took her hand briefly. "But doan yuh wurrie none. 'Enry gonna hab accidan walkin down t'Tulips. Mebbe at dat Snake Sheah."

"Think a minute, Jefferson. That's not right to hurt Marse Henry."

He smiled at her. "Carrie, yuh a good Christ'n an fergibs dose who does yuh evil. But I nebbah do. Marse 'Enry need punishin foah de evil he 'flictin on yuh in d'night."

Aware that Jefferson's strength gave reality to his threat, Carrie saw her only course was correcting his belief. "Jefferson, listen to me. Listen, Jefferson. Henry's not doing any evil on me. I go to his bed because I want to. Do you understand? Because I want to."

Jefferson's face moved from disbelief to shock, then disgust. "Carrie, yuh a low slut."

Shocked at his accusation, Carrie stepped back, wordless, as if struck.

"An all de worser on 'Enry," spat out Jefferson, "foah tempin' yuh t'id. Carrie, yuh is anodder . . . anodder Jezebel."

Henry had run back. "Carrie, here's water. Sit down for a while. Get cleaned up. That was quick thinking. Good thing the rifle was loaded. If you didn't give us that alarm, the fire . . ." He switched from gratitude to fury. "C'mon Jefferson. We're going back to Miss Hackett right now. I won't have you here one more minute. Get your things together. We're leaving now."

Jefferson pulled a bundle of tied-up clothes from his shed. Carrie realized he had tied them before the fire, and saw that Henry did not spot this.

"Marse Henry," Carrie tried to get him to notice Jefferson's bundle.

"Carrie, I'll stay at Tulips tonight." Henry was focused on Jefferson. "Be back in the morning for coffee." He turned to go.

"Marse Henry?" He turned back for her question. "Marse Henry, let me . . . let me get you something to eat before you go."

"No time. I want to be there before pitch dark. We're going right now." For Jefferson, Henry reinforced his words with an arm pointed toward the path down.

Drained of the energy that buoyed her during the fire, Carrie could hardly move, let alone think clearly. Never before had *slut* or *Jezebel* been thrown at her. Did she deserve that for sleeping with Henry? She could blurt out the truth about the fire, but she knew what that could bring down on Jefferson. She remembered stories about Jefferson's owner: if she did not shield Jefferson, he might become desperate enough to attack Henry right here. But if she let them walk away, she risked Henry being forced off Snake Sheer. She watched their receding backs in despair. She had the same feeling as when she threw off the cistern lid to fight the fire and saw no water.

She caught up with them well down the trail. She carried a towel-covered basket. "Marse." She was breathing hard from running.

"Marse Henry." They stopped. "I brought you some hoe cakes to eat on the trail. Here, Jefferson." She slipped out a piece and handed it to him. She reached under the towel again. "Oh, this one feels too crumbly for you to carry, Marse Henry. I don't want to hold you up." She looked at Jefferson. "Go ahead, Jefferson. I'll have to get the one below for Marse Henry. He can catch up."

Jefferson moved off, his mouth full of hoe cake. Carrie threw back the towel to answer Henry's raised eyebrows at her impertinent directions. She sieved disheveled hair out of her eyes and glanced at the soot her hair left on her hands. "I must look like a Huron in war paint," she whooped loudly. Her voice became a boy playing Indian games. "Ugh, me think Uncas keep tomahawk ready, 'cause Magua want him scalp." She laughed. Henry moved pistol from basket to his belt.

"It's loaded," she mouthed silently, as her fingers mimed a pushed figure falling, falling.

Plowing with Greek, My Life
HL Hollis

Rereading my earlier description of Audie Ann, I feel compelled to return to her because I am nagged by fear that I did not do her justice. Despite being crippled and deaf she was never a recluse. In point of fact, she was an active member of the family, a trusted confidante, a shrewd observer of the wider world, possessed of an unpredictable and sometimes impolitic sense of humor.

That description, though entirely accurate, I believe, does not satisfy me. I must add that Audie Ann was endowed with an unusual facility for guiding by query. You answered her questions, perhaps at first mostly out of courtesy, and gradually saw some action, now your own idea, must be the obvious choice. Bill will assure you that's how he decided on medical school; Dory, how she chose between returning to law school and becoming Mrs. Micah Henderson; Crotia, that she should take seriously gathering and recording old settlers' stories; and I, that I must delay no longer in making my best friend also my wife.

Do not imagine Audie Ann a cipher devoid of judgment. Perhaps I can condense an illustration. Because the Lutheran liturgy is, of course, mostly prescribed, she could follow church services easily in the hymnal. When the pastor entered the pulpit for the sermon, she turned, in my early childhood, to read from some collection of printed sermons she'd brought along. As we children got older, however, Solomon's facility with handtalk inspired my brother Marcus to translate on the spot (I should say, in the pew). He became so fluent that I learned to watch him as I listened to Pastor because on occasion Marcus inserted a turn of phrase better than the original.

On a Sunday when some travel mishap delayed our pastor's return, a ministerial candidate substituted—a very young and unprepossessing candidate. Granted, our instant disappointment was premature and unfair. But first impressions, it transpired, proved too true.

He ill-advisedly chose as sermon text the uncompromising imperatives toward the end of Matthew 5 (Resist not evil; turn the other cheek; give your cloak, etc.), difficult enough for preachers blessed with unusual sagacity, of which he was not one. Instead, he belonged to the homiletical school founded, or floundered, on the conviction that sincerity redeems a paucity of content. He preached a painfully elementary sermon, haltingly delivered.

Worse—perhaps no one had forewarned him; perhaps seeing his words become motions mesmerized him—as he preached he kept watching Audie and Marcus. But Audie Ann followed Marcus's faithful translation only for a short time, then signed to him, "This is awful. Save yourself the trouble." Shaking her head, she turned away from Marcus to face the pulpit, her arms folded across her chest, obviously in eager anticipation of the amen.

The poor man's knees must have entered the pulpit as castanets anyway, and Audie Ann's rejection surpassed his courage. He terminated the sermon as ungracefully as he initiated it, at least bestowing the virtue of extreme brevity.

At home during dinner, Father commented genially on Audie's summary rejection, but she did not retreat. "Even I could give a better sermon."

Mama as usual issued cautions about little ears. Father as usual ignored such entreaties and turned to his sister. "I agree: a yard-axe of a preacher and probably the worst sermon I can recall. But Audie, be fair. That text is hard. What would you do with it if you could stand in the pulpit?"

"I'd preach a sermon worth listening to," was her prompt answer. She quickly specified, with jabs at her plate to separate food, what she would have done. Intro (water glass), four main heads (chicken morsel, green beans, mashed potato, sweet potato), a complementary text (applesauce), conclusion (dessert plate). The floor open, Dory sharpened the intro, Bill collapsed four points to three, I submitted a better complementary text, Crotia added flourishes which Marcus reworded for greater concision, and Annie happily approved.

My aunt flashed Father an impish grin. "Maybe Lutherans should require that women and children preach? You know, that boy-minister reminded me of the story about the young preacher and the farm girls." She glanced at Mother's end of the table. "But I'll wait until later on the porch."

One of the rare points of (very muted) contention between Aunt Audie and her sister-in-law was Audie's practice of paying little attention to her audience's composition when she embarked on one of her anecdotes fit only for mature listeners. Her repertoire of what some might consider rather coarse stories seemed infinite. I never ascertained their origin. A reference to "the porch later" was a sure sign where older children might head after dinner for discreet eavesdropping while Mama was busy shepherding children with tender ears.

The begats in Genesis are different from the plots in Thucydides. One is genealogy, the other, history, and I aspire here to history, or at least biography.

In point of fact I would be more complacent about my labors on family history were I less cognizant of two troubling lacunae: Hollis antecedents in England and my father's Quachasee years.

About the former, I once gathered enough courage to write to a professional genealogist in London, seeking assistance or, in the extremity, advice. After a delay so protracted I forgot my inquiry, his terse reply—the very paper reeked of supercilious impatience and condescension—made my face burn. He humbly begged me (he, about as supplicant as John D. Rockefeller) always to bear foremost in mind the probably scores of men baptized Peter Hollis in late seventeenth-century England. Perhaps tens of them emigrated. Tracking down *my* Peter Hollis would require, as I surely might grasp on even cursory consideration, certain basic facts, of which I possessed too few. That being the case, et cetera, et cetera.

My father's many years on the Quachasee farm also present frustrations. What documents would a single man leave from such mountain farming? A deed? Yes, but bloodless. A diary? Unthinkable; remember that my father was of the generation following Samuel B, the compulsive diarist. Letters? Unlikely. His most plausible regular correspondents lived within a half day's walk.

The only paper records I am aware of are his meticulously detailed records of weather and his careful documentation of horticultural experiments and animal breeding. His weather records are devoid of human references but filled with notations about dates of plant maturation, flowering in relation to temperatures, and wind's havoc on trees. One may brighten, as I at first did, at some human reference, to Cora, or Julia, or Audrey, only to see those are names he gave to various new varieties he developed.

These pages demonstrate that Father was a determined experimentalist and innovator from his earliest farming years. Small wonder that when he moved down to Tulips he gave this farm a reputation in the area for its fruit and its bacon. I put my own record books alongside his with considerable humility. But they give little hint of his thinking.

After Father's sudden death, I belatedly thought to supplement the paucity of written record by oral recollection. Crotia-like, I sat down in a quiet corner with Judge Bright, pencil and paper in hand. I possess those yellowed pages still, and copy them here.

Q. Did you [John P. Bright] visit Father up on the Quachasee farm?

A. Yes, regularly. I always enjoyed those visits.

Q. What was it like to live up there so out of the way?

A. I suspect you're imagining a penurious, hairy, eccentric recluse, eking out a cheerless existence on barely-ground corn meal and gristly bear meat. [I may have colored a bit at the truth of the Judge's suspicion, because he kindly rescued me by quickly going on.] The sun was your clock, the seasons your calendar; you grew what you ate, you made what you used, and what you did not grow or make, you tried to compensate for or did without. You were prudent to exercise common sense around fire, guns, and mules.

Q. But corn and hogs don't make a healthy diet, and tools wear out.

A. Your Father lived much better than you imagine. He learned the native plants and paled in a very large garden plot so I hardly ever ate a meal there without, in season, a large salad of greens well dressed. Some of my most memorable meals were up there.

Q. Edie [our longtime cook] was there too? I did not think she was that old.

A. She was not. Your father was very fortunate. He discovered that the knobs and ridges around the head of the Quachasee created a highly localized climate, substantially milder than that just a few miles away. Perfect for a large orchard—Tulips' reputation got well started up there. Once he learned how to graft limbs—and he became very skilled at it, as you know—he was always experimenting.

Q. But to keep going one needs a market. Was there some road I don't know about? Some route to get fruit to market?

A. No, no road. But his apple brandy in small kegs fit a pack mule. It caught on with the far-flung, little-noticed immigrant merchant network that connected large cities with, say, Moses Lipschultz in Clayton. Herr Schmidt, the cabinet-maker—you remember him?— was also an enthusiastic middleman.

Q. I never guessed that. But apples are only once a year in the fall, right?

A. True. But Quachasee tree-cuttings were a spring product requested far beyond Clayton. A mare going to Doc Sexton went loaded with bare-root young fruit trees to be delivered along the way. Demand always exceeded supply.

Q. All that business takes time to build. How did he eat in the meantime? Wasn't it difficult to get started?

A. Yes, but not so difficult as you imagine. The first year or so, the hogs just ran loose to feed on mast. The cornfield looked terrible rough to a lawyer's eye, with some girdled trees yet to cut down, but the soil was still rich without fertilizer. And I wager you don't know about that huge mountainside of fine ginseng up beyond Quachasee. Still there, I'd guess, if a laurel slick hasn't taken over. I happened to have a client, dead now, who raved about your father's seng. Paid a very high price for it, and sold it again for even higher.

After the first year, Henry never let his hogs run wild. Kept them penned in so he could breed them selectively. You've seen his records; he gave a lot of thought to that and conferred with the few men around who were doing likewise. A little piglet in a poke can fit in a mule's pack, once your father was known for good stock. Same story as apples. Tulips' reputation for bacon and hams did not begin here at Tulips.

Q. Wasn't it isolated up there?

A. Visitors appeared almost never.

Q. Was Father ever lonely?

A. He never complained of loneliness in my recollection. He was extremely busy.

Q. How did Father occupy himself after a day of farm work?

A. He always had book requests.

We were in familiar territory, so here I concluded my questioning.

Books Father requested and books he devoured. He spoke of Dickens's characters as if he hailed them yesterday in Ginners Ford. Trollop's inventions were old friends. Bronte's people lived the next valley yonder, and heirs, aspirants, or mere pretenders to the Crown skulked just across the state line in North Carolina, along with a great many London scoundrels.

Once, scanning shelves, I retrieved from its topmost location a copy of Shakespeare's comedies more worn than most. Its pages were much stained, spotted with what looked like culinary ingredients. I enjoyed the thought of Father mixing Shylock and Oberon with cornbread. When I showed this to him in amusement, he took the book from me, more deeply moved than I anticipated. Soon after, he gave me a brand-new replacement. The stained copy summarily disappeared. Only after his death did I locate it deep in his desk and shelved it in a place of honor.

That place of honor needs justification, I suspect, because it so lacks ostentation, being a narrow, yard-high bookcase devoid of ornament. What in my eye gives it high honor is its status, along with the hall clock, as among the few goods my grandfather, Samuel B, carried with him here to Tennessee. Father remembered hearing as a boy that it was in the family several generations already in Virginia. The "T" for an earlier Tulips and "H" for a previous Hollis scribed inconspicuously in the back, he once pointed out to me, as I have to my grandchildren.

Subsequent to my father's furniture tutorial, whenever on sleeting days I ventured up to the attic to play, I always examined the retired furniture stored there, searching like a keen-eyed Mohican scout for secret marks. I did find them, only once. They were on an odd, creaky chair with seat so low it fit perfectly a little boy's short legs. Father received my excited report with deflating calm.

The cushion (or "piller" to some around here) for the chair's seat nevertheless intrigued me enough that I brought it down to show Mama. The pillow's needlework depicted a whale and an elephant (perhaps also another large beast, though my memory grows hazy here) along with a white barn, their apparent residence. Since my experience with large mammals was intensive but not extensive, I quizzed my distracted mother at length about the pillow's threadbare menagerie.

When I then conveyed my new knowledge to my father, emphasizing the peculiarities of these beasts, he corrected me. "No, they're more like us than you think." It took me years to recognize the congruence of that answer with Father's kindly treatment of our stock.

My mother at last tired of having a worn-out pillow intruding in her space, and ordered its return to the attic, where it must be still. That storage, however, skirts a subject of some delicacy, for the Tulips attic is space that violates my wife's need for order. To dampen marital discord, decades ago she absolved herself of future responsibility by declaring the attic a male realm and thus a male duty. This, proving her perspicacity, has meant that for years it has languished a duty unaddressed. Reader, mark here a lesson about procrastination.

I have just returned from risking attic steps, decades of dust, and intimidating spider webs in search of The Pillow. It and the short-legged chair, however, must be tucked away somewhere well out of sight, for I could not easily lay hands on them. Caroline's worried calls soon brought me back to more hospitable spaces. These lines will remind me to try again when I feel more fit and persevering.

QUACHASEE
WHC

When Henry's crew gathered for a meal at dusk, perching on stumps and stones or sprawled at the porch edge, their mud-stained clothes and fatigue made them hard to differentiate. Henry, though equally as dirty and tired, entered the cabin and sat in the sole chair for many miles around. Carrie served him there, resting at intervals on a crude three-legged stool, her knees higher than her hips. That's where she hunched, rubbing the small of her back, when she looked up to see Henry studying her. "That stool ain't right," he said, but no more.

Hoping to dispatch many birds with the same stone, Henry went down the valley. At the Mercantile, a replacement honing stone; at the kitchen house, spices from Lilly's cache; at Audie's room, hand signs (and Audie's slate) to cheer her; at his stepmother's sitting room, a courtesy call; at Sam's office or the barn, quick word about a chair.

Down to the last item on his list, he found Sam lounging in the big barn while he directed a hired man pushing conveyances around. "Hello, brother, what you doing with the gig?"

"What the hell it look like, Henry? We're movin' th'damn thaing back outta th'way. Don' rightly need hit. No pint in ruinatin a fancy rig when a wagon don' discomfit nobody t'ride. Gotta mine fer sellin hit."

"But Father bought this for Audie. It's a lot better slung for her than that farm wagon," Henry protested.

"Tain't so, brother. Anyways she don' go nowhurs much. Now what d'ye want, 'cept interferin?"

"I thought I'd tell you before I borrow some chair you're not using."

"Ye got a cheer; seed hit go up thar wit' m'own eyes. Ye sell hit off fer cash money?"

"No, Sam. I took one chair up, so I have one chair there."

"Wal? Don' need no lavish a cheers. Cain't sit in two cheers the same time, ken ye?"

"Maybe, Sam, I could have chairs in different places, alternate sitting like rich farmers do at Tulips."

"I jes' cain't abide damn foolishness. Who ye got sittin' wit' ye?" Sam scowled. "Ye ain't a-givin thet damn Carrie airs, is ye? Gotta straighen her out, brother. Audie Ann jes spiled her rotten. Gettin her likeness took. Readin with her, even read after thet Shakespeare. Lettin her think to whar she white. Ain't fittin. Cousin Caleb's right. Niggers is niggers."

Henry's smile vanished. "I don't agree with you about Carrie. And as a matter of fact, I just invited Audie Ann to come up to my place for a visit. You know she can't sit there comfortably on a stool."

"Audie Ann, huh? In plain sight, with them wavin arms and wild faces? How ye gonna git her up . . ." Sam checked himself and almost chuckled. "'Long's the vexin's all yourn, brother, I ain't contrary. Set hyar. I'll see ifen I ken fine a cheer we ain't usin." He went to the house and after a long delay returned with a ladderback Henry remembered seeing years before, a solitary discard, stored far back in the attic. Sam blew a cloud of dust off the age-darkened wood. "Ain't got nary nother." He met Henry's stony look with a scowl. "Don' be choicey; this'un fit at yournses."

Back at the Quachasee cabin just after dark, Henry warmed his hands at the fire a moment before loosening the straps over his shoulders. "You should be prepared: Audie Ann is coming up for a few days. I told her I'd come back for her fortnight if the weather is decent. She can ride the mare if I walk right beside her."

Carrie gave a little cry of pleasure. "I wanted her here so much to see the farm, see what you've done, Marse, but it . . . wasn't my place . . ." She broke off and hid her gratitude by busying herself with a pot of soup she'd kept hot for Henry.

"Got something." Henry eased the chair down. He put his hand on its back. It wobbled. "What the?" He moved the chair harder. It wobbled more. "Floor isn't flat here?" He moved the chair. It wobbled a lot. He sat down on it, moved to a new spot. The chair tilted. "Damnation. I ask Sam for a 'settin cheer' and he gives me a sorry rocker. Look at this." Henry rocked back and forth in vexation. "Hauled this thing all the way up here on my back, and look at this thing, a bucking mule. How could you use this?"

Carrie stared. "You brought that up for me?"

Henry rocked roughly back and forth, avoiding her eyes. "I don't like you standing at the table like a . . . Look at the rock in this thing. If

Sam were here I'd throw it at him. You can't use this." She watched his vigorous rocking a minute more. "I think we *can* use this," she declared. She straddled his lap, her hands gripping the chair's uprights to trap his face between her arms.

The next morning while she cleaned a pot boiled to burned, Henry took the chair out to saw off uneven legs. Tests on the cabin floor required repeated trips, but by the time the pot hung clean, he declared satisfaction. "No rocking."

"But isn't it awful low?"

"Well, I guess it is. But no rocking at least."

"We'd better check." She closed the cabin door.

"Did I get it right?" he smiled as she rose.

"Think so, but I can't be sure without . . . trying it some more . . . I mean later, *later.*"

"If we were in New York, I could patent this and go into manufacturing, get us rich."

"Or sportin houses in New Orleans. But how would you advertise?"

"That might be hard, I guess."

"And you'd have to measure every customer like a tailor."

"Seems like I'd have to measure every pair of customers. Be a little embarrassing, I guess. Maybe I'd better stop now."

"Not with the using." Carrie opened the door to carry burned soup for the hogs.

On his next trip down the valley, Henry went on to Gerhardt Schmidt's shop in Ginners Ford to buy a new chair. Carrie perched on a stool only when the cabin door stood wide open. The Old Chair and the New Chair faced the table. Carrie never straightened them without breathing her mother's *Child, a chair is a mark of civilization.* The Low Chair stood alone at the hearth, where Spooks thought it a fine place to take off the chill at a small fire.

❧

In October, Henry went down the mountain for Audie Ann. Dispiriting overcast threatened rain, but she was eager to travel. On the trail she kept a sharp eye; as they got higher, from time to time she asked Henry to stop so she could survey the panorama. Under clearing skies Henry gave her an abbreviated tour of the farm. At the cabin he helped her off the mare and retrieved her crutch. She and Carrie soon flashed language back and forth rapid fire as if they sat at Tulips. The difference was that cooking interrupted Carrie, and Audie Ann stopped sometimes just to study the serried ranks of ridges beyond the fields, delight obvious on her face. Carrie brought food out to Henry and Audie Ann on the porch.

Afterwards, Audie Ann wanted to talk, though her hands moved much too fast for Henry. "She says," Carrie reported, "Solomon and she have never gotten this far up. So this is a special treat, to see the mountains close, and to be with us." Audie Ann retrieved her slate to write two words for emphasis. "Perfect contentment." Carrie said the same, even after three days of preparing the usual meals for the hired men and something special for the table where Audie Ann and Henry sat.

On the day set for Audie's return, Henry came in from the field early. As he waited on the porch, Audie Ann beckoned him inside. She hugged Carrie, then moved her attention to Henry, making motions Henry recognized. "She wants you to translate just in case I've forgotten too much," said Henry, as if Carrie didn't know. Staring intently at Carrie, Audie Ann moved hands and arms in rapid sequence.

Carrie hesitated. "She says . . . Oh, now I'm the one who's nearly forgotten some things, it's been so long since I was at Tulips," Carrie muttered. Audie Ann made an admonitory face, but Carrie still hesitated. "She says . . . says . . . that you . . . she . . . I . . . sees." Carrie stammered false starts.

"What does she say? I don't get it all."

"She says . . ." Carrie laughed in embarrassed confusion. More motions on both sides. In the midst, Audie Ann held her slate up and pointed to Henry.

He intervened. "I know she's saying that if you don't translate, she will write it all. She's saying that she sees you and I . . . we . . . what?"

Carrie turned briefly to Henry. "That you and I . . . that we are lovers. How could she know? Do you want me to tell her she's wrong?"

She looked back at Audie Ann. "She reads my mind. She says she can't hear what other people do, so she can see what other people don't. She knows she's right. Calls us . . . man . . . and wife."

"No point in denying it to Audie," answered Henry. He put his arm around Carrie and pulled her unmistakably close.

Audie Ann pointed to his arm approvingly, her hands and arms moving rapidly. "She's still too fast for me," complained Henry.

"She says," Carrie picked up, "that this is what she wanted to happen. She says that—Oh, she's going to make me cry—that seeing us makes her so happy . . . but lonesome. She would only be willing to lose me to you, and you to me. She says not to worry about Tulips because she will never tell anyone there. She knows that . . ."

Carrie paused while Audie Ann wrote *Sam* and *Caleb* on her slate for Henry. "Yes, Sam and Caleb are bad—no, evil—men, and will try to hurt us if they know. She says I must stay here, far away from Tulips. She wants to come up to visit whenever you have time to help her travel."

❧

"Mister Hollis, not to speak outta turn, but ken I ax what ye be plannin'?" Lem took the chance for quiet words as they sat with midmorning coffee and cornbread. "Sun's warm 'nuf now, but right soon cole gonna a-come on, an hit's gonna be mighty shivery fer us'un sleepin' in them thar sheds." He brushed crumbs away. "I reckon a man could do hit," he speculated, "ifen ye kept a monstrous fire the night long, but thet'd be a heapa wood. The more time choppin firewood, the less fer work t'git ye ahead. So hits work er warm, one. Then too, Hilpert and Jake ain't got coats fer when nippy come on."

Henry nodded. He knew that on chilly mornings Hilpert and Jake wore every garment in their bags. He sipped. "I'd just like to get two or three more weeks with this gang."

"Then what, Mister Hollis?"

"We'll close down and everyone goes home."

"Ev'un?" Lem cleared his throat. "Don' git me wrong, Mister Hollis. My woman sure like t'see me back—long as thar's cash money in m'pocket. Ye don' want a couple'a men through? Or mebbe ye jes fixin t'head down t'Tulips right soon?"

"No, this is home now. I'll stay here, see what I can get done alone."

Lem nodded. "I own thet. Sometimes a body alone git a heap more done then ye'd reckon. No offense, Mister Hollis, but ifen ye stayin hyar, keep the gal t'cook. I tell Jake thet I ain't never ate on nary place I work like I ate since she come. Ye done one smart thaing, yessir. 'Sides," he winked, "mebbe she get chilled 'nuff sleepin 'lone for to come keep ye warm."

"Two or three weeks, Lem. We need to make the time count. If the weather just holds."

It didn't. Sleeting rain and icy wind some days later made fieldwork an endurance trial. Halfway through the morning, Henry squished out of the muddy puddle left by a pulled stump, shaking his head in disgust. Jake shifted the chaw in his cheek. "This hyar field gettin right sobby."

Lem had a glum face. "Hit's a-gonna weather up."

Henry surveyed the darkening sky. "I'd say this wet sticks for a while."

"Yessir, nigh onto a week, Mister Hollis. Mebbe more. Two year past it blowed three week. When it git to rainin this time a year, hit most generally don' fancy stoppin."

"All right, all right. No point in shaking our fists at God. Pass the word: let's pack up and get out. We're done here this season."

Sleet came down harder as the men drove the teams to the sheds, packed their gear. Henry hurried to the cabin. He leaned inside, hand on the door. "Carrie, need some hot coffee quick's you can."

"Right away, Marse. What's happening?"

"Closing down and sending the gang home."

"What?" Carrie could not conceal her dismay.

Henry winced as a gust stuck his wet pants to his legs. "We're all cold and wet. Need coffee bad. I'm sending everyone down. Be here alone from now on. Told you before."

He pulled the door closed, missing Carrie's anguished whisper. "No, you didn't tell me you'll be here alone."

Hastened by sleet, the men packed slapdash and soon disappeared, Henry with them to authorize pay in Ginners Ford and to visit Audie.

He returned the next morning, despite wind-driven flurries and clouds so low they snagged on the bare tree branches at ridges. As he approached the cabin Carrie was stretching sodden bedding on a line strung under the porch roof. "What on earth?"

"Canvas leaked." Carrie didn't look at him.

"You didn't sleep out here?"

"Yes, Marse, started to. But it got too wet, so I sat by the fire last night."

"Why didn't you go to bed?"

"The leak soaked my bed through, Marse."

Gusts repeatedly blew sheets of water onto the porch. "Carrie, I'm too wet and freezing to stand out here talking." He plunged into the cabin and shivered dripping by the fireplace, trying to unfasten his coat. "Fingers so cold I can't even work the buttons," he grumbled to himself, now shaking uncontrollably.

"Here." Carrie took charge of his coat, then his shirt. "Marse Henry, you're soaked clear through. Why, you're wet to the skin, Marse Henry. Take that off now." She became a flurry of action: prodding the fire, offering towels, producing dry clothes, pouring hot coffee. "You could catch a deathly cold," her scold not sufficient to hide her concern.

Vigorous rubbing, roaring fire, and steaming coffee gradually took effect. Henry could huddle on the Low Chair at the hearth without shaking like the ague. Carrie poured more scalding coffee and began collecting his sodden clothes. "What's that?" She pointed to a large, lumpy oil-cloth bag Henry threw from his back when he walked in.

"Your mother went nursing with Aunt Sally, so I asked Diana to pack up your warm things. What's that?" He pointed to a similar bag on the table.

"I got my things together so I can leave when you tell me to, Marse Henry."

He frowned.

"You said you're gonna work here *alone* over the winter, Marse," she explained, "so I got ready to go."

"You think I'd say, you're leaving? Right now? Get out?"

"Mama heard that three different times, Marse Henry." Her voice almost went into a wail before she steadied herself. "I heard it myself two of the times." She dashed a knuckle fiercely at her cheeks.

Henry stared at the fire while he sipped the coffee. Slowly he put the cup down. "Carrie, we haven't understood each other very well. Partly, I see, it's my fault. So let's get down to Mister Christopher Bechler's gold dollar, as Cousin Hurley used to say. All right?"

"Yes, Marse Henry."

"Number one. I am not Marse to you. I'm Henry at night. I'm Henry in the day. I'm Henry in between. Agreed?"

"Yes, Marse . . . Yes, Henry."

"Number two. When I told the gang I would be working alone, my *I* included you. I thought you knew that, but I see I forgot your life before. My *I* includes Carrie. Agreed?

"Yes, Marse, I mean Henry. I understand your words, Henry, but it's hard to get my mind all around them."

"When you think on it later, remember what I'm saying now. When I say *I*, that means we. We means you and I, now and in the future. Agreed?"

She stared at him, with the slightest nod.

"Then there's number three. Your bed's never outside. Our bed is always in there." He pointed to the back room. "Agreed?"

Her answer came as a gush of tears, and a tight hug. She moved back enough to brush off his shirt. "Don't know where that wet could come from. I cried myself dry last night, thinking I lost you."

She knelt on the floor beside the Low Chair. "I'm still tryin to get my mind 'round this. So Marse . . . I mean, so Henry," she said, "your 'I' means both of us. And my bed's always in there with you?"

"That's what I said. That means, not incidentally, that your *I* means me, too. You did agree, didn't you?"

"Marse . . . I mean, Henry, I agreed. I agreed with all my heart." She pressed his hand to her chest for a long time.

Then she looked up with a little smile. It was shy or it might have been sly. "But Marse—Henry, I still have a question. If my bed, our bed, is in there, what'll I do if I'm wanting you here in front of the fire?"

"In that case you bring quilts from there in here," he instructed around a grin he could barely swallow, "and put them down in front of the fire." Which she did. Many times that week. As Lem had predicted, the weather blew for days, too miserable to attempt anything outside more than feeding the stock.

Plowing with Greek, My Life
HL Hollis

Sometime in my early years (I am unable to date it more exactly), I conceived the idea that if Bill collected scientific curiosities, and Crotia collected archaic and unfashionable words she wanted to revive, I, too, should commence some assemblage of ephemera. Ben, one of the hired men who tended to repairs around the house and yard, spoke a mountain brogue so clotted that on occasion Mama, in exasperated frustration, turned to me for translation. Consequently, I thought so highly of my abilities that I decided to preserve on paper the unusual coinages I heard from him and those like him.

One thing progressed to another, and gradually I embarked on a larger collection of all the old mountain talk and grammar I heard. Crotia became a fellow investigator and longtime collaborator; she still sends me notes on possible entries she has run across. Imagining that in time my collection could make a small contribution to some future scholarly history of our American language, I set as my goal to print a modest lexicon. I kept delaying closure, however, because I kept discovering new candidates, long failing to recognize the penalty of my additions. I must now depend on Crotia's firm promises to bring the lexicon to print.

My project much interested Father. He recommended people I should listen to with special care, and himself dictated a great many entries from his memory, something I welcomed all the more because my collection proved stimulus, nearly the only stimulus, that prompted him to reminisce about mountain characters he encountered long before my birth.

One day, for example, as we rested in the shade at the edge of a field for our quartering time, one of the hired men, Wade Slater, used an unusual phrase that caught my ear. I was patting pockets for pencil and paper when another of the men objected to the phrase's sentiment, and without warning languid drawls became furious insults.

The exchange escalated so precipitously I feared a brawl right there (an awkward, expensive damper on harvesting), but Father, apparently oblivious to impending fracas, observed that Wade's phrase happened to remind him of Doc, a mule dealer located far beyond Claytown. (I believe I mentioned him earlier.) Whether "Doc" was title, nickname, or surname, I cannot tell you. Many people traded in mules, of course, but Doc gained a wide reputation for his ability to recall every mule he ever saw. With a knowledge of mules both encyclopedic and intuitive, he seemed instantly to understand mules and they him. Bring him the cussedest, orneryest mule in God's creation, and Doc soon converted it to docile cooperation. Either that or he would confide to the owner with utmost seriousness, "This is a frampold mule. This mule-Lucifer has an evil in it that in a man-Lucifer would lead to murder, so you must confine evil as you would put a murderer in prison."

Father recalled that if you asked Doc how he secured such rapport, he would answer impatiently as if his means were transparent. "Andy here," or whatever the name (Doc was peculiarly insistent that animals bear a proper name, one name at a minimum, two even better) "Andy here appreciates a thorough scratching on the face at midday," or "Billy Bob hates being shouted at; he prefers very quiet conversation first thing in the morning." Most people considered Doc a sure candidate for the state hospital. In point of fact, though, there were those who, like Father, put Doc's advice into practice and testified to its efficacy, while admitting in the next breath the man suffered from loose screws too numerous to count.

This much about Doc I had heard from Father before, but as the crew disputants glowered at each other, Father embroidered and embellished. Doc's uncanny animal rapport included a curious deduction: his unswerving conviction that God forbade mixing. Colors on buildings, materials in clothing, garden flowers, book bindings, forest trees—each and every to its own kind, and own kind only. Against mixing he outdid Moses down from Sinai. No ladies being about, Father gave rather earthy examples of Doc's preaching, and soon even the most bloody-minded of the crew was laughing at Doc's theatricality and absurdity.

Bill's response was perplexed cross-examination. "How can somebody breed animals and never mix male and female?" I, as usual, had loitered with Sexton's rhetoric instead of leaping ahead to a crucial biological contradiction.

"Oh, Doc knew male and female are commanded to be fruitful and multiply, so *that* mixing is permitted." Father stood up, the signal he considered his rest (which, of course, was our rest), sufficient.

But Bill could not let go of the problem. "How could he breed mules and not see he's mixing horses and donkeys?"

"He *did* see. He believed mules bore God's curse from conception, punishment for a shameful act," said Father, motioning to Wilber, the laziest man on the crew, to get on his feet.

"But . . ." Even then Bill did not have much use for theological constructs in the natural world, and could engage Father in furious debates. "That's a stupid . . ."

Marcus interrupted Bill with a new question. "What about people? What did Doc think of mixing human races, white and black?"

Father answered only by shaking his head as he headed back to the field.

"Pretty soon, no mules, and stupid marriage laws," Bill hooted. "Nobody was dumb enough to believe that mixing stuff, were they?"

Father stopped and turned around. "No, in the end I didn't."

"In the *end*?" Bill snorted at anyone granting Doc even initial credence, and I braced for another father-son battle. But Father reproved him a great deal more gently than I expected. "You'd need to know the circumstances."

In this rare instance I wish my sister had been present, for, to my present-day frustration, as we worked our way down the rows, nobody asked Father, as Crotia assuredly would have, to describe in detail the "circumstances." Typically, he volunteered no elaboration. Later, when I tried to reopen the topic by telling him I thought several of the men close to easing out knives, he nodded grave agreement, and added that years ago Judge Bright gave good advice: when a meeting becomes unproductively contentious, stop and tell a good story, preferably a long good story. He recounted a number of instructive examples from the Judge's experience. (I shall record them some other time, when not so fatigued.) We became so involved in those examples that neither Father nor I returned to the "circumstances."

Wade Slater's original phrase, occasion for all this? I lost it.

I am intrigued to discover here that the process of recording a story is something like viewing a photograph of a familiar scene. You may notice in the photograph telling patterns and details you never noticed before. In this instance, I discern symmetry I long overlooked. Father diverted the hired hands about to fight, to be diverted in turn by Marcus from yet another argument with Bill. That symmetry is evidence of the similarity between Father and Marcus, both inclined to keep the peace—not, I must add, out of weakness, but from strength of character.

A further thought occurs to me only now, decades delayed. At the time, when Marcus asked about mixing people, about mixing races, I assumed he posed a hypothetical question to distract Father's attention from Bill's objections. Now I believe Marcus had another reason only he yet knew, something I must explain in more detail when I can muster more energy.

QUACHASEE
WHC

For three weeks Carrie fought down nausea every morning and dread every evening. In her mind's ear she heard the low voices of neighborhood aunties trading stories in the evening shadows of Sally's cabin.

I heared ob a marse, he sleep wid a gal an when she makin' a baby, he jes go an get 'nodder gal foah de tiam. He say de fas'er dey breed, de fas'er he ken sell off de chillens.

It turr'ble, turr'ble. Mah sista near die. When Marse fine out, he has she beat so bad, she lose de chile. An when he hear, he say, "good." He doan wan his wife fine ou'.

Oh, ye-ah, she tole he, an de nex day, de nex day, *he send she up to de city t'sell she.*

She gettin too big t'hide it. Mebbe he tink she be puttin' on fat, but den he foun out, an near trow a fit. Say it not his, no ma'am, not his; she sleepin wid 'nodder man. He hauls she straight to de ugly ole o'erseer. Say, "heah, yuh poke dis slut. I dun wid she." An he fine he 'nodder gal.

Carrie tried to explain away her nausea, but "something I ate" could not be repeated often. She tried to hold in her thickening body, but she knew Henry always watched her appreciatively when she undressed. She could find no way to conceal her condition from him indefinitely.

One evening, as their breathing slowed before the fire, Carrie lowered close to his ear. "Henry, I think I'm carrying your child." There. It was said. She lifted herself, arms straight to his shoulders, knowing it was a sight he enjoyed, hoping it might distract his response.

"That's not too surprising"—the sight of her prompted his further thrust—"considering how often I have known you."

She reciprocated his movement unmistakably. "You're not angry with me?"

"Why should I be angry?"

"Well for one thing, pretty soon I'll be big as a house." She stopped short of, *and you won't want me, and maybe send me back to Tulips, look for someone else.*

Henry put each forefinger on her nipples. "So that's it. I've been wondering what's been worrying you sick." He pressed one finger. "You won't be as big as you think." He pressed the other finger. "Then you'll be back to your usual self." He spread both hands. "And in the meantime we can enjoy ourselves."

Relieved of the immense weight of tales from the neighborhood aunties, Carrie bent to kiss him, silently thanking her mother for her promise.

❧

"Carrie!" shrieked Sally from the stoop of her cabin. "Marse 'Enry say he brings yuh down de nex tiam he cum." She enveloped Carrie in an auntie hug, then kept her gripped at arm's length. "Let ole Sally see yuh, gal." She eyed Carrie up and down. "Lookin' good. Real good. Uhm-hmm. Sompin up dere agreein' wid yuh, foah sho. Solomon say, Carrie's cookin taste 'most as good as Lilly's."

Carrie struck a smiling pose. When Sally looked again, her eyes narrowed. "Yuh bigged, gal?"

"Yes'm."

"Mm-hm." Sally did not release her grip. "Who de fadder?" Her smile had faded.

Carrie saw she had unexpectedly slid onto thin and treacherous ice. Of the men who worked up the Quachasee, Sally would count three candidates. She, and a good many other servant women, angled unsuccessfully for Solomon, so jealousy ran high in that quarter. The combative Lucia considered Zeke firmly spoken for. Carrie refused any association with the disgraced Jefferson. Forthright honesty offered the only way out.

"Henry," she said quietly, realizing too late that here she must include *Marse.*

"Solomon, I 'spect? Mebbe Zeke?" Carrie's brief answer had not registered with Sally.

"No, Aunt Sally, I don't steal a man from another woman."

"Not Jefferson mebbe?"

"Can't be Jefferson, Aunt Sally." Carrie consciously held her eyes. "He and I aren't even friends. Never slept with him. I told you the truth, the only man I've ever been with is Henry, Marse Henry."

"Marse . . . 'Enry? Oh chile. Mah poor Carrie. But doan yuh feel no shame. It Marse 'Enry whut mus' face Almigh'y God. I know it ha'd. Do he hur' yuh real bad?"

She wrapped Carrie in another hug. "Caleb, he jes 'boud kilt Magdalene. Cum in one night, big stick in he han. She say no and he make she lie down. Hits ha'd. She say no, an he hits she 'gain. Still say no, and he hits. Till she bleedin bad. She hurtin so, she gib up, an he takes she rough. He still takin she. Ebben wen dey say he mebbe gonna marry purty lil Miss Alice, dat nebbah stop 'im. Ebbah tiam, he hab dat stick an stan i'in de conah so she know whut happen iffen she say no. An he ain't happy iffen she jes lay dere. When she doan act hot he reach foah de stick, an she know, she know."

Sick at the news of Magdalene, and taken aback that Sally thought Henry could be so brutish, Carrie spoke firmly. "Aunt Sally, Henry isn't Caleb."

"Dey cousins, ain't dey? He white, ain't he? He a marse, ain't he? Look whut his broder, Sam, do ebbah tiam Elvira 'way."

"But Sam and Henry are only stepbrothers."

"Dey hab de same fadder."

"Yes, but Henry's not Sam."

"I ax yuh 'gain: he a marse, ain't he?"

Only one way out of this hole. "Aunt Sally, he's never hurt me. Ever. In any way."

"He givin' yuh tings so yuh sleeps wid he?" Sally's disdain wounded.

"Never, Aunt Sally, you know I'm not like that. I go to his bed because I want to."

Sally released Carrie with a start. "Yuh bin goin in de marse's bed free?"

Carrie quailed. She took a deep breath. "Aunt Sally, I sleep with Henry because I love him. That's why I'm carrying his child, our child."

"Lord, Carrie, I doan know whut t'say." She stood stock-still for a long moment. Then, "Whut Lilly tink?"

Carrie shook her head. "I was on my way to the kitchen house. Haven't seen Mama yet."

"I prayin' foah yuh, chile."

In the Tulips kitchen Carrie did what she knew suited her mother. After exclamations and hugs, she went straight to the point. "Mama, I want to tell you that I'm carrying Henry's child. He never hurt me. I sleep in his bed because I love him."

Lilly sank down in a chair, and stared bleakly up at her daughter. "Jefferson's been boasting . . . you were his woman up there, . . . I was worrying you were going to tell me . . . But this?"

"Mama, would you rather have Jefferson the father?"

"Of course not. He's strong as an ox and about as bright. But Mister Henry . . ."

"What's the matter?"

"He owns you."

"But Mama, he's never talked like that to me."

"Huh. Child, you answer me straight now. Has he ever, in broad daylight, looked you straight in the eye, and said, 'Carrie, I love you'? Tell me honest."

"Well . . . no. But does a man have to say that for it to be true? Don't his actions matter so that you know in your heart?"

"You're in dreamland, child. Sleep with him if he gives you no choice. And carry his child if God gives it to you. But don't love him, Carrie, don't love him."

"But you told me you loved Etienne in New Orleans, Etienne Thibeaux."

"I loved him. And he broke my heart. I told you about that so you wouldn't make the same mistake and have the same grief."

Carrie retreated and regrouped. "What about my father in Nashville? You didn't want to leave him."

"What choice did I have? Henkel owned me. I was grateful for his kindness. I wanted to stay with him, yes. And look what it got me."

"It got me."

"And I thank God every night for you. But that's not what we're talking about."

"But, Mama, Henry's a kind man. You know him. He's so gentle and considerate. He even says—"

Lilly cut her off. "I can say the same about Etienne and Henkel." She went to the work table. "Gentleman, both of 'em. Kind. Considerate. But did that keep 'em from selling me off?" She brought the biggest skillet down on another pan with a mighty crash. "No. Etienne had tears in his eyes when he told me I had to go. You think that did any good? He knew he owned me and could do what he wanted with property. But for God Almighty I'd have drowned myself and never seen you."

Lilly began throwing bacon into the skillet. "I wanted to tell you before you went up there: whatever happens, *don't* love Mister Henry. He's *Marse* Henry. He *owns* you. I didn't because I was afraid I'd put ideas into your head that wouldn't be there if I kept my mouth closed. So I told you to take care of yourself. And now look what happens."

"Mama, I did take care of myself. I'm happier than I've ever been. Would you rather never in your life have loved someone the way you loved Etienne?"

"Do you want your heart broken 'til you'd rather die?"

"You're not answering me, Mama."

"You're not answering *me*. Don't go perplexing things." She turned to her daughter, defeated. "It's too late to make you not love him. He's a marse; he'll break your heart soon enough. When's the child coming? You can't have that baby up the Quachasee, no woman anywhere close and Henry just ignoring you."

"Mama, he would never do that."

"I keep telling you, he's a marse. You don't listen. Could you come down here when you think you're close?"

"And have Marse Sam and Miz Elvira see a baby with Henry Hollis all over its little face? And have Elvira take it out on every woman at Tulips? And Sam . . . no telling what he'd do. . . . But it would be fun to see Elvira's eyes pop out." Carrie began giggling at the thought. Soon Lilly joined her. But the laughter ended in tears and a long embrace that meant Sam angrily rejected his bacon as too damn burnt.

❧

Henry lounged by the fire while Bright cleaned his rifle. Carrie joined them, a book in hand. "Marse John, these tales you brought me . . . by," Carrie flipped to the title page, "this Hawthorne, they take some thought. To tell you the truth, I'm not sure I like them. Maybe I don't understand people up north. But I thank you for bringing the book."

"Perhaps you'll like the stories better after they've fermented some." Bright searched at his feet for the rag he was using. "By the way, Cook Carrie, d'you consider me a good friend?"

She looked at him, bewildered. "Of course, Marse John. How could I not?"

"Then," he sighted down the bore, "I suggest you drop the *Marse* John. Spooks will be fine."

"I," she put her hand briefly on his arm. "That's so. . ." Her voice went husky. "I just can't talk about it now."

Spooks stood to give her a quick buss. Henry responded with a mock reprimand. "Now friend, I'll thank you not to go messing with the cook. But maybe this is a good time, Mister Bright, to ask you to be godfather for the newest Hollis when he or she arrives in the spring."

"I will be honored, old friend." He turned to Carrie. "I will be honored, dear friend." He turned back to Henry. "What will my godchild be named?"

"Can't say. Remember the Hollis tradition. The mother chooses a boy's name, and the father chooses a girl's. And neither gives any hint until the baby appears."

Spooks nodded. "As I think Erasmus wrote, 'May the child's exit be as pleasant and easy as its entrance.' I hoped you would ask me to be godfather."

That nettled Henry. "This seems like old news to you, Spooks."

Spooks turned on him the John Patterson Bright half-smile opposing attorneys were learning to recognize—and fear. "Uncas, remember, brave warrior, that Hawkeye has eyes to see and ears to hear. And also mind to consider. Yes, Uncas is clever. He leaves no tracks. But Uncas is too clever. Leaving no tracks is proof of tracks."

"Hawkeye must explain his riddles."

"Examine the signs, old friend. We track a young man, vigorous and at ease in the world, and see he lives in close proximity to a young woman. We see she is cheerful and unstinting when she throws herself beside him into a heavy yoke. She cooks delicious dishes; she also nourishes his mind. Does our quarry notice? No. Something is amiss."

Spooks again sighted down his rifle. "Her form, unaided by expensive clothes, would lure any man with eyes. But does our quarry notice?

No. Something is very amiss. If not love, where is lust? She seems a log before him, not a woman. Something is greatly amiss. Hawkeye tracks with eyes, and also with mind. Eyes see no tracks. Mind knows no tracks show tracks."

"No proof."

"Not a confession, no. Circumstantial evidence? Overwhelming. Besides, you did slip once, Mister Hollis."

"Slip?" Henry's pride showed.

"On the porch with Carrie serving dinner. You asked if she saved some gingerbread, please. Carrie guaranteed you she saved lots for you. She smiled at you with bright eyes. But she never served you a bit of gingerbread. Not on the porch, that is."

Carrie flushed and looked down.

"Please forgive me, my dear," Spooks pleaded. "I assure you these intimacies I share only with my two closest friends. I was simply waiting to see how long before you told me what I knew."

"Mister John Patterson Bright," ordered Henry, "tell me to hire you when I need a real smart lawyerman."

Even a real smart lawyerman could not solve the quandary about where to deliver the baby. Nor could Audrey. In her joy at the news, Audie had so many questions the sun was low when Henry left her. As he walked home, it occurred to him that for prudence he should have a long talk with Dr. Symes, fast gaining approval among younger wives in Ginners Ford; he should also borrow a book or two from Symes. As was customary, he set up a place in one of the sheds for Aunt Sary, famous for fetching babies; she promised to come stay shortly before Carrie was to be brought to bed.

Carrie miscalculated. The morning after they said goodbye to Spooks, off for a long trial in Knoxville—a good month and half before she thought she was due—the first sharp pangs ended breakfast. Late that afternoon Henry, a little atremble, washed the bright-eyed baby. Everything went generally the way Dr. Symes' book said it should. "It's a boy," he announced. "What shall we name him, mother?"

"John Henry Hollis. We'll call him Harry."

Little surprised Eusenius Berkemeier. Ordained a Lutheran minister of the Gospel thirty years before by his father and grandfather, he learned from the Pastor Berkemeier before him, and from the *Herr Pastor* Berkemeier before him. As a boy in his father's parsonage, as a seminary student, as a minister himself, he saw much and heard more. So when Henry interrupted Berkemeier's study in Ephesians for Sunday's sermon, the pastor greeted him warmly. (It was, after all, only Tuesday). When Henry asked diffidently whether Pastor would please baptize his newborn son in a private way, Berkemeier immediately responded with a firm "Of course. The sooner the baptism the better."

Berkemeier well remembered Henry as a boy. It was easy to remember the few really bright boys eager to learn. Of course it was also easy to remember Henry's stepbrothers, that pack of godless rascals. An odd lot, differing remarkably, some were, in physical appearance. *That,* too, was easy to remember. New to Bethel Church and casting about for a conversation topic while getting acquainted with one of his oldest parishioners, he had mentioned how unlike some of the Hollis boys were.

She winked as she spoke around her pipe stem. "Them's Knoxville boys."

Thinking he misheard, he bent closer to her.

She took the pipe from her toothless mouth. "If ye gone 'way to Knoxville t'make new laws in the legis'ture thar, ain't nobody t'mind yer bed, an—"

"Ma," her son had hastily interrupted, "Ye gonna embarrass Pastor with them ole stories. He's ourn brand new pastor, Ma. He ain't used to hearin . . . Pastor, Ma gits kinda mix up of a time, ye know."

Different as some were in stature or eye color, the Hollis boys were identical in being eager sinners, glorying in their misdeeds, utterly immune to pastoral remonstrance. Well, God is not mocked. They were, sadly, in their graves now, all save the reprobate Sam.

They did not get their wicked ways from their father, though Samuel B was as stiff-necked a man as Berkemeier had ever known. A man whose vision knew no shades of gray. He chastised his wayward progeny severely after their escapades (though punishment had no discernible effect). And yet Samuel B, urged on by his pastor, offered his sons forgiveness ten times over.

But when it came to his most promising, most obedient son, Samuel provoked that catastrophic argument. Berkemeier had tried his best to patch things over, to counsel patience, urge forgiveness for hot words, but Samuel B wouldn't hear of it. Only after years of Berkemeier urging at least a gesture of peace, did Samuel offer that land. Yes, it was a large tract, but inaccessible, raw and remote. *Why not offer Tulips itself?*

"You have read Luther's Catechism." In Henry's case this was a statement, not a question.

Berkemeier recalled that the class seating went Hoffman, Hollis, Nuechterlein: the cadaverous Hoffman boy, much more interested in tearing the wings off captured insects than in the Trinity, then Henry, then Betsy Nuechterlein, perpetually fingering her ringlets while she "reviewed" the Commandments. Yet Henry had evaded the temptation of both ringlets and dismemberment to be the outstanding student of his group. Berkemeier still mourned his failure in urging Henry toward holy ministry.

"You remember the meaning of baptism."

"Yes, Pastor. 'It effects the forgiveness of sins, delivers from death and the devil, and confers everlasting salvation upon all who believe it, as the words and promises of God declare.'"

"Indeed." Berkemeier did not alter his tone as he added, "Henry, be careful you are not puffed up that God blessed you with an excellent memory for the catechism. Now tell me, when was the child born?"

He continued down his mental list, part of his mind still indulging his memories. "Does the child's mother also desire the child to be baptized?"

He realized he had skipped a standard question. "Who is the child's mother?"

"Caroline LaCroix, Pastor."

Berkemeier thought for a moment, puzzled, unable to recall any LaCroix. He hesitated. It was hardly the first time one of his congregation had reversed the sequence of wedding and children. Yes, as Luther taught, there is Law and there is Gospel. But knowing when to use which is not easy. Surely one does no good by so alienating Henry with stern pronouncements that he recants his decision to bring his son for baptism. Berkemeier eased into the next question. "You will marry the mother?"

"I would if I could."

"Henry, you are not delaying marriage to be sure of a competency, are you? Lately I have admonished some young people who postponed marriage for material reasons instead of trusting the Lord to provide."

"No, Pastor. I can't marry her because the law won't let me."

Berkemeier shook his head, uncertain if he had heard correctly.

"It wouldn't be legal."

It wouldn't be legal wrenched Berkemeier's attention fully to the young man facing him. He always wondered why the papists required private confession in a booth; in *his* pastoral experience, men volunteered anguished confession even in barnyards. He looked at Henry expectantly for clarification. *Not legal?* Did the boy lie with another man's wife?

"She's a servant from Tulips, Pastor."

At least not adultery. Berkemeier tried to conceal his relief and his confusion. A servant, a slave?

"Carrie. Lilly's daughter. She told me you examined her on the catechism yourself at Tulips. But Tennessee law says I can't marry her, doesn't it?"

"Carrie at Tulips?" The one in the class who seemed aloof from the others, perhaps because she's the lightest servant I know, he added to himself. "When you said Caroline LaCroix, I did not make the connection I . . . should have. Of course I know Carrie." As you marvel how God has combined such beauty with intelligence, Berkemeier thought to himself, you understand more clearly how mired in sin are our institutions.

Pastor Berkemeier knew Tennessee marital statutes as well as any jurist. He also knew local custom by which men—even, sad to say, a few of his own parishioners—fathered children in slave cabins, then laughingly denied responsibility. But here sat a man brought up a good Lutheran, ready to marry a slave, a girl firmly lodged in the pastor's memory for her questions. Questions that had inspired a series of his sermons on Abraham, Isaiah and the burning bush. And yet they could not legally marry. Sin piled atop sin.

"You're correct about what the law dictates, Henry." He continued slowly, trying to foresee the implications of what he must say as a shepherd faithful to his flock and to his Lord.

"You know that our Tennessee Lutheran Synod adopted a resolution against slavery, the only substantive matter on which I differed from your sainted father."

Henry shrugged. "I could never figure out why he was so adamant on that."

Berkemeier sighed. "Samuel B pointed to slavery as an accepted reality mentioned in both Testaments, as indeed it is. But I could never convince him that 'slave' in the time of Saint Paul was not the same as 'slave' now in Tennessee. The majority in Synod felt slavery today is a different thing from that, and a great evil."

After a pause he resumed. "And so do I," he added with a firmness stemming from regret—perhaps more than mere regret—that he always found some reasonable excuse not to denounce slavery by name directly from the pulpit.

He stopped for thought, then forged ahead again. "As Christians we are to give to Caesar what is Caesar's. But that command is not much help, I admit, when we are convinced, convinced by Scripture alone, the Lutheran principle, mind you, that Caesar is wrong. But . . ." He trailed off in thought. His decision crystallized. "Your dear sister, as wise and God-fearing a woman as I know, would make an admirable godmother. The remarkable Solomon is to carry her to the church anyway so she can care for the vestments. Bring Carrie and the child to the church, with a godfather, late next Tuesday afternoon. We shall baptize the child as is commanded, and no man may stop us."

Late Tuesday afternoon Pastor Eusenius Berkemeier stood erect in his black ministerial robe, his shock of white hair a little askew, stood in the echoing little country church, stood with Henry, Carrie holding the baby, with Audie Ann, and Bright, and Solomon too. Sunlight streamed in low-angled shafts through the windows, lighting bits of floating dust. Berkemeier followed the Book of Forms to the letter, abbreviating nothing, raising his eyes from time to time to hold the rapt attention of the little group gathered before him. At intervals he paused by forethought, and patiently held the book for Audie to read the words he had spoken.

Then with an experienced motion, he welcomed the placid baby into his arm as securely as he sheltered hundreds before. He shook back a cuff and dipped a hand into the clear water to let tiny beads glisten on the child's silken hair. He made the prescribed signs of the cross and sonorously declared John . . . Henry . . . Hollis baptized in the name of the *Father* . . . trickles of water . . . *the Son* . . . the child smiled at his touch . . *and the Holy Spirit*. Hearing, Berkemeier did, his hallowed words echoing back in time . . . *Nahmen . . . Vater . . . Sohn . . . und Heilige Geist . . . nomine Patris . . . Fillii . . . et Spiritus Sancti.*

He returned the baby to Carrie's arms. But then he did something not found specified in even the most inclusive Lutheran Book of Forms. Something he had never done before. Something he prayed about much. Something that, when in his last hours he reflected somberly on the mistakes he had made, despairing of his ministerial errors in commission and in omission, he was satisfied to have done in that little church, though thankful he never had occasion to repeat.

He closed the service book and gave it to Audie. He gestured for the parents to kneel. He reached one hand to rest atop Henry's head, and the other to rest on Carrie's. Then he prayed aloud. If the straight-backed pews, those long-suffering experts on liturgical forms, if the empty pews surely suspected that Pastor borrowed freely from words normally appointed for Holy Matrimony, then they were not wrong. The pastor implored God's rich blessing on the union of these *both* His children. And on their child, just sealed by baptism as God's own. He pleaded with such fervent urgency that tears ran down Carrie's cheeks. Henry's *Thank you, Pastor* came out later in a strangled voice.

And after he saw the unusual party out the door, Pastor Eusenius Berkemeier, now feeling much more than his age, was compelled to the altar for another prayer, for forgiveness if he had done wrong, for strength if he had done right.

Baptized he was, *John Henry Hollis.*

But *Harry* heard his mother's lullabies.

Harry smiled at the feel of his father's rough whiskers teasing him.

Harry heard Lilly coo when she came up the week Sam and Elvira visited in Knoxville. Lilly became less stiff with Mister Henry as she found she must compete with him for baby-holding time.

Harry. Audie Ann had a special sign for him the many times she visited to fuss over him. She smiled even when her nephew contracted colic, she undisturbed by the crying that drove Harry's parents, reluctantly (and relieved), to fieldwork.

Harry heard few other voices. His father elected to get along alone— other than several extra hands for butchering and harvest days—the better to adhere to convictions about slavery firmed in long discussions with Spooks, and the better to preserve his independence. Carrie welcomed Henry's decision. If the price of solitude was her fieldwork, she thought it penny for a pound.

Plowing with Greek, My Life
HL Hollis

Two decades ago, our Robert stopped here between University and Army. He had a spring in his step, buoyed by just besting his Aunt Crotia in one of their alliteration contests, exhilarated by that patriotic fervor of 1917, ennobled by the promises of a worthy young woman. What young man could fail to be in fine form?

He had recently wrestled with an Army questionnaire documenting family background, and complained boisterously to us about Hollis genealogy. Bereft we are, he cried, of murderers, cattle rustlers and traitors; we fail to produce a mere forger, swindler or pickpocket. Solid, stolid Lutheran farmers, that's all the Hollis genes generate. It's the bee's knees how we do it. We march forward carrying the banner of Propagation, Property, Propriety and Propinquity We are, he laughingly warned, Proponents of the Placid and Prosaic.

Hold on, I objected. You forgot Proletarian. And Placid does not fit. Your grandfather's stepbrothers, hellions all, rode unerringly to early graves. More recent still is the tragedy of my brother Marcus and Josie White.

I had from time to time previously alluded to that sad story in a fragmentary way, intending at some point to provide a coherent narrative. Robert's expiring military leave made that evening the appropriate time. The story so fascinated Robert, always susceptible to family lore, that he asked me to write it down, which I did, and sent it to him at Camp Dix before he left for France. No new facts change the story, so I insert here what I wrote for Robert.

Reading through it now, I see that I should preface it with an identification. My father's lifelong friend, more of a brother, was John P. Bright, inside the family, Judge Bright, though my father— and only my father—used his boyhood nickname, Spooks.

"Judge" was an honorific, somewhat like certain Confederate "colonels." In antebellum days John Bright had apparently onces erved very briefly as a judge. Upon learning this, my mother adopted the title, revered in her Coyner family of jurists, and insisted her children use it without fail. In point of fact, we children had little trouble remembering the title, for Bright's speech and gravitas seemed to fit the title precisely. And, as we grew older, to recognize the frequent twinkle in his eye, well, that made our relationship all the more special.

My father also enjoyed, as did we all, the company of Mrs. John Bright. (My careless mistake there, for which she would gently but firmly chastise me: she styled herself proudly as Mrs. Lydia Bright.) Originally from Philadelphia, she was an exceptional woman, sensitive to social wrongs, and firm in her commitments to fairness and justice for all God's creatures. As children we called her Aunt Lydia. My sister Dorinda, who saw in Lydia Bright a model of life and conviction, has put on paper an eloquent appreciation of her. I must remember to request a copy to include here, for she powerfully influenced the Hollis family as long as I can remember.

Father (Henry) and John Bright (Spooks) apparently grew up inseparable, and as boys and young men together went through so much, including the war years, that it sometimes seemed they used a unique vocabulary. That is to say, the words sounded familiar, unremarkable, but many were freighted with special connotations related to shared experiences to such extent that they belonged to a different language. The closest analog I ever (inadvertently) observed was private conversation between a long-married husband and wife who had, decades before, endured heartbreaking loss, the deaths of all their children in a single catastrophic accident.

Because of the lifelong friendship between these two men as well as our Hollis admiration for Mrs. Lydia Bright, the Hollis family and the Bright family grew exceptionally close. Tulips, sprawling and commodious, became the Bright's summer home, their welcome residency so extended that Judge Bright had to return alone regularly to Knoxville for his work. During those summers I came to know and admire their younger daughter, Caroline, and, to my good fortune, managed to lure her into marrying me. Such is the explanation for how my children have grandfathers who knew each other as young boys and ever remained bosom friends.

During a University recess I arrived home to discover chaos and uproar. The precipitant was Henrietta Haeckle, neighborhood busybody. Without invitation, she served up her juicy gossip: credible witnesses observed my brother Marcus on a lonely road embracing and kissing Josie White so passionately as to leave no question of their intimacy. Or so she claimed.

Marcus, third in line after Dory, everyone recognized as the sunniest, most sweet-tempered, open-hearted, and very likely most gifted of us all. With him there could be no sibling rivalries, something I can't see how to explain, but in point of fact, everyone in the family loved Marcus in a special way.

Josie White came from the most established, accomplished, respected family in town—the most respected *colored* family in town. The White family story begins with a singular character, Ramses White, a wealthy Tidewater planter of Rabelaisian inclinations. He immigrated to Tennessee, bringing with him a large retinue, including many slaves, a little before Samuel B arrived. Ramses expected to be a leading figure in the county. But his promise ended abruptly when he was fatally gored while caring for a prized bull. His will freed his slaves. Most drifted back east. Alton, however, adopted his former master's surname, stayed, and married. He fathered a son, Amos, roughly a contemporary of my father.

In many places Amos and his family would have been the Whites. Ginners Ford knew them as the Colored Whites. Josie's older brother I envied for his good looks—and also for his baseball skills. Even as a boy he possessed an uncommon dignity; he went to Ohio for college, then to Meharry in Nashville, and on to further medical education before setting up a practice in Memphis. Josie, too, attended college in Ohio. She was from the same mold as her brother, displayed similar aspirations and gifts: very pretty, very funny, very smart, a potent combination indeed.

Once Haeckle was definitely gone, Father sent for Marcus, occupied that afternoon at the old Haney place. In the meantime chaos reigned. Father was so furious that Crotia saw him strike a favorite mare, something unimaginable for him. Mother was beside herself, crying her eyes out. My sisters were thoroughly upset. They all knew Josie, as one does in a small town, admired her gifts, and wished her the best. They also felt personally demeaned that their own brother could mistreat a colored girl, particularly as promising a girl as Josie, the way some white boys did on the sly, boys from families we did not associate with.

Into this confusion walked Marcus, assuming he was sent for because I'd just come home, hugging me and laughing for the joy of seeing me again, the way he always did. Father cut him off with a growl. "Miz Haeckle says you were making time with Josie White down along the river trace. Is that true, boy? Tell me straight now."

We all held our breaths, convinced, hoping, that Marcus would squelch the rumor with an *absolutely not, you know Haeckle the Cackle*, and we'd all whoop because we *did* know the Hen's Cackle.

"Is that true, boy?"

"Yessir."

Mama just wailed, Crotia and Dory had tears in their eyes, little Annie started sniffling loudly. Father pointed Marcus to his office— few family matters were *that* serious—and slammed the door behind them so hard the walls shook.

We all heard him roaring at Marcus. (You must understand: Father almost never roared at anyone, least of all his own children.) Sometimes we heard Marcus' voice, very low and brief, but Father always cut him off with more roaring. His own son, with the Hollis name, from a Christian family, taking advantage of his position, using a fine girl like Josie for his own pleasure, taking advantage of the way people here think of her color, treating her the way white trash would treat her. You read the Gospels and then abuse one of God's children like this? Shameful. Not to be tolerated. Never in a Hollis. Think of how kindly Amos White always treats you, and this is the way you repay him? Misleading his only daughter? You know how hard he works to get his children educated. On and on. Dory and Crotia fled to the barn, from which they could still hear Father, though at least they couldn't distinguish the words.

Then as if on a switch, the roaring ceased. Silence. The door opened, and Father stepped out. "Bill, would you run, tell Ben to bring round the buggy quick as he can. I'm taking Marcus to catch the next cars. We don't have any time to spare."

We were aghast, imagining that Father was casting Marcus out disowned, though in point of fact as he came out of the office Marcus looked more dazed than disowned. As they dashed off with Father's Lucy trotting finely, we could hear in the far distance the faint squeal of cars' wheels rounding the curve before the straightaway leading in to Ginners Ford. Our uncertainty when we again heard Lucy's trot was whether they had caught the cars. That Father was alone answered our question. As he came closer he saluted us with an arm raised in victory. He told us with a grin that he had driven close alongside the cars so that Marcus mounted the car steps directly from the buggy, just as the cars were picking up speed.

(At some other place I must elaborate on Father's penchant for daringly close connections with railroad transportation, for it revealed a side of his personality not otherwise apparent. It was a predilection bequeathed only to Marcus.)

When our faces still had questions, he added, as if incidentally, that Marcus went to Knoxville to consult Judge Bright, an "explanation" that only increased the mystery.

What in the world transpired? I cannot give you quotations verbatim because I wasn't inside Father's office, much less with paper and pen in hand, but I know the gist from Marcus's subsequent reprise. Father's fury, said Marcus, seemed without bounds. Only the need for a breath forced a brief pause in Father's explosions.

Marcus took the chance to explain. Father, I could never *use* Josie. I respect her. In fact I love her.

You love her, boy?

Yessir.

She's very pretty. Could go a long way on her looks alone. I don't condone it, but I understand a damn quick infatuation.

Nossir. We've loved each other a long time.

We? You think Josie loves you?

Yessir.

How d'you know?

She says she does. She says she'll marry me.

So we're on to marrying, are we, boy?

When I love her, and she loves me, isn't that the proper thing, the honorable thing, instead of hiding?

Not legal for you to marry Josie.

Not in Tennessee, but we could go to some state where it is legal.

Then you think you could come back here?

Nossir. We know we'd have to live there.

And in six months she misses her family so much she wishes she never met you.

We've talked about our families. It'll be hard. But at least when we're married, we'll have each other. Father, we don't want to be always hiding. We hate it.

When we're married. Not *if* we're married?

Yessir.

Father turned and looked up at the bookshelves, looked so long Marcus knew boiler pressure was rising for a catastrophic explosion. He considered bolting from the office, from Tulips. Then Father swung his chair back around, fast. He glared intently at Marcus.

You're certain, boy?"

Yessir.

Certain without reservation, about marrying, and Josie certain too?

Marcus believed the explosion was inevitable, but braced to face it bravely. Yessir, I'm certain of myself, and of Josie too.

Well, Father stood up, if that's the way you two feel, there isn't a moment to lose. You must consult Spooks in Knoxville at once to know in what jurisdiction you can legally marry. Father's tone and manner were as if the question was when to commence planting the bottom land fields. Thunderstruck, Marcus stammered something about Mama, but Father waved him off. "I shall look after Mama." No more reliable sign of order's return existed at Tulips. To Mama, Father's word was law.

Marcus took the cars to Knoxville and the Brights. The Brights' youngest daughter, my Caroline, was at home there when Marcus arrived at the door, and has clear recollection of sensing from his face and confusion that something momentous had happened, but he would not tell her anything until he consulted her father, the Judge.

John Patterson Bright. A man you would ardently desire at your side in any contest. Both quick-witted and judicious. So preternaturally observant he seemed clairvoyant. Impossible to rattle, a trait I observed often, though here is not the place for the manifold examples I could relate.

He was a much-respected attorney, someone who did not suffer fools gladly, who by position tended to defend the standing order. Small wonder that Marcus feared Judge Bright's reaction to his news. He told me he jittered on the stoop outside the door five minutes without knocking, his gut in cramps, and almost fled. But once Caroline took him to her father's study, Judge Bright heard out calmly his stammered questions. To Marcus's astonishment, he said that he didn't know Josie, was sorry not to, but if Marcus loved and admired her, Judge Bright needed to know no more, and looked forward to her acquaintance.

After such reassurance, the rest could only be anticlimactic. The Judge set to work systematically consulting many legal tomes, compiled a list of states permitting marriage without reference to race, and supplied citation after citation about Tennessee prohibition. Then, without hesitation or fanfare, he sat down and wrote a large cheque in favor of Marcus, an advance wedding gift to travel on. Marcus, his head in a whirl, brought Judge Bright's list back to Tulips where he and Josie—Father insisted she be included—held intense conferences with Father. They ultimately decided to slip off to New York state to be married, and to live.

Meanwhile, the rest of us felt pulled this way and that. My narrative might be more satisfyingly suspenseful were I to report that Father called the whole family together and gave a rousing little speech. "We don't turn our backs on a Hollis who needs help. We circle our wagons, we face out, watching for who is friend and who is foe."

Those sentences, however, require a dramatic license I do not have in my pocket—though I'm certain my sister Crotia has applied for one. In point of fact, someone who did not know better might have assumed from Father's firm responses at every point along the way that he long before rehearsed for such an unprecedented trial as this. He never gave us directions how to act, at least not in words, though the unruffled way he maintained his customary schedule was eloquent instruction indeed. Since he apparently took for granted that we all would welcome Josie to Tulips as Marcus's fiancee, so did we welcome her.

Dory remembers fretting how her beau, Micah Henderson, would react to the news. Maybe he'd fade away, like one of Crotia's admirers, who did, in fact, initiate some deprecating comments, condemning such a connection as Marcus planned. Crotia cut him off midsentence, decisively terminating his cant. He likely did not grasp her "four-book nitwit" but perhaps "pusillanimous knave" penetrated slightly. She erupted with such magnificent outrage that Annie, eavesdropping from the top of the back stairs (as little sisters have no doubt eavesdropped since Tulips contained a back stairs), got so worked up she started applauding loudly. Crotia's admirer summarily disappeared (to her undisguised satisfaction). Dory should never have worried a second about Micah, for that was not to be the only storm in which Mike Henderson stood a stout oak.

Here a confession to amplify the historical record and to document my admiration for Caroline Bright ever since we met, according to our mothers, before about age one. Playtime individualism turned to cooperation developed into esteem which matured to love and we came to private understandings, she and I. Under Marcus' new circumstances, however, I believed I should give her freedom to change her mind. (Modern reader: exercise charity about the aberrations of a dundering fool in an earlier, less enlightened age.) When I wrote to her—a rather incoherent epistle, I confess— Caroline's more reasoned and courageous reply came from Knoxville by return mail. The paper is now fragile, for I have unfolded it to re-read on every wedding anniversary, and by now can quote it from memory.

> *Dearest Harry, if you'll have me there, I'm at your side come hell or high water. That's not ladylike, but that's what I know.*
>
> *Now that I have written that first, I can say I see that if I let Marcus's choice damage my relationship with the Hollis family, my parents' disappointment in me would be so intense I could hardly face them. After Marcus left us, both Father and Mama spoke in such praise that his ears must have glowed cherry red. They admired him so, in fact, that I became nettled they said nothing about his brother, my dear Harry. In my dudgeon, I ventured that I felt just a little sorry for your father.*
>
> *That brought conversation to a screeching stop. Mother looked at Father with a question on her face. I'd swear he shook his head. Then she took my hand as if I were about five years old. "Caroline, if you knew Henry Hollis as long as we have, you'd realize that we've all been through a great deal together in times past. So we all want to help each other. We must do whatever we can."*
>
> *Harry, I think we don't know our parents. Is it because we're still young, and our fathers are so much older? We should talk about this the next time you are here.*

Darling Harry, can't we get married soon? I'm available for that ceremony as soon as you can arrange it.

Your Caroline

(Modern reader: grant that the fool, though dundering, was not an idiot; the mutually desired ceremony occurred in a few months).

Meanwhile, Marcus compiled a list of five or six cities in New York to reconnoiter thoroughly. Josie agreed he should go, pick a place, and after he settled in, she'd come to marry him. With Marcus gone, we returned to familiar routines and concerns.

Then one night long after dark a frantic Amos White pounded on the door with news that Josie collapsed, gravely ill. Despite the hour, Father roused Ben and sent him off posthaste to fetch Dr. Payne. He went himself to the Whites. Dory, who had grown very fond of Josie, went along in case she could help somehow. They didn't return until the next morning—with devastating news: Josie died. Apparently she found she was with child, and, shamed, consulted old Mabel, notorious as a doctoress, but something went terribly wrong.

Believe me, Tulips fell into more disarray at the news than when we first heard about Marcus. Father walked off and did not return by sunset, Mother frantic about his whereabouts. At length Dory and I organized teams of children, friends, and neighbors to search for him, without quick success. Well after midnight, Bill and I found him, in a place we least expected, coming down the Quachasee trace.

He apologized repeatedly about causing worry; he had forgotten how late the moon rose that night, light essential on a rough road flanked by precipitous dropoffs. Bill questioned him incredulously. "You went all the way up there?"

"Seeking solace," Father explained. His face said he found none.

Bill asked whether Father had built three tabernacles up there. Referring to Peter with Jesus on the Mount constituted unkind sarcasm, of course, but demonstrated Bill's exhaustion and worry about Father. Looking back at it now as a father myself, I imagine Father's grief over Josie could have been tempered by relief that Marcus's life would be easier without such a fraught marriage. But in point of fact Father remained more undone than I ever saw him.

He said he could never forgive himself for failing to foresee and forestall what happened to Josie.

Bill argued with him vigorously, absolving him of any responsibility for Josie's death. Father shook his head, rejecting Bill's arguments without articulating his objections. At length he said his guilt consisted in "wishing, not working."

To this day I cannot specify to what he referred. Neither can Bill (less prone now as an old man, I should add, to hide under a crusty exterior his concern for people). But as usual Father did not enlighten us, saying no more as we stumbled back to Tulips by lantern. Nevertheless, that phrase has stayed with me these many decades for its wide applicability. I have commended it often to all my children. It is so easy to go on wishing but not working for some good end.

Complications accumulated. Our telegrams to Marcus failed to reach him before the funeral. At the church the Whites attended, the young preacher, barely out of training, solved all problems by strict adherence to rules. He was adamant: a just God punished Josie for her terrible sin. That sin meant burial was forbidden in the church cemetery, hallowed ground. God had spoken.

When Father learned of this new debacle, he unhesitatingly announced an unprecedented solution. "Alright, if her parents don't object, we'll bury Josie in the Hollis graveyard. That's where she belongs anyhow." About the family graveyard, who could argue with Henry Hollis, the only man alive who had known virtually everyone interred there?

In that graveyard, as those who have seen it may recall, is a small section to one side where in the old days Hollis slaves were buried, next to which is a sort of dividing, vacant aisle, then the Hollis family graves. Delegating me to carry some stakes and a hammer, Father led the way to the graveyard, and unhesitatingly crossed the dividing aisle to stand in a vacant place on the family side. He looked around thoughtfully, then directed me to drive stakes precisely where he stood.

But when the men he hired to dig the grave saw the stakes, they came hustling back to Tulips for my father. "We'z believin' that some-uns mistook, Mister Hollis, puttin down them thar stakes, an we dint wanna spile the grass. Dint wanna dig no hole in the wrong spot. Mebbe some sumbitch put in differen stakes 'stead of yourn."

Father responded with puzzled curiosity. "Why, Slater, you sure? Are the stakes square-sawn, with a small scrap of white cloth tied at the top?"

"Wal, yessir. But, Mister Hollis, but them stakes cain't be rightly sitiated."

"Why is that?"

"Becuz . . . wal . . . becuz . . . Mister Hollis, to be speakin plain, them stakes ain't in the nigger kerner, whur they orter be."

Father became conciliatory. "Boys, I'm sorry to have troubled you. I figured to pay double because we need the grave dug neat and fast. But since you don't find the place fitting, Slater, I understand you won't dig. Perhaps I can find someone else for double pay."

"Double, ye say, Mister Hollis? Double? Wal-sir." They consulted with a look and exchanged nods. "We sure ken use the work, yessir. We wuz jes needin sartain we diggin right."

"And now you know?"

"Yessir, yessir. At them stakes. We havin ye thet grave dug out right quick jes whur ye marked 'er."

Even that didn't satisfy Father. He went to our pastor at the time, a good man, Pastor C. C. Schmitt. Father told him, "At the funeral, that Methodist minister will preach nothing but doom and damnation. We need a sound Lutheran at the graveside to stress Christ's love and the Resurrection." (I have this from Schmitt after Father's death.)

Still fairly young in the ministry, Pastor Schmitt felt he should defend even a Methodist minister, at least one Father labeled a pathetic jackass. Schmitt hemmed. Schmitt hawed. He said Josie White wasn't a member of his Lutheran congregation. He said he didn't want to butt in where he wasn't invited. He said he hardly knew her family. He said she appeared guilty of a monstrous sin. He said he wouldn't want it to look like he was condoning such a thing. He said pretty much everything but *no*.

Father listened to this screen courteously, but no one could mistake his response. "Pastor, you're from up in Pennsylvania, so you don't fully understand the social situation here. Besides, I was taught Jesus Christ on the Cross wasn't just for little sins. If I have to read the graveside service out of the book myself, I'll do it. But if I have to do that, then, Pastor, I recommend you find an easier place to preach Christ's Death and Resurrection and God's forgiveness, because you are obviously failing God's call to do that here in Ginners Ford."

"Mister Hollis, with the help of the Holy Spirit, I am always ready to preach Christ and the Resurrection, in season and out.

Father nodded. "With the help of the Holy Spirit, in season and out is eleven o'clock tomorrow morning. I'll see you there."

Thinking it my duty to represent Marcus and the rest of the family at the funeral, I had steeled myself to sit up in front of the African Methodist church, but Father shook his head. "I shall do that with Dory and Crotia. Audie Ann is going with Solomon. She doesn't like fussing over her. You sit in back with them and translate."

I did so, Solomon too overwhelmed by grief to attempt the task. Even I had trouble concentrating because the more Audie understood, the more vehemently she objected. "He's so wrong. This is not Christian." As Father predicted, the Methodist minister preached doom and damnation; to my incredulity he explicitly pronounced Josie fittingly punished by God for her great transgression. Audie became so agitated that Solomon even put his arm on her shoulder. I feared she might rise and cause a scene, but the minister shortly finished, though with a prayer as bleak and unmerciful as his sermon.

At the Amen, before anyone could rise, Devon Burke stood and started to sing, something that, as I could see from the minister's face, took him unawares. Later, when I spoke of this to Father, he only smiled and said, "Bet you don't have a voice at the University as good as Devon's." (He was correct. Devon Burke was blessed with the most powerful and expressive bass I've ever heard anywhere.) He sang "Abide with Me," then, without pause, he moved into "Swing Low," except that he changed the "me" to "her." *Comin for to carry her home.*

I listened, and tried to translate for Aunt Audie Ann, while we wept along with the whole congregation. Striking, how much power music has.

After the funeral, the Reverend slunk off (he decamped soon to Memphis). Pastor Schmitt met us all at the grave. He conducted the burial service there with great dignity and warm empathy. He included extended, eloquent remarks on God's infinite compassion for His children even when they make terrible mistakes, and warned that we judge not, lest we, too, be judged. Perhaps unaccustomed to audible amens and yessirs, he spoke admirably, and Father later told him so with what was for Father great effusion. Years later Pastor Schmitt volunteered to me he grew about ten years more a theologian and a pastor in those two days.

The very next morning (recall Father was then in his seventies) he left to console Marcus in New York. Marcus later wrote me a letter, which I still possess. "Father gave me great solace, speaking from his heart of his own life." I wasn't certain what that meant, though I could not ask on cold paper. I might have in person, but, Marcus, now estranged from Tennessee, elected to stay in New York. He did well at a business in Utica. There, Mama and Dory at his side, he died a few years after Father, from a lingering malaise the doctors could not diagnose. I think Mama never recovered from her grief. Or Josie's parents from theirs either.

The story includes a sequel, perhaps farce after tragedy, though it might have eventuated as tragedy compounded. Father learned of ugly talk among the class of men who loitered at the Mercantile and idled at the Livery. Some were vocal about Josie's burial, condemning Father's role, which, after all, was hardly a secret. When the indefatigable Henrietta Haeckle carrried this to Tulips, Father promptly told Mama he must go to town on an errand. Suspecting trouble from his grim look, and knowing dissuasion impossible, Mama appealed to Dory. What she thought Dory could possibly do, I have no idea, but Mama's plea illustrates her helplessness in such cases. Dory knew Father would firmly decline her company, and anyway, she and Crotia had previously promised to escort Aunt Audie Ann on a shopping expedition.

Ben Holman, always next to me in alphabetical order at school, worked that morning at the Mercantile, opening crates outside at the side of the store, and saw Dory and Audie Ann come to Miz Hawkins's little shop, just across from the Mercantile. Ben favored Audie, even learned her hand talk for hello and goodbye, so he went over to help her down from the buggy while Dory carried in some parcels, the yard goods, she explained, they needed to match in color.

As Ben attacked another crate, he saw my father drive up to the Mercantile porch. Ben told me that my father didn't jump down from the buggy and stride off on errands as he usually did. Instead he stood there in front of the Mercantile porch, where the usual bunch of loafers and rough fellows sat. Father looked at them and they looked at Father. No one said anything, until he spoke, loudly enough to carry easily.

"Nace Johns, I came into town special to see you. Word is, you and your good friend Wilber there are saying you're gonna teach that damn Hollis a lesson. I know you don't have courage enough to come talk to me at Tulips. So I came to town to hear you say what lesson you have in mind."

In the following silence Father cupped an ear. "Nace, I'm getting deaf in my old age. You'll have to speak up. What say you?"

Only silence.

Father took a different tack. "Mister Wade Slater, that Nace Johns is sitting right nigh you, so you must have heard him. Can you tell me what he said? That damned Hollis would like to know." Father again cupped his ear and leaned forward.

"I believe he dint say nuthin, Mister Hollis."

"Nuthin! Nuthin? Is he dead, Mister Wade?"

"He breathin, look like, Mister Hollis."

"Mister Wade, he's not asleep, is he?"

"Not lessen he sleepin wit' his eyes open."

"Well maybe Wilber there has something to say?" After a long silence Father cupped his ear again. "Eh, Wade?"

"Guess not, Mister Hollis."

Father raised his voice. "Nace Johns, you're a damned sorry coward and Wilber Tabbet even sorrier." He backed up, still watching the Mercantile, climbed onto the buggy, and sat there for a time looking at the men, nobody saying anything. Then he called, "Mister Wade, it occurs to me I'd be grateful for a small favor from you."

"Ifen I ken, Mister Hollis."

"If either of those two pathetic excuses for men ever finds their tongues, would you send them along to Tulips, please. Maybe they might find enough gumption to talk to a woman, like my little sister, Miss Audie Ann. I imagine she'd like a word with them. Don't have to send word ahead. I'm sure Miss Audie'll see 'em, even greet 'em, from a good ways away. If they ever work up the courage."

Audie Ann, as everyone there knew full well, could pick off a man on the road easily from the Tulips porch.

"You won't forget to say about visiting Miss Audie Ann, Wade?"

"Nossir."

"Thank you, Mister Wade, thank you kindly." Father drove off at a slow walk.

He was out of sight when Audie Ann and Dory came out of Miz Hawkins's with their parcels and left. Ben said the porch crowd broke up very much sooner than ordinarily.

After her shopping trip to town, unusual for Audie Ann, she wasn't on the Tulips porch to greet any man Wade Slater sent. She languished sick for weeks, didn't appear out of her room until early afternoons, and looked pretty peaked when she ventured downstairs. We children feared for her health, though she, the most impaired among us, customarily despised any hint of inactivity.

Then one night, at full moon, gunfire and distant shouting woke the whole family in the middle of the night. All the children came tumbling downstairs in a sleepy fright, to be met in the front hall by Father, fully dressed.

"Go back to bed," he ordered. "All that noise came from Solomon. I asked him to keep an eye on the graveyard. We've seen some sign of skunks and varmits there. Sounds like he got 'em. Go back to bed, I say. All is well. Get back to sleep."

Dory looked around. "Where's Audie Ann?"

Father seemed to find this a dumb question. "Why, Dory, when you're deaf, you sleep right through commotion."

It wasn't Father's way to be casual about his sister, so a suspicious Dory went upstairs and then slipped across to Audie's room. In the moonlight, she could be certain without a lamp that Audie Ann wasn't there; in point of fact, her bed was not even faintly rumpled. Dory drafted Crotia to help her stay awake. They heard Father go out soon, and, just as the hall clock struck three, heard him return with Audie Ann, her thump-and-drag obvious, even if she tried to tread lightly.

The girls forced themselves to keep watch, though they heard nothing unusual. At first light Dory hightailed it to the cemetery. She found shovels and cans of black paint scattered about, the paint all leaked out through a multitude of neat round holes, not unlike those on the shovels.

She carried samples to the house, where she found Father in jovial spirits and Audie Ann in restored health, enjoying an early breakfast. Father examined Dory's evidence—rather casually, she thought. "Solomon says that last night he fired some buckshot at a whole family of skunks trying to move in. But I wonder who would have left trash like this?" He put down his coffee to free his hands. "Audie, what do you make of this?" he asked, but Audie Ann just shook her head, the personification of innocent perplexity.

Dory thought she didn't need a Pinkerton for this mystery. Audie Ann, with Solomon as her ears, watched nights at the cemetery for someone aiming to desecrate Josie's grave. A person or persons did come, but departed quickly, leaving ruined shovels and drained paint cans in exchange for some small lead they took away.

I'm not certain this story will dissuade those convinced Hollis history is entirely dull, but it's all we have, so it must suffice.

That's what I wrote to Robert all of twenty years ago now, in 1917. Josie lay then in her grave undisturbed, waiting for her Lord and Savior, as she does to this day, next to my brother Marcus. And not far from our Robert, back home from a field in France.

Dory came again today, saying her place is lonesome with Mike gone, which I understand, for I, too, miss Mike more than I can easily say. She, I, we all lost a great bulwark when God took him home with so little warning.

Dory and Caroline conspire: they won't tell me outright, but they arrange so that one or the other is always here. I don't require that, not yet, but I don't protest much because their sorority may help them both when I'm gone.

I asked Dory to read some of what I've been writing. She complimented me on my recollections of Audie Ann, I'm relieved to record. Dory did, though, gently remind me that she and Crotia also took shooting lessons from Audie Ann. When I concentrated on my own early shooting experience, my sisters' lessons and accomplishments slipped from my attention, self-absorption about which the Ancients had more than a few things to say.

Dory generously went on to read some of what I wrote about our brother Marcus and Josie White. At the part about her shopping the day Father went to town to face Nace Johns, she interjected she was relieved I did not mention anything about the gun in her purse since it might give her granddaughters wrong ideas.

The gun! In her purse! I'm glad I had emptied my coffee cup by then or stains would have spoiled a favorite hand-pieced quilt. After I recovered to a degree from my shock, Dory explained that Audie Ann slipped the pistol into her bag as they were leaving the house. They heard Father telling Mama he was going into town, which Dory correctly took as a sign of trouble.

I could not have been more astonished. In my perturbation, I spoke out with insufficient control. I fear I sounded too adamant in my inquiry. Why had I never known this until this very minute?

Before I could take back my words or at least my tone, Dory nailed me. "You mean, Big Brother, why were you, Herodotus Lucius Hollis, the eldest son and custodian of all family secrets, not kept instantly informed of every detail at all times?"

Dory is slow to wrath and was soon smiling. "I guess, Brother, it's because you were only the oldest son, not the oldest daughter."

From inside Miz Hawkins' store they heard Father drive up to the Mercantile and watched through the open door. "I knew that if bad trouble started, I should shoot the most dangerous first: men with guns but no brains. That meant Wilber Tabbet. You remember how Wilber loved to carry that cheap owlhead pistol, and he came from the Tabbet branch with all those first cousins marrying, let alone outright incest. Figured I should eliminate that threat first thing."

Marveling at such cold calculation, I admitted I couldn't have done that.

Dory shot me the Sibling Pity look, so I braced for the candor one accepts only from a beloved sister.

"You're right, HL. Your soft heart always got in the way, even when you were little. Remember how you tried to hide you weren't disposing of the kitten litters? Don't forget Marcus's black cat caper."

(The barn kittens shouldn't detain us. I'll try later to mention Marcus's black cats.)

Over fresh coffee we traded more of our memories about Marcus as I reminded her, and she reminded me, of incidents the other had forgotten, we both still sensible of our great loss, though so long ago.

QUACHASEE
WHC

Sent by Carrie to walk the farm, her transparent excuse to force a day's break from barn construction in January, Henry eased around a rock outcropping high on the ridge, on his way toward the next boundary marker.

Rifle shot. Close. High-pitched zing. Rock fragments burst from a boulder above him. Crouching, he scuttled from cover to cover until well away from the rock shower.

"Damn. Who go thar?" a rough voice challenged.

"Hold fiah, stranger, hold fiah," Henry shouted, peering through a bush from behind a boulder.

"Show yerself, dammit," returned the voice.

"I dasn't. Not withouten ye do."

"The hell. Ye crope on me. Show yerself, cow'rd."

Such impatient shouting revealed the rifleman's position. Henry stayed down and silent. Thank Spooks for scaring Carrie with all that talk about how territorial and aggressive tusk boars have gotten; otherwise she wouldn't have insisted he carry a rifle.

"Show yerself, I say, er I'll fiah agin an destroy ye."

Henry glimpsed the stranger rising, looking in a wrong direction, bringing up a hand to shade his eyes. *Uncas knows one hand for the eyes means he can't shoot*, whispered Henry to himself as he rose, rifle at his shoulder, finger on its trigger. "Hyar, stranger. Hyar."

"God damn. Should'a knowed ye be sneakin back'a bresh." Audibly chagrined to be taken at such disadvantage, the man whirled and, rifle barrel down now, approached Henry.

Henry lowered his rifle only slightly. "Now jes quile down an behave yerself. I don' call to mine seein ye afore. 'Low ye travelin' through. Wha'cher bis'ness?"

Unkempt, the stocky stranger fit his voice. "Sumbitch. I'm not beholden to ye. My bis'ness is ye trespassin my land." He stopped about ten paces from Henry, where rocks made footing more difficult. "Name 'a Arkwright. Ye 'member thet: Arkwright." He seemed to be working himself into a rage. "Arkwright, I'm tellin ye. Who the hell be ye?"

"Name 'a Hollis. Remember thet. Hollis. Hollis, I'm tellin ye."

"Don't sass me none, poacher. This hyar's my land. Ye's poachin."

"Nossir. I'm standin on my land. Own hit ridge t'ridge. One ridge's right yander."

"No sech, ye goddamn liar. This hyar land mine. All a'hit. Bought me hit half yahr past."

"Don' want no ruction hyar, Arkwright. Check the courthouse."

"Hit's my land," screamed Arkwright as he began picking his way through the rocks toward Henry.

"Arkwright, I'm tellin ye flat-footed, ye's mistook." Henry raised his rifle again, aimed straight at the man. "Now ye hav'ta quit hyar. Turn 'roun an git offen my land. Yourn mus' be a valley o'er. Ifen ye neighbor me a'tall."

The man came on, his progress slowed only by bad footing.

"Mister Arkwright, one more step an' I fiah. Nigh as ye is, I'll blow ye all to flinders. Ye finacious daid."

At that, Arkwright stopped. "Ye not a-gonna shoot no neighbor?" His tone spoke aggrieved feelings.

"Yessir, sartain sure will." Henry's eyes did not leave his gun sights. "Lessen ye turn 'round and git offen my land. Keep thet right hand shy'a thet rifle, Arkwright, an git movin."

"Dammit, Hollis, this hyar ain't th'end," Arkwright roared as he turned around. "I'm gonna see my lawyerman. He'll court ye sure."

"'Til then, keep goin up, o'er the ridge. I'll jes walk wit' ye. Wanna make sartain sure no trespasser don' lose hisn way."

"Lef' m'coat down thar. Hit's store-boughten." Arkwright returned to his wheedling tone.

"Glad t'hear hit. Got me a mule thet need a blanket now cole come on. Left, Arkwright, uphill."

"Goddamn bastard."

"Don' slow walkin like thet, Arkwright. Ye need offen my land afore sundown." Close to the ridge, Henry nearly caught up with Arkwright so that the man could not get out of his sight too quickly over the brow. He stood watch from the ridge top until Arkwright dropped well down and into the trees.

"Silhouette on a ridge's a right easy target," he muttered to himself as he moved to an outcropping he remembered from when he and Spooks played Uncas and Deerslayer here; a hole surrounded by boulders, it offered protection on all sides. There he watched several hours, even long after he heard shots far in the distance, perhaps Arkwright's rifle. *I don't think Deerslayer could have done any better*, he told himself as he trudged homeward in twilight, *even if I can't hit the side of a barn*.

❧

"Ma-ma. Ma-ma." Henry exaggerated the syllables separately, clearly, his face close to Harry's. Carrie kissed them both. "I see now how you taught Audie Ann. You're so patient."

"Ma-ma," urged Henry. "Ma-ma."

"That child is not going to say a word for months, Henry. My mother says so. Aunt Sally says so. He's way too young."

"He acts the way Audie Ann acted when she hadn't learned some hand sign Mama made up for us." Henry mouthed the prompts, smiling at Harry as he carried him.

"Give him to me, Henry. He's going to be screaming hungry in a minute."

At his transfer, the child objected and put his hands out for his father. When his mother ignored him, he began crying, extending his arms to Henry. "Mama," he cried.

Henry laughed triumphantly and pointed to Carrie. "No, that's Mama over there."

"If I'm Mama, who are you?" Carrie asked Henry as she capitulated to the boy's demands and returned him to his father.

That evening after chores, Henry again played with the child while Carrie finished cleaning up. "Mama," the boy smiled.

"Well, sir, what shall we do about you, Master Harry?" questioned Henry aloud, knowing that in the excitement over the boy's first words he never answered Carrie's question, knowing that Carrie also listened to his musings.

"Things steal up on us, don't they? Just when you think there's plenty of time to figure everything out. They don't give you time. You say an answer quick, and then you find one thing after another follows from that answer, things you didn't think about or even know about when you gave the answer. I said, 'Yes, I want her with me' about a girl, and one thing after another, and here is Harry, saying 'Mama.'"

The child looked up. "Mama."

Henry pointed to Carrie, turning the boy's head. "Mama. There's Mama. But what am I? It's an early move on the checkerboard. If this move is to teach you to call me 'Marse Henry,' then somewhere down the line is maybe the move when you ask Mama who your papa is, which would cut my heart deep."

He paused to wipe the baby's mouth. "Or if this move is that I teach you 'Papa,' maybe that leads, who knows how many moves ahead, to the move where you come out with 'Papa' for the wrong ears, and there's hell to pay.

"But the rules don't let us skip a move. And the fact is, Master Harry, that I am your father. So it has to be 'Papa'. And we'll make up the strategy for future moves as we go along. 'Pa-pa.'" He pointed to himself.

❧

Cycles of planting and harvest. Once so silent, the cabin filled with the boy's chatter. "He's a strange child," Carrie told Henry. "He'll be talking so fast he can hardly get the words out, and then he'll stop and sit. Just when I worry he's in some kind of spell, he smiles to himself and starts talking again with questions about everything."

Evenings, Harry climbed into Henry's lap to help turn the pages as Henry read and reread stories for him. He listened to nearly anything: newspaper reporting, Henry's hog records, *Aesop's Fables*, political speeches. When his father tired and put him down, the boy toddled to the Low Chair, painstakingly spread out on the seat the latest papers from Spooks, and gravely announced he would "read his own paper." His parents exchanged amused glances, and urged him to find interesting stories.

Leaning over "his" newspaper on the chair seat one evening, Harry asked, "Papa, what's a tar . . . if?"

Henry looked up from his grafting records for the orchard. "A tar . . . if? I don't—oh, a *tariff*. A tariff is a government tax on imports, on things that come from outside the United States." Carrie glanced up from her novel. "Tariffs? Why are you two talking about tariffs?"

"Well, Mama," Harry patiently explained the obvious, "it says here that tariffs will rise, but I didn't know whether that's good or bad because I didn't know what a tariff is."

"Where does it say tariffs will rise?" Henry puzzled.

"In my newspaper."

"Why don't you bring that over here and read it to me?"

The boy cheerfully complied.

"You've got a good memory, son," smiled Henry, recalling a previous evening when, the boy on his lap, he read aloud from the same article. "Maybe you should go help Mama read her book."

Harry happily trotted over, climbed on Carrie's lap. "Where should I start, Mama?" She winked at Henry over the boy's head, and put a finger on the page. Her face changed to consternation at Harry's voice. "The . . . strange man . . . jumped from the . . . horse and . . . pounded on the door." By then Henry was looking over Carrie's shoulder. "Open the door, you black . . . guards. Papa," Harry looked up from the book, "what's a . . . black guard?"

"Hard to believe." Spooks whispered as he listened to Harry plow down a column of *De Bow's Review,* fresh from Spooks' saddlebag. "But there is no possibility he is doing this by memory. Have you tried numbers?" he asked in a low tone. Carrie shook her head.

"Thank you, boy," he interrupted. "Master Harry," he tousled the boy's hair. "How many fingers do you have?"

"Ten," the boy mumbled, still reading in a whisper.

"How many toes?"

"Ten."

"Well, if you put together all the fingers and all the toes in this room, how many would that be?"

Harry stopped reading to consider the question briefly. "I don't know." He spoke slowly, apparently frustrated.

"That's all right." Spooks eased back in his chair. "It's not important."

"I don't know the word for eight tens."

"I think it's eighty, son."

"Eighty? Oh." His face brightened in discovery. "Eight-ty, and nine-ty and ten-ty."

"Not exactly. Ten-ty is called one hundred, and then you start again, one hundred and one, a hundred and two."

"No eleven-ty?"

"No, a hundred and ten. But look. If I have ten fingers and I do this," Spooks made a show of pulling fingers off and held up the back of his hands with three fingers bent into a palm, "so I lose three fingers, how many do I have left?"

Still laughing at Spooks' grimaced finger pulling, the boy shouted, "Seven."

Spooks casually put his hands in his pockets. "What if I took away six from the ten?"

"Four," answered Harry. "Can you pull off your fingers again?"

"I will if you help me solve a puzzle. If your mother has ten eggs and she wants to give exactly the same number of eggs to you and to Papa and to me, how many should she give each of us?"

Harry shook his head. "She can't do that."

"No, I thought not," answered Spooks, leaning back and again relaxing

"Unless she wanted to give part of an egg, and that would be all runny and hard to clean up." Harry giggled at such an idea.

"Yes, truly a mess," Spooks agreed.

❦

"Lo dere in de house? Carrie?" Solomon bore spices from Lilly. As he sat before a low fire, sipping from a mug Carrie offered, he dispensed news about Tulips people and of other farms far below.

Speaking of Audie, Solomon switched unthinkingly to hand talk. "Sam and The Witch get more hostile to her by the day."

"Henry and I told her she could come live up here."

Solomon shook his head. "She's grateful for that, of course, but with all due respect, her rooms at Tulips are larger than this whole cabin.

More important, much as she enjoys your company, she doesn't want to impose on you. I think, though, at bottom is her determination to act as watchman for Tulips. She doesn't trust Sam with his hands on Tulips. He's unconscionably lazy and chronically short of money. Furthermore, an important detail: if she lived way up here, she and I could not enjoy as much time together as we do now."

"No, and up here there's not much privacy," conceded Carrie. "But you tell her again that if Tulips gets impossible, come here. What's the news from the cabins out back?"

Solomon shook his head dolefully as he shifted out of hand talk. "Trubble an 'fliction, Carrie. Betty gone."

"Betty? Serena's girl? At Caleb's?" Carrie's apprehension mounted swiftly. "What's happened?"

"Marse Caleb lent huh t'Marse Sam whiles Miz Elvira 'way las mon, de whole mon. Yuh knows whut dat mean. But Marse Sam sen huh back di-reck. I 'spect it 'cause she say no t'Marse Sam. An when Betty say no, it no. She strong."

"Why's Betty gone? She run away?"

"No, she ken' run 'cause'a huh lil' boy, Joe. Aftah Sam tells Caleb 'bou'id, Caleb tells Betty he gonna sell off Joe 'less she co'p'rate, but she dint tink nuttin ob id 'cause he use t'be good t'she."

"Oh, Solomon, don't tell me."

"Yessum. Caleb sen Betty to wok oud in de field. She dint wanna leave her Joe. Caleb lies. He say, doan worry 'bou'id. So she go oud. An aftah she oud dere, some spekalater fum Atlanta cum by de big house, an Caleb jes 'boud pays he t'take de boy. So wen Betty cum in, her Joe gone. She make sech a ruckus, Caleb calls men—he need tree a'dem—to sen huh west t'sell huh so she nebbah fine huh boy. Caleb laugh an makes sho all de dahkies know, so dey see whud happen iffen dey doan 'bey ordahs. Now lil Joe gone, an Betty gone, and Serena doan wanna lib no moh."

"If he were here now, I'd kill him or make him kill me," Carrie spat out. She hurled her mug into the fireplace, where it shattered against the stone, the liquid hissing in the fire.

"Yuh gots Lilly's spirit, Carrie. When she fine oud, an heered Caleb 'n Sam at Tulips laughin 'bou'id, she step oudda de kitchen t'face 'em. Sally wuz dere an heered id. Lilly calls dem 'bou' ebbah cuss word Sally know, an a whole bunch Sally nebbah heered affoah. Caleb get so mad he grab huh, an say he gonna trash huh bad. But Lilly kick he in de privates, hard, so he scrunch up, an she run into de big house. She goes straigh t'de big cab'ned in de dinin room. Yuh knows de one."

Carrie nodded. "With all of Elvira's best china that means more to her than anyone's life," she sneered.

"Yeh, dad'un. Lilly wok de top 'way fum de wall so id fall down on de face. Id mash up de wood, mash up de glass fron', mash up near all de plates. Sam, an Sally right ahind he, come runnin in at all de c'motion, he screamin he gonna hab huh beat neah daid. She jes tells he, 'membahs de burnin in yore pants. Id ken burn 'gain—only *dis* time, dat burnin, id las' long's yuh lib."

Carrie smirked briefly. "I think I know where the burning came from. What did Sam say?"

"Sam nebbah say much. When Elvira come home, he tells huh de cab'net jes fall idself. Sally say he hab t'spen pow'rful, ohderin all new tings fum Nashville. Cause Miz Elvira buy de bes, yuh know. An Sam hate t'spen money, yuh knows dat too."

"That doesn't bring back Betty, or her boy."

Tears came to Solomon's eyes. "Carrie, I couldn' do nuttin 'bou'id. I wah gone den, way up at Marse Abner's, an—"

"I wasn't blaming you," Carrie assured him. "Caleb would have killed you if you tried to interfere. The man is the devil's helper. No, the devil himself."

Harry wandered in from playing on the porch. Carrie pulled him to hold close in her lap. "Betty's Joe was only a couple of years older."

Solomon nodded sad agreement. "He a good boy. I used t'lahk de way he laugh." With a sad smile Solomon drained his mug and put it on the table. "Where Marse Henry is? I greets 'im 'fore I goes back down de valley."

❦

In helpless rage, Carrie brooded for days over Betty and her Joe. Carrie knew both from servants' holiday celebrations. Betty, her mother, Serena, her whole family, had come down to Caleb from Marse Ennis, Marse Samuel's younger brother. The family had been with Marse Ennis for decades. In fact Serena was Caleb's nurse. When his mother died young, she helped raise him, seeing him unscathed through one boyhood scrape after another. But none of that mattered when Caleb inherited the farm and its servants. He assigned both Serena and Betty to the field crew bossed by a servant notorious for driving his crew, his fellow servants, mercilessly from first dim light to last dusk.

Now one man, one evil man, had destroyed so many lives—Betty's, her boy's, her man's, her mother's. One evil marse. He had the power, could call in helpers to prevent any resistance. Carrie went back again and again to Solomon's telling. *Betty dint wanna leave her boy, but Caleb lie.* It was so easy for a marse to lie. No servant could correct a marse.

Day after day for many weeks, Carrie could not escape it. A marse's lie and so many people hurt. She was still preoccupied when Spooks stopped in to say hello-and-goodbye on a quick hunting trip. After Spooks left, Henry was in high spirits.

"I was telling him that Harry is learning too fast for me to keep ahead of him, and Spooks suggested I think about sending him away to a special school Spooks heard of in Boston. They have other students like Harry."

Her attention dragged from mourning Betty and her Joe, Carrie spoke in alarm. "Boston? But that's so far away."

"It'd be for the boy's own good," answered Henry. "I guess Cousin Hurley must know businessmen in Boston. He'd write me letters of introduction." He opened a box of papers and began poking through them. "I think I've got Cousin Hurley's new address; his firm moved."

Carrie tried to calm herself, but the questions, the pleas, tumbled out. "There's got to be a good school closer than Boston. Maybe in North Carolina. Maybe Pastor Berkemeier could teach him."

"I'm sure there are closer schools. But the close ones would never take him once they found out who his parents are. I don't want to ask Berkemeier. He's trying to get that mission church going out near Hopewell. The road is misery so he can't take a buggy; he's not a young man any more."

Carrie's panic overwhelmed her. She crossed the room quickly to face Henry. "Then where are you taking my boy?"

"Boston is a long way," Henry admitted. "It'd be hard. I'd miss him during school months. But I have to think of what's best for him. When the time comes, I could take Harry with me to Boston to prospect for schools there. But that's a ways off. Don't worry about it. Right now I'd better feed the stock."

Henry left for the barn. Then it came to her. Henry's *Don't worry about it* was what Caleb told Betty. It was all lies. The more she thought of Betty and her boy, the more certain she was.

In panic she lifted the boy. She bolted outside. She slipped quietly past the barn. She ran as fast as she could past the young orchard. She flew through the open field into the refuge of the uncleared forest. Once she was well in the woods, the ground sloped up. Further, and the slope became steadily steeper. She forced herself to keep going, but her heart hammered in her chest. It was impossible to keep going fast, carrying a fidgeting boy who wanted to be put down. Yet walking at his speed, they would be easy to catch.

Winded, her legs trembling from exertion, Carrie glanced back the way she came, traced her faint trail on the ground, just as Spooks had explained tracking. Her heart sank. No matter if she went fast as the wind, someone like Spooks could always follow them, catch them. They could not escape. Not in this life.

Despairing and out of breath, she sank down at the base of a huge tree, and leaned back gratefully against the trunk. Massive root buttresses protruded from the ground on each side of her like armrests on some giant's chair, enfolding her. As her breathing gradually slowed she recognized the place. Henry had once brought her up here.

Trees filled her life—from lone oaks to dense, dark forests, lines of trees as field borders, saplings as anticipated shade for new dwellings, trees offering their fruit—but nothing like this open grove of magnificent ancient maples and beeches, spaced far enough for long vistas, but close enough their dense canopy prevented any brush below, as if caretakers had carefully groomed this park. The tree trunks were so large no single human's arms could encircle them. Their lowest limbs were so high, their trunks' diameters so large, they were unclimbable.

The trees were here long before the oldest person she knew was born. They promised to stand yet long after she and then her boy were gone. Wise in their silence, they offered their trunks as unyielding support, their dense crowns as protection overhead.

The scale of the enormous trees calmed her. The mute giants offered space to realize the vast eternities within which she, they all, lived. She rose and walked among the giants. Here the lying marse, the betrayed, brokenhearted mother, the stolen boy: these did not disappear, but they no longer possessed all of her mind.

The boy stood, legs wide, head far back, staring up in rapture. Just like his father. Henry had ordered a special, expensive book, of troublesome size for Spooks to ferry up. It was filled with drawings of European cathedrals, their massive columns, impossible heights, bracings that leaped daringly overhead, delicately framed openings. She and Henry had spent many evenings absorbed in the drawings. When she voiced their loss at never seeing the cathedrals in person, Henry had brought her up here, as close, he said, as they could come in America to such majestic spaces.

Imagine, he told her, celestial choirs filling the space with hymns of all the ages. Imagine the music swelling so that you feel it in your bones like you feel thunder or a waterfall. Imagine holy ones in robes from different centuries processing past the towering columns of beech, one after another, and another, far into the distance, into eternity.

The Patriarchs, Henry called the grove. He even named individual trees. Adam, Cain, Enoch, Seth, Enos, Methuselah, Noah, Shem, Ham, Japheth, Abraham. And Isaac. Isaac: the boy who went so trustingly when God ordered Abraham to make a sacrifice. Isaac: who kept asking practical questions, to which the answer was always "the Lord will provide."

Carrie saw shafts of setting sunlight pierce the leafy canopy here and there to set a branch or trunk or patch of grass instantly aflame in brilliant orange and red, as if lighting the way for the procession as it wound its way up the mountain.

"Mama, did you bring my blanket?" The boy lay on the ground to stare up the trunk. "This tree goes up to touch the clouds."

The Lord will provide. Pastor Berkemeier repeated that answer with special emphasis when he taught them about Isaac and Abraham. *Isaac looks for the wood, the fire, and keeps asking, where's the sacrifice? And Abraham's answer is always the same.*

"Mama, I'm hungry. Did you bring our supper?"

Sometimes you wonder if the Lord will provide, if He actually keeps promises. She had tried Pastor's patience by questioning. But he listened, even nodded sympathetically with her examples, while the rest of the class fidgeted and whispered.

"Mama, we need a book about trees, *big* trees. Did you bring one to read to us?"

Carrie, we are God's children. Remember what it means to be children. Think of Hallie's little Washington, how he cries sometimes even when Hallie is trying to help him. He doesn't understand what his mama is doing, that she's looking out for him, even when it doesn't seem so. Little Wash can't understand. He's just a child. That's how we are with God.

The boy walked to a nearby tree, still looking up. Carrie started to call him back, then let him go. Pastor had spoken so earnestly. *Carrie, we're just children with God. I don't understand it, I admit. How could I understand God?*

Harry began working his way around the tree, moving out of her sight without a backward glance. *I don't ever expect to see a burning bush, Carrie, but that's not the point of the story.* The boy came around the other side. "Mama, I think we should come up to these trees every day. Don't they make you feel good?"

He started around another tree and came out the far side grinning. "Let's go find Papa and show him these *big* trees, Mama." He reached for her hand. "Let's go back to find Papa."

Find Papa? Go back? *The point of the story is that God takes care of us, Carrie. All of us. God will provide, even though we can't see how.* She took the boy's outstretched hand. In dread, she walked back the way she came. *Lord have mercy.*

Henry appeared at the edge of the High Field. The boy wrenched his hand from her tight grip and ran ahead to be swooped up by his father. *Christ have mercy.*

"Papa, we saw trees so big I can't put my arms around them, and they're so tall I get dizzy and fall over if I keep trying to see their top."

"That grove is the closest thing we have to a cathedral, Harry, a huge old church." Henry put the boy down to walk with them back to the cabin.

Lord have mercy.

"Carrie, I was coming up to the Patriarchs because it was the last place to look for you. Why would you go off without saying anything?"

"You said Harry is *your* son."

"Well, isn't he?"

"You said you were going to take him away."

Henry stopped and turned to face her. "He's my son," he said curtly. "I should know what's good for his education."

She raised her head. "He's my child too."

Henry looked at her impatiently, shook his head. "Yes, of course, but we have to think what's best for the boy."

"We? You never asked me."

"It's pretty obvious, what's best."

"Obvious to you. Not to me."

"Carrie, think about it some. I've spent a lot of time weighing this. I'm not complaining about the time. I *ought* to be thinking about what's best for my son."

"Your son?"

Between them, Harry covered his ears to shut out the rising volume of adult voices above him. "I can't hear you. Anyway, I'm God's child," he began chanting. "I can't hear you. Anyway, I'm God's child."

Glaring at Carrie, Henry finally became aware of Harry. He yanked one of his son's hands away from his ear. "Stop that noise."

The boy looked up in pain. "I don't like it when you two shout. That's not polite. Besides you told me I'm God's child." He pulled helplessly to ease Henry's hard grip as tears filled his eyes. "That's what you told me," he sobbed. "You said I'm God's child."

"That's diff . . ." Henry began, then stopped. After a pause he reached down to lift the boy to his chest. "Of course you're God's child. I'm just sharing you with Him."

"And Mama too?"

"Well . . . yes, Mama is sharing you too."

"Then why are you and Mama shouting?"

"We're not shout . . . ," snapped Henry. A long pause. "Well, son, that's a good question." He began walking again toward the cabin. After a time he held Harry so he could look at him face to face. "Here's some advice, son. When you're worried angry, keep your mouth shut so you don't say things out of your worry you don't mean."

He turned to Carrie with a softened voice. "What made you go to the Patriarchs?"

"You did. And Caleb. Solomon told me Caleb punished Betty by selling her and her boy Joe to different dealers to separate them."

"Are you sure?" Henry began, then made a helpless gesture. "It's probably true. Caleb only gets more evil with age." After many more steps. "Are you saying I'm another Caleb?"

She did not answer.

Henry stopped short and touched her face. She flinched. "Carrie, our first winter up here, you remember what I told you? I'm never Marse Henry to you; I'm Henry."

She did not answer.

"I'm still Henry."

Carrie looked him in the eye. "You could go back to being *Marse* Henry any time you want, and there isn't anything I could do. You could lie to me and sell Harry away from me, and I could never stop you. You could send me back to Tulips without Harry, and I'd have to go."

"But Carrie—"

She cut him off. "I wouldn't have any say. Marse, you *know* I wouldn't have any say."

Henry's eyes lingered at the twilight on the mountain ridges before he faced her. "Legally, you're right. But Spooks would say, even a lawyer knows there's got to be more than the law here." He turned back to the mountains again. "I don't think I've ever told you about Charity and Prudence, have I? Sisters. Friends of mine in New York. Smart and pretty, both of them. I . . . well, I loved them."

She didn't speak, her face unsoftened.

Henry kept his eyes on the deepening shadows. "They hated slavery. Would not abide it. And they said being women, being subject to men, was just another kind of slavery. I used to try to debate with them, but they were better at arguing. Besides, they were on the right side. Even I saw that after a time. I admitted it to them—just before they died, both of them. Young. After they were gone, there was no reason to stay in New York."

He turned to look at Carrie. "You're right," he said firmly. "*Legally* I could go back to being Marse Henry any time I wanted to, and you hant no law stopping me." He spoke lower and more slowly. "But I wouldn't be Henry Hollis then. You have to trust me to be me."

"You don't know how hard that is."

"I think I do."

"No, you don't. You're white. You're free. You're a man. You *can't* know how hard it is."

Henry sighed. "That's what Pru always said."

"Mama, why are you crying?" Harry tugged her hand.

"Because she needs hugging," answered Henry. He lifted the boy to Carrie's arms. "Can you give her a big hug all the way home?"

Dorinda Hollis Henderson to Crotia Hollis Warden

Collection of Lewis Hollis Warden

December 14, 1938

Dear Sister,

Yesterday I spent the whole day at Tulips to give Caroline a little rest from nursing. She needs it. She's worn out. HL is just skin and bones. Bill doesn't know what keeps him going anymore. I think it's his writing. He showed me his recollections about Marcus and Josie. I'd rather he hadn't. It brought back what I don't want to remember. Except one thing I never want to forget: the first time I told Mike about Josie and Marcus and our family. I was just a little uncertain how he

Alright, I'll start again and be honest. I half-thought Mike might just walk away. You know how ugly the talk was about Marcus and Josie. But then to have him calmly say, "Your daddy's right. Tell Marcus I'm with him if he needs help with the no 'counts in town." He kept talking a little and I realized he wasn't just saying that because of me; he had thought about this race stuff on his own, and decided it just wasn't right. I knew then I could <u>never ever</u> marry anyone else.

HL didn't suspect how I feel about remembering Josie—just as well—and asked me to read the account he wrote decades ago for his dear Robert (another terrible story it hurts to remember; such a fine young man). So I read it. Oh, Sister.

HL sanitized the White antecedents. He does say Ramses White was a "Rabelaisian character." Huh. Dionysian would be more like it—and that's just hiding behind dictionary words, according to Samuel B's stories that Father told me. Ramses came out to the frontier looking for freedom. Freedom to act like a Persian pasha, complete with his own

266

seraglio. The bull-goring that killed him wasn't a farm accident; Ramses was trying to repeat some ancient fertility ceremony, but the bull hadn't read the script. And most of the slaves he so generously emancipated (only in his will) were his own children by a half-dozen slave mothers. That's a lot for "Rabelaisian" to cover, but I didn't say a word. Not that Amos was to blame for any of that.

After I finished reading, HL began saying things about Josie that made no sense. Lucky I held my tongue, thought maybe he wasn't remembering right because of his pain. Then I realized that HL thinks Josie could not wait, and was pregnant by Marcus!

After all these years I shouldn't be so upset. Can't help it. I close my eyes and it's still so clear. Sitting at Josie's bedside while she gets weaker and weaker. Her mother crying. Father pleading with her to name the men; at least he could get them charged later with rape. She weakly shaking her head. "Rebecca Jordan" was all she would whisper. We knew what she meant. Three wives made widows, but still a rape case never close to a courthouse. And they were all white.

HL thinks Father went to the Mercantile because of Josie's burial! I started to tell him about my pistol, but it upset him so, I stopped. He's slipping away fast enough as it is. If he weren't so frail, I'd have set him down and told him straight out.

HL, here's what really happened: Our shopping was a blind. Audie gave the orders. When trouble starts from the Mercantile porch, she plugs Nace. Wilber is mine. If he runs for it, weasel that he is, Crotia gets him at the back door. And HL, your sanctimonious, Bible-quoting Miz Hawkins didn't even blink when Audie unwrapped her long "yard-goods" package. "Dammit all, Miss Audrey, don't just wound the bastards."

Sister, can you imagine HL's face if I'd told him? Poor Brother. I had no heart to do it to him. If the facts about Josie didn't kill him, realizing he doesn't know all the family stories would.

It gets worse. HL went on, and I saw he believes the whole thing started with Haeckle's busybodying, has no inkling how far ahead of everybody else Audie was. Well, I admit I'd be in the dark too if Josie hadn't told me about Solomon, sliding through the woods as usual like a phantom, seeing them, and telling Audie. You remember when Haeckle came to dump her gossip on Tulips. Everyone in the house was thunderstruck, too upset to notice Audie didn't seem concerned. I should have known right then that it was weeks past when she sat in the porch corner with Marcus and sent Solomon to Josie: Leave Tenn. and get married.

Give you credit, Sister. I haven't forgotten you had the intuition that Father somehow had proof Nace and Wilber at least helped rape Josie, and he was <u>looking</u> for a chance to do what no jury would. I wasn't sure then, I admit. But I remember—you must too—Audie's tears on the way home. "I wish I could have shot him." I won't speak for you and the back door, but if Wilber had reached into his pocket, I would have dropped him without a pang. I'd still do it, even without knowing what Father must have known. Guess the whole truth will never out.

Vengeance is the Lord's, I know. Still, I hope they're roasting hot in Hell right now. They've got to be. It still makes me shaking-furious. What is the matter with people?

For my health and Christ's sake I should get off this topic.

Will the same damnable business always be with us? When Annie was here yesterday, I told her about HL's confusion. Annie said she has confusion enough herself. Last Friday late, her Rick came all the way down from Chicago to bring home a special friend, the girl he's been writing a lot about. Looks serious.

Crotia, she's <u>Italian</u>, her parents right off the boat. She's born on this side, but still speaks it. Everything you could hope for—smart, pretty, <u>very</u> pretty, pleasant, polite—but oh boy, sure not Hollis. Jet black hair. Beautiful clear skin, but a lot darker than Josie's. You can hear it from her first words: she didn't grow up anywhere around here.

When they all got home from G. Ford, Rick took her out to see the barns. While they were gone, Annie and Garth just looked at each other dumbfounded. Garth — you know his temper — started growling he just might lock Rick out of the house for the scandal of his dark woman.

Annie told me she remembered Marcus and Josie. She remembered you calling that slimy Carl Smith a pusillanimous knave. She decided she wasn't going to have her Hollis family ashamed of her. Our timid Annie took off her apron, put on her coat and hat. When Garth asked what the hell she was doing, she said that if he locked the door, she wanted to be on the outside with Rick and his girlfriend. Garth swallowed hard a couple times, but no more door-locking talk.

On Saturday they all had a fine time getting acquainted. Annie said they honestly enjoyed talking with her. When Rick and his girl left on Sunday, Annie invited her to come back real soon. Rick promised early in the spring. I told you it looks serious. Garth even gave her a hug!

I told Annie, Father would be proud of her, and I am too. I always hoped I'd have that courage if one of mine brought home someone like Rick's girl. Annie said it all made her think a Josie even today would be a horrible fight. (She's right, of course.) She had Father's example to follow, but she wonders, where'd Father find his example to follow?

I know he told you it was those sisters he fell in love with in New York. But <u>why</u> were they so influential for him? What caused Father to be open to different ideas? Was it maybe his mother, who must have been pretty unusual, teaching her children a silent language she made up? I puzzle over this a lot, partly because I don't want to lose what Father had.

While Annie was here, I opened the mail with your note and your Mtn. Springs column, the one about the woman who keeps getting pregnant. Annie and I read it together, fresh out of the envelope. Then we looked at each other and both of us burst out laughing: Mrs. Bates! Daisy Jane Bates, for sure. Laughed ourselves silly.

Don't worry, Crotia, no one else could guess. Even we weren't positive until you put in she said her <u>four</u> books were plenty.

We liked that you didn't get all feminine coy about human bodies. How come (Annie asked this) our brothers can't talk about sex? Bill's the exception, but he's an M.D. and an atheist besides. QED. All the rest seem like they're from a different time. Why this male prudery? You remember Mama wanted us children to think roosters were hens with fancy feathers, and called bulls "boy-cows." But Father—I can still hear him describing the crazy mule dealer's fucking cane, you and little Annie right beside me, taking it all in. 19th century mother. 20th century father. So you'd expect Hollis girls to blush, and Hollis boys aren't shy. But it's usually the opposite. Have you noticed too? Tell me sometime if you can explain it.

Love from your admiring sister.

Dory

QUACHASEE
WHC

Henry swung hard. The axe cut deep. He swung again, full arm and handle length. A big maple chip flew out. Another swing, another chip. The spell of bad winter weather had seemed endless. He could study his breeding records only so long. Working hard outside satisfies a man. Felling trees helps a man think. He still argued in his head with Carrie. Not that she ever again brought up him stealing the boy, not since that terrible day last fall. He kept coming back to it nevertheless. How could she ever imagine he might revert to *Marse* Henry? Why wasn't she grateful for what he did for her?

He stretched to increase leverage, pleased he profited from sleeting days by honing the double-bladed ax so sharp he could shave with it. He brought the axe up far and fast for another solid blow. But without warning the handle was too light. *Clank, ssss, clunk.* He saw the ax head skitter through dead leaves on the ground ten feet away.

Mentally he rehearsed that *clank, ssss, clunk,* his eyes scanning nearby trees. Clank? A ricochet off that trunk where bark hung deeply gashed. Ssss? He put his finger to the bridge of his nose. It came away blood-stained. The blade just missed his face. Clunk? He noted with respect the force with which the axe head tore up the frosted ground when it landed.

A close call, Henry. It could have got you. He jammed head back on handle, returned to the barn for wedges, and soon finished felling the tree. The High Field became that much bigger. He turned to chopping off limbs and dragging them clear.

As he worked, his imagination wouldn't leave him alone. Only a slight deviation in the ricochet and he saw himself on the ground, this time not rising, like after he acted out Uncas's death. He saw Carrie searching, then running with a cry to his body. He tried to formulate some nice things people could justify saying about him. He could hear the reassurance of Pastor Berkemeier's confident, dignified funeral sermon. But what then? The Pearly Gates, which he could not picture. Reunions: his parents, Emily Jo, Riti, Pru, Isaiah.

271

In his imagination he saw Carrie closing the door and leaving the Quachasee cabin forever. But then he froze. She wouldn't leave alone or freely. She would be taken away as property, a slave, a valuable asset in his estate to be liquidated. And Harry too. That's what Pru blistered him for back in the city: a slave mother's child is a slave, even if the father is free or is white. Why hadn't he put that with Carrie and the boy before?

He narrowed the focus, as if under a magnifying glass; he could make out an unknown hand closing on Carrie's arm as she pulled Henry along. Henry put the axe down. He must concentrate. The question isn't whether he could go back to being *Marse* to Carrie. Sooner or later Carrie would realize that. The real problem is someone else being master to her and the boy. That's what needs correction. Not now, though. At this moment, there was nothing to do about it. Besides, trees need felling. He chopped on, with care.

❧

Henry waited until Carrie had cleared the dishes and Spooks had asked detailed questions about the spices Carrie used in her stew.

"I think I need your legal help, Mister Bright."

Instantly serious, Spooks turned to him sharply. "What's the trouble?"

"Nothing, right now. Is there a government reason I can't sign some paper that makes Carrie legally a free woman, and Harry free, too, I mean officially, in court?"

Carrie abruptly ceased her washing, hurriedly dried her hands, and returned to the table. Standing behind Henry's chair, her hands on his shoulders, she leaned over and kissed the top of his head, then returned to the dishes, brushing her eyes with the drying cloth.

Spooks spoke slowly, thoughtfully. "That matter is a little more complicated recently. I looked into it a couple of months ago for a client down in . . . well, a client." He paused, apparently to recall the client's question, then said, "Why don't we take things just one step at a time? First is proof you legally do own Carrie. I assume you didn't buy her from your father, so there's no bill of sale. Did your father write anything about his gift to you? Then no one can object you're giving away what you never owned in the first place."

Henry's face fell. "He told me once he would give me servants for this farm. But I decided I was happier farming by myself, and just put off that subject. When Carrie came up here, I . . . well I wasn't sure she'd stay. Father was dying. In the confusion . . . the answer is there's nothing I know of on paper about Carrie."

Spooks bit his lips. "In that case formal ownership most likely fell to Sam. I know all is not light and laughter between you two."

"Huh," huffed Carrie. "After he and Elvira made Audie Ann eat her meals alone in her own room?"

"But there shouldn't be any reason Sam wouldn't give you a letter to document the gift from your father."

"I hate asking him for a favor." Henry glanced at Carrie. "But I have to."

"Mornin, Brother." Henry tried not to be hearty in the Tulips doorway. "Lookin like I mebbe could use some hep."

Sam grunted, but did not lift his eyes from the disarray on his desk.

"Spooks bin telling me I orter hav my bus'ness in better order. So I wen' a-through bunch'a papers, but I don' have no bill'a sale or note'a transfer showin no ownership 'bout Carrie."

"No, ye don' have no papers."

"Father tole me clear he be givin me servants fer Quachasee." Henry stepped fully into the room.

"Don' sound right t'me."

"What wit' all the commotion'a goin up the Quachasee an' then thet spell, Father musta bin fergettin to writ out some kinda doc'ment. Gen'ly he was verra careful 'bout thet sorta thin."

"Yessir, the ole man, whenever he was livin, was kerfuller wit' papers nor me. He ne'er wrote no paper 'bout givin ye nary sarvants."

"Well, you write me some paper thet'll show the transfer?"

"No."

"Father said, 'I'll tell Sam the same, 'case the Lord takes me sudden.'"

"Yer mis-rememberin," Sam corrected. "The ole man ne'er tole me thet. I guess thet show he nary meant t'give Carrie nohow."

You're a bare-faced liar, Henry almost burst out. He closed the door and pushed his fists deep into his pockets. "Alright, I'll buy her from ye then."

"No."

"Name the price."

"No."

"Jes' tell me the price."

"No."

"What the hell? Ye don't . . . she ain't even here."

"Wal, now, Henry coulda took Alice Pruitt e'en if she ne'er growed her nary no tits. An then he'da got alla her pa's money when thet damn fancy trotter a-run wild an pitch Emmer's buggy inta thet tree. But, no, my smart li'l stepbro'er hed 'nother i-dear. My 'membrance is near to yesterday. Anybody could see damned well I fixt m'mine on thet nice piece'a ass. But, no, Henry always figgered the old man favored him, so Henry worked hit to git thet Carrie up the Quachasee fer hisself."

"That isn't true," Henry protested.

"Seed it wit' m' own eyes. She ain't fer sale nohow."

"Brother, you've got to believe me."

"She *ain't fer sale.* Made up m' mine long time past. Hell'll freeze o'er 'fore Henry Hollis git legal ownership. Tole my lawyerman: make up special paper sayin Carrie belong t'Sam, an she gits sold in Memphis ifen I die."

He rose and sidestepped toward the fireplace. "But I hain't agonna take her 'way from Henry *now.* Fact is, I want my li'l brother t'enjoy Carrie. To the mostest. Hain't nothin like a tasty dish'a ass t'perk up his tard soljer."

Sam broke off at Henry's tight face. "What ain't ye approvin', Brother? Betcha ye saw lotta bare ass up north."

He picked up a heavy poker to sight along it. "I ain't takin her 'way now, Henry, 'cause e'er time Carrie be yer mare, bent over, on some good, strong table say, her legs nice an wide, yer big soljer goin in an out, 'boutta ex–plode, e'er time I want ye obliged t'tell yerself, 'Henry, ye'd best stay *real, real* healthy, cause ifen y'die, Sam be right hyar in yer place.' So pound away on'er, brother, an ever time y'do hit, think'a Brother Sam doin hit." He looked up to leer at Henry while he grasped the poker with both hands.

Despite the poker, Henry gathered himself for a rush. Instead the door suddenly opened wide. His stepmother walked in, trailed by Audie Ann with her thump-and-scrape gait. The once-empty space between Sam and Henry was now clogged by the door, two women, and Audie's crutch. Audie Ann stepped close to wrap him in a long hug. Sarah exclaimed about a party at Chestnut Hill next week where many young people would gather. As she listed the most eligible guests, Sam slipped out.

Audie Ann took his arm and marched him to her shooting range to see the clever action on a new pistol. He nearly seized one of her weapons, but calmed himself enough to grasp that Sam shot dead would mean Henry hanged, unable to protect Carrie and the boy. Hot anger cooled to determined fury. He left for home, resolved never again to talk to Sam.

❧

Spooks brought fish and stayed for dinner. Afterwards, Henry said that Sam, typically greedy, would not surrender formal ownership of an asset. "But I've been telling Carrie," he went on, "that we'd better have a plan in case I'm killed or die somehow. Don't ever go running to Tulips for help, no matter what. Never. You pack some things, and the boy, and . . . and . . ."

"And what, Henry?"

"Could she come to you, Spooks?"

Bright looked uncomfortable. "In a desperate case, of course." He paused to consider. "Tennessee law, though, forbids assistance to runaways. And as a member of the Bar . . . But," he brightened, "why don't I buy her from Sam, then transfer title to you?"

Henry shook his head. "Sam won't sell."

Harry cried out from a bad dream, and Carrie went to comfort him. In her absence, Spooks spoke low to Henry. "Why're you so sure Sam won't sell?"

"He wants her at Tulips."

"But Elvira has never cared about food."

"Not Elvira. Sam wants Carrie. He wants her to . . . use her."

"Why didn't you say so sooner?"

"And frighten Carrie even more?"

Spooks leaned back in his chair. "Since Sam is . . . intransigent, there's no reason to bother with the next problem about freeing slaves."

"The next problem?"

Spooks nodded unhappily. "According to Tennessee law, should a resident owner ill-advisedly free a slave, he must post bond equal to the slave's value, and the freed slave must leave the state."

"But then . . . there'd be no point . . . in . . . freeing Carrie." Henry slowly caught up with the implications.

"Presumably that's what the legislature, in its infinite wisdom, intended."

Carrie returned with the sleepy Harry in her arms. Spooks looked at mother and child speculatively before he turned to Henry. "Mister Hollis, I ask you now, sir. Does that child look like he has white parents? I could be sure of it. Is it possible that the well-spoken woman caring for him is his nurse, Miss . . . of course! we bow to Cooper: Miss Cora Munro, charged with conveying him to his father, Henry Hollis, who might be in Canada on business? Perhaps the recent epidemic in Tennessee left the poor child motherless."

"But what if I get stopped and people don't believe me?" Carrie objected.

Spooks focused on the ceiling. "If she were stopped, Miss Cora Munro would, I presume, be outraged by such presumption. Should legal authorities detain her, however, it might be necessary for her to submit the elegant letter written by Mister Hollis attesting to her employment and instructions."

"But I don't have cash money to buy a ticket to anywhere."

"Speaking of money, Uncas," Spooks's eyes shifted to Henry, "an interesting thing happened to me recently. A client, *former* client, not a pleasant fellow, ignored the bill I sent him. Kept ignoring it. I just forgot about it. Too much irritation. Then last week he came in and paid up, in gold, no less. I've been planning to put that windfall in your care and custody, old friend, to keep safe here in your cabin, while I wait for some good investment to come up. Think you could oblige me?"

"That's so generous, just like you. But Spooks," Carrie persisted, "you move around so much, you forget: I haven't gone anywhere since I came to Tulips. I've never been to Claytown. Even with cash money, I have no idea how to get up north, let alone Canada."

"Now my friend, Henry, here," Spooks spoke to the door, "sometimes gets restless, has been thinking of looking for a bigger farm in Canada;

he tires of heat. I half remember he asked me to find out about the best route to Canada. I intend to inquire, and write out directions for him. It is possible he might show them to other people. I have no control of that."

"It'd be so risky."

"Yes, it would be." Spooks turned to Carrie. "Would Tulips be better?"

She shuddered. "But anyone would see that a woman dressed like this," Carrie brushed at dirt on her skirt, "isn't a rich child's nurse."

Caught up short, Spooks sighed. "You're right. Ahh, the treacherous mysteries of women's fashion."

Silence of the stymied, until Carrie exclaimed, "Audie Ann."

"What about Audie Ann?" asked Henry.

"She'd help get some proper dresses, I think. Spooks, you can carry my note to her, please."

❧

In several months, the big trunk in the corner held a new bag stuffed with several new dresses too fancy for a farm wife, too plain for a wealthy city woman. Probably just about right for a woman who cared for a wealthy family's child.

On a subsequent trip, Spooks assured his hosts that he had a system to stay current with travel advice. "Once you get to the new cars, they say traveling's a lot easier. I hear they plan to extend the rails from Chattanooga all the way up to Elizabethton."

He bought an immigrant guide book, complete with maps, including basic instructions for those unversed in American railroad travel, and inscribed the fly leaf, "For your trip, Henry." Carrie read until she memorized it, just as she memorized the revised itineraries he brought. She thought she was ready if she ever needed to pull the small bag of gold coins from behind the loose rock in the chimney.

❧

"Mister Spooks, I know the names of all the patriarchs." Harry and Spooks idled on the porch out of the cook's way.

"Which patriarchs, Master Harry?"

"Those *big* trees on the mountain. Mama likes to go up there. She says it's a lot easier now that I can walk the whole way myself. We even take a basket with food. Mama says she feels closer to God up there. She likes Isaac best. Sometimes Papa comes too."

"And what does Papa do there?"

"Jus' talks. And gives Mama hugs. Look at this, Mister Spooks." Harry offered a paper with a line of his painstakingly-printed numbers:

4 9 16 25 36 49 64 81 100 121 144 169 196

Spooks scanned the sheet. "Aha. You've been doing squares, haven't you?"

"But look how they get bigger."

"Yessir. By consecutive odd numbers. Curious, isn't it?"

Harry nodded.

"Now Master Harry, can you think of a number that can only be divided by itself?"

The boy hardly paused. "One hundred and one."

"That's pretty fast. How about numbers before that?"

"Only divided by itself? Two, three, five, seven, eleven, thirteen, seventeen, nineteen, twenty-three, twenty, ah, nine . . ."

"Alright, alright," laughed Spooks. "I guess my question was too easy. What's the *biggest* number you can think of that can only be divided by itself?" He saw Carrie coming out from the hearth, a stirring spoon still in her hand. "You think about that while I talk to your mother."

"You're doing numbers?" Carrie spoke in a low voice. "Spooks, I'm defeated. Sending him to a Boston school would be like sending him to China. I could not endure it. But he needs a teacher."

"Next time I come, I have a note to myself to bring up a bigger dictionary and a geometry book. Maybe a medical book with pictures." Spooks leaned back in his chair as his eyes ran over the rafters. "I think the best teacher I ever knew," he mused, "never 'taught' me a thing. He only asked questions. Questions about everything. And not only questions he knew the answer to. Turns out, I was well ahead of my classmates when I showed up at the college. You can ask questions, Carrie."

"Nine hundred ninety-one, Mr. Spooks, but there are bigger ones, too," said Harry, moving inside and toward the table. "I'm hungry."

Plowing with Greek, My Life
HL Hollis

My brother Marcus stays so in my mind, I cannot easily leave off writing about him. Laughter is what I chiefly recall, which made the Josie tragedy all the more affecting. We older children remember a long list of practical jokes he dreamed up, ingenious and elaborate stunts. Of his inspirations, the most outstanding was one Bill christened the Black Cat Caper, an escapade which still makes me smile—though I concede that, cat-like, it resolutely evaded direction and control.

As a birthday gift, Marcus received a miniature printing set. With this he produced ephemera to pin up through the house. CORPSES BOUGHT. MIDNIGHT ONLY. HELP NEEDY SCIENCE decorated Bill's door. THIS PROPERTY FOR SALE BY NEIGHBOR Marcus affixed to the door of Dory's and Crotia's room.

By happy inspiration he once ran off many copies of a handbill posted on a moonless night throughout Ginners Ford. (Should you be curious as a cat, search Tulips for the copy of *Alice in Wonderland*, into which one of the handbills is folded at the illustration of the Cheshire Cat.)

WANTED TO BUY

BLACK CATS

The handbill's headline parades over explanatory text something as follows: The Universally recognized *Pheline, Tabbi & Perr Inc.* of Atlanta, Georgia, USA, having recently completed all arrangements to produce black cats for fur commercially in Mesopotamia, MUST acquire stock, to wit, <u>BLACK CATS</u>. Consequent to a unique similarity in climate with Mesopotamia, east Tennessee mountains are the ONLY area in America from which the cats can originate. Accordingly, *PT&P*'s Supervising Agent, Mr. A. Kanine, will disembark in Ginners Ford from the 1:28 cars on such and such a Saturday (Scratch on your calendars!). He will be authorized and prepared to pay out immediate CASH ($ On the Spot!) for Black

Cats, a special bonus to the seller offering the most quantity of quality. Proffered cats must be healthy, their BLACK fur in excellent condition, tendered one to a crate. Crates must measure (in each of three directions) ONE CUBIT, the Mesopotamian standard. Above all, cats must be BLACK, with NO evidence of any other color. [A price schedule at the handbill's bottom—Toms, Pregnant, Yearlings, Unweened Kittens, etc.—completed this modest proposal.]

Some smiles we anticipated. Gales of laughter we hoped for. Recognition of those clever Hollis boys we dreamed of. All were dreams, vain dreams.

The very morning the sun first shone on the posted handbills, Dr. Payne quarantined Tulips. He suspected Baby Lowe had contracted a contagious disease. (N.B. I must ask Bill if he remembers what false alarm Dr. Payne sounded.) Readers can imagine our crestfallen faces when, finally released from quarantine, we were smugly informed by town chums we had missed the crucial first rungs on the ladder to unimaginable wealth. A far cry from admiring recognition, gales of laughter, or smiles.

In point of fact, during our absence the cat handbill created an electrifying effect where no one went hungry but many jingled little in their pockets. Now a cash crop lurked in every barn, prowled every alley. A novel line of commerce sprang up, with innovative aspirants. Even desiccated old maids cast disdainful eyes on tawny pets, but mercilessly shooed black mousers out the door at sunset and, in anticipation of multiplying profits, listened hopefully for night-prowling toms.

Tearful juvenile reports of catnapping deluged Sheriff Bascombe. Some children countered conscience and cupidity, torn between an oft-stroked pet and the temptation to convert Tabby into candy via Cat Buyer Kanine. Other children, long the affectionate masters of cats every color but black, struggled with the temptation to envy.

Canny townspeople descended on unsuspecting farmers in distant valleys, offering as much as a nickel for black cats. They counted as pittance against profit the expense of maintaining their stock until Buyer Kanine's arrival. Better-informed farmers viewed cats, at least black ones, like innkeepers greeting rich travelers, and offered bowls of fresh milk to fatten feral felines, thickening their fur.

Alarmed by the mischief he wrought, Marcus patrolled town, suggesting to some the handbill was a swindle, intimating to others the company was a fraud, advising still others the agent was a phantom. But Marcus preached as a prophet in his own country.

He grew sufficiently apprehensive that he confessed the Black Cat Caper to Father (and necessarily to Judge Bright, fortuitously visiting then). Marcus shamed his fellow conspirators, Bill and me, to accompany him for what I could call a cat-harsis. Given an old man's memory, I cannot produce a near-stenographic report, but to the best of my recollection, the proceedings evolved as follows.

As spokesman, Marcus gave a detailed confession. In point of fact I thought honesty did not quite require his confession be so complete—at least when he specified my height as crucial to reach high for nailing handbills. Guilty, we awaited sentencing.

Instead of meting out punishment, however, Father posed a question, one, moreover, we never anticipated: "What counts as a black cat?"

Precisely what Marcus stammered I don't recall. Most likely, possessing black fur.

"What about a mixed cat, some black fur and some white?" Father persisted.

Marcus referred to the handbill: all fur had to be black.

"But," objected Father, "how about a black cat like the one in the barn, HL's favorite, Eloise, black except just one white paw?"

Marcus anticipated some trap in the offing, but plunged heedlessly ahead. "No, a white paw in a black cat disqualifies it from being a black cat."

More intently now, Father pressed him further. "How about a hypothetical kitten in Eloise's litter; let's say the kitten is all black, no white paw. Do we then have your black cat?"

Bill, budding scientist, was just learning a little genetics and could not resist. "No. Somewhere down the line of litters that white paw will show up. So the kitten can't qualify as black. The book I'm reading says it's a kind of pollution in the genetic pool."

"Pollution!" Father burst out. He turned to Bright. "We can't even talk about cats without floundering on black and pollution." He crashed a hand down on a side table not reinforced for that. "We're all still in Doc Sexton's barn. The wretched business will outlive us," he motioned to us boys, "and them too." He rose in his agitation and seemed to gather himself to continue.

But a calm Judge Bright intervened swiftly. "Old friend, Doc Sexton lives only if we allow it. Take a seat, please, while I proceed with cross examination."

Perhaps ten or fifteen seconds. But in that brief interval, words, topic, mood shifted, and shifted again, far too fast for me to understand; that is, I followed, but I did not see where we were going. It has taken me years to tease out different strands, and I still can't unravel them to my satisfaction. First of course was the cat confession, traumatic enough. But just below the surface, something (cats? pollution? Doc Sexton? Hollis pride? some unknown?) triggered in Father a kind of response we almost never witnessed, but the Judge comprehended. And rebuked. Then there was Judge Bright, drawing on his courtroom experience, asserting control and for some reason directing the proceedings in a different direction.

"Marcus," asked the Judge, "do you know if the Mercantile has seen any trade in colorant, say, lampblack, these days?"

The question took us aback because only the day before, Jimmy Brixton, one of our cronies who worked after school stocking at the Mercantile, complained about his mother's blows over how he had dirtied his good shirt, the result actually not of carelessness but of being sent to confirm in the most remote Mercantile storage that they were sold out of lampblack. This we reported to the Judge.

He nodded and threw an aside at Bill. "As a budding scientist, you should investigate how lampblack can offset genes. And remind me later, please, that you surely need a less tendentious book on genetics." Then, without hurry, but also without pause, he interrogated the three of us: did any Hollis anticipate pecuniary gain in this escapade? We boys stoutly (and truthfully) denied any prospect—Bill adding, it didn't seem fair when chronic idlers on the Mercantile porch at first promised to pay immediately half the company's advertised rate for cats caught. But, on delivery, they refused to pay more than a dime a head, take it or leave it. A "rotten, dirty swindle," was Bill's phrase.

"Duplicitous is perhaps a more elegant characterization, Bill," answered the Judge. "But, gentlemen, we must not stray from an essential point: the buyers are guaranteed to lose every single dime they paid out?"

At assent from each of us, the Judge sighed ominously, and turned with grave face to Father. "Our laws against fraud require a lengthy stay in unpleasant prisons. This Black Cat Case could well attract lawyers whose fees can bankrupt mountain farmers."

At this news, Bill and Marcus looked pretty fragile; I thought I kept a pretty good face, but, I grant you, I had no mirror. Father nodded solemnly as the Judge proceeded. "Complications abound here, all issuing from apparently *deliberate handbill fraud.*" He looked at each of us in turn, square in the eye.

"Antecedent to all these matters, however, is the question that shall occupy me all the way home." He paused. Silence continued interminably. (When I mentioned this to Bill on a recent visit, his memory coincided with mine. "Damn near wet my pants.")

Finally the Judge sighed deeply as he turned back to Father. "Old Friend, why did neither of us think of something half as clever when we were boys?" Then his face betrayed him. "Could there be sweeter justice than all those dimes squandered by the Mercantile loafers?"

He and Father began laughing so hard they wiped their eyes repeatedly. We pieced together between the Judge's renewed spasms of laughter that no prankster could be liable for the avaricious credulity of the willfully ignorant. Between wheezes the Judge managed to gasp, "I wonder if handbills will appear stating the whole thing a comical invention."

That very night a FRAUD!! handbill went up in the darkened town, nailed very high.

Too late. Marcus had become a cat Cassandra. The more strongly he warned, the more tenaciously cat entrepreneurs clung to their fur futures. They indignantly tore down even the highest FRAUD!! warnings as a plot to depress demand long enough for the rich bastards in town to make a killing.

At last came the Saturday appointed. Ford Street in front of the station filled with sellers, easily identifiable by cubital crates, though a Tennessee "cubit" turned out to be an imprecise measure. Sellers could be identified by scratches on hands and arms, and by, in certain instances, a dusky skin tone.

The 1:28 arrived. Amid the locomotive's hissings and clamor a lone passenger swung down and reached up for his bags. The 1:28 departed. The solitary passenger, with two heavy drummer's cases, emerged from the cloud of steam. At last. The crowd, solidly four people deep, quickly surrounded him.

He was not, however, Kanine. He said. The crowd knew better than to be misled by such persiflage. Jostled about, the presumed Kanine claimed his name was Klopp. Kenneth Klopp, he persisted. No, not Kanine. Always Klopp, Kenneth, baptized Kenneth Klopp, K-l-o-double-p, Klopp.

Terrified by the crowd, he insisted he hated cats, in particular black cats, never bought a cat his whole life, never so much as petted black cats. He plead ignorance of cubits equalling his aversion to cats, asserted he was merely a shoe drummer from Cincinnati, not Atlanta, abjectly confessed he drew this territory because of an inferior sales record—for shoes, not cats. He got off in Ginners Ford only because he slept through his intended stop at Claytown, which he would never do again, though he meant no reflection on this lovely town.

Notwithstanding his loudest protests, his humble appeals, his glistening forehead, the close-pressed crowd compelled him to open his cases right there on the platform. Shoe samples, shoe catalogs, soiled collars and drawers, plus a near empty bottle of rotgut that went rolling aimlessly and unretrieved along the platform. No bulging bags of coin, no thick bundles of bills. No money whatsoever. Only then were skeptics, most of them, satisfied. Not Mr. A. Kanine.

The frustrated crowd then turned to, or on, Station Agent Quincy Adams Hower. Quince was a quick-thinking agent. As the station house filled with people, he swiftly dropped into place the thick steel rods angling from floor to his stout office door. He answered inquiries only from behind the heavy grill at his counter window.

He pointed out the 1:28 had arrived. It dropped one passenger, two cases. The 1:28 had now departed. No other cars were scheduled for the day. Therefore, Quince reasoned, no other passengers could arrive this day. Maybe, Quince speculated, yer Kanine dint come 'cause he ain't ne'er comin, 'cause he don' ex-ist. Quince slid the frosted glass down, swung an even heavier interior grill into place and clicked its stout locks, one, two, three, four.

Quince's words sank in only slowly, given certain thick heads leading the crowd and better heads too far back to hear well. But finally, with a whoosh, the Great Cat Bubble deflated. (I heard tell it was last seen, dragged by a mangy dog, along the road toward Seymour.)

Loud then were lamentations in Zion. Bitter were tears in Gilead. Disappointed sellers threw open their crates summarily, entertaining town dogs. One enraged vendor imprudently emptied his crates of premium black cats over a half-full rain barrel. When kind-hearted spectators fished furious felines from the barrel, the water was black but the cats sopping messes of multihued fur.

Another fellow was particularly slow to grasp the unwelcome intelligence, consequent to hoisting a jug too enthusiastically while waiting for the 1:28. Once he comprehended the situation (to the extent his fevered brain allowed), he angrily drove his wagon not-quite-straight into the river, liquidating his substantial inventory. A hole at ford's edge upset the wagon. Crates and felines floated off. Outraged yowls slowly receded downstream.

Several Hollis boys were later hailed in the *Herald* as modest heroes for quick-wittedly pulling the drunken driver to safety. That brief journalistic notice was the solitary public record of the Black Cat Caper. What Ginners Ford resident would enjoy noising abroad the gullibility or attempted fraud revealed there?

In the aftermath, the Mercantile crowd's exploitation of the town's boys came to light. Humiliated (and poorer, for they invested a great many dimes beyond recovery), they converted embarrassment to fury, swearing to unmask the handbill villain. Surmise and suspicion substituted for substance; consensus connected Cat and Culprit with Hollis. Since the worst possible denigration of a man had to do with race, certain in the Mercantile porch crowd could never mention "Hollis" without preceding it with "nigger-lovin."

We Hollises generally ignored this as the sort of response one should anticipate from porch denizens. In retrospect, though, I am puzzled, because compared to our neighbors, we sought no more (or less) contact with Negroes in our area, and all this occurred before Marcus and Josie. So I conclude raw feelings about the Black Cat Caper explain the epithet.

Dory has read this now, and, ever judicious, cautions me of confusing my own awareness with origin; the epithet may have been common long before I first heard it. That's theoretically possible, but I remain impressed by the cat moguls' outrage, strong enough that Father issued orders: for the time being no Hollis goes to town unless three Hollises go to town together.

Storms do blow over, however gradually. In this case, though, conversations about black cats evaporated literally overnight. Saunders Ledley, bank vice-president, scion of the bank founder, slipped away unnoticed on a dark and stormy night, accompanied by his secretary, a much younger woman of enticing eyes and voluptuous figure. Each of the travelers carried a large valise, one containing the bank's cash, the other, new tropical-weight clothes. Saunders neglected to leave word how his wife might reach him.

I must not conclude without mentioning the one person in town who intuited the truth of the Black Cat Caper from whisker to tail. He was Gerhardt Schmidt, the cabinetmaker. Soon after the cat handbill appeared, Schmidt advertised his shop by hanging outside a model cage, cubitally cubical, a masterpiece of ornate woodworking. *Die Schwartze Katze* was carved on its door.

When Marcus admired his craftsmanship, Schmidt whipped out a sharp chisel and with deft strokes carved a simple tulip above the lettering. He finished with a wink at Marcus. Marcus protested the implication, but Schmidt jovially overrode him. Vy, he inquired cheerfully, do not Hollises any cages order? Vy? Because Hollises know in Katzen no market is. Vy do dey dis know? Ve can guess, ya wohl. Some months later, Schmidt presented the model cage to Marcus in gratitude, he said, for the business and the entertainment provided him by the Mesopotamian venture. (That cage has since diverted and fascinated several generations of children, so the hoax tale twitched a long tail.)

Herr Schmidt, as my father always addressed him, was a strange and wonderful bird in the Ginners Ford aviary (to soar above cats for a moment). He somehow became separated from a larger migration, that of the "Forty-Eighters," meaning, my father explained, refugees from a German revolution crushed in that year. His fractured English supplied much material for our dinner entertainment. Somehow he wound up in Ginners Ford, a brilliant eccentric woodworker. If demand sometimes slackened, perhaps because of his notoriety for fashioning beautiful pieces closer to his inner light than customer specifications, he tinkered skillfully with nearly anything mechanical. A good ding zat to Hollises vas, for

Herr Schmidt became the Tulips horologist, the only one Father allowed to nurse our tall clock.

He did not reminisce publicly about his military experience, I suspect because he left to fight in the Union rather than Confederate army. He read widely in literature not otherwise found in Ginners Ford, never losing an insurrectionist spirit. He was the most eloquent, outspoken, and principled critic of social institutions I ever knew in person.

I include this excessive detail because it assists, I believe, in characterizing my father. Friends are an important index to a man, and Gerhardt Schmidt was someone with whom Father manifestly enjoyed talking. My own reaction, I confess, was slightly ambivalent. Schmidt's intelligence and manual dexterity awed me, but in point of fact I found conversation with him unnerving. When I spoke he studied me so quizzically that somehow I felt I was a jigsaw piece he sought to fit into the puzzle.

Nevertheless as a boy I visited him whenever we went to town, eager to hear him hold forth. His shop occupied a building not far from the livery barn. One day a commotion outside interrupted our conversation. From Schmidt's door we witnessed a fight under way at the barn, unremarkable among those reprobates. Herr Schmidt made some observation. I could not understand his German, but his tone needed no translation. I replied that the fight looked to be a bloody one. Herr Schmidt nodded. "Ven your vadder dere vit de dark woman vas . . ." He grimaced and shook his head.

"Audie Ann?" I burst out. Herr Schmidt looked at me sharply, and I saw first denial, then, perhaps, dismay. "Dis, you not know?"

My "no" I wanted to retract instantly, for instead of prompting him to say more, it made him shake his head. "Nein? Den ist not my blace you to tell." He abruptly abandoned the door for workbench and spokeshave, his now stony face forbidding all questions.

That evening at supper, I brought up the fight, risking Mama's reprimand for my proximity. Collecting my resolve, I turned to Father. "Herr Schmidt said you might know from personal experience something about fighting there."

Father lifted his eyebrows high, then sought Dory's attention. Especially in her late girlhood, she often found it trying to be patient with Mama. I sometimes thought Father occupied Dory to ease contentiousness between mother and daughter. In any event, father and daughter enjoyed remarkable compatibility. Father turned to Dory. "Your Honor," he boomed with a public-speaking voice, "plaintiff hereby petitions for a summary judgment: alleged fighting at the livery barn would constitute a case of such poor judgment as to be summarily ruled unimaginable for a Hollis."

In a similar voice, without missing a beat, Dory announced her ruling. "Very poor judgment. Mister Hollis would have had to be drunk." Since it was widely known that Father accepted only one companionable sip of whatever mountain brew offered him, an inebriated Henry Hollis exceeded imagination. Allegations of his livery barn fighting—and my hopes of solving Herr Schmidt's small mystery—were thus out of order.

Dory's response prompted Marcus to describe an encounter (what was rightly known as a licker scrape). Two men, their hostility spurred by poor liquor, had progressed so in their cups that they could remain upright only by clutching each other in a clumsy dance.

That brought to Father's memory an encounter between adversaries who had previously sampled Wade Slater's white mule with excessive indulgence. One of them went for his knife, but discovered he had lost it. As substitute he pulled off his belt. Massive buckle and decorative metal studs made it capable of disfiguring lacerations. Denied customary reinforcement, however, crucial trouser buttons failed catastrophically. His pants slithered ingloriously toward his ankles.

"But then everyone could see his *underthings*!" exclaimed little Annie, just learning to be conscious of her appearance.

"If he wore any," Dory interjected before Mama could issue her usual caution.

Grinning broadly at his daughters, Father resumed his narrative. One hand to hold up half-mast pants left the combatant only one hand for both defense and offense. He elected to kick free of his impediment. But in his kicking he lost his balance, tripped, and pitched head-first onto a rock harder than his skull.

Father turned to Dory. "He *did* wear drawers." Long pause. "But they needed mending badly." He shifted to Annie. "And they hadn't been washed for too long."

Over her wrinkled nose and loud "Eww," Father continued. The belt-threatened pugilist meanwhile tried to escape on a nearby nag, but, befuddled, lost the reins. His steed, rudderless yet urged into motion by hard kicks, bolted inside for its stall. The barn door lintel swept rider off into dust and ordure.

While both combatants were supine, unresponsive to many buckets of cold water, wags nailed belt to one side of the barn door, pants to the other, and reins to the lintel.

My father told that story, I now suspect, to steer us away from the disturbing side of livery barn fights that I gradually became aware of through tales told in undertones by older boys during school recess. Usurping church and court, barn loafers sometimes arrogated prurient oversight of others' behavior.

A couple cohabiting without benefit of clergy was at particular risk should they incautiously pass. The man might be pulled down for a disfiguring beating and the woman dragged into the barn to have her clothes torn off, or far worse. Ordinarily I lament the Passing of the Old Order, but the livery's demise at the hands, or wheels, of the automobile distresses me not one whit.

QUACHASEE
WHC

Prideful of their son's gifts, Henry and Carrie planned to abandon their usual seclusion, at least for a few hours. All three would go down the valley to show off Harry's reading to Lilly and Audie Ann. Go first to the Lone Barn, isolated in a field a half mile from Tulips. With Uncas-like stealth, Henry would then slip into the kitchen house. He could bring Lilly and Audie Ann to the barn to visit with Carrie and Harry while he went on for supplies from Ginners Ford.

Their planning was wasted. In the Tulips kitchen, Henry learned that Elvira was gone to Knoxville, Sam in tow; she supervised her sister nursing an ailing uncle. With the way now clear, Carrie brought the boy openly to the kitchen, where Lilly made him near sick on cake. Audie Ann came out to hug her godson, speaking excitedly around him with her hands.

Henry hitched Earl to the wagon he kept at the Lone Barn. As he passed Tulips, Carrie waved him down. She wanted to add three more items to his list. As she began to dictate, she remembered still another. "Just c'mon with me," he ordered brusquely. He pointed to the seat beside him. "We'll get through faster."

Carrie hesitated. "That's not a good—"

Henry cut her off. "It'll be all right this once. Jump up."

Carrie hesitated. Henry insisted. She turned and rushed back to the house, calling over her shoulder, "Be right there." Henry fumed mightily to Earl, even though Carrie soon came running out. Henry felt so put upon that he flicked reins before she was fully in her seat. Seeing Audie Ann's shawl in Carrie's lap, Henry could not resist unkind comments about female vanity, abuse she absorbed silently.

As they passed the old abandoned mill on the outskirts of town she pleaded, "Henry, stop just a minute, so I can climb into the back. There's plenty of straw to sit on."

Still in surly humor, Henry curtly refused, extending an arm to keep her on the bench. "Stay right here. Nothin to worry about. We'll be fine."

As they turned into Ford Street, though, Mrs. Burkhart and her cousin Gertie began to acknowledge his salute, then saw Carrie clearly and turned their heads. "Ole biddies," muttered Henry.

The usual group of idlers in front of the livery barn inspected them as they approached. Sinister laughs and hog calls erupted as Henry's wagon came close. A falsetto voice sang out. Nigger-lover-nigger-lover-nigger-lover.

Henry pulled Earl to a sharp stop. He climbed off the wagon deliberately, tied the mule to a post in no hurry, then turned to face the growing crowd. "Gentlemen, who's singing that poor tune?"

"Me, you goddamn poacher." Arkwright thrust his way to the front.

"Ahh. The shagnasty Arkwright. Should'a knowed that high, squeaky voice. But Arkwright, yer lookin kinda weasly ain't ye? Ye look to pindling along."

"I'm feelin fine, Hollis, so good I'm a-gonna do what I had orter done up thet mountain. An then my boys ken use yer bitch fer enertainmen in the barn." He turned to grin at those behind him. "She a-gonna be my specialest treat fer ye, boys."

Henry was mock concern. "Arkwright, ye bin sickly? Ye lookin t'me like ye on the down go. Mebbe ye got thin blood?"

Arkwright moved aggressively forward. Several men began to follow him, but others blocked them. "Fair fight, one on one."

The crowd spread out as every man sought an unobstructed view to assess impending action.

"Thet Arkwright, he no taller then the next man, but he powerful burly. An dog-mean."

"An touchous, seem like. An fightified."

"Yessir, he all fire an tow. He have weight so he good to overbear. But he hard-favored, I believe."

"He as hard favored as his pappy, but he'a nat'ral fighter, an he good to mean. Fortnight past he drug a man clean acrost t'yard."

"Drug acrost t'yard? Don' sound like too turrible."

"Drug by his *year*. Tore hit clear off."

"O'er near Clayton, he jes gouge out a man's eye. Right fronta' the man's ole lady."

"Ark shouldn't a done thet nohow. Not right fronta' the man's woman."

"Not the fers time neither."

"Skinny 'un like thet Hollis feller don' have hardly no chance agin a body built like Arkwright."

"Nary no chance a'tall. He shoulda kept drivin. Ole Ark's gonna jounce thet fella, beat him to a pulp fer sure."

"Feller like thet got to have a lotta sand t'stan upta Arkwright."

"Don' take sand; hit take stupid."

"Jest keep in mine thet I git fers turn on thet nice piece sittin 'pon the wagon."

"Boys, this serious. I bin watchin ole Ark faut fer a long spell, an everwhen he spit his 'baccy plug out like thet, he mad. An he gonna take thet mad out dreckly on t'other fella. Name 'a Hollis, y'say?"

"Hollis *was* his name."

"Somebody better fine the doctorman now so he git hyar in time."

"We agonna need us a buryin'man, not no doctorman."

"Girl looks white ta'me. Yer mistook 'bout who go firs. Hits me, right hyar."

"Hot damn. Evern Ark charges right off wit' thet kinda roar, he know he got his man, an thar ain't no stoppin 'im. Hollis'l be maimed soon 'nuf."

"I'm not in no line ahind ye fer thet piece. I dun tole ye: nigger er white, I firs on'er, an ye know hit."

"Thet's the end'a hit, boys. We seen this afore a bunch'a times. Now Ole Ark'll git his man down an thet's . . ."

"Jes like I bin a-thinkin. Them as has longer arm, they ken stay clear an mess up Ark's nose."

"Watch out, Ark, ye don' a-wanna try thet."

"Lordy. Ark's nose. It stuck-pig bleedin."

"*Two* stuck-pig, look like. He maybe have trouble seein, being thet he bleedin so."

"Ole Ark's tough. Thet Hollis were jes' lucky oncet. Ark'll make him regretfulest he start this ever."

"Seem t'me Ark's a mite dobbly."

"Hollis were lucky, fer sure, 'least right off, but Ark ain't fightin smart now."

"C'mon, Ark."

"Ark ain't pullin no knife, is he?"

"Cain't be no knife. They fittin fist an skull, ain't they?"

"Ark, whar ye g'win?"

"What'd I tell ye? Yer face bleedin so bad ye cain't see nothin. Yer righ' set to get run inta thet tree. "

"His haid din' hurt thet tree none."

"Not Ark's. His haid too hard to think straight, seem like."

"Guess thet's hit. Might's wail go do sumpin else."

"She-it. I woulda had some barn fun wit' thet piece."

"Yer soundin jes' like ole Ark. He evern woulda, coulda."

"Seem t'me thet tree joggle jes a mite when Ark's haid hit."

"I sees thet too. Coupla leafs dropt. He movin?"

"Huh. Not doodley squat."

"Wal, thet's done o'er an finish."

"Boys, Ark's bad off. He need someun t'doctor him up. Hep me git 'im inside."

Henry reached down, picked a knife from Arkwright's limp hand and tossed it in the dirt at onlookers' feet. With a single jerk he untied Earl. He jumped to his seat wagon, nodded a brisk salute to Herr Schmidt at his shop door with a large framer's chisel in each hand, and drove back up the street at a fast trot.

As they passed Mrs. Burkhart he raised his hat. When she did not acknowledge him, he added a wave. "Isaiah was right about one thing."

"What're you talking about?" asked Carrie.

"Isaiah Choker. My friend in New York. He told me I was going to get murdered some dark night if I didn't take lessons to protect myself, lessons from Black Jim at The Speared Fish."

"Speared . . . what? You're not talking right. Arkwright get you in the head?"

"Not hard. I never wrote home about The Speared Fish. For good reason. A low dive down at the docks on the river. Black Jim kept order. The Fish catered mostly to sailors and fishermen. Tough crowd.

Black Jim said, always go for the nose. Everything you have. On the nose. But funny I never needed his lessons until I'm back in Tennessee."

As they again passed the abandoned mill, she motioned to his bloody knuckles. "Hurt bad?"

"Most of the blood is his." Henry's euphoria was wearing off fast as he shook his hand to loosen muscles. "What's hurt bad is pride in my judgment. That was a damn-fool thing to do. You were right. I should never have put you in such danger."

"Me! He wanted to kill you."

"Yes, he did," Henry agreed quietly.

"You shouldn't fight with your back to me. Fight from the side."

Henry puzzled. "The side?"

"The way you stood I couldn't have gotten him until you were down, hurt bad or dead."

"And what would you do then?"

Carrie eased back the shawl in her lap just enough to show her right hand's grip on a long-barreled pistol.

"Audie Ann's?"

"Um-hmm."

"So that's why you ran back in before we left."

"You sure were grumpy."

"Jury wouldn't take five minutes if you shot Arkwright, you know."

"You think I'd care about that if he'd killed you?"

Despite Carrie's pleas, once they reached Tulips he returned alone to Ginners Ford for their supplies, though with one of Audie Ann's pistols in his belt. As he promised, he detoured to avoid the livery barn, but news of his earlier appearance had sped down the street. He bought in near silence, oversaw a very nervous store boy finish loading, and drove away without delay.

His purchases considerably exceeded what Earl could carry. They stayed the night in the Lone Barn, then returned to the farm early the next morning. Henry unpacked Earl there and, pistol still in his belt, left for the second load.

In deepening twilight he made his way back up the valley with Earl. Fatigued, his eyes down to pick his footing, he was very late seeing the figure in a long dark coat slip out from behind a tree to block the way. Henry leapt at the man's throat with both hands. The figure stumbled back with a muffled cry. Earl's shying gave Henry a moment of cover, but only a moment. Another figure behind him closed with a club. Collapsing on the trail before all went black, he barely felt the steel edge at his throat.

❧

As dusk became dark, a worried Carrie gave the boy his supper, and read to him. After putting him to bed, she went outside, her eyes and ears straining for any sign of Henry leading the mule. The sliver of rising moon decided her. She went in, lit a lantern, roused Harry. Flickering lantern in one hand, and the sleepy, stumbling boy's hand in the other, she started down the trail.

"Don't hurt my arm, Mama," Harry protested as she hurried him over a rough patch of rock and root. The lantern made weird shadows in the woods. Ominous noises sounded from the sides of the valley. A terrifying apparition loomed out of the darkness. Earl on his leisurely amble home. Convinced now something terrible had happened, Carrie caught his dragging lead rope, tied him to a tree, and scrambled on, occasionally putting down the lantern to lift Harry over rough spots, confusing creek and path so repeatedly her skirt hem became waterlogged.

She came upon Henry almost before she distinguished the sprawl on the ground. He lay in such a pool of blood she thought of butchering days.

"What happened to Papa?"

"I guess he hurt himself, Harry. You need to sit over there to keep out of the way. Here, I'll put the lantern right beside you, while I help Papa."

Her ear to his chest, she could hear his heart faintly. Tearing at her skirt, she made swabs she soaked in the creek to clean the terrifying gash at his throat. More torn strips made bandages to staunch the oozing blood. She was startled by Harry's voice. "Will Papa die and go to heaven?"

"He won't if I can help him."

"Good. You help him, Mama."

She worked on. Harry fell asleep. The moon sliver disappeared. The lantern hissed, went out. Henry's skin felt cold. Carrie lay down in the bloody leaves beside him and tried to give his body her warmth.

At first light, she was not certain she heard his heartbeat. She changed the blood-soaked bandages and, with steadily stronger light decided he lived still, but she wanted to scream. She could not move his body and support his head at the same time; yet, unless she held his head when she moved him, her bandages at his neck quickly showed bright red. His breathing seemed slower. Mercifully, Harry slept on. Terrified that Henry was slipping away, she knelt beside him. Better in the night, because then she could believe that when light came she could do something. When the light came it showed only her helplessness.

Carrie heard Harry stir and begin to play a game with himself in a soft voice. "Hello, Mr. Spooks. I've been praying you would come."

Carrie hardly glanced up. "That's right, Harry. You say your morning prayer."

"We have a big problem with Papa."

Carrie spoke as she untied a bandage. "Harry, you just sit right there while I work on Papa's bandages."

"I think Mama and God need help. And I don't know what can help so I'm worried. Can you do something for Papa? He's leaking way too much blood."

"Harry, you just play right there, alright?" Bent over Henry, Carrie saw boots step close beside her, heard a familiar voice. "Hello, Master Harry." A hand on her shoulder. "What happened?"

She told Spooks what she knew, with an abrupt warning when he began moving Henry. He felt at the bandages silently, glancing at Carrie. "Don't stand up in front of the boy," he advised in a low tone, "you'll scare him half to death. Take him home for some food and get washed up. Bring back clean bandages and a sharp needle with the finest thread you have. You can sew the cut closed. I once saw Doc McCaffee sew up a gashed cow. It was just like sewing cloth. "

"What if Henry dies while I'm gone?" Carrie whispered around the knot in her throat.

Spooks spoke gently. "Unless he's conscious, it makes no difference. If he does die, I won't wait here. I'll come up immediately. You'll need a head start to get away."

"I can't leave him," she protested.

"Remember what he told you so many times."

"Yes, but—"

"Mama, aren't you hungry? I am." Her son's needs decided her. She took the boy's hand and started up the trail. After they reached Earl, they moved much faster, Harry riding the mule's pack.

"You're all bloody, Mama," Harry announced. She nodded without looking down; she could feel the stiff cakes of blood, mud and forest floor dried to her skirt as she walked.

At the cabin, she put food out for Harry, and unloaded Earl, leaving the supplies where they dropped. She fed the animals in a rush, then ran to the spring, where she plunged in as she stripped. She hurried back to the cabin for clean clothes, and threw worn out material on the table to sort frantically for bandage-makings. Briefly she considered retrieving her traveling dresses and the gold coins, ready for flight, but feared that anticipating a catastrophe would cause it. She refused even to look at the trunk or the loose chimney stone.

The boy once again astride Earl, she led the mule back down the path. She remembered her frights in the pitch dark the previous night, but this daylight trip was worse in its way, for she dreaded at every turn she would see Spooks hurrying toward her.

He still sat beside Henry, their shadows on the other side of them now.

"Mister Spooks," sang out Harry, "you are just like the angel Gabriel keeping watch over Papa while Mama and I went home for more bandages to keep blood inside Papa."

Spooks looked up in surprise. "Master Harry, thank you. Nobody has ever called me an angel before, let alone the archangel Gabriel." He turned to Carrie. "No change," he reported in a low voice.

"Can you go for a doctor?"

"I could, but it would be fruitless. I happen to know that Doc Jarvis just started his annual six-day drunk and the new man is off to Chattanooga, courting."

"Could we somehow get him home for proper nursing?"

"Been debating that. We might kill him getting him on Earl. Maybe he's best off here. Didn't think I'd ever wish the drought holds. Why don't we see if we can get him off the ground onto pine needles and leaves? Nurse him right here. Couldn't have clean water much closer."

With great effort and the slowest movements possible, they eased Henry onto a blanket over piled-up pine needles. He never stirred.

Carrie brought out thread and needle while Spooks eased bandages back.

"Good." Harry followed their progress cheerfully, "you can sew Papa together and keep the blood inside." Carrie turned so he would not see her face as she worked the needle. She let out a deep sigh as she tied the last knot.

"How long is it since you slept?" Spooks asked.

"I can't remember."

"You've been up and down that trail too many times to count. Better stretch out on a blanket. I'll watch Harry." The boy fell asleep before she. Spooks woke them mid-afternoon. "One of us needs to go before it's too dark. Lantern and food and more blankets."

Henry gave a loud sigh, then seemed not to take in a fresh breath. "Mama, has Papa stopped breathing?" asked Harry in alarm.

With stricken face Spooks put his ear on Henry's chest. "No, his heart is still going. I think he's breathing very quietly."

Carrie realized that she had been holding her breath for Spooks' report. She pulled her son close to reassure him—and herself.

"Leave the boy here so you can move faster," Spooks suggested. "And bring that travel plan back with you. We can go over it again."

In lantern light, they reviewed the plan step by step, Spooks adding instructions especially for the first, most risky, legs. He asked Carrie to repeat the sequence by memory, but she made hash of it.

"Spooks, I can't do it. I'm so tired and scared. If he dies I don't have strength to leave."

"You must. For your son and yourself—and for Henry."

"I'm so afraid I'll make a stupid mistake."

"I'd come with you now, except that Arkwright—and Sam—would use that to prove I was the one who murdered Henry. Case closed."

"Murdered Henry? But you're his best friend."

"Oldest story around, Carrie. Two bosom friends quarrel bitterly over a beautiful woman. In a rage one kills the other and runs off with the woman. You've read that, Carrie."

"But I thought it only happened in books."

"The happy stories are only in books. The bad ones are in both. I would have to hang Arkwright first, then come on."

"To Canada?"

"Of course. Surely you realize . . ." He stopped abruptly. "Carrie, you must believe me. More than anything I want to enjoy Henry's company and your company right here on your farm."

Spooks began building a small fire, its solace as welcome as its warmth. Staring into the flames, Carrie tried to untangle her confused thoughts. "How do you know Arkwright did this?"

"Logical candidate. Wanted revenge. His reputation suffered mightily at the livery barn. Plus this." Spooks pulled from his pocket a button attached to a flap of black cloth. "Found it in the leaves while you were gone. I think Henry tore it off someone's coat before they got him from behind. Arkwright's best friend always wears a black coat."

"It's not much proof."

"True, but somewhere there's a torn coat missing a button."

"At the livery barn, every man has torn clothes."

"Too bad I can't take you with me when I walk around town. I'll need eyes that repair clothes."

Harry slept in an awkward position. Carrie straightened him, then turned back to Spooks. "Can we get some help to move Henry to the cabin at least?"

Spooks hesitated, then spoke, weighing alternatives. "If we don't get help, Henry could die. If we do get help, Henry could still die, but Sam might be tipped off, and you'd have terrible trouble leaving with Harry. It's your choice."

Carrie shook her head at her quandary. "He's here and he's alive. Let's keep him here."

Spooks nodded acceptance. After a time he yawned. "No point in both of us staying up. Wake me when the moon rises."

They watched in shifts for two days. Then, late in the afternoon, Henry opened his eyes slightly. He said nothing, but managed to swallow the corn mush Carrie spooned to his mouth. Several days later, the sky threatening thunderstorms, they fashioned a crude litter of thin saplings and canvas. They harnessed the forward end to the placid Earl; Spooks carried the back end wheelbarrow fashion. When, after many stops to rest, they finally reached the cabin, the bandages at Henry's neck showed bright red against his startlingly pale face. Henry gave Spooks's hand the faintest squeeze and feebly made the signs for "home," then "die," and closed his eyes.

Perhaps Henry lived because Spook kept bedside watch through long nights, murmuring of boyhood times. Perhaps he lived because Carrie spooned fortifying soups to his mouth at any sign he would swallow them. Perhaps because Harry, playing on the floor beside Henry's bed, looked up at his father and solemnly announced, "God is not going to take you to heaven now because He knows how lonesome Mama and I would be."

When finally optimistic about Henry's recovery, Spooks went down the trail to pacify clients. Solomon appeared, and helped with farm chores. When she was not creating new soups, Carrie read to the boy at Henry's side.

While Henry and the boy dozed, she went back over Spooks' words that night on the trail. *Two bosom friends quarrel over* . . . Carrie searched her memory for the faintest evidence of competition between Spooks and Henry. Nothing. Then she pondered Spooks' unfinished *Surely you realize*. That, she decided, was a door best kept bolted and barred.

❧

Henry sat up in bed, a rebellious convalescent, when Spooks dropped into the low chair nearby. He examined Henry's neck critically. "Carrie knows her needlework. No pus? All Doc Jarvis talks about is pus. Laudable pus. He seems to think it's a sign of healing."

"I *am* healing, confound it," Henry exploded. "Carrie won't believe me and keeps me in bed. You tell her. Maybe she'll believe you."

Spooks changed the subject. "Arkwright saved me a lot of trouble. He and a couple of men tried to set up an ambush for old man Henson on the other side of Arkwright's land. Some squabble Arkwright invented over boundaries. But Henson and his sons did patrols. Cooper's own Hawkeye could have done no better, Henry. They spotted Arkwright from above and prepared for him. When Arkwright tried to spring his trap, they sprang theirs, and with witnesses. Henson wounded, but Arkwright and two friends dead."

Spooks held up the torn strip of black cloth with a button. "The sheriff laid the bodies out behind the jail before they buried 'em. The bodies laid out made it easy for me."

Henry asked the question with his eyes.

"Yessir: cloth and tear and button all match. Guilty as charged. But Henry, that doesn't mean what you think. You'd better stay clear of Ginners Ford as long as you can. Your livery barn name has spread some into town. Maybe if you stay away, people will forget."

"I've already decided I'll never go back there. We'll go to Claytown from now on, even if it's twice as far."

"Wherever you go, Uncas, go alone. Listen, old friend," he persisted to smother Henry's protest boiling up. "I'm not telling you about what's right or wrong. I'm not telling you about a man's honor. I'm just thinking about protecting people that I . . . well, people I think highly of. If you drive into town and Carrie is sitting up there with you on the seat like she's your lawful wife, that's right and fitting to *you*. It's right and fitting to *me*. But it just inflames the low element. They think you're giving dangerous aspirations to them niggers. So they git kinda hostile. 'Cause if the niggers git uppity, why our whole civ-li-zation totters. Tain't nary a body 'round thet don' a-know all thet twicet o'er."

He sniffed appreciatively and called to the main room. "Carrie, I hope the smell of your cooking doesn't get out of this cabin much, 'cause it'll bring in every critter for miles, and I'll have to shoot 'em all to keep my share."

Plowing with Greek, My Life
HL Hollis

Sleep comes tardily these nights. In consequence I have too much time then. I pray, of course, for peace, for justice, for stronger faith, for courage facing the end, and for Caroline, the children. While the clock increases the hours, my mind devolves to questions I would have liked to ask previous generations.

"Peter Hollis, you say? Good day, sir. I am your grandson's grandson. Can you tell me, sir, why you made the arduous journey from England to Carolina? What did you think of it on your arrival? I beg your pardon, sir, but I ask because I wonder if I will recognize any of myself in you."

I think I know my grandfather, Samuel B, well through his diaries. Would speaking to him in person change my view, especially of him as an old man? In his last years, Samuel B's diary, once filled with admirably succinct summaries of correspondence with, say, Cousin Hurley, was reduced to bare memoranda, such as "Rec'd report from Cous. Hurley." Was that evidence of a mind and hand grown weary, or an indication of information or opinions about which Samuel B desired no record?

The number of my questions increases exponentially when I consider my diary-less father. What do you recall of your mother? What caused your departure from Tennessee? Were you apprehensive about living all alone at the Quachasee farm? Other questions also occur to me, questions I concede I could never have actually posed: Father, what impelled you, in your fifties and inured to solitude, to fetch home a wife? In fact a *young* wife, by whom you could, like patriarchs of old, beget sons and daughters in abundance, who will in turn beget sons and daughters unnumbered?

I am chagrined I did not ask my questions in timely fashion. Of course in the Glorious Hereafter there should be time a-plenty for such researches, assuming I shall still care then about these matters. (Reader, from what I gather, you should not depend on me to stealthily add my findings to the margins of these pages.)

Why is it so intimidating to ask your father questions about himself? It *is* hard. I recognize that in my sons, and try to offset it with family stories; such tales bore them, which of course predestines my grandchildren to complain that their fathers offered them nothing. (I persist incorrigibly in my alternating generations theory.) Reluctance to ask questions of one's father is reinforced if he is much more senior than usual. When boys at school teased me about having a granddaddy as daddy, I fought my tormentors to silence (helped by Marcus, I should confess), but to myself I had to admit the truth.

I reflect much about fathers and sons these days. It's a complex subject—as if Israelites and Greeks did not plumb its depths eons before it occurred to me. A father knows his son from the son's earliest minute, and unless he is pretty unobservant or excessively prideful, he appraises the son's strengths and foibles better than the son. In point of fact he shares with the son the frame of reference which is the son's whole life.

Also sharing that same frame of reference, the son understandably imagines he knows his father as his father knows him. Consequently the son easily assumes without deliberation that since he has known his father his whole life, he has known his father for his father's whole life, though, of course, once you formulate it this way, the fallacy becomes embarrassingly obvious.

Everyone knows of the proverbial son who at twenty thinks his father an idiot and at forty finds him grown unaccountably sage, but even as a young lad I recognized in Father a wise man. I knew it from observing him conduct the farm and its businesses, from listening to the many people who sought his advice and assistance. That, however, didn't make it easy to ask him questions. I did not inquire. He did not volunteer. I'm poorer for it.

Even when beset by Crotia's interrogations, he possessed a persistent reticence. She characterizes him as a melancholy man, but I disagree emphatically, having seen him laughing so hard his eyes shone wet. I have observed him talking with back-mountain people, trading straight-faced, outrageously tall tales until the weaker man cracked a smile. If neither man did, why, then they recognized their secret affinity, their superiority to the common herd.

Father adhered to an oral tradition which required a manly man be laconic. A steady stream of patter numbered the speaker among shopkeepers, schoolteachers, and drummers, men with soft hands and no hat line from the sun. For a manly man to boast was barely short of spitting on the flag. In consequence a man waited until someone asked him many questions before he offered the least about himself. When he did speak, his pride lay in the tersest answer.

A woman could talk all day, maybe should, but a manly man gained status by silence. Father wasn't melancholy, he was reticent. A good example is the scar on Father's neck, in fact, clear across his throat. Something terrible occurred. My brother issues a flat pronouncement from his medical training and experience: anyone slashed like that should, in Bill's words, never expect to stay on sod's green side. Yet Father volunteered no explanation. Something about him—not forbiddance, not sternness, not lack of tenderness, but some aura of intense privacy—prevented his sons from inquiring.

Usually one of the youngest of us, innocent of social nuance, full of curiosity about everything, climbed to Father's lap, looked up and touched the scar. "Does it hurt?"

"No, it's only a scar."

"What's a scar?"

"A cut that fixed itself."

"How did you get cut?"

Then the older children held their breaths, trying not to show their attention. "A bad man cut me," Father always answered.

"Why?"

"I protected someone I loved."

"Oh. Did you protect Mama?"

"No, before I knew Mama."

"What happened to the bad man?"

"He's dead."

"Did you make him dead?"

"No, someone else did."

"Who?"

"I did not know him."

Crotia once plotted the perfect scar strategy. She planted herself in front of Father, and spoke in her most winning way. "I want to write a good story. I think it should be about your scar. I made a bet with Dory. I bet her a nickel you will tell me your scar story so I can write it down."

Father feigned worry. "Crotia! As much as a nickel?"

She nodded solemnly. "If I lose I won't be able to buy any sweets for ever so long."

"I am concerned," Father teased with his inclination for alliteration, "about a curious candy-less calamity."

"Calamitous. Catastrophic. Cataclysmic. But contingent."

"Contingent? You mean I must help you out?"

"Yes, you must. I knew you would." Crotia dug into a pocket to retrieve her pencil.

Father also searched a pocket. "Here, Dory," he flipped her a nickel. "I believe Crotia owes you this. She can work off her debt to me with a bucket of peach ice cream."

After Father's death, Crotia badgered Mama for the real story, but Mama just shook her head. "When I asked him once, years ago, he said, 'My dear, that's from a life I'm no longer living.' I knew from his tone he'd never tell me more."

Crotia theorizes (in this case, Dory seems to agree, at least some of the time) that Father and Audie Ann and Judge Bright formed a kind of inner circle. The three often kept subtly apart from everybody else, even using hand talk we children didn't know or was too rapid for us to catch.

In point of fact Bill gets mighty impatient with such theories, and even more with the theoretician. "Crotia, since you write for a newspaper, a putative journalist, shouldn't you report what's true instead of making things up?"

"Bill, is your 'true' in uppercase or lowercase? But never mind, I know you're trying to dodge my question about Father and Audie Ann and Judge Bright."

"Crotia, when three elderly people are besieged by a screaming mob of children, of course they'll withdraw."

She never backs down easily. "No, Bill, it was more than that. It was like they were a kind of . . . well, a kind of inner guard."

"Twaddle, Crotia, twaddle. What were they guarding? Everybody, except Mama the way she told it, grows up with someone. That doesn't give them something to guard. You forget their age, Crotia. Ancient. Like us, approaching senility. Actually, seems to me *some* of us have already gone over the edge."

He fixes her with raised brow and gimlet eye. "Would you choose to be with those grandsons of yours every evening? No. You'd hide. You'd even hide with me. Well, maybe you would. If you didn't have any other choice. And then some dingbat daughter comes along and purely out of her imagination concocts the claim you're part of a conspiracy to conceal something."

"Bill, this dingbat daughter did not say there was any conspiracy. And remember that Papa and the Judge and Aunt Lydia always called Caroline, HL's Caroline, they always called her Caroline, never Carrie."

"Crotia, what are you prattling about?"

"You misspoke, didn't you, Bill? You meant to say, 'Of whom are you speaking?' didn't you? Don't pretend to be so obtuse, Bill. You need to protect your reputation as a smart doctor, remember? I'm not prattling. I'm talking about a specific woman, who is the Judge's and Aunt Lydia's youngest daughter, who is HL's wife, who is your very own sister-in-law, who is Caroline Bright Hollis, who is right now out in a hot kitchen cooking a fine meal for you to eat without noticing it, much less thanking her for it."

"Crotia, believe me, I am grateful for the fine cooking. But I think you let yourself go astray in your irritation."

"Bill, if senility hasn't got you, do a differential diagnosis, or whatever you call it. You know the facts: the Judge and Aunt Lydia name their son Henry, after Papa. They name their first daughter Audrey, after Aunt Audie. And then comes their last child and what do they do? They name her Caroline, and never call her Carrie, always Caroline. Now tell me why that is."

"You tell me, Crotia. You're just dying to."

"Alright I will. They name her Caroline maybe because that's the name of the woman Papa loved before Mama, and they knew her, and they always say Caroline, never Carrie, to keep them separate. And don't you roll your eyes at me, Mister Smarty Pants."

Bill rolls his eyes in a special way for his sister. "Crotia, your support for that is about as thin as a . . . as a spider web."

"I'm shocked at your scientific carelessness, Bill. Keep in mind how adhesive a spider web is. It sticks no matter how you brush it off. Doctor Hollis, haven't you ever looked at some patient, and known, just known by intuition, what's wrong? Admit it. You're a strong man. You can do it."

"Of course I have. When I was too young and too arrogant to know better. You know why I learned to keep that diagnosis to myself? It was always wrong. Wrong, spelled D-U-M-B. Crotia, you don't have a shred of evidence for this Caroline story."

"Tell me why those three people were the only ones to call the little girl Caroline."

"Because that was her name, for God's sake."

"You don't even believe in God."

"We were talking about Caroline."

"*I* was. *You* wanted to talk about God.

So they go, back and forth, but not much forward.

QUACHASEE
WHC

Clearing the table after a birthday meal for Henry, Carrie accidentally tapped a spoon against one of the rarely used best glasses, a small set Henry had brought from New York in case he'd forgotten an important person on his list for homecoming gifts. The bell-like ring fell away slowly. Without looking up, Harry began singing at its pitch. *Si l'amour vous si fort, faut plein d'argent dans poche.* Carrie joined him, as she had made her mother join her in the dark days of the Dinkins farm.

She tapped the glass again for the pleasure of the sound. Remembering *his* mother's lessons, Henry tried humming a third below. Badly out of practice, he hit nearly a halftone flat. The boy quickly turned to him with a pained expression become a smile as his father slid up to pitch. Again Carrie tapped the glass. Henry sounded an octave well below, then tried to whistle the octave above. "No, Papa," came the quick reproof. Again, a pained expression until Henry quavered to pitch. The parents exchanged a look. Carrie put the glass away with the others. The boy returned to Spooks' puzzle, Henry to his hog-breeding records.

He stared at his neat print, however, without seeing. That shift, from slightly pained to affirming smile, stirred memory of his mother's face, teaching his sister Emily Jo and him to sing duets before he could run, as his father marveled in reminiscence. Louisa, his father later told him, loved music. More than reading, more than clothes, more even than eating. She spent whole days with her hammer dulcimer. Henry wondered whether his childhood pride exaggerated her virtuosity. Then he recalled seeing the blur of her hammers. Even her fast tempo music was unmarred by the wrong notes other players made, filling the room with glorious sound. He remembered people who told him about listening—"give me the overall shivers"—when his mother played years before.

Perhaps her music explained part of her devastation when it became obvious that Audie Ann, miraculously recovered from the fever, did not hear the dulcimer any more—did not hear anything. When they understood the only sounds she could make were harsh screeches. Even duets Emily Jo and Henry sang to cheer up their mother only made her eyes redder and her voice sadder.

Until, that is, Louisa came upon him instructing a rapt Audie Ann, giving her directions by his gestures, his face, posture. And Audie understood. His mother seemed to stop crying midsob. She resolutely set aside her dulcimer to focus on a silent language. Enlisting Emily Jo and Henry, urging them with intense concentration, she bent their collective energy to talking without sound. Soon they constructed a basic vocabulary, sufficient for a young child. They settled on rules for coinage. Henry and Emily became so at ease without a sounded word that they used the silent language even when Audie Ann wasn't present, rapidly expanding its vocabulary and syntax.

Sometimes they unthinkingly responded soundlessly to their father, instantly raising Samuel's ire. Louisa, however, intervened, intimidating even Tulips' patriarch by her fierce defense of her children and their language. She was determined her youngest child be included in the hearing world. Anyone who referred to "poor" Audie Ann discovered in the shy, deferential Louisa a she-bear with cub.

The children were secure in their silent language, Audie Ann absorbing more daily, when, without warning, the angels came for Emily Jo, then their mother, hurrying them away so quickly that Henry could talk with his dying mother only once. Numbed by fright and grief, he promised, and promised yet again, yes, he would keep teaching Audie Ann, yes, he would look out for her, yes, always.

Henry could not remember any other time his father seemed so staggered by loss. He stayed locked in his office for days. Years had passed before he gave away Louisa's dresses—only hours before Sarah became his third wife. Little Henry watched wide-eyed as Sally—she must've been younger than Carrie then—struggled to carry Louisa's remaining things up the steep staircase to the attic. The attic, where Sarah boasted she never went.

Tuesday morning, Elvira always met with the Ginners Ford church ladies. Tuesday morning, Sam always went with her, not to the church, of course, but to Ford Street for leisurely gossiping and gaping. Tuesday morning, Henry slipped into the Tulips kitchen. Lilly soon walked to the main house, then reappeared at the door with a nod. The attic stairs proved less steep than Henry remembered, the storage not so jumbled, the load he carried away not as heavy as he feared.

At the Quachasee cabin he unwound the cloth wrapping. "My mother's dulcimer," he explained. "But I never needed to tune it." He kept sounding strings, using Harry's face as much as his own ear for the adjustment. Years before, Sally hurriedly jammed sheet music inside the wrappings before she carried the bundle to the attic, but Henry had only begun then to read music, not just shape notes. Now parents and boy worked together, detectives puzzling out the code.

Henry suspected Carrie and he kept up with their son mostly because they recognized the tune after a few notes and could extrapolate beyond, matching ear, string, notation. His hammers never blurred like Louisa's, but with the boy on a spare set, they played simple tunes happily. The boy also used a hammer on his own, picking out *Guègue Solingaie, balliez chimlà, m'asis li, oui, m'a dis li,* and other songs Carrie taught him. Then he picked out pleasing sequences unlike any Henry ever heard.

"I wish," he told Carrie, "that my mother could see her grandson play, could even give him some lessons."

"I hope you can give his children lessons," she answered. "I used to read about grandfathers and wish I had one. You'll be a wonderful grandfather, Henry."

❧

"I could have carried the water for you," Henry said at the cabin porch as Carrie lowered full buckets of water and Harry proudly set down a miniature pail sloshed near empty on the way from the spring.

"I know, but you're tired too." She grinned. "How come de boss man, he doan jes run sum crik by de cabin dohr?"

How come indeed? Spooks appeared with fresh fish. Henry sought a consultant while Spooks gutted. When as boys they found the ground too muddy for fending off Magua and his Hurons, they played canal engineers, linking puddles by channels gouged cross country to float their twig craft vast distances, even over mountains. Henry's challenge now seemed simpler. They calculated fall, volume, gate design.

Henry constructed a header box at the spring, then began chipping out lengthwise channels in sections of tree trunks. Connected to the header box, each trunk in place made shorter the trip with heavy buckets. As reservoir, a large barrel, carried from Clayton precariously strapped above Earl's back, completed the new system. A water supply bubbled at the end of the porch, also a handy place to keep crocks cool, for Henry built a miniature spring house through which the water flowed after the barrel filled. A creek did run right by the cabin door.

Spooks arrived to celebrate the first official fill of the porch barrel. "Henry, you've got enough volume for a pounding mill, I think."

"That's next. But one thing at a time," laughed Henry.

Carrie ceremoniously watered a cutting. Spooks took a long drink. "My Papa is smart," Harry declared, and exuberantly emptied his pail over his head.

"Henry, it's just like when you wrote about a new reservoir opening in Manhattan."

"The reservoir I remember, but not writing about it. Did you read that letter?"

"I read every letter you wrote to Audie Ann. She told me to. So we could talk about them."

"I didn't know that. You read every letter?"

Carrie nodded. "I near memorized them. I think I was partial to you years before I ever met you."

"No wonder I never saw a chance," laughed Spooks and threw a dipper-full of the new water at Henry.

Harry stopped drawing circles on the slate Spooks brought him and walked to his mother, her book close to the lamp. "Mama, I don't feel very good." Carrie put her hand on his forehead, flashed an alarmed look over his head to Henry, and tucked him into bed with assurance he would feel better after a night's sleep. In the morning he looked far worse. Henry took buckets to the spring for the coolest water to sponge the boy's flushed face and arms.

That day Carrie read to him as he lay in bed. The next day she did not, for he seemed to want most to sleep. At supper, which she ate standing up, the easier to go back and forth to Harry's tick by the fire, Carrie burst out, "If he isn't better in the morning, can you get a doctor?"

Henry shoved back his plate. "Good moon tonight. I'll go get him now." She kissed him, helped him pull on a warm coat. He didn't return until well after sunrise, alone. "I finally found the new doctor. He was out at a farm looking after a sick family, so I went there for him. Got lost for a while when thick clouds covered the moon, but I found him. He said he attended so many sick people"—Henry did not say, "dying people," as the doctor had—"that he couldn't come all the way up here for just one patient, no matter what I paid him."

Carrie flashed an angry face which Henry understood was meant for the doctor.

"He's a decent man, Carrie," Henry answered her. "Just at the end of his rope. He said if it got worse, come back and he'd try to make the trip if I bring a mule. I even stopped by Aunt Jane, the root woman, but she's too sick herself to walk. The doctor gave me this to try." Henry took a brown bottle out of his pocket.

As Carrie poured out the vile-smelling liquid, Henry saw her hand tremble. By noon she needed to lie down when she wasn't tending Harry. That evening she stayed in bed herself. Henry carried many more buckets of water now, for he required the coldest possible and threw out what had warmed in the cabin.

The brown bottle emptied without effect, but Henry could not search again for the doctor. There was no time. He nursed day and night. Coaxed food, fetched a cool drink, sponged feverish bodies, rinsed soiled bed clothes. Sat too numb to page yet again through the prayer book. Watched.

Henry forgot whether he saw dawn or dusk, whether he slept or woke. Dozing, he dreamed terrifying nightmares. Charity trampled again in the street; Isaiah hammering from inside his coffin; Pru's hallucinations of the Devil watching her. In the worst, Doc Sexton held a fiery scepter aloft, his black beard smoldering. *Young Hollis knew: when you allow together two kinds in the generative act, the fruit is flawed, Sir. The young are doomed by guilty progenitors, by an unnatural act, Sir.* The nightmare returned so often that Henry wondered. Was he being punished? Had he incurred God's wrath by a forbidden act?

Incline thine ear, O Lord, and answer me,
  for I am poor and needy. . . .

He read psalm after psalm, sharing King David's despair. Returning from the spring, remembering how he nursed, and lost, Isaiah, then Pru, then Riti, he understood he would also lose those he loved here.

Thou art my God; be gracious to me, O Lord,
  for to Thee do I cry all the day . . .

He dropped to his knees to pray yet again, rising only when he thought he heard Carrie's call. He rushed into the cabin, but both she and the boy slept their usual febrile slumber.

Give ear, O Lord, to my prayer;
  hearken to my cry of supplication.

Late in the evening he again sponged Harry off, and slipped a clean night shirt on him.

In the day of my trouble I call on thee . . .

Harry smiled. "Papa." Henry put his hand at his son's side. The boy took Henry's little finger as he had done as a baby. He held it tightly and looked steadily at his father. He slowly closed his eyes. His grip gradually loosened. Exactly like sleep, but Henry knew it wasn't.

Too shattered for tears, he kept his finger in that loose grasp until long after midnight when he heard Carrie stir. He brought the lamp to her bed. She looked up anxiously. "Harry?"

Wordless, Henry shook his head slowly. With a look of despair, she turned her face to the wall. She, too, Henry foresaw, would leave him, despite his agonized prayers. Everything he could do failed.

Henry marked a small rectangle in the ground frost. There on the knoll in sight of both cabin and spring, he dug a grave. In the crudest of coffins—hardly a box even, but he had no time to do more—he lay his son and closed the lid. Mechanically he read prayers. Numbly he shoveled earth to fill in the hole. Grieving, he left the tools readily at hand outside when he returned to the cabin and Carrie.

He passed the tools when he went to feed the stock; dirt still clung to the shovel. He passed the tools when he labored awkwardly in the yard over steaming kettle, over block and battling stick; rains washed the shovel clean. He passed the tools when he went to chop more wood to keep the fire roaring; weather roughed the handles.

Little by little Carrie improved. He put the tools away.

❧

Carrie wanted to visit the knoll, but Henry dissuaded her until, working quietly late at night by firelight, he fashioned a headstone from a stout slab of oak, and laboriously carved letters in it.

J. H. HOLLIS

He brought Carrie to sit on the porch in the sun, wrapped in an extravagant cocoon of blankets. She took his hand and held it long to her cheek. When time came to work the fields, she urged him to go, though at first he came back every hour. She mended.

Spooks came whistling up the trail, his saddle bags stuffed with gifts for his godson. He looked first in the fields for Henry, swearing jovially he would never again go abroad for a client, no matter how prestigious the commission. Henry's news so shocked him that he fled back down the valley. Returning the next day, he sat for hours with Carrie in silent sympathy.

Solomon, alerted by Spooks, slipped out of the woods a few days later to join Carrie by the fire, his eyes brimming. He returned the next sunny day with an unlooked-for visitor, Audie Ann, whom he had carried much of the way. Audie summarized everything with the most elementary hand talk, snapping an imaginary horizontal stick grasped between closed hands: broken. Irretrievably broken.

Carrie grew better, but not whole. She answered Henry's questions in a voice so soft he heard only by straining. Even her smile spoke sadness She never laughed. In the evenings he might look up from reading to see her sitting immobile, tears coursing her cheeks. She paid so little attention to dress that Henry collected a pile of garments worn too often; over her halfhearted protests, he washed them himself. She resumed meal preparation, but proved so slow and heedless that Henry accustomed himself to cooking. She ate what he prepared without comment. She initiated no effort to prepare game Spooks brought, so the men attempted simplified versions of her best dishes. The three rarely discussed a book, for Carrie never read and the men did not want to exclude her.

When Henry came in from the fields he most often found her on the knoll near the headstone. He marked out a space large enough to hold an aisle around three graves. As the evening light lengthened, they wordlessly enclosed a graveyard with a dry-laid rock wall. Starting with the excess stone from the pile Carrie once collected for the chimney, they brought the wall to more than waist high, with a gap for an entry. Henry contrived a wooden gate.

He brought Pastor Berkemeier up to hallow the little cemetery, to say prayers at Harry's grave, thanking God for Harry's time here and imploring His solace on those left behind. Encouraged by Carrie's close attention to Berkemeier's prayers and his readings from

Scripture, heartened that Carrie worked diligently on the wall, Henry then noticed she focused on nothing else. She cut cloth for clothes she never sewed. She assembled ingredients for dishes she never cooked. She opened books she never read. At any time Henry might turn to see her silently weeping.

Winter work followed harvest, though Henry tried to find more things he could do inside, reluctant to leave Carrie alone all day. While Carrie sat at the grave, he made a careful search for any of Audie's pistols she might have. He brought together the powder and stored it in a shed. After he thought Carrie studied high beams in the barn, he painstakingly sorted through the store room to collect and hide all rope, though a glance at the harness rack ruled such precautions futile. If despair overwhelmed her, he could not prevent her from self-harm.

Plowing with Greek, My Life
HL Hollis

I am sore with unusual aches this evening, in consequence of my prolonged visit to the Hollis graveyard with Gerald, one of Dory's grandsons. (I can blame my aches on no one but myself, for Bill and dear Caroline gave ample warning to someone too stubborn to hear.) Now that leaves have all fallen, I aimed to clean around the markers, a job postponed earlier because of my condition. The unseasonably warm temperatures and clear skies lured me to the task, despite it seeming distinctly un-Christmas-y. We worked the morning there, or rather, Gerald worked while I "supervised," an old man basking in the sun, breathing elegies.

Gerald took obvious satisfaction in slashing down tall grass obscuring a few low gravestones. "Don't want to lose anybody," he said respectfully. His concern brought again to my mind the tiny graveyard up at Father's high Quachasee farm. I don't know of a more beautiful spot at which to rest until Eternity, though it must have been a heap of trouble for the living to convey the deceased up there. Even today the way is steep, the road rough, the distance long. What could have compelled bereaved survivors to that effort? The difficulties surely explain why only two graves are inside the stone fence. The gravestones read "J. H. Hollis" and "C. LaCroix Hollis." Neither includes any dates.

Those facts are easy. Explanations are another matter entirely. I can identify neither a J. H. Hollis nor a C. LaCroix Hollis in family records. LaCroix has a somewhat exotic sound to it in East Tennessee, but I have never run across it within the family—or elsewhere in this vicinity.

Years ago I became acquainted with Tom Cross, old as Methuselah, who was for many decades a fixture at the county courthouse. Tom had a remarkable memory. I found that one could ask a junior clerk to look up land records on some parcel, but it was usually faster—and more interesting—to ask Tom. He could give accurate names and dates right out of his head. He was nearly as well versed about who married whom and the children they had. I should return to him at greater length for his memory's role in cutting short the political aspirations of certain scoundrels in the county. Here I record simply that Old Tom could not recall ever seeing a county document with the name LaCroix.

Mama could shed no light on these graves, and Crotia, averse to physical exertion already as a child, never ventured up there so that the graves prompted her questions for Father. Consequently this remains a mystery I have for years puzzled over fruitlessly, albeit patiently, assuming that someday the answer may appear unbidden, like another unexpected, essential entry for my "almost-done" lexicon of mountain speech. I might speculate that those graves date to the original settlers on the Quachasee farm, but that family was headed by Obediah Oppdyke. Sitting ruminatively today in the sun, I conceded (to myself) that just as I won't live to see my lexicon in print, so also with definitive solution to my gravestone mystery.

Father, too, urged meticulous graveyard maintenance. Twice a year he organized us children, and we all trooped over, Audie Ann driving a dog cart. We weeded, raked, pruned and planted, each according to his capacities. Father's six stepbrothers, a sister, and his parents are buried there. Crotia sought details, scandalous or at least melodramatic, on every one.

Late in the morning Mother brought a hamper down and we picnicked, which Father always closed with the same prayer, a forgiving prayer, I realized when older. He always prayed that whatever good was done by those who rested there might inspire their descendants to conduct their lives faithful to God and generous to the memory of the dead.

I said the same prayer with Gerald when he finished.

QUACHASEE
WHC

Henry hoped spring shades of green working up the mountainsides would lift Carrie's spirits. They didn't. In the lull after the planting, he repeatedly proposed that he bring Audie Ann up again for a visit. She always shook her head with some transparent excuse. Knowing that his sister grieved, Henry went down to Tulips to see her, leaving before first light so he could be back by dusk. After sitting with the desolate Audie Ann, he went on to the kitchen house. As soon as Lilly saw his face she seemed to hold her breath. "What new grief do you lay on me?"

"Carrie is well in body, but not in spirit." He described her lassitude and crying spells. "She used to be proud of what she put on the table; now she doesn't notice whether I eat at all." He hesitated. "She used to want me to touch her a lot, Lilly. Now she flinches if I do. So I don't. I'm not complaining. I just want her to be happy again. I ask her what I can do for her and she says, Nothing. Would it do any good for you to talk with her?"

Sagging, Lilly turned back to the big table. "She's her own woman now. But maybe a mother's talk can't harm. Next week Miz Elvira is going to Knoxville again, and Mister Sam with her. I'll come up some day then. I guess I won't tell Carrie you asked me to come."

"It wouldn't make any difference if you did, Lilly."

❧

From her seat on the wall around Harry's grave, Carrie saw Lilly toiling up the trail and met her in front of the cabin. As they embraced, she murmured, "I didn't feel so good this winter." Lilly stood with her for a time, then asked, "Aren't you going to ask your mother in, Carrie?" As the two entered the cabin, Lilly glanced at the cold hearth. "What're you cooking for dinner, child?"

Carrie avoided her eyes. "Haven't started, Mama."

"Here, I'll help you. What're you planning to fix?"

"Been so busy this morning, I haven't thought much about it."

Lilly surveyed the cabin's disorder. "I'll pick up a little for you, then how about if I bake something simple and quick? Henry always liked fresh biscuits."

"All right, Mama." Carrie was too close to tears to say more.

Once she worked at the table, Lilly began again. "Henry says you're still grieving hard for the boy." She kept working and talking. She spoke of how thankful Carrie must be for God's many blessings. No woman could ask for a finer man than Henry; imagine being trapped with his brother Sam or his cousin Caleb. Her health is back, when she could have died too. Quachasee is a beautiful place to live, with no one telling her to do this or do that. Lilly spoke of the Good Lord and how He does not spare those He loves; in affliction one must be confident of God's care. Harry is gone to a better place to be with Jesus. In the end Carrie will be united with him, only without any pain or tears. She still spoke of God's love as she slid golden biscuits onto a plate.

And Carrie still wept. "I know all that, Mama, I tell myself that every day, but it doesn't make me any happier."

"Carrie," her mother said firmly, "you need to get hold of yourself, a strong hold."

"I know," Carrie sobbed. "But I can't."

"Why in heaven's name not, daughter?"

"Oh Mama, it's so hard. You don't know what it's like to lose a child."

Lilly moved a chair to sit closely facing Carrie. "You're right. I don't know about losing one child. I lost three. Three children I carried for Etienne, and not one lived more than six months."

"Mama, you never told me that before."

"Why should a mother load all her past grief on her daughter? Etienne bought me as a toy. But then his wife couldn't have children, so he was determined to have children by me. I disappointed him. He gambled me away the night after I lost the third child."

This time, Carrie embraced Lilly. Her mother wept tears of her own. "It's hard to see God's justice sometimes. I lost one man because I couldn't have his child. And another man because I could." She wiped tears with an apron and searched a shelf. "How do you cook? You don't have hardly any of the spices I taught you."

Carrie looked down, shame-faced. "It's hard to cook when all you can do is cry."

"A woman can cry and cook. I have, and a lot of other women, too. You're lucky Peddler Mordecai came by Tulips just last week; he's near as good as old Moishe used to be. I'll ask Solomon to carry up some things." She sat down to make a list, speaking as she wrote. "Black pepper. You remember the day . . . Ginger . . . you told me you loved Henry and were carrying his child? White pepper."

Carrie nodded. "I went home low because I knew I disappointed you. I kept asking myself if I had made some terrible mistake. But, Mama, it was Harry I was carrying, remember that."

"Cayenne pepper. I do. Basil. And before that it was Henry you were loving. Nutmeg. Remember *that*. Oregano. In my mind I can see you standing across the big table asking me, would you rather have never loved Etienne so you wouldn't have your heart broken? Coriander."

"Oh, Mama, I was so young and so arrogant. That was cruel. I'm ashamed. I didn't have any idea what I was saying."

"Sage. Probably you didn't," Lilly granted with a small smile. "I'm not young and I hope I'm humble, but I need to ask you the same questions to think on. Thyme. Would you rather never have loved Henry, to be where you are now? Mustard. Would you rather never have borne your boy so you wouldn't have your heart broken? Cloves. You think about that some instead of weeping. Paprika. Now does your man never come in to eat? Anise. He needs a real cook, daughter. Nutmeg . . . I already put down. It's your shame, how thin he is. Cumin. Oh, I near forgot some tamarind for you to try."

List tucked into a pocket, Lilly disappeared into the woods. Carrie did not talk with Henry about the visit. He surmised, sadly, it had done her no good.

❧

Now that days felt summer, a body could stand in the spring pool without ice-numb legs. Early one morning Henry said he decided to build a better cold house there. At the spring he dropped tools, pulled off his shirt and plunged in. The cold water shocked him, but he warmed as the sun rose higher. Preoccupied, he did not look up from his work when footsteps approached.

"Henry, I brought you late breakfast." Carrie stood on the bank, her dress clean, her hair neatly gathered by a ribbon. "Come and eat,

Henry." She held up a basket. He climbed out of the water with great splashes.

"Ooof. What a sopping wet mess you are. Sit there and I'll feed you." She perched on a log to dispense breakfast, starting with fresh biscuits and smoked ham. He ate as she dipped again into the basket. After he shook his head gratefully to her offer of more, she reached again into the basket to bring out one of Harry's alphabet blocks. "You missed this one, Henry," she said gently. "You didn't destroy the others, did you?" She touched his arm lightly.

Remorseful at her discovery, he shook his head. "I couldn't make myself do it."

"Good. We'll need them." She returned to the basket again, this time to retrieve an outsized square of gingerbread. "Now, this," she said with a smile that could have been shy or it could have been sly, "you get only if you say please." She held it high above her head in the hand opposite Henry.

❧

Almost from the time Henry first sponged her off, Julia Lilly LaCroix Hollis smiled with a face so flawless she looked like a china doll. On the porch, Spooks teased Carrie at her description of the new baby napping inside, reminding her that every mother finds her child perfect, no matter how initially misshapen. But when Carrie deposited Julia in his lap he apologized handsomely for his jokes, and became a most loyal attendant.

Several trips up the valley later Spooks drew from his bag the yard-long dress of gossamer fabric fastened with barely visible stitchery. The dress with "JLH" intricately embroidered in an elaborate medallion set within the lace. The dress that brought uncharacteristic tears to Lilly's eyes as she assured her daughter she had seen fine christening wraps, but never one as fine as this. The dress the baby wore when Pastor Berkemeier took her from Carrie for baptism in the quiet little country church, where John Patterson Bright and Audrey Ann Hollis again stood by as godparents, and Solomon Haller as joyful witness.

Lilly boasted of her namesake, and took every chance to visit her, making light of breathing heavily after the long uphill climb. A minute or two to catch her breath was a very small price to hold a granddaughter who smiled so beautifully every time she recognized a visitor. At every departure Lilly slipped a yarn bracelet scented with lavender on Julia's wrist. "That's so she remembers me."

⚜

Solomon appeared silently at the cabin door, his whole shirt dark from sweat, so upset he dropped unconsciously into hand talk. "Carrie, I must bring you bad news. Lilly died last night in her sleep. I heard the news from Short John by accident. I decided I must tell you as soon as I could get here so that you can be at your mother's burial at daybreak tomorrow morning."

A shocked Carrie quickly sounded the horn to bring Henry in from the field. While she gathered a few traveling things, Solomon carried the news to Henry. When the men reached the porch, she stood waiting with Julia in her arms.

"Henry, I think I must go. I want to take Julia," she paused to gather an explanation, "so when she's grown I can tell her she saw her grandmother's burying, even if she can't remember it. You won't object to me taking our daughter, Henry, please?"

Henry hesitated with a grave face before he nodded. "Sam and Elvira will have some excuse to stay away. Sally can keep you both out of sight." He came up on the porch to put his arm around her shoulders. "I'm so sorry. Do you want me to go with you?"

Only that brought tears to her eyes. She shook her head decisively, reflecting the alarm visible in Solomon's face. Henry saw them off with kisses and a wave. He turned to a harness needing repairs.

To his bewilderment Carrie was back on the porch in several hours, a small piece of paper in her hand. "Jim met us on the trail with Audie's note. He said she thought Sam or Caleb might search him. She wrote it like a riddle. I came back to make sure you read this the same way I do."

Henry took the paper and haltingly spoke the hasty scrawl.

"Magua prepares sharp knives. For Cora to leave the warm fireside of Uncas is to be cold forever."

He looked up, worry on his face. "She's saying, if you go down, they'll force you to stay. You'll never come back here."

"But I never said goodbye to Mama."

"If you go down, Julia may have no chance to say goodbye to *her* mama."

The baby began fussing. "Julia's hungry," said Carrie as she began unfastening her top.

As they sat on the porch that evening, Henry read aloud from Stark's prayer book, and the comforting words in Romans 8. Then he reminisced about Lilly, ending with the last pie she gave him to carry up the Quachasee trail. "Of course, you have many more memories, and a lot more interesting," he conceded.

"Mama always anchored me. Even when we got sold off, twice, I don't remember being truly scared. I always knew Mama would take care of things. And she always did. I wish I could have known her in New Orleans. But all I have is my imagination and memory. I don't have a single likeness of her to show Julia some day."

"At least you could show Julia her grandmother's legacy in food. Think of all the special dishes Lilly cooked. Haven't you written out directions in that little book you first brought up here?"

"That's only a few."

"Don't you remember more?"

So Carrie honored her mother by recalling the dishes that won Lilly most acclaim, and writing notes about their production. Henry cannily advised that the recipes surely needed kitchen verification—and more essential, taste guarantees.

A month after the burial, Solomon ferried Audie Ann up the valley. They brought what Solomon quick-wittedly took charge of in Lilly's loft, barely ahead of Sam's rude rummaging, though the whole did not fill two hands. Audie also brought a copy of Pastor Berkemeier's grave-side sermon; she had written it out from the notes Pastor lent her.

Audie almost forgot to add a footnote of unsurprising news: Elvira quickly installed in Lilly's kitchen a girl who struggled to boil an egg. After all, as Elvira said, food was food, nothing to display, dwell on, or dawdle over. She had always scorned a dauncy eater.

A fuller report from Tulips might also have noted a small change in tone there. After Lilly's burial both Sam and Elvira went about in much improved spirits, though for different reasons. Elvira was pleased that a hapless girl in the kitchen removed the faintest hint of her mistress's inadequacies. Sam missed the savory dishes he once wolfed down without comment, but nevertheless looked ahead with a lighter heart. Surely a hex maker's death cancelled the hex.

❧

After Julia, Carrie miscarried twice. She and Henry worried, wanting a son. Then, the summer that Julia turned three, Henry held up George Bright Hollis, screaming so forcefully that little Julia burst into sympathetic tears. For the successful pregnancy Carrie credited furniture; she spoke facetiously of naming the boy Lowe Chair Hollis. When Henry later took the chair to the barn for repair but gave fieldwork priority, she reinstalled it at the hearth, despite its creaks.

Another son, Edward John Hollis, arrived not so long before the evenings that Spooks, Henry, and Carrie stayed up late discussing reports of uncompromising politicians, of armed volunteers to defend the state's rights. To Carrie's relief, Henry shook his head in vehement disagreement. "Usually I read that newspaperman Brownlow, and think he's plain rabid, but this time he's right on target. What's driving this secession talk is the almighty dollar, as usual. Plantation owners need cotton for profit and slaves for cotton, so they invent fancy theories about states' rights to protect their wallets. The war with Mexico smelled bad enough, but at least we got land. This can't come to any good."

Spooks described the fiery secessionist who argued that any Bright male truly loyal to his ancestors must raise a company and volunteer to lead it. "How did you reason with him?" Carrie marveled.

"Couldn't. Finally said I preferred my fishing rod to a saber," answered Spooks. "He tried to shame me. Told me my family's sacred honor required defending the sovereign state of Tennessee from federal aggression. I told him federal aggression hadn't stopped the fish from biting. I'm sorry for him, or rather, for his widow. When he played soldier, drilling, he helped load a field piece. More enthusiasm than skill. It blew up. No battlefield glory, just useless death. I hope it wasn't the first glimpse of waste to come."

Henry agreed. "I wish someone would explain, Mister Lawyerman, if this state referendum on secession is genuine, how come the governor does one thing after another to pull Tennessee out of the Union even before a vote? That's no democracy."

After Lilly died, Carrie never left the farm. Henry or Solomon brought Audie Ann at intervals to delight in the children and in the mountain views. But Carrie always declined Henry's offers to take her to some nearby town, even when he promised they could appear separately. "Henry, everything I want is here—you, the children, the cathedral up the mountain, this precious place." She motioned at the ridges, the fields, the spring. Her eyes stopped at the wall around the graveyard.

"Wouldn't you like to see places you read about?"

"I'm happy with just the reading. You forget that I'm only property. Owned by Marse Sam Hollis, Junior, of Tulips, Ginners Ford, Tennessee, just a slave wench called Carrie, nothing more. You know what hell my life would be if I were at Tulips, Henry." She gave him a hard, fixed stare until he had to nod assent.

"Besides, going down the valley only tells me how alone I am. Now that Mama is gone, who can I talk to there? I mean, talk to as equals, like ordinary people, plain folks. White people won't because they think I'm *not* white. Servants won't because they think I *am* white."

She stepped close to hug Henry. "Think of all I've got. You and the children, and Spooks and Audie Ann. Solomon. Sally. The Patriarchs up the mountain. I think of Mama's life and know how lucky I am."

She stepped back to see Henry's face. "Why in the world would I ever think of going someplace else? I just pray you never have to go down the valley for longer than overnight, because I don't sleep while you're gone. I can't help it. I sit up with the lantern lit."

Henry rarely went anywhere overnight. Except in deep winter, when he left the farm only in direst necessity, by leaving before first light he could usually be back by nightfall. Had he appeared in Claytown at closer intervals, or had Claytown been less accustomed to mountain eccentrics, people there might have remarked more on a solitary, taciturn figure, on foot with a pack mule, who sold efficiently, who bought and loaded from a neat list, never stopped for any liquid refreshment, and said little more than a polite *Good day* to anyone before he disappeared.

In compensation he wrote regularly to New York City booksellers he once patronized in person. A stream of print, a slow stream, but a steady one, flowed from New York to Tennessee, then eddied at the law office of John Patterson Bright, Esquire. From there, sooner or later, books and papers moved up the valley in a pocket or saddlebag. Sophisticated New Yorkers might smirk about the lag between the latest literary sensation and readers in the Quachasee cabin. But sophisticated New Yorkers might recognize the thoughtful winter evening discussions in that cabin. A library so laboriously acquired meant reading slowly to last, carefully to meditate on, and repeatedly to cherish.

❧

When Henry retrieved the dulcimer from a loft corner, Julia became an apt fellow student, just as she quickly learned his code symbols for hog breeding to help with his recordkeeping. Saying that he feared his faculties were unchallenged, Henry dug out the papers on which Lilly had written song lyrics for Carrie to teach her children. *Si l'amour vous si fort, faut plein d'argent dans poche.* He asked Spooks to ferry up a fat French dictionary and frowned over the entries. How could that make sense? He wrote down more stanzas as Carrie dictated. Did she misremember? Could his spelling be so far off? "Two possibilities, Henry," Spooks grinned. "Either New Orleans French is pretty different, or our little cherub Edward here cheerfully sings filthy ditties, so salacious no publisher dares print them in a dictionary."

Each year the first time the family saw the ole woman pickin her geese, mantling the mountaintops with snow, was signal for standing the children against the previous wall marks and boisterous new recording of their growth. In the dark of early morning hours, though, Carrie confessed deep fears. The annual custom might arouse some malignant power to swoop down on them once again, stealing their happiness.

Henry urged trust in Almighty God. He went down the valley for an urgent conference with Pastor Berkemeier, who, frail as he was, toiled up to the high cabin with, as he told Carrie, the two God-given essentials, Word and Sacrament. These both he dispensed in his kindly, confident way. On his downward trip Berkemeier breathed prayers on behalf of this loving and lovable family that so needed God's protecting arm for its future.

Carrie felt much strengthened by his visit. Nevertheless, to make the children's growth marks less visible, Henry transferred the family history to the freakishly dark wood of a bedroom doorpost, where only a close lamp revealed the penciled lines, names, and dates.

The growth-marks ritual, coupled with the Advent lessons that Henry, following Berkemeier's list, read from the big Bible: these were more than enough to make the children study the wall calendar in breathless anticipation of Christmas. Henry fashioned tree ornaments, selected an evergreen to stand a small distance from the porch, and carefully cleared for fire hazard around its base. He consulted privately with each child in excited conferences about what gifts they should give to siblings and mother. He pulled from hiding certain items he had picked up on various trips to Claytown. He spent much time in solitary construction of ziggerboos, flipperdingers, bull-roarers, and even more ingenious toys of his own invention. He was patient tutor for the intricate rules governing the first to say "Christmas Gift." And he served as enthusiastic adviser to the chef regarding choice of dishes for the hallowed eve and day. He carefully reviewed the Gospel accounts he would read aloud. Then on Christmas Eve, to the children's oohs and ahhs, he began the celebration outside by lighting candles in the evergreen's boughs—always with a full bucket of water close at hand. With good reason, Carrie called him Belsnickel.

As winter loosened, Henry gave up on New Orleans French and turned to self-instruction in Latin. Pointing out that conversation would create more discipline and variety, he coaxed Carrie into joining him. They practiced orations in the evenings and the language of the latifundia during the day. The children's alert teasing at any lapse into English became a powerful incentive to memorize vocabulary. Laughter rang again in the high Quachasee Valley.

Plowing with Greek, My Life
HL Hollis

Some years ago I answered inquiries about family history from distant kin on the Coyner side. Their city importunity took me aback, but I did sympathize with their genealogical problems, a consequence of fragmentary Coyner records. By contrast, I have enjoyed the benefit of Grandfather's notations, reinforced by congregational registers. I believe I have previously written that Samuel B helped found Bethel Church early last century. Though he grumbled mightily to his diary (and I hope only there) about blockheaded fellow congregants from German immigrant families, he always remained an active churchman, as was my father, and as I have tried to be. In church lists the Hollis name turns up frequently. My grandfather's oldest son appears in the baptismal records, as does my youngest son's youngest.

These church records interlock satisfyingly with gravestones at the Tulips graveyard. Compared to the Coyner side, I possess an embarrassment of genealogical riches and only a small puzzle: Pastor Eusenius Berkemeier in the 1850s recorded in brief memoranda the baptism of four Hollis children who are absent from other registries. I note, though, some of those lists are not complete, thus names may have been lost in the previous century. Further, one must recall the horrifyingly swift deaths then of newborns, sprouting like proverbial grass and too soon withering in the wind.

I feel overwhelmed by my family's kind attention. My son Peter sends me Montaigne's *Essays*. Why have I never looked at Montaigne before? Did the man know every Latin author? I enjoy reading him and play at reconstructing his library by his citations. So inspired, I diverted myself by going back through these pages and mentally inserting in my sentences parentheses for classical references and quotations. That, though, is a pedant's pleasure no longer permitted in American prose, even in scribblings such as these. Were I to attempt it here, I can see Dory's frown and sense Crotia's impatience at thus clogging narrative's flow.

The tall clock downstairs gathers itself. In the slumbering house I hear the clock's gears murmuring to one another in shared anticipation. Its drive train spurs the laggards. Its escapement remonstrates with the impetuous. Now it gathers itself for maximum exertion, to mark midnight in a pitch so low I don't differentiate between hearing and feeling. It tolls with intervals so prolonged all but the most attentive or anxious may lose count. The strike mechanism whirs louder than the movement. The hammers strike. Solemn, unhurried, and inexorable.

The whirring stops. The hammers fall silent. The hands jerkily advance. Heavy lead weights lower a fraction closer to the case floor, a fraction closer to time's end. And I release held breath into a new day.

The very house timbers resonate with the clock's vibrations, another reason I cannot reside any other place. I ruminate on my father toiling late on his accounts, also hearing the clock, counting each strike as I do, and surely thinking of *his* father listening to the same clock, counting the strikes from his sickbed with breathless attention until God took him beyond all counting.

Tulips' gravitational pull is manifest in unpredictable places. On one side of a doorway to the backstairs is my grandfather's record of his children's growth. On the opposite post is my father's record of his children's heights, a pre-Christmas ritual as consistent as clock strikes. As a small child, my sister Annie called these marks "family stairs," and that became their name among us, just as most of us Hollis children honor the tradition with our own children, as many of them do with *theirs*. I have never seen Bill as furious as he was a few years ago when an overzealous painter blithely obliterated his family tree to "freshen" their pantry door.

My own marks for the next generation ascend the door trim next to my father's. I have feelings identical to my father's as he reviewed the lines he inscribed, though perhaps his advanced age made him more sentimental than I, to judge from the tears in his eyes when I once unexpectedly found him studying the doorpost. Mostly to cover my awkwardness in coming on him, I inquired what occupied him. "Trying to remember," he answered.

As am I.

QUACHASEE

WHC

Carrie watched as two boys, so young they held hands, eased out of the tree cover and walked hesitantly toward the cabin. From the tone of the dogs' barking, she knew other strangers, grownups, remained in the woods.

"What you want?" she called sharply, backing up to the porch.

"Please, ma'am, us not trubble yuh none," pleaded the older boy. "Ken yuh spar sumpin t'et?"

"Mebbe."

The boys came slowly closer. Rail thin, their clothes in tatters.

"Wen yuh las' et?" she called.

"Yes'dey mornin', ma'am, a li'l."

"Law, chile, yuh hungry!"

"Yessum, I is."

"Hows manya' yuh's beck in d'woods?"

Alarm at being found out, then a pause as they looked at each other for support. "'Bout seben, ma'am." Shy or frightened or both.

"Dey dint jes leaves yuh, an' goes on?"

The older boy quickly looked back as if to check, but the younger one shook his head in stout conviction. "Mama promise she not g'win nowhere. 'Sides, Billy nebbah walk fas, an I ken."

Carrie whistled in the dogs, then turned back to the boys. "Whur yuh g'win?"

The boys again looked at each other briefly before the older one answered, his eyes on the ground. "Doan rightly know, ma'am."

Carrie smiled at the younger boy. "Whut yuh called?"

"Joe."

"Well, Joe, yuh's a growed up boy: walkin long, an' not tard, ain't yuh?"

"Yessum, I is." He detached his hand from the older boy's.

"Hows yuh walkin hungry an' doan knows whur yuh g'win?"

"We walkin t'sumplace free," he declared with a proud smile.

"Joe!" Cautious reprimand from the older boy.

Joe looked up defiantly. "Id true."

"All right, boys." Carrie's guess was confirmed. "You go tell your people back there to come on. I've got a little food to spare, wherever you're going."

The boys returned ahead of the group that straggled in. A pretty girl carrying a very light-skinned baby. An older woman with a child on each hand. Three men, one gray-bearded. The youngest man wore no shirt; his stiff movements could only mean pain. At a respectful distance from the porch they eased to the ground. The shirtless man grimaced. As he lowered himself, part of his back became visible from the porch. Carrie saw long, oozing open wounds.

Staying on his feet, the gray-haired man pulled off his battered hat. "Miz, we ken et jes 'bout any ting yuh ken spare. De chillens too hungry t'walk moh. An we mus be 'long quick."

Carrie nodded at the girl with the baby. "Some marse messin' with her. Then he near killed her man with a whippin. So you gonna run for it, all one time, mebbe get to Union soldiers."

The old man hesitated, rubbing his forehead slowly, deliberating with himself. Then, "Yessum, yuh 'bout right. Dint figger dey be aftah us s'soon, or de chillens move s'slow, or de chile take s'sick. Affoah de valley wen we near ketched, a fren say, take dis trail up heah t' 'scape. But dey's dogs trackin."

After briefly watching the mother vainly enticing her baby to take a nipple, Carrie hurried inside. She reappeared with a hot kettle of stew, assigning Julia and George to bring bowls and spoons. The three wound their way through the group, ladling out portions and refills until they emptied the kettle. George, at first tight beside his mother, found children close to his own size fascinating and sat with his bowl beside them, talking shyly to them.

Carrie sent Julia to the spring house while she returned to the cabin. As the older woman collected empty bowls, Carrie handed a sack and a jug to the gray-haired man. "Meal, and milk for the children. It's a long way yet, Uncle . . ."

"I's Zachariah, from . . . mebbe id bettah yuh nebbah heered moh. But I sho tank yuh, ma'am."

She looked up to see Henry coming in from the High Field for dinner, and hurried to meet him. He stopped, waited until she reached him.

"What's this?" He didn't smile.

"They're runaways, Henry. A beat-up man, little children, and a baby real sick if it isn't already dead. Sounds like bounty hunters with dogs are after 'em. I guess they won't make it. Henry, I gave 'em your dinner."

Henry's face spoke his strong disapproval.

"I'd feed 'em the last thing in the kitchen," she shot back. "You think I forget who I am?"

Stone-faced, he walked past her toward the cabin, she trailing. As he approached, the whole group rose, watching him silently. Zachariah broke the silence. "Marse, we tank yuh foah de res' an de stew. We nebbah trubble yuh no moh. We movin 'long d'rekly."

Henry did not smile or nod acknowledgement. "Where you from?" he demanded.

Before Zachariah could answer, Carrie cut in. "Where you headed?"

He bit his lip. "To say de trut', Miz, we a mite los'. I usta hab a fren in Scottville, but . . ." his voice trailed off.

In the silence, from far down the trail came the barely audible baying of a dog. As they listened, baying turned to bawling.

Carrie stepped in front of Henry. "Sounds like you don't have much time, Uncle. That hound just picked up your scent. I'll tell you what a good friend who hunts all over these mountains tells me. Take that trail up over the ridge. On the other side, going down, you come to a fork. Send just one of your people, *one*, the man who can run, send him down the left fork until he comes soon to a creek. He'd better not cross the creek, but run back fast as he can and follow you down the right fork." She reached to shake his right arm. "The *right* fork. You understand?"

"Yessem."

"When you come to a creek on the right fork, don't cross it, any of you, don't cross it. Walk in the water, *only in the water*, upstream for a while, maybe 'til you find a granddaddy beech tree. Stay in the water, *in the water*, until that tree. Then *after* the tree, strike off down and swing around to find the trail going down again, and keep going. The trail will fork. You always take the right fork except at an empty, old shanty. You go left there. Maybe you'll know the country close to Scottville. You got all that, Uncle?"

"Yessem. I unnerstan 'xactly wad yuh sayin. Das one clever plan. God bless yuh, Miz. If we get ketched, nobody wuz home at dis heah cabin an we slip by in de woods. Yuh mus'bin workin oud 'way sumplace."

He waved the group on, carrying one of the children so they could all move faster. Soon the only evidence of their stop was the stack of empty bowls on the porch floor. Carrie stood watching the party move up the trail, urging them faster with her body.

"I don't like those children," scowled George.

"Why?" asked Henry.

"'Cause they wouldn't play with me. They said I'm white, so they can't play with me." He held out an arm to inspect it. "I'm not white. Nobody's white 'cept Flora and her chicks."

Julia was no more approving. "They sure didn't have any manners when they ate. I could hardly understand some of 'em. The older woman asked me if it's Ohio on the other side of the mountain. Mama, what disease is on that man's back?"

"That's not a disease," Carrie snapped. "They whipped him 'til his whole back was bloody, and then rubbed on salt or something so the pain is worse."

"Who would do *that?*" cried Julia.

"Ask your . . ." Carrie began, motioning to Henry, when the faint bawling of dogs preempted the family's attention. Henry held up his hand for silence. Unmistakable, and coming closer as they listened. "Sounds like visitors," he grimaced.

"Mister Spooks coming, Papa?" whooped George as he balanced a small pile of bowls.

"No, son, some people we've never seen before." He took a deep breath. "Alright. Julia, I need you to find some cloth that's a little bigger than the front window. George, get out the old shotgun."

"With the children here?" Carrie questioned in a skeptical tone.

"*I* didn't ask to get into this," answered Henry stiffly. "But we're in it and we need to get out. In one piece. All of us." He turned to the children. "Julia, George, when our visitors come, you stay out of sight.

I don't want to see you. I don't want to hear you. Don't wake Edward. Not a whisper. From either of you. Not one word. Understand, George? Not one word. What did I just say, George?"

"Not one word," he mouthed soundlessly.

Henry issued detailed instructions, ran a rehearsal, adjusted instructions before a repeated quick rehearsal. Then he idled on the front porch while George played with a top. Dogs sounded again, very close on the trail. Henry did not call their hounds back when they loped off to investigate. He pointed George inside, then pulled the door almost closed and slouched against the latch-side doorpost.

Furious barking. A distant voice. "Hello, th'house, thar."

"What's yer business, stranger?" Henry shouted.

"Call off yourn dawgs, th'house. Don' want no dawg fight, an good hounds git bloodied."

Henry whistled and shouted. The din subsided. Four men emerged from the woods. One held the leashes of several hounds. Two carried rifles. The fourth wore brought-on clothes, most prominently, a black felt derby. A pistol glinted at his belt.

Unmoving, Henry watched them approach, then warned, "Thet's 'bout fer 'nuff, strangers. What y'all wanin?"

The city man halted only reluctantly. "Niggers. I'm Netzler. You must'a heard of me. We track run'way niggers."

Henry said nothing.

"I know niggers came up this way."

Henry gave no sign of hearing.

Netzler stepped forward and exploded angrily. "Dogs got their scent clear all the way up here. Ain't that right, Brown?" He glanced at the man holding the leashes but did not wait for an answer. He glowered at Henry. "You must'a seen 'em. Which way they go?"

"Don' recall me sayin I seed nobody, Nezer. Mebbe I jes disremember."

"It's Netzler. What kinda game you playin?" he sneered. "I know those niggers come up here and I bet they stopped here to rest." He cut himself short to smile tight-lipped. "You know what I think? I reckon you got 'em hid here, an figure to take 'em in to get the re-ward yourself."

"Hain't got nary niggers hyar, Nezer."

"It's *Netzler*. We gonna search this house, then the barn. We'll find niggers, and fodder our horses need."

"Hain't got nary fodder nuther, Nuzer. Bad 'nough y'all be on my land. Latch string ain't out fer y'all nohow. Best go down now an not ne'er come back hyar."

"Martin, Jimmy," Netzler barked. They leveled their weapons at Henry while Netzler wrenched his pistol free. "It's *Netzler*, dammit."

Henry did not change his slouch as he addressed Jimmy and Martin. "Boys, lissenin to Nuzer Dammit, y'all forgettin' manners. Some body 'tother likely git kilt."

"Seem to me that body is you. And for the last time it's *Netzler*."

"Mebbe so, Nuzer. But the body thet shoots me is gonna be most pintedly daid afore I hit groun." Henry gradually stood full upright and eased slowly to one side, exposing more of the doorway behind him. Through the narrow slit by the barely opened door protruded a rifle's long barrel; it centered on Netzler. A slight motion of the cloth covering the far open window, and a muzzle appeared, pointed at Jimmy. Another barrel slid low through the doorway slit. It pointed high at first, then slowly, ominously, came down to line up with Martin.

"Goddam, ye crazy fool," burst out Brown, the dog handler. "Netzler, ye lost yer . . ." He raised his hands, palms empty, for the cabin, then swung back to Netzler. "Ye not on no flatlands plantation, nohow. This hyar is moun'ins, dammit, an ye gonna git us'n all kilt." He stepped even with Netzler—though at a calculated distance—and spoke to the cabin. "Frens, this hyar man," he motioned disparagingly at Netzler, "he a . . . he a damn ferriner. Ye ken know by his speechin'. I'm still larnin him good manners," his shoulders drooped, "but he slow. Jimmy, Martin, Put down them damn guns. Down, goddammit. Ye wanna be daid, man? Down."

He turned back to Henry, more relaxed once Jimmy and Martin had hesitantly lowered their weapons. "Now, fren, I regrets fer trespassin. I dint know this hyar trace rightly. You'unses the upperest cabin on hit. I was up nigh hyar oncet sanging, but thet's twenty year past. Mebbe we'uns got the wrong sow by the ear."

He stopped to mop his forehead. "Hit's sweltery, ain' hit? Raised up overyan in Armeny, I wuz. Got close kin yander still. Mebbe ye knowed Jeb Pickett. He's my couz oncet removed. An John Lazard o'er thar, he kin too, by my woman's fambly." He mopped his wet forehead again.

"Anyhows, we not be troublin ye none. But ifen ye happen to sight the party we'uns trackin, er tryin to track—an, fren, I not sayin ye did see 'em or ye gonna see 'em—but if ye mighta seed 'em, be mighty obliged fer news."

"Wal, my fren," Henry stooped to scratch a dog's ear. "Seein as how ye growed up in Armery and is kin at the Picketts. An Nuzer is a ferriner. Now thet I put m'mine t'hit, I mighta seed a party goin o'er the gap a whiles back. Could be they come by hyar. Mebbe movin' fas. Mighta spoke 'bout headin fer Claytown, left fork yonder." He motioned vaguely toward the closest ridge.

"*Left* fork, ye say," Brown looked meaningfully at Netzler, then back at Henry. "Beholden to ye, fren. Now we be movin' on, an not be nary no trouble."

Henry nodded placidly. "Growin up in Armery, ye git nigh these parts much, huntin?"

"Jes res yerself some, Nezer," muttered Brown. To Henry he replied, "Nossir. We used to hunt more on t'other side of Armery. As good huntin' as any ever on this yearth."

"Any ba'ar usin o'er thar?"

Netzler threw up his hands in vexation. Brown bent to tousle his restless dogs, and to partly hide his low-voiced translation for Netzler. "He jes askin 'bout ba'ar sign t'track 'em."

He straightened. "Yessir, they usin tother side'a Flat Knob mostly. Ye still see 'em usin hyar?"

"Mebbe. But the trace up thar is give up to be the worstest trace t'hunt ba'ar. Better t'be huntin e'en in some laurel hell whar ye cain't see an ye cain't move. Up thar, ye cain't crope up on 'em a'tall. Havta look sharp, cause thar's some place thet's right na'ar an crooked betwixt rocks. Y'know, ba'ars 'ill clum er fight, one."

Brown nodded at the commonplace, an experienced hunter's affirmation of prey behavior.

"An up thar ye cain't tree 'em 'cause ain't no tree fer 'em t'clum. So they jest a-waitin ye. Dawgs has to go one by one, an a ba'ar ken jes swat em as dawgs snugger in, e'en a pow'rful Plotz hound, an jes destroy 'em afore a hunter ken come up to fiah. Fak is, a ba'ar ken be on a hunter hisself afore he know hit."

"Thet the worstest sitiation ye ken face, ain't it?"

Henry nodded, adding as an afterthought, "A ba'ar, mebbe a hunter man too, could stand off a whole big army, seem like."

Brown pursed his lips thoughtfully and nodded. "Specially if thet man bear a good rifle."

"Oh, the rifle don' hev t'be thet good nether, my fren. Nossir. An ifen thar's e'en jes two a 'em—man on the pass, an t'other outta sight up on clifts above—then one 'tother might give a pecka trouble, y'know, *no matter what* a man huntin."

"I knows places like thet, fren. Say, ye wouldn't have seed ifen the party thet *mighta* gone past hyar, they carry a rifle wit' 'em?"

"Wal," Henry pondered. "No, I cain't rightly say thet *ever one*'a 'em carry a rifle. Nossir."

Brown stood up. "Damn. How many wuz thar?"

"Oh, I dint count."

"Three or twenty?" Netzler snorted derisively.

"Wal, if hit be put thet way, I'd hev t'say more'n less." Henry kept his eyes on Brown.

"More?" Netzler could not contain himself.

Henry's eyes flicked only briefly over Netzler in annoyance. "Don' contrary me none, Nezer."

"But they dint *all* have rifles?" As he tried to retrieve the conversation, Brown made silencing motions at Netzler.

"Nossir, they sartain dint," agreed Henry. "Some'a 'em only carry pistol guns thet ken shoot off a whole bunch afore reloadin." He paused, then continued languidly. "I guess the onliest one with a sword wuz the soljerman."

"A soldier with a sword!" repeated Netzler incredulously.

Henry looked off in the distance at crows cawing. "The resta'em coulda borne scythe blades 'stead a rifles. A course, in them na'ar passes, what yer fren—Nuzer, Neser . . ."

"Goddammit, the name is *Netzler*. Something wrong with your hearing, or your brain?""

"Nuzer, Nezer, Goddammit, everwhat hisn name," continued Henry, unruffled, "what thet igorant feller don' know is, a scythe blade be a fine weapon. Scyth blade kin slice a man's inners to mush quicker then ye kin git a long barrel up t'fiah. Don' make no sound goin in." He smiled. "Ner comin out neither. Least thet's what some people says." Henry's drowsy eyes sought Brown's face. "I 'spect they's right, *if a body know what I mean*."

"I think this hyar body *do* know what ye mean, fren," said Brown slowly. He straightened up and pulled together the leashes of his dogs. "An I know whur I'm a-headin me from hyar."

"Where?" demanded Netzler.

"Home. Di-reck'ly, cause hits a fer piece. Remember, I wuz walkin wit' t'dawgs whilst ye wuz ridin."

"Keep tracking, Brown." Netzler waved his pistol menacingly. "Can't go home now."

"The hell I cain't. An put thet damn toy away," Brown retorted. "Like my fren hyar say," Brown thumbed at Henry, "ye shoot me," he motioned to the unmoving cabin muzzles all now pointed at Netzler, "an ye be real daid afore I hit groun. Daider then four o'clock daid. Nezer, I tell ye, this is all the far I wan' t'go."

Netzler held his pistol pointed, but Brown regarded him contemptuously. "Ole Brown, hyar, he's jes' a poor feller what lissens to dawgs, but he not crazy. Ye tole me we wuz after two, three beat-up niggers we could took up fer easy cash money. An hit twarn't so. Thar's a gang'a 'em. Carryin real mean weapons. Might could be some goddam Union raidin' party, fer all I know, jes layin a trap."

Pushing the pistol aside, he brought his face close to Netzler's. "We go up thar," he pointed to the ridges, "an sartain sure we not come back nohow. Them's the nastiest hills in four counties. We hogs to the knife. No time to shit or squeal."

Brown pulled on the trackers' leashes. "I'm a-goin' to home, Nezer, an if ye ever knowed what good fer ye—sun's down soon—ye'll git, too, afore ye benighted. 'Member them clifts right nigh thet trail we clum? No moon t'night, so hit dark. Right easy t'go o'er. Hit's a quick way t'die, but hit hain't no good way. Tain't no bounty big 'nuff hit worth my life."

As he turned, Brown saluted Henry. "Wish ye well, my fren. Real nice meetin y'all." He waved to include the guns in the cabin. "Come fren an' go along." He half-loped back down the trace.

Jimmy and Martin turned to follow Brown and his dogs, but Netzler held up his hand. "I'm not done here, boys. I'm thinkin this all is just a trick. We see rifle barrels, but we don't see who's holding 'em. Most likely just women and children. They couldn't fire at nobody." He turned to Henry. "Ain't that so, Mister can't-hear-right?"

Henry hardly shifted his slouch or his tone. "Ye mebbe true, Nuzer. A'course, I 'spect thet some'un who cheeps on everthin, like ye do,

Nuzer, thet kinda torn down man would brung up two boys what ain't usta shootin no rifle reg'lar-like, 'cause they ne'er own nary rifle theirselfs, an cain't ne'er practice. Ain't I right, Nuzer?"

"No, I ain't cheap."

"Jimmy," Henry turned from Netzler. "Jimmy, Nezer hyar tole ye'll make good cash money outta t're-ward bounty. But, Jimmy, Nezer dint tell ye what he pay ifen thar *ain't no bounty.* Right, Jimmy? Wal, yer pay, hit nuttin. He not payin frum hisn own pocket. Thet's cheap Nezer fer ye."

"Goddammit man, can't you hear or are you too dumb to understand plain English? Not Nuzer. It's Netzler. NETZLER. And I'm not cheap."

"Then Nezer, ye ken 'splain t'Jimmy hyar why he ain't gittin no pay fer all his trip a hull day. Or, mebbe we ken have us'en a leetle shootin match t'see how cheap Nezer is. Take thet fancy water jug offen yourn belt, Nezer, an' throw hit high fer a ta'git. Hit store-boughten an shiny yet, but don' worry fer hit. Neither them boys ken hit the thaing. Mebbe ye don' care t'show how them boys cain't hardly shoot an' ye really is as cheap as it look?"

"It's Netzler, I keep telling you, dammit. You belong in some institution. This'll show you how cheap I ain't." He yanked his canteen savagely from its strap. "Ready, Jimmy?" Without waiting for Jimmy's reply, he threw the canteen high, paying no attention to the angle of the bright sun.

Facing the sun, Jimmy fired, but the canteen landed unscathed near Netzler's feet.

"How cheap ye ain't?" Henry broke the silence. "Wal, don' fret on hit, Nezer. Ole Martin's a dead-eye sartain, ain't he? Nezer everly hires him the bestest, don' he?"

Netzler threw again. Martin fired. Netzler swore. The canteen landed near Jimmy.

Henry chuckled. "Now Jimmy, this Nizzer here, he trow an 'spect ye to hit 'er whilst lookin di-rect in t'sun. Jimmy, why don' *ye* give 'er a trow an we see ifen Nizzer ken knock 'er down wit' thet toy pistol. He like t'carry hit, but ken he use hit er is hit jes' fer show?"

Glaring at Netzler, Jimmy seized the canteen and gave it a tremendous heave. Netzler got in three wild shots before his pistol jammed. As the shiny canteen floated high and whole against the deep blue sky, a sharp report from the cabin door made Henry duck instinctively. The punctured canteen instantly jerked upward, then tumbled down eccentrically.

George appeared in the now-open cabin doorway, half-dragging a rifle nearly as long as he was tall.

After a pause Henry addressed him loudly. "Thet's a decent shot, boy. 'Least fer a young'un."

He turned to the three men in the yard. "M'youngest boy, Nizzer. He jes larnin a rifle. M'older boys," he waved at the two barrels now leveled from the window, "they might as like t'practice on thet dumb hat yer fixy 'bout, Nuzer. Now y'all git offen my land afore the gen-u-wine shootin start, alla ye."

Martin and Jimmy were already sprinting for the cover of dense forest, and even Netzler moved with impressive speed, pulling off his derby as he ran.

"Don't celebrate too soon," said Henry as he guided George back inside. "Rest your weapons, but keep 'em close. I'll go up to the Witch's Nose to make sure they really are leaving.

"They were pushing their horses so hard," he reported on his return, "I almost missed seeing them." He hugged George and Julia with each arm. "I guess it'll be a while before you'll shoot like *that*. You keep that canteen as trophy, even if it can't hold water now."

❦

After the evening meal, Henry pulled the Bible from its shelf as usual. He paged slowly through the Gospels, scanning for a passage, then read aloud.

> *When the Son of Man comes in His glory, and all the holy angels with Him, then He will sit on the throne of His glory.*
> *All the nations will be gathered before Him and He will separate them one from another, as a shepherd divides his sheep from the goats.*
> *Then the King will say to those on His right hand, "Come, you blessed of My Father, inherit the kingdom prepared for you from the foundation of the world.*
> *"For I was hungry and you gave Me food. I was thirsty and you gave Me drink. I was a stranger and you took Me in.*
> *"I was naked and you clothed Me. I was sick and you visited Me. I was in prison and you came to Me."*

Then the righteous will answer Him, saying, "Lord, when did we see You hungry and feed you, or thirsty and give You drink?

"When did we see You a stranger and take You in, or naked and clothe You?"

And the King will answer and say to them, "Assuredly, I say to you, inasmuch as you did it to one of the least of these My brethren, you did it to Me."

As he returned the Bible to its shelf he gave Carrie's bowed head a kiss.

❧

Hearing George's prayers at bedtime, Carrie saw small tears in his eyes. "Too much excitement today?" She gave the boy a hug.

"Papa told lies, and God heard him," he whispered.

"When did he tell lies?"

"To those men."

When Henry returned from a late check of the barn, Carrie caught him before he snuffed the lantern. "Better talk to George. He worries that God will punish you for telling lies."

Frowning, he climbed to the loft, put down the lantern, and knelt beside George. "Now, son, what's worrying you?"

"Oh Papa," he popped up, sleepless. "You said those people we fed had rifles, and they were going to Claytown, and there were twenty-four of them, and you pretended I shot the water bottle instead of Mama shooting it, and those were all lies, and Julia thinks so too, and you said we have to always tell the truth, and God hears us when we lie, and . . ."

"You've got sharp ears, boy. That's what I said. God doesn't want to hear lies, but He also wants us to be good to our neighbors. I said some things that weren't true because those were bad men. They were chasing the people you gave food to, and would hurt them if they caught them. So I tried to say what I hoped would keep them apart. Sometimes, to help people, grownups have to say things that aren't literally true, and God doesn't punish them. But you don't have to worry about that until you're grown up. Does that make you feel better?"

George half-nodded as he lay down again.

Julia lifted her head. "Why did you talk that way to those men? Mama says that's ignorant talk."

"So that it'd sound as if we've always lived up here in the mountains."

"But we have."

"*You* have. Not your mother and I."

"Weren't you scared when they pointed guns at you?"

"Only a fool wouldn't be. But I depended on your mother and you and George to do what I told you. And you did."

George popped up again. "Yer likely git kilt."

"No, George," corrected Julia in a superior tone. "You could have been killed."

Since she lay too far away for George's punch to reach her, he went to a new question. "Papa, what's a nigger? That bad man talked about niggers."

Henry snuffed the lantern. "We can talk about that in the morning. Now it's time to go to sleep."

On the porch in the bright moonlight, Henry broke the silence. "Seems like two days since this morning." He paused, then added, "That was a nice shot on the canteen. I wasn't expecting it. What made you fire?"

"Couldn't resist. It was just like years ago with Audie back of the barn. Audie would have about killed me if I missed a simple hanger like that."

"A hanger?"

"That's what she calls 'em when you catch one at the very top, just before it starts to drop—when you have to lead more—just hanging there for you in the blue sky."

"Still, it was a nice shot. I couldn't have done it."

"Not with your eyes. But I could never have stayed as calm as you on the porch. And how did you know to say what I wanted you to say when I pushed George out the door?"

Henry didn't answer for some time. Then, "I guess I just knew without thinking much about it. Mebbe we're like the old couple: been together so long that one knows what the other is going to say before they say it."

"I noticed the gray at your temples," teased Carrie. "Sometimes I worry that we don't talk as much as we used to. But then I think, Henry doesn't always have to tell me what he's thinking because somehow I already know."

"I guess I was too rough about the runaways this morning," Henry said. "You caught me when I was in deep thinking about some grafting. I should have remembered that Bible passage sooner."

She, too, was silent a long time. "Next time Spooks is up, I'll have to tell him I was wrong. I remember when he told us how some lawyers mispronounce a witness's name during a trial to rattle him on the stand. I thought he was making things up. But now I know it works. Only trouble was it got me giggling so much, I was afraid Netzler'd see the rifle wasn't always steady."

After another silence her tone was more somber. "I looked at those runaways and knew they could be me and the children."

"But they weren't. You should think of other things."

"Like what to tell George tomorrow? He won't forget his question. First it will be, what's a nigger? And then, what's a slave? And then, why're niggers slaves? And then, are we slaves? And then, are you a slave? And then, why not?"

"I guess here is one mother who knows her son's head pretty well."

"Not *his* head, Henry. *My* head. I pestered Mama with just those questions when I must have been about George's age."

"A smart woman, your mother. Do you remember how she answered you?"

"I remember exactly, like a lot of things she told me. She said some people call a lowdown, worthless, stupid person a nigger, but since I was too young to figure out who was lowdown, worthless, and stupid, I'd sure better not call anybody a nigger, 'least not before I checked with her."

"That's what I'll tell George."

"What'll you say when he asks what color he is?"

"I'll tell him . . . he is . . . the color he is," Henry rehearsed. "God makes people . . . all kinds of colors. Only God knows why. And his mama and papa are . . . glad God made him. . . . Think that will satisfy him for now?"

"Maybe. But remember that Julia'll be listening, even if she's pretending not to."

"Yup," he sighed. "It gets harder and harder."

A cloud passed over the moon, then left it unobscured. Carrie held out her arm to study its shadow. "When I see how bright the moonlight is, the first thing I think is, good, that'll make walking at night easier for them. I pray they can rest safely somewhere yet tonight."

Henry put his hands on her shoulders and she reached up to squeeze them. "Listen, Henry, dear Henry. I have to tell you that I'm proud of you for standing up to those slave catchers, and doing it so cleverly."

"I don't want to have to try that again."

"Be thankful we're up here instead of on some main road down the valley."

"It looks like even up here I could get you into as big a mess as at the livery barn."

"The livery barn was pride. This was Christian courage for the least of them. You did right, Henry, and I love you for it."

SLAVE NARRATIVES

Federal Writer's Project, Number 320010.

EUNICE RANTWELL, born 1851

Interview with Mrs. James Jamieson, May 5, 1937
Place: Asheville, North Carolina

Yessum, ole Eunice ken 'membahs dem slave deys. I wah jes a chile back den, but I ken recalls id, yessum. I borned on a siz'ble fahm ovah in Tenn'ssee, good ways fum heah. Id near a town nobody in Carolina neber know, call' Ginners Ford.

My mama die wen I wah borned, so my aunt brung me up dere. An one dey de Massa, dat Marse Sam, cum walkin by de cabins, an he see me. He stops an say t'mah aunt, "Dat chile plenty big t'hep Miz Ann." Miz Ann he sister. So dat's whut I does. I de pussonal maid foah Miz Ann. Dat mah wok. She need hep bad 'cause she hab a lame foot, so she only walks wif a big ole crutch. An she deaf'n dumb, so she ken' heah nuttin' a'tall. But she reads lot a'book. Make mah mine ache jes t'tink ob all dem book. She try t'teach me t'read, too, yessum she do. But I dint hab no maturity yet, an ken' keep no mine t'id.

I 'spect Marse Sam nebber wan t'see Miz Ann 'round, 'cause he'n Missus, he wife, dey move Miz Ann way t'de back conah ob de house. Dey say she hab t'take she meals in she room. Lots a'lady, dey'd make big fuss 'bout dat, but Miz Ann doan make no fuss a'tall. Mebbe she sees de new room good foah she, 'cause dere's no commoshun dere, an' she ken sleep late mohnins, de ways she lahk. I's de one dat carry huh food fum de kichen, an de dishes back. An does erran's foah she. Miz Ann jes so kind t'me, she let me sleep wif mah aunt; she nebbah make me stay in huh room late nights. She a real lady, I tell you, a real, God-fearin' lady, an I admires she fer dat.

Fum time t'time I hep huh pack tings t'go visit huh othah broth'r, Marse Henry, an his wife an chillens on dere fahm way high up on de moun'in. Miz Ann sho did lahk dat. She jes lub dem chillens. I nebah goes up myselves wif huh 'cause huh othah broth'r, Marse Henry, he alwuz come down de moun'in wif a mule t'gets she, an fetches she back. I stays at Tulips.

Yessum, I 'membahs wen I fust goes up t'de big house at Tulips. Lahk yestedey. I tells yuh, I scared. I nebbah bin a place wif a diff'ren room foah neah ebbadin'. Dere's a clock dere dat go clear up t'de ceilin. Ebbah time id hit, I jumps. I ain't nebbar seed somepin lahk dat afoah. I usta stan front'a dat clock an jes watch dem two hand go 'roun ta'straigh' up—I din' harly tell time den— an I know id gonna boom out. I jes' know'd. But den id booms. I jumps an'ways.

No, ma'am, I nebbah heah 'bout no ha'd pun'shmen, 'least nuttin worse den whut som mama gib a chile. Yuh know, a mama sumtiam mus' wallup a chile, on accounta he misbehavin. She habda do id. De chile need dat t'growup right. Mebbe iffen pun'shmen happen, lahk yuh says, some man done whut he tole not to.

Yessum, I 'membahs heerin 'bout run'ways. Jest a few. I doan know wy dey does dat. Dey not tinkin' right. I nebbah runs 'way m'self. Hab no reason, not a'Tulips. I doan 'membahs nobody runnin fum our place. I tink id fum some uder place a good ways fum we, so none'a us nebbah heers 'bou'id.

I growed up fas. Miz Ann used t'point how high mah dress gettin up mah laig, an shakes huh haid. She usta make Massa fine me a new dress. He'd do id, an I'd hab me a right purty'un, too. But den *id* gets too short too, an he say, "Doan worry, Eunice, I gets yuh nodder one." He do, too, an id be eben purtier. He mighty good to Eunice, I tells yuh. He puts he arm 'round me and gibs me hugs, jes fam'ly.

Missus, he wife, say I ole 'nuff now t'go wok in de field. She want a white maid foah de house. But he say, "Eunice heah, she jes part ob fambly." 'Cause dat's wha' we was, jes all fambly. He tells she, "W'man, why yuh wanna be puttin on airs wid sum wide maid? Eunice not good 'nuff foah yuh? She orter stay in de house t'be close." Dey goes dis ways 'n dat ways.

'Bout den de wahr, it done, an Massa say we's all free. I dint hardly know whut dat mean, free. My aunt, she say, "C'mon, gal, we leavin heah. It not safe foah yuh heah." An I say, "Wad you talkin 'bout? No place safer den heah wid Massa. We fambly." I argues wid she. My ole Aunt say I doan know wad I talkin 'bout, an she do. She my aunt, an she make me leaves dere, an go 'long t'Nor'Car'lina.

We lived some tebble, wurried times den, yessum. Real ha'd. 'Course, aftah a whiles I reconcile mah mine t'Car'lina. Still, iffen de ha'd times comes, den I tinks back an wisht I ain't nebbah lef' Massa an Tenn'ssee. He a true fren t'Eunice.

QUACHASEE
WHC

Henry was back at the cabin porch already at mid-morning, to Carrie's surprise. "That was fast. You finished the orchard pruning already?"

"No, I couldn't keep working there with what's on my mind."

"Sounds serious enough for seconds of this poor coffee we've got. Sit and I'll get some warm."

When Carrie returned with full cups, Henry was moving about, almost pacing. He barely started sipping his cup before he put it aside. "Those slave catchers just walked in on us. Netzler would have been trouble if Brown, the dog-man, hadn't been along to warn him off. It'd be more than canteen target shooting."

"So that's what you've been lying awake about."

"You wouldn't know I'm lying awake if you weren't lying awake too."

Carrie made a wry face. "But that lying awake doesn't give me any notion what I could do about another Nezerdammit."

"Well, pruning gave me an idea. We need to pull up the drawbridge. Let the ridges go back to doing their work."

Carrie's face showed how completely Henry had lost her.

Henry's forefinger swept the horizon. "We've got steep ridges all around us. Right?"

"That's what I've loved ever since you first brought me up here. They're like walls all around."

"Except there." Henry's finger stabbed at the trail down the valley. "That's where we've been lowering and widening the drawbridge ever since Lem's crew started work on it to bring up Elvira's cow."

"I remember how shocked you were when I suggested that."

Henry was too absorbed to reminisce. "I'm not blaming you. I had a good trail in mind since the first time I came up here. But we've made it *too* good for the situation we're facing now."

"So the trail is our drawbridge." Carrie's face said comprehension, then fell. "Now I'm lost. How do you raise a drawbridge when it's a trail on solid ground?"

"That's what came to me in the orchard. I walked that trail in my mind, looking at all the places we've fixed. There are a lot of them—keeping laurel cut back, clearing rocks out of the way, log bridges, cutting down trees—you know, all the work we've done over the years. A lot of that work we can undo if we want."

"You can't grow trees quick."

"No, but the log bridges could disappear."

"Henry, you worked so hard on them."

"I'd rather lose that work than see Netzler again, wouldn't you?"

Carrie nodded. "Of course. But the trail that brings Netzler also brings Audie Ann and Spooks. Guess we need a drawbridge we can lower for friends and raise against everybody else."

"I've been worrying that," answered Henry. "I'm not certain, but I think I could make sections of the trail very hard to follow, and still leave ways to go around them. Not a nigh way; it'd be . . . I guess you'd call it a 'long cut.' But I need to make sure before I start anything."

Carrie rose, picking up Henry's nearly untouched cup. "I know Henry Hollis won't rest until he's started checking. I'll get some cornbread for you to take along. Try to be back before dark, so I don't worry."

Henry did return before dark, dog-tired, his face and arms bloody from long scratches. One look at him and the boys stopped playing with a favorite jiggerboo, and Julia immediately sought a clean cloth to moisten.

"What I need," he explained to Julia, who was wiping blood off his neck, "is a trace that's not very inviting, and if you do start on it, looks for sure it's gonna wind you up in the rough—but doesn't, of course."

"Exactly," she said, her eyes sparkling. "I understand. I think I could help."

Henry smiled to avoid spoken response while he reflected. The lifting of heart-wrenching worry with that offering of gingerbread at the spring. The beautiful baby baptized in the ornate "JLH" christening dress. The porch child, still too young to be allowed alone in the yard. The little girl, tongue sticking from the corner of her mouth, doggedly mastering her ABC's with pencil and paper. Now this confident offer of help.

"No harm in taking her along when you go," observed Carrie. "Her eyesight is a lot better for seeing distances. And she'll have sense enough to keep you out of the thickety places, so you don't come home so scratched up."

❧

"Mama, we found the perfect routes," Julia announced even before she was up on the porch. "They're hard to spot and once you're on them, they look like they'll only take you into terrible roughs."

"I hope you're right, daughter, because you are a wreck," Carrie surveyed the triumphant pathfinder. "You still have stickers all over your back, and twigs in your hair. But I guess all you need is a general combing out."

Henry interrupted plaintively. "Could the combing and currying wait until after we eat? We're both famished."

Supper. De-snagging. Bed. All accompanied by Julia's detailed description of the terrain they encountered. Once in the loft, however, she was asleep as soon as she lay down.

Henry too fell into bed very early, though Carrie found him awake again when she slipped in beside him. "Not often I've seen her so excited," she said in a low voice. "Was she any help to you?"

Henry rolled over to be close to her ear. "She was not a help," he answered. "She was essential. I could never have done what we did without her. You were right. But it's more than just her sight. She has a feel for how the land lays. Talking over alternatives with her is almost like talking with Spooks, except our goal was the opposite of getting somewhere efficiently. We even studied some at Snake Sheer. She's her mother at that edge. I remember the first time we came up you scared me half to death standing close to that edge."

"You didn't let her get as close as I was?"

"Girl turned mother and the world looks different," teased Henry. "Anyhow I think there are places where small powder charges could bring down a lot of rock, just obliterate the old trail. We'd really raise the drawbridge."

Carrie sat straight up. "Henry, you could get killed trying that. Powder blowing up rocks—you don't know the first thing."

"You're wrong there. I do know the first thing."

"What?" Carrie demanded.

"I know I don't know much about powder, except powder in guns. And rocks aren't guns. So I'd have to ask someone who knows. But could we talk about it in the morning? Julia ran me ragged today, and now I can't stay awake." Henry's eyelids drooped. In a few seconds he was snoring very softly.

The next morning Carrie was soon after him about using powder on the trail. He did not argue with her. "I'm not looking to get myself killed. I need advice from an expert. You remember after some fruit tree deliveries near Clayton, I told you I ran into Carter Fineman. We helped each other with arithmetic problems in school back when I was a lot smaller than he was. When I came back from New York he was long gone North and I lost track of him."

"I do remember. Wasn't he the one you said was terribly hurt and came home to recover what he could?"

"That's the man. He was hurt working for a canal construction company, so I got the idea he maybe knows something about using powder to clear rocks. I thought I'd at least ask him. I know for sure he's a good Union man, dead set against secession, disgusted with the government. Next week when I go down the valley, I may look him up again."

Carter Fineman was the expert he needed, Henry reported to Carrie. He knew powder. He even volunteered to go to Snake Sheer to see for himself. Pronounced the job trifling. A little push on the rock face above, and a big stretch of trail gone. Happy to do it, partly to return the large favor he long owed Samuel B, something involving a scrape Carter got in as a young'un. Powder was all Carter needed, not readily available because of military needs. Best come back in mebbe a month or two or three.

Carrie heard all this secondhand. The gregarious Carter never sat on the cabin porch. A flask of Henry's fruit fermentation in his bag, Carter did not notice his exclusion, nor suspect the cause: his undamable stream of canal-building stories, always horrific accidents, always with powder. Carter's most oft-told centered on a damned Irishman, so dumb he learned from a wheelbarrow how to walk upright. The Irishman was careless rigging fuses. The charge went off as Carter strolled up to check it. Carter survived, but not nine Irish. "Damned, dumb, dead Irishmen," said Carter, waving his hand dismissively. His left hand. His right hand was missing, as was his right arm, and eye and ear.

In a month or so Henry left before sunrise with a young pig for a buyer down the valley. When he returned dusk was just giving way to dark. Carrie greeted him with relief. "I was starting to wonder if I should worry." She poked at the fire below a kettle.

Henry answered with a smile. "Did you hear the explosions?"

"What explosions?" She turned from the hearth. "You weren't working with that Carter? You promised not to be involved."

"I kept my promise. I wasn't involved. Carter did the whole thing himself. Wouldn't let me touch a thing." Henry thought he need not rehash Carter's growls about damned Irish. Nor mention Carter's manic glee at each explosion. "He knew what he was doing. He dropped rock on the trail with little charges so as to block it completely without sending a whole landslide down that people might be able to walk over."

Solomon appeared. He and Henry went off with axes and long saw. They returned dragging, but looking pleased. "Carrie," said Solomon with a broad grin, "we wuz ball-hootin lahk yuh neber seed. Dem log bridges slide down de mountain lahk dey greased." For the listening children he shot his hand down from above his shoulder to waist height in log imitation. "Dat drawed bridge Marse Henry talk 'bout, it raise way up now."

Henry nodded. "There's still the back way, the high trail, of course, but it's so long and unpromising before you get to us. And," he emphasized with satisfaction, "there's that great stretch of scree on it below Pinter's Knob. Horses hate it, and trails that are obvious in brush just disappear in that moving rock."

"Papa," Julia had been listening closely, "why is scree called scree?"

Henry was caught up short. "I have no idea. I learned the word from Spooks. Ask him the next time he's here. I gave him a map of the new route."

"Julia, I don't know," was Spooks' answer as he sat with the family for an evening meal. "A natural philosophy course I took long ago when I was young and handsome said the word for that kind of loose rock is scree, and I just accepted it. You see the value of simple questions. I must read further at home." He pulled paper from his pocket to scribble a reminder before he continued.

"Incidentally, Miss Julia, your new route is tiresome indeed, about half again as long as the old one, I think. But I'm sure the Mohicans would congratulate you on your choices. They would note admiringly that all the key turnoffs are at places with mostly rocky ground, so less chance to leave telltale hoof marks for the perfidious Hurons. This cabin is now as nearly hidden as I can imagine."

Talk turned to the war and hopes the Union forces would move south from Kentucky to Tennessee. Spooks spread out his map, and they all agreed that for early relief, they were too far from the Mississippi, the logical route to channel a Union drive south. Attention would go first to the Vicksburg bottleneck.

"Spooks, aren't you wary of the conscription law?" asked Carrie. "From what I read you could get taken up."

"I am," Spooks admitted. "I've resigned the bar and almost shut down my office to keep a lower silhouette. Fortunately this immediate area is heavily Union. A lot of people share Henry's view that rich planters are all behind this. Oligopoly would be a good word for you to tease, Miss Julia. O-l-i-g-o-p-o-l-y. Anyway with Union feelings strong I'm hoping I'm not forced to buy my way out. I talked with a man—Henry you may remember him, his . . hmm, well he should remain nameless. He'll go for pay. He promises to desert first chance, as he's already done twice. So I wouldn't be helping the Rebs much. With all the chaos, there may be just enough water for a lone fish to swim through."

"Who's fishing?" asked Julia as Spooks extended his hand to wiggle it fish-like through low water.

"That, Miss Julia, is the crux of the question. The Confederate Congress sees the enthusiasm of first-year enlistments is long gone, and the generals must have an army. So the Congress passes a conscription law, trying their best to forget all their past rhetoric about federalism and states' rights. You've read those speeches I brought up?"

Bright waited for Julia's nod before continuing. "There is such resistance to the draft that governors establish Home Guards to enforce it. Around here, though, Union sympathy is so strong that many of the Home Guards are Union men, so they enforce the law, but only against men they know have Confederate sympathies. Not exactly what the governor had in mind. The slackers fight the Home Guard."

He turned from Julia to Henry, though Julia still listened intently. "You're lucky, Uncas, old friend, to be well clear of Tulips these days. Some hotheads say it's the same as a flatlands plantation, even if Tulips is a ways below the twenty-slave rule. Sam had a scare coming home one night. He barely outran a group of masked riders; claims he had some shots go close by him. So he finds it expedient to spend much time in Knoxville with Elvira's sister."

"What does he do in a town," Henry wondered, "with no farm to mismanage? Just sit all day? He never read much."

"You can be sure he's up to no good." Carrie nearly spat the words, then softened her tone. "But is Tulips in danger?"

"I think not. At least not yet. Audie is too famous for her marksmanship and respected for her courage against so much adversity, and for her kindness. Still, one can never be sure. I talked with her the other day. She's let it be known she patrols at night with Solomon carrying that fancy rifle for her. Samuel B could not protect the homeplace better. I doubt you'll see much of her up here for a while."

"What I don't understand," Julia interrupted, "if there are so many Union people, how can secession succeed?"

"Because," explained Spooks patiently, "where you live, Julia, happens to be a mountain region anomaly. Another good word for you to consider. A-n-o-m-a-l-y. Now west of here the Home Guard is more Confederate men, so the Union men scouting out back in the mountains, the so-called Regulators, put up a good fight, I'm told. Near pitched battles that aren't shams, and the Home Guards don't always win. Unholy chaos. Which I try to use to my advantage. But so will other men. And our advantages may conflict in unfortunate ways."

"Murky water for your swimming." Carrie imitated his wiggled hand.

"Murky indeed. On a clearer note, I have been meaning to ask, Miss Cora, if it would be acceptable for me to bring a friend up to visit sometime, despite your raised drawbridge. A good friend would like to see a high mountain homestead like yours. I have told many stories about you all. May we come up for the day sometime?"

"Shame on you for thinking you must ask ahead. You know any friend of yours is welcome here. Bring him up."

"I thought I'd better ask because he's a she. Miz Lydia Davies. She's the widow of a former client."

Carrie's response was only slightly delayed by her surprise. "All the better. The only woman who ever comes to visit here is Audie Ann."

"Our visit may not be as soon as I'd like. A full moon would be best if we are delayed going back, considering Julia's new route. And I'm not certain whether this moon will be during good weather. I believe Miz Davies is an early riser, so we should be here before midday."

"Come ahead when the weather is fine. You know the raised drawbridge wasn't meant against you."

The Civil War in the Upper South
A Review of Strategies & Campaigns

By Lt. Gen. Archibald Gaint, III

U.S.M.C. (Retired)

Military Affairs Press

Bethesda Md, 1928

Tennessee
West to East, 1861 to 1862

As we turn briefly to the montane region of extreme eastern Tennessee and western North Carolina, military action and impact may be quickly summarized. The armies of both North and South avoided this difficult terrain. Absence of population centers or foci of commerce, industry or transportation (compare with, e.g., Knoxville on the southwest periphery) meant there existed here no productive targets to attack or essential resources to defend. As a result no actions that were part of a grand strategy disturbed the somnolence of these forbidding mountains and isolated valleys.

Neither side maintained a headquarters or even a subordinate command center that covered this area in any but the most nominal sense. One cannot speak of a conventional chain of command, for reconnaissance information and reports going one way, and commands going the other were not passed along (much less retained for the later diligent military historian).

What military action occurred was of limited scope and negligible consequence. Neither side assigned promising young officers here to gain experience useful in other campaigns. In fact, Federal, and to a less extent, Confederate, commands "promoted" incompetent and out-of-favor officers to this backwater, presumably to limit their damage or punish them. As a result, the officer corps on both sides was universally thought to possess little experience, competence or authority. Indeed, some Confederate officers were elected by those they nominally commanded.

More formally-organized troops (almost a euphemism), small in number, were encumbered by irregulars, jobbers and camp followers. Almost without exception the ranks were poorly trained and equipped with a miscellaneous assortment of light arms that must have been a curious sight on the parade ground, and surely presented problems in precluding interchangeability. Since logistics was a concept virtually unknown, shortages of ammunition and rations were treated with resignation as inevitable. A retired U.S. Army officer, graduate of West Point, with extensive experience under fire during the Mexican War, filed a highly confidential report in which he devastatingly characterized the units he inspected in 1861 as "rabbits carrying pea-shooters, incapable of offensive attack and most likely to trip each other running in retreat if called to defend."

From time to time, loosely-organized forces did engage in light skirmishes when they encountered, usually by chance, some opposition. Though certain reports imbued these accidental brushes with epic proportions, the historian, from a less parochial perspective, must describe the actual engagements as perhaps thrilling for some participants, but partial, brief and indecisive for all concerned. Those involved learned little they applied to any subsequent action.

Col. Dennis Crushing (U.S. Army, Ret.), now of Asheville, N.C., who has studied this theater most intensely and is intimately familiar with its geography, is surely correct in characterizing military action along Tennessee's mountainous border with North Carolina as a fly on the elephant's ear.

QUACHASEE
WHC

Julia stood at the door, her nose reddened from early morning chill. "Mootoo got out'n gone."

"Confound that brute." Henry looked up from the harness he was repairing. "Come spring, Mootoo turns rogish. Shoulda ended the problem last January." He stood, dumping tools and harness on the floor. "Gone far?"

"Busted through the fence, outta sight."

"Sure had other things I wanted done this morning," he complained. "Must have gone up to the bald on Stony, just like before. Won't want to come back either."

"I can help you." George reached eagerly for his coat.

Carrie intercepted him. "You're not going anywhere, boy, until that sprain in your ankle is healed for good. If you couldn't limp from here to the spring to open the water gate yesterday, you sure can't make it all the way up to the bald to chase a critter today."

Henry almost intervened. Childhood ills and accidents perturbed Carrie as they never had before they lost Harry. Then he reconsidered; a malingering George *had* manipulated his mother's concern. He grinned at George. "Well, son, don't get sulled. You did yourself in, didn't you?" He turned to his daughter. "Julia, come with me so I don't run my legs off." Belatedly he looked at Carrie. "You don't need her right now, do you?"

"I do need her for some stitching." Julia's face showed mute disappointment, and Carrie relented. "She can do that some day that's not so fine. Julia, you change to that gray dress with all the mends. And Henry, see if you can stay clear of the rough up there since she's with you. Wait a minute and I'll make up some hoe cakes and beans to keep you walking. Maybe you should take a rifle. We can use game if you see any."

After a glum check of broken fence, Henry followed tracks pointed up toward the nearest bald, a grass bald by their good fortune, a knob-top meadow fire-cleared by lightning or perhaps Cherokee, now only grass and stunted shrub. Henry walked at a good pace, but slow enough he could enjoy sun warmth and bird songs. For Julia he fingered swelling on twigs. "Watch as we go higher. Every foot up and you'll see fewer buds. We'll be lucky at the top if the grass has even started to green. Be thankful that we're not headed to a wooly top."

"Papa, were there once sheep up there, that some balds are called wooly?"

"For sure, never sheep. People who only look at laurel thickets from a distance call them wooly. People who look at laurel thickets up close call 'em laurel hells. Small wonder. You know how hard they are to get through."

"I know *I* can't. Only big hogs and bears. Birds. Ants too, I guess."

The bald produced fresh tracks at the lick log, but no Mootoo. Henry stared across to Razorback Ridge. "You don't think that dumb critter remembered the salt lick over on Razorback?" He glanced at Julia, remembering Carrie's warnings. Razorback meant tough going, and then a long, slow way home driving the steer.

Julia read his face. "I'm not tired, Papa. We have to find Mootoo."

Down, sometimes slip-and-slide down. Up, sometimes grab-a-bush-and-pull up. In the bald near Razorback's top, they found the salt lick easily, but no steer and no new clues. Henry declared the hunt over for the day. Before retracing their route, they relaxed on sun-baked rocks while they finished Carrie's rations. Julia jumped up, listening intently. She motioned to her father. He rose silently, his hands cupped behind his ears. At first nothing; then, on the wind, a long drawn-out *moo*, so faint and distant an inopportune bird twittering would have drowned it out.

"That's Mootoo," Julia declared.

"Maybe," Henry conceded. "Could be the fool critter just found out there's no way out of Battle Hollow."

"What's that?" Julia buckled the leather bag, ready to press on.

"All the way down there, you follow a clear trail that keeps rising so you're sure you're going to ease right over a gap up ahead. Turn a hard corner and you drop into a bowl. Good soil. Right pretty. Until you notice you're fenced in—rock cliffs or slope so steep a man needs five arms and a rope to get up. No way out except for birds and squirrels. Haven't been there since Spooks and I explored it when we were about your age. Ole man Hilton used to live there. All alone. Ran us out with birdshot."

"What happened to him?" Julia started jumping down the steep, long slope toward the trail.

"Died there, of cussedness, we thought. He'd been dead for a year, looked like, before anyone found him. People only went there for arrowheads and spear points. Used to be some of the biggest, most beautifully made spearpoints I ever saw, right out on the ground, mixed in with a lot of bones. People talked about a big Cherokee battle there. Maybe some raiding party ran in there by mistake and had to fight with their backs to the wall. You wonder who won." Henry stopped talking to keep his daughter's pace.

Far down, they easily found the trail Henry remembered. After several turns they saw ahead the high profile of a cliff jutting from the right. Henry motioned to it. "We turn past that cliff, and the trail just ends. That's where ole Mootoo—"

He broke off at the sound of cantering hooves behind them. Seizing Julia by the shoulders he hurriedly pushed her off the trail and behind twin hempines with massive trunks. Crouched there, Henry had a clear view. A hard-ridden horse appeared. The man in the saddle wore a blue military coat and held upright a staff flying a small Union flag. Behind him clung a younger man, hardly more than a boy, with long blond hair. His grimace presumably spoke for the wound soaking blood through his pant leg.

The rider reined in just beyond Henry. He picked the flagstaff out of its saddle foot and threw it as a spear far into the brush, then turned in the saddle. "Bill, I'm gonna set ye down hyar, ride on to bring hep back."

Bill shook his head. "Hiram, don' do thet. They'll kill me if ye don' git back in time."

Hiram forced Bill's hands off his waist. "Hain't got no choice. Two's too much fer the hoss." He stood in the stirrups, turned, and shoved Bill hard. With a cry sounding despair as much as pain, Bill fell heavily to the trail. Hiram spurred his horse.

"Holp me, Hiram. They'll kill me sure after what we done to 'em." Bill pulled himself to his feet by a tree trunk, and started to limp after the disappearing horse, but soon fell and lay unmoving. Hoof clatter died away. Birds began chirping again.

"Shouldn't we be good Samaritans, Papa?" whispered Julia.

Henry looked down at her. Only a few days ago he had read the Gospel parable aloud at the table. Here was surely a stranger in dire need. He started to agree when they heard distant, heavy gunfire. He stood up full to listen, Julia beside him. "Isn't it getting closer?" he whispered.

Motionless, they listened, holding their breaths.

"I think so," she said. "Closer now. And fast, I think. What's happening?"

Henry puzzled. Then he knew with certainty. Knew from the days Deerslayer and Uncas reconnoitered this land, tracking the route of the Hurons being driven back foot by foot by the Mohicans, in serious straits but not dire, only to find themselves boxed into a blind hollow with no exit except death.

"He needs bandages and water, Papa."

The firing sounded closer. The parable's Samaritan traveled alone, not with a young daughter, and made no promises to his wife before he set out. Gunfire closer still, maybe heavier. And the Samaritan hadn't offered succor amid lethal crossfire.

"Julia, listen careful. We've gotta run hard and right now. Stay close. Stay quiet. But if you fall or can't keep up, you yell at me. Holler loud until I stop. You hear?"

She nodded calmly. "Where're we headed?"

"Up 'n outta here." He gripped the rifle barrel firmly and charged uphill as fast as he could, back along the trail's line, but always angling higher above it. The firing clearer still, steadily closer to where they left the trail, but Henry ran up, ever up, bulling through brush when forced to, trying not to let branches slap back at Julia. The steep grade left him gasping for breath. Sweat poured down his face despite the cool air. Trying to ignore his pounding heart, Henry drove up as fast as he could make his legs move. Several times he glanced behind him. Julia, long-legged, her skirt tied up somehow, stayed close at his heels, though she too gasped for air. The firing sounded even with them now, but far below.

A huge, impenetrable thicket blocked their trajectory. Henry started directly uphill, but found the slope far too steep for running or even walking. He reversed in a switchback, now abreast and moving with the firing, but gaining altitude with every step. He no longer heard shouting, but gunshots were still clear. Ahead he saw a great rock outcropping against a blue sky, and angled up still steeper, even though his labored gasping would give his position away to anyone within earshot. He reached the outcropping, worked his way up its near side, stumbled over a boulder, and collapsed, fighting for breath.

His heart still racing, he made himself sit up. He sleeved the sweat out of his eyes, and looked back for Julia. No sign of her. He almost cried out. He clearly remembered her right behind him just before the outcropping when they had struggled with a clothes-snagging windfall. Even in a skirt she was fleet. What could have happened to her?

He started to call, hesitated at the danger, then called, heedless, his hands at his mouth to direct his voice back down the way they came. "Julia." Louder, "Julia."

No answer. He stood, and risked exposure with a full shout down the mountain. "Julia."

"Up here, Papa."

Henry whirled around. She, too, rested beside the outcropping, but far above him. She pantomimed that she had gone the long way around, and come down from the highest rocks. He struggled up to give her a hug, his intended reprimand forgotten.

She returned his embrace only briefly, and beckoned him to follow her still higher, then along the uppermost outcropping. They were at the highest point on the ridge, the land sloping precipitously away both in front of and behind them. She stopped at a cleft between two massive boulders.

"Look, Papa. They're like toy soldiers. Or ants down there." Henry lay on a rock and cautiously eased his head out between the boulders. Far below them, much farther below than he would have guessed, lay Battle Hollow, its miniature cabin in a little field just beginning to green. He thrust his head out further, no longer so afraid of being spotted, felt Julia squeezed beside him, also watching.

Henry made out ant figures coming out of the woods, a compact mass moving steadily amid much gunfire. "What're they doing? Your eyes are a lot better than mine."

"Union men. In retreat. Not a rout; a very orderly retreat, looks like," she answered promptly.

Henry wondered if she might have listened much more closely than he had realized to Spooks describing battle tactics late into the evening.

"Some casualties, though."

Henry could distinguish tiny ants left on the ground as the compact body of ants moved closer to the cabin. Some larger ants went ahead quickly to the cabin, then even faster along the hollow's walls. Easy to spot because of the intermittent blinding light that located them.

"They carrying message mirrors? What are those bright flashes?" he puzzled aloud.

"Swords in the sun, Papa. The mounted officers carry swords. They've been racing back and forth, figuring out they're trapped in the hollow, no outlet, just like you said. They have to make a stand behind those huge cottonwoods. No other alternative. Good choice for cover. Do have to worry about their ammunition supply though."

How carefully she had listened to Spooks. Henry rubbed his eyes and squinted. Ants were coming out of the woods now toward the downed trunks, but most of them soon stopped moving. Fire from behind the cottonwood trunks must be devastating.

"Those big logs are good cover, but . . . look, Papa. There. Two, no three, Union men, trying to climb that cliff."

"Where?" Henry could not distinguish them until he saw a falling figure whose coat caught on a tree branch so that he swung limply back and forth as the tree swayed ominously. Then the whole tree with the caught soldier came crashing in stages down the cliff face, dragging with it other trees and loose rocks.

"Now they're getting outflanked at those logs. Casualties piling up. Aren't they in real trouble, Papa?"

"Terrible trouble," Henry answered. "No way to retreat."

"One, no, two officers must be at least wounded, 'cause I can't see them any more. What else can they do?"

Henry could spot a white flag waving back and forth at the cabin. "See that?" he asked Julia and felt her answering nod. "Only alternative when it's hopeless," he added. "No point in every man dead." The distant firing slowly stopped. Another white flag came out of the woods. The two white flags moved toward each other. "There'll be a parley over terms and then surrender," he predicted.

The flag coming from the woods suddenly went down to the earth. Instantly there was much firing. The other flag waved back and forth, then it fell.

"What the . . . ?"

"I'm not sure," answered Julia. "But it looked like the Sesesh got Union men out to the parley, then canceled the truce all of a sudden so they could shoot Union soldiers who left their rifles. Could that be? That's not fair, is it?"

Henry shook his head in wonder. "It's war." He strained to distinguish details so far below them. He thought he saw a wagon, perhaps with a load of men, come out of the woods and stop at the old cabin.

"Papa, I think they have that boy from the trail; I think I saw his long hair. . . . They're carrying all those men to the cabin. . . . must all be wounded. . . . Looks like they're making the cabin into a hospital for wounded . . . Oh, no, no."

Flames leaped out of the windows and door, shot up the roof and raced along the rotten wood shakes. In another instant the whole cabin erupted afire, sending a large smoke column slowly skyward. Henry felt Julia press into him, but there was no room between the boulders to put his arm around her. "Don't look," he counseled quietly.

Out in the field Henry could discern tiny figures scurrying among immobile humps on the ground. Occasional faint pistol shots.

"War booty, Papa. Boots are what they want most." Julia had ignored his suggestion. Another pistol shot. "And making sure the men they rob are dead. What's that Sesesh officer on the horse doing?"

"Dunno." Henry followed the glinting sword as it moved to one group, then to another around the field. "Maybe giving orders they're just ignoring?"

"He's pointing back where they came from," Julia offered. "I don't see . . . Do you hear bugling, Papa?" She stopped abruptly to listen.

Henry nodded. Bugling and intense firing from the woods.

"It's Union men, Papa. Now is the merciless hunter in turn unpitied prey."

"Looks like you're right. Now *they're* in trouble."

More heavy firing. Many of the ants in the field who started toward the cabin had stopped moving.

"The Rebs are trapped. No way out."

In frustration Henry rubbed his eyes yet again. "Isn't that a Reb white flag? But I don't see one on the Union side."

"Me either," answered Julia. "It looks like they just keep firing and there's no way to retreat. Except . . do you think he'll make it, Papa? Over there. No, there. Look for a big bush, then follow a line straight up the cliff. Look for the Reb climbing . . . The bush to the left of the cabin. See him?"

After much searching, Henry spotted him. A long-limbed figure going up the cliff with amazing agility. But he was increasingly exposed because small trees rooted in cliff crevices still had not sprouted leaves. Nevertheless he reached so high before he was hit that he fell in spectacular twists and turns.

"Papa, aren't those Union officers using telescopes to search the cliffs? They're working this way."

The cabin roof collapsed into the flaming structure, adding spectacular sparks to the smoke column lazily drifting in their direction. Horrified by the burning cabin, Henry was lost in a swirl of emotions.

Officers with telescopes. Henry snapped to consciousness. He jerked his head back from the lookout, pulling Julia with him. "You sure those are telescopes, like what Spooks brought up once to show us?"

At her nod he began scrambling to his feet. "We need outta here before they get to this side and spot us. They'll shoot everybody they see without asking questions. Keep low so you don't show up against the sky. You go first. Head for that knob over there. Fast as you can."

The knob. A very short breather. He picked a towering pine and they were off again. She moved so smoothly through the forest that Henry, encumbered by his rifle, doubled over for limbs she simply ran under, and feeling his age, barely kept up.

The pine. Another pause for breath. A new landmark and they raced on. After they were over one ridge, the firing sounded much fainter. Down into a narrow valley, mostly sliding, then up a ridge, hands-and-knees steep. The firing had become inaudible or ceased.

Long shadows preceded them as they approached a high bare spot. Julia jumped up on a rock, looked around and nodded. "I thought this seemed familiar. Now I see the way. We'll get back down by the Witch's Nose. Papa, how can you know without any trails? We swung the long way around and crossed our path, in case anyone followed us."

Henry nodded. She had been silent while he stared back during their stops for rest. Sentinel too, he now realized, and wisely done. She moved off ahead, confident of their direction. As he came exhausted out of the woods, she was already waiting by the barn. She pointed to their fenced lot. Mootoo stared at them in bovine placidity.

Carrie came out of the barn to walk toward the cabin with him. "That critter, that damned critter, slunk back this afternoon," she said in a low voice. "I could have shot him." Then louder for Julia, "And you two been climbing for nothing all day long. You both need a big supper. I already fed the boy and the baby. George was real cross at first about having to stay home."

"Good thing he wasn't with us," answered Henry.

Carrie caught his grim tone and inspected Henry and Julia more carefully in the dusk, noticing for the first time their clothing's muddy knees and tears. Julia's skirt had burrs all over one side; she pulled it to inspect the scratches on her calves. Carrie's voice rose. "Henry, what happened?"

"Mootoo wasn't at the bald, of course." Henry decided he need not mention the desperate race up the mountain, certainly not his panic when he thought he left Julia behind. "So we looked down into Battle Hollow. No Mootoo, but we stumbled into seeing a . . . battle. But way below us," he assured her.

"A battle?"

"Sesesh soldiers trapping Union men and giving them no quarter, and then Union soldiers giving no quarter to Sesesh," explained Julia matter-of-factly as she let her skirt drop.

Carrie wheeled on Henry. "Is that true?"

He nodded.

"And you let your daughter watch it? You said you'd take care of her." Carrie put an arm around Julia.

Henry stood without excuse. He remembered his fright when he looked back for Julia and saw nothing. And the fire devouring the cabin with the wounded men. How could he deny being a delinquent father?

Julia extricated herself from her mother's arm. "Mama, nobody could have shot us. We climbed so high I saw hawks circling—way *below* us."

"But a battle. And watching a battle."

"Mama," Julia instructed, "it's war. It's not pretty. War is hell. People are shits. And hell and shitty people are what we saw today."

"Julia Lilly LaCroix Hollis, I'll not have any daughter of mine using language like that."

"But Mama," Julia objected, "those are exactly the words that Mister Spooks used with you and Papa the last time he ate here. And you agreed with him."

Carrie did not retreat. "He was talking to your father and me. Not to you, supposed to be asleep. And child, Spooks saying it doesn't give you a ticket to repeat it. I've got half a mind, more than half a mind, to . . ."

"Carrie, Carrie." Henry gathered himself to intervene. "Julia saw what she saw. It's me you need to fault." He turned to Julia. "Spooks is right. But remember the Catechism says the same thing in different words. So quote the Catechism, not Spooks. I don't want strangers to think my daughter isn't a lady. And Julia, you don't need to tell George what you saw. . . . We could use something to eat, don't you think?"

After Carrie cleared the dishes, the family stayed at the table. Henry brought down the big Bible and read aloud.

> *I will lift up mine eyes unto the hills, from whence cometh my help.*
> *My help cometh from the Lord, which made heaven and earth. . . .*
>
> *The Lord shall preserve thee from all evil; he shall preserve thy soul.*
> *The Lord shall preserve thy going out and thy coming in from this time forth, and even for evermore.*

George slumped with drooping eyelids by the time Henry finished, but Julia's eyes shone still alert. "Thank you, Papa," she whispered in his ear when he hugged each child, headed for bed. Henry dropped into bed himself not long after the children. But when Carrie slipped under the covers he was staring at the rafters.

"Still at Battle Hollow?" she asked.

"Can't get it out of my mind."

"Henry, I'm sorry I barked at you when you came in. But you do forget Julia is partly a girl yet, even if her body is getting womanly."

"The reason I forget is because she's just like her mother. When she sees evil, she stares at it, not a blink. She doesn't run from the rattler. She stands and watches it. Studying. It's so obvious—she's calculating just how to overpower it. And she's been listening to Spooks talk about military tactics a lot closer than I thought."

"Was it so bad?"

"Worse than anything I've ever . . . We were too high to see faces or all the blood, thank God. Too far to hear shouts and screams. Carrie, they murdered the prisoners in cold blood. Burned the wounded men alive. And then came retribution. They got trapped themselves. What did Julia say? From some poem, I guess. 'Now is the merciless hunter in turn unpitied prey.' None of those Rebs got out alive."

"Remember Julia's eyesight is better than yours. I know you kept her hidden, but she might have caught glimpses."

"Yes," Henry acknowledged, deciding he need not say more.

"She told me she wanted to be a good Samaritan, but you held her back just in time. No saving that boy."

"Not a chance. Hard to imagine so many men who saw this morning's sunrise, but never saw the same sun set."

"Think of all the mothers and wives and sweethearts who will never see their men at the door again. You did right talking to Julia about Spooks' language. I jumped on her too quick. I want to keep her protected, but that's all the more reason for her to know war is hell and people are shits."

"She knows it plenty well from today."

"If you'd stayed home it would have been a perfect day. George moped around a while, then decided he'd get Edward to start talking. Played all day with him, so patient. Edward watching him with bright eyes, the way Harry used to. I think he said 'Mama.'"

"I wish Julia had stayed home. I wish *I* had stayed home and just enjoyed the children."

"Henry, what did I do to deserve children I'm so proud of? I hope my mama felt half as proud of me."

"I know she did. I still remember her look at me in Tulips' kitchen when we went down there after we first slept together in this cabin."

"Henry, she figured you were raping me the way Cousin Caleb or your brother Sam might have. No, the way they for sure would have if you hadn't kept me here."

"When she looked at me, yes. I know that. I even knew it then. But when she looked at you, her face said what she told me once, I guess not long before she died. I was leaving for up here, and she gave me a fresh pie of course, and whispered, 'Henry,' I think it was the only time she didn't call me Mister Hollis, she said, 'Henry, you take good care of my beautiful baby.'"

Carrie sniffled. "Now you've made me cry," she smiled. "I'm just as proud of my children, our children. But I worry how to protect them. I worry and worry, and can't see how. Tell me honest. How far do you think Battle Hollow is from here?"

"Not far for an eagle, but on the ground it's hard country between here and there. I'm certain nobody followed us. I took the long way, and both of us watched for trackers."

Carrie re-arranged the quilt over them. Neither broke the silence. After a long time, Henry said, "I know what you're thinking. We all stay put. Even with the bridge up. The Quachasee doesn't seem as far away from everything as it used to."

Plowing with Greek, My Life

HL Hollis

Tulips, January 6, 1939

Christmas, this year with both cheer and tears, is come and gone. I regret my situation threw Advent preparations chiefly on Caroline, already much burdened by my care. Reflecting on that, I realized that my boyhood memories of Christmas all connect with holiday details Mama organized. Father was too much a Christian to emulate Dickens' Scrooge, but I cannot recall him much engaged in holiday hilarity. Though he sometimes spoke of Christmases past in this very house, the recollections seemed to make him pensive. Perhaps, though, I misconstrued and he was in fact resisting the commercialization of Christ's birth already visible to some degree then. I'm not certain. Another question for when I am past heaven's portals.

Definitive. As in *definitive* decision. I have always relished *definitive* for its sound, those quick-marching vowels in succession. By some mental quirk, I can recall time and place when I consciously first heard *definitive*. In point of fact, it concerned Dory. Already as a little boy, I held my sister Dorinda in such high regard that I assumed she must one day be my wife. Mama's shocked contradiction and her flustered reaction to my claims propelled me in outrage to Father. He listened sympathetically, and firmly concurred: Dory will make a *splendid* wife. He confided, however, that in his experience women usually prefer to be consulted first, and in a leisurely way. Moreover, they value "please" prior to some joint enterprise. He counseled I wait some before a *definitive* decision to marry Dory.

I understood the gist of his response (his advice about women seemed then, as it does still, particularly prudent), but *splendid* wife and *definitive* conclusion perplexed me as I wrestled with words.

Splendid seemed some derivative of *splinter*, and the second syllable of *definitive* intimated a piscine connection, but the context supported neither interpretation.

All this trivia comes back to me today in the aftermath of Dory's visit, a visit I expect (happy anticipation, not of laying on obligation). After consulting Father, I deferred a *definitive* decision about marrying Dory. But only rarely—and usually to my sorrow—have I wavered in my respect for her perspicuity. I ignored her most carelessly when she pronounced my old rope too frayed for hayloft swinging, and predicted pain with Dr. Payne. Pronouncement and prediction proved prescient.

When she visited, Dory advised me to chronicle in these pages how I ventured off to Vanderbilt University for Classics, and returned home for farming. Despite my hesitation about substituting such self-absorption for family memoir, a suggestion from Dory is one I have learned to follow.

I wrote earlier that during his solitary Quachasee farming Father taught himself Latin to ward off loneliness. He persevered at Tulips, drafting us children as fellow students. He it was who began me on Greek letters. He then cajoled our pastor, Helmut Haenschke, to tutor me in Greek. In those days a scholarly pastor of a small country congregation enjoyed ample time for intensive language study, perfectly justifiable to explicate God's Word. Such was Haenschke. After theology he most loved Greek, never calling me HL, always, with special emphasis, Herodotus. To Father's request he responded generously. Yes indeed, he would try tutoring Herodotus in Greek, beginning with Herodotus the Greek. From Herodotus, Haenschke eased me into Homer, with a knack for what sections would hook a boy. I read happily through one to the next.

As he later confessed, Haenschke originally hoped to dispatch two birds with the same alphabet. He encouraged me to follow him as a Grecophile. He also encouraged me to follow as a Lutheran minister, urging me to listen for God's call. I did listen, and God may in fact have called, but if so I missed it; at the time I imagined God speaks at theatrical volume with magisterial sonority.

My father took a keen interest in my lessons—sometimes, I thought, too keen an interest, making certain I did not slight Greek for a dime Western. To be honest, he also arranged time off from farm work so I could sit with my books. That offended some hired men who, despite their exquisite expertise in sloth, believed to their core in the value of physical labor as beneficial to the character—of children. The sight of an "idle" Dory grappling with Herr Schmidt's uncompromising German lessons on the Tulips porch disturbed one hired man sufficiently to unburden himself. He burst out that no darter a'his be ketched relaxen in shade when thar's alwuz sumpin in the kitchen needin doin. A female like thet got no call t'be larnen some ferrin speaken.

Father's agreement startled me initially. "Wilber, yer mebbe right. Yessir, mebbe right. Mebbe Dory be better barefoot an no drawers, waitin' fer her uncles to big her so she don' hafta play w'carnhusk doll nary no more." Flattered by Mr. Hollis's unusual concurrence, Wilber missed allusions to his own family.

Installed at the University, I caused at first a minor sensation, since I could declaim by the yard. How could this raw bumpkin off a back mountain farm be fluent in Greek? I soon, however, received comeuppance, for the Greek that university scholars considered important was philology. In consequence I found myself back at the quick draw contest with Audie Ann's pistols. As farm boys generally do, I buckled down to the task. I learned what Haenschke hadn't taught me, but after a time I saw that Greek without stories failed to elicit the same pleasure.

Close to the juncture I was to decide either to go on to some graduate studies in Classics or to a Lutheran ministerial seminary, Father slipped while helping to haul feed sacks into the barn ahead of rain. To ease his back pain he lay much of the time on the day bed in his office. For a normally active man—considering his age, an abnormally active man—to be bedridden was so unusual, even alarming, that I made a quick visit from Nashville to check on him.

From that trip, a curious, indelible fragment that, I concede, fits with nothing else here. I proceed nevertheless.

To divert Father, I brought him whatever mail the day produced. After one such delivery, I had just exited when a small cry turned me around. Father sat up with an open envelope and a page torn from a newspaper on his lap, his face in anguish. I attributed his pain at first to a muscle spasm, but then he said, "Julia died. In Columbus."

Mystified, I just started to inquire particulars of this Julia-in-Columbus when Mama called urgent instructions. Dr. Payne had turned into our lane and I must meet him. Dr. Payne's concern (privately expressed to me), trips for medicine, and assiduous efforts to ease Father's pain—the immediate problems dominated our attention. All else faded.

Curious it is, how one's mind functions, or fails to. At the time I was so focused on Father's alarming condition that this Julia dropped from my consciousness. Now, decades later, here she is back, a nagging but unsolvable mystery. I recall the name mostly because it is my sister Dory's middle name, one to which I have been so partial that my older daughter is Julia. But "Julia in Columbus" leaves me blank. Julia who? Columbus, as in Ohio?

I assume she was another of the tangential figures, often peculiar, even eccentric, from Father's past we occasionally caught sight of. Figures such as Carter Fineman, whose biography went all the way back to the day of canal building, when he was horribly maimed in a blasting accident.

His life long despaired of, he nevertheless survived and returned to Ginners Ford. He appeared at the Tulips porch from time to time. Father always welcomed him with the challenge of some obstructing field rock too large to drag away. Inconvenient rocks delighted Fineman. He would set to work, alone with his dynamite and fuses. Everyone was ordered a far distance away. In due course there would be a muffled WUMP, followed by what sounded like a high-pitched giggle.

Fineman would have a celebratory drink on our porch, where Father paid him immediately, always complaining jovially that Carter should pay Tulips for providing the rock—and later telling us privately that if Fineman deferred his bill Father might well wind up owing the sum to the man's estate.

Another (now obvious) characteristic of the aging mind approaching senility is the propensity to derail itself at the slightest opportunity. So much for Julia of Columbus and Carter Fineman.

After his mishap, Father asked me to send a wire about it to the Brights in Knoxville, which alarmed us further. Was he preparing for his demise? The Judge came promptly on the cars, and spent many hours talking privately with Father and Aunt Audie Ann. (Remember, the Brights were by then also my in-laws.)

Apparently for old times' sake, the two men decided to go up to Father's abandoned farmstead at the high head of the Quachasee Valley.

We all were aghast. It seemed so imprudent. We considered Father in no condition to travel anywhere, let alone to such a remote destination. We also understood our opinion would have no effect. (We were correct on both counts.) Caroline urged me to go along in case they needed help (after all, her father, Judge Bright, was no younger than my father), but, as we anticipated, both men rejected the idea. For two old men, up and back constituted an exhausting all-day trip.

In point of fact, the day following, Father was in such pain that getting out of bed was beyond him. Caroline and I helped Judge Bright to the station with a trunk full of papers Father wanted him to have, and he returned to Knoxville. After that, Father seemed to decline a hair more every day. Dr. Payne's diagnosis was "exhaustion and debilitation of superannuation." Caroline's apt translation: doctors have no cure.

Mama thus faced a frightening prospect, for, active as she was in family care, she lived in a cocoon Father continuously wove. He had always relieved her of any farm managerial or financial matters. Without him, in addition to the prospect of raising some still-young children alone, she, a city woman, faced the challenges of managing a large farm with a thriving orchard, and with reputation for swine breeding as well, in addition to various other enterprises.

Distraught, Mama pleaded that I stay on at Tulips for a time. This was small sacrifice for us—me and my new wife. Caroline had always looked forward to her long summer residencies at Tulips and now the farm fit her like a glove. Better yet (this may embarrass, alarm, disgust, or bore our great-grandchildren, but so be it) now her delicious kiss in the barn could be unhurried as she ignored with blithe impunity my sister Annie's teases and ululations.

I settled satisfied into my farming role until I overheard a lawyer in town lamenting Father's decline. "And look at Hollis's oldest boy. Gets a fancy education, and all he does with it is come home to farm." The lawyer's comment stung so that I repeated it to Father as he lay vainly trying to find any comfortable position—in retrospect, not the best timing for any patient's patient ruminations.

Father demonstrated that by a reaction both immediate and fierce. "What else can you expect from a scrivener's soul? Thom is educated in law, but ignorant about life. He's the kind of lawyer who knows 'party of the first part,' but has never thought seriously about how people face death."

He grimaced as he tried a different position on the chaise. "I've noticed that failing in some professional people—even in people who read a lot. They'll tell you everything about a novel except what it's saying." He winced as he shifted again. "Try asking your mother about some novel she's just taken those exhaustive notes on, and then listen really closely to her answers."

I believe that Father meant Thom confused training with education. The only way to waste an education is to stop thinking. I needed farming to appreciate my Greeks, and I needed the Ancients to appreciate farming. We both know firsthand about sowing and reaping. Mutatis mutandis, veterans of the War and my Greek warriors.

I must write later about Mama and her fiction reading.

Curiously, while I plowed my way into farming, Father miraculously recovered much, though not all, of his mobility. No longer essential as a substitute at Tulips, I had to plot my own course. I came to a *definitive* decision. Since I didn't know anything I preferred to tilling the soil and to reading Greek for the stories, why do otherwise?

After a time, one of my professors wrote to me about an opening for an instructor in Greek. I replied, with thanks, that it would allow me no time to farm. Perhaps a year on, Father proposed to purchase an adjacent farm and add it to Tulips, to which I said, with thanks, that so much Tulips land would allow me no time for Greek. He nodded as if he anticipated my answer. "You won't be richer, but you'll be a better man for it." About the former he forecast correctly, and, I hope, about the latter as well.

COLUMBUS
SENTINEL

Formerly

OHIO FREEDMAN'S ADVOCATE

Sept. 12, 1891

Obituaries

LAMPERT, JULIA HOLLIS

Our community, indeed, we may say, our city, has endured an incalculable loss in the shocking, tragic death of Julia LaCroix Hollis Lampert on Monday last. She expired of injuries inflicted under mysterious circumstances by unknown assailants while returning to her home Sunday evening after attending a meeting devoted to improving the lot of our youth.

She is mourned by her husband, Lawrence, and her children, Lilly Lampert Andrews of Cleveland, Harry Hollis Lampert, and Audrey Ann Lampert of Columbus, and also by her brothers, George Hollis of Chicago, and Edward Hollis of California.

Solemn funeral services were held at St. Andrew's Episcopal Church, where she was long a faithful member, active in its charitable endeavors. The crowd of sorrowing mourners at her funeral was so immense that many had to stand outside the commodious sanctuary. The orderly, dignified procession to the cemetery was many blocks long, distinguished by the prominence of personages in attendance. An eloquent and affecting eulogy was given by the Rev. Aubrey Martin. (*Text of the eulogy is printed elsewhere in this issue. Ed.*)

With her husband, Mrs. Lampert founded and ran the Cuyahoga School, which has served Negro children seeking preparation for admission to institutions of higher education. She assisted her husband with teaching duties, as well as assuming daily management of the School, a difficult task she made appear easy by her superlative talent for administration and by her unflagging energy. The School's graduates give evidence by their attainments of Mrs. Lampert's unwavering conviction that they could, that they must, be credits to our Race.

She stated that her work to aid the next generation honored her mother, who had sacrificed her private preference for the well-being of her children.

Mrs. Lampert was a founder and the president of what was originally the Women's Improvement Society (now the Columbus Negro Women's Club), thereby putting Columbus in the vanguard among sister cities in the mobilization of this force for civic good. Her capabilities and her extensive correspondence with like-minded women around the country would, her friends know, have soon put her in position to take a leading role in the wider coalescence of this most promising movement.

She was the originator and chief moving spirit of the annual Expositions formerly held in Columbus to display and advertise the progress and capabilities of area Freedmen and others in the years since Emancipation. She was one of the group of far-sighted women who founded Columbus Independent Hospital, which refused no patient for any reason, and welcomed on its staff physicians turned away from other city hospitals for no professional cause.

Most recently she and a few other courageous ladies urged state legislators to take statutory action against the unspeakable horrors of lynching, and to repeal laws banning marriage between members of different races.

Julia Lampert was born in 1850 in old Tennessee. She was educated at home and at the Erie Ladies Seminary, a very progressive institution, regrettably now closed, located in Cleveland. She was an omnivorous reader, a habit she imbibed from her parents. She had been well schooled in

Latin by her parents. Her reading, coupled with a capacious memory, gave her the ability to be enviably at ease when conversing even with Columbus leaders who boasted of college degrees. This writer can easily recall the embarrassment on the face of a (now deceased) eminent and influential Most Reverend when Mrs. Lampert, in the process of eloquently refuting his willfully misconceived claims about the favorable treatment of Negroes in the state of Ohio, politely but firmly also corrected some of his incidental allusions in classical mythology.

Mrs. Lampert was a skilled raconteur, with an inexhaustible repertory of illustrative stories, often gleaned from her girlhood, growing up at her birthplace, a small, very removed east Tennessee mountain farm which her parents built with their own hands. She was proud of this upbringing, even though she knew it gave certain enemies of her race in this city an excuse for ad hominem attacks on her as one exceeding her station.

She explained that on that small mountain farm her parents taught her lessons she could not forget, lessons she judiciously applied in our own time. To current voices who would make our brothers and sisters chiefly hewers of wood and drawers of water, she spoke eloquently about the necessity of, as she put it, also being alive above the shoulders. And to distinguished leaders who speak mostly of educating our gifted and talented, her advice, to the chagrin of some, was that every child needs to learn by experience that calluses and perspiration are necessary and honorable in attaining a meritorious station in life.

Those who knew her best must agree her advocacy was distinguished by its respectful and reasoned approach, an approach, however, that did not exclude tenacity and on occasion, a dash of audacity. Perhaps her finest triumph was at the tumultuous mass meeting only a few years ago to consider response to a tragic provocation that had recently occurred not far from Columbus, a shameful outrage which regular readers of this paper will painfully recall. Memory of the meeting is indelible for this writer, supported by verbatim stenographic notes.

At the meeting, various people spoke, well aware that a low element of the city was gathering that same evening at no great distance. A few of the speakers could only voice despair. Many hotly urged action. A few, extreme action. The mood was so volatile that the chief of the city's police, in attendance out of concern for public order, sent urgently for armed reinforcements.

At Mrs. Lampert's turn, she told a story deliberately lengthy and detailed. (She explained later to intimates that long ago a family friend had advised her to calm a meeting becoming tense by telling a long, interesting story.) The story she chose was from her girlhood, when her isolated family faced armed men who accused them of harboring fugitives escaping the lash, an engrossing tale which she related in her usual dramatic and humorous style.

The family averted a catastrophic outcome by a combination of her father's quick-witted guile, and her mother's phenomenal marksmanship. To the audience's delight, Mrs. Lampert held aloft a bullet-punctured canteen as evidence from those days.

Mrs. Lampert proceeded to a penetrating analysis of the situation at hand, and a persuasive recommendation of tactics. By the time she finished, many tempers had cooled to a degree. Rash voices were stilled. The meeting heeded her sound advice.

Mrs. Lampert was always happiest at home as dutiful wife. She cherished her maternal status and rejoiced as only a mother can in the signal achievements of her offspring, while secretly sorrowing in her mother's heart about the separation that maturation inevitably brings.

In the privacy of her home life, Julia Lampert revealed to privileged friends talents even they could not have anticipated. Within the domestic circle, she sometimes entertained with French Creole songs and the old-fashioned hammer dulcimer, reflections of her New Orleans and her mountain roots respectively. Those mountain roots were further revealed by her little-known but astonishing dexterity with firearms.

When requested to write this notice, I felt honored, and accepted the task gladly as a public tribute I could pay to a loyal and talented friend, but my spirit fails me now when I see how feeble is this effort to do justice to her memory.

During these difficult times, when we, released from cruel servitude, with boundless hopes and aspirations, now find ominous threats and unwarranted limitations wherever we turn, we can ill afford to lose the rare qualities of leadership that Mrs. Lampert provided. We must mourn for her family in their loss of beloved consort and vigilant mother, and mourn for ourselves in our loss of a staunch friend and wise counselor.

We hope to see reports soon that Mrs. Lampert's assailants are arrested and await speedy justice, *whoever they may be*, and call on the mayor and the police to effect this end.

A.G.

QUACHASEE

WHC

The moon waxed again. The weather finally cleared. Carrie discussed preparations for Spooks and his friend over the supper table. "Isn't it just like Spooks to help an old widow lady get out to satisfy a wish."

"I remember he was very respectful of old people even when we were boys," answered Henry. "I remember because he corrected me a couple of times when I made some fun I shouldn't have; he wasn't joking."

The dogs barked at the stranger traveling with Spooks, so everyone came on the porch to see the two mounted figures ride out of the woods. As they trotted into the clearing, Julia breathed a "Mama!"

A little closer, and Carrie's pleasant anticipation turned to apprehension. At mere yards from the porch, Henry whistled quietly. "Thet ain't no ole widder lady," he muttered just loud enough for Carrie to hear. "An look at Spooks. Haven't seen him this gussied up in . . . Think thar's sompin goin on hyar?"

Now acutely sensitive about the limitations of her best dress, Carrie stood trying to smile a welcome. "Wave to the pretty lady," she urged Edward and George as she pulled the boys in front of her skirt.

"The pretty lady wears funny clothes," George declared, to Carrie's relief not in his usual clarion voice.

"That's called a riding dress." Its cut, cloth, and colors took Carrie back to her Nashville girlhood, luxuriating in the fashionable dresses Henkel ordered for Lilly. Carrie could still feel the green velvet trimmings on one she often begged her mother to wear. When the shocking message came that mother and daughter were sold, and would be leaving in a few hours, Lilly decreed they abandon everything, in fact ordered Carrie to empty wardrobes in disarray onto Henkel's bed, topped with the laciest underthings. She sorted

381

ruthlessly through Carrie's clothes, her face so forbidding that Carrie dared not beg for favorites. Come to pick them up, Dinkins' man was astonished to find no huge trunk. They walked away with him in clothes so plain Carrie shrank on the street. Only at Tulips, upon Miz Sarah's orders, had their wardrobes improved. Even then Carrie had seen nothing as elaborate as what their mounted visitor now wore.

Spooks dismounted while still reining in. He helped the lady alight gracefully from her well-groomed mare. Carrie noted the elaborate tooling on her saddle. Her clothes complemented her coloring. Carrie's spirits did not rise at the realization the widow lady must be hardly older than she. With a light laugh, the lady swept from her head the broad-brimmed hat trailing ribbons, and looked expectantly at the porch.

"Miz Davies," began Spooks, "here stand my favorite scholars, Julia and George. And Edward, a little bashful behind his mother's skirt. Henry and Carrie you recognize, I'm sure, from my description."

Miz Davies tossed her hat on the porch and stepped up with a radiant smile and a clasp for Carrie with both hands. "Mister Bright has told me so much about you and this beautiful place."

"I'm afraid you'll be disappointed," began Carrie.

"No, I find Mister Bright too restrained in his praise. The mountains remind me of Vermont. I loved to visit my grandparents there partly because they lived high in a narrow valley just like . . ." She drifted off as she surveyed the distant successive ridges and mountains.

"Want me to show you Daisy and Lazy?" offered George. "They're in the barn."

"Now son, let's be a little more considerate to a guest," interposed Henry. "Let her rest a while."

"I'd love to see Daisy and Lazy, George," answered Miz Davies in an enthusiastic tone. "I've been sitting all morning and need to walk. Julia, you'll come too?" She locked elbows with the girl and off they went, George's excited soprano jabbering at full speed, Julia answering their guest's cheerful questions, Edward trying hard to keep up despite his very short legs.

"Spooks, you fooled us." Henry clapped him on the shoulder as the children and guest disappeared into the barn. "You told us you wanted to bring up a widder lady, and I thought you meant some old crow in black who pined for one last look at mountains."

"She's a fancy lady for plain folks," added Carrie quietly, self-consciously smoothing her skirt.

"Not too fancy to go to the barn first thing," Spooks objected. "I'm afraid I'm partly to blame," he added. "She worried about over-dressing, but I encouraged her to wear . . . well, to wear what she hasn't had much chance to wear recently."

"Guess we'll forgive her," said Henry with a glance at Carrie.

Spooks hurried on. "Her late husband was a fine man, friend as well as client. He went up to Philadelphia to nurse a drunkard brother there, met Lydia and persuaded her to marry him. Buried his brother and came back with her. He argued hard against secession, but when it came, a lot of his kinfolk in Charlotte pestered him. He ultimately decided he had to go their way, but he took sick and died in camp before he fired a shot."

The barn party visitors reappeared quickly. "Papa," said Julia, "Edgar is acting funny. You'd better look at him."

"I saw him first," declared George.

"Did not," replied Julia.

"Then you'd better all come with me to look again," placated Henry, as he and Spooks headed for the barn. Julia and George followed closely, but Edward chose to inspect the stranger from the safety of his mother's skirts.

"Come out of the sun, Miz Davies," said Carrie. "I'll get you something cool to drink on the porch."

"It *is* warm in the sun. But you must call me Lydia."

"Thank you, Miz Lydia. Would you like to sit here or inside?"

Lydia Davies smiled at Carrie. "Why, *Miz* Hollis, I think the porch is perfect.

Carrie hesitated, then looked down. "I'm not really . . . Henry and I can't get . . ."

"Mister Bright told me just a little about you, in confidence of course. He knows my abolitionist sympathies." She smiled. "To me, you're Miz Hollis. But I'd rather have you call me Lydia, so I can call you Carrie."

Carrie unhesitatingly took her outstretched hand, remembering how similar in spirit Spooks' very first greeting to "Cook Carrie" had once been.

"Mister Bright said he did not tell you much about me. Maybe that's because I'm a fish out of water. Philadelphia girl in Tennessee. But I'm used to the feeling. My father was a Friend, but my mother was not. So when he married her, the Meeting excluded him. Edward, would you like to sit on my lap?"

Edward shook his head.

"So I have some idea about having feet in two camps. In Philadelphia many of my friends belonged to the Hicksites. My father quit working for a man who wanted to trade cotton."

Edward changed his mind and climbed up to her lap.

"I wouldn't have married a Southerner except that Mister Davies told me on his honor that he didn't—and would not—own slaves. He said East Tennessee is different from what I imagined. And it is, to a degree. But who ever thought there would be actual war?"

George came running in, breathless with news. "Edgar got a burr under his halter. That's why he kept shaking his head."

Lydia patted the chair beside her. "George, come sit here and tell me what you do all day. You have lots of energy."

Carrie went inside to brush coals from the dutch oven. After a time Lydia appeared in the doorway, a boy at each hand. "What a wonderful, snug cabin. I envy you. Everything in its place and everything at hand. Do you have a spare apron so I can help?"

"Oh, Julia will be along in a minute," answered Carrie, reluctant to impose on a guest for help with her introductory meal.

"Here's one," trumpeted George, triumphantly pulling a ragged, stained apron from its hiding place in a cupboard.

"Oh, George, son, we can't have—"

"Thank you, George," said Lydia. "Just what I need. You think we ought to set the table while your mother tends the fire?"

❧

"That dish tasted even better than Mister Bright predicted, Carrie." Lydia sighed as she silently declined Julia's offer of another helping.

"She didn't believe me, Carrie," Spooks grinned. "After all, what can men know about food? We eat it only to fill up. We never notice how it tastes."

"Mister Spooks, you didn't bring Killdeer with you," interrupted George impatiently. "Deerslayer should always carry Killdeer with him, ready to shoot."

"Deerslayer depends on Uncas," volunteered Julia, giving her brother a reprimanding look.

"What's this? Deerslayer? Un-cas?" Lydia asked the children.

"You know, like in the book," George instructed hurriedly. "Deerslayer and Uncas. Mister Spooks is Deerslayer, and Papa is Uncas. Like in the book. You know."

"Which book, George?" asked Lydia.

In the limelight, George faltered. "The Mohican."

"It's called The Last of the Mohicans," corrected Julia, "by James F. Cooper."

George gave Julia a murderous look, then turned back to Lydia. "Don't you remember?"

"George, I'm afraid you're ahead of me," Lydia smiled. "When I was your age, I liked other books. Can you tell me what happens in this Mohican book?"

"Well," George took a deep breath. "There are a lot of big words, and even some French words. An some parts are hard, so I jus skip 'em."

"What's the story, George?" Carrie prompted.

"Well, Deerslayer, he lived a long time ago up north, has a rifle called Killdeer that never misses when he shoots a deer, or when the bad Indians . . ."

"The Hurons," interjected Julia in a whisper. George waved her away.

"And his best friend is Uncas; he's the last man in his Indian family."

"Deerslayer and Uncas. What happens to them?" smiled Lydia.

"They're in a war. And the bad Indians, the Hurons, capture two sisters."

"Cora and Alice. They're stepsisters, and both beautiful. Cora has some African blood through her mother," elaborated Julia.

"I'm telling the story," George cut her off. "And Deerslayer and Uncas have to rescue them from Magua, he's a bad Indian, and they do, but he gets them again, so Deerslayer and Uncas have to follow them by tracking their trail and they have to paddle their canoes really hard to get away from the bad Indians, but when they find the sisters, Magua kills Uncas, but Deerslayer shoots with Killdeer and that's the end of Magua. He's dead."

"You forgot the Hurons kill Cora," added Julia.

"Sounds like I'd rather be Alice," laughed Lydia.

"No, you wouldn't," corrected Julia. "Alice is dull. Every time she's in real danger, all she does is swoon or fall asleep."

"So I should be Cora?"

George shook his head. "No! Mama is Cora. Mister Spooks said that's what he and Papa used to call her, Cora. Nobody else wants to be Alice, so you can be her. You want to see the book?"

"George, I think you've told Miz Lydia everything she wanted to know about shooting Indians," laughed Carrie.

Henry intervened more directively. "What I want you to do now is check that Edgar is alright."

Though obviously reluctant to abandon the spotlight, George did ease out the door when Henry added, "Now, son."

In the pause after he left, Lydia smiled to herself. "No one has informed me before that my education is so incomplete. I shall have to get a copy." She looked at Julia. "Now help me get this straight. Mister Bright was Deerslayer?"

Julia nodded. "Deerslayer is also called Hawkeye after he has to shoot some Indians."

"Alright, Hawkeye, with his Killdeer which never misses a Huron." She inspected Spooks in amused appraisal. "And Uncas," she glanced at Henry, "is the last Mohican." She gestured graciously to Carrie. "And Cora is the beautiful woman with African blood he tries to rescue. Are they in love?"

Julia nodded vigorously, but Spooks was cautious. "That literary point is open to debate, I'm afraid. Cooper isn't as explicit as some readers," he grinned at Julia, "would prefer. Thanks to the evil Magua, we can never know whether they would have gotten together somehow and lived happily ever after."

"I think they would have," declared Julia.

"Miss Julia," challenged Bright, "marshal your evidence. Why do you think so?"

Before she could respond, George stood wide-eyed at the door. "Papa, there's a *big* storm in the sky."

Henry rose, scanned the clouds, then signaled Spooks and Julia. "He's right. We'd better get the stock in and close up all the buildings tight. Hard to run after eating."

The wind howled, trees bent far, and large drops splattered as they dashed back to the porch, laughing in triumph at having just beaten the rain. Soon, they all retreated inside; any watcher on the porch risked thorough soaking. The storm's ferocity quieted even George. He sat happily close to Lydia and reread about Hawkeye and Uncas while the grownups talked, their words drowned out from time to time by heavy thunder, the crash of a huge limb, or a whole tree blown down.

Though the wind eased, the deluge persisted. Henry caught Carrie's eye, then shook his head. She nodded. Henry turned to Lydia. "Your misfortune is our gain. With a storm like this I'm afraid you'll have to stay the night."

Lydia looked up from George's book. "Courtesy compels me to say how much I lament such a frightful imposition." She smiled mischievously. "But since I'm among good friends, I can say what I really think. That's *wonderful* news. I'm enjoying myself so much I'd be sorry to leave this afternoon."

At a break in the storm just before dark, the women stood on the porch while the men checked the barns. Lydia gestured to the cemetery wall. "Is that where your Harry lies?" she asked softly.

Carrie nodded, but the familiar catch in her throat kept her mute.

Lydia added, "I hope you don't mind Mister Bright telling me. He was trying to give me solace, I think. I, too, laid a little one in a private place. Leaving him makes the decision to go back north so hard. But I *must* go. My sister has children. Maybe as an aunt I can be some use to somebody."

The two women stood sorrowing, comforting arms at each other's waists. To avoid tears, Carrie changed the subject. "Isn't it risky being a northern woman living without a man in the house? I don't think I'd be that brave."

Lydia laughed dismissively. "Not bravery. Inertia. The Sesesh don't bother me because my husband went to fight and die for Jeff Davis, damn him. Union people leave me alone because I'm from the North. Mister Bright keeps warning me, though, that the balance of forces may collapse any time. I've made up my mind to leave as soon as I can find a guide I trust."

❦

In the evening, after Julia and Henry entertained the cabin with doubled hammers on the dulcimer, Lydia spoke up. "Julia, I know enough music to hear you have talent. Keep working on it."

Spooks chimed in. "You've been reading the *Odyssey*, Julia, which I studied too long ago to remember accurately. I recall a Euripides, but is he the faithful shepherd or the man that Ulysses slays right when he steps off the returning boat?"

Julia gave him a conspirator's grin. "Ulysses doesn't slay anyone when he steps off the boat. As you know very well. I think Eumaeus is his faithful shepherd."

"Ah yes, now it comes back to me," said Spooks with a wink. "Have you told George the Cyclops story?"

Julia shook her head.

"He'd enjoy it, I think. About the right amount of mayhem. Next time I'm here he can tell me the story. Right, George? A good test for you and for your teacher."

Carrie shooed reluctant children up to bed, then glanced about apologetically. "It may be snug, Lydia, but it isn't very big for guests. The men must do with hay in the barn loft. I'm afraid you'll have to share a bed with me. " She called strict orders up the ladder, forbidding Julia to tell George and Edward after dark about the Cyclops.

"I'm sorry to deny you your husband beside you," said Lydia in a low tone as Carrie brushed coals carefully back on the hearth. "It took me months to get used to not having Tom there."

"I know what you mean. If Henry's gone, I sit up the night. Can't sleep. Maybe it's different for men. Spooks's always lived alone."

"So he tells me. You've known him a long time?"

"Nearly half my life, come to think of it."

"Did you meet him here?"

"The first time he came up, looking for Henry. Just a girl trying to cook. I've only known him here. If I imagine his house, all I see is a room with rows and rows of books."

"His library. That's the only room in his house I've seen. He uses it as his office." She slowly placed a small bag on the bed, seemingly in deep thought. "What's he like? When he's up here, I mean."

"The same as this evening." The question puzzled Carrie. "The children are so happy to see him. So is Henry. So am I. But of course, we don't see many visitors here." She went to the window and pulled the curtain closed. When she noticed Lydia watching, she smiled wryly. "At Tulips I always longed for curtains in the kitchenhouse loft, but Elvira kept a tight purse. So up here I enjoy pulling them closed, even though the window is small and there's no one around for miles and miles."

"I'm for curtains, too," replied Lydia, though she seemed preoccupied by a different topic. "It's so hard," she continued, "to judge people. To know if they're genuinely what they seem. Like in Philadelphia when I first met Mister Davies. He seemed kind, considerate, so persuasive. My brother inquired confidentially about Mister Davies' affairs."

She unclasped and shook out her hair. "But financial things don't tell you about the person, do they? I tried not to be some flighty schoolgirl about him. I told him I could never marry someone who owned slaves. He pledged his honor that he didn't and never would. Said his first wife felt the same way. She died only a year after their wedding."

Carrie felt that Lydia wanted to say more, so she tried to help. "I'm sorry I didn't meet Mister Davies. He never came up here with Spooks."

Sitting on the bed, Lydia searched in her little bag with a deepening frown as she asked. "Did Mister Bright tell you about when he gave me my husband's papers?"

"No. He wouldn't. Henry says a reputable lawyer never, ever talks about other clients."

"And Mister Bright is a very conscientious lawyer, I think I know that much. . . . He was very careful about Tom's things he brought me. . . . But I'm getting ahead of myself. When we got word that Tom was deathly sick in camp, I went to nurse him myself. Didn't care what the 'ladies' thought. But I got there only a few hours before he died. I'm not even sure he recognized me."

"He must have. Your voice, your touch."

"I wanted to think so very much. . . . You know, I was sure I brought a hairbrush with me." She shook the bag in irritation as she continued. "A little while after we buried Tom, Mister Bright brought me a small pouch of papers, things Tom left with him for me . . . in case. I welcomed them so, because I didn't have many mementos of him."

Carrie picked a brush from the bed. "This isn't mine. It must be what you're looking for."

Lydia took it with a chagrined look of thanks, sat on the bed and began brushing her hair. After many strokes, "When I read his diary I discovered that before his first marriage he . . . forced himself on a slave woman, even fathered a child by her. Then just before his first wedding he sold off both of them." She stopped brushing and turned to face Carrie. "*Sold* them. I felt like a club had struck me."

"If it's any consolation," Carrie offered, "he wasn't alone. That's what my father did."

"I can't get over the horror of such things. Cold-blooded severing of paternal bonds."

"I never thought of my father as a real father. I never called him that."

Lydia put her brush down, and stood to pace about the small space. "How could he stand to have his own child not call him father? I'm sure I could not be so forgiving."

"I wasn't talking about forgiveness. I'll never forgive him for how he treated my mother. I think she came to love him by the time he sold us. He didn't even see us to say goodbye."

"Carrie, how can men do such things? Painted sepulchers. Outwardly so respectable and polite. Inwardly a mass of corruption. When I read it, read it in my husband's own hand, I was so angry. Partly at myself."

She picked up the hairbrush, then put it down again. "How could I have deceived myself so? I thought I loved him. I gladly married him. I gave myself to him happily. And then this. It enraged me so I didn't eat or sleep for days."

"I know the rage you mean."

"I forget you don't just hear or read about it. You live it." She shook her head. "How can you be so calm?"

"I'm only calm," Carrie answered slowly, "when I don't think on it. Sometimes I get so angry I want to do things that frighten me. If I didn't have these mountain walls around to keep out the world, I don't know what would happen. I tell myself we have to accept what God gives us. But it's so hard. I've prayed long about it. If we're all God's children, why does God punish some of us so? What have my sweet babies done to deserve this? Why is God so angry with us?"

"I can't believe God is punishing you." Lydia's voice became very stern. "That's not a God *I* want to pray to. God is a loving God."

"I try to be thankful. For having a place like this, hidden away in the hills, where almost nobody comes to remind me I'm just property, not legally Henry's wife. And I *am* thankful. But then I think, what will happen to the children? They can't stay here forever. Maybe the war will change things."

"We can't go back to where we were, not after . . ."

"No. Not after so much blood. Well, you see, I'm not so calm as you think," Carrie said, as she opened a trunk and pulled out a fresh nightgown. "Try this for size. I know I could not be calm reading terrible things from someone I had loved. I'd tear the pages into little bits. I'd throw the book into the fire."

"That's what I almost did." Lydia took the gown absent-mindedly. "But I decided to know the whole terrible truth. After a while I was glad I did. I found some solace. After his marriage, he saw what an unforgivable thing he had done, selling the woman and his own son. He tried to trace them, to buy them back, to free them. But they'd been resold again and again. West Tennessee, then Alabama, then Texas, and then the trail ran out. He never found them. He filled pages with regret, with remorse, but of course that didn't change anything."

"If the girl was good-looking, she probably got sold quick and quiet. Anyone would have a hard time following my mother."

"And the child. They weigh heavy on my conscience. I even thought of looking myself. Not personally, of course. What chance would a woman have? Mister Bright said if Tom found it impossible before the war, it'd be the same now. He says he never guessed any of this at the time. But I don't know if he's telling me . . ."

"I imagine your husband never flaunted the woman and son. Unless he brought them into the house, the way my father did, Spooks would never have seen them."

"Sometimes my mind just goes around and around." Lydia finally held the gown up against herself. "This is so thoughtful of you. It will serve nicely, and the stitching is so pretty. Did you do it?" She admired the gown, but returned to her topic. "You see why I ask about Mister Bright? You understand why I'm so very afraid, what a man seems to be isn't what he is."

"I understand. You sound like my mama."

Lydia put a hand on Carrie's shoulder. "Forgive me for asking this. You've known Mister Bright a long time. Is it possible you're such good friends that you don't . . . see. . . a less attractive side?"

Her head to one side, Carrie considered. "It's possible. My mama warned me that a white gentleman always has feet of clay. I can still remember her voice when she said that and the way she banged the heavy skillet down. She knew a lot more of the world than I ever will."

"Mister Bright told me she was a rare woman."

"She was, and I learned to listen to her. So at every chance I tried to watch the two gentlemen I knew, Henry and Spooks, looking for the clay. But I've never found it."

Carrie pulled her nightgown from its peg. "I don't mean I think they're perfect. They're sinners like the rest of us. But I've never seen a shadow of some other side, at least not a side more terrible than what I can see in myself sometimes."

She went over to the candle on its shelf. "But remember," she added, "I've been up here so long I don't know many people. Only the people I love. Maybe if I lived in town, I'd see different."

Carrie turned to Lydia. "Should I snuff the candle?"

Lydia nodded. In the dim light of fireplace coals, she burst out, "Tell me, Carrie, if your . . . your circumstances were . . . different, I mean, if you didn't know Henry, and Mister Bright asked you to marry him, would you?"

Grateful for the very low light, Carrie could not say, *I've wondered about that ever since Spooks and I thought Henry might die on the trail,* but she realized silence or even hesitation would be misinterpreted, so she spoke immediately, feeling out her answer as she went along. "That's hard to answer. . . . If I didn't have Henry and the children, . . . how would I know Spooks? . . . But I do see what you want to know. . . . Well, if I didn't have Henry, if he didn't exist, or the children either— and those are big ifs—and I somehow met Spooks, and he somehow asked me to marry him—and those are big somehows—why, if that happened, I'd feel honored. And grateful. And happy beyond words."

"I cannot imagine higher praise."

"But you don't believe me."

Lydia pulled the borrowed nightgown over her. "I do believe you, but I was so terribly wrong once. I wish I knew him better to set my mind easy. Carrie, I'm the outsider in my neighborhood. My Sesesh neighbors would love to crucify me. They know I pleaded with Mister Davies not to go to fight for something I believe is horrible, a damning sin. They think Thomas Davies is a glorious martyr for the Confederate cause. They didn't see Tom gloriously martyred on a filthy cot in the mud of a forgotten, bedraggled camp, out of his head delirious, dying for absolutely nothing."

Lydia stopped to control her voice. "I hope I didn't wake the children." She got into bed and pulled up the quilt. "With my Sesesh neighbors, it's not easy for Widow Davies to spend time privately with a single gentleman and not have vicious tongues wag. Even when Mister Bright calls about lawyerly things he brings someone with him as chaperone."

"I wish I could help you more," said Carrie as she got into bed, trying not to crowd her guest.

"You've helped so much already. A woman's ear is such a godsend. I can't write my heart to my sister in Pennsylvania. Mister Bright warned me that letters don't get through, or worse, are opened and read. . . . Isn't it a comfort to listen to rain on the roof?"

❧

The morning dawned with no leftover trace of storm in the sky. At early light, Henry and Carrie met alone on the porch.

"Success for Spooks?" Henry whispered.

"Don't know. They need more time alone together. But she plans to go north in two or three weeks."

"I guess you told her Spooks is a good man, and that's all we can do," said Henry. "I'll go open the water gate."

"While you're up there at the gate, think on how many favors we owe Spooks."

When Henry returned, he found everyone eating breakfast. He followed his hearty greeting with a subdued tone. "Lydia, I'm sorry to be the bearer of bad news. I checked the new trail. After all that rain, it's a slippery mess. Down further, there'll be impassable places because of deep, deep mud. It's just not safe for a lady on a pony. Not safe a'tall. I believe you'd better wait at least a day, let things dry out."

Lydia apologized, embarrassed to be a burden, concerned that she be underfoot.

Carrie waved this all aside, and turned to Spooks. He had greeted Henry's announcement with a surprised look but said nothing. "For those who like to look at mountains, it's a beautiful morning. Why don't you take Lydia up to the Witch's Nose?"

She smiled for Lydia, "If you go slowly, you can take your horses most of the way so it doesn't weary you much. In fact, we'll pack you a little lunch. The day stays fine, you must go on up to the top."

"Will that trail be safe?" inquired Lydia.

"For certain," Henry answered quickly. "You see . . . that . . trail . . is . . .ah, ah . . . more protected and—"

"It drains a lot better," Carrie cut in, "so it stays dry."

"I can come and show you the way," shouted George excitedly.

"No, son, I need you to help check all the fruit trees after that storm."

"Awww, Papa. Edward should help."

"You know what to look for, and I need your sharp eyes after all that wind. Edward isn't near big enough to look close at grafts."

"Julia could help you."

"Except," Carrie promptly corrected him, "that I need her in the house today." She scanned the wall. "George, where did you put that basket you used yesterday? I told you to put it back on the peg. I need it for their lunch."

"I'll find it, Mama," said a smiling Julia.

❧

The visitors came back into view as the sun just touched the west ridge. George, on watch for several hours, ran out to greet them—and ride on Spook's horse the short way back.

"Did'cha do any hunting?" George aimed an imaginary rifle. "Pow."

"George, we did a great deal of hunting." Lydia leveled her own imaginary weapon. "That's why we went, I now understand. Pow."

"Wha'cha hunting? Deer?"

"Oh yes, a very special one," said Spooks, smiling over the boy's head.

"Find any?"

"Indeed we did," Lydia answered. "My deer looked promising from a distance, and at close range I took more than a mild fancy to him. Pow." She lowered her rifle.

"How 'bout you, Mister Spooks?"

"My quarry proved much more elusive, but the day became very satisfying as it unfolded. Pow."

"Well, where're the deer to dress? Didn'tcha bring 'em back with you, Mister Spooks?"

"We did, though our deer are somewhat metaphorical. Now, George, can I trust you to take both horses gently to the barn? I'll be along directly to help you unsaddle them."

At the cabin, George's voice rang out. "They hunted deer, and Mister Spooks got one and Miz Lydia got another one. . . . I think."

Spooks slipped over to Lydia's mare and helped her down.

"Thank you, John." She took off her hat and looked up at her hosts on the porch. "What a glorious day. And what sublime views! I owe you thanks, Carrie, for the suggestion, and I owe . . . Mister Bright," she turned to Spooks, "for being such a trusty guide," she took his arm, "as in so many matters."

❧

Lydia sat with Edward, who found his voice to tell her in precise detail no one could hurry how many things he counted every day and what he fed his pet turtles. Julia and Carrie cleared the table. Henry and

Spooks sat on the porch within earshot through the open door. Edward wound down and dozed in Lydia's lap.

"That is a contented child," laughed Lydia. "But no more than I after such a day. It doesn't seem right to be so happy in the midst of a terrible war."

Spooks came inside, stood behind her chair, and rested his hands on her shoulders. "Should we tell our friends what they already know?"

"Already know?" Lydia faltered, putting a hand over his.

Spooks nodded to Carrie.

Without looking up from a wash bucket, she answered. "Lydia, you are very discreet, but one small slip gave you away."

Julia broke in with a grin. "When you came back from your hunting trip and thanked Mister Spooks for helping you down, you called him 'John,' not Mister Bright."

"An when you come in," Henry picked up from the cabin door, "Spooks heped y'down but y'held onta him a heep longer then y'woulda if he'd a-bin only Mister Bright."

Lydia colored as she smiled. "I didn't anticipate my actions were so closely observed."

"Don' need nary no lawyerman for't. A pretty lady an a bachelor man down from a picnic at Witch's Nose, wal, e'en a mountain farmer ken figger thet un."

"I'd say, especially a mountain farmer, Mister Hollis."

Spooks gave Lydia a quick kiss. "Don't take it amiss, dear. Uncas has been waiting near an eternity to retaliate for my unwise observations about gingerbread when I was young and cheeky."

"Durned right I bin a-waitin."

"Now we're all going to stop right there," Carrie spoke firmly, refusing Julia's questioning look.

"I suspect that's wise," agreed Lydia. "In the storm last evening I forgot to show you something I brought with me." She went to a saddlebag Spooks had left in a corner. "When I was staying with my grandparents way up in the Vermont mountains, the biggest treat anyone could bring was a fashion book. So I brought one with me. Would you like to see it?"

Carrie and Julia certainly would. They ignored the men's teasing. George shuttled between the unexciting pictures on his mother's lap and Spooks's conversation with his father.

A wartime wedding: quickly arranged, small and quiet. The second time Lydia rode the mountain trail, she dressed much more plainly. With a wide smile, Henry bussed her. Carrie happily hailed her as Miz Bright, and fondly embraced her as Lydia. She brought with her a bag of promised yard goods and another fashion book.

She came frequently after that, until Spooks informed his hosts on a solitary trip that she was in the family way and would be staying home for some months. He carried with him things Carrie requested: instructions and material to embroider the cushion she recently fashioned for the Low Chair.

Dorinda Hollis Henderson to Crotia Hollis Warden

Collection of Lewis Hollis Warden

September 20, 1915

Dear Sister,

I'm resting a bit in the kitchen with a tiny sip of home brew. It's in a coffee cup. Just in case some bigmouth, another Haeckle the Cackle, shows up without warning. I spread an old newspaper on the table to soak up spilled tomato, so I had to reread it around the spills. It's stale news, I know, but I still grieve again at so many innocent people killed when that Lusitania sank. Horrible. As long as Mr. Wilson keeps us out of the war, I'd vote for him. If only Tennessee was smart enough to let women vote. I'm on a county committee about that, but some silly women just want their husbands to do all their thinking.

No politics today, just canning. Put up 82 jars. Getting them down to the cellar was a big job itself. I do hate those steep stairs, Crotia. Someday I'm going to trip and land at the bottom in a pond of tomato and broken glass. Broken neck too. You just make sure they get my gravestone right. "Well Stewed in Her Own Tomatoes." Don't let 'em misspell tomatoes, Crotia. They're sure to, you know, since it's in stone.

It's now or never to write you about an unusual visitor last week.

HL happens to go to G. Ford on some business. Happens to pass the station when the 2:37, the short dog, comes through. Happens to notice an elderly gentleman getting off. City-dressed, but too dignified to be a drummer. Looks around like he's lost. Quince pretends he's too busy with freight to help, so HL asks the stranger if he needs directions. He politely answers, yes, says he's on vacation, looking to enjoy the mountains in the fall. Picked G. Ford on the map, didn't know it's so, well, tiny, no offense intended. Can HL please recommend lodgings for a few nights' stay?

Of course, since Lester closed his place (I did write you about that, didn't I?), you know lodging in G. Ford is unwashed towels, critters between dirty sheets, muddy coffee with soured cream and bad breakfast grits from a hungover (would you accept 'slattern'?) cook.

HL takes pity on him, invites him to put up at Tulips. Plenty of room, for sure. The stranger checks Quince's schedule board. Next down cars at 2:11 a.m. (assuming the crew doesn't stop in Trenton for some of Rafe's homebrew, which the board doesn't mention). Stranger accepts HL's offer.

He says he should introduce himself. So they shake hands. HL says, "Hollis, H. L. Hollis" about the same time the stranger is saying, "Hollis, E. J. Hollis." They're both amazed. They check names. Herodotus Lucius Hollis. Edward John Hollis. They check spelling. H-o-l-l-i-s, twice. They check Hollis origins. England to Virginia, twice. HL says if they go back far enough they must be related somehow, but his guest warns him that going back in families is dangerous. You find things you might not want to know. HL agrees, thinking of that Hollis coal-black sheep, Caleb. (By the way I'm glad WHC could use my gossip about Caleb's sons, those low-down skunks.)

Anyhow, on the way to Tulips, the visitor Hollis asks all kinds of questions. Crops & stock & mountains, seems much interested in local churches & clergy. Of course HL can wear your ear off on all of those, so they don't get back to family.

I'm at Tulips helping Caroline & the girls with canning. Tomatoes. More tomatoes.

What adjective would WHC use to amplify the noun? An <u>attractive array</u> of tomatoes? A <u>wholesome harvest</u> of tomatoes? A <u>bounteous blessing</u> of tomatoes? A <u>surprising surfeit</u> of tomatoes? A <u>gagging glut</u> of tomatoes? I don't rightly know what WHC'd say. I do know what I'd say. <u>Too damn many</u> tomatoes.

Anyway, we are taking a sit-down when HL rolls up with his guest, HL without any thought of course that we're all dressed pretty rough, for canning tomatoes. But the new Hollis smooths things over as if he does this every day. Which, it turns out, he maybe does because he introduces himself as Pastor Edward Hollis. So we have a double unexpected: another Hollis and a minister at that. HL doesn't waste any time finding out this new Hollis is a <u>Lutheran</u> pastor.

Or so he <u>says</u>. Maybe the heat and tomatoes got me, but I happened to notice that he hesitates a bit when he tells us about a brother and sister. That somehow brought to my mind how trusting HL can be. You know, bad as Mama sometimes. Pay for the Brooklyn Bridge if the seller spoke a little Greek to him. I wonder if this stranger could be some con man, picking up his clues from us as he goes along, and we're ripe tomatoes ready for the cooking down.

I am staying the night at Tulips anyway—Mike gone with James to Knoxville—so there's plenty of time to listen to the maybe-fake Preacher Hollis talk. He asks more questions than talks, and I suspicion that's a bad sign. He can feed us back all the information HL gives him to sound like he knows the family.

Comes time for supper. Caroline asks "Pastor" Hollis to say the blessing. He leaves a long silence, then clears his throat and his first sentence is "Lord God, we plead for your infinite mercy." Crotia, it may be sacrilege, but all I can think of is Emmaus and "By His breaking of bread they knew him." I nearly look to see if Father is at his place, the similarity is so close.

I always thought all that introductory habit was Father's invention, but now I bet he got it from his father, who copied <u>his</u> father, and so on back generations until you get two brothers who both pick it up, but one goes west and stops at the mountains, while the other keeps going west past the mountains. And each brother passes down the silence, the throat clearing and the Lord God we plead.

There. I know what you're thinking about me. As credulous as HL about smooth-talking strangers. For once I've out-Crotiaed Crotia. But Sister, if you looked at HL Hollis and Pastor Edward Hollis facing each other across the table, you'd agree they've got to be related somewhere well short of Adam. Compared to HL, Pastor is a little shorter build. But same profile, same head shape. Of course he doesn't have HL's farmer's sunburn. But he talks with the same hitches all the Hollises have, except you and Marcus. Even some of the same mannerisms.

When I get him to talk, he's not a four-book preacher. Went to the seminary in Philadelphia and then had a church in California but now he's executive secretary of a new Lutheran charity home for orphans and chronically ill patients. He notices HL's Greek NT sitting out, which not many people have on their table, so HL explains how Father started him learning Greek as a boy. That leads Pastor to tell us how his mother started him learning Latin when he was a boy and how he still remembers his pride when he found he could count to 22 in Latin — he was counting soldiers on parade. Preparing for the seminary, he had to pick up Greek and German. HL kindly mentions my German from Herr Schmidt and the University, and we're just having a grand gab, droppin in ferrin words every other sentence. Wish you'd been there.

HL leaves openings for him to talk about his parents or grandparents, to see if we can figure out a relationship, but he never takes up on it. He does say his wife died last year. Has an older brother in Chicago, and an Ohio sister who was killed in a robbery. He talks most about his two sons in California, a doctor and a teacher, and their children.

An old member of his congregation, a Union veteran, was with troops that spent time in these mountains during the war and always praised their beauty, so when his congregation gave him a going-away purse he decided to take a trip east, combine it with seeing family.

He says a man on the cars between Claytown and G. Ford told him of a fine view from the head of a narrow valley, perhaps called Quach-something? Of course we guess it must be Quachasee. Yes, we say, you can see mountains from a good many places, but the Quachasee head is an extra fine lookout. Edward says since he's come this far, he'd like to go look for himself if someone can give him directions. HL's Daniel volunteers to show him the way. I go along on spur of the moment. Alright, I admit it. I wanted to escape the damnation of tomatoes. We take a picnic lunch.

Pastor's shoes aren't the best for hiking, but he doesn't complain, though he's puffing on the steep stretches. He treats the cliff drop-offs sensibly — just respectful, not scared stiff. It's been so long, I forget how beautiful the little farm is up there. In fact, Father's buildings distract Pastor from the mountains. He guesses what all the buildings are without asking. Looks in every shed. Goes into the cabin. I forgot it's just two rooms. Enough for a bachelor in a pinch, but no more. He stands for a long time at that little cemetery, even says a prayer there. He wipes his eyes when he steps away, says it's a fine place to await the Resurrection. I think the same. I'd like to rest there myself if it weren't for the Henderson plot.

Back at Tulips, he must be worn out, but is fine company. Says he read up some on the war in Tenn, so he knows Union troops raided farms, sometimes burning buildings or at least stealing stores and stock. We tell him how Caleb's whole place was burned down. Anyway, Pastor likes the Quachasee so much he goes up there again the next day, alone. Knows the way by then; of course it's either all uphill or all downhill, and look out for the drop-offs.

HL wants to introduce our own Pastor Hollis at Church on Sunday, but when they study timetables, they see he couldn't meet his Ohio nieces and nephews when he promised.

What intrigues me most is that some day, years and years ago, two brothers head west out of Virginia. At some point they part company, with a tearful handshake or maybe a snarl, who knows. Then you wait some generations. And you have Edward who is still so much a Hollis he could be a half-brother easy. I wish you could have met him. He wrote out his California address, but I just now see I left that paper at Tulips. I promise to send it on in my next letter for sure. I warned him you would write him, and he seemed to welcome the idea. So write him.

Next week there's a potluck at church. I have to figure out something to take instead of my usual. I'm not looking forward to it. There's no getting out of having words with Ginny Hanes. She's going after Lucy Titcomb, our new organist at Bethel. Why? Because Lucy gives piano lessons weekdays, and told Ginny's daughter that she is wasting her money because she doesn't practice. (Lucy was too generous, in my opinion; the problem is lack of the slightest musical talent.) Ginny knows this as well as anybody, but can't face the truth and gets insulted. She's the bell cow for a little herd of bovine followers that sits together and sings loud to fight the organ. Every hymn they lag on purpose way behind Lucy's tempo. Puts Lucy nearly in tears.

They want to drive her out. They will, too, at the rate they're going. Lucy is the best we've had in years, everyone but Ginny and her herd agrees. That shrew has blocked arteries to the brain—sorry, this child of God is reluctant to accept blessings. She nearly wrecked the Ladies Aid two years ago over nobody remembers what. You remember how peculiar her mother and aunts were. Lord help us, it runs true in the family. Contrarious, ever'una 'em. Sister, the women in that family should be in your "Mtn Springs News" sometime. Guess you'll never be short of subjects.

The other day I was hankering for some of Helen Coates' dinner rolls. You remember she gave each of us the recipe when we were complaining to her about Edie's hardtack. I used to make them regularly. Proportions have to be just right or you get very ordinary rolls. Wouldn't you know it, I've lost the copy she gave me. Do you still have yours?

This has gotten a lot longer than I thought. Just looked at the clock, horrified. If I don't start something on the stove quick, I'm in trouble. Mike never complains, but I'd have a guilty conscience. He works so hard.

Heard from Annie last week. Had a sick spell again, a worry, but she's better now.

No news from Lowe in a long time; guess he's too busy with his flatlands girl.

Mike & I got a good laugh out of the last column you sent. Keep the columns coming and write me soon. I know you'll have lots of stories about Lew. Don't spoil a perfectly nice little boy, Crotia.

Your loving sister,

Dory

QUACHASEE
WHC

Carrie knew something was amiss because Spooks arrived at the cabin unusually soon after the dogs yipped. "You want Henry?" she called from the porch.

"Both of you, absent juvenile auditors," Spooks answered as he swung off the steaming horse. "Hello, Master Edward, want a ride?" He lifted Edward into the saddle and walked with Carrie at a quick gait to where Henry, Julia, and George hoed in the High Field. Spooks moved a little way deeper into the woods for shade, and tethered the horse to a tree. At his unspoken signal, Carrie sent Julia and George to the cabin to punch down rising dough.

Spooks skipped pleasantries. "Lydia developed some private connections with certain Union officers, Philadelphia men. Found out their troops may be coming this way. Ordered me to ride up to tell you. They covered Clifton yesterday. That's just twenty miles away," he explained to Carrie. "They're short of rations so they do a lot of foraging on these patrols."

A wry face. "Doesn't help the Union reputation when you steal from friend as well as foe. They're looking for Sesesh scouting out as well as foraging. Generally raising hell. Looks like they've got informers. Some places they ride in like thunder, hardly say a word. Burn every building clear to the ground. Stock they don't take, they shoot and butcher on the spot."

He slapped a fly successfully and continued without triumph. "They skip a few places, but not many. Some owners they treat mighty hard. Your drawbridge has worked well so far. But using informers has been very effective for the army. They been seen carrying hand-drawn maps. Have gotten to places that surprise me. You should know that your risk has gone way up. Some informers have ancient scores to settle."

Henry nodded, resolute. "If they come to steal, my rifle'll be ready for 'em."

"Uncas is a brave warrior, but perhaps this time guile is better. From what I've heard, resistance isn't wise." Bright glanced at Carrie, quickly rolled his eyes, then looked back at Henry. "It's war, Henry. You fire at 'em, you're automatically Sesesh. How can they think otherwise? Makes things a lot worse."

"Man has a right to protect his home and family. Don't need a lawyer to know that. These mountains make good defense. One man can throttle up an army."

Spooks nodded. "A few passes here one man can hold by himself easy. But the Quachasee isn't one of 'em. And, pardon my saying, Henry, but your eyesight doesn't make a good sniper."

"A man has rights," insisted Henry with a dark face.

"Henry," snapped Spooks, then halted with a deep breath. He slowly drew a line in the dirt with his boot toe. "Henry," his voice light, his manner cheerful, "you're right. You can exercise your rights as a free, native-born Tennessean. After all, we tried to set up our own State of Franklin here when North Carolina got forgetful. Maybe you could do it again, just East Tennessee, in the Union like West Virginia. There's talk of it. We could elect you governor."

He flashed Henry a crooked grin. "There is a little problem, though. The troops haven't read up on your rights as much as you have. So standing for your rights means your property gets burned to ashes. Standing for your rights means your sons get shot down like dogs, and your womenfolk get carnally used until they're discarded off a cliff edge like offal. By all means exercise your rights."

"What d'you expect me to do? Send 'em an invitation?"

"They don't need one, believe me. I'd take some of your smokehouse up the mountain. Not so much that any fool can see what you've done. Take some chickens, but leave the crowing roosters here. Henry, I assume you've made all your fruit liquor deliveries."

Henry nodded.

"Best make sure there's not some drop left in a forgotten keg. In fact, hide any empty kegs if you can."

He turned to address Carrie. "Lydia suggests you wear rags and make sure your face looks like it hasn't been close to soap for a month. Julia—"

"Julia, we keep completely out of sight," said Carrie firmly.

Spooks agreed in evident relief. "She's gotten too freshly womanly to take a chance. Pray the officers want control. Henry, you'd like regular troops in clean, new uniforms come to visit. Their discipline seems best, from what we hear."

Tired of urging on an unmoving steed, Edward called, "what you talkin 'bout?"

Spooks answered as he walked back to him. "Why, Master Edward, nothing much. Only pillage, rape, and murder."

"What's that?"

"Converting defeat into disaster."

"Defeat?"

"You know about de feet. How many you have?"

"Two." Such a simple question insulted Edward. "Everyone has two."

"In Latin?"

"Duo."

"Have you looked at your horse, sir? Just duo feet, or maybe tres?" Spooks swung Edward down without waiting for an answer, untethered the horse, and mounted. "Now you count." He looked over Edward to his parents. "When this is all over we must have a debate about rights. Women's rights, don't you think?" With a wave he rode away at a trot.

Wordless, they returned to the cabin. There Henry began dividing stores. By nightfall they positioned a cache well concealed within an extensive yellow patch George and Julia had found up the mountain. While skirting the impenetrable laurel thicket, the children, berry picking, had noticed a concealed entrance to a bear-bored tunnel and ventured in, Julia tying bright yarn flags to show their way back out.

One path meandered deep into the thicket until it opened into an unexpected clearing, further protected by massive rock outcroppings. Henry had pronounced the spot good as a cave for protection, better even, because the highest rock gave a good view in all directions.

They brought up the most valuable piglets in pokes to a hasty enclosure, staked the mules there and slept close by, feeling as secure as if protected by thick high ramparts. Henry diverted the children with stories he had heard of hunters as experienced as Spooks who attempted a yellow patch only to be lost for days. Carrie distracted them with memories of her first brush and bark shelter at the farm, though she broke off at Edward's "Is that where Papa slept too?"

They now followed a novel routine, though a routine it remained. Every morning they led Edgar and Ellis down for water. Carrie did minimal cooking while Henry and Julia hastily tended the animals left on the farm. Then they hurried away. Henry insisted on working the fields and on keeping both rifles, loaded, close at hand. Carrie insisted on being with the children helping Henry.

After a week, they all complained of cold food and of aching muscles in the morning, despite the pine needles Julia carried into the thicket as cushioning. Edward missed the chickens and cows. George whined about watching the high trail down into the valley, at Henry's repeated orders, for any sign of soldiers. When Henry suggested to Carrie privately they should move back the next day, she agreed without hesitation.

As they gathered at the edge of the High Field for mid-morning rest, Edward looked up and calmly announced, "There are the soldiers. I'll count them in Latin. Unus, duo, tres. . ." He went on counting as the family hastily moved deeper into the trees to watch mounted troops successively silhouetted as they crossed the ridge above on the High Trail.

"Octo, novem, decim . . ."

Henry growled. "So they figured out the way. Maybe we should ambush them." He picked up his rifle and practice-aimed it toward the cabin. Carrie lifted the other rifle, steadying it against a tree the better to aim accurately.

"Viginti, viginti unus, viginti duo. Mama, I can count to twenty-two in Latin."

Henry looked at Carrie and shook his head with a grim expression. "This isn't like dumb Netzler and his gang. I can't fast-talk twenty-two real soldiers. We've got no choice: retreat right away to the yellow patch."

As she nodded, Carrie handed her rifle to Julia. "I'll try going down to meet them."

"*Meet* them?" Henry's voice rose with incredulity.

"I can't bear the thought of sitting up in the yellow patch and watching the smoke when they burn everything that we've worked so hard for. But I need to go alone."

"That's pushing luck."

"More than taunting Netzler about his name?"

"That was worth a try."

"So is this."

"Without a weapon?"

"I don't dare carry one. I've got to be a dithering woman."

"I can go with you, Mama," said Julia as she passed the rifle to George.

Her parents locked eyes and wordlessly rejected her offer.

Edward had been peering around trees to get a better view of visitors. "Mama, I think I could count even more than viginti duo soldiers if they ever come to see us again." Both parents' eyes swept the boy, then met.

"A dithering, manless woman with a talkative, friendly little boy," muttered Carrie as she ran hands through her hair to leave it in wild disarray, and rubbed dirt on her dress and face.

"It's dangerous," said Henry. "I wouldn't ask you to do that."

"About as dangerous as standing alone on the porch to face four armed men."

"Those were four idiots. These are professionals. The farm isn't worth your life."

"It's not *worth* my life. It *is* my life." She held out her hand for Edward to take. "They're wearing uniforms. Twenty-two men must have officers. All I can do is try to shame them into not burning everything down. If they leave, send Jingles. I won't let him in if it's not safe, and he'll come back to you."

As she hurried toward the cabin, she warned the boy about not talking when grownups were busy. From the porch she watched as the last of the troops reached the bottom of the treacherous path from the ridge. They paused, milling at the edge of the woods, then came on fast, so fast that Edward could not recount them. The first to reach the cabin did not even slow. Dogs in their way they rode down. The churning stream divided and flowed around the cabin, reining in only when men and horses engulfed the outbuildings.

Watching the blur—powerful mounts, clean uniforms, shiny weapons—Carrie imagined Henry and her aiming two rifles to repulse twenty-two heavily armed men. *Merciful Lord, we'd be dead already.*

One of the last riders, stocky, unshaven, with no neck and a dirty uniform, pulled up directly in front of the porch. "Well, lookee what we got here, our re-ward after one helluva ride." He took a long swig from his canteen. "A real temptin dish." Another swig. "It's still early in the mornin, but 'specially after a ride that hellacious, you takes what's on the table." He tilted the canteen again.

Carrie sought Edward's hand. *Was he slurring his words? What if they've been drinking?* Her heart sank. *Henry was right. The only choice in face of overwhelming force is retreat. I'm lost and I've sacrificed Edward.*

"UN-fortunately, when you got a fresh new lieutenant, it's business 'fore pleasure." Another swig. The soldier pulled crumpled papers from a pocket. "Now, the map, we don' need anymore." He dropped the top sheet and studied another. "Our reliable information is, hmm, that Hen-ry Holl-is lives here with a house full'a slaves." The soldier recapped his canteen with theatrical deliberation.

"Where's Hollis?" he suddenly barked.

Carrie looked around slowly. "Ain't heah, look lahk."

"You mean he's hidin in the woods."

She scratched her head. "No food foah 'im in dem woods. I 'spect he lef couppa deys 'go."

"You're lyin. He's hidin. But he made a *big* mistake leaving you in plain sight. Who're you?"

"Me?" She shrugged and searched the ground for an answer. Finally, "Jes de housekeepa."

"Yeah. An' I'm jes de green recruit. That your kid?"

She inspected Edward as if he had just appeared. "Well, I tinks so." She nodded lethargically.

"Hey kid, where's your daddy?"

Edward gripped Carrie's skirt.

"Speak up, kid. I asked you a question, dammit. *Where's your daddy?*"

"I . . ." Edward hesitated at conflicting imperatives. "He's . . ."

A clean-shaven man, young, in a fresh uniform with more stripes, rode from behind the cabin. He spoke in a rush. "For your own good, ma'am, we need straight answers, no delaying. You have liquor hidden in any building?"

Carrie shook her head.

Narrowed eyes. "Any weapons? Guns, pistols, a hunting rifle?"

Again Carrie's mute negative.

"I hope you're not lying. Who are you, ma'am?"

"Hollis's whore," the short, dirty man snorted. "Says she's just the housekeeper. With looks like that! *Bed* keeper is more like it. Hollis must've been tipped off. She says he's gone. Too bad. I had a nice run going. Shot one Reb before noon the last nine days."

He pointed at Edward. "You won't get anything outta her—until we string up the boy." He smiled unpleasantly. "Did that a coupla months ago, Lieutenant, before you arrived. Got the mama to sing long and loud. Fack is, she give away her whole fam'ly. But it turned out her boy choked on the rope and died. Too bad."

He chuckled without humor, and gestured toward the water barrel fed by the log sluice. "What's in there, nigger?"

"Yuh talkin t'me, mister soldierman?" Carrie stared wide-eyed at the barrel as if she had never noticed it before. "Mebbe watah, I guess."

He drew his pistol and fired. Water spurted from a hole. Carrie looked up at him in surprise. "It sho look lahk watah."

"Could be a whole arsenal in there."

Carrie nodded agreeably. "Yassuh, I 'spect so. 'Specially de powder. It stoh real good in watah."

The man seemed not to hear her jibe, perhaps because he was occupied in bringing at hand a coiled rope with one end worked into a noose. "Kid, let go of your mama's hand and come over here. I want to see if I get better answers from your mama when I try this loop on your neck. Com'on. Get over here."

"Stow the rope, Corporal. Stow it. Now." The lieutenant spoke stiffly. "Corporal: four men. Go through the barn for Sesesh. Sabers hard into the hay to the hilt. Move on it, Corporal."

As the corporal slowly rode off, the younger officer turned back to her. "Let's start all over again," he said in a tired voice. He paused. "Good mornin, ma'am. I'm Lieutenant Colfax. Your name, ma'am?"

"Caroline LaCroix, Lieutenant Colfax. LaCroix is capital L, capital C. And a final x, sir, like your name, but silent."

"Miz LaCroix, you're certain Hollis isn't here?"

"Yes sir. Very certain. Why do you look for him?"

"Need to ask him a few questions. He's been named as a Reb leader."

"Lieutenant Colfax, your informer is mistaken. Probably malicious. Mister Hollis is a Union man. Wouldn't fight for Sesesh."

"That's what they all say."

"Even if he's Reb," Carrie persisted, "he's too old for long marches. Eyesight is too bad to shoot well."

Lieutenant Colfax pursed his lips. "I'll know that when I see him." He raised his voice. "Anderson, take Gerber and Fairfax around the edges of the fields. See if anyone is hiding in there. On the double." The man galloped off. "Is that your boy, ma'am?"

Aware he had adult attention at last, Edward stepped forward. "I can count. You have twenty-two soldiers."

Colfax's smile froze. "Your mama tell you to count us?"

"'Course not." Edward burst out, pride injured, now an indignant child. "I count all by myself. Can *you* count all the way to twenty-two?" he demanded.

"Sometimes," the lieutenant seemed to relax. "When I try hard."

"In Latin?" Edward challenged, "Like tres, quattro."

"Quinque," his eyebrows raised, the lieutenant picked up. "Sex, septem."

"Octo, novem, decim, undecim."

"Yes, and all the way up to octodecim and novemdecim," added the lieutenant casually, watching for Edward to fall into his trap.

"No, you're wrong," cried Edward triumphantly. "You can't count right. You can't count right. It's duodeviginti, undeviginti, viginti."

"Think you're a pretty smart fella, don't you?" replied the lieutenant. "Who taught you that, your daddy?"

"No! Mama did. She can read Latin. It's hard. Can *you*?" Edward challenged.

"I used to." The lieutenant's eyes switched to Carrie. "The cabin is empty, ma'am." More observation than question. Carrie's hopes revived.

"Yes, Lieutenant."

Colfax sighed. "Have to check, ma'am. Brawley, Peters," he shouted, motioning to the cabin. Carrie stepped out of the doorway to allow access. "Lieutenant, would you kindly ask your men to scrape their boots before they go in? I just washed the floor."

Brawley and Peters dismounted and looked at Colfax. An amused look on his face, he nodded. "You heard what the lady says."

Pistols drawn, the two men scuffed their feet on the steps, tiptoed in and tiptoed out. "Nothin, sir."

"Did you check under the bed and up the chimney?" Carrie covered her dare with a smile.

"Yes, ma'am," answered Brawley, grinning. "But no fresh coffee."

"You didn't tell me you were coming this early."

Peters was not looking for coffee. "Lieutenant, there's a *lot* of books in there. Could be Reb stuff for all I know."

Colfax turned to Carrie. "Is that true, ma'am?"

"The books, yes. I'm not certain what constitutes Reb stuff, Lieutenant. Would Mister Shakespeare and Mister Dickens be Reb stuff?"

"Not to my mind. Can you read, ma'am?"

"Tolerably well, Lieutenant."

"What do you read?"

"About anything I can get. I keep going back to Shakespeare."

"'If we shadows have offended, think but this, and all is mended,'" began the lieutenant, watching her intently.

"'That you have but slumbered here while these visions did appear.' I wish that were so, Lieutenant. But I'm wide awake, your men make poor fairies, and the corporal is an especially rotten Oberon."

The last jab brought a smile. "Ma'am, you bring to mind 'And then will I swear beauty is itself black and all they foul that thy complexion lack.'"

"I don't remember any mention of the dark lady mothering a little boy, Lieutenant, and anyway . . ." Before she could continue, intense firing echoed from the High Field. It ceased as abruptly as it had begun.

Dear God, no. Henry must not have gone to the yellow patch after all. He must have been goaded beyond reason at the sight of troops on his farm. Henry, oh my dear Henry. Carrie closed her eyes in despair. When she opened them she saw Colfax studying her suspiciously. Edward took her hand and whimpered. She bent to comfort him—and to hide her face, which had said far too much.

"Mama, are the soldiers hunting deer?"

"I don't know, Edward." When she stood, she looked up expressionless at Colfax.

He stared at her, no longer a Shakespeare-quoting young man teasing a little boy and a fellow Bard-lover. "You're afraid the firing means they've found Hollis."

"Not at all, Lieutenant. My boy feeds a fawn out there as a pet. I'm afraid your men mistook it for your enemy. Edward will be heart-broken."

Remembering a story Julia invented for him, Edward was solemn. "Lucky is my favorite deer."

"We'll see, ma'am."

Anderson galloped back. "Nothing there, sir."

"Then what the hell was all that firing?"

Anderson shook his head in disgust. "Gawd-damn, I'm tired'a green replacements. That dumb-dutch Gerber sees Rebs behind everything. Had us firing at a tree. Damn near cut it down with lead, and not even a squirrel."

As he listened, Colfax did not look at Anderson, but kept predator's eyes on Carrie. She tried to seem coolly disinterested.

"You know you're no longer a slave, ma'am," Colfax's voice became much warmer. "You're a free person by presidential proclamation. You can leave here anytime you want. We're here to help you."

"Yes, Lieutenant, I'm aware of that. This is my home. I've no desire to leave my home."

Edward fidgeted, ready to enter the conversation. "Mister Soldier, can you cut a card in half with your pistol? Aunt Audie—"

"Edward," Carrie shushed him, "Don't bother the lieutenant. He's very busy."

"But he's just sitting there."

The lieutenant smiled, again a pleasant young man.

"Hush, Edward, he's sitting there to chase chimera."

"What's that?"

The lieutenant winked at Carrie as he spoke to Edward. "Why, son, a chimera is an imaginary entity which—" he could not finish because of the commotion as his men reassembled, their mounts laden with hams, chickens, pigs, and bulging sacks. Carrie did her best to sound horrified. "Your men are taking everything."

"Orders, ma'am."

"Lieutenant Colfax, you told me I'm free."

"That's correct, ma'am. You are free, by presidential order."

"What you meant is, I'm free to go hungry."

Colfax looked away.

"Lieutenant," Carrie persisted, "is it better to be free and dead of starvation, or a slave but alive?"

The lieutenant considered. "We debated something like that once at the college."

"I'm not debating it, Lieutenant. I'm living it."

"It's war, ma'am."

"War on women and little children, Lieutenant?"

As he searched for an answer, the corporal came around the corner, pulling Daisy and Lazy, both mooing loudly.

"Lieutenant, if your men steal the cows, where will my boy get milk? Is he to starve too?"

Colfax decided. "Corporal, you know our orders are to move fast. We can't be slowed down by stock."

"Well, all right." The corporal reached for his carbine. "I'll just shoot 'em here."

"No, Corporal, they'll die soon enough."

"Well, dammit, do we burn the place down?"

"Corporal, we use fire only in case of resistance. Have you encountered any resistance— except for the cows?"

He muttered something inaudible.

"Corporal?"

"No."

"Corporal!"

"No, *sir*."

"Then prepare to move out. We have more calls to make today. Just as precaution, detail three men for the usual special duty. Corporal, three *reliable* men this time. Sample their canteens, Corporal."

As the corporal called orders, Colfax moved his mount back closer to Carrie. "I wish we could meet in different circumstances."

"When you're not thieving, Lieutenant?"

He smiled. "And you're not so impertinent, Miz LaCroix. Goodbye, Edward. Mind your mother, boy. She's a clever woman."

Edward gave him a little wave.

Lieutenant responded with a crisp salute. "Corporal," he shouted, "move out."

Motioning to the track winding downwards, the corporal glared at Carrie. "Nigger, is this the way to Ginners Ford?"

"Carrie is my name. No, you can't get there from here that way. The only trail out is the way you arrived."

"That goddamn trail again? It's more like mountain climbing than a trail. You sure, nigger? Cause if you're lyin', we'll burn this whole damn place down."

"Corporal, what possible hypothesis could I propose to impede your departure, when your egress is so eagerly anticipated?"

"What the hell you talkin about?" The corporal stared. "You sure talk funny for a nigger." He shook his head. "But I still bet you're hot on the sheets."

The lieutenant's broad smile disappeared. "Move, Corporal. Move out, I tell you. Now." The troops left as fast as they had come.

Carrie listened until she could no longer hear creaking leather or hooves clipping against stones. Drained, she sank down on the steps. The men stole so much. But she had been as clever as she knew. Her family still had roofs over their heads and over the stock. Edward stood holding her hand, counting the soldiers as they appeared one by one silhouetted at the top of the ridge. "Duodiviginti. Undeviginti. Where is diviginti?"

Carrie was not listening to the boy. She heard wind in the trees, an eagle scream in the distance. The fields lay as peaceful as always. Getting through the winter would mean some hungry times, but they could make it. She knew they could.

She shook herself mentally. Hiding helpless up the mountain all this time, Henry would be worried, even if he saw no billowing smoke. She must give him the good news without delay. She hugged Edward. "Can you be a big boy and stay on the porch while I go up for Papa?"

"Yes, Mama."

"You stay right on the porch, Edward. Don't go in the yard. No games in the yard or the barn. We'll be right back. No games. You hear, Edward?"

"Yes, Mama." He looked up at her, puzzled. "The soldiers hiding out there are playing games, aren't they?"

Carrie froze. "Edward, are soldiers hiding?" She adjusted her grip on him to restrain his arms. "Now don't point, Edward. Just tell me, do you see soldiers?" She lifted him so he could see out over her shoulder, but he didn't respond.

"Tell me in a very soft voice, Edward."

He still said nothing.

"Edward?"

"Duo, tres. Tres soldiers behind bushes, Mama," he whispered. "They're off their horses. Isn't it unfriendly if I don't wave?"

"No, *they* will wave if they want to be friendly."

Holding him, she turned this way and that, as if comforting him. Quick looks out the corners of her eyes. Yes. Unguarded flash, reflection off shiny metal. Yes. Patch of white, skin visible when breeze stirred leaves.

She sat down hard. Thus does pride indeed go before fall. *Three reliable men.* Who is so clever now, Miss Clever Caroline? She had nearly led them straight to Henry, guided them to her whole family. She thought she tricked Colfax to let down his guard, and here he succeeded more at that trick with his *She's a clever woman.* Huh. Her stupidity, her gullible vanity now mortified her. In her shame she wanted to hide.

"Mama, what do we do now?"

"We collect our thoughts, Edward."

"Where did our thoughts go?"

Wherever her thoughts had wandered, she must start thinking hard again. She told the lieutenant she was a housekeeper alone with her little son. What would that woman do? She walked with Edward slowly to the smokehouse and looked in. "Pretty empty, Mama," Edward pronounced. They visited other outbuildings for Edward's repetitious pronouncement.

She took him back to the porch, sat on the steps and put an apron to her face as if she were weeping. "Edward, it's very important for you to come sit beside me."

"Will the soldiers see us?"

"Yes, but it's rude to stare at them or wave. Now could you hum some hymns for me?"

"Which ones?"

"Your favorites, Edward."

So Edward sat by his mother and hummed. From time to time she put her arms around him, then returned the apron to her face. When he twice hummed every hymn he knew, and some he didn't, she persuaded Edward to put his head in her lap for a little nap. He woke as the sun approached the western ridge. She despaired of any strategy to keep him on the steps.

Edward looked up. "They're leaving now, Mama." Because she did not lift her head for a moment, she almost missed Edward's answering wave to the last soldier who mounted his horse in plain view and rode after the others.

Carrie took no chance. She sat on the steps until nearly dark, seeming disconsolate, though she had to be unusually short with Edward. Finally, she went in. At arm's length she lit a single candle, and waited. There was no sniper shot through the window, only silence.

Before long she heard Jingles scratching at the door. She let him in, told Edward to play with him and slipped out into the darkness to stand and wait. After a long interval a shadow appeared. A touch. Fierce hugs.

"Oh, Henry, I thought I had planned out my moves. But one thing after another didn't go the way I thought," Carrie confessed. "And I didn't think far enough ahead. Didn't dream they'd leave spies behind. But I couldn't warn you without them catching on."

"They thought they could fool us by all that commotion of leaving."

"How did you catch on?"

"I didn't," Henry admitted. "The children did. Edward counted them in and Julia counted them out. Julia only counted nineteen. So we

needed to find three. We spotted them easy from behind and above."
He left unsaid Julia's calm, her sharp eyes, and her stealth.

"Henry, I'm afraid to stay here tonight. What if some of them slip back without their officers?"

"We'll sleep together up on the mountain." They returned to the laurel thicket the same night Brawley reported to Lieutenant Andrew Colfax that the "real good-lookin woman who could pass for white in my town," had stared into the smokehouse, and then sat on the cabin porch, crying for hours.

I thought she had more pluck than to just sit and cry, but that damn Gleason did strip her smokehouse.

✍

They camped in the laurel thicket for nearly a week more, watching their farm below. Henry slipped down at night to tend Daisy and Lazy. The soldiers never returned. When hard rain left everything sodden, they moved back by silent agreement.

They picked up standing customs, slightly modified. Henry still took his rifle with him to the fields, but did not always keep it loaded. Carrie still noted a dog's bark, but did not stand listening, frozen and breathless, if she heard an unusual sound. Edward still told and retold his counting to viginti duo, but forgot chimera. George happily gave up dull lookout duties, but found his assigned hoe no more satisfying. Julia sought private clarification from her mother about girls and soldiers, but was happy not to search out promising mounds of pine needles.

Once again Henry and Carrie sat on the porch in the twilight to enjoy the cool evening air sliding down the mountain, Carrie on the steps leaning against Henry's shins. The children asleep or at least quiet in bed, Henry broke a long silence.

"That was a brave thing you did with the soldiers, and I admire you for it."

Carrie shook her head. She remembered gullibility rather than courage. "If the Corporal had been the Lieutenant, this whole farm would have been ashes, and we'd have all been dead."

"But, in fact, Colfax was the lieutenant. And what he said was true. You *are* a free woman. You could leave and Sam couldn't stop you."

"Um-hmm. Henry, would you try to persuade me not to leave?"

"You know that."

She reached for his hand and laughed ruefully. "Lieutenant Colfax wanted so much to tell me I could go. And vain Carrie thought he told her because he hoped she'd go off with him."

"That's what I'd hope if my name were Lieutenant Colfax."

"Believe me, he was a lot smarter than I was. But you know what I told him? This is my home. Slave or free, I've no wish to leave."

"You didn't go on, tell him Mister Lincoln got things mixed up?"

"How's that?"

"That it's you who owns Henry Hollis."

LETTERS FROM SOLDIERS

OF THE MINNESOTA REGIMENTS SERVING IN THE GRAND ARMY OF THE REPUBLIC DURING THE INSURRECTION

COLLECTED ON THE OCCASION OF THE 50TH ANNUAL ENCAMPMENT OF THE MINNESOTA G.A.R.

Printed by Webb Bros.
Minneapolis Minn

1916

Camp Lincoln, near Claytown, Tenn. August 6, 1863

Dearest Nancy.

Don't believe that you and Baby Tom are ever far from my thots, even when I cannot write to you. Our regiment has been on the move so much the last ten days, in early hours or at night, on and off the cars so, there has been no time to write the letter my sweet wife deserves.

This camp is in far east Tenn. Our Minnesota 5th and the Wisconsin 3rd came from Nashville over the mountains to the Sequachie Valley. It was pretty poor country. We crossed the Sequachie and came to the Tennessee Valley, crossed that and kept going east, the country getting poorer every mile. The people fit the country. I don't see how they can keep body and soul together in these mountains. Towns here make our Northfield seem like a big city. There are whole farms on land so steep or creek flats so narrow that in Minn. no one would claim it except maybe as a woodlot. You remember how I worried whether we did the right thing buying our land in Minn. After coming here I don't worry any more. So, you see, the war is good for one thing at least.

The letter you sent on July 24 came yesterday, balm for a lonesome soldier. I and Charles Furgeson were out on picket duty all day, so John brought our letters out to us. Wasn't that just like him? Charles tried opening his out there, but the wind took it out of his hand and he had to chase it clear across the wet field, not looking very soldier-like. He did recapture it. But by then his prize was torn and wet, so spoilt he could hardly read it. I took the lesson and tucked your letter under my shirt until I came in last night and could enjoy it in a place where there was no wind to blow it away.

The heat here is so bad I am sending my heavy coat and some other things to you in a box. It was either that or throw all away. May it one day be something of times long past, when your husband went off to fight a righteous battle, before he came home never again from you to part.

There are a lot of Union men living here in east Tennessee. The problem is they're mixed together with Sesesh, so you don't know who is which. A man can smile, say he's for Lincoln, and his Reb son can be drawing a bead on you from the barn loft. So we're real careful about barns. We always drive our sabers hilt-deep into the hay. Sometimes we just burn down the whole barn and smoke the Sesesh out.

The colonel has been sending out parties every day, partly to punish the Sesesh and scare them, partly to gather edibles. We're short on rations, but collect good victuals as we go. We got new mounts before we left Nashville, well-fed stock. I think if I saw 25 or 30 rough soldiers ride fast up to our door the way we ride, all set to mow down anybody who gets in the way—why, Nan, I'd want to run for sure. Except that it would be too late to run.

There aren't so many colored here as further west. Mostly they're dressed in rags, and need soap even if their skin is black. The ones I've talked to are about as ignorant as their masters. Colfax, though, had a different experience. He was patrolling. They stopped at a farm so far up in the mountains and the going so bad that he would have missed it for sure if he did not have a detailed map from an informer. He was told the farm was down between steep high ridges. Colfax thanked his lucky stars he had not tried to take wagons. They barely made it mounted. Says they never would have made it with wheels.

By the way, Colfax has had his difficulties with this informer, but hadn't made up his mind what to do. His problem was solved this week when someone found the informer with a pitchfork through him—planted by a Union man, to go by the flag on the handle.

Anyhow, Colfax got all the way to this farm—nothing for miles and miles around—and found the rooster had flown the coop. Someone had tipped off the owner, who made a quick retreat. Where, God only knows in these mountains. The trip had taken so long Colfax wasn't going to waste time looking for one man.

The informer had told Colfax that he'd also find a slave woman and her children on the place. All he found was a woman and her little boy. The boy was so white it was obvious his father wasn't a slave. Colfax nearly fell off his horse when the boy began counting in Latin—and way beyond 1-2-3. Who could have expected that? The boy said his mother taught him.

Then she began quoting Shakespeare, somebody Colfax reads every chance he gets, so he was tickled to find a fellow admirer. She wasn't just leading him on either. He tested her some without showing it, and she knew Shakespeare by heart. He says if he hadn't been told the woman was a slave, he never would have thought she wasn't white. She was so well spoke he said he could have met her at his parents' home back in Albany. He's still singing her praise today. We've all been teasing him about finding some just slightly dark lady to take home to Minnesota with him. (Guess you'd better not mention that to Abby Admunson next time you see her.)

You hear and see things like this, it makes you know this war is for the Right, and God will help us prevail.

I sent you money out of my pay to give Leonard Spencer back the four dollars you owed him. Use the rest to settle with Sumner Price. Then he won't have an excuse to come to your door. Everyone expects us to be here several more weeks at least, looking for Sesesh, trying to rid the place of Jeff Davis's friends. But don't worry about me. It's dull work and not much real fighting. Chances are slim that I'll run into a lady as fetching as Colfax's Miz Caroline up in the mountains. If I do, I'll tell her I'm already taken, don't you think?

All of our marching agrees with my health. I feel much better than when we were in camp at Cairo. My weight is up to 149 pounds.

There's talk of us getting a furlough once we clear this country, and are back in Nashville. But it's only talk. You know that the first chance I'll be there to pester my sweet Nancy.

Your Abner

QUACHASEE
WHC

No surplus, but enough. Carrie took her portion last, the bottom of the pot. Henry ladled his own plate thoughtfully. Julia often returned some of what she first served herself. Following Spooks' directions, Julia and George ranged widely in search of wild berry patches. There was yet another reason to greet Spooks gladly: he came laden with chickens or game or some gift from Lydia's stores, with her apologies, for she was again with child. Spooks always asked Carrie to cook some supper with what he brought, but they all knew he brought much more than he ate.

In Bible reading for the family, Henry returned frequently to the five loaves and two small fishes; in time there was good reason to feature that miracle. An unusually bountiful harvest guaranteed they'd get through the winter.

They drilled each other on Latin in the evenings. Edward seemed to inhale the language. Henry read while the others played tense checkers matches or charades. If Spooks visited, after the evening meal he unfolded his war map and they debated how much longer the Sesesh could survive, with Sherman pushing into Georgia, Grant battering in Virginia. They traded weather observations and talked books, plotting how to acquire more installments of Southworth's *Hidden Hand.*

By spring, conversation centered on the end of the war, the shocking assassination, and the new president. Soon a familiar theme was Spooks' increasingly vehement condemnation of Johnson's pardons granted to former Sesech. "Maybe we don't need to throw them all in prison, but we don't need to ignore their treason." He became so animated that usual roles switched and Henry became the calming one. "Try a small farm, friend. You never get rich, but you don't starve either."

He plowed and planted whistling. Carrie nearly replaced all the chickens she lost to foraging troops. In warm air the two could sit comfortably on the porch again to chat in quiet murmurs out of children's earshot, or just rest in companionable silence.

"Henry, with slavery gone and Brownlow trying to prosecute old Sesesh, does that mean laws are changed, so I could be your legal wife?"

"Figured to ask Spooks just that, next time he's up. Unless you want me to make a special trip to see him."

She shook her head. A little later she stroked his leg. "Another thing, Henry."

"Hmm?"

"Can you fix the Low Chair so it doesn't creak so? I'm afraid it'll wake the children."

"You didn't notice I fixed it already."

"Can we test it?"

"Well, I dunno." Henry's tone started dubious but ended nearly in a grin.

She lifted her face. "Come here and you'll know."

A mess of fish in his creel, Spooks rode up to a noisy greeting from dogs and children. He listened through a short speech in Latin from Edward, prompted only slightly. He warned George about the dangers of growing too fast. He quizzed Julia on the Constitution.

Tasty fish enjoyed, Henry waited until Carrie could join them on the porch before he raised their question. "Carrie and I couldn't get married before, but now she's free. Sam can't interfere, right? So can't we be legally married?"

Spooks rubbed his jaw. "You're right about Sam, of course; he's out of the picture. But slave status wasn't the only impediment. I don't know the current law; there's such confusion. I'll look into it."

Several weeks later Spooks found Henry and George in the High Field. Sending George to the cabin with the crusted dish from Lydia, he drew Henry into the shade at the edge of the field. "You farmers just love the sun. Any hunter will tell you sun is bad for the bile, but I'm afraid you farmers are outnumbering us."

Henry answered in kind, aware Spooks was killing time until George was out of earshot. Then, "Did you have time to find out about marriage law?"

"If you don't mind, I'll tell you and Carrie at the same time. I stopped here first to warn you in case you're thinking that now the war is over you can take your family to town. Don't. We've got peace that isn't peaceful. It was bad enough when there were so many men scouting out. Raising the drawbridge was a smart move. That helped a lot to keep you clear of men avoiding draft officers."

"No conscription now," Henry observed.

"No conscription, but a lot of unhappy people, a lot of movement."

"How unfortunate, that marse has to pay wages all of a sudden," agreed Henry.

"It's even more chaos than that, Henry. People who were slaves from birth see they're free now and can leave. So they leave. For where? They don't know exactly. They're just trying on their travelin' shoes to see how they fit."

"I can believe that," laughed Henry. "Remember Solomon years ago, when you arranged for Audie to buy him from ole Jeb Rinker. First thing Solomon does is light out to see the mighty Mississippi. With Audie owning him, he was free for all intents and purposes, but he didn't *feel* free, he told me, until he could go wherever he wanted."

Bright nodded. "Think of thousands, hundreds of thousands, of Solomons now. Problem is, the gangs of slaves the farmers used to depend on suddenly aren't dependable. That upsets some people who happen to be white. They claim the law isn't working. Which generally means a bunch of new laws to protect white interests."

Henry wrinkled his nose in distaste.

"Talk of it already. I don't know if better minds will be able to head that off." Bright shook his head. "What's also getting too obvious is that a bunch of the men who were mustered out didn't go home as they were supposed to. The war taught 'em to kill people, and they'd just as soon keep at it. So they're skulking about, looking for any opportunity in the chaos."

"The only time I leave is for supplies or deliveries. Got a trip coming up soon. I was thinking of taking Julia with me. Just so she gets some experience away from the farm."

Spooks shook his head vigorously. "Please don't. If you have any fruit tree deliveries yet, put 'em off. Now is a good time for you, and especially the women, to stay real quiet up here. Keep the drawbridge raised. It's worked so far. Maybe it will keep working."

"Deerslayer," asked Henry quietly, "are there Hurons close by?"

"Honestly, I don't know," answered Spooks. "But I think Uncas would do well to watch for sign. He should have weapons at hand whenever he leaves the cabin. Don't depend entirely on isolation, old friend. Some scoundrels have been hiding in these mountains for years now and know their way around. Or they talk to those who do."

Henry nodded gravely.

"I'm sorry I don't have much for Carrie's cook pot; Lydia was adamant about warning you as soon as I could. She's found some menacing notes under the back door, so now she keeps a big pistol handy, even if it's never loaded and she can barely hold it steady with two hands."

Henry smiled at the image. "She needs to visit Audie Ann."

After the meal, the children lingered with Spooks, but Carrie was firm in sending them outside to play.

The door was barely closed before Henry spoke up. "Don't leave us in suspense about the next installment on marriage law, Spooks. What did you find out?"

Spooks cleared his throat. "Question: in the state of Tennessee may a man undeniably of the white race now marry a woman who is not so identified? Simple question, but with all the confusion these days, the answer is not simple. Henry, you might get one of your Lutheran preachers to pronounce you man and wife; after all, some of 'em never acquiesced to slavery, though this gets even more sensitive than slavery itself."

A perplexed frown on his face, he elaborated. "You're not inquiring about clerical action, but government recognition. That's what's so uncertain."

At the noise of children's excited voices and dogs outside, Carrie rose and moved to the door with a frown and murmured apology.

"Court will recess briefly while the bailiff investigates the commotion outside the chambers involving male child about four feet tall, and young dog."

Once Carrie returned from the porch and stern words for George, Spooks grinned. "The bailiff having performed admirably, the court shall now reconvene, noting that the lot of the middle child and his young dog is a hard one."

His face returned to a frown. "I'm sorry to bear the news when it isn't encouraging. People whose opinions I value agree that trying to get a marriage recognized would precipitate a court test. In today's conditions, a court case is a match on fatwood. Even if you won, maybe especially if you won, you would be personally exposed to disturbing threats, at the very least."

"Isn't there any place we can get married without a problem?"

"Not, I believe, in the enlightened state of Tennessee. There are fewer impediments in a northern or western jurisdiction, say, New York or California; I don't have access to current sources for full research. There remains the significant question whether even in such states the court of public opinion would accept the marriage."

Spooks glanced out the window in annoyance. "Henry, does that egg-sucking dog bark at his shadow? What poor excuse for a hunter have you inflicted on George?"

Henry rose and went out to silence the dog. As soon as he stepped off the porch, Spooks spoke rapidly to Carrie. "While he's gone: I need to tell you that bad men are loose, my dear. Deserters, drifters, dissolute: no officers, no discipline, no scruples. Maybe worse, some of them know these mountains as well as I do. Henry might not be able to get in from the fields in time to help you. He may anticipate that and want to stay by the cabin all day. Which means no field work and a poor harvest."

Spooks hesitated a moment, worry apparent on his face. "To speak plainly, he's a damned poor shot and my brave old friend doesn't always assess threats prudently. You stood off the U.S. Army with light losses. Plan a strategy for vermin."

Carrie was nodding acknowledgment as Henry returned. He persuaded a reluctant Spooks to stay the night, but conversation lagged; all seemed deep in private thought. As Spooks left before sunup the next morning, Carrie slipped a note into his bag. "Would you give this to Audie Ann? I think you'll approve," she said. "And ask Solomon to see her real soon?"

The sun said late afternoon when Solomon materialized from the woods. Carrie greeted him with a silent nod. She accepted the cloth-covered basket he offered, and he was immediately gone, enveloped by trees.

After Spooks' visit, Henry carried one of the rifles, loaded, with him to the fields each morning. Carrie began sending Julia out to work with Henry and George. Early one afternoon she heard one of the dogs bark insistently in the distance. When the rest joined in, she knew they were not after a squirrel or coon. She stopped to listen intently. The barking ceased mid-yap, without an antiphonal concluding yip. She watched at the door briefly, then went inside.

When she returned, Edward looked with an infectious smile at the shawl she had thrown over her shoulders. Julia had cut it from the skirt of one of the now-unnecessary travel dresses. "Are you playing dress-up, Mama? But you need to wash your face; it's very dirty. You didn't comb your hair, like you say to do every morning. You look like you fought your hair all night long."

She did not reply until they heard approaching hooves. "Edward, some men are coming. They won't be friendly, and you must do exactly what I tell you."

Three men with drawn pistols rode fast into the yard on abused horses. They wore mismatched parts of different uniforms. One jumped down and ran quickly to the outbuildings. Carrie heard him bashing in the smokehouse door that always bound on its hinges.

She stayed just inside the cabin doorway, her left hand clutching the shawl at her throat. Two men pushed their mounts closer to the cabin. Unshaven, clothes filthy, boots falling apart. The tall man mopped his neck with a ragged, dirty bandana.

"Whar's Hollis?"

"Ain't hyar."

"Whar'd he go?"

"Away, fer good, mebbe. What y'all done with them dawgs?"

The short man smiled. "They ain't gonna bother us none."

"Who *is* hyar?" the tall man demanded.

Carrie hesitated.

"Woman, I axt yeh a question. Who's hyar?"

She nodded toward Edward. "Me 'n him."

The short man bellowed, "Joe, fine anythin?"

A boy's voice came from behind the cabin. "Nothin much yet, 'cept food. Narya dropa good stuff t'drink."

The men urged their horses still closer, more relaxed now. They holstered pistols, but kept their hands close.

"Why don' yeh step outta thet door so yeh cain't reach no rifle jes inside."

"Tain't no rifle." Carrie moved listlessly into the bright sunshine on the porch. The tall man whistled and spoke to the short one while eyeing Carrie. "Now Al, they dint tell us Hollis kept him a purty piece up hyar, did they? Mighty glad t'see thet."

The short one smiled. "An' I bet I know what yeh got in mine."

"Yup. We ain't got us no piece since, what were hit? Three days past, hit was. We overdue, ain't we, Al?"

They dismounted, but one after the other, so Carrie was always in their surveillance. One after the other, they pulled sabers from saddle-mounted scabbards. "Now, woman, this ken be real easy er kinda hard. Depends on yeh, mostly." They held sabers high.

Edward gripped Carrie's skirt. "Mama."

"Why don' yeh sen' thet kid inside so he don' git huht. Might fright him to see Mama wit'a man a-top'er."

"Mighty glad yeh thought'a thet, mister." She hurriedly guided the boy toward the door. "Close it, Edward."

"Maybe yeh meanin to cup'rate."

Carrie smiled and shifted her hips. "'Low y'all lookin fer enertainmen."

"We sure is, an we got yeh in mine." Eyes fixed on her, they dropped reins and moved toward the porch.

"Thet's good, cause it gits kinda lonesome up hyar. Bring sumpin t'drink, I hope? How big this hyar party gonna be?"

"A real private party, woman. Jes yeh an us three. Nobody else invited. Fact is, I 'spect nobody else 'round."

"Thet's the bes' news since y'all come." Carrie released the shawl she had clutched to her with her left hand. It dropped over her right forearm. "Mebbe this be what y'all lookin fer?"

"Holy shit. Look at them tits, Al. Hit were a longest way, but hyar the promised land."

Carrie simpered. "Not yet, but mebbe close."

"Al, my pants is bustin. We gonna be hyar a long, long time."

Carrie cupped her left hand under her breast. "I sure hope y'all right 'bout thet. Which one a'yeh gonna be firs'?"

Their eyes fixed on Carrie's left hand, the two men started up the steps, throwing their sabers aside on the porch floor. The sound of the sabers clattering on the floor almost covered two quiet pops. The men dropped like stones, blood spurting from small holes in their faces.

"Hey, what's goin on?" Joe ran in from the barn. "Yeh gettin' ass afore me? Hey, yeh promise las time . . . "

Carrie turned to the corner of the cabin. Her revolver only clicked. Squeeze, click. Squeeze, click. She leaped to the door and heaved against it for the rifle inside. Edward had drawn in the latch string. She fumbled at the handle. "Edward, open . . ."

"What th'hell?" Joe stared from the end of the porch and reached to unlimber his carbine strap. A shot sounded in the distance. A thud from the wall above Carrie's head.

Young Joe had been playing soldier only two weeks. In his inexperience he swung full away to meet the new threat. He never saw the saber scooped from the floor as it came down a cleaver, again and again and again and again and again.

Breathing hard, Carrie threw the bloody saber aside, and looked up. Henry was running in, Julia outpacing him, George at a distance. Before they reached the cabin, she persuaded Edward to unlatch the door. She slipped in for a long pin to refasten her shawl, and to insist the boy stay inside.

"You all right?" Winded, Henry could barely stand.

"No. Yes. No."

"Is that all of them?"

"They said there's no one else around."

"If they were just scouts from a bigger group," Henry wheezed, "the others find the bodies here, they'll want revenge. We'll go back to the old camp in the thicket." He turned to a dazed George staring at the bloody mound once Joe. "Go back up the mountain with the mules. Stay up there. You, too, Julia."

Julia, though, was already on her way to fetch a large tow bag for Joe's remains. Her efficient aid silenced her father's orders to go back at once. She helped lift bodies onto the horses. She retrieved scattered gear. She scrubbed the puddles of blood off the porch as if her daily chore. She remembered to search for the dogs, and piled up dead brush to hide their bodies. With frantic haste, the family urged the horses into the trees. From there they could move more slowly up the mountainside to tie the three horses in a dense stand of fir.

When they reached their old camp, Carrie slumped down, staring at the ground, but seeing nothing. Julia had brought the lunch basket from the cabin and passed it around, though no one ate much. Edward soon began crying over the dead dogs. George suddenly started to shake. Dry-eyed, Julia sat next to him and held him close. Henry went to watch the farm far below from a boulder that gave good cover.

He returned with a shrug and spoke gently to Carrie. "Nothing down there. I'll get the horses, string them on one lead line and go bury bodies and gear. It'll take me a good while. George is too upset to help, and I want Julia to stay here with you. I'll leave you these pistols. Full moon tonight, but I'll give you an owl hoot when I'm back so you don't shoot me in the shadows."

At last a soft owl hoot close by in the dark. The boys slept. Protected by a boulder, Julia stood guard, a pistol in each hand. Propped beside her leg, the sharp scythe blade she remembered from the barn. Henry dropped down beside Carrie. "I took everything off the horses and led them to the top of the high trail toward Claytown. They'll keep going downhill."

"You bury the bodies?"

"Yes, but not very deep. I guess bears and coons will find 'em. Maybe that's not bad."

He put his arm over Carrie's shoulder. She put her rifle down and finally let herself sob into his shoulder, so hard she gasped for breath. Henry held her tightly. When he started to loosen an arm, she pulled it around her again.

Quieter, she whispered, "How did you know to come?"

"Never heard dogs quit barking the way ours did. Figured we had bad trouble. But I knew I better not come charging blind without knowing how many there were."

She sought his arm again.

"I'm sorry, Carrie. It almost made me too late. They forced you to . . . expose yourself, didn't they?"

"No."

"I couldn't fire because you were behind 'em. But I thought I saw them make you—"

"They didn't make me. I just did it."

"You what?"

"Henry, they were fixin' to bust me no matter I was dressed like the Queen of Sheba or naked as a jay bird."

"I know that, but why . . . ?"

"Best thing to distract a man is a naked woman, and my hand shook so bad I knew I'd miss if they weren't close right in front of me."

"I wanted to fire sooner, but was terrified I'd hit you. Cursed my bad eyes."

"You saw plenty good enough today, Henry." She began to shake and sob again. Much later he spread a blanket for her, and took Julia's place as sentinel. At first light he slipped down to feed the animals, returning straightaway. During the day he slept, Carrie dozed fitfully and Julia kept watch with the boys.

Late the following day they heard dogs, and spotted Spooks approaching the cabin far below. They set out to meet him. Henry sent Julia ahead, running down the mountain sure-footed as a goat. By the time the rest appeared, he knew all the details, including Carrie's choice of an old shawl to protect her dress from all the blood.

Spooks greeted them with grave ruefulness. "Looks like my timing is off. I rode up to tell you that yesterday Union regulars came through in a great sweep. Shot or captured a bunch of the scum. Put the fear of the flag in a bunch more. Lydia says she hears some firing squads tomorrow should produce more respect for law and order."

He smiled as if he had never heard Julia's account. "If you'll have me, I'd like to stay a few days, just to be out and hunt. Lydia suggested it. In fact she threatened to come herself if I didn't, but she still has too much Quaker in her to pull a trigger without remorse. So I can hunt while Henry catches up on barn chores."

Edward looked up at him. "Whacha huntin, Mister Spooks?"

"Common vermin, Master Edward."

"What's a vermin?"

"A bipedal mammal, usually hirsute, of only rudimentary intelligence and low antecedents. Smells worse than a bear. Travels in small packs."

"Oh." Edward considered this from a practical side. "Can you eat 'em?"

"Whew. You wouldn't want to, they're so rank."

"Will you bring me the skin after you shoot it?"

Spooks shook his head. "Their hide isn't usually worth troubling, Master Edward."

For days Hawkeye stalked vermin. At the cabin they heard the distinctive crack of Killdeer, sometimes more than once, far in the distance. To a disappointed Edward, Hawkeye reported the day's bag too inferior to show off as trophies. To a drawn-faced Carrie, Spooks reported his hunt should help her sleep better.

When at last he went down the valley, he left his dog at the cabin, and said he would ask Solomon to bring up several more. After his departure, the family found most reassurance in sticking together, with weapons, through their workday.

In the evenings, Carrie stayed up late. When she went to bed her reluctance to snuff the last bedside lamp was so apparent that Henry told her he would do it later. He woke in the small hours to find her staring sleepless up at the loft floor. When she did fall asleep she moaned and thrashed so that he had to wake her. "I can't get my mind free of the vermin." she whispered. "They keep coming up the steps after me, getting closer and closer."

A smiling Solomon appeared with more dogs, and stayed a bit for quiet talk with Carrie. A different Solomon, face creased with worry, went back to report to her friends.

In a few days, Spooks reappeared.

"Huntin for vermin, again, Mr. Spooks?" Edward asked. "Can you shoot vermin with both hands? You've got Kildeer, so why do you need that extra rifle?"

Spooks smiled at him, then addressed his parents. "Old friends, my spirits have been low lately. Lydia thought I would benefit from being outside, maybe hunting in the mountains, if I can impose on your hospitality again. Henry, I know you need to stay close to home these days, but Lydia pointed out that I would hunt most efficiently with a guide. So I wonder if I might borrow Julia? She has, after all, been tutored by Miss Audie Ann. I brought along a rifle that I think would fit her about right. It's a loan from Lydia, so it's hardly been fired."

Julia was not hesitant in exchanging hoe for rifle. She nodded patiently when Spooks perfunctorily reviewed its features. "Where're we huntin?" she asked.

"A necessary question, but the answer depends on what we hunt. I suggest our prey be the elusive vermin, which range widely in the day but tend to seek shelter at night. For more efficiency we should pursue in an organized fashion. If I may borrow your stick, Master George?"

He took the stick and began scratching in the dirt while he spoke to Julia. "You have this territory in your mind's eye, I've noticed. So if I say we could seek our quarry between Knowles Knob, here, and Double Top, here," he drew the two promontories, "then work our way gradually southward past Howard's Cove toward your infamous Battle Hollow," he drew a circle, "do you have the appropriate landmarks in mind?"

Julia studied the dirt drawing for a minute, then nodded.

Spooks turned to Henry. "Just as I anticipated. Great warrior, we shall see you as the sun falls below yonder ridge. Julia, I have some refreshments in my bag should you crave them." As they walked off, Spooks instructed, "Now, Julia, when two woodsmen hunt together, you will appreciate that it is essential each know where the other is, so one . . ."

Those left on the farm returned to work, listening intently for Kildeer. They heard nothing more than birds and the wind in the trees. To a disappointed Edward that evening Spooks wondered if the vermin had left for other parts. The next day saw the same report as the first, and the following two days likewise.

Edward lost patience. "Mister Spooks, can vermin fly? Maybe they're like birds. Papa says some birds just fly east or south or somewhere to stay warm in the winter. If the vermin flew away, then you can't find 'em to shoot 'em."

Spooks grinned despite his obvious fatigue. "Master Edward, a perceptive analysis: if they are not there one cannot find them. My invaluable assistant and I checked many a possible lair for the elusive vermin, and have come up empty."

After Carrie urged the children off to bed, the adults stayed on the far end of the porch, out of the children's earshot. Spooks turned to Carrie. "We've covered the map. Julia and I looked right and left, up and down, in front and behind, but, believe me, dear friend, no vermin did we find."

"Spooks, I thank you many times over for your care. That was the kindest thing you could ever have done for me."

"Thank Julia. Mister James Fenimore Cooper, I now see, left a major flaw; he never mentioned a Julia in his stories. I'll leave that rifle for her to practice with. We dared not shoot while we hunted, for fear you would hear and think we found something. Carrie, believe me, there was nothing to find."

After Spooks left, Carrie doused the light when she went to bed, but still moved alarmingly in her sleep. Henry woke her and held her close. "It's not like after Harry died," she whispered. "Sometimes I hear the dogs barking, and I get cold, I'm so scared. Just want to run somewhere."

"Where to?"

"As far as I can, clear to California."

"Maybe it would help if we just moved to California."

"You've thought of that too?"

"You saw the last papers Spooks brought up. Full of California."

"Gold. Silver. People getting rich. No guerrillas and bushwhackers. No vermin."

Henry hesitated. "I assumed you'd never leave Harry's grave."

"You'd have been right a month ago. But I see more clearly than ever that I have three living children to care for. I used to think as long as I stayed here, I had you and the children with the ridges all around us. Maybe everything would be fine. Now I can't put my mind at rest anymore. At least not here. Maybe I could in California."

"It'd be hard to leave here."

"The best place I know. 'Course I don't know many places. They make California sound beautiful. Maybe the children could have a future there. Maybe my nightmares wouldn't be so bad there. Maybe we could get married there . . . if you still wanted to."

The tightening of his hands gave her his answer about marriage. "I've thought of it enough to ask Spooks to be on the lookout for guidebooks next time he's in Nashville," Henry added.

❧

Spooks's saddlebags bulged with solid shapes. *The Youth's Companion* occupied the children on the porch. The adults sat inside at the table, reading snippets of advice or description from books and pamphlets to each other. "It sounds too good to be true," exclaimed Carrie.

"Maybe that means it isn't," Henry grumbled.

"Should have known: what you want to learn most is what they don't talk about." Spooks looked up in frustration. "The climate may be ideal for consumptives, but we still don't know what it's like for . . ."

"People like me," finished Carrie softly. "They're not going to talk about that in books. You'd have to go and see for yourself."

"A long trip just for bad news," observed Spooks. Henry nodded.

"Well, I think Henry should go to check." Carrie was resolute.

"And leave you here alone?" Spooks's frown deepened.

"Alone with your nightmares?" Henry was even more dubious.

Carrie shook off the questions. "I'll cry myself to sleep some nights and have to sit up some nights with a light to keep the vermin out of my head. And worry about Edward getting at the rifle by the door." She took a deep breath. "But there's got to be a better place for us and the children. Pretty soon we'll be saying we're too old to travel that far. Henry, you could go as soon as the crops are in."

Henry turned to Spooks. "I guess I should at least look."

"Sounds like you two have done a lot more thinking than you let on. If you need cash, I could lend you some for a while."

Henry worked maniacally the next two months, tending crops, making deferred repairs, stockpiling supplies. The stack of firewood stood fit for Maine. The barn overflowed for all seven lean years. Carrie told him she and the children could care for themselves, but still he worked like two men, until the last week before his trip. Carrie woke him repeatedly those nights.

Pulled from deep sleep yet again, he drowsily croaked, "Woman, what has gotten into you?"

"You." She shushed him with her free hand over his mouth and bent down to whisper close to his ear. "I'm making sure you don't have anything left for loose women in California. And remember to come back."

❦

Henry remembered. Before the first buds swelled, he whistled his way down the High Trail. His valise stained and threadbare. His face thinner. His hems frayed. But happily back, manhandling the joyous children, listening to Edward's excited report of a pet turtle who understood Latin, hugging Carrie so closely, with hands so indiscreet, that she twisted away with an embarrassed laugh. At the table he told them of seeing mountains that made Tennessee's look like hills, of rivers so wide they seemed like lakes, of deserts so parched, of sea so ceaseless, of horizons so boundless.

Edward slid off Julia's lap. "When can we go to California?"

"Whenever your mother decides."

All eyes turned to Carrie, but Henry rescued her with a last round of little gifts from the very bottom of his valise. Then he entertained the children late by narrating his route on a map much frayed at its folds. Carrie ordered bedtime and wondered about sitting on the porch, the evening agreeably warm for early spring. After fending off more questions from Edward, she joined Henry there, sitting on the steps, leaning against his legs.

"Julia has changed so much," observed Henry. "From a distance I thought she was you. Where did she learn to do that with her hair? Almost as pretty as her mother."

"You didn't notice how high George's pants are."

"I did. He'll be a tall one. But what about his crying spells?"

"They got worse after you left. Even Julia couldn't help him. But one day when it poured rain all day, I made him help cook. It rained the whole week, and he cooked the whole week. When the sun came I could hardly get him outside. That boy is a natural in the kitchen."

"Like his mother and grandmother."

"Better. He can imagine tastes and how different flavors will affect each other."

"Can Julia cook?"

"When she gets a chance. But she took care of the farm. Tomorrow you should push her a little and see how strong she is. I think she rivals Spooks with her rifle barking squirrels. And she does amazing things on your dulcimer."

"I saw Edward reading by himself."

"Fast. Almost as well as Harry."

They sat silently. Henry saw Carrie pass her hand over her face. His fingers found her cheeks wet. "Your crying spells?"

She shook her head. "I'm so happy to have you here," she sniffled.

"That's silly. You knew I would come home."

"Maybe in my heart, but not in my head. One night I lay in bed wanting you inside me and worrying, what would I do if you didn't come back. I don't own anything but the clothes on my back, and I'm not sure I own them. I'd be penniless with three children."

"You'd have this farm. But what about the vermin?"

"They're still coming after me, at least sometimes. It was hard when you were gone, Henry. And I worry about the children so. That bothers me as much as the vermin. I worry about the children's future here."

"Maybe we could change that in California."

"Are things really better there? Be honest with me, Henry."

"I saw some things I didn't like, but I guess that's anywhere with human beings and sin. There are so many kinds of people there."

"It's not just either white or black?"

"No. Colors, countries, languages. They do have laws about marriage. Got a new word: mis-ceg-en-ation. I went to a courthouse and asked about it. Fellow there told me, 'Mister, the law says I can't marry a mixed couple, but it don't tell me how to decide if somebody isn't white, and I tell ya, my eyesight is damn poor. I follow the law strict: I just decide all the people I marry together here are white.'"

Henry caressed Carrie's cheek before continuing. "Another thing, out there everything is booming. If a man can keep from catching gold fever, seems like he'll do all right. I even attended an English service at a Lutheran church."

"You think we ought to go? I don't want to make you leave."

"I hate to think of leaving here. It's so beautiful and so private."

"Me too. Seems like I've lived my whole life here."

"But they spoiled it for us here, didn't they?"

"Yes."

"You want to go, Carrie?"

She stood up to face him. "As soon as we can."

Plowing with Greek, My Life
HL Hollis

Dorinda was here again yesterday. I had previously complained to her how difficult I find it to capture on paper the essence of a person or a relationship. Yesterday Dory brought with her some notes she made years ago after a conversation with Father, one that she found instructive and wanted to remember. It is such a revealing "snapshot" of my father's interaction with his eldest daughter, their mutual enjoyment of verbal sparring, that I have tried to reconstruct the conversation here using her notes as a framework.

First I must mention that Dory returned from her initial year at Vanderbilt in triumph. She was the first woman from this county to be admitted to that institution, and she did the county proud, to toot her horn a mite. She had gotten much interested in a history course there. Happening to read that Tennessee produced many thousands of men for the Confederate army, but more men for the Union army than any other southern state, she thought to ask Father if he or his closest friend, Judge Bright, ever contemplated going North to fight for the Union.

Father answered without hesitation. "Spooks is a very skilled marksman. Thoroughly familiar with all types of firearms. You've watched him when he's up here in the summer. His accuracy isn't always as good as Audie's, but with a rifle at long range he's hard to beat. Remember that match last summer when they had to keep moving the targets farther away? You remember how Ben kept muttering under his breath every time he had to go out and move the target again. What was he muttering? I'm forgetting."

"What you're forgetting is to answer my question. Did Judge Bright join the Union army during the war?"

"It was a difficult choice for many in Tennessee: which army to join."

"No doubt. That's why I'm asking. Did he join the Union or the Confederate army?"

"Spooks has lots of family in both Carolinas. Virginia too. Almost all of them put on a gray uniform."

"You're not making it easy, Father."

"What do you want made easy?"

"Did he join his cousins and uncles in gray uniforms?"

"No, he didn't. It's an interesting question. How strong do you think bonds of kin ought to be, Dory? Did they ever talk about that in any of your classes?"

"Not that I recall. They did talk about the tactic of changing the subject."

"Sounds like a good course."

"It would be for some gentlemen I know. Father, *why* did the Judge not join his family in gray uniforms?"

"He told me he thought they were engaged in an insurrection against a legitimate government. Do you think that's sound reasoning in this case?"

"Father, why do I always have to be the one keeping us on track?"

"What track is that, daughter? Anyway, it's good to stay on track, isn't it?"

"Yes, that's why I'm asking you. Judge Bright didn't join the Rebel army, so he joined the Union army?"

"You specified that, not I."

"It's a war, so it's one side or the other."

"That's your assumption, not my statement."

"So, Father, the Judge was neutral?"

"No."

"But he did not join the Union army? Father, you are evading me when I'm trying to ask you why he did not join the Union army."

"It didn't sound that way to me. You asked *if* he joined the Union army."

"All right, *why* did he not join the Union army?"

"Because he could not stand the thought of aiming lethal fire at maybe his own blood kin."

"Was that the only reason?"

"No."

"What were the other reasons?"

"He did not want to be bound by Army discipline and orders if he became aware of a situation he could rectify privately and immediately."

"That's understandable. War makes for very difficult situations."

"It does. Should I tell you about it?"

"Please do—after you have fully answered my question."

"Which was? My memory isn't as good as it used to be."

"I think it's plenty good when you want it to be."

"Which is actually when *you* want it to be."

"Regardless, Father, did *you*—not the Judge, but Henry Hollis—did he, you, ever consider going up north to join the Union army?"

"Yes, of course."

"Aha. Now we're getting somewhere."

"Where's somewhere?"

"There."

"Where is There?"

"Somewhere, I guess. Now, Father, why didn't you go?"

"To there or somewhere? I couldn't go there because I don't know where it is. Do you know where somewhere is, daughter?"

"It's there, of course. But what I want to know is *why* you didn't join the army."

"For one thing, I recognized my poor eyesight meant I'd be of use mostly to stop bullets. A tree would do just as well. Your Aunt Audie wanted to go. She would have made a fantastic sniper. The army didn't want women snipers, though. What do you think, Dory? You are much in favor of women's rights—the franchise, married women's property, women in the professions like medicine and law, in the army—that kind of thing. Should women be soldiers? Or don't you favor that?"

"Father, I favor not changing the subject. What other reasons meant you didn't go?"

"I am not aware I said there were any other reasons."

"You said, 'For one thing.' That implies an aggregate, from which you first chose your poor vision, which would be better, you know, if you always wore your best glasses. But vision leaves other reasons to explain."

"You're parsing words pretty close, daughter. Am I going to regret sending you to the university and maybe law school you've been thinking about without raising a whisper at the dinner table? By the way, should women be judges? Even on the Supreme Court?"

"Father, that is a smoke screen of questions. All of them should be ruled out of order as irrelevant."

"In American jurisprudence, the prosecuting attorney cannot also be the judge."

"Correction conceded. I rephrase the question. Were there other reasons to stay home?"

"Yes."

"Please state the other reasons."

"Slavecatchers. Bushwackers. Jayhawkers. Men scouting out, or claiming to. Too much action by irregulars and no-goods right here in this county. I thought unless I could make a real contribution in the military I should stay close to protect people I felt responsible for."

"Aunt Audie Ann."

"Yes." After a long pause, Father began grinning.

"Father, I don't like the looks of that. Why are you smiling?"

"Because, Miss Prosecuting Attorney, you eagerly executed an early, elementary error in examination."

"Father, I am not in one of your alliteration contests. I don't see any error in examination."

"You forgot 'early' and 'elementary.'"

"Even with them, I don't see any mistakes."

Father's grin widened. "Counsel, you prompted my answer. So you limited my answer to your disadvantage. You closed doors prematurely. You said Audie Ann was the person I felt responsible for, with a question mark. I could answer, yes, and nothing more. A good lawyer, like Judge Bright, would first ask, 'Who were the person or persons for whom you felt responsible?' That way the cross examiner leaves open the door to possibilities he . . . or she, I suppose, was previously not even aware of."

Chagrined to be caught out, Dory tried a correction. "Alright, Father, please name all the persons for whom you felt responsible."

"Dorinda Julia! No, you can't go back now. You asked already and I agreed I felt responsible for Audie Ann."

"Well, anyway, isn't it correct to say that the Quachasee farm kept you so isolated you could be nearly unaware of the war?"

"No."

"Well . . . ?"

"Well what?"

"Your Honor," in frustration Dory appealed to her little sister nearby, a rapt Annie. "This witness is being uncooperative and evasive."

"Your Honor," Father followed with his own appeal, "the record will show the witness answered the question, the question verifiably posed, as fully and directly as possible. The record will show this: Question: 'Is the assumption correct?' Answer: 'No.' Your Honor, that is a direct and honest answer, surely not evasive, as alleged. (Now, Annie, you need to say, 'Sustained,' in a bored voice.")
Annie's "Sustained" could not be bored. She loved watching Father and Dory in verbal exchange.

Down but not out, Dory tried to limp on. "If Quachasee isolation did not leave you unaware of the war, did you ever consider leaving for some place even farther away?"

"Oh, yes. Leaving these mountains would have been very hard."

"Would the witness please answer the question?"

"Which was?"

"Which was, did you ever consider leaving?"

"Yes. The Hollis family has been here for several generations, and the family graveyard is here. Can you imagine a stronger bond to an area?"

"Would the witness please answer the question, which was, 'did you ever consider leaving?'"

"Yes."

"Would the witness answer the question, please."

"The witness did—thrice."

"Oh. Oh, you *did* consider moving. Alright, I'll be careful with my questions now. How many places did you consider as alternatives to Tennessee?"

"Just one."

"The name of that one place?"

"California."

"Oh, I can understand that. No ice to slip on. Orange trees in the winter. Father you have that smile again. What did I do wrong this time?"

"You assumed California's climate attracted me. A smart lawyer would have first asked why I considered California."

"Too late to go back? Thought so. Alright then, California. Really, Father? California? It's so far. Would you have taken Audie Ann? What about Tulips?"

"Your Honor," Father turned to Annie, "we respectfully petition for discharge of this witness. Opposing counsel is now engaged in nothing more than a flagrantly obvious fishing expedition. Or should it be obviously flagrant fishing fiasco?"

"Father!"

"I think I like 'fiasco' better than 'expedition.' Annie, you need to say, 'Witness dismissed,' then rap the table."

"Fiasco. Fishing. Flagrant. Witness dismissed," complied Annie, using her shoe as gavel.

Father sank back into his book, though not before grinning advice to a protesting Dory that good lawyers weigh venues scrupulously. Or rather, with considerable cautious care.

446

QUACHASEE
WHC

They could not take animals to California, said Henry; he would go down to Claytown to look after selling the stock. He rejected assistants because he expected to be gone overnight, but that very evening George spotted him striding up the trail.

"Jeremiah heard from friends in Ginners Ford that Sam died a few days ago," the perplexed Henry reported to Carrie. "He's buried now. I hope the Lord is merciful. So I'm left without brothers. But Jeremiah mentioned strange rumors."

"About what?"

"It was hard to ask much because it already raised eyebrows that I'm Sam's brother but didn't know he's buried. I had to tell them that I decided never to talk with Sam after an argument years ago."

"Isn't there anybody else to ask?"

"I started to go to Tulips, but met Janth Nugent, who asked me so many questions I couldn't answer that he kept giving me an odd look, and I saw other people coming, so I ducked off the road. I took the high trace out to Spooks's place, but he's in Knoxville. Lydia said she'll send him up as soon as he gets back. She hadn't heard the rumors. I didn't want to get more questions from anybody so I just came home."

"The rumors that bad?"

"Yes, from the hints I heard. But I don't know what's true."

What, though, was true? Answering that question amid malicious hyperbole and uncharitable speculation confounded even those who heard with their own ears and confused even those who saw with their own eyes. Indefatigable inquirers, such as Henrietta Haeckle, established pretty conclusively that Elvira Hollis invited Hilde Endicott and Maggie Em Washburn to coffee at Tulips. Since Elvira was not close to either Hilde or Maggie, one might suspect that the invitation was related to that monstrous crate from Nashville, the one Jake at the station said near killed his back.

Elvira did serve her guests on new china shipped from Nashville; too bad the coffee was reheated and the rolls were yesterday's. Then, as she was known to do, she invited her guests to "see"—she might have meant "envy"—the covers she chose for one of the guest bedrooms upstairs in the Old House wing. As she approached the bedroom door, Elvira described to the least detail her arduous search for an exact replica of what she had admired at a very fashionable house in Knoxville. She ended her account (so effectively on cue one might have thought it rehearsed) by throwing open the door with a flourish to allow her guests to appreciate her success. Crowding the doorway, the three women peered expectantly in at the high four-poster bed.

Elvira's new bedcovers did not, however, display to full advantage. Obscuring them was Elvira's new maid, Lucy. Her skirts thrown up, Lucy was swinging her hips rhythmically while moaning encouragingly. Close behind her, firmly grasping her plump bare bottom, stood Mr. Sam Hollis, his trousers around his ankles, in the very instant of delivering his seed to a receptive orifice. Contorted by spasm, Sam turned toward the three women, utter disbelief on his face.

With superb reflexes, Elvira jerked the door closed before Sam could open his mouth. She shepherded her shocked guests back downstairs, where, yesterday's coffee forgotten, they made flustered exits. Elvira sent Jim, the handyman, upstairs to investigate a strange noise. While Jim poked about ineffectually, she excavated a valise and efficiently began packing some favorite things, nearly elated at being so unexpectedly freed.

In the new, worrisome circumstances at war's end, Elvira had lately felt acutely the desirability of plotting out defensive legal strategy in person with legal counsel and her sister in Knoxville. Her liberation from Tulips and Sam was therefore most timely, all the more so given her frustration at having scoured the countryside to find Lucy, a white maid. Sending a wire ahead, she descended from the cars in Knoxville late that very evening, resolved never to return.

Lucy Mercer, too preoccupied by her exertions to hear the door, nevertheless caught sight of the three women in a mirror. There she also glimpsed Sam's face slacken as he fell to the floor, striking his head on the way down successively against the many sharp protuberances of an ornate maple wardrobe. Her balance upset by the unexpected removal of lateral pressure, she tumbled in disarray atop Sam, forcing his neck at an alarming angle. Demonstrating presence of mind nearly equal to Elvira's, Lucy rose and ran to her room without a glance back. She threw her possessions into a go-poke and hastily left Tulips via a little-used back trace whose solitude suited her. At Ginners Ford she did not dally.

Jim, the handyman summoned by Elvira, shambled upstairs in his own sweet time to scope out the cause for the clatterment Elvira reported. After a leisurely survey of rooms normally off-limits to him, he discovered Sam unmoving on a bedroom floor. An experienced trapper, Jim recognized a broken neck. He ran for the doctor. His run was slow, though, for he knew the summons he carried was a formality.

In careful reconstruction, Jim came to the only conclusion possible: after sitting on the bed while putting on his shirt, Sam rose to pull on his pants, but lost his balance. No man 'live, hit don' happen to, some time 'tother. What prob'ly kilt him, he a-bang his haid on thet fancy wardrobe, mebbe four, five time, an hit creck his nek.

In days following, women of the Church Ladies' Association whispered Hilde Endicott's shocked accounts of Elvira's humiliation. Men at the Mercantile dispersed Jim's morbidly humorous account of Sam's fatal trouser accident. (No one repeated Lucy's account because she kept her own counsel on her way to Charlotte, where her sister ran a profitable boarding house of sullied reputation.)

Those who selflessly assumed reportorial responsibility thus found themselves with conflicting accounts not easily reconciled. One fact, though, seemed unassailable: Sam Hollis was dead.

Spooks arrived at the cabin as Henry and the children finished barn chores. He greeted the children fondly with penny candies, but as they walked to the cabin he all but required they stay outside to play. Disappointed at the exclusion from grown-up conversation, Edward resisted. "You just want us outside so we can't hear what you're telling Papa and Mama."

Spooks tousled his hair. "Your allegations, Sir, though prompted by resentment, are not wholly without merit. The subordinate, outraged, must accede to arbitrary and capricious exercise of power."

"What's that mean?"

"Means we stay outside," grumbled Julia, taking his hand.

Once inside, Henry was too curious to sit down. "Is it true that Elvira didn't go to the funeral?"

"She sent a competent cousin, name of Haines, with proper power of attorney to handle everything. Many remarked on her absence, but most of the ladies found it entirely fitting."

Horrified, Carrie could not believe the news. "She didn't go to Sam's funeral?"

"She withdrew to her sister in Knoxville."

"Her *husband's* funeral?"

"For lawyers, it's flagrante delicto. For normal people, it's three unimpeachable witnesses to Sam playing stud with a maid's mare."

Spooks looked sharply at Henry's slight nod. "Did you know about his predilections?"

"I knew he, ah, was, ah, partial to that game."

So that's why you never play it, thought Carrie.

"The farm needs running, and Elvira can't run it from Knoxville." Henry clearly wanted to move on. "When does she come back?"

"Now here's something more down my row than Sam's proclivities. Jesse Belter has been Sam's lawyer ever since I decided I should decline any work from slave owners. After Sam's death, Jesse showed me the papers—all public record now."

He sat down as Carrie handed him coffee. "Couldn't we predict Sam would encumber Tulips so he could game in Knoxville?"

"You mean he borrowed money to gamble?" Carrie voice rose with anger. "I just knew he would be up to no good in Knoxville. You mean creditors could take away Tulips?"

Spooks nodded. "Buzzards circle already. It might be a close thing to clear the debt off Tulips."

"Oh, Henry." Carrie's face spoke her dismay. "Your father must be rolling over in his coffin. He loved this land. And he's buried . . . How could Tulips leave the family?"

"I can still hear him: 'Henry, whatever you do, keep the land.' Well, Spooks, can Elvira fight off the creditors?"

"It won't be Elvira. Years ago your father hired an attorney by the name of Dinkins. Dead now. I knew him, didn't much like him, but he was smart. Dinkins drew up the most cleverly devious arrangements I've ever seen."

Carrie broke in abruptly. "*Erastus* Dinkins?"

"Erastus Dinkins, yes. How did you know him?"

Her anger boiled up so that her speech came in jerks. "He's the one who bought Mama and me from Henkel in Nashville. Put us in a little cabin back of a house way out of town. He'd come every once in awhile for a meal in the evening. Sent word ahead. Mama wouldn't let me into the big house those times. She cried every time after he left. She didn't want me to see all the bruises he gave her."

Spooks sat back, his eyebrows high. "I'm glad I said right off I didn't like him."

"'Didn't much like him!' You should *hate* him. I did. I think Mama got worried because he kept asking her to bring me up to the house with her for—he called 'em bedroom games." *And pretty soon the asking would be ordering, so Mama was ready to poison him*, Carrie remembered. "But Miz Dinkins came busting into our cabin one day, and right after that we got sold to Tulips. Never saw Dinkins again."

"A great credit to the Bar, Erastus Dinkins. No honor, but smart. His documents for Tulips are a masterpiece in certain ways. But you don't need me to explain strategies that interest lawyers."

Henry grimaced. "I never aimed to be a lawyer. All I need to know is that since Sam's only son died years ago in that horrible hog-butchering accident, Tulips must go to his widow."

"Except for Dinkins' documents. Elvira's cut out. She could challenge the arrangements. I think there are excellent grounds to do so. I'd like the case; it'd be interesting. But Elvira refuses to consider it. Her cousin told me she doesn't want to hear a word about Tulips."

Spooks mouthed a silent *please* to Carrie offering coffee, and leaned back in his chair. "Cousin Haines intrigues me. He has too much free time up here, is bored, likes more than a bit of brew, and welcomes a sympathizing ear. So I learn a good deal. Elvira and her sister had a thriving Knoxville business. Did you know that?"

"No, but it makes some sense," said Henry. "Homely as a mud fence, but I thought she was smarter and a lot more energetic than Sam. What did they sell? Thread and soap?"

"No. They traded in slaves. Their specialty was women for domestic work. Made a lot of money at it."

"Slavers!" Carrie burst out. "I thought she and Sam made a deal she wouldn't do that. So her 'sickly sister' was a—"

"A cover," nodded Bright. "For trading trips way beyond Knoxville. The sisters started just after Samuel B died and you two came up here. No coincidence, I suspect. Holt and Hollis. They became quite familiar at the chancery court to protect their interests as married women. Cousin Haines showed me an old flyer. Wet nurses, maids, cooks, nurses for the elderly. They didn't try to compete with the big traders on the order of Franklin and Armfield. Just carved out a corner for their specialty. Elvira kept it quiet around Ginners Ford because Sam kicked. Invested the proceeds in Knoxville real estate."

"No way to prosecute her?" asked Henry while Carrie glowered.

Bright shook his head. "Anyway, with Emancipation, that whole business went to hell. The one bright spot is that she has her hands full with some federal action regarding flagrantly illegal steps she took to coerce the services of former slave women. Otherwise, the sisters are sitting pretty because of their real estate in Knoxville."

"I feel like I should spit out something awful I bit into," said Henry. "My father would have thrown her out of the house if he had known what she was going to be up to. Once when I was a boy he took me along on some business west of here. We met a slaver's big coffle on the road. You could smell 'em before we saw 'em. Godawful stench— poor people must have been in chains for weeks; couldn't wash or even attend to the necessaries. I keep mules and cows cleaner. The head man was in a wagon at the end, with more slave women and children. Greeted us as calmly as if he were driving hogs to the market."

Henry glanced at Carrie, then after a moment continued. "He told my father he had a likely high yeller girl in the wagon for sale. When my father shook his head, the slaver offered to let him use the girl off the side of the road, wouldn't charge him anything, but that might change his mind about buying. Pulled the girl up front. She had a big black eye, bad bruises on her arm. My father just rode away without a word."

Henry put his arm over Carrie's shoulders. "After we had gone a ways, my father heaved up his whole breakfast. Maybe revulsion or maybe just indigestion. We stopped at a creek for him to wash, and he said he should have been sick right on the trader. 'Boy,' he told me, 'in the Hereafter you're going to see the line of people down at the gates of Hell. Watch careful and you'll see slavers are at the front of that line.'"

"But Henry," objected Carrie firmly, "Samuel B *owned* slaves."

Henry nodded. "If you said you were against slavery, he would argue with you. I could never fit it all together."

"We alone are completely rational and ever consistent," observed Spooks. "Still, slave traders could not exist without legal slavery."

"Nor slavery without traders," declared Carrie. "If I had been at Tulips and known about Elvira, I would have shot her with a clean conscience."

"Shot her?" mused Spooks. "How war does lower the bar on casual violence."

"That depends on where you're sitting," Carrie retorted. "Slavery did a lot more than the war to lower the bar on casual violence."

An electric moment of silence. Carrie so rarely corrected Spooks. He broke the silence with a sad look. "You're right, of course. My mind is in such confusion these days. I was convinced for so long that slavery was the fever. Get rid of the fever and the patient is free of disease. But now I see how wrong I was. Slavery was just a manifestation of the real malaise. The disease is far more deeply embedded than I assumed. And Dr. Bright has no idea how to eradicate it, for it may suffuse the whole body."

The three sat grieving until Henry shook himself. "I'll never see her again. Audie Ann and Mother: two women for a big house."

Bright shook his head. "Except that they are there only temporarily. Dinkins' document forestalls any claim to house or land they file to legitimate their occupancy. They've got no place to live. There *were* timber tracts to provide their support, but Sam got his hands, illegally, on those. Squandered the proceeds on gaming. Gone, most of it."

Henry threw up his hands. "I'm lost now. Where does Tulips go?"

"To you."

"But, Spooks, we're set to leave for California. Why can't I just sell off everything but the family burial ground, and split the money with my sister and stepmother."

"A problem there. To liquidate, you'd have to challenge Dinkins' arrangements. Jarndyce and Jarndyce. Tulips would be another Bleak House. The lawyers alone do well. You may ultimately win, but 'ultimately' could be longer than . . . a Dickens novel."

"Damn. Why can't I just decline it?"

"You can decline, of course. But there are certain complications." Bright raised fingers to tick off points. "One, you'd be passing up an enviable inheritance. Two, declining wouldn't help Audie Ann and your stepmother. And three, Tulips then goes to your cousin Caleb."

"Caleb!" Carrie stood up with a start. Childhood terror rushed back as she remembered Caleb visiting Tulips when his father came to consult Samuel B. Too restless a boy to stay inside, he was soon out, looking for mischief. When he spotted her, Carrie had ducked into the barn to avoid him, but he came in after her, cat after a mouse. Desperately she slipped from shadow to shadow, her heart pounding. Then she slipped around a corner and ran right into his greedy hands.

She had fought with all her strength, but he was bigger, stronger. He groped her. Grinning, he tore off her clothes while she fought. He was opening his pants when they heard Ennis calling. "Boy, you come right now, else you're gonna walk home and get a lickin besides."

Ennis stood up from her on the ground. "Next time, nigger girl, next time," he sneered before he ran off to his father.

Her clothes torn to tatters, Carrie had waited in the barn, sobbing and shaking, until darkness could hide her nakedness as she fled to the kitchen house.

"Caleb can *not* get Tulips," she told Spooks.

"To be honest, Carrie, things don't look good," warned Bright. "Somehow Caleb got wind that he may be heir. He figures Henry is a hermit who won't leave Quachasee. He boasts this will be a repeat of when he took Alice Pruitt away from Henry."

Carrie shook her head, her arms akimbo. "Huh. He didn't steal Alice from Henry, and he can *not* get Tulips."

"Even if he does," Spooks tried to deflect her rising anger. "he's not enough of a manager to make it pay off its debts. Give him time and he's sure to lose it anyhow. Look at what he did with the Pruitt's Chestnut Hill holdings. He could have been the richest man in the county. But the documents are unequivocal: should Henry decline, Ennis' oldest male heir—that's Caleb—receives Tulips."

"He always made fun of Audie Ann talking with her hands." Henry spoke angrily. "I got licked once when I tried to stop him. I wasn't big enough yet. He won't take care of her, or Sarah either."

"How big is his brood now?" asked Bright. "Four with Alice Pruitt in four years before she died. Two from Jenny Clemson before she died. Emily Kate is on her third already."

"Plus all the colored babies," snapped Carrie.

"Too many to count," agreed Bright. "And a few extra white ones, from what I hear. Anyway, he has so many legitimate white children he says he needs the whole house. So he claims he'll just put Audie Ann and your stepmother out to board on what's left from Sam's embezzlement, though you don't need accountants to see they'll starve on that."

In her agitation Carrie paced the floor. "Caleb can *not* get Tulips."

Henry stared at the table in thought. "Maybe I'll take the inheritance after all, and move down to Tulips and Audie Ann and Mother, take Carrie and the children there. It's a big place. Plenty of room."

Spooks made an indecipherable noise. He stretched, rubbed his chin, sighed, and rubbed his chin again. "Would you accept some very non-legal counsel, Uncas?"

Henry did not lift his eyes from the table. Spooks continued softly. "Think slow, old friend, about moving everyone down. Tulips isn't like up here, hidden away where no one goes. It's on the main road."

Henry made a dismissive gesture.

Bright did not raise his voice, but his tone became firmer. "Everyone knows Tulips. A farm that large hires men as essential labor. It buys in substantial quantities and it sells at least some on the local market. I'd guess it's the third biggest property in the county. If Sam hadn't been so lazy, and if he had treated his hands better, it would be the top producer. That means Tulips' owner stands out in the community."

Henry shook his head.

"Whether you like it or not, Henry, Tulips' owner is a big fish. Of course a lot depends on the pond. You and I know this pond is no 'count. But the frogs in the pond think it's almost as important as Knoxville. So they want their big fish to act like a Knoxville big fish. Tulips is important for their own self-esteem."

He lifted his cup. "Carrie and the children at Tulips: that's not what they want from their big fish. They're likely to make that unpleasantly obvious."

Spooks sipped quickly from his cup, then continued. "I suppose you could leave Carrie and the children up here at Quachasee and be a bachelor at Tulips. But there'd be no man here to work the farm. No man in case there's trouble."

"What trouble?" asked Carried quietly.

Spooks sighed. "I'm mortified by my failure to anticipate the new reality, even more by the reality itself. I used to think that if we could only get over the wretched slavery business, we could live in peace and quiet. I was completely wrong. I admit it. The vermin, along with a bunch of people I thought would know better, they think freed slaves need to be kept in their place."

He stopped, then carried on unhappily. "I can't just pass over what Lydia tells me from Tennessee papers—we're awash in newspapers, so she can send reports north to influential people in Washington."

He paused a long time before he went on. "You do need to know. Over near Memphis, a mob burned down the place where a man lived with a woman, lived with her for twenty years. She was almost white, but not quite. Next county to that, they butchered a black man who lived with a white woman, made her and their children watch. Another man with a woman born free was maybe luckier, maybe not. The mob just tarred 'em. Ran 'em out of town. But on the way a gang dragged the woman into the bushes and now she isn't right in the body or in the head."

He turned to Carrie with a pained look. "There's more. Too much more. Of course you can always say, That's west Tennessee, a long way from east Tennessee mountains. I hate to tell you these things, believe me, but you need to know them."

Tears in her eyes, she put a hand on his forearm. "Those things would be hard to say for anyone who has feeling. I thank you."

"My thanks, too, friend," a shaken Henry joined in. "But that makes it even harder to know what to do."

Bright nodded. "I wish you had more time to decide. Tulips won't run itself, not when creditors demand evidence of solvency. Sam's foreman, Eli, is in charge right now, but he lies, and the creditors know it. They also know your stepmother can't take over; Jesse says her mind is usually confused. That leaves Audie Ann. Running the place would be utterly beyond her, bless her. Creditor know that too."

He rose to leave. "You two have a lot to talk about."

Even a small farm left no time to talk until after dark. In the dusk Carrie brought out a chair to place next to Henry's on the porch. After a time Henry spoke. "You're right. Caleb can't take over Tulips. He won't care about Mother and Audie Ann. But I have you and the children to think about. I can't go to Tulips and leave you up here mostly alone. I feel trapped."

"Me too. I just get my man back, and now this. I knew that when you were gone it'd be hard. And it was. You were only gone a few months. I can't live up here alone the rest of my life, not after the vermin."

Henry put a hand on her shoulder. "Maybe we could at least try having you all at Tulips. Audie Ann and Mother will never object. In fact we'll have the opposite problem. Audie'll spoil the children rotten."

"She would. I'd love to give her the chance. But what about the big fish in the pond? Even penny-pinching Sam knew to throw a party once in a while. What happens when you invite people to Tulips?"

Henry shrugged, but Carrie would not let the topic go. "Do I stay in the kitchen, you ready to explode when you hear whispers about 'that woman' out back? Or should I be all dressed up, standing beside you, waiting for people who won't take my hand because they want to spit on it?"

"Those kind of people don't matter."

"They do at Tulips."

"Maybe I could be friendly, but not have parties," offered Henry.

"Spooks says it doesn't work that way."

"He could be wrong, you know."

Carrie rose to tend the fire under a pot, but returned immediately. "You know he isn't. But even if he were completely off about the big fish, what about the children? Julia is about ready in her mind to leave home."

She overrode his unvoiced dissent. "Henry, she's not so far from my age when they sent me up here alone to cook for you and Lem's crew. Count the years."

She waited for him to recollect, then went on. "As soon as she or the boys step away from Tulips they're in trouble. The white children won't accept them. The older white boys will think they have a right to Julia, alone or in a gang. And the lowest white girls will think George is a thrill and try to seduce him. Colored children won't be friends because they say our three look white, talk white, and think white. And they'll be right."

Henry started to object, but Carrie cut him off. "No, Henry, on this I'm sure, because I remember it happening to me. Our children will listen to children who were slaves, and think—they'll think it, even if they don't have the words to say it—those children are mostly ignorant and hopeless. Remember how Julia and George reacted to those runaways being chased by Netzler Dammit."

Henry went to the little cold house at the end of the porch to refill his glass, then returned to sit down heavily and stare at the floor. "You remember that too."

"Um-hmm. It took me years to see that's why Mama always kept me right beside her. You remember the deal she made with your father—if he would put me to be Audie's maid, she would make Tulip's dining room famous."

Henry looked up in surprise. "What? I never heard that before. You sure? Anyway, she still needed to worry about Sam bothering you."

"Elvira watched him like a hawk. Mama told me later that's why Elvira wanted me sent up here as cook. Besides Mama carried a blade in her sleeve as a last resort."

"I didn't know that either."

"There's a lot you don't know. There's a lot neither of us knows. Like where will they find someone to love? How can they be as lucky as I was?"

Henry corrected her. "As we were."

Carrie gripped his arm, but kept going. "Do they pass and marry white? What happens if they're found out? And what could the boys do for a living when they grow up? Working season after season for wages that'll barely buy food, let alone books? Spooks says that devil Dinkins wrapped up Tulips so our boys could never inherit it."

Henry opened his palms in appeal. "You know I'd buy them land so they could be independent."

"Yes, I know you would, no matter if it beggared you, and I love you for it. The boys would have fine farms." Carrie put her hands on his. "But then what? A fine farm makes envy even worse. And what about after you're gone? The vermin come when the boys are away in the day to rape their wives, or at night to burn them out?"

Henry held his bowed head in his hands. "When the bed was bad on the road to California, I'd lie awake thinking about these same things, hoping I could make them go away if we moved. I have to look after you and the children. If that means we have to leave, we leave."

Carrie shook her head. "But remember your promises. You promised your mother you'd always look after Audie. You promised your father you'd look after your stepmother. And then there are the promises that come with just being a Hollis. Your father worked all his life to build Tulips to hand on to future generations. Your whole family is buried there."

"I know all that. What am I supposed to do?"

"Honestly, I don't know." She leaned over and kissed his cheek. "We need to sleep on it."

They slept only fitfully. A few nights later, the moon halfway across, Carrie felt Henry roll over. "You awake too?" she whispered.

"Too much to think about. Elvira. Sam. Dinkins. Caleb. Damn the whole lot. And what am I going to do for Audie Ann and Mother? What am I going to do for you and the children? I just go in circles."

"Henry, we have loved each other so much, and how does it come to this?"

"I'm afraid that's a, a . . ."

"Non sequitur? But what have we done wrong?"

"Pride, I guess. We thought, I thought, we could escape the world."

"That's what I wanted. To stay up here as escape."

"But then the soldiers came."

"The war was supposed to end it. But now I feel trapped in the only place that used to make me feel free. I have to leave, Henry. The children have to leave. And you have to stay for Audie Ann, and your stepmother. And your father's work."

"Yes."

"Can you forgive me for going?"

"You have no choice. Can you forgive me for staying?"

"You have no choice."

"Will you go to California?"

"No, it's so far. But mostly because I'd always remember that you and I planned to be together there. Aunt Sally's boy went to Ohio. Solomon says he writes it's at least some better than Tennessee."

"Where in Ohio?"

"He's in Cleveland. Isn't that by Lake Erie?"

"Yes."

"Henry, I don't even know where I'm going. How can I go without you?"

"How can I stay without you?" His fingers found wet on her cheeks. "Will you come back?"

"I have to make myself so hard, so resolute just to leave that I can't even think now of coming back."

"When will you leave?"

"Soon, or my small courage will just dribble away. I need to sew some new clothes for the children so they look presentable."

"What do you want to take with you?"

"I came here with only my clothes, and that's all I'll take away."

"No."

"Henry, you wouldn't deny me . . ."

"I mean, no, you'll also take money with you, enough to be comfortable for a time. Spooks was going to lend me cash to move to California. It will work just as well in Ohio."

She wept harder as she pulled herself close to him. "I don't know how to tell the children."

"Let me do that."

In the morning he did, taking each child in turn to speak about the need to move for their future. The hardest part came when they realized he was not leaving with them. Determined not to lie, he answered each child's tearful inquiries as best he could. "Only God knows the future. I promise I'll write to you. I hope you write to me, please."

He went down the valley and brought back Aunt Sally to help Carrie and Julia with sewing. Because he thought to enter a store in Clayton, newly opened by Moses Lipschultz, assembling new wardrobes progressed faster than Carrie expected. She took the children to Tulips for goodbyes to Audie Ann. When they returned, she wept much of the night, but the sun rose on her at sewing.

Henry remembered Carrie's urgency during the wild nights right before he left for California. Now she sewed late long after he went to bed, and lay beside him without touching him. He understood she hardened herself for leaving, and let her be.

Spooks and Lydia came up with their children and stayed overnight, making such a crowd that the men and boys all slept in the barn. So much hubbub prevented intimate conversation inside, but Lydia once followed Carrie, bound for the hen house to hide tears. In the yard, Lydia put an arm around Carrie. "How can I ever thank you for giving me John when I was set to go north forever?"

"The question is, how can I thank you for . . . for so much?" Carrie pulled herself together with a struggle. "Sometime you tell your husband, please, that there is no man except Henry that I have ever admired and loved as much as John Bright. From the first time I met him he did more for me than anyone deserves. And you have been just like him."

Another week, clothes packed, most stock sent to Tulips, Henry spoke of several mares to carry them to the railroad, but Carrie refused. "I walked up here. I'll walk away from here. But having Edgar for our bags would make it easier for the children. I'll go out the High Trail and leave Edgar at Claytown Livery."

"You're avoiding Tulips."

"Tulips and Ginners Ford both."

"You think I'll forget."

"Henry, please don't make me cry, or I'll never be able to do what I need to."

Low clouds were pearly. The very highest clouds showed faint rose. Doves had just begun a tentative cooing. A rooster's first crowing turned to a squawk as Henry stepped out the door for a soon start. He saw Julia already leading Edgar from the barn. Carrie checked a list against parcels George carried from the cabin. Julia intuitively saw the logic of mule packing. She and Henry pronounced Edgar ready. Carrie looked haggard. The children's eyes shone wet.

Henry hugged each child. "Remember you're baptized Christians. Remember your name is Hollis, a good name. Remember me. Take care of your mother. Remember . . ." He faltered, and the children, tears on their cheeks, crowded into his arms.

When he straightened up, Carrie stood a little apart and avoided his eyes. "It's a long way," she said. "We need to start."

Henry nodded and passed Edgar's lead to George. Julia took Edward's hand. Carrie led the way up the slope. Henry watched as they disappeared into the woods, where Edward and Julia looked back and waved. He returned their wave and kept watching until their silhouettes appeared up on the ridge. He waved with his full arm and hat. Maybe they waved back, but his eyes blurred so, he was not sure. Soon they disappeared down the other side. He sat on the porch the rest of the day, watching the ridge.

The next morning he closed the cabin securely, and went down the valley to Tulips.

Plowing with Greek, My Life
HL Hollis

Tulips, January 16, 1939

Since I missed this month's Holy Communion when I didn't feel up to church, Pastor Herkimer visited yesterday with prayers and private Communion. (I prefer to explain his presence thus rather than hint at some Lutheran version of last rites.)

Pastor and I exchanged observations about prayer. I told him about a dinner years ago when I served as lay delegate at the church convention in Nashville. Some pastors there reminisced about a seminary professor so God-smitten he sometimes prayed the night through. I confessed to Herkimer that even in my current straits I could not find enough about which to pray that long. He speculated the supplicant professor recited psalms, something my upbringing did not fully qualify as prayer.

Prayer and psalm my father distinguished in his customary practice every evening before anyone dared leave the dining table. Psalms he read. Prayer, though, he spoke ex tempore, for Father did not hesitate to include a current problem or even a person seated at the table.

Though anything but formulaic, Father's prayers always began with "Lord, for your infinite mercy we plead," and ended so predictably that Bill, impatient with piety, welcomed the first words of his unvarying conclusion with a sigh of relief. I can quote Father still: "Lord, we plead for your guiding and protecting hand over those of our beloved who make their way in far places among strangers and enemies." While I did not fully share Bill's impatience (he was already half out of his chair when Father reached "among strangers"), I did wonder why Father petitioned so generously on behalf of beloved who wandered. At the time the whole family sat securely situated around the dining room table. Later, my own children grown and gone, I found Father's closing sentence slipped unsolicited into my own prayers.

I thought today to inquire of Herkimer if he recognized those words from some prayer book. He did not, though perhaps his memory-search suffered from impatience to get to our Greek reading, the agreed-on chapter of John. His Greek is, frankly, a little shaky (he would agree), for his schedule makes diligent study hard to fit in. The automobile shortens transit time for pastoral calls, but, aware of that, parishioners expect more visits.

Further, church clubs and societies multiply like rabbits. Fight fire with fire, I remember one visiting expert telling us; for instance, with so many tempting secular alternatives, we must sponsor a young people's group to keep our youth in church. Since the youngest generation mostly baffles me, I stay neutral about church societies.

It all does incite my speculation, though, about how, at my age, Father coped internally, surrounded by children, his own children, barely as old as my grandchildren are. He never complained, at least in my hearing, though when he bounced one of the younger children on his knee, I thought his mind sometimes seemed someplace far away.

Herkimer is the third pastor I have known at Bethel church. Following Berkemeier, who was before my time, I have known Haenschke, Schmitt, and Herkimer. We have been blessed by faithful shepherds. I have listened for seven decades with reasonable attention to their sermons, which in my memory are now considerably shorter than in my boyhood. Brevity is not necessarily an improvement, though I am cognizant everyone expects the aged to equate change with decay.

Sixty years ago God was correct (small wonder) in neglecting to issue an unmistakable summons for that boy Hollis to enter the ministry. I'd have been a better preacher than the average, but not a better pastor. In point of fact I lack the patience with human weakness essential to heal souls. I was certainly pleased some decades past to meet serendipitously a Hollis from another branch of the family who did hear God's call to the ministry so clearly that he acted on it. (I believe Crotia, that sleuth supreme, is in occasional correspondence with the Rev. Edward J. Hollis in California.)

Years ago I scoured Bethel's archives for any sermons by Eusenius Berkemeier, who preached to my grandfather and to my father. Among other things, I wondered whether Berkemeier ever questioned slavery from the pulpit, but I found no homiletical equivalent of the smoking gun.

To conclude from the written record, he apparently did what all but a few saints did (and do). He rationalized a prevailing social practice inherently repugnant to the Gospel, thereby becoming at ease with it. Should I condemn him? I waver, according to which Gospel I am reading. Surely my grandchildren and their progeny will fault me for my moral obtuseness in some controversy of my own time. If, in defense, I wish they will know all the relevant facts about me, I must assume Berkemeier hoped the same.

QUACHASEE
WHC

Tulips left Henry no time to brood. Sam had ignored orchard pruning. His hogs resembled stock just driven in from the wild. Roofs leaked, windows lacked glass, railings rotted, flues were obstructed. Barn doors hung stiff on frozen hinges. A dead tree leaned hard on the Big Shed or vice versa. Worst, the tall clock in the front hall stood silent.

Eli Richards, Sam's overseer, seemed all thumbs when Henry tried to teach him fruit tree grafting; his appraisal of hog qualities for breeding was not merely ignorant, but wrongheaded. Henry discovered disconcerting gaps between Richard's reports and facts he observed. But Eli had friends at the livery barn. Henry bided his time. Sooner than he expected he had in hand irrefutable proof of brazen theft. He called Richards up to the porch, where Audie was cleaning pistols, and displayed his evidence. He gave Richards a choice: the sheriff or immediate, permanent relocation. Eli left for Alabama on the evening cars.

Henry took on the foreman's role himself, but it consumed all his energy. A property as large as Tulips was much more challenging than his Quachasee farm. The scale of Tulips' many auxiliary enterprises complicated its operation. Small details of field soils and topography at Tulips spelled the difference between adequate and excellent harvest. A reasonable repayment plan staved off Sam's creditors, but Henry recognized vultures who allowed no room for mistakes.

Feeling he neglected Audie Ann during his Quachasee years, he also needed time for her. Their conversations became the bright spot in his day. But without Carrie to translate, he found conversation exhausting; worse than merely rusty, his hand talk needed relearning. Sarah, their stepmother, had aged prematurely; she slipped in and out of coherence. Perhaps his father had seen signs of this before he died. She now required patience he could barely muster.

Frequent visits with the Brights nearby bolstered him. He found in Lydia a friend who was as compatible as Spooks. He envied Spooks' domestic tranquility. Then a prestigious law firm, of counsel to large corporations, invited Spooks to head their Knoxville office, an offer a man with a growing family could not refuse. The Brights moved to Knoxville.

Henry wearied on like a blindered mule at a sweep, treading at a steady pace, one round, then the next, head down, following the path until the end of the day. He paused only when an envelope with a Cleveland postmark arrived in the mail. Then, no matter who or what job waited, he disappeared into his bedroom. Usually multiple sheets burst from the envelope, some with Carrie's free script, some with Julia's careful hand, George's impatient scrawl, Edward's enthusiastic printing and drawings.

I don't know what I would do without your money, dear Henry. . . .

Dearest Papa, Miss Baker, the head of the Ladies Academy, says I am so far ahead of the other girls my age that she put me in an advanced class and asked me to help with the youngest girls. Some of them come from very small towns to board here. . . .

Papa, I hat schul, but Mama says you would make me go the same as her . . . .

Dere Pap, Today I drew a pikcher of Moo-To. Julia maid one of Edgar, but I like mine beter. I wil sen it to you. . . .

❦

To keep Tulips running, he needed to establish his presence in Ginners Ford. That proved less fraught than he feared. He had avoided the town so long that many people he dealt with there believed he had recently returned to claim his inheritance after decades in New York City. For the social responsibilities incurred by the owner of Tulips he began sponsoring an annual shooting contest. It proved immensely popular. Audie Ann could be the star, and he the conscientious host in the background tending to detail. He offered little about himself and let people think what they chose.

Neighborhood mothers chose to think, Henry discovered, that a single man in possession of a large farm must be in want of a wife. Henry learned to accept invitations only from Tessie Linder, who had no daughters.

Henry first met Tessie by accident when her buggy developed a small problem close to Tulips. She seemed grateful for his aid. He in turn appreciated her pleasant overtures to Audie Ann. Though Tessie was not especially favored in looks, she dressed well, and treated him in a casually flirtatious manner which reminded him of Pru so long ago in Brooklyn.

I wrote out a fresh book of Mama's recipes for George. You were right; her recipes are her best memorial. We have found some people here in Cleveland pretty much like us, Henry. They also wrestle with the memory of non sequiturs. I'm cooking for a nice family now, so I don't have to dig so deep into what you gave me. . . .

Dearest Papa, I have loving and loyal friends at the Ladies Academy. I am teaching Luther's Catechism to Edward, as I promised you I would. I'm also painting pictures for him so he doesn't forget living in the mountains. . . .

Papa, on Saturdays I work in the kitchen at a fancy place downtown. The head cook is from New Orleans and he didn't know a recipe Mama gave me. . .

Deer Papa, Julia makes me pictures about the viginti duo soldiers. I'm reading Aesop's Fables. Do you kno the one about . . .

Initially wary, Henry came to enjoy his Linder evenings. Tessie and her husband, Herbert, had just recently moved to Ginners Ford. He was the managing partner for St. Louis capitalists behind the new mill, and Henry came to consider him an astute businessman. Tessie was ever soft-spoken, considerate, educated. She engaged guests in stimulating conversation. Gradually Henry accepted Tessie's increasingly frequent invitations almost automatically. After one interesting evening, he sank into bed suddenly aware of how many hours he had not worried about Carrie or Audie Ann or Tulips.

Baking sun on a Sunday afternoon made it a good time for Henry to sit in deepest shade on the porch with Audie Ann and Solomon. She touched Henry's shoulder to get his attention; her hands and face moved. "Tell me again why Carrie went to Ohio."

"The rogue soldiers stuck hard in her mind. And she worried, we both worried, about the children's future here."

"Too white, too black here?" She watched his face.

He nodded.

"Will she come back?"

"I don't know."

"You miss them?"

"More than I can say."

"She stop loving you?"

"I don't think so."

"You begged her to return?"

"It isn't that easy."

"No, only in books."

He nodded with a pained smile.

"You think it unmanly to beg?"

He shook his head.

"Who does begging harm?"

"Maybe no one."

"Oh, dear Solomon, what would I do without you? I was just thinking how good a cool drink would be, and you read my mind as usual."

Audie Ann's questions came back to Henry as he went about the farm. He had never begged Carrie. Should he now? Nothing physical kept him from appearing at Carrie's door. He knew her reasoning as if his own, as in fact it was. But maybe they acted too soon. A school for colored children opened recently in Ginners Ford. Just one teacher for fifty or sixty children, but the bright ones could learn something at least. In the last election a few colored men voted without trouble, at least not violent trouble. Sally's sons had scraped together some money to buy the old Lyman place; shabby buildings and exhausted land, but you have to start somewhere.

He listened to himself as he knew Carrie would listen. He could not fully convince himself. But Gerhardt Schmidt voiced a different opinion when he picked up Audie Ann's rocker for repair. Gerhardt's view of war never wavered. "A terrible vaste, Henry. Ven you a man zee bleed, de blood all red ist, not black or vhite. Beeple in dis down." He rotated his forefinger at his temple. "But Henry, in Ginners Vord new beeple ve zee. Dey maybe here change." Gerhardt was right: new roads, the planned railroad spur, the mill. They all brought outsiders, like the Linders, outsiders with new ideas.

Should he tell Carrie that? This wasn't Alabama or West Tennessee. Maybe the mountains did make people more independent. He weighed the evidence, guarding against misplaced optimism. Or pessimism.

Henry, I used part of what you sent to get some new clothes for Julia. She never complains, I knew you would want me to. She is so pretty I alternate pride and worry and try to think what you would say. . . .

Dearest Papa, thank you, thank you for the new dresses. Girls at school weren't making fun of me, but it is very agreeable to be as fashionable as I now am. . . .

Papa, the head cook uses fish in a lot of recipes I know for beef or pork . . . Mama has written out a book of old recipes for me. I like the ones that use spices I don't usually use. . . .

Dear Papa, my teacher used some Latin today that was wrong, so I told her . . .

Plowing with Greek, My Life
HL Hollis

Tulips, January 24, 1939

Lately I have counted in the night as the clock strikes one, two, even three. I try to stay as still as I can, for Caroline is too conscientious in looking after me for my nocturnal restlessness to cause her loss of precious sleep. It is a comfort to reach across and touch her in the night, so I'm grateful she has chosen so far to sleep in our bed.

In point of fact the night leaves me far too much time to think. Every fall of my life here at Tulips, as we finished harvesting I wondered whether I would be around to plant the next spring. It is rank superstition, pagan at that, but I always figured that if I got seed into the ground, somehow that meant I would be around to take in the crops. Now it wonders me if I will make it till planting.

To escape the Three O'clock Dreads, I tried mentally walking through Tulips, room by room. Colors, furniture, windows, even floor creaks. I mentally retrieved the shifting cadences of Audie Ann's thump and scrape as she approached a door or stairs.

That went so well I somehow thought to try the same for Father's Quachasee farm, as perhaps he also did, lying some sleepless night here at Tulips. Though the Quachasee place is much smaller and simpler, I found troubling gaps in my mental picture.

Fretting on those, I could not recall Father ever taking me up there. I went many times, but always with Mike Henderson, hunting. Forest was reclaiming fields already then. In season we prowled the orchard, gleaning fruit overlooked by birds and bears. In warm weather Mike and I took a quick dip in the springs pool; we needed hot sun for the water temperature to be barely tolerable. We paid our respects at the little cemetery, and admired the surrounding wall, of such exceptionally precise rock work that I wish the mason had left his mark or signature there.

These memories, however, are all associated with Mike, whose marriage to Dory confirmed his status as my brother. I recall being with Father at so many other places about these mountains, where associations with place sometimes drew an anecdote from him. There is no equivalent for the Quachasee.

(Perhaps—something I dread to contemplate—my illness has advanced to affect my mental faculties, or perhaps it is the medicine. I must press Bill on his next visit.)

Even though he rarely visited the Quachasee once he settled at Tulips, I believe Father retained a strong affinity for his Quachasee farm. My evidence is twofold. First, his efforts, when work was slack for our crew, to get an old path up to the cabin cleared of the many occlusive rocks and debris that had, one after another, gradually fallen on it. Second, the pains he always took to ensure the buildings stayed in excellent repair.

Occasionally I questioned the prudence of spending funds on buildings no longer used. Father consistently overruled me. Actually I should say he ignored me. Perhaps had I invested as much effort in those buildings as he when living there, I too would be loath to see them go to rack and ruin. For whatever reason, my father always retained a soft spot for the locus of his solitary years up in that remote valley.

Last night, when I heard the clock strike one, I experimented with a different strategy for insomnia. I counted sheep, or at least livestock in this neighborhood. That census proved too easy. It moved me, though, to the subject of land.

Land led to Crops led to Cultivation led to Plowing led to Furrows: how many furrows it took my father to work across the high field at the Quachasee place. That prompted me to estimate how far one walks to plow that field. Multiplying by the years Father was there gave me a distance so astronomical I at first assumed arithmetical errors.

Impressed, I did the same for other fields, thinking to aggregate a total I could compare to the circumference of the earth. But I fell asleep before the clock sounded two. I believe I was then cutting a long furrow far westward of California, closing on Hawaii.

In this morning's light I conclude it unwise to spend even dark hours reviewing how much of a life is spent on the mundane and repetitive—my plowing and pruning, Caroline's dishwashing and housecleaning.

I told her this, and her response was as I expected, a sensible, daylight response. "You can't eat off dirty dishes." And you can't sow an unturned field.

Bergman & Co.
Rare Books, Autographs, Letters, Maps
Est. 1919
347 Archer Ave.
Cincinnati, Ohio

Auction Lot 63
Misc. Unidentified Family Corr. 1868

Envelopes are Postmarked, Ginners Ford, Tenn
Letters all Addressed: "Dear Sister"
Signed: Various given names

July 12, '68

Dear Sister,

So relieved to have you back and safe. When you first told me about Horace years ago, I dint know being a mining engineer means you haul your wife off to god-forsaken places for months at a time. I wish I was there. I'd push Horace out of your bed, and we could lie in each others arms and say whats in our hearts.

After you left, Herbert did decide to go into business with the St. Louis men. He's the partner on the spot, to buy land, build a mill, get the operation running and then sell out and go build another one some place else. It sounded good. Then I found out their first mill would be far east in Tennessee, a town so tiny it didn't show up on <u>any</u> map. I just wept buckets when Herbert first brought me here. I wanted to go right back to St. Louis, except Herbert had worked <u>so</u> hard to find us the best house in town. I told myself, Tessie Linder, if your sister can follow <u>her</u> husband all the way to South America, you can stick it out in Ginners Ford, Tennessee.

But I was going to need a <u>lunatic</u> asylum unless I adopted some project! Then a letter came from Jaimie. Right away I knew—our little sister shouldn't stay in mourning forever. She needed a new husband!

I kept a likeness of the unknown man in my head. But where oh where could I find him? The last straw was a gentleman— old, rich, childless and looking for a wife. <u>Perfect!</u> Then I noticed he never wore shoes. He told me he didn't abide 'em on his feet on account shoes wasn't "jes nach'rul." When I told him his hat wasn't natural either, he said hats "wuz diff'ren—the Good Lord put hair on a man's haid, so a hat be jes heppin' what God give a man." But feets is bare, he said. His sure were. And his prospects, too, as far as I'm concerned.

I was giving up when someone spoke of a bachelor man on a huge farm. Fair game. All the mothers in town tried, but missed. He never, ever, came to any party.

You know me. When other women give up is when the game gets interesting. The ladies here have <u>such</u> <u>limited</u> imaginations. After all it wasn't <u>so</u> hard to have my little buggy break down right at his lane. I dint have a choice but to walk up to the house, a damsel in distress, to beg Sir Henry to rescue me. I expected some broken-down shack, so my spirits went up when I saw the house, about the largest one around, with new shingles. I could hear the chime of a clock inside—it reminded me of Uncle John's tall clock when we were little girls. Well, I said to myself, Tessie, all you need is your knight.

I found him—he rode a rocking chair as his mighty charger— on the porch with his sister who is a deaf-mute—a kind soul warned me about her. Sir Henry was just what I was looking for—not too young, but not feeble old. You and I have both kissed frogs a lot uglier to find our prince. He was perfectly hospitable—his sister ordered an old darkie servant to bring a cool glass for me. The sister is terribly crippled. Sir Henry right away went down to look at the buggy while I stayed on the porch and "talked" with the sister by writing on a little slate she keeps close.

Anyhow Sir Henry fixed the buggy quick—too quick. But of course as a frail female—you know how frail I am—I was so unnerved by my accident that I needed him to drive me home with a mare tied behind for his return. And of course I drove out again the next day to thank him for rescuing a helpless woman—and to make him agree to come to a little party I organized. I coaxed him some and teased him more, and he said maybe.

He did come! Of course I made over him. I don't think he said more than six words the whole evening, but he was attentive. After that, it was so easy. You taught me how years ago. First the frequent visits with small gifts for Sir Henry's sister, and confidences with her about how much we valued his company. Then invitations to private suppers, with just Herbert and I. Then small parties including couples and several unattached ladies—of inferior qualifications. (I remembered your strategy—to set off your moon you make sure the sky has only bitsy stars.) Once we trained him used to us, I wrote Jaimie to come for a long visit. And leave her mourning black at home.

She came! She conquered! (I don't think it's fair that you two got the looks in the family.) To introduce her here, I invited the town banker over. All his wife can talk about is her precious Saunders, the boy-genius. She's a country mouse with no idea how to dress. Of course I never dreamed how much nicer Jaimie's gown would look in that comparison. I also invited the Haeckles. Henrietta is the sort who needs to pull her corsets tighter.

Jaimie just breathed it all in as if they were royalty. Of course, where she sat, men had to notice her fine figure. Her jonquil silk looked as good in the candlelight as I predicted. Herbert heard Ledley tell himself—I predicted this too—Banker Ledley said, Damn, that's one fine woman, several times. Sir Henry's eyes said he noticed.

Tomorrow evening I am having a little house party. Clay Dunne, one of Herbert's business partners will be here from St. Louis with his Minnie (who deserves to be called Biggie). I've invited Sir Henry for overnight.

Yesterday Jaimie and I spent the entire day taking in seams on her white gown. We were giggling like schoolgirls when she tried it on, it's so snug. Today Jaimie is practicing a bit on the piano that Herbert thinks is too expensive. I noticed that Annmarie Thom down the road has the smallest piano bench I have ever seen — it isn't much wider than a stool — so I traded benches with her during Jaimie's stay. To turn pages while Jaimie plays, Sir Henry will have to sit <u>very</u> close on that bench.

At the end of the evening the ladies will retire and I shall tell Sir Henry which is his room when the gentlemen have finished their drinks. Of course I must not get mixed up and <u>accidentally</u> direct him to Jaimie's room. Of course not. I could never be <u>that</u> careless, could I?

Herbert came in just now. He sends his love, of course. He is in a good mood because he says the original mill design uses materials that are much stronger (and more expensive) than they have to be, so he figured out a way to build cheaper and faster. He says it's only fair his savings on materials go into his pocket because he spotted the mistake. He also says we will be able to leave months before his partners expected. Oh, I do so hope he's right. I also hope Sir Henry is up to some jousting tomorrow night.

Your loving sister,

Tessie

QUACHASEE

WHC

"Friends," Tessie Linder's voice was, as on Henry's previous visits, soft and well-modulated, "this is my sister, Jaimie Post. Sister, I want you to meet our good friends, the Ledleys and the Haeckles. And this," her eyes came to Henry, and, he thought, stayed there, "is Mister Hollis. Jaimie, I'm sure you'll enjoy their company as much as we do. You'll be seeing them again while you're here, because they're special to Herbert and I."

Henry vaguely recalled Tessie had mentioned her sister's visit. Still, Jaimie caught him off guard. He would have predicted Tessie's sister to be pleasant company, easy to talk to. He would not have predicted Tessie's sister to be so attractive and yet so unconscious of it. She seemed pleased to share a sofa with mousy Constance Ledley, listening raptly to her interminable stories about little Saunders. She skillfully parried fat Henrietta Haeckle's rude prying. Jaimie seemed oblivious to the way her yellow dress reflected the candlelight and set off her perfectly plaited hair.

"Damn, that's one fine woman." Ledley spoke under his breath at the other end of the room. Henry was of the same mind a week later when Tessie invited him for dinner with her, the Simes, and the Gunthers. The occasion brought more chance to chat amiably and inconsequentially with her while other guests long occupied Herbert and Tessie.

He did not debate with himself when a boy brought the note to Tulips. *Mr. Hollis, I want some friends from St. Louis to meet you. Since the party will be so interesting, no one will leave early. Come Friday evening for dinner and stay overnight here. Please say Yes.*

On Friday evening, Tessie introduced him to the Dunns, associated with Herbert in the new mill. Jaimie Post wore a white dress fitted so snugly that Henry had to make a conscious effort not to stare. She greeted him cordially and asked him sensible questions, followed his answers closely. When Tessie requested music, Jaimie acquiesced without coyness, and sang well, accompanying herself confidently on the piano. At least so it seemed to Henry, though he told himself the last time he heard anything similar was decades ago in New York City.

Over a late supper, Jaimie listened diffidently as Linder and Dunn argued without animus over editorials in Memphis and St. Louis newspapers. She spoke to Henry of concerts she attended a few months ago, and how she cried and cried over *Great Expectations*. After the meal, she sat with Henry on the parlor's small sofa and teased him pleasantly about his long silences, bringing her face, and her perfume, close to him several times.

Clay Dunn poured himself another glass. "You know the war was a terrible thing, but it's turning out good for us, woke us up, at least some of us. We're booming like we never did before the war." He paused for a deep swallow. "The only trouble is, last month I needed to get out of that St. Louis city heat, so I stopped at my favorite cool place. *Biergarten*, the Dutch call 'em. Looked up and saw a white man sitting with a black woman as calm as a cat with cream. I mean, she was light-skinned and all, but if you looked real close you knew. Some generations back there was African blood. I kinda stared at the two of 'em, the way they assumed this is acceptable nowadays in decent society. Just didn't like it."

Tessie picked up. "I know. It's like crossing a horse and a donkey. They don't belong together. Our uncle gave Jamie and I a donkey when we were little girls. A wonderful little pet. Took us everywhere, always so patient. Then we graduated to horses. What glorious, glorious rides. So we learned: donkeys and horses are different. You shouldn't mix them. If you do, you only get mules. Ugly beasts. Recalcitrant. Troublemakers." Herbert chimed in with forceful agreement. Tessie and Dunn piled on more examples.

Henry's eyes flitted among them, every sense now alert. He noted tones of voice, watched for covert signals. The conversation became more animated, more denunciatory. Yet Henry could hear nothing aimed at him. He saw no surreptitious glances.

When Clay went on to describe a white woman with a black man, Minnie Dunn shuddered in revulsion. "I don't care how common or low she is, all I can think of is, how can she do that, throw herself away so?" Minnie turned to bring the silent Henry into the conversation. "I'm sure you get that feeling, too, Mister Hollis."

Henry stared into his glass. Were they well aware of Carrie? Did they know of Solomon with Audie? Were they playing with him maliciously? No, he finally decided, their convictions were so hardened they simply assumed he felt the same way. Fuming, he recalled Spooks' advice from long ago. When you need to relax a meeting, especially one not going the way you'd like, stop everything with a slow-told tale, a good tale with many details.

He sipped from his glass, then cleared his throat. "Years ago, from time to time, I used to visit a mule dealer with a big place, a lot of fine buildings, out way past Claytown."

Henry started to sip again, then put the glass aside to free his hands. "The dealer was a great big fellow, always dressed in black, only black; hat to boots, all black. His barn," Henry's arms spoke its large size, "painted all white. Every board. Even the trim, the door hardware," Henry's hand jiggled the handles, "all white. He dressed his black men in black and his white men in white. One or the other, never both. Some people thought he was maybe a mite peculiar."

"I can't imagine why, Mister Hollis." Tessie followed him raptly, ready to laugh at a punch line.

"His mental condition was a question because other things also made you wonder. Before he greeted you, he always turned a complete revolution, turned all way around. Always to the left." Henry's forefinger made circles.

"Every time I went there I found him reading. He maybe owned more books than I do. When he finished books, he just strowed them all over the floor. Chaos."

"Sounds like he needed a wife," laughed Minnie Dunn.

"Or bookshelves," answered Henry. "He had neither. But once he said something about searching for a book, and I looked closer at the scatteration and finally understood. He *did* group them. By color of the cover. Over here, all the red covers. The few green over there. All the black ones in that corner. All the leather-bound thrown there."

His listeners chuckled, and Henry continued. "Sexton was his name, and he never said, 'I think' or 'I agree.' Always 'Doc Sexton thinks.'"

"He sounds off in the head," Linder snorted.

"That's what my father always thought. Anyhow from time to time, something happened"—Henry decided to skip the fucking cane and generative acts—"something would prompt him to start preaching. Didn't need a pulpit. Start wherever he stood. Deep thundering voice. Moses down from Sinai, or maybe a Jeremiah."

"Old Testament for sure," offered Linder. "Tough to sleep through."

"He had his own way to keep his audience. He would turn himself completely around, and whenever in the circuit he faced someone, he would demand to know if they were with him."

"How could you keep from laughing? I would have at least giggled," Tessie smiled.

"Some of his preaching could make you laugh. Mostly he preached fire and brimstone. In that voice it could make your hair stand up. Sooner or later he'd be sure to decree that mating horses and donkeys to produce mules constituted an unnatural act, guaranteed to receive God's punishment. Infertility, the least of it. Sexton preached death on any mixing. Colors, animals, plants, people. Mixing was unnatural, a violation of God's order." Henry switched to a theatrical bass. "Someday God will punish you."

"Well, maybe he wasn't mad. I agree with him about mixing," Tessie's smile had vanished.

"Turned out, he *was* mad. A true raving lunatic. If anyone had question about his mental condition, came the day he burned down his whole place, building by building, everything. All burned to the ground."

"Oh, Henry, why didn't someone stop the poor man?"

"Couldn't. He had a couple of pistols in his belt. Anybody with water got close, he'd start firing. Nearly killed one Good Samaritan. All the while he kept preaching against pollution. Even burned down that huge white barn, screaming, 'Pollution, pollution, pollution.'"

"Then what happened to him?"

"Why, he burned the barn down from the inside."

"With him in it?"

Henry nodded. "All his stock too. People said the sounds his animals made while being burned to death were just unbearable."

The women made soft sounds of sympathy.

"After that," Henry concluded, "no more sermons."

"I guess you didn't miss them," said Linder with a laugh.

"In one way, no. At first his preaching bothered me some. I wasted a lot of time worrying about whether he might be right about mixing. Then I talked to an old friend, a smart lawyer. He just laughed at me. Said I got my examples from Sexton, and Sexton had been breeding mules so long, that's all he could think of. My friend pointed to his dogs. His best hunting dogs were crosses, every last one of 'em."

"But Henry, people aren't dogs," said Tessie without a smile.

"No ma'am, you're right," Henry conceded. "But they ain't donkeys an hosses, neither."

Linder laughed. "He's got you, Tessie. That's what happens when you invite a rabid abolitionist into the house."

Henry shook his head. "No, I never had enough courage to be an abolitionist. But I'm sure we're better off with slavery gone."

Clay Dunn thumped down his empty glass. "Right you are about that. I once took the time to cost out building and running one of our mills with slaves. Can't be done. Economics won't work. Much cheaper with free labor. You escape initial investment and all kinds of side costs."

Henry waited him out. "I didn't mean dollar costs. I think slavery poisoned people."

Ever the alert hostess, Tessie interrupted smoothly with a light laugh. "That's why we like you people in these mountains. You think so independently. I'm on your side, Henry. I think we can get along just fine without slavery. Of course people aren't mules. They don't have four legs. But I do think of their limits when I see someone who is mixed. Don't you, Henry? Now admit it."

Henry felt his anger rising. "Miz Linder, I know someone you'd call mixed who reads Latin, memorizes Shakespeare, and points to weak spots in Dickens' latest."

"You could predict that, Henry," said Dunn. "Your man is half white. And that *white* ability, that *white* competence, is just going to come out. But the *white* side is always dragged back by the black side."

Linder sounded more conciliatory. "You've been away up north too long, Hollis, I'm afraid."

"It doesn't seem so long." Henry could not concede now. "Most of the time I just wonder why we can't mind our own business, leave other folks alone."

"That would be fine, Henry." Linder no longer sounded conciliatory. "Except this isn't just folks getting along. We're talking about the future of our American civilization. To move ahead, to boom big, we need to make sure we're breeding the best characteristics."

Jaimie looked up, speaking in her usual gentle voice. "No one asked what I think," she said smiling. "I think our silent mountain man has been teasing you gentlemen. Taking a position just to get your dander up." She touched his arm lightly. "He knows, we all know, gentlemen in Tennessee will do everything they can to protect the purity of Southern white women from pollution."

She smiled at Henry. "I can always depend on the gentleman in the community for the courtesy a true lady deserves."

"Oh, not *merely* gentlemen's courteshy," responded Dunn, "never *merely* gen'men's courteshy. Also their admiration, endless admiration, for her charmsss . . . and her . . . charmsss . . . and her admiration and her—"

"You shouldn't have taken that last glass, you silly man," laughed Jaimie, winking at Henry. "I think this conversation has gotten far too serious." Henry wanted to argue on, but she moved quickly to the piano and began to play.

When Jaimie asked him to sit beside her and turn pages, he did so mechanically, noting as if from a distance that the unusually short bench forced them to sit hip to hip, that her dress's neckline at his angle seemed startlingly lower than at supper.

Tessie clapped her hands, said the hour grew late. The ladies must retire for their beauty sleep. Herbert would serve the gentlemen a toddy. They could stay up as long as they liked. She turned to Henry. "Your room is all ready for you. I had your little bag put up there for you. It's upstairs, the third door on your right. Can you remember that, Henry? On the right. The third door. Sleep well everybody," she called gaily.

Linder served drinks so strong and large that Henry covertly dumped his onto a potted fern. As drained as his glass, he excused himself, went upstairs, counted doors. At the third he knocked perfunctorily, turned the knob, pushed the door wide, and walked in.

An embarrassing, an inexplicable blunder. He entered a room softly illuminated, candles on each side of a freestanding full-length mirror. At the foot of the mirror rested his bag. Facing away from him, Jaimie stood at the mirror, brushing her long hair. From her shoulders to her ankles, her bare back was a line of graceful curves. The mirror's reflection confirmed that the slipping decolletage's shapely promise earlier downstairs was no artful illusion.

Jaimie did not start or cringe as he entered, but brushed on without pause, her carriage as erect as if she were receiving guests in the parlor.

"How nice that you did not take forever downstairs, dear Henry." She tossed the brush on a chair and pulled her hair over her shoulder so that from her tight grasp at her nape it fell free down her back nearly to her waist. She looked over her shoulder at Henry with an arch smile. "Would Doc Sexton advise the mare is suitable for mounting?" She turned and moved slowly toward him, her elbows high to hold her hair. "But first you should close the door."

So he closed the door.

And quickly eased back down the stairs. Linder and Dunn still sipped their drinks. Neither heard Henry let himself out the back way. Rather than try to saddle his mare in the dark barn, he walked home by moonlight in confusion and sorrow. The luscious Jaimie was desirable, available, impossible. And how could he urge Carrie to return to Tulips after listening to the people he had believed would improve things for her? Was he a Peter in the High Priest's courtyard, remorseful after failing miserably before the cock crowed to defend those he loved? He went back over his words, relieved at some, realizing too late what he should have said in place of others. The road stretched long. Once home he fell asleep immediately.

That afternoon a boy brought his horse and bag. There was no note. As he sat with Audie Ann that evening, he turned to her. "I can't beg Carrie."

"Why not?"

"She might come. Then I'd have betrayed her." To be sure his handtalk was correct, he also wrote it on her slate.

Audie read the slate, erased it slowly. She looked at his haggard face sadly, then kissed his forehead.

Henry, I have a new job now, cooking for a very wealthy family that moved here from Boston. You could fit the whole Quachasee cabin and porch into their kitchen . . . the children seem to be getting along well, as you can read in their letters. . . . People have made us welcome, especially at church. Some of them were born free; they're leaders here. Henry, I remember telling you there could be no happy place for me at Tulips. I still think I saw right. I think I see there could be no happy place for you with these people here.

A few weeks later, as the new mill building neared completion, substitute beams, Linder's silent revision of the engineer's specifications, failed catastrophically. The mill roof collapsed without warning. Five men died, including Herbert Linder.

Henry wrote a condolence letter to Tessie, but discovered she had left to stay with her sister in Baltimore. Without an address, the letter sat on Henry's desk until he threw it into the stove. He hardly noticed how rarely anyone troubled him with a social invitation.

Plowing with Greek, My Life

HL Hollis

January 30, 1939

Given the many shelves of books at Tulips, most of us children took
early to reading, each with his or her own taste. Dory favored
biography; Marcus read everything; Bill, science; Crotia, romantic
novels, including many now exiled to well-deserved obscurity. We
always knew when she retrieved some old-fashioned novel because
without warning she spouted stilted phrases and archaic words. (As
did Mama from time to time, though much less consciously.)
*Habiliment*s. Crotia loved *habiliments. Forsooth*. She once even
tried *forsooth*, but only once because Bill hounded her about it. He
greets her with it still, in the same sepulchral, long-drawn-out howl.
For-s—o—o—o—th.

We could also ascertain Crotia's current reading from clues in the
latest story she composed, sometimes with crayon stick figures,
later, colored-pencil illustrations. The identity of her inspiration
usually shone like an illuminated sign. Her ambition, I admit
guiltily, faced much sibling ridicule. Father, however, always
encouraged her, perhaps as implicit reproof to her philistine
siblings. He quizzed her exhaustively about her characters'
motivations, and inquired closely about their probable fates after
The End.

Crotia once announced at the dinner table that her friend Beth's
grandmother said a lady named Post came to town a long time ago
and *set her cap* for Father. Crotia looked across the table at Father.
"How did you defend Tulips?" she asked, a reporter in hot pursuit
of leads.

Father, however, demanded to know whether Miz Haeckle (Beth's
grandmother Crotia quoted) had actually used the phrase *set her
cap*. Crotia squirmed a bit, forced to admit the phrase might be her
own more satisfactorily archaic substitute. "Miz Haeckle said the
Post lady tried to snag you and Tulips down to your last thin dime."

His suspicions confirmed, Father relaxed. "Now *that* sounds like Henrietta Haeckle." As I may have written previously, Father occasionally referred to her as the Hen's Cackle.

That peripheral matter settled, Crotia bored in for substance. "Well, Father, is it true? Did the Post lady try to snag you and Tulips to your last thin dime?"

His forehead creased, Father looked vacantly into the distance, seeming to search remote recesses of his memory. "The Post lady," he puzzled just loud enough for Crotia to hear. He buttered toast slowly, I suspect to increase suspense. "Post? Perhaps Jaimie . . . Post? Miss Jaimie Post?" Dramatic jam succeeded butter, as Crotia and Dory exchanged quick looks that Father surely noticed—he possessed a special sense for juvenile signals—but chose this time to ignore.

"Jaimie Post. It must have been Jaimie Post." Father returned to the present. He cleared his throat. "Let's assume, Crotia, just for discussion's sake, you know, that Miz Haeckle is right about Miss Jaimie Post wanting to snag me and Tulips. Let's assume Jaimie Post was after all that Hollis gold you and I buried nineteen paces behind the old kitchen house." Crotia leaned casually toward Dory to nudge her surreptitiously. Father again seemed to pretend he didn't notice, chewed his toast without haste, and puzzled on. "Then what was her strategy to accomplish this goal?"

He dawdled with another piece of toast. "Crotia, your novels should provide some help here."

"Not hardly," interjected Bill, our resident skeptic. "They're all made-up stuff."

"But they can be a useful spur to the imagination. Even better than a tall mirror. Now Crotia, don't the novels say that in these circumstances, the unscrupulous plotter would turn to a surfeit of spiritous liquids in hopes of affecting her victim's judgment? Or even rendering him insensible?"

"Mister Hollis, the tender ears . . ." Mama cautioned. Father, as usual, didn't hear the usual caution.

"Oh yes," agreed Crotia. "Huge bottles of very strong spiritous liquids." She considered the matter thoughtfully. "But that would not work on a smart man, who knows full well that trick by low ladies."

"So the Post lady would go get a pitchfork," jibed Bill, who had little use for such deliberations.

Father lifted a fork to examine it. "But that's not very subtle, is it? Too big to hide under her coat, I think. Well, Crotia, we're stuck. What shall Miss Jaimie Post choose?"

"I think," said Crotia, "she would try some dresses with necks lower," she hesitated, then finished in a rush, "than they should be."

"Crotia, what have you been reading?" came from Mother, whose attention was engaged partially, but clearly not fully, by one of our youngest siblings attempting a cup of some liquid.

"Right, Crotia," concurred Father. "We could predict that dress with a scandalous neck. That v-e-r-y low-necked dress is a requirement, don't you think?"

Crotia nodded solemnly.

"These tactics usually come in threes, don't they?" Marcus had been following silently up to this point. "So you need a third weapon, and it has to be the most dangerous weapon. But after liquor and too much skin, I don't know what the third would be."

Any dullard could see Crotia was reeling through her novels for suggestions. She shook her head, defeated.

Dory it was who came to the rescue. "Unsubtle invitations to illicit carnal knowledge," she said in a calm voice.

"Guess you're right," Father conceded. "But those are pretty fancy words for Doc Sexton's barn, Dory," he half-objected.

Dory waved her hand in dismissal. "The tender ears . . ." She nodded to Mother steering the cup.

"Well, Crotia, we've got this one pretty well wrapped up now, don't you think?" Father was brisk good cheer. "Spiritous liquids, a shockingly low-necked dress, and unsubtle invitations. Isn't this *The End*?"

"No-o," objected Bill. "What happens to the Post lady?" He was always systematic in his dissections.

"Oh," Crotia disdained the plodding of junior scientists. "That Post lady goes away to use her wiles on some poor rich man in Charleston, marries him, and makes his life miserable while she drains his accounts."

"Well done, Crotia." Father thumped the tabletop as he rose. "Could not have written a better story myself."

Thus dismissed, we went off to our several pursuits.

I have reported this incidental vignette as accurately as I can for two reasons. One is to give later generations a glimpse of how the eccentricities of Hollis table conversations could go. The other I have commented on previously, so I shall be brief here. I do not recall any of us at the time noticing that, as happened so predictably, Father stealthily evaded Crotia's initial question. Her query was lost in the effort to decide the proper details for Crotia's story of drunken attempted seduction. Meanwhile Jaimie Post— whoever she was, we never learned—slipped away, in Crotia's editing, bound for Charleston to find there some easy mark.

QUACHASEE
WHC

Another harvest. Winter work. Spring planting. Henry heard Audie Ann's gun in back and went to watch. She emptied a revolver at a target. There seemed to be only one hole. She saw him, grinned triumphantly, and put down the new revolver to free her hands for talk. "I wonder if Carrie can still do that."

"I wonder too."

"I miss her terribly."

Henry pointed to himself in agreement.

"Will she ever come back?"

"I don't know."

"Is it wrong to ask?"

He shrugged, but a resolution formed. Solomon planned to visit Sally's boys in Ohio again. When he stopped at Tulips for the small leather wallet Henry asked him to carry, they walked in the yard, talking for some time.

In a month Solomon again stood on the porch. Again they walked in the yard. "Marse 'Enry, I 'most dint rec'nize Miss Julia, she sech a fine lady. Carrie sen me by her 'Cad'my and I sees her out wid all kind'a white lady, so dress up. Dos chillens verra po-lite t' ole Solomon, yessuh. George's one fine cook. An Edward, whoo-ee, he smart. They all talks so eddicated, jes lahk you an Carrie. I proud t'know 'em." He paused at a darker thought.

"Marse 'Enry, I waits till de chillens gone, an den I ax Carrie, I ax huh, 'yuh e'er gonna cum back t' Tenn'ssee?' She start cryin. She verra truble in huh mine. She say, 'Oh Solomon, it so hard. But I ken' go back. Mah chillens, dere lifes, be heah.' I ne'er argue wid huh, lahk you say, Marse 'Enry. She sho appreciate dat wallet. I tink tings wuz a lil' tight dere jes den. But, Marse 'Enry, I hab money lef o'er fum mah travels. I guess I fogits t'bring id back t'yuh."

"Keep it, Solomon, you'll need it on your next trip."

❧

Evenings grew so warm everyone lingered on the porch, swatting the bugs. Conversation low and slow. Spooks was taking depositions preparatory to a case in Wyndham, so he came up from Knoxville for the duration, took quarters in Wyndham. He sat on the porch regularly, though each time he rode away worry-lines on his face were deeper. Finally one evening after Audie Ann went in when dusk precluded hand talk, Spooks cleared his throat, a hand on the table between the men for the bottle and glasses Henry offered.

"Uncas, old friend, I seek a candid word with you that I hope you won't take amiss."

"Speak up."

"I worry. About you."

"No need, friend."

"I believe there *is* need. Item one: the hall clock. It has stood silent for many months and you never talk of summoning Herr Schmidt. Item two: your appearance. You never dressed particularly well, pardon me, but in the past few months your clothes look like you've slept in 'em. They're owned, but rented. Wrinkledy. Plain tackey. When did you last shave more than once a fortnight? Item three: your spectacles. Instead of replacing the new pair you broke, you went back to being blind in your old ones."

He sipped from his glass as Henry gave no response. "Item four: the farm. You're not making timely decisions; I won't list the many subheads here. Item five: liquor. You have begun drinking too much."

A last sip to drain his glass. "From the audience seating, when the curtain rises, the set, costumes, props, and actions all say one thing. Our hero is going downhill, and going down fast. That's a drama I would sit for only reluctantly. Uncas, what can I do to intervene?"

After long silence, a chair creaked, followed by clink of glass.

"You're right, Spooks, and brave to speak. We're in the last act, though it looks to be long and dull. I'm afraid we neglected to read the script to the end before the first curtain went up. The leading lady has made her final exit. In fact she is committed to a different drama, different house. I don't leave this stage as long as Audie is on. It appears I've already said all the lines assigned to me."

Another long silence, but no glass clink.

"Henry, would you do an old friend a favor before you take your bow?"

"Can't contract in this context."

"You're not a lawyer."

"What's the favor?"

"Take a trip. Chicago. New York. If that's too far, St. Louis, Memphis, Nashville."

"Spooks, I'd be a rube in those cities, just wouldn't be comfortable."

"Well, maybe go to some mountain resort. I know you wouldn't go to Bersheeba Springs because of all its slaver and rebel associations. But you could try the new Blue Valley Springs Resort. People tell me it's the nicest hotel in East Tennessee. Might do you good."

"You're too smart to believe that drivel about special waters at springs."

"It's not the waters I have in mind," replied Bright. "It's people,"

Again, after a long silence, the creak of the chair and clink of glass.

"I'll meditate on it. Like a refill?"

"My head won't take it, Henry. I need sleep for tomorrow. Good night."

"Good night, friend."

In the morning Henry startled a puffy-eyed Edie by appearing unusually early for breakfast. He carried a long list of tasks requiring attention before his intended trip East on business.

Dorinda Hollis Henderson to Crotia Hollis Warden

Collection of Lewis Hollis Warden

February 3, 1939

Dear Sister,

Visited HL today as usual. He's just a faint shadow now, poor man. He was pretty cheerful when I was there, but Caroline says his mood can go very dark and back to sunshine in the same afternoon. Small wonder. Bill predicts HL will just slow down more and more until the end — but he also warns us he's made poor predictions in the past.

Caroline and I talked some about funeral arrangements, but she hasn't made any firm decisions. I think it's good she's at least thinking about it now because when the time comes there's such a rush it's hard to think straight. I told her I'd have done some small things different for Mike's funeral if I had had time to think, so I hope she takes the hint.

Brother Lowe sent a get-well letter to HL. I admit I suggested it. Now I wish I hadn't. I'm positive I wrote "terminal cancer" to Lowe, but he writes as if HL has a bad cold. Another, "worser," thing, Crotia, I don't know if it's Memphis or that odd cutting of a wife he has or something else, but he can get going so about the "darkies," it's just shameful. You'd never guess he's a son of Henry Hollis.

I try to be charitable and think he doesn't know how he sounds. But Sister, I'm afraid he <u>does</u> know and doesn't <u>care</u> if he sounds so hateful. It's as if Edie never fed him everything he ate all those years growing up at Tulips, and he never noticed Solomon and Audie taking such loving care of each other. I'm just afraid he'll get on to that topic in some "comforting" letter to HL. Some comfort!

What Lowe needs is a copy of that interview manuscript you did years ago and then put away — wisely, I thought, and think. Or maybe it wasn't wise, and we all — Lowe included — should have had the facts about Carrie and their children years ago.

I'm plumb flusterated this mornin thet I cain't make up m'mine. Lowe's shameful letter and what to do about it. And your questions about your well-aged manuscript.

Crotia, I need to say one thing loud and clear. You've done some wonderful work about life in Mtn Springs. But this Hollis manuscript is the best work you've ever done. Period. Couple of periods. . . I can hear Father's voice true, and see him peering around with that near-sighted look. The same with Spooks; I get a vivid sense from your work of his kindliness and his courtliness. And Audie's thump with slow, slow drag. Especially her questions. It's all there. So I think if you've got those three right, even though I never met her, you've got to have Carrie right, too.

But as you say, getting the full story isn't the same as an order to send it to the printer. I still think, when Mother was alive, you did the right thing to put the manuscript aside. About releasing it now, I go back and forth. Tell 'em the truth and let 'em stew. Or Father's advice to me on something (I forget now what), first, Dory, do no harm. Which should I tell you?

About showing some parts to HL now as a diversion for him, I'm dubious. He might be elated to see big gaps in Hollis history filled in. Or he might be crushed by seeing what he didn't guess all these years. And seeing it done better than he ever could have, to be blunt about it. I'm not sure which, and that makes me lean hard toward doing nothing with the manuscript in his last weeks — or days.

I think the bigger question is what provisions you make for someday publishing your work. I know that for years you've been teasing especially Bill and sometimes HL, by dangling snippets in front of them. Catnip they perversely refuse to recognize as catnip. But seriously, Crotia, you need to settle on a trigger for releasing your hard work. I'm pretty certain

Father had a trigger of his own in mind. He just neglected to figure in a sick mule. That would have been catastrophic if you had not done all those interviews years ago with Father and Audie Ann and the Brights.

Crotia, this letter is an incoherent mish-mash if there ever was one. But I don't have time to straighten it out, nor fix my brain either, which is what really needs organizing. I just have to get something, anything, into the oven NOW for tonight's church supper.

You wrote you were hoping a neighbor could drive you to Tulips for a visit with HL soon. As they say — and I got this from you — it would pleasure me for you to come and set a spell happen you to pass.

Your admiring sister,

Dory

QUACHASEE

WHC

Henry tipped back in his rocker on the long porch, pride of the Blue Valley Sulphur Springs Resort. Waiting for dinner on his first day of his first vacation was time for reflection and appraisal. What value should he place on the various elements he had encountered during a long day?

Gibbs—owner, manager, whatever he was—the man who checked him in. Supercilious and dressed like a fop. It's true, Henry conceded to himself, that before he left Tulips he should have stopped at Lipschultz's clothing shop. Well, there was not time. For that, or for replacing a shabby valise either.

His room. Not a garret, but its view of the mountains was no better than from Tulips. At least it promised quiet.

Glasses clinking inside at the bar, musicians noisily tuning up at the pavilion close by, ceaseless promenade of self-absorbed young couples who kept blocking his view of the moonlit mountains. What a bother.

"Emenities." Lord help us, that was its spelling in a flyer at the front desk. What was Gibb's line? "Mister ah Hollis, many guests find bathing in the sulphur waters is highly beneficial for complaints of the back. The salubrious effects on digestion, Mister ah Hollis, of drinking the waters directly, undisturbed by the agitation resultant from transportation, is well attested to." Had Gibbs memorized the vapid puffery of the resort's advertising? Maybe he had written it? When Henry told him the water stank, the man's face was a mule swallowing medicine, a visage so entertaining that Henry had some regret cutting Gibbs off gruffly when he started up like an automaton, shilling sightseeing expeditions and private rooms for discreet gambling.

Henry had assumed he'd dine at his own table. But Gibbs shook his head. "It's our practice, Mister ah Hollis, to intermingle guests together at the tables so they have easy opportunity to enjoy each other's company. It's a bit daring to require no prior introductions.

But, Mister ah Hollis, most of our guests—they come from the best circles in our major cities, you are surely aware—they leave our resort fully convinced by our custom."

Gibbs had told him the dining room served at seven. Henry pulled out his pocket watch. Five to seven. High time to be at the dining room door, among the first in line. His stomach chastised him. He had taken down cars from Ginners Ford to a junction in the middle of nowhere, and waited alone hours for the up-bound cars on a different line. No food available at any stop.

His mood did not lighten at the dining room doors when he discovered that not a single guest sat in the dining room at seven o'clock. His hasty retreat was cut off by a waiter who asked his name, checked it on a list. Riding a tumbrel, Henry followed the man—was he smiling or smirking?—across an echoing room to a seat at an empty table for four. He memorized the menu card, fiddled with the cutlery, played with reflections in the empty glasses, and was back to the menu card before the waiter returned to complete the table with Mrs. Sherman Field, Miss Elizabeth Coyner, and Mr. Clinton Barton.

Henry quickly learned that Barton called Richmond home, had never met the two charming ladies before this very minute. The two charming ladies, also new arrivals, were from Nashville. They could hardly be less alike. Mrs. Field: large, florid, loquacious, imperious; to Henry she was immediately "General" Field. Miss Coyner: her much younger and much trimmer, also much more reserved, cousin.

While Barton engaged Miss Coyner, General Field pressed on Henry a detailed history in a hoarse voice she apparently thought discreet. Miss Coyner, she reported, grew up her aged father's sole companion, but the learned judge recently died, an act General Field seemed to find inconsiderate and irresponsible. Nevertheless, she selflessly volunteered to guide the now-orphaned Miss Coyner into society to "meet people." "People" obviously meant eligible men. To that end, she sacrificed the company of her doting husband and talented children in order to chaperone Miss Coyner here. So many *distinguished* guests. Such *luxurious appointments*. And especially the *guests!*

She beamed encouragement at her cousin, who seemed a little dazed by Barton's assiduous attentions. "I believe my plan is working nicely," the General rasped at Henry. Then, without warning, he was no longer a fellow guest in prospect of dinner, but the subject of a prolonged inquisition.

He was relieved when their waiter finally arrived, eager to please but inexperienced. The women ordered the chicken; he served them the fish. General Field sent hers back with voluble indignation. Miss Coyner accepted hers with an encouraging smile. "I'll have the chicken some other time. You're new at this, aren't you?"

"Fust day, ma'am." Beads of sweat ran down his temples despite a cool breeze through the dining room.

"It's hard, isn't it?"

"Ha'des' ting I e'er do."

"Don't worry, you'll get the hang of it; I'm sure you will."

"I hopesso, yessum."

The General gave her meal unwavering attention, a focus Henry realized he should have predicted from the multiple rolls under her chin. Freed of her questioning, he studied her cousin, Miss Coyner. Somewhere in her twenties, he decided, svelte, certainly compared to the General's ponderous bulk. Blonde hair framed her face well. Attractive features; only a nose a little too long kept her from being head-turning. Barton did most of the talking, which apparently suited both of them. Henry decided General Field should easily succeed in her campaign, unless she stumbled over her own ambition.

Dessert. Guests began rising. Barton asked if Miss Coyner would care for a walk in the garden. She hesitated, her eyes on her older cousin in a look that Henry could not decipher. General Field urged Miss Coyner out, reinforcing her whispers with unsubtle jerks of her head and hand signals the tablecloth hardly concealed. Miss Coyner finally left with Barton. There was so much, Henry saw, to embarrass her, but what exactly, he wondered, caused her deep blushes?

He escorted General Field to the lobby, then continued out the front doors to take again one of the many rockers lining the colonnaded porch. Declining the waiter's offer of refreshment from the cart displaying many bottles, he settled himself to review his trip balance sheet, as Cousin Hurley had taught him so many years ago.

Manager Gibbs: debit.

Room: debit.

Food: his dinner was an urgent reminder to encourage Edie, Tulips' cook. He must stir her imagination and ambition. She was in a deep rut, not having had a good apprenticeship, as well as far too few occasions—Henry accepted responsibility—where she could shine for sit-down dinner guests.

Young crowd: debit.

Emenities: debit; no, a credit for the coinage.

Guests: a mixed entry, for in fairness he had hardly spoken a word to Miss Coyner and Mr. Barton; given General Field, though, debit loomed large.

Totals: quickly done. No need for an audit. This bankruptcy required no verification from some green-eyeshade clerk.

Henry considered leaving in the morning, but decided that would dishonor all the commotion at Tulips his trip preparation had caused. He resolved to keep the original plan—two weeks, no less. But no more.

Plowing with Greek, My Life

HL Hollis

Feb. 2, 1939

This morning I woke with the intention of writing a small section on a continuing minor but chronic vexation through Hollis generations, the patronizing attitude of hotel front desk staff upon ascertaining that we hail from deep in the mountains of east Tennessee. I had worked out some paragraphs on the subject in my head during the small hours of the morning.

The subject remains my intent, filled as it is with amusing anecdotes from successive generations. But as the morning unfolds, I find I do not have the strength today to pursue the topic as it should be. So here I make merely notes, to be properly explicated when I feel up to it.

I. Grandsons and grandnephews at church youth assembly, Knoxville, 1936.

II. Son Peter, checking in to Palmer House, Chicago.

III. Nashville hotel during church convention. "You have a farmer's sunburn, but you don't talk like a farmer."

IV. Father's encounter with Mr.(?) Gibbs(?) at Blue Valley (defunct) resort.

V. Shirts and collar styles. Failure in 1933 of Moses Lipschultz & Son, a loss of fashion polestar for this region.

QUACHASEE
WHC

As he sat again on the Blue Mountain porch after breakfast, Henry went back over his first dinner, and that harrowing interrogation by General Fields. All had been customarily superficial at first. She had oozed solicitude for her cousin, Miss Coyner. But then she resettled ample haunches in her seat. She turned to Henry.

"Mister Hollis, tell me about yourself." Her peremptory tone startled, then offended, him. Before he could open his mouth, she added, "I'm told you're an educated man, someone who can communicate in good English instead of that dreadful mountain dialect. You enjoy a luxurious ancestral plantation—Tulips, isn't that its name? very poetic, I think—not a far distance from here, which you have greatly enlarged."

When he began demurral, she shook a warning finger at him. "Oh, Mister Hollis, I know this from very reliable sources. I understand you own many, many acres of extremely valuable land and ever so many heads of purebred cattle, which routinely win prizes, so they fetch *very* pretty prices."

She loomed closer. Henry was assailed by perfume he disliked. "You see, Mister Hollis, I already know a great deal about you, don't I?"

Henry heard laughing. He had almost forgotten Pru's laugh. Here she was, ascerbic as ever. *Oh-oh-oh Henry, you pulled a good'un outta the river this time. Safer to buy oysters, you know. But is this a bloated fish or some rotting trash your line hooked? Put it down, hard. See if it flops around.*

"No, ma'am." He shrugged. "Guess them tole ye wrong 'bout Hollis."

"Wrong?" Her voice rose enough to merit brief scrutiny from adjacent tables.

"Thet right, ma'am. Wrong. Oh, the talkin part 'most right. But we'uns hyar ken unnerstan ferriners like ye."

"Mister Hollis, I'm afraid you mistake me. I'm not a ferriner . . . foreigner."

"Well I swan. I'd'a never knowed."

"I'm a Nashville girl."

"But then, ma'am, why nobody thar teached ye En'lish?"

"Mister Hollis, I understand English perfectly well."

"Purty poor teachers, if you ax me. They done ye."

"Mister Hollis, I speak English, not some ignorant dialect."

"I'm bumfuddled. But I got me an i-dear. Thet thar waiterman, he ain't brung nary no food to ate yet, so thar's time t'play us'uns sum word game. Ye willin? *I* give out a word an *ye* makes a sentence usin hit. Then *I* has t'make a sentence usin hit. Ye unnerstan?"

"I think I comprehend, at least in part. You are to challenge me with a word? Alright, what is your word?"

"Summers, ma'am."

"That's much too easy, Mister Hollis, especially for someone who likes word games—and usually wins, if I may say so."

"Summers, ma'am."

"Summers? My sentence is 'I could stay whole summers at this resort.' Now what is *your* sentence with summers?"

"Summers in the Bible is the 'xact passage I needin fer this preachin."

What? Summers in the Bible? Oh-oh. Somewhere *becomes* sum whurs. *And* sum whurs *becomes* summers. *Henry, that's pretty good for a man who can't seem to remember punch lines. But she isn't half clever enough for this.*

"What?" The General furrowed her brow. "Summers what? That hardly makes sense, Mister Hollis."

"Make sense t'me, ma'am. But how 'bout sum differen word? How 'bout spang?"

"You must mean sprang, past tense of spring?"

No ma'am. Spang is what I said. Or, being as how we'uns in S's, how 'bout staving? Thet 'minds me'a strow."

Forget it, Henry. You're way over her little head. She'll call foul any minute now.

"Mister Hollis, you are not playing fairly. Those words aren't in my dictionary, I'm sure."

"*My* dict'nary has 'em, Miz Field, 'Pears to me thet ye ruin' back. I'm eddicated to unnerstan yourn En'lish, but ye ain't eddicated to unnerstan my En'lish."

Now Henry, calm down. Remember how McClary and his shillelagh used to throw you out when you got riled up.

"I 'spect we ken jower 'bout words night long, Miz Field, but thet not never no mind. Ye axt me 'bout cows."

"Yes indeed." General Field straightened, once again a sleuth. "Reliable sources tell me you own many purebred cows."

"Wal, thar's a heapa 'em," Henry conceded. "But nary none is pure. In a common way, ourn cows is crossbred. Has t'be so's to git long laig on one side an short laig on t'other."

She stared, confounded. "You're saying your cows have short legs on one side and long legs on the other?"

"Yes ma'am, thet what I sayin. Ye dint hear hyar?"

Henry, be polite. She's got a basic problem. She's stupid.

"I've never seen an animal with legs of different length. But it would be helpful on these steep mountain sides. I would have trouble walking on them myself."

"Yes ma'am, I ken see *ye'd* have plentya trouble flanderin 'round a moun'in. Like to creel an ankle. But ourn cow don' have nary trouble."

She eyed him suspiciously. "How can I be certain you are not just joking with me, Mister Hollis?"

"'Pon my honor, ma'am," replied Henry. "Ye seed pitchers'a them ani-mules down in Austral'a, them as called keng'roos. But mebbe in Nashville ye don' git proper pitchers?"

He waited in vain for an answer, then continued. "Man from Nashville—since ye from Nashville ye probly know 'im, name'a Smith? No? Wal I hev t'ax him if he know ye; he prob'ly do, 'cause he run wit' *all kinda* peoples, he not partic'lar—well, thet man come out hyar. He give up t'be the bestest t'advice us. We'uns tole him we do everwhat he want. An he say, cross breed to git cows wit' short front laigs an long hinder laigs. Like them keng'roo hoppers. Only they cows."

The General nodded thoughtfully.

Henry's face sorrowed. "But them cows dint work out good. A-comin home downhill, ifen they try head-fers to spy out the way, wit' them short laigs in front an long laigs ahind, why they good to tumble, bust their necks. So we train 'em to *back* down hill, but wit' no eyes ahind, thet'd like as not git stuck a-runnin into a tree or sum rock. Dint have the strenth t'git 'way"

A brighter thought lit his face. "Powerful clumers, though. Ye'd be 'mazed how quick they raised them hill. But the onliest place they go were up, y'know. They turned t'hit."

He shook his head in recollection of problems. "Thusly the moun'in knob git too crowded fer feedin. 'Til they git t'gether theirself an figgered out which uns for to hove off of a night. Leastways thet cause of good aten fer ba'ars 'n painters."

"Mister Hollis. I concede I am confused. I thought I was following you, at least partly, but now you referred to painters. Am I to understand that you coat certain of your cows with some kind of paint?"

"Oh no, ma'am. A painter ain't no painter, no ma'am."

"If a painter isn't a painter, what *is* a painter."

"Why ifen a painter *is* a painter." Henry conveyed patience sorely tried. "What else could a painter be?"

"But Mister Hollis, first you say a painter ain't—isn't—a painter, then you say a painter *is* a painter. I am utterly confounded."

"Yes ma'am. Thet's 'cause ye mebbe dint larn En'lish rightly. A painter ain't no painter brushin paint ifen a painter be a mountain lion, a'course. Them an ba'ars is back in the hills."

Henry adopted an encouraging tone. "Now, some city body like ye is wond'ren: what is a ba'ar. Now a ba'ar, wal . . . hit's right yonder." He pointed at the entrance door, smiling in satisfaction at an example so close at hand. "Anigh thet door, thet big black 'un standin up an sniffen t'wind fer yer scent."

"I believe that frightful beast was imported by a taxidermist from somewhere in the West, where they keep dangerous wild animals."

"No ma'am. Thet ba'ar, thet'un were kilt hyar two year since. Hit tore up three, four severe big Plott hound an two man afore they destroy hit. Turr'ble ruction, yonder in under Giffords Knob."

Henry, scare the bejesus outta this pathetic city girl.

"That very bear by the door lived in these mountains?"

"Thet's the fack I tryin t'tell ye. Ye ken spy Pilot Knob from whur ye sittin, I figger. But I don' advise walkin thar, not with nary no coat, an dresses thet hardly cover ye."

The General smoothed her dress as her eyes widened. "I had no idea we are in the midst of such dangerous . . . Gibbs did not give us the least warning." She paused, but only briefly. "Did I understand you to mention mountain lions? Perhaps that was a misplaced attempt at humor. I know lions are found only in Africa." She smiled, apparently complacent in her convictions.

A waiter stopped with a large platter of appetizers for the table of four.

Henry spoke around him to answer the General, who was easing the platter closer to her. "Yes ma'am. Africa lions is. I don' wanna be biggety, but we'uns has Tennessee lions. Mountain lions, mountain screamers. Some as calls 'em cougars. Some as calls 'em painters, like I tole ye. Stalks people, they do. Go fer yer neck."

Mrs. Field's pudgy fingers toyed with her heavy necklace. "Gibbs should have warned us not to venture out in the garden with such dangerous beasts prowling about."

"Tain't nary painters in this hyar garden. Res' yerself. Mebbe we had orter talk 'bout yer chillums."

"Do you mean children?"

"Chillums is what I says, yes ma'am."

"Children."

"Chillums."

The General hesitated. "That's certainly kind of you, Mister Hollis, to ask, I think, about my children. They *are* very exceptional, if I do say so. Especially my Billy, who is at the very head of his class. And my Emily is just very unique. Everyone agrees she has prodigious musical talent." She stopped herself with obvious effort.

"But," she straightened in her chair, "I also want very much to hear much more about your valuable cows. Herds, is it not? Your diale— your accent—is such that I am not always certain of the line between fact and jocular fiction."

She sighed. "I suppose I can only be certain you're joking when you begin telling me about something like . . . growing a fifth leg on your cows." She tittered to herself.

"Oh no, ma'am, I'm telling of the truth, sartain. I sure not peddle sum store-boughten story t'a lady as smart and eddicated as ye."

Henry paused while the General smiled at the compliment, then he conceded, "a'course we did *try* fifth laigs, yes ma'am. Not many people knows 'bout thet, 'cept really smart ladies. *Them* cows was downright failure."

He made a quick motion with his palm through the air. "Fast. A boy-cow, five-laigged, like as not could beat any mule at a mile without hardly tryin! Stand t'reason. Thet extry laig meant they wuz plum 'xactly one laig faster. Thet twenty-five percents!"

Henry thought he heard a sudden cough from Miss Coyner; when he turned toward her, she was blushing and had covered all but her eyes with her napkin. "So sorry . . . That appetizer . . . it's spicey hot . . . so incautious of me . . . I shall recover. . . . Please continue your conversation."

The General seemed more concerned with cows than with her cousin. "Am I misconstruing your words again? What could be wrong with a fast runner? After all, there are horse races for speed, I believe."

"But yer unrememberin thet mules disfavor cows. An when a mule seed a cow run thet fast, lot fas'er then a mule ken, hit jes a-killed mule spirit. They sooner starve as come outta t'barn an show theirselves, they so 'shamed."

Henry shook his head in defeat. "Thet's why, whensomever ye lookin outin them pasture fields hyar, ye don' spy nary five-laigged cows, usually, leastwise not on no farm wit' mule."

He smiled to reinforce his observation, then demanded, "Ye hasn't seed any five-laig cows hyar, has you, ma'am?"

"I? Seen five-legged cows here? Not that I recall, Mr. Hollis."

"*Now* ye knows why," Henry beamed.

Miss Coyner again coughed into her napkin, and again apologized, her blush testifying to her embarrassment at her disruption.

The General was unrelenting in pursuit of the facts about cows. "Mr. Hollis, I still wonder if this is just a story you tell to mislead city people and have a laugh at our expense."

"Sartain not, ma'am." Henry face showed his shock at such suspicion. "No raison t'misdoubt Henry Hollis. I ain't 'bout ta green out ye. Now, I *will* tell you *this* jes betwixt me an ye." He leaned closer and used a stage whisper to keep his secret-sharing confidential. "Ifen ye hear some body 'tother talkin 'bout crossin the side short-laig cow with the front short-laig cow, why *then* ye ken know fer a fack *thet* is a joke on ye city folk." He finished sternly. "Don' never trust 'im. "

He sat back satisfied, a man who had fulfilled his duty. "Jes keep thet in mind, an nobody ken pull nary no joke on ye. Got thet?"

The General nodded slowly.

"Even a poor body on a mountain farm know it tain't practical. If ye try t'cross them cow, ye know what ye git?" he demanded.

Henry waited until she moved her head somewhere between a nod and a shake.

"Ye right! Ye'd make a good farmer's woman," he congratulated her. "Specially fer a man what cain't stan jarrin an mouthin. Now, them crosst cow has sech a rotary action walkin, why the milk in theirn udders, hit gets so churned, hit turn to butter right in theirn udders. Then ye in a *real* tight fix. Caint hardly milk butter, ken ye?"

When this did not produce agreement, he paused at a new thought, a complication previously unconsidered. "Miz Field, ye *has* milked cow, a'course?"

"Certainly not. See here, Mr. Hollis, do I look like a country milk-maid?"

"Wal, Miz Field," Henry craned his neck, moved his head closer for intense examination, then at more distance for different perspectives. "Now thet ye mention hit, no, ma'am. Ye'd mebbe co-lapse the stool."

Henry, be careful. She blushing under all that powder. Sooner or later she'll catch on. Better get off cows.

"Miz Field, mebbe we orter speak'a lan' ye ax 'bout."

"Land, did you say? I would indeed prefer that. I would like you to describe your acreage."

"Ak-ridge?" Henry shook his head. "Wal, ma'am, thet's shootin purty high fer jes a farmer. I'm like the body which he be satisfied when he got corn enough to bread 'im and hog 'nough t'meat 'im through the winner."

"You are being too modest, Mister Hollis. I was told by a reliable source that you own at least two thousand acres of land that is appreciating rapidly."

Henry shook his head sorrowfully. "Dunno who tole ye thet, but he jes' a-joshin ye, ma'am."

"What? Mister Hollis, good authority—"

"I a-own a heap more'n thet."

"More than two thousand?" Her voice rose again to indiscretion. Adjacent tables again turned, this time for a more prolonged appraisal of the obese woman and the lanky man with sun-burned face above an old-fashioned collar.

"Shh, ma'am. I keep it kinda private. I do own me a big boundary'a land. The best part, hit run up steep. Tother part hit run down steep. So ifen ye squash hit all out flat-like, hit's way more'n t'deed say."

"Mister Hollis, I still think you're much too modest about your land holdings."

"Hit's a wide scope a land I own, hit is. Leetle bit a huckleberry timber. There's a rimption of oak an chestnut. But they like as grow sideways on them steep slope. Boards ye git from thet timber is real short. Make the houses turrible small. Tulips ain't 'xactly a plan-ta-tion nigh ta some pitcher ye seed, sum gi-normous white place thet have high colyums out front'a hit."

He moved his hands from spread wide to thumb and forefinger nearly touching. "Mine's jes leet-tel. In a valley so na'ar 'twixt two knobs hit nary sees no sun. Fack is, we-uns hedta build a mirra top'a the mountain t'check what the sun look like."

Smiling proudly, he assured the General, "Wit' thet big mirra' up thar now, we'uns ken put in *winders* t'light them rooms."

General Field paused, perhaps puzzling over mirra and winders, then sought more familiar interrogative terrain. "That's rather like what Mister Dolan over thar . . . over there says about his house, and I know for a fact he winters in Italy." She eyed him narrowly. "Tell me, when were you last thar?"

"Ne'er, ma'am." Henry answered cheerfully. "Man like me's hardly smart 'nough t'walk t'hyar, let alone walkin fer a place like Eye-taly." He lowered his voice for a confidence. "Thet thar Eye-taly, it more'n coup'l holler 'way, ain't hit? Don' thet Mister Dol-mans git 'nough winter hyar, thet he has to walk all thet ways fer more? Seem kinda pecul'ar t'me. Ye think, ma'am?"

He suddenly sat upright, obviously abashed. "Say, I fergits my manners," he apologized. "I had orter ax *ye*. When was *yourn* las walk t'Europe?" Then he could not resist adding, "Did ye really walk all thet way in them thar fancy slippers? Mebbe ye use some good ole workin boot?"

The appetizer platter was empty. What saved the General, Henry realized now, was the arrival of her chicken plate.

Look at it this way, Henry. With all your worries, you haven't had this much genuine entertainment for years. You needed those laughs. Good for the soul. Admit it or you'll be a dour old man. And don't forget, Uncas will be one up on Hawkeye for a decade at least. Of all places, Hawkeye sent you to a marriage market. Could have been worse, though. You'll always remember the fat General Field, and you'll have to chuckle every time you do.

Plowing with Greek, My Life
HL Hollis

February 4, 1939

Some days ago, writing about Crotia's imaginative construction of the Jaimie Post story, I became too fatigued to continue as I intended. I am falling behind in my intentions to elaborate on some topics, so instead of opening a new topic, I return to the woman we never met, the marriageable Jaimie Post.

Crotia was summarizing the story, with some new hypothesis of Miss Post's destination, when little Annie piped up from across the table. "What about Father and Mother?"

What about Father and Mother, indeed. Much depends upon whom you ask. The logical sources are Father and Mother. But when approached, as you can be certain Crotia did repeatedly, Father's reply was a consistent "That is your mother's to disclose." When then pressed, Mama always had some reason not to delve into details just then. She was too busy, too tired, too involved with a book, had too many people around for privacy. In short, as Dory puts it, "She had a bad case of too's."

So what about Father and Mother? When pressed by Annie, Crotia thought so hard for an answer she scrunched up her face. Then her eyes popped open. "I know," she proclaimed with a beatific smile. "Love at first sight. They saw each other and saw love."

Bill's booing earned Mama's warning frown for its lack of refinement. Even Father pursed his lips, dissatisfied. "Crotia, first-sight-love is pretty used up. One book after another: always love at first sight, then impediment, followed by new impediment, and still more impedimentia, before amor vincit omnia."

First-sight-love was Crotia's answer to many an awkward impasse in her early story plots, so it should not have surprised us that it reared its head here. But, years ago, Crotia always met her critics with the clairvoyant's certitude. "Just because it's in books doesn't mean it never happens. I think, for Father and Mother, love at first sight."

Crotia fabricated a fairy-tale castle in the clouds, turreted and crenellated, a handsome archer behind every merlon, complete with Prince crossing the drawbridge to seek his Cinderella, locked in a high chamber. Or the reverse. Depended on the day of the week, phase of the moon, the rotation of a planet, or some similar sign that guided superstitious farmers and junior writers in these parts.

Bill's barnyard term for this I shouldn't repeat. (The tender ears of children, you recall.) He in fact thought Annie's question irrelevant. What about Father and Mother? Well, he would say, what about them? Father was male. Mother was female. They interacted the way many males and females do.

Marcus tended to stand back a bit, the better to see the problem whole. What, he asked, was a busy farmer, with his hands deep in many different enterprises, who wanted some task finished to greet every sunset, what was he doing frittering away his time at a vacation resort as crops were close to harvest? And why would a young woman, who so consistently preferred the calm and secure order of her city home, nevertheless forsake it for the bustle of a crowded, fashionable summer resort? Crowds and surprises were inimical to this woman.

Dory, too, weighed in. Consider: a taciturn farmer and businessman, widely judged prudent and sagacious, of mature years, deliberate in decision-making, little versed in forms of flirtation. Consider: a bookish city woman, half his age, with no interest in small talk and repartee; given to excruciating self-doubt and crippling indecision; for whom placid routine was essential. Does this sound like a promising pairing?

For years now we have fiddled with this puzzle, turning the parts this way and that, inside out and upside down. We never get closer to making a complete picture, much less bringing it into focus.

QUACHASEE

WHC

Following his arrival day's resolutions, Henry made himself act like a typical resort guest, except of course that typical guests do not have Pru at hand.

Henry, those spring waters are gen-u-wine repulsive. But otherwise this place is just like Sexton's barn. They even make a fetish of white paint. And look out for the whales and elephants in your way. Law, there are eligible bachelors everywhere.

No wonder General Field brought her cousin here, despite stiff competition. Anxious mothers shepherded their daughters as young men circled. Most of the young ladies were pretty. A few beautiful.

You've been on the farm too long, Henry. Stylish is not the same as pretty. Miss Corcoran is pretty, I grant you. She does look much like Alice Pruitt. Same tiny waist and dresses to match her eyes. But Henry, the same painted rosebuds I warned you about before. Miss Lorca, now, she's in a category by herself. Been years since I've seen a woman that beautiful.

Henry enjoyed watching from a distance. But when pretty Miss Corcoran was seated at his table—by mistake, he suspected—she treated a harassed waiter imperiously. Pru was offended. Henry was disappointed. Not a gentle Alice Pruitt after all.

I know we're sneaking down this little side corridor because you spotted General Field coming at us on the main route, Henry. If it's any consolation, Mr. Fifield, Mr. Sims and jolly Mr. Bridges are all doing the same thing—but they saw her before you did with those bad eyes of yours, so they didn't have to duck down so. This is just ridiculous at our age, Henry.

As his resort days went by, Henry gradually modified his initial judgment. Many of the guests, he grudgingly came to admit, did not pay the slightest attention to the marriage market. In fact, he gradually noted, confounded, how much he enjoyed himself. His dinner companions changed with each meal, by the resort's custom. He sat with intelligent men on vacation from interesting responsibilities, who voiced well-considered, thought-provoking opinions. Their wives were often gracious, cultured ladies. They appeared to find appealing his grave reserve, a reserve partly habit and partly clamped on himself fearful of revealing his exhilaration at such congenial and stimulating company. Guests as gauche and climbing as General Field were the exception, indeed the object of covert derision.

He appeared a little late the evening he was assigned to a table with Miss Coyner, timid Mr. Thaddeus Lynch, who agreed with everyone, and the dreaded General. He might have skipped dinner once he saw his table assignment, but he was hungry after a long walk. Henry took his seat just as the General had concluded new orders for her cousin; he heard only Miss Coyner's demurral. "No, Cousin Sukie, I'm not made for crusades. I'm happy minding my own little world." She avoided Henry's questioning eyes, but the General had worked up a head of steam that required release.

"Mis-ter Hollis. I was just *implo-o-ring* Miss Coyner to reinforce our campaign to isolate an interloper." She nodded, too energetically, toward a table near the garden doors.

His stomach growling, Henry had little patience. "Inner-loper? We orter guard the garden door? In or out? Ye think I orter git me a fireplace poker? Don' have no other weapon." He craned around the dining room. "Don' see no inner-loper yet. Crupin up like some painter? What he look like? Big's a ba'ar?"

"Surely, Mister Hollis, you *must* be aware. Miss Lorca there. I have it on excellent authority that Spanish ancestry does *not* explain the woman's dark complexion."

Pru was more than offended. *Damnation, man, this blob of blubber just exudes poison. Stomach can wait. Do something.*

Henry's eyes lingered on Miss Lorca, beautiful as ever, sharing animated conversation with other guests. "I dint know we hafta explain . . . her complexion, ye say? She don' look sick t'me. Light's not s'good, though. Mebbe ye'd better ax Mr. Abel an' the Cones sittin wit'er."

"That would serve no purpose, considering those men."

"Why, ma'am, I bet they see good. Better'n me with these specs. Must see real good. I heered tell thet either one'a them men could a-put this whole re-sort in his coat pocket with lotsa room left o'er. And thet young Abel she talkin at is s'pose t'take o'er from his daddy t'en-tire bus'ness. He cain't hardly do thet lessen he got real good eye."

"Mis-ter Hollis." She sounded as if his dim-wittedness surpassed belief. "This is not a question of eyes. Surely even a mountain farmer with so many strange cows must be aware that Cone is Cohen and Abel is Abelstein, no matter how much money they've made. They're . . ." She stopped abruptly. "We shall deal with them later. Right now our concern is Miss—that Lorca woman."

She turned to, or on, Mr. Lynch, who had the poor judgment to nod confirmation at Henry's appraisal of the Cone fortune. "Mister Lynch, surely *you* understand why that woman does not deserve to be here. I see she is about to walk in the garden. I for one can*not* enjoy the garden with her there. You and my dear cousin can perambulate without me—*if* you can appreciate *very dark* flowers."

Henry and Lynch rose as the General did; but Henry leaned close. "Be sartain t'check Genesis, ma'am."

She stared at him in hurried perplexity.

"In the Bible, ma'am," he flung at her formidable backside. "Summers in the Bible is thet story 'bout Cone n' Abel."

Excusing himself to Miss Coyner and Lynch, he sought cleaner air on the porch. There he imagined standing with Miss Lorca facing the General and her ilk. Miss Lorca became Carrie on his arm at the dining room door. He saw seated guests glance up in their customary covert appraisal of a new arrival. Would gatekeepers like the General glare at them, at her? He realized that he had not worried about Carrie for days.

He was just beginning to ponder the state of his mind when Chambliss Chambers appeared at the porch door, coming out to his customary rocker. Chambers, his stout cane at his side, often sat out there, apparently nursing a game leg. He usually sat seemingly half asleep, hat tipped over his eyes. Uncas knew a ruse: Chambers missed nothing. He seemed to find Henry compatible company. Henry dropped into the empty rocker beside Chambers, who nodded silent greetings as he lit his evening cigar.

Flashes of approaching lightning silhouetted the mountains. Miss Corcoran strolled by on the arm of Hubert Porter, who, the General reverently reported, personified Old Money. "Hope they pick up umbrellas. Don't want to drown," murmured Chambers as his eyes followed their backs.

Henry turned to him with a questioning look.

"Carry your nose so high, it can't help but fill up with rain water."

Henry developed a slight crinkle at his eyes. "Ye cain't see ground, so like to step into some meadow muffin thet stinks yer shoe."

Chambers almost smiled, ⌐   faced as he watched
Porter and Corcoran move ou⌐   was about to broach
Miss Lorca when Marilou, Chambe⌐.   ⌐   ⌐stled up and took an
adjacent rocker, so intent on a mission she ⌐ ⌐ld barely spare greeting
for Henry, much less find a seat for their daughter, awkward in her
early adolescence.

Marilou spoke at a discreet volume, but urgently. "Mister Chambers,
you know Mister Abel, and, I think, Mister Cone, too. I'll thank you to
tell them both, they should not be paying attention to that Lorca
woman."

Chambers turned toward her with a surprised, quizzical look.

She continued smoothly. "They're undermining our determination to
show that woman her African blood pollutes the atmosphere here and
is not welcome at this establishment."

Chambers blinked at her several times, slow as an old turtle, then
turned again to the mountains. "Miz Chambers, I don't figure to do
that."

"Mis-ter Chambers, you're balking me."

"Which I regret, my dear," he answered without apparent concern.
"But Abel and Cone are intelligent enough to notice that Miss Lorca is
surely the most beautiful and engaging single lady here. They're also
plenty old enough to judge people without my help."

"Just like a man," hissed his wife. "Count good looks and forget
everything else."

"A baseless allegation, my dear," drawled Chambers. He inspected his
cigar. "I might say, highly insulting allegation, if I didn't know you're
always a true lady, aren't you?" He gave her a prolonged, silent stare.
"Besides, in addition to her very good looks, Miss Lorca has always
acted ladylike that I've seen."

"How she *acts* and what she *is*," Marilou Chambers bit off the words,
"are two different things."

"Gen'ly, I measure the is from the acts," Chambers responded
impassively.

"Mis-ter Chambers. If you won't say something, I will."

Chambers had apparently anticipated this, for his answer came almost
a continuation of her sentence. "And about the time you do," there
was no hurry or change in his tone, "will be just 'bout the time we

pack up and go home for good to dear ole Eustis, Georgia, where the dogs can sleep in crossroads all afternoon, some days at least."

He exhaled a long stream of smoke nearly in her face. She fanned furiously.

"That horrible cigar . . . Mis-ter Chambers. . . I . . . That woman . . ." she sputtered, but apparently thought better of an open row on the porch. Without a glance at Henry, she rose and flounced off, daughter one step behind.

Chambers turned to Henry with a twisted smile. "Hollis, sometimes I envy your solitary state. Seems to me since the war our women have just gotten rabid. They can't let go. We men, we knew we fought as hard as we could, and saw with our own eyes that we got whipped. No shame in it when we gave it our best. Took the hate out of us."

While inspecting his cigar, he continued. "Marilou didn't see the war. Not until Sherman's men came through. Burned her father's warehouse. The secret warehouse with hoarded cotton appreciating every day. Now she's death on Yankees and nigrahs both."

He used his cigar as pointer. "She thinks the world of you, Hollis, despite her rudeness just now. For which I do apologize," he added out of the corner of his mouth. "But, damn, if you walked onto this sacred porch, and you had on your arm some woman she thought wasn't as white as this porch, she'd cut you dead. The women think they're the gatekeepers for this porch and everywhere else."

"The war didn't change as much as it should have." Henry's tone was neither a flaming declaration nor an interrogatory. He met Chambers' sharp look without a blink.

Chambers studied him in silence for long enough that Henry wondered which way, if at all, their exchange would go. "It was a long war." Henry recalled offering an arm when Chambers had hesitated at a step. "Gettysburg," he had murmured, accepting the aid.

Chambers continued after another silence. "The war did change how I see some things," Chambers finally allowed. "Boyhood friends and I volunteered right after Sumter—seems like centuries ago. Comrades in arms, you know, fighting for our Georgia home, all that romantic claptrap. Millville Bridge. You've never heard of it. We took terrible losses. Several of us were promoted quick to fill the grievous holes. Didn't take a week before my old friends turned tyrants. Sudden power did it. When I tried to reason with them, warn them, they couldn't even see what I was talking about." He carefully shaped his cigar ash.

"Little later I wrangled a short furlough. Someone had to clean up the godawful paper mess after my blessed mother died. At home I started watching the women. Damned if I didn't see the same thing as my old friends showed. *In my own house.* The women were so proud of being 'true southern ladies,' they couldn't see they had been corrupted by power, corrupted by owning slaves. Domestic despots everywhere you looked." He shook his head in despair.

"Even my beautiful little twin girls were picking it up. Bit by bit. I called 'em pinafore tyrants. See a black face—any black face—and they couldn't resist. Started acting like God. I figured we'd have to move abroad after the war to escape it." Chambers blew a long jet of blue smoke which hung along with silence in the air.

"Fever took both of them." Another cloud of smoke and silence. "You aren't shocked at my vicious attack on the true southern lady." It wasn't a question.

Henry looked at the mountains. "Years ago several New York girls taught me about southern ladies and their slaves—servants, they wanted to call 'em."

"You were damned lucky."

Henry added, "I didn't have Europe as a possibility. I tried mountain isolation instead, but it didn't work."

"How many generations, Hollis, until we get past this insanity?" demanded Chambers. "Three? Six? Never?"

He rose suddenly without farewell, took his cane and limped off into the shadows. "Dammit, dammit, dammit, dammit."

That night Henry had trouble sleeping. He debated leaving the resort in the morning. What good, though, would that do? He could not go around the dining room announcing to each table he was leaving because he didn't approve of their opinions. Apart from the zealous gatekeepers like Marilou Chambers and Sukie Field, he had no idea what most guests thought of Miss Lorca. Perhaps if he stayed he might share a table with Miss Lorca and let his presence declare his mind.

Gibbs was unsurprised when Henry intimated that assignment to Miss Lorca's table would be welcome. But no one seemed to notice the several times Henry was seated with her. His gesture was inadequate, but he was at a loss for more.

Sitting in his usual chair on the porch Chambers hailed Henry to apologize for leaving him so abruptly on the porch evening last. "I grieve for my twins."

Henry nodded. "I know that grief."

"A hard fellowship," Chambers got in before he was hailed by Eldon Lister, who wanted certain very specific details about Chambers' bank in Eustice.

Evenings later, Marilou Chambers again took a chair to join her husband and Henry as they enjoyed the evening air on the long porch. She turned unsmiling to Henry. "Mister Hollis, I see you were sitting with that Lorca woman at dinner. Probably Gibbs' assignment?"

"Miss Lorca? Yes indeed," Henry enthused, so Gibbs could not be blamed. "Miss Lorca is more adept at word play than anyone I've ever met. She can deliver clever puns quicker than I can remember them. Did you talk with her?"

"I did not." She sniffed. "Vaudeville tricks in addition to her questionable background."

"Why, Miz Chambers, you have a gift for language too. I admire minds so nimble as yours."

She shifted her address to her husband. "She's gone, Mister Chambers, even though you men refused to lift one finger to do what you should have." Triumph slipped into her tone. "We've rid the resort of that woman and her false pretenses."

Chambers slowly exhaled a long plume of blue smoke, then spoke languidly. "Before you take credit, Miz Chambers, you might talk to Gibbs. You would learn that Miss Lorca departed on the exact day she established when she arrived, not an hour before. And since Gibbs is fawning, supercilious, stupid, *and* oleanginous, you might also learn that the Abels checked out early." Another blue plume. "They're returning to Baltimore for a surprise social announcement." A pause and again a plume of cigar smoke. "Its import you may find disagreeable."

For a long moment Marilou Chambers looked as if she had been slapped. Then she narrowed her eyes. "I don't believe you."

"A fine example of conjugal trust, ma'am. What is our friend, Hollis here, to make of matrimony? Perhaps that's why he's not attached." He winked broadly at Henry.

"Never mind, Miz Chambers. It's your privilege to disbelieve, as well as to spread ill-founded gossip at odds with the religion you profess. But as you doubt, consult the obsequious Gibbs. He is the man to question. He loves to talk. What he loves most to talk about are matters he correctly assures you must be strictly confidential. Ask unctuous, indiscreet Gibbs."

"Mis-ter Chambers, you know I can't do that."

"And precisely why is that, dear?" Chambers inquired of his wife's retreating back.

Another blue cloud before he turned to Henry. "Hollis, sometimes I regret promising my dear old mother I'd never play poker. I do believe I'd flourish at poker."

AMID POTTED PALMS

Portraits of Colorful Figures From
A Famous New Orleans Inn, Recalled by Its Owner

Toussaint & Sons Printers
New Orleans

Chapter Eight: The General Manager

No sir, the chair is not claimed. Please have a seat. I shall be gratified by your company. I find myself alone this evening, quite alone. Allow me to introduce myself, sir. H. H. Gibbs. Yes sir, Horace Horatio Gibbs. People call me Gibbs. As you can see there from my card, sir, I am associated with the Blue Valley Sulphur Springs Resort Hotel in Tennessee, with the double n, s, *and* e.

But I am not here in New Orleans on business, sir. No, sir. I am seeking relaxation and respite. Relaxation and respite is always my goal in January when our resort is closed. Closed for the weather, for we are located high in the mountains of far eastern Tennessee.

Most salubrious. People come from all over the country to regain their health while they enjoy our magnificent mountain views. And no miasma. No miasma whatsoever. Our air is utterly pure, being of a superior elevation. Furthermore, the health benefits of our springs are well attested to. As a result we have a very large clientele, a very refined clientele, I assure you.

Of course there is the odd guest who doesn't fit the rule. Inevitably. For instance, I am at my usual post in the lobby when in walks an old man with a valise so worn you'd think he carried it all the way to California. And back. His collar. I wish you could have seen his collar. You have not beheld the like in twenty years. He should donate it. But even darkies would not wear something like that.

He isn't used to wearing it. He keeps running his finger inside to loosen it. Once he stretches his neck some, and I catch a glimpse of a scar clear across his throat. Clear across, sir. Gibbs, I say to myself, be careful of this man, very careful. This man may be one of those maiming mountain fighters one hears about.

In our Guest Register, he scrawls out the name of his hometown, a place I have never even heard of. I am at a loss. Happily, one of my staff knows that area and its residents very well, and is able to furnish me with abundant details about this individual. To maintain our standards, sir. We must be careful about the standing of guests—all strictly confidential, of course.

He inquires what entertainment is available at the resort. He sounds like a prosecuting attorney, complete with subpoena. Of course, I am pleasant and helpful. That is Gibbs. Always helpful and pleasant. It's the same when this man is cross-examining me most closely. I tell him about the healthful properties of our spring waters. It stinks: that is his only response. It may be slightly odiferous, but its powerful healing properties have no credit with this man. All he can say is, it stinks. So I begin describing our many other opportunities for diversion. From the look on his face, you'd think I am peddling rags and scrap.

The only time he perks up is when I mention dining. Gibbs intuits the explanation without a spoken word. He hasn't eaten since breakfast. His collar tells me why. Someone in that collar has never ridden the cars before and he wasn't quick enough to figure how to get a lunch there.

While we are conversing, our grand floor clock—standing in its special alcove, a prominent feature of our lobby, sir, and justly so—the clock strikes the hour, strikes it in all of its majestic solemnity. As I always tell our guests, if that clock's tolling doesn't speak to you of eternity, you just don't know reverence. You just don't.

Our new guest turns to look at it, as he should. I take the opportunity to inform him the clock is of the finest Philadelphia manufacture, purchased expressly for the Blue Valley lobby at immense expense. Our new guest turns back around to me and shrugs. Well sir, he says to me, well sir, guess I've got the granddaddy to that clock in my front hall. Except *my* clock strikes slower and lower. That's what he says to me. His exact words. Can you imagine such fabrication?

Perhaps, sir, you may be aware that among those of us who deal with the public, we occasionally bestow a secret sobriquet, a private sobriquet, on an unusual guest. A sobriquet, sir. A nickname, sir, a nickname. This man needs a sobriquet. For this man it could be Hayseed. Hayseed, it is.

I have no sooner gotten our Hayseed sent off to his room when a new guest, a female guest, parades in from the omnibus. This guest is very rotund indeed. Her circularity is so pronounced that it strains its circumference. She possesses, however, only a very small head. She keeps turning it this way and that to spy around her. Honestly, when I see her the only thing I can think of is a huge battleship and an admiral perched way up in the crow's nest, I understand sailors call it, though this crow could not possibly fly.

She is halfway across the lobby before I can see she is in convoy, as I believe nautical men use the expression. She is in company with another lady, a lovely young lady, with thick blonde hair, an enviable golden crown. Alongside the ponderous battleship wallowing in the ocean swell, she is a trim yacht, a very pretty yacht slicing through the waves.

When I was a boy, my uncle owned a rowboat I loved. He called her—a boat of course must always be a she—he called her Miss C. So that's what I call the Admiral's cousin, Miss C. One glance at them, and someone as experienced as Gibbs knows. The Admiral in her battleship has given armed escort to the Miss C, ensuring she reaches the resort safely, where she is to rendezvous with eligible gentlemen of the sort not available in such abundance back in dull old Nashville. And the Miss C sails only reluctantly, though not entirely devoid of hope.

The little convoy steams off to their rooms. A dilemma now challenges me. What table am I to assign the Admiral in the dining room? Such a person I strongly suspect I must not inflict on other guests. Then my eye happens to fall on the Guest Book in front of me. I notice our Hayseed's name. Truly, it is God's finger writing on the wall, H-A-Y-Of course! I put our Hayseed and the Admiral and Miss C at the same table.

To make a foursome I solve yet another festering problem. Barton, the Richmond drummer. As a sales reward in his company he won seven days—that is six nights—at the resort. You may be assured I never, ever go around telling guests about this, even though it *is* a tall feather in our cap to have a well-known Richmond company select Blue Valley as a prize. But Blue Valley is not a drummers' hotel. Never will be a drummers' hotel as long as Gibbs is in charge, I assure you. What a wonderful quartet I now form: all my odd guests at the same table to entertain each other—or not—their very first night.

I am sure our Hayseed will depart shortly. He will break his reservation. Against our stated policy. We ignore the revenue loss, sir.

We desire only satisfied guests. However some stubbornness on his part intervenes. He stays on and thusly becomes part of new developments. Developments most unusual.

One such development, sir, is an amusing episode with the Admiral and the Hayseed. Quite humorous, if I do say so. One evening I am walking in the garden at dusk. It's my customary practice. Knowledge of Gibbs' presence assures mothers that proprieties will always be observed at Blue Valley. Always proprieties. Of course one must exercise some discretion about what one sees in the garden and what one doesn't see. That is why Gibbs, and Gibbs alone, does the evening perambulation, regular as a faithful sentry. Only incidentally, it is also fine relaxation after the rigors of the day.

As I stroll in the garden I hear nearby sounds of apparent feminine distress. Just when I am hastening expeditiously to lend all the assistance at my command, I see, in tableaux as it were, the Admiral on the ground and Drummer Barton and Miss C bending over her solicitously. She is moaning most piteously, having tripped and fallen. Hayseed, who has apparently also heard the cries, comes rushing up from the opposite direction.

Something says to me, Gibbs, the Admiral has ample assistance. Something tells me, Gibbs, stay back and see what eventuates. So I watch in the shadows from a little distance. Barton and Hayseed set to work. By prodigious effort they right the capsized battleship. Once upright, the Admiral clings to Hayseed's arm, to regain her sealegs. But a curious thing happens. Instead of also taking Barton's arm as extra assurance, she orders him to follow with Miss C.

The battleship proceeds slowly, buffeted by any wave. Listing badly. Poor Hayseed must keep the battleship afloat, taxing his capacity. Finally they reach an intersection of paths. The Admiral sends up signal flags. She commands Barton and Miss C go ahead. They must summon medical aid to await her arrival. She directs them to the Circle Path.

That is the wrong way, of course. I see they will take much, much longer than necessary to get to the lobby. Gibbs considers intervening with accurate directions, but, uncertain where we are headed, Gibbs delays a bit. Barton and Miss C disappear on the very circuitous Circle Path.

You can imagine my astonishment now, sir. The Admiral stops. The Admiral straightens up. She stands without Hayseed's aid. She puts her dress to rights. She pats Hayseed's arm. Thank you, she says to him, thank you so much for your help. My cousin, confides the Admiral, is awkward and shy. She needs to be alone with Barton, but she doesn't know how to arrange that. So I did it for her.

Gibbs, I say to myself, Gibbs, what a fox is this Admiral, a clever old fox. Miss C and drummer Barton will take an eternity on the meandering Circle Path.

But! There is a *double* joke! The Admiral thinks she is tricking Barton and Miss C. The real joke is instead on the Admiral. Yes, on the *Admiral.* She has the wrong man for Miss C. Barton is only a drummer. Not a penny in his pocket. Not an ambition in his heart. He dreams only of idling with a sweet young thing and a drink at his elbow. As they say, a Bird and a Bottle. Barton's daily goal, his yearly goal, his life goal: a Bird and a Bottle. The minute the Admiral tries to collar him, Barton will abscond.

He does exactly that, even sooner than I predict. The very next morning. Before breakfast. Gone on the early omnibus for the first cars back to Richmond. I hear him tell Miss C—she is down well before breakfast to see him off—he tells her he is called away on urgent business. I say to myself, Gibbs, his urgent business is escaping the Admiral, that's what his urgent business is.

Miss C is disconsolate about his departure. Even Hayseed notices. He, too, is out early as if to milk the hogs and feed his valuable cows. In this instance, he is to take a buggy up to the Old Baldy Lookout. The most sublime views from there, sir. I always tell our guests, it is just as sermon in itself to go there. If you cannot recognize God's handiwork from Old Baldy, why, you just can't. Hayseed observes that Barton has departed. He knows the Admiral is still on the invalid list. With brash temerity, he invites Miss C to join him to see Old Baldy!

Well. The next thing you know, Hayseed elects the rowboat excursion down the river to the falls. A most picturesque excursion. A most picturesque falls. I always tell my guests, if you cannot be awed by the thunder of that water coursing over the rock, why then you are simply beyond awe. Simply beyond. Our river trip is a whole-day trip. For an extra charge. It is an excellent moneymaker for the resort, if I do say so. Our Hayseed takes the trip—with a passenger: Miss C!

By then the Admiral is getting much the wiser. She recovers from her damaged ankle, a miracle worthy of a pilgrimage to some holy place in Spain. She requires me to put Hayseed at other tables for dinner. But from her crow's nest, the Admiral has locked the barn door too late. She finally sees what is perfectly obvious to Gibbs from the very day they arrived: Hayseed has always had fantastical designs on Miss C.

First he shoulders aside Barton. Then he outmaneuvers the Admiral. So he has the quarry defenseless.

The next day he takes Miss C for a trip up to Kings Knob. Another sermon in itself, sir. They leave while the Admiral is searching for Mr. Carlyle, I believe. By the middle of the afternoon the Admiral has ascertained from assiduous cross-examination of certain of our staff the whereabouts of Miss C. By late afternoon the Admiral is steaming up the veranda. The Admiral is steaming down the veranda. Mr. Carlyle is quite forgotten. She keeps sharp lookout on the road to Kings Knob. The sun goes below the yardarm. She sits. She stands. She sits. But always she is keeping a lookout on the road to Kings Knob.

Gibbs, I say to myself, observe with strict attention. You must not miss the Great Sea Battle. In fact that deduction does not require my customary perspicacity. Even less alert guests guess the same. Word spreads, for the Admiral has achieved a certain notoriety, shall we say, a substantial notoriety she has brought on herself by her improprieties, sir. More and more guests come out to sit on our renowned porch instead of entering the dining room to enjoy our usual sumptuous repast.

Some think they discern the clop-clop of a distant horse. Conversation dies proportionate to the nearing sound of what may be Hayseed's buggy. All eyes fasten onto the road. Hayseed's buggy materializes in the dusk. He reins in. The porch is silent.

Hayseed no more than hands Miss C down from her seat than the Admiral orders battle stations. She attacks. She fires her heaviest guns. Boom! She is astonished! Boom! She is scandalized! Boom! His failing as a gentleman! Boom! His threat to a young lady's reputation! Boom! Negating her devoted chaperonage! Boom! How dare he!

Withering fire, I tell you, simply withering. Hot and heavy. The Admiral pours it on. But there is no answering fire, sir, none whatsoever. Finally Hayseed lets fly a single sniper shot.

Cousin Sukie, he says, you must be careful of your ankle.

That's all Hayseed says. No more. And so quickly, many of our guests on the verandah miss it: What did he say? Too far away to make out what he said. Didn't hear.

He hands Miss C up to the porch and goes back to retrieve a bundle from the buggy. The Admiral follows Miss C into the lobby. How dare he, she thunders, how dare he call me Cousin Sukie?

Then the Admiral turns. She turns on me! Gibbs, how could you possibly have let a farmer like that into your resort? You have failed your duty, Gibbs. Failed your duty to your guests.

It is all so sudden. So unjustified. I admit I am taken temporarily off guard by such an unwarranted attack. I am gathering myself to return a scathing rebuke, justifiably scathing, sir, when I am cruelly denied my date in court. Denied without redress. Duty precludes a response because I am needed without delay in our dining room. The press of guests coming in simultaneously from our porch once the Great Sea Battle is over requires my presence. My fate is most unfair, but, as always, I put duty first. That is what people expect from Gibbs.

Our Hayseed departs the next day, as scheduled. When he comes down to the lobby he is again carrying that disgraceful valise. I try to express some pleasantries as best I am able. I motion to his valise. Well sir, I say, you travel light, sir. But he shakes his head. No, Gibbs, he says to me, this old valise is heavy compared to a young lady's baggage.

I think that is a very strange thing to say, don't you?

QUACHASEE
WHC

Excursions, naps, the dining room. Life at the Blue Valley Sulphur Springs Resort flowed ever on, though at the rate of sorghum molasses in winter. Departing guests exited reluctantly. Arriving guests entered expectantly. For each arrival, the General, as authoritative as an R. G. Dun agent, offered a detailed financial summary over dinner. To offset the bad taste she left, Henry wandered about the large garden with its arbors, fountains, statuary, and paved walks—the only resort feature he wished he could take home, that pleasant garden.

There one evening he came upon the General feigning an injury to bring Barton and Miss Coyner together. Unashamed, she even admitted it outright to Henry. She added, "Oh, Mr. Hollis. I owe you an apology. I secretly suspected your five-legged cows was a fable you mountain people tell city visitors. But I have been observing closely, Mr. Hollis, and I see you are correct! Whenever there are mules, you do not see five-legged cows."

Second thoughts tempered Henry's amusement, especially sympathy for Miss Coyner, humiliated daily by her cousin's ignorant forwardness. Miss Coyner and he, Henry decided, shared the same predicament, urged to Blue Valley by well-meaning friends. Granted, he could enjoy his stay much more than she. What must it be like to face the General's public grotesqueries here every day, morning to night?

The question recurred the morning on the porch when he witnessed Miss Coyner say hasty farewells to a valise-carrying Barton, who all the while peered nervously about like a rabbit, then hopped into the omnibus, closed the door hastily, to slink back in his seat as he disappeared down the hill in small dust spirals.

She turned, saw Henry, and explained her presence at the early hour. "Mister Barton was called back to Richmond on urgent business and cannot return. I'm so sorry for him. Cousin Sukie and Mister Barton and I were planning to go up to Old Baldy today. But I am now a general without troops. I must look after Cousin Sukie. She is in such discomfort. Seeing Old Baldy was high on my, our, list."

On impulse Henry pointed to Clinell, just driving over from the barns. "Looks like he's bringing the buggy I reserved to go up to Old Baldy myself. Miss Coyner, the Blue Mountain doctor will take good care of Cousin Sukie.. Why don't you escape a bit?" After very little urging, he handed her up, and they set off, Henry smiling to himself as they passed the front door: Gibbs's face did in fact bear an uncanny resemblance to a mule taking medicine.

Once committed to the trip, Miss Libby, for that is what she told him to call her, was pleasant company, much less reserved than at the dinner table. She told him of growing up in Nashville, her only companion her father, an elderly man already at her birth. She described her late father, Judge Herodotus Lucius Coyner, whom she admired unreservedly. She asked many questions about Henry's farm, something needing explanation for one reared in the city.

Chatting comfortably, they reached Old Baldy Lookout surprisingly soon. After they absorbed the views, Henry retrieved the hamper packed for him in the resort kitchen. Miss Libby divided it deftly, worrying his share was too little. As she tidied up wrappings, he poked around in the buggy.

"What are you looking for, Mister Hollis?" she called.

"Livery man said he'd throw in a loose tarpaulin in case it rains." Henry pointed to large thunderheads spreading overhead. Before the brief deluge they found cover under a rock overhang, using the tarpaulin to sit on. The limited projection of the ledge above forced them to sit rather close together, but Miss Libby feared he'd get wet, then chilled, then ill, his vacation ruined. When the rain passed, she rose with a smile to help repack. Her only artifice, if artifice, was in revealing no artifice.

Back at the resort, she went up to dress for dinner. At the desk Henry asked Gibbs to seat him at Miss Coyner's table that evening. He braced for at least a swallowed smirk, but saw no muscle move in the man's face. "I trust Gen . . . ah, I trust Miz Field may be joining us as well."

Miss Libby appeared, however, without Cousin Sukie. To Henry's polite inquiry, Miss Libby blushed with an embarrassed laugh. "To tell you the truth, Mister Hollis, I did not stop in to check on her. I'm afraid I'm savoring my freedom. Cousin Sukie is so ready to get me married off to some young man. Well, she has such a good heart. That

Mister Barton was pleasant, but he boasted to me he never read a book through. And I—"

"And you're a reader. I suspected so from your speech."

She laughed again, though ruefully. "Stilted, isn't it? Cousin Sukie always tells me not to talk that way, but it's hard after a girlhood of many book friends and few children friends."

"Have you read *Great Expectations*, Miss Libby?"

She had, though without tears. As the others at their table were engrossed in each other, Henry and Miss Libby debated Dickens amiably through dinner. Rising after dessert, Miss Libby confessed, "I am duty bound to tell Cousin Sukie of Mister Barton's departure." She paused, her eyes scanning the room. "That, however, will precipitate her appearance down here tomorrow, going about like a roaring lion to do good. She will pick out another young man, like Mister Wilder there, who makes such silly jokes and has those awful sideburns."

She again glanced across the room, then quickly lowered her head. "Oh dear, he's coming this way. Oh dear. I'm trapped."

Henry saw resigned despair on her face. "Miss Libby, my arm." She took it automatically. He wheeled briskly with her, cut Wilder off decisively, and headed to the river walk at a pace not to be mistaken as a meander in search of company. His third visit, but this time, with Miss Libby at his side, it seemed more attractive than previously. She pointed out picturesque views and stayed ever alert for protruding roots hazardous in the fading light.

The next day Henry went alone to Kings Knob Lookout, a tiresomely long drive for an attraction, he concluded, not worth the effort. That evening, from a distance he observed General Field at the dining room door leaning on a cane, surveying the room for quarry. Henry knew that look from shooting parties. She lacked only a good hunting dog.

He found he was assigned again to the General's table, but she said little to him over dinner, too preoccupied with plotting range and trajectory for various tables. She hardly put a spoon in her dessert before she rose, beckoning to her cousin. "Come, my dear. I want to introduce you to Mister Thistle. He just arrived today, and I fear his waiter was much more efficient than our incompetent boy, whom I shall have to report to Gibbs. Come, dear, right now."

Miss Coyner blushed deeply, and Henry saw in her eyes the same look as in a snared rabbit's. Instinctively he rose between the two women, standing very straight to be as tall over General Field as possible. "You must pardon me, Gen, ah, Miz Field, but Miss Coyner promised to accompany me in the, in the garden before dusk. She is curious, I believe, about how certain plants, ah, achieve reproduction."

General Field blinked confusion. "Promised? Reproduction?"

Henry extended his arm. When Miss Libby took it, he nodded to General Field. As he remembered from their first dinner, she deferred instinctively to male authority.

"But . . . but . . . Mister Hollis, when will she . . .?"

His elbow a secure hold on Miss Libby's hand, he led her off at a smart pace. As they reached the garden door she brought her free hand to his arm as well. "Mister Hollis," she murmured, "that was the kindest thing you could have done for me. I admire your quick wit. I dreaded the evening, and instead I have you." She paused at the door. "Oh, Mister Hollis, I am confounded at my apparent presumption. In my confusion I did not see where my tongue carried me."

He tightened his arm to keep her hand engaged and did not look back. Neither, he noticed, did she. After a walk out at a quick pace, they drifted back through the garden to rocking chairs on the long porch. A chilling breeze came off the mountains. Miss Libby slipped away and returned with a throw for Henry's shoulders and a cup of hot chocolate. She smiled at his thanks. "That's little enough for your gallant rescue of a maiden in distress." Folding her skirt under her, she sat down on the steps by his feet. Unconsciously he expected her to lean against his knees. She sat up straight. "I must conjure some equally clever stratagem to avoid my fate tomorrow. I must have something for Cousin Sukie."

"Well, maybe you could tell her," Henry began ticking off possible alternatives, "that you're going to another knob top that Gibbs touts. Or you're to play some games of shuttlecock. Or perhaps to go down the river to the falls. Boat down, wagon ride back, the trip takes most of a day, according to Gibbs."

"The river and falls trip. What a wonderful excuse. Gibbs urged that on us when we checked in. A boat trip would be a perfect excuse for me. Sukie is mortally afraid of water, won't go near boats. I cannot tell you how grateful I am, now to be twice rescued."

Miss Libby paused. "But if I tell her that," she mused aloud, "I must have in mind a good place to hide the whole day."

Henry recognized too late the terrain of Battle Hollow. "Why, in the boat; they all seat two."

"You'd actually take me in the boat?"

After the disappointment of Kings Knob, he had weighed the river excursion without decision. "My pleasure, Miss Libby."

"I've read about boats for years, but have never been on one."

"A parasol will be useful against the sun, I think. We should leave from the landing at nine."

∾

Complete with parasol and large handbag, she was waiting before nine. Henry decided she told the truth about her inexperience, for she attempted to board in such lubberly fashion the boat boy's grin widened in eager anticipation of capsize. Another wailing woman whose waterlogged dress revealed her legs and clung tight to her bosom.

"Wait!" Henry took command. "First the parasol. Thank you. Now the bag. Thank you. Now in you go." He disregarded her extended hand, grasped her waist, and half-lifted her to the stern seat. As she arranged her things, he sat midship, took the oars, and signaled shove-off to the disappointed boy.

"Whither our course, Captain?" Miss Libby cried merrily.

"Only two choices." As a test he gripped the oars firmly and rowed hard upstream. It required strict attention and unflagging effort. Fifty yards, and he shipped his oars. The boat swung around so forcefully its gunwales nearly shipped water; they saw the boy signaling to go downstream. Henry let the current take charge.

Miss Libby, who grasped his experiment, nodded. "How much less work it takes to follow the river flow."

Henry rowed only enough to stay clear of snags and sandbars. Miss Libby, under the parasol, fished in her bag and, with Henry's consent, read aloud from Longfellow. At a well-screened spot on shore, he pulled to the bank and told her he would stay in the boat, but she might like to stretch her legs. She gave him a grateful look, and did not shrink when twice again he took her waist to help her out and back. As they drifted on she doled out lunch from the basket the resort provided, sitting very still, attentive to his needs.

"Mister Hollis, I owe you much. I did not conceive this could be so peaceful or the water so clear. We see everything on the bottom as we slide past. We are swept silently, swiftly, inexorably along, always ignorant of what lies around the next bend."

Henry smiled tolerantly.

"Too poetical for a sensible man, I'm sure. All right, in the novel, we catch on a snag, capsize, and I drown in a foot of water to universal grief. Or . . . I know: a sudden freshet sweeps us over the rushing falls from which only you swim out. So all across the country, singers with more zeal than talent hammer on mistuned pianos a terrible, lachrymose song, Libby O'er the Falls."

"Why are you always the victim?"

"Because in novels that's what happens to women."

"And in real life?"

"In real life, as far as I can see, nothing very dramatic happens, unless you unwisely choose to row upstream. You adjust your expectations to the speed of the current."

At the landing, now well practiced, they reversed the boarding drill to disembark, and walked the path to the foot of the falls. Transfixed by the water thundering down, Miss Libby shook her head. "Mister Hollis," she shouted above the roar. "I find I prefer waterfalls only in novels. In real life, I am a silent-current person."

The wagon back to the resort carried other excursionists, all of them apparently—too-apparently—courting couples. Miss Libby seemed much ill at ease, and said little. Henry was content with silence.

Back at the resort, Henry lingered on the porch, trying to organize his thoughts. One, it was stimulating to be with a variety of people again. Spooks was right after all. Two, socializing became so easy when all the guests sitting down were white and all the waiters standing up were colored. What a relief not to be somewhere in between, always trying to foresee consequences. Maybe old age loomed. Maybe he should ship oars and go with the current. Three, how pleasant again to be looked after by an appreciative, sensitive woman. Four, Miss Libby was intelligent, if sometimes a bit pedantic. And, five, quite attractive, with trim ankles, a slim waist, and a firm high bosom.

He heard Spooks ask, "And where, old friend Uncas, do your five points lead?"

"Gotta track the Hurons to find out, I guess," he answered as he watched the beginning of the early evening porch promenade.

When Miss Libby came down for dinner and saw Henry sitting on a lobby divan, she was still flustered. "It has been a trying day for you, Mister Hollis. I do want to apologize for the return from the falls. I had no expectation that after all your kindnesses, you would be subjected to such disagreeable company."

Henry looked at her amused, "Why, any farmer knows whales and elephants must circle 'round. Buffalo, too." Seeing her confusion, he changed the subject to avoid explanation. "Is Cousin Sukie's ankle still bothering her?" he inquired.

"Cousin Sukie is put out with me." Apparently Miss Libby fumed from a recent argument. "I say I am enjoying myself here, and she says I am wasting my time on—" she stopped abruptly, coloring.

He finished her sentence, "on a man too elderly to be eligible?"

Miss Libby's blush deepened. "Mister Hollis, my impulsive candor about my cousin's opinion, only my cousin's opinion, is now a great embarrassment to me. She takes time from her own family to be here, and means well, I'm sure."

Henry rose. "Miss Libby, we're early for dinner. It's cooler to wait in the little gazebo at the edge of the garden." As they walked through the garden she stammered, "Mister Hollis, I writhe at my indiscretion," and fell silent.

At the gazebo, she began again. "Mister Hollis, my indiscreet tongue has so embarrassed me. My cousin Sukie—"

"She's right, ain't she? Hollis *is* old enough to be your father. You could ask whether you would marry him anyway."

"Mister Hollis, I am . . . astonished . . . and . . . flattered, . . . really . . . and . . ." Miss Libby began slowly, then let her words dangle as she looked over the valley below. Then, without turning her head toward him, "Yes, Mister Hollis, I will marry you."

Henry felt a brief pang at his "would" and her "will." He felt the river current's force. The boat spun around. He shipped his oars. He let the current carry him inexorably to his fate. As she seemed to expect, he bussed her cheek. Then she took his arm and went in with him to find their respective tables for dinner.

Early the next afternoon, as Cousin Sukie searched the far end of the porch for Mr. Thistle, Henry accepted his buggy from Clinell at the barn, drove briskly in, stopped but a moment at the porch steps to hand Miss Libby smartly up. He tipped the horse lightly with the whip and they were gone. Cousin Sukie still searched.

Henry drove again up to Kings Knob Lookout. The way was shorter and view better than he recalled. As they looked out over the successive ridges before them, Miss Libby put her mind at ease by verifying that Mister Hollis was a Christian, long active in his Lutheran congregation, that he drank spirituous liquors only sparingly, never gambled.

He wrote out the law firm address for John Patterson Bright in Knoxville should some cousin, perhaps also in law, think it best to inquire about him. He said she must keep her property in her own name, and described his more-than-satisfactory debt repayment progress. He drew rough sketches of Tulips, specifying Audie Ann's quarters, describing in detail his beloved sister's burdens. Other than Audie Ann's area, he said, she could redecorate Tulips as she saw fit, assuming reasonable economy.

She listened with strict attention. When he finished and asked what else she might want to know about him, she shook her head. "You are admirably forthcoming, Mister Hollis. A woman could not ask for more."

After a pause, her tone became rueful. "You must see I am far from a romantic person, Mister Hollis. I received your proposal with . . . nothing short of amazement . . . and gratitude, but I confess I did not distinguish the pealing bells many novels intimate ladies in my position hear."

"Well," inquired Henry, "if Miss Libby did not hear pealing bells, what *did* Miss Libby hear?"

"I heard voices, Mister Hollis. Oh, that makes me sound demented, doesn't it? I should say I remembered voices, like my father's voice and how I enjoyed talking with him over dinner. I also remembered my cousin Hazel's voice back in Nashville with her everlasting instructions about what to say at her dinner parties so I am more marriageable. And Sukie's voice evaluating different men here, and how wrong I thought she was about all of them, including you."

She hesitated, then continued. "I certainly remembered your voice, from the first evening we arrived. I'm sure you have no recollection. That evening I was overwhelmed by the realization I had made a great mistake, as I so often do. I realized I should never have listened to Sukie. She had painted such a picture of the people we would meet. I was dubious. Then we sat down with Mister Barton and he proved me right. How limited a man."

She fiddled nervously with ribbons hanging from her hat. "Mister Barton talked for both of us, so all I had to do was nod or shake my head. I had one ear free to listen to you and Sukie. I was amazed to hear you tell the most hilarious tales about cows. I had thought only humorists in books could spin such yarns. But you: one story after another. You seemed to have an unlimited repertoire of tales."

"They were pretty ordinary," Henry protested.

"Maybe to you, but I found them enormously entertaining. I wanted to laugh out loud. In fact I did, to my great embarrassment."

Henry's polite attention became a grin of memory retrieved. "Not choking on spicey hot appetizers?"

Libby's confession was smiling. "Not the appetizers. Thank the Blue Valley Resort for its oversize napkins or I would have had no cover."

She was back at her hat ribbon, but continued earnestly. "I assure you I was so grateful to be amused, even if I had to hide it. It was such a disappointment when the waiter brought our food. Possibly you have noticed, eating is very important to Sukie."

"Hog happy in swill," murmured Henry.

Libby appeared not to hear. Perhaps she was apprehensive about the confession she now felt compelled to make. "I must not be truly a kind person, Mister Hollis, for I'm afraid I enjoyed how you made fun of Sukie without her realizing it. So later, instead of falling asleep in tears at my terrible mistake, I fell asleep laughing at your stories. That's what I heard instead of pealing bells, Mister Hollis. I hope it does not disqualify me."

"Miss Libby," said Henry after a long pause, "you have before you your equivalent in the romantic department. Perhaps two injured halves can make nearly one whole person. I—"

Miss Libby interrupted him earnestly. "Mister Hollis, I am inexperienced in the world, but from my reading I gather that at this point in intimate conversation, a man seeking a woman's hand feels obligated to regretfully confess whatever were his former attachments. I have always considered such confessions deplorable, and unlikely to contribute to conjugal happiness. Do you not agree?"

Henry looked at her in surprise, then continued with a grin. "Miss Libby, you can't back out when Barkus is willing. When do we wed?" Miss Libby ventured that long engagements seemed inexplicable, and a showy wedding in no way to her taste. Henry pronounced himself of exactly like mind. They soon settled on a fortnight hence in Nashville. She touched Henry's cheek gently several times as she spoke. It was for Henry a sensation so familiar and so missed that when she rose restless from their boulder seat, he stood too and took her hand.

Dusk fell on their way home. Covered by the deepening shadows, Miss Libby broke the silence with false starts. "Mister Hollis, you are aware that I have lived a very sheltered and solitary life so far. . . . Not only was I an only child, but my mother died when I was very young. . . . I have not had many girl friends or woman friends I could discreetly consult on certain matters. . . . I have read a good deal . . . I know that many matters are not discussed in the books accessible to me. . . . Perhaps it would have been easier had my father's library been that of a physician rather than of a jurist."

"Miss Libby," he demanded, "what on earth are you talking about?"

She swallowed hard. "Well, as a single lady, I know I am woefully ignorant of the, of the physical side of marriage." Another hard swallow. "And what I want to say is that I will be so grateful if you exercise your exemplary patience in teaching me what I need to know to be a truly satisfactory wife, on the physical side, I mean."

They trotted along in silence, both looking straight ahead. Overhanging trees cast deeper shadows. "Mister Hollis," Libby faltered at last. "Have I been so terribly indiscreet as to disgust or shock you?" Her voice faded. "I thought I should always . . . be candid . . . with . . . you." She ended hardly above a whisper.

Henry turned and kissed her full on the mouth. She gave a little gasp as he turned away to slow the horse from trot to walk. When he turned back, her lips responded immediately, and she put her hand over his. She followed his hands without resistance as they moved from her waist to her breasts.

When, after a lengthy interval, he gave attention to the horse, he spoke matter-of-factly. "That's a good plan. All I ask is that when we are together at home alone, I'd like you to be covered, not upholstered. The rest of it, given your candor, we can make up as we go along, if that's agreeable." He felt her assenting nod at his side.

By the time they saw the resort, the evening porch lantern ritual was nearly over, the glow revealing an unusual number of guests still in rockers. Then Henry recognized the General's elephantine figure—her arm high completed the silhouette by resembling a searching trunk—laboriously descending the porch steps. She was on him even as he handed Libby out of the buggy. Her attack's volume and ferocity amused him, but, aware of the audience in rocking chairs, he tried to resist retaliatory urges.

The General was far beyond caution. Her voice as she followed Libby inside carried clearly in the summer evening air. "Gibbs should have told me. That's his duty here. He should have known: that man was not fit for polite society from the time he tried to trick me about painters. How dare that man call me Cousin Sukie? Just tell me that, Libby Coyner."

Even in the silence the answering voice sounded faint, receding.

The General boomed again. "*Marry* him? Marry *him*? Two weeks? Remember your trousseau! . . . It's . . . He's . . . IMPOSSIBLE."

❧

Back at Tulips, Henry made a point to visit Lipschultz & Son Clothing to refresh his wardrobe. On the day appointed, he appeared in Nashville. Henry stood with Libby before her uncle, yet another Judge Coyner. Shortly he carried away marriage documents tucked in a new valise. He carried away receipts for cartage of crates and barrels. He carried away a bride.

Plowing with Greek, My Life
HL Hollis

Tulips, February 5, 1939

Yesterday my sister Crotia came all the way over the mountain to visit with me. Her company buoyed my spirits, for I was a little down.

Today, my brother Bill, William Hollis, M.D., gave me his medical once-over, ignoring my grumbles about his professional inscrutability. After his exam, over coffee, he smothered my complaints by marveling about the changes in his practice wrought by the telephone, recalling the primitive wire communication he and I once set up between the house and the barn.

As further exercise in such nostalgia I reminded him of the time a magazine article on medical education prompted my idealization of autopsies. A crow, whose insatiable curiosity led to swift end in old Ben's snare, provided our corpse. With board and purloined knives, I started in, Bill my assistant. Before long I assisted Bill. Further dissection and I said I needed some fresh air outside. He looked up bewildered. "But HL, we're already outside."

From my earliest years I was familiar, if a little queasily, with hog butchering. But intensive, prolonged exploration of once-living bodies was somehow beyond me. Thus terminated my last dissection.

We both read avidly, but he snorted at my preferences. "Why don't you read science instead of only fiction?" We both learned Latin, but typically I needed a tutor; he absorbed it solitarily out of scientific curiosity.

In point of fact Bill knows I attempt these reminiscences. I believe he approves, though he fears I give excessive credence to Crotia's romanticizing the past. He alluded to that yesterday. I anticipated his customary rejection of Crotia's "vapors," but he selected a different tack. "Crotia can talk all day about our parents, but it never occurs to her to ask why a young woman would need a father figure so badly she'd marry one. Or to ask how a man that old sired so many offspring."

Prior to that instant, his questions occurred to me no more than to Crotia (something I did not confess). In consequence I temporized; I theorized most children unconsciously assume they issue from immaculate conception. I feared again sliding from primary investigator to assistant; soon I would find it essential to break off for fresh air. I did some fast arithmetic. "He was fifty-five at my birth. That doesn't seem utterly superhuman."

"And seventy-four when Lowe arrived." Bill consistently bested me doing sums. "That's older than you are, HL."

I inquired of my learned brother how he explained this.

"Human reproduction requires a fertile couple, tumescence, penetration, the ejaculation of viable sperm, and subsequent connection with a viable egg."

When I thanked him for that valuable insight, he relented, barely. "You remember that ornate, freestanding mirror that used to be in their bedroom? Near six feet tall. Dory has it now."

In point of fact, I do recall that Victorian monument, complete with its obsolete candle stands. Father commissioned it of Herr Schmitt, had specified its design in unusual detail. (Herr Schmitt also fabricated the elaborate bedstead in their room, but that is a different story.) Even without Bill's prompting, I could place the mirror in that bedroom, connected by a doorway to Father's office.

Bill inquired if I ever noticed lines of sight. From Father's chair at his desk in the office, you could look through the door into the bedroom, and, in the reflection of the mirror, see Mama's big wardrobe .

I shrugged off such obscure, or I should say, reflective trivia.

Bill, however, persisted in a way I should have noticed. "I tumbled to that when I read somewhere about angles of incidence and was testing it out. One day I moved the mirror to experiment with a different angle. The next day it was back as always. So I started changing it regularly. The longest it stayed where I put it was seventy-two hours."

I considered that a real puzzle.

"So did I, at age ten," Bill assented. Coffee fortified, he took his leave.

Meditation on angles of incidence still preoccupied me when Dory kindly visited later. Rashly I admitted to her I never previously considered our parents in biological terms. She bestowed on me her Sibling Pity Look, consistently her reaction when I am dense.

"You don't remember," she asked, "that every day at the end of her work after supper, Mama always, without fail, changed clothes?"

Of course I remember. For evenings she always changed into a sort of loose dress. It was her leisure costume after a day's labor in the household.

"You noticed that under that dress she never wore a corset?"

I confessed my inobservation.

"Boys," she regarded me with the Sibling Pity Look.

To save face, I casually reminded Dory that Father had observed his fifty-sixth birthday when she was conceived.

"But remember Mama was twenty-four," Dory immediately replied.

I told her that conception at twenty-four seemed hardly remarkable to me.

Sibling Pity appeared yet again. "HL, don't be a prude. Surely you remember Caroline at twenty-four in your bed?"

I do. Well enough that here I think it wise to terminate this discussion, whether to the relief, frustration, or amusement of my great-grandchildren, I cannot know.

QUACHASEE
WHC

Tulips and Ginners Ford welcomed Mister Hollis's new wife variously. Curiosity was mixed with relief that a mistress of Tulips properly completed the town's social order. Men were pleased she was pretty; women, that she was not beautiful. Both remarked on her youth.

Old timers on the Mercantile's porch chewed and spat and chewed and nodded agreement with Clinton Tuxen, the sage who by seniority occupied the chair once rocked by Lem Shetcliffe. "I dunno, but some'a y'all orta go up t'Tulips an check thet wail thar. Sompin funny in thet thar warter they drinkin. Gits them Hollis men de-rail. Firs' ole Samuel marry thet young Sarah when he dint need nary third wife nohow, an hit kilt him. Then his son Sam alwuz want t'take his young female sarvants backside up—mebbe got use' t'hit 'cause his woman's frontside so damn homely—and hit kilt *him*. An now the las' son, he brung home a young-un hisself, when he too ole fer *any* side. All them Hollis men, they cain't see plain fac'. Take 'er up or take 'er down, a flibbergidget filly ain't no mare."

Clinton Tuxen erred. Henry Hollis chose well in Libby as wife. At Tulips she bloomed. She took competent charge of the household. She restored order, renewed wardrobes, banished dirt, and coached Edie on her cooking. Herr Schmidt repaired the tall clock so it chimed as solemnly as of old. Libby treated Audie Ann with deference and sororal affection. She learned much hand language, and, as with Henry, a shared love of books increased their bond.

Confounding the experts lounging at the Mercantile, nine months from her wedding day, Libby presented Henry with a son. Given the Hollis mothers' prerogatives, she named him Herodotus Lucius Hollis to honor her father. She often called him Harry. Henry consistently shortened his name to HL.

Libby Hollis chose well in Henry as husband. On her wedding night she encountered much that was unexpected . Beyond astonishing male anatomy and physiology, she discovered most strikingly her own ardent temperament regarding the physical side of marriage. What she once steeled herself to endure as wifely duty became essential to her contentment.

A husband as advanced in years as Henry might thus become a concern. But Libby Hollis was quick at self-tutorial. She readily grasped where duty and inclination happily coincided. She paid rapt attention to Henry's discreet hints—lessons, some of them, originating in less-reputable quarters of New Orleans. Libby assumed such information as gratifyingly innate in mature males as their physiological features. She learned well, and practiced imaginatively.

Ordinarily soon after the evening meal Henry retired to his office. This pleasant space Libby Hollis refurbished. She commissioned inside shutters on the windows to admit the mountain breeze but provide nighttime privacy. She had a door cut from the office to their adjoining bedroom. She specified large, decisive bolts, as certain experts on the Mercantile porch predicted. But these secured not the opening between office and bedroom, but the doors to the hall.

Clinton Tuxen nodded confidently at rumors from the depot of new furniture for Tulips. Boys, hit's the old story; give the woman two bits an' she run through yourn whole pocket, stuffin the homeplace. Goddamn useless geegaws. Nuthin ken stop'er. Nuthin on God's yearth. Geegaws, ever-lastin geegaws.

Tulips' new furniture in the office and bedroom eventually included, as gift from Libby, a Wooton desk from Indianapolis, fit for any office, even if this desk was the Ordinary Model. A well-upholstered chaise welcomed napping. In the bedroom, pride of place went to the bed, Henry's wedding gift, done by Gerhardt Schmidt in black walnut and beech. Its monumental headboard Herr Schmidt decorated with tulip sprays. Corner posts supporting the canopy displayed bas-relief flowers intermixed with Latin letters. Not far from a large wardrobe stood a tall, pivoting mirror with old-fashioned candle holders at the sides. In a corner, a chair, also fabricated by Herr Schmidt, its unusually short legs specified by Henry to the fraction.

Geegaws in decoration or geegaws on personal adornment were conspicuously lacking. After her evening domestic duties, Libby Hollis usually joined her husband in his office, though only after a brief stop at her bedroom wardrobe to follow conscientiously Mister Hollis's preferences differentiating dress and upholstery. Whatever the vagaries of current fashion, her unvarying at-home evening attire featured a loose white cotton wrap, closed collar-high in front by large buttons. To her children, when she came to hear bedtime prayers or nurse childhood illnesses, her dress made her an ethereal figure, who seemed to float like a ministering angel. To Henry, when she firmly bolted the hall door, her gaping dress made her seem considerably more corporeal, though no less ministering.

Henry Hollis's vigor into old age astonished and confounded many, for Libby Hollis conceived like clockwork. Herodotus Lucius eventually counted as first of nine. After each delivery, Libby organized a large christening party.

There Henry received with equanimity the polite toasts inside and less delicate cheers outside. He responded consistently with a little speech neighbors learned to predict. In his speech, the grateful father always included a bewildering but amusing excursus on the potential running speed of five-legged cows. He habitually reminded all of their debt to Miz Hollis for her strenuous labors, an acknowledgement that prompted the hostess's modest blushes as well as guests' grateful applause.

On the way home, though, celebrants varied in reaction. Older guests sometimes fell into resentful contentiousness, for a citing of Hollis example could lead to spousal recrimination. Others, younger guests, went home chuckling at the double-entendre the old gentleman inadvertently fell into, literally referring to his wife's birthing. No one recognized that Libby's blushes responded to her husband's very private joke, a reference to her most pleasant exertions behind the bolted office door.

By then Clinton Tuxen had long passed on, his place on the Mercantile porch taken by others no less sagacious.

Henry's children knew him at Tulips as a loving figure rather than a forbidding despot, not a pa, but a grandpa, though they ostracized or fought any playmate whose language implied that. The eldermost later fondly recalled his limitless patience in teaching their youngest siblings to talk. The more romantic described him as having a slightly melancholy air. All of them remembered strict examinations on Luther's Catechism. All wondered about the heavy scar on their father's neck. None recalled a satisfactory answer to account for it.

As they matured, particularly the older children became aware their parents were indeed much odder than most. (They had as yet only a faint inkling that therefore they themselves were odder than most.)

The older children discussed their father surprisingly often, though without consensus.

An analysis that found much support was offered by Marcus, who argued that their father's mind was like his desk. Locked by a single key, essential for any access. Inside, he divided his mind into cunningly-divided compartments. One compartment was for New York and whatever was associated with that. Another compartment was his years on the farm at the head of the Quachasee, and those associations. A third compartment was for his years and family at Tulips. Father, said Marcus, consciously or unconsciously observed walls around each compartment. Just as, in his desk, he kept one door with its compartments closed while he tended to the compartments in the other side.

Bill, whose taste excluded Wooton desks, tolerated such musings only out of sibling affection. "You can put brain tissue under a microscope, but you can't put a mind there. We don't know what Father was really thinking, and we can't know. In fact he may not always have known himself. Do *you* know for certain what pushes you?"

Once Bill warmed to his subject, he often continued. "Remember how old he was. A generation, two generations, older than all our friends' fathers. And think of the responsibilities he carried. A sister—deaf and crippled—a stepmother, family graves right down the lane. Just think of one building, this damn house, for instance. It's an albatross around your neck. And because you're a Hollis, you can't escape."

Dory and HL, and Crotia, too, as young adults had opinions then, but none fully convinced the others—or themselves.

None of Henry's children questioned his affection. Or occasional displays of conviction. His reaction on overhearing his oldest son mistreating Edie, forever their cook, was savage. HL told the story to his children, nieces, nephews, and grandchildren so often, so earnestly, that it became the "Edie Story," prominent in the family canon.

Few of the children noticed that from time to time Henry received envelopes postmarked Ohio. If anyone asked, he said these contained greetings and obscure references from an old friend who also knew Judge Bright years ago. When still young, his eldest daughter looked over his shoulder as he read one letter at his desk. "That's Latin, isn't it?" she asked. "Yes, it is, Dory," he answered, refolding the paper, and offered no more.

Once read, the letters went forthwith into an elaborately marbled box, shelved deep in the complex recesses of the Wooton desk. The box was distinguished by a label printed in Henry's crabbed hand.

IN CASE OF MY INCAPACITATION OR DEATH.
TO GO WITHOUT DELAY AND UNOPENED TO
JOHN PATTERSON BRIGHT
Henry Hollis

Inside, the papers rested sealed into envelopes within sealed envelopes. On top of the envelopes lay a single sheet. *Deerslayer, burn these, please. Uncas.*

Plowing with Greek, My Life

HL Hollis

Tulips, February 17, 1939

Today's mail includes a letter from my youngest brother, Lowe. It is thoughtful of him when he is so rushed he mistakenly signed it *L. J. Hollis*. One reason for his rush is the imminent opening of his third store. He also has new duties at the church they joined. Elizabeth, he says, was not happy with their previous (Lutheran) connections—too old-fashioned, I gather—and has friends at the new church. Reporting the success of his business, Lowe writes an aside about the need to "discourage colored customers."

The letter as gesture is kind; as news, it is so distressing I wish he'd never written. Lowe was only a little boy when Father was killed, and as he grew up Marcus and I tried conscientiously, to the degree he permitted, to be as much of a father to him as we could. This letter says all too clearly I pretty much failed in that duty. Tomorrow I must summon energy enough for a tactful reply mentioning our father and our cook, Edie. Lowe does not grasp what being a Hollis means. I shall ask Caroline to send a copy of these family memories to Lowe and Elizabeth. Their children may know very little of Hollis ways.

Tulips, February 24, 1939

The past few days have been too occupied with being nursed and doctored. I had no energy to write about family. Today, still feeling decrepit, I decided not to write, but to review past work. Having now done that, I can hardly find enough spirit to scratch out any more lines. I see I attempted something far beyond my abilities.

My intention was to write out information my grandchildren's grandchildren will need to understand Crotia's stories, and along the way record something about family members I have known. The former rests in a satisfying stack of papers. That turned out to be the easy part. It is the latter that so disappoints me. I thought to write a family history and instead I embarrass the family with this mishmash. I never aspired to Montaigne, but too much of this sounds like the radio soap operas that Gracie listens to in the kitchen. I can hear the organ music swelling to conclude today's thrilling episode in a Tennessee never-never land where wise fathers and loving mothers guide good-hearted, if occasionally wayward, children. People jump from one exciting occurrence to another, so there's always suspense about what will happen next.

It wasn't like that. I have reconnoitered the past and can describe the lay of that land. A few mountain knobs rise high, embodiment of laughter, high spirits, and rejoicing. Some chasms plunge deep in grief and terrible despair. These preclude any bucolic scene.

Dominant, though, is vast, level plain, and more level plain, and yet more plain. Made for plodding from one day to the next to the next. When I search my memory, what I see best is unrelenting toil. No 'counts existed a-plenty, of course, determinedly lackadaisical in pursuit of all save sloth. Most people, though, whether the poor or the better off—that's all we saw—most people recognized that they needed to hoe their own row. And they did. They worked. From the day they could pull weeds, though they couldn't yet hoe, they worked. To the day they lay down and died, they worked. They plowed. They washed dishes.

This puts me at a loss. If the suspenseful drama of a soap opera is not honest or accurate, if you aim to write truthfully about ordinary people with their dogged perseverance to endure monotony, how do you do it? How do you write without being so monotonous no one who values his time will read?

I don't know how to do that, as is embarrassingly obvious here. I thought it should be possible for me to set down in coherent order at least a guide to the family I knew. How wrong I was. I should not have started.

Tulips, February 26, 1939

Yesterday Crotia visited again, a touching gesture. Even with the new highway, it is not so easy to get here from her place. She brought her usual good spirits. Crotia has always loved high drama. Crotia has always been high drama. I suspect she came expecting to say a final, heart-wrenching goodbye. I'm not ready for that. I told her I'll call her long-distance in the middle of the night, gripping the telephone with one hand while the Angel of Death tugs at my other.

When she saw with her own eyes I was not about to expire forthwith, she sat to catch up on the details of family news. Naturally our conversation devolved to our pride in respective grandchildren, those we hope and pray will finish this century in triumph and courageously begin the next.

Crotia has always been a loyal, loving sister. I made a kind of confession. I told her I see now that without her teasing of Father, which made me so impatient at the time, I'd know even less about him than I do.

Tulips, February 27, 1939

Jimmy, one of Dory's grandsons, stopped here a few days ago to inquire if I needed any errands run. I took advantage of his energy. (I envy his youth more than I can say, but who am I to rail at God?) I asked him, when he finds time, to go up to Father's old farm at the head of the Quachasee. I wanted him to study with fresh eyes the two graveyard markers.

Today he unexpectedly dropped in to tell me he had already been up there. (Dory is rightly proud of him.) He cleverly thought to take rubbings of the gravestones. Fresh eyes, indeed, for I never thought to do that. The rubbings, though fine reproductions, reveal nothing new. As an afterthought, he said, he went into the cabin. Chuckling, he said he could tell it was a Hollis place because of the "family stairs" on the back room doorpost.

I was somewhat befuddled because of just waking from a nap, and I told him I have been in that cabin countless times. I know there is no such thing. I spoke sharper than I meant to, I'm sorry to say, and owe him apology. Jimmy inherited his grandmother's tact and forbearance. He took no offense, in fact kindly excused my previous inattention as understandable. The doorpost wood has aged so dark, he said, the marks are extremely hard to make out. As he entered, by chance sunlight shone through the one window at just the right angle for him to barely notice the penciling. By foresight he brought along a flashlight with an intense beam, which enabled him to see adequately.

I guessed it must be more of the damn graffiti that trespassing hunters have left over the years, but Jimmy said no. The marks, he claims, go up the post with names and dates in the 1850s and '60s. He knows the marks here at Tulips, and those his grandmother kept on the pantry door at the Henderson house, so the Quachasee marks seemed more of the same. He took no notes, but said he'll make a copy the next time he's there.

What Jimmy finds just interesting, I find baffling. What children would be growing up on Father's isolated Quachasee farm? All sorts of hypotheses offer themselves. Some lines of conjecture are pretty outlandish, but lately I have too much time for idle speculation. I must be careful or I might sound like Crotia.

The solution is to go look for myself. I am resolved to do so as soon as I can muster the energy, I hope when this cold rain clears to sunshine.

Knoxville, September 1939.

My darling husband did telephone Crotia. But he could not revisit the Quachasee. The good Lord released him from pain on March 3, 1939. He died holding my hand, trying to comfort me. He wanted me to add to this. I cannot. It reminds me too much of what I have lost.

Caroline Bright Hollis

QUACHASEE
WHC

Just after HL's thirteenth birthday, Henry drove to check the maturing cornfield at the old Haney place. He saw Solomon seated in the shade ahead, easily distinguished by his thick hair, gone entirely white. As Henry approached, Solomon stood up creakily and motioned. Henry reined in sharply. "Are you all right? I'll take you back to Tulips so Audie can give you some of your medicine."

"I alrigh, Marse. I jes sittin heah t'tell yuh sompin priv'it."

Surprised, Henry waited expectantly.

"Sally fadin, look lahk."

Henry bowed his head silently. "I knew she ailed, but thought she would recover. She always has. I have such fond memories of her. The thought of her going soon makes the ground move. Why didn't you come to the house with the news?"

Solomon shook his head. "Yuh 'membehs Lilly an' Sally wuz bes frens. So Carrie come down quick fum Ohio t'see huh a las' tiam. Mebbe yuh knows dat."

"No, Solomon, I didn't know that. Did you tell Audie?"

"Nossuh. Figgah id be a su'prise t'cheer she up."

Henry nodded agreement. "Tell you what." He reached into a pocket for a memo book and a pencil. He wrote, *Carrie, I'll be at the Quachasee spring on Thursday morning. Henry.* He tore it out, then shook his head, went to a new page, and wrote *Cora: Q. Spring, Thurs morn about 11? Please. Uncas.* He handed the new page to Solomon. "Can you give this to Carrie?"

"Yessuh. I carry sum note back t'yuh?"

"Only if she tells you to. Thanks for your trouble."

"Pleased t'be carryin' sum note fum yuh t'she. Mighty glad."

"Would it be welcome if Audie and I stopped in to see Aunt Sally this afternoon?"

"Yessuh. She weak, but she happy t'see yuh."

That evening, Solomon materialized as soundlessly as usual on the Tulips porch. He slipped into Henry's hand a paper with a single word: *Cora.*

Henry turned to Libby, shelling peas with Audie Ann. "My dear, on Thursday, I must go up the Quachasee to speak with someone about, well, about boundaries."

"All alone? Shouldn't someone go with you? I would come myself except . . ."

"Certainly not in your condition," smiled Henry. "Rest easy. I know the way with my eyes shut."

❧

Henry arrived at the spring early, but Carrie already sat waiting. He grimaced as he got out of the buggy, stiff after the long, rough ride.

She nodded knowingly. "Try walking."

"Carrie, if you'd told me, I'd have sent a mare for you."

She smiled. "I know you would have. You were always kind. Except about that pile of chimney stone." Smile became a grin.

"I didn't know you well then," he protested.

Her grin widened. "The Old Testament 'know'?" She extended her hand, which he took and pulled her to standing.

"The years haven't made you less forward. Why did you walk here?"

"Because I wanted to come back the High Trail we took when we left. It's gotten longer and a lot steeper," she added with a wry laugh. She pointed to the cabin. "It's still in good shape."

Henry slowly examined the panorama from one side to the other. "Looks so. I haven't been here much since you left."

"Since I left? It looks like you were just here," Carrie protested. "How could you stay away?"

He shrugged. "I didn't have the strength of mind to come back, Carrie. I send young Tom up once a month. He's happy for the money. I'll remember to tell him he's done a good job."

Carrie pointed. "He even mows in the graveyard."

Side by side they walked to the rock wall. "I told Tom to do that every trip before he does anything else."

Looking over the wall they examined the polished stone marker.

"You ordered that and sent it up."

Henry nodded. "Had to do something after Tom said my old wood marker was just rotted crumbles."

She bowed her head into Henry's chest. He put his hands on her shoulders. "Such a bright, loving boy," she whispered. "Henry, promise that if I die before you I can be buried here. I just want to lie here with our boy."

Henry's voice became husky. "Of course I promise. You know, though, I'm likely to go first. I'll leave instructions, but I can't guarantee they'll be followed unless Spooks is still around."

She walked a few steps away, then returned to stand with her back to the wall. She started to raise herself to sit on the wall, then gave it up as too high for her. Henry stepped over, put his hands at her waist and aided her jump. Seated atop the wall, she leaned to kiss his forehead. "Henry, you been working in the fields? You're still strong for an old man."

When he did not answer, she began looking around, up at the mountains. "It's even more beautiful than I remembered. And listen. Henry, really listen. Was it this quiet when we were here? There's only the wind."

They watched two deer pick their way daintily through the old orchard and across the Low Field, long gone to grass. Carrie pointed out a hawk doing slow spirals high above a ridge. "In Ohio what they call hills are only rises. Pathetic, most of 'em." They watched the hawk disappear behind the ridge. "Henry, why did you sign your note *Uncas*?"

"No important reason," he replied. "Maybe nostalgia for when Spooks saw you were Cora."

Carrie wasn't satisfied. "I thought you remembered how we wondered why Cooper didn't let Uncas and Cora live happily ever after."

"I do remember wondering that. Guess when you're old it's easier to see Cooper wrote stories that weren't fiction."

"A lot of things get easier to see when you're old, but some get harder to see." She held out her arms. "Henry, can you help me down, please?"

Again he put his hands on her waist. She held his shoulders and eased down. They stood regarding each other at arm's length. Perhaps Carrie read his eyes. "You're used to a young wife, Henry, still strong, without the wrinkles and stoop. Years ago I could have jumped that wall faster than you."

She silenced the beginning of Henry's reply. "Don't even try to flatter me, Henry. I know I'm not a girl anymore. Or even the woman who walked out of here. But you." She looked at him critically. "Hair gone nearly white, which makes you look distinguished. Thicker glasses. But you haven't gone to fat. Is she taking good care of you?"

"As well as I let her."

"As good as I did?" Carrie grinned at her own daring.

"Almost." He shared her grin.

"Do you remember to say 'please' to her?"

His grin vanished. "Carrie, I have only said that to one woman in my life."

"At least you've got someone to inherit Tulips."

"Never my goal."

"What was your goal, Henry?" she asked, cocking her head inquisitively to one side.

He did not answer for a long time. "The sad fact is that I didn't have a clear goal, let alone a noble one. I suppose I was getting tired of fighting. I just went with the river current."

"You're getting old, Henry Hollis. You wouldn't have accepted that when you lived up here."

Henry conceded her point silently and she relented. "'Course, I've gotten old too. Old enough to know all about going with the river current. It's a lot easier, isn't it?" She watched the hawk as it soared back into view. "You visited Sally the other day. She'll be gone soon. Solomon doesn't look at all well to me. After he goes there won't be anyone at Tulips who remembers us together."

"Audie Ann," he corrected, "but of course, she—"

"Doesn't talk. Will you be relieved to have no witnesses around?" She watched the hawk spiral high until it was only a speck.

Henry objected in the mildest tone. "You saw the stone marker. If you die first there'll be another, and your name on it."

"Henry, I'm sorry." She grasped his arm in apology "I'm upset to see Sally dying. Spooks would certainly have ruled that question out of order. Speaking of Spooks, I haven't had a letter from him in several months. How is he, and Lydia?"

"They're thriving, though he's too lame to roam the mountains the way he used to. We still see 'em most of every summer when they come up from Knoxville. You'd be proud of your namesake, their younger girl. I wish you could meet her; a fireball, that girl. They'll be disappointed they missed you."

Tears welled in Carrie's eyes. "They're still the best friends I have, except for Henry Hollis."

They both watched hawks soaring in thermals for many minutes.

Finally Henry asked, "Has George opened his restaurant in Chicago?"

"With a French partner. They call it LaCroix. New Orleans food. Uses some of Mama's recipes that you told me to write out after she died. He works terrible hours, but says the place is so popular they need more room."

"Guess I shouldn't have worried that he might not amount to much because he would never stay with a job. Do you get any hint of a lady on his horizon?"

"He wrote once that he's sweet on his partner's daughter. I wondered if he was telling me he's passing. But he never says right out. He sends fancy recipes sometimes for me to try."

"And cooking has always been what you love."

Carrie corrected him quickly. "I liked cooking, but the loves of my life were Henry Hollis and our children." Her voice faltered. "Oh, Henry, you know leaving here was the hardest thing I ever did?"

"Yes. And staying was the hardest thing I ever did," he answered with a sad smile.

She acknowledged his quiet declaration with a gentle touch on his cheek. "I tuck things—papers and pictures—into Starck's prayer book you gave me when I left here. Julia will get it when I die." She hesitated. "I'm nervous sometimes. Paper is so fragile. I wish I could leave the children something more solid from you."

Henry's smile steadily broadened as he settled on an idea. "The next time Andy goes up to Cleveland to see his sister I'll send along the original Low Chair to you."

"How could he carry that?" she protested, though her smile could have been shy or it could have been sly.

"We'll figure something out."

They walked up the faint trace toward the cabin, Henry quickly taking her arm when she lurched a bit at a misstep.

"Henry, let's stop here. I thought I could sit on the porch steps and lean against your knees the way I used to. But I better not. Already it's bringing back more than I can bear." They turned to look at the cabin's view.

"It's so beautiful," she breathed as she reverted to the cabin. "I can almost see Harry playing on the porch, and asking me questions I couldn't answer."

She glanced down the trail. "And Mama coming up from Tulips to visit us."

Facing Henry, she asked, "You remember when I was so sick after Harry died, and just wanted to die?" It was not really a question.

Henry reached to give her a hug, which she accepted willingly, but she had more to tell him, and finally pulled away to continue.

"Mama came up that trail and saw right through me, saw I was mostly feeling sorry, not for my dead child, but for myself. She asked me hard questions."

"After all she had been through, she was pretty tough," Henry agreed ruefully. "Scared me, and a lot of other people, I think."

"I've thought of her question many times: would you rather never have loved Henry so that you would not have the grief of losing your son? When I think of it now, I make the question bigger. Would I rather have never loved Henry and lived up here and had precious children up here so that I never had the grief of having to leave here— and Henry too."

"And how do you answer?" murmured Henry.

"My loss, my grief, they were real," she said earnestly. "Those were wounds that never really healed. Just like my beautiful little boy's death." After a long pause she continued in an equally firm voice, "But I don't regret my loving Henry."

"Thank you," Henry managed before they both studied the serried ridges and misted valleys.

After they had looked for a long time at familiar mountains, Carrie turned to Henry, dabbing her eyes. "I'm so glad you asked me here."

"You shouldn't thank me. I couldn't have done otherwise. Why didn't you write that you were coming?"

"I didn't think at first that Sally wouldn't live on, the way she always has. I came too fast to write—" Carrie broke off. "Henry," she demanded, "why can't a woman even lie decently to the man she loves? I wasn't sure how things were at Tulips and—"

"And you weren't sure I'd welcome a visit. And I didn't invite you to Tulips because I thought being there would be painful for you. But mostly because I wanted to see Quachasee with you beside me."

"We still think alike sometimes."

"When we leave, I'll take you back in the buggy. We can stop and see Audie Ann. Solomon and I haven't told her about you being here, so you can be a surprise."

Carrie shook her head. Tears glistened on her checks. "No, Henry, I've thought a lot about visiting Audie. We had such good times and she taught me so much. But still, I can't see her. It would be way too much reminder of what I lost."

She wiped her cheeks with her palms. "And you know perfectly well you shouldn't give me a ride, Henry. Someone is sure to see us, and— what did Spooks used to call 'em? the vermin—they'd be all over you tomorrow."

"I don't care about them."

She stared steadily at him. "After the fight at the livery barn I remember looking at you with your bleeding knuckles, and being so proud of you. And also knowing that sometimes you can be so dumb. You haven't changed a bit, have you? Same Henry, ready to tell the world to go to hell, and the devil with the consequences. That's what could've gotten you killed when you made me ride with you into Ginners Ford."

"But you covered me from your lap."

"Couldn't this time. I won't let you do that to your Tulips family. But let's not argue today, please, Henry. Please. We should talk about happy things. You do hear from Julia, don't you?"

He smiled at the thought. "She writes so faithfully I feel like she's next door. I can almost hear her little ones." Then he paused with a slight frown. "But even reading between the lines I can't get a focused impression of her husband, her Lawrence. You wrote about him when they married. But what's he really like?"

"He's a good man, who wants what's right and is determined to help get there. Teaching is almost a holy calling to raise the race."

Carrie hesitated, then made a wry face. "Sometimes, though, just between us, Lawrence is a little stuffy. Julia is good for him; he needs someone he loves to laugh at him from time to time. Like you needed. And she does. He gets angry because he's seen so many doors closed when he wanted higher degrees in education. He's real dark, Henry."

Henry shrugged, and Carrie struggled to explain. "His family . . . they were ignorant sharecroppers . . . dirt poor. Had the ambition whipped out of 'em umpteen generations back. He didn't learn to read until he was *fifteen*, Henry. Everything was a struggle for him. He can't really understand Edward."

"Who read from the cradle and had Spooks."

She nodded. "Edward had Spooks, but mostly he had his father always writing him letters full of advice and encouragement. You had confidence in him and he knew that."

Carrie cut off Henry when he seemed about to reject her praise. "I saw it, Henry; I know that's true. He knew he had a loving father, even if you were back in Tennessee. You were a father I never had, and certainly more than Lawrence ever had. Lawrence's father was a drunk who walked out on eleven children, so Lawrence thinks Edward had it easy. But you know Edward worked hard for where he is."

"It wasn't his fault that Spooks paid his room and books at the seminary." Henry grinned in recollection. "Did I ever tell you what Spooks called it?"

He finger-wrote high in the space before him. "The Reverend Eusenius Berkemeier Memorial Fund to Support Indigent Upper Quachasee Valley Ministerial Students Who Count in Latin."

"Just like Spooks to make a joke to cover a good deed," Carrie laughed. "He did get the Berkemeier part right."

"I remember Edward writing that your stories about Berkemeier were what sent him into the ministry."

"That and Julia's catechism teaching."

"I try to read her letters between the lines, but I can't tell if Julia feels caught between a black husband and an almost-white brother."

"Of course she's caught. We're all caught, Henry. Every one of us. That's our lives. Julia's proud of her Lawrence, but she's read some of Edward's sermons he's sent her, and she told me she knows full well that Edward's congregation will listen to him say things they'd never hear from someone like her husband. And Edward does say them. So she's proud of both of them."

"And I'm especially proud of her."

"An important thing is she knows that. She never forgets that you always took, and take, her seriously. Pru in New York did that to you, didn't she? Do you treat your new daughters the same?"

At his slow nod, she continued. "You realize Julia's the one who told Edward to go away to college and the seminary? She said, 'On one condition.'"

"I never heard that. What condition?"

"That he never lie if anyone asked him. She isn't easy on him. Every time he writes some good news from California, she writes back, 'You didn't lie, did you?'"

"How does he answer that?"

"She always gets a telegram back: 'No stop I didn't stop.' Except after his John was baptized, he wrote Julia that he told his wife about his family in Tennessee."

"And?"

"He wrote that he wished he'd told his wife sooner." Carrie paused a long time, as if waiting for Henry to speak. When he said nothing, she turned to face him. "Have you told your wife about the nigger whore you kept up here?"

His face anguished, Henry choked out, "Is that really what you think I did . . . just kept a . . . some woman here?"

"Yes, that's what I think. Before dawn when my bed is cold and empty and I know I'm going to die alone soon, that's what I think. I lie there and remember back that you nearly raped me by the spring over there when you knew I was only property. You knew it was no account if I didn't want you. If I had screamed, no difference. You could've laughed and cut my wind, forced yourself into me no matter if it even killed me. Be honest with yourself, Henry Hollis."

Henry shook his head, but slowly. *And when you come panting to your mare? Will she be tethered, unable to escape?*

Carrie continued, but in a much gentler voice. "And then the sun comes up and I try to be as honest with myself as I want you to be with yourself. And I remember how I fancied you long before I came sashaying down that path with a lunch basket and that gingerbread. Oh, how I wanted you to take that gingerbread, and a whole lot more."

Her voice hardened again. "But you couldn't know that. I was just a slave girl who must be hot because she's got some nigger blood."

She dabbed at her eyes with a sleeve cuff. "Oh Henry, in the day, I ask myself, Why in the world did you leave? I tell myself I could be here still, and you would be with me—I know you would be—until we're both buried over there with Harry."

Her eyes stayed long on the tiny graveyard. "But at night I know: every time I'd come onto that porch I'd see the two men with their sabers, grinning as they come up to rape me. And I'd be worried sick about the children. Mama was right. The child kicks inside so hard sometimes it takes your breath, but you laugh because you think the kicking will be over soon. What you don't know is the kicking keeps on until you lie down to die."

She brushed her eyes again. "But I still want to know. Have you told your wife about me and your children, who all loved you, up here?"

Henry looked at her steadily. "Libby is a kind woman. She works hard. She grew up alone with her father, who knew everything about the law and nothing whatever about human beings the law applied to. So she never learned much about people. She reads a great deal. She can talk about almost any novel you want. Tell you the plot and name the characters." He sighed with a slight shake of his head. "She knows their stories, but in a way she doesn't grasp them. I don't think she feels them."

He paused, searching for words. "She devotes herself to her children . . . to me. For her . . . something is important, is good or bad, depending on how it affects her immediate family, because Tulips and Tulips people remain her whole world. She doesn't see, doesn't imagine, beyond that. She would never understand *those* people," he motioned toward the cabin, "or feel their choices."

He sighed again. "So, no, I have not told her. The children, I want to tell when they're a little older."

"You ashamed of us, Henry?"

His face spoke vehement disagreement, though his voice stayed mild. He shook his head. "I'll go to my grave with the scar that says I'm not ashamed of you."

She reached to touch his neck softly in acknowledgment. Yet she persisted. "Not ashamed of us, but not proud enough of us to tell everyone."

"Carrie, you know I don't want the world to be the way it is."

Track and Sign

Lewis Gates Warden

After Julia filled one of her longest letters to Henry with Carrie's collapse and sudden death in Cleveland;

After a neighbor's ailing mule kicked a doctoring Henry, killing him instantly in the midst of retelling a favorite Doc Sexton tale;

After Solomon was found dead, apparently of his chronic heart problems, lying in the orchard next to a ladder necessary to glean the fruit most out of reach;

After Audie Ann slipped away from her handicaps as mutely as she coped with them her life long, and was buried, according to her detailed map, in a corner of the Hollis graveyard, a corner with Solomon's fresh grave;

After cancer claimed a still-young Libby;

After Herodotus Lucius, the family chronicler, wrote his last page, nagged that something essential had escaped him;

After his sisters Dorinda and Crotia, returning from their brother's burial, were both killed by a drunk driver, one of Caleb's grandsons;

After an antique clock "expert" pronounced the sole salvage for Samuel B's stilled clock was replacement of the worn-out works by a slide-in digital unit with choice of four electronic chime tunes;

After an empty, derelict Tulips burned to the ground, the flames lighting an untilled field of the lovely flowers that gave the place its name, plants that, over countless seasons of untended propagation, had mixed promiscuously to produce unusual strains, so exotic or so variously sized or so resistant to common perils as to confound even a Doc Sexton;

Even after all this was forever gone, faint track and sign still remain.

The track and sign, however, demand luck as well as patience to decipher. It is as if the wily Hurons, ever duplicitous, have walked backwards in their moccasins, dropped enticing fragments on dead-end trails, straightened branches surreptitiously bent by their captives to guide rescue. Impatient pursuers, not fully conversant with wilderness ways, are easily led astray. The tenacity, the keen eye, the light tread of some new Uncas is required, but is rarely at hand to discern the meaning of half-hidden sign.

❦

A PBS *Antiques Road Show* expert from New York, filmed at the show's stop in Columbus, Ohio, exclaims over treasures brought in by a handsome, well-dressed young woman who speaks with crisp diction, in command of her facts. Her chair and paintings, she explains, have been in the family from Civil War times, and came to her at her mother's death.

The expert begins with the chair. He identifies it without hesitation. Perhaps eighteenth century, more likely early nineteenth century, made in Maryland or Virginia. Chairs like this, he explains, were the work of skilled slaves. Usually anonymous, the makers sometimes did leave their marks. He turns the chair over so the camera can zoom in on what he points out as the maker's initials, a T faintly incised on the inside of one leg, and an H on another.

He admits, though, that proportions and scale stump him. If the seat is so low for a child, why is the back so tall? Why would someone apparently shorten the legs? Multiple repairs suggest hard use and a very heavy occupant; the seat is not wide enough to imagine two adults occupying it side by side.

The cushion tied at its corners to the seat, he says, appears fashioned specifically for this chair; it is old, but not as old as the chair. Its figures in needlepoint are unusual; a leisured mistress, not slave women, generally produced decorative stitching such as this. The cushion's four panels just don't connect with the Midwest. Why is the barn white, not red? And a whale, an elephant, and what looks like it could be a buffalo? Not typical American farm animals.

The New York expert then turns with quickened pace to the three modest-sized paintings done, according to family story, by the owner's great-great-grandmother, whose origins were in Tennessee. Charming folk-art, these are farm scenes, depicting a field with workers, perhaps slaves, though the workers are not dark. The mule-riding man may be the overseer. The depictions are painted by an untrained hand, valuing narrative over precision in perspective and proportion. The almost childlike innocence and vibrant color beguile the expert.

He lingers on the picture showing soldiers in blue uniforms riding down a mountainside to a farm. He wonders if this depicts a Union party freeing slaves. The woman and child awaiting the soldiers, however, are white and appear apprehensive about their rescuers. On the painting's back—the expert swivels the frame—there is the only marking: XXII. A date? He shrugs. Eighteen twenty-two is too early; nineteen twenty-two, too late. Perhaps this was originally the twenty-second in a series of paintings? Wrapping things up, he says that if he showed these items in his gallery, considering their provenance and their good condition, he would put a price, conservatively . . . he pauses for suspense, then names a figure in five digits.

After her ritual exclamation for the camera, a rather calm exclamation in this case, the owner points out a detail the appraiser did not mention. The background mountain profile is identical in all three paintings. It must be the same farm. Horizon is so distinctive she speculates that if she could find like mountains today she could locate the farm and know her forebear's exact origins. The expert politely corrects her. The painter surely cribbed the backdrop from some stock scene. The owner shakes her head, but then the audio is turned off and their lips move while the appraisal flashes on the screen just ahead of a cut to a visitor with Rookwood pottery.

Harold and Betty Hollis, of Chattanooga, share a fascination with Hollis family genealogy—they both grew up near Ginners Ford—though their precise interests are conveniently different. Beverly focuses on the Tennessee Hollis family, and is patiently constructing a genealogical chart. It has gotten so large, jokes Harold, that they'll need a even bigger RV for their winters in Florida. Harold concentrates on the early Hollis family in Virginia. Their RV has multiple stickers from their trips to the Chesapeake. Recently they were inspired to create a family website, the better to disseminate their work, but also to categorize and stay in touch with informants.

Many of the names of their original respondents could be quickly discarded as unconnected to "their" Hollis. A latter-day Hawkeye, however, pauses thoughtfully at an "Andrew Hollis, Ann Arbor, Michigan," who reports that his aunt in Detroit retains (very protective) custody of a tattered Lutheran prayer book; in its pages are stuck small repetitious portraits from a Knoxville studio, some handwritten letters in simple Latin, and a much-creased, 19th century map tracing a route between eastern Tennessee and California.

Andrew's cousin, an M.D.-Ph.D. in Ann Arbor, writes that she hopes career pressure will soon ease enough to allow her attendance at the annual Tennessee Hollis reunion she learned of from Harold's Hollis family website. She would like to locate there volunteers for DNA studies, more persuasive to a natural scientist than oral tradition.

❧

God, look at these damn photos—all Hollis ancestors.

Allison (Missy) Elizabeth Hollis, junior at an expensive private college in Tennessee, fidgets absentmindedly with her nose studs while she flips the pages of a little family history book she sweet-talked a reluctant uncle into express mailing for a course paper due very soon. To open the book fully on her desk she shoves aside a white pharmacy bag, charged on her father's credit card. It worked fuckin cool: I just told him either I get the card or I can't buy contraceptives and he knows what *that* means.

Dad pissed me off, I mean, *truly* pissed me off with more of his Memphis Hollis shit. So I dropped the bomb on the phone about who I partied with, and can you believe it, Dad shows up at Darrin's apartment the next day to offer him a car if he'd get lost. Like, duh, he's some kid with a basketball and dragging pants, right out of the friggin ghetto. Get real, Mr. L. J. Hollis IV. *Fuck off, man* was Darrin's answer. He's pre-med from Dallas, parents both doctors. The wheels they gave him—god, I love that car—he keeps them at home so he can concentrate on classes here.

Goodbye, Memphis. Noshit, after that visit I couldn't move in with Darrin fast enough. Made fuckin sure to send Mom a shot from my phone. Darrin's front door, no text, just the street numbers big on the door. It's so cool to be "such a disappointment" to your parents.

That's all my parents think about—living up to the high holy Hollis name in Memphis—the right house on the right street in the right suburb, with the right clothes in the right car to go to the right schools, the right church, the right clubs, until you get into the right college to get laid by the right guys to find the right husband, to get the right house on the right street, in the right suburb.

No way. Been there, done that. Goodbye, mindless Memphis. Except maybe to drop in some time with Darrin for the fuckin hell of it. It's so cool, the contrast between black skin and natural blond cornrows.

Hell-yes, Darrin's parents are up tight about their precious son living with me. They keep calling him so that Darrin takes the phone into the bathroom and closes the door. But they're too smart to offer me a car. I'd blow 'em off, of course. It'd take me, what? Ten seconds max, maybe less. They're afraid a girlfriend's gonna keep Darrin from his classes. Hell, no frickin chance of that with him.

But I have to say most of the time they're pretty relaxed and nice—his mom even wears her hair in an Afro—nothing like my stuffy Mr. and Mrs. L. J. Hollis-don't-forget-the-frickin-IV, of Memphis, Tennessee, with the drugstore chain they sold out to big boys from New York.

So that's my theme song: Goodbye, goddamn Memphis. Grandpa Hollis always talks like the Hollises were in Memphis since creation, like they came up river from New Orleans. Maybe originally Huguenot refugees from France.

Look at Uncle Tim's book, Gramps. It's right here in pictures. See it? The Hollis clan came from *east* Tennessee—frickin hillbillies—no cotton, no plantation mansion, just ugly, plain houses and sagging, sad cabins, one-field farms and bony-mule teams.

Look at the photos in the book, Dad. Go-odbye, goddamn Memphis. They're grainy, the photos, but you can see the Poor in the mountain people. Tired. Old. And damn sour. Killjoys, they look like. Even when they dress up to have their portraits taken, like these two women with a book on a table—*one* book—they don't smile. They obviously didn't joke around, those mountain Hollises. One book, no music, and certainly no sex.

Well, they must have gotten *some* sex, or Hollises wouldn't still be around. But all you have to do is see the faces in the photos and you know. Creeps you out, those faces. They need a little weed, bad. No laughing for them. Look at the faces, man. The only reason they had sex was to get kids. Sex with all their clothes on. Missionary style. While they were praying. Anything to keep their minds off enjoying what they were doing.

Out on those farms at least they had animals around to tell them what sex is. They put the cows with bulls. And mares with—what is it? donkeys, I guess, if you want mules. Or maybe the other way around, I forget. Anyway, not in Memphis. Hollises moved to Memphis and moved away from the last thought of sex. Memphis Hollises are frickin freaked out by real sex.

Giving the mirror a glance for the purple streak in her hair, Allison (Missy) Elizabeth Hollis is pleased to know she and Darrin are the first generation that is honest—so help me—about great sex, finally liberated. So go-odbye, goddamn Memphis.

❧

The New York Times runs a capsule review, with endorsing stars, of a new small Manhattan restaurant, Chez Lacroix. The chef/owner is one of a long line of men, all talented cooks, in his family. Some signature recipes go back generations. The restaurant entrance gives pride of place to a cleverly illuminated plexiglass cube displaying a tattered, stained book passed down from father to son since the 1850s. Patrons waiting for tables are diverted by pages of handwritten recipes. "Cursive is neat and legible, orthography sometimes inconsistent, quantification always unconventional, results consistently excellent."

❧

Patient trolling of eBay will turn up FarmGleaner, a vendor with self-imposed limits: treasures from rural estate sales within a hundred miles of the border between Tennessee and North Carolina. Among FarmGleaner's offerings is "Large, hand-carved Headboard w/ Footboard, mostly in walnut." Illustrations taken by an inexpert photographer include distracting flash reflection off the varnished dark wood. The photos at least demonstrate the predominate motif is floral, intertwined tulips. The centered medallion features an elaborate letter H. A frieze of whales swims sedately along the top of the headboard. Patient photographic reconnaissance vindicates the vendor's claim that Latin phrases adorn the heavy corner posts. *Tempus Fugit, Carpe Diem,* and *Viresque Acquirit Eundo* are most easily deciphered, phrases

FarmGleaner helpfully translates as Time Is Fleeting, Seize the Opportunity, and It Gathers as It Proceeds.

The name G. Schmidt is plainly visible carved in the back, but there are no other identifying marks or date. FarmGleaner touts the bed set as one-of-a-kind folk art, therefore difficult to date, but he strongly suggests antebellum origin as justification for his price.

Inquiry by telephone reveals the vendor may negotiate. He has carried this gem in his inventory much longer than expected. Had the central monogram been S, he says, he would have sold it long ago. A lot more customers, as he now sees, have names beginning with S than H.

❧

Jeffrey Hollis, Associate Professor of Political Science at Falling Water State University, Wisconsin, wins teaching awards so customarily it seems easy. To hearten students puzzling over uncooperative data, he tells the story of his own failed undergraduate research for a senior honors paper. He conducted an ambitious survey of racial attitudes among Hollis family members living within one hundred miles of Ginners Ford, Tennessee, "a wide spot in the road in east Tennessee, propped up economically by tourists at the national park." His respondents sorted readily into two groups. Publicly he calls them Traditionalists and Progressives. Privately, he calls them Rednecks and Good Guys.

"The best honors thesis back then would have won a prize big enough for me to escape crop work that summer, so I sweat blood on explanatory correlations. Man, I looked at age and gender and birth order and occupation, education, income, politics. I looked at everything: the car they drove, military experience, residence, mobility, religion.

"But no bingo. Nothing clicked. All I had was data. So no prize, and sweaty crop work that summer. Hang. I know there is some correlation somewhere to explain it. I just could not come up with the right question."

An Uncas, to whom subtleties separating friend and foe mean life or death, could easily explain that enmity divided the Hollis tribe into two clans, the Wolf Clan, descended through Caleb Hollis, and the Eagle Clan, sprung from Caleb's cousin, Henry Hollis. That recognition would have meant the honors thesis prize for Jeffrey Hollis (unknowingly a member of the Eagle Clan), though likely Jeffrey's success then would have made him less of a teacher now.

❦

SA Today, the monthly newsletter of the upscale Sheltering Arms, the premier retirement/assisted-living/nursing home complex in Knoxville, carries on its front page, as usual, a photo of Sharon N. Willis, CEO. This time she appears with the newest resident, a dyspeptic Mrs. Phyllis Henderson, along with her son, Dr. M. L. "Mike" Henderson, a cardiac surgeon in Nashville. Standing stalwart between CEO Willis and the Hendersons is an exceptionally tall antique floor clock.

On an inside page Dr. Henderson explains the remarkable clock has been in the family ever since its construction by an itinerant German immigrant high in the Tennessee mountains. As a special birthday gift for his mother, Dr. Henderson personally rebuilt the cunningly designed works, machining new parts for originals when necessary. In the process he had to learn nearly as much about clocks as he knew about hearts, though clocks and hearts are, he observes, much alike in many ways.

Despite the lofty ceilings at Sheltering Arms, the height of the Henderson clock would have required removal of its top scrollwork to fit the apartment, something Mrs. Henderson could not countenance, reports the newsletter. At the suggestion of Mrs. Audrey Ann Shelton, Mrs. Henderson's daughter, the family therefore decided to place the clock on temporary loan in the Sheltering Arms lobby, so that other residents as well as Mrs. Henderson may enjoy its "bright tinkling chime" as they pass through to the SA dining room.

Space limitation in the publication may explain omission of certain details, in particular the contentious objections of neighbors below, beside, and above Mrs. Henderson's unit when she first moved in with her clock and its dirgelike, resonating strike every hour, a feature she was not inclined to silence.

Such articles about residents always close with a quote from CEO Willis; in this case, she observes, "A much-cherished heirloom, Mrs. Henderson does not have to part with the clock at SA." Newsletter readers must decide for themselves whether the cherished heirloom is the clock or Mrs. Henderson.

Urban professionals with expensive sports vehicles are delighted to pay astonishing sums and drive many hours to read *The Economist* amid intense seclusion at a picturesque, primitive, high mountain cabin.

"It's where the national park boundary sort of jogs around it, so no neighbors except bears. And cougars or panthers—the old timers call 'em painters. Way up at the head of the Quachasee Valley, which even a lot of locals have never heard of. The road up is only two tracks in the grass or rocks. Hairy, man. Sheer drop-offs and a l-o-n-g way down; no guard rails, of course. I tell Marcy, Close your eyes and hold on. You need four-wheel drive. Even then you wonder whether you'll make it.

"How did those people get stuff up there? On their backs? Imagine getting that fireplace rock together without any machinery. That's muscle building for sure.

"We've only met the owners on the phone. Seem like nice people, lawyers in Chattanooga, inherited the place. They did a great job of restoring the cabin, replacing a few rotting sills, tuck pointing, that sort of thing, but the stone work is all original, the sort where you're on a list and you wait for years to pay a fortune when they get to you.

"You can tell they're proud of the place. Even apologize the inside isn't quite authentic because it's painted inside. They didn't have a choice; it was already painted when they got it. They told us the story. A big dust-up in the family, I guess. One of the boys in the family used the place as a hunting shack, and in 1939—they all remember the date because it was one helluva fight—he took paint up. Wanted to brighten the inside. Didn't tell anyone beforehand. Some people in the family wouldn't talk to him for decades. I'd say that's taking interior decorating pur-ty serious.

"Anyhow, we get up there and put on our hiking shoes. Every time we go, we see something new. Found a neat spring they still get water from. It runs into a pool about hip deep, stones on the bottom to keep you out of mud. Huge trees hang over it. Some old stumps the size of tables to sit on. Thick grass like a carpet. Marcy thinks it's the most romantic spot she's ever seen. Me too. On a hot day, all you hear is water running over the rocks, and the wind. You expect to see a satyr step out of the woods with his pipes and some gorgeous babe, ready to take a dip and do what satyrs do.

Quachasee

When I say that, Marcy agrees—until I suggest we ought to follow suit, give the place a proper initiation. Gotta be a first time and it can be us, I tell her. But nope. She's a city girl. No alfresco sex, not even skinny-dipping, so the place stays as virgin as when we come.

"No electricity, no television, no cell phone reception: nothing. The kids won't go because it's so bor-ring. So we love it. We're not telling many of our friends, or it'll get too popular.

"Oh yeah, we found a tiny cemetery, a stone wall circling just two graves. The markers obviously weren't made up there; somebody went to a lot of trouble to bring in carved gravestones. Matching stones, but I can't figure them out. They are both marked Hollis, which is a common name around there. But one is J. H. Hollis and the other is C. LaCroix Hollis. Not just C. L., but C. LaCroix Hollis. English and French. A real melting pot right in East Tennessee.

"Marcy looks at those gravestones in such a lonely place, and gets all teary-eyed. But I just say, 'Hey, things were rough back then.'"

Acknowledgements

On legal advice I risk insulting the intelligence of readers by stating this book is not history, but fiction. There is no Quachasee, no Hollis family centered on a homeplace called Tulips, and no LaCroix mother and daughter. Actual events or personages referred to are used only to produce a sheen of verisimilitude. It's a novel, for cryin' out loud.

For the telling of this tale, I drew on nearly subliminal memories from decades of reading and teaching American history, standing on the shoulders of many giants.

I owe particular debt to Noel C. Fisher, *War at Every Door: Partisan Politics and Guerilla Violence in East Tennessee, 1860-1869* (University of North Carolina Press); to Margalit Fox, *Talking Hands: What Sign Language Reveals About the Mind* (Simon & Schuster); to David Greene, *Of Farming and Classics* (University of Chicago Press); to Stephanie E. Jones-Rogers, *They Were Her Property: White Women as Slave Owners in the American South* (Yale University Press); to Peggy Pascoe, *What Comes Naturally: Miscegenation Law and the Making of Race in America* (Oxford University Press); and to Joshua D. Rothchild, *The Ledger and the Chain: How Domestic Slave Traders Shaped America* (Basic Books).

For the speech of rural ante-bellum slaves, a fraught matter, I relied on individuals who in the 1930s interviewed former enslaved men and women, and reported what they heard.

The snippets of old Creole songs are from Mina Monroe, *Bayou Ballads* (G. Schirmer)

The recent, encyclopedic, authoritative *Dictionary of Southern Appalachian English*, by Michael B. Montgomery and Jennifer K. N. Heinmiller (University of North Carolina Press) is vastly more than HL Hollis and Crotia Hollis Warden aspired to, but it is a work to which they would have proudly contributed. They surely would have consulted the dictionary as frequently, as admiringly, and as gratefully as I have.

Of course none of these authorities are responsible for my possible misreadings.

Appreciation

As I struggled with shaping this story I have been fortunate to have readers profligate in forbearance, and generous in kindly candor.

James Lawton Haney, of Marion, North Carolina, expert in Church history, Russian icons and Carolinian mountain past, answered my first questions when I floundered, and continued over the years until I finally came to my last.

Audrey and John Eyler, a literary scholar and a historian of medicine, provided much encouragement early on by remarkably tactful suggestions on a first draft so primitive I cringe to recall it. Then, with infinite patience, they assessed subsequent drafts.

Seth Graebner took precious vacation time to catch his father's blunders large and small. His familiarity with *Nota Bene* word processing and his tolerance for endless e-mails and telephone calls at all hours were essential.

Later drafts benefitted from keen-eyed reading by Patricia Albjerg Graham and Meg Graham Peterson, as well as Linda J. Mack, Lorraine Buckner, and Jane Lamm Carroll.

With her imaginative marginalia Eileen Bartos went well beyond conscientious copy-editing. Steve Semken of Ice Cube Press shepherded the manuscript through production.

Customarily, a writer's spouse is finally acknowledged here. Muse, editor, researcher, or proofreader: common alternatives for a spouse. Margaret, however, evaded them. Except, compelled by incredulity at my ignorance, several tutorials on matters medical. But she and I both knew these pages would not exist without her cheerful forbearance about my resolve to take up this tale, and her steady confidence that in time—my time—I would tell it. Smiling to myself, I looked forward to very public gratitude sure to embarrass her.

Instead I must write that Margaret K. Graebner died just short of having in hand a finished book. Words fail.